Tot Taylor is a writer, composer and art curator.
He is co-founder of Riflemaker gallery and lectures at Sotheby's Institute.
The Story of John Nightly is his debut novel. He lives and works
in London.

THE STORY OF JOHN NIGHTLY

Pop's Forgotten Genius

Tot Taylor

Unbound

This edition first published in 2017

Unbound
6th Floor Mutual House, 70 Conduit Street, London W1S 2GF

www.unbound.com

While every effort has been made to trace the owners of copyright material reproduced herein,
the publisher would like to apologise for any omissions and will be pleased to incorporate
missing acknowledgments in any further editions. For legal purposes the full list of credits and
acknowledgements on pp. 864–878 constitutes an extension of this copyright page.

Endpaper image, 'Everyman' © David Jones, engraving, 1929. Used by kind permission

Text design by Julian Balme at Vegas Design

A CIP record for this book is available from the British Library

ISBN 978-1-78352-320-7 (trade hbk)
ISBN 978-1-78352-321-4 (ebook)
ISBN 978-1-78352-322-1 (limited edition)

Printed in Great Britain by Clays, Ltd, St Ives Plc

Dear Reader,

The book you are holding came about in a rather different way to most others. It was funded directly by readers through a new website: Unbound. Unbound is the creation of three writers. We started the company because we believed there had to be a better deal for both writers and readers. On the Unbound website, authors share the ideas for the books they want to write directly with readers. If enough of you support the book by pledging for it in advance, we produce a beautifully bound special subscribers' edition and distribute a regular edition and e-book wherever books are sold, in shops and online.

This new way of publishing is actually a very old idea (Samuel Johnson funded his dictionary this way). We're just using the internet to build each writer a network of patrons. At the back of this book, you'll find the names of all the people who made it happen.

Publishing in this way means readers are no longer just passive consumers of the books they buy, and authors are free to write the books they really want. They get a much fairer return too – half the profits their books generate, rather than a tiny percentage of the cover price.

If you're not yet a subscriber, we hope that you'll want to join our publishing revolution and have your name listed in one of our books in the future. To get you started, here is a £5 discount on your first pledge. Just visit unbound.com, make your pledge and type **nightly5** in the promo code box when you check out.

Thank you for your support,

Dan, Justin, and John
Founders, Unbound

For Kristina

'These scenes made me a painter'

John Constable (1776–1837)

Cambridge Evening News. Friday, 2 January 1966.

Last Friday evening, at the Eagle public house in Lion Yard, Cambridge four-piece the Everyman beat seven other contenders from the East Anglia area to win the final of the *Melody Maker's* National Beat Contest, becoming all-out winners with their rendition of the group's own composition, 'Zigging & Zagging'.

The judges – local MP Marius Johnston, publican John Nightingale, BBC television's Sefton Johns, and Mr Jonathan Sands from DJS Records in London – praised the group's energetic live performance and also the vocal and songwriting talents of their lead singer, John Nightly. They singled out for particular praise the wistful ballad 'Wave Orange Love', written by Mr Nightly about a childhood trip to the seaside. Mr Sands described it as being 'as good as Leonard Bernstein' and said he felt certain that a career in pop music lay ahead for the Everyman. Mr Nightly's father, John, an engineer at Pye in Newmarket Road, told the *News* that his son had always shown an aptitude for music, being able to pick out a tune from a very early age. The group's drummer, John Hilton, said that the £1,000 prize money would come in 'very handy indeed' and would be spent on much needed new equipment and stage outfits. The Everyman are due to play at the Dorothy Ballroom on Friday, 16 January supporting the Graham Bond Organisation.
Tickets: 2/6s on the door.
'Around Cambridge' by John Gardner, showbiz editor.

Cambridge Evening News. Friday, 9 January 1966.

After winning the *Melody Maker's* National Beat Contest at the Eagle public house last Friday night, local beat combo the Everyman have parted company with their lead singer, John Nightly. Mr Nightly, of Meadow Road, Grantchester, who also played rhythm guitar and organ with the group, announced he was leaving to 'concentrate on a solo career in London'. The group's drummer, John Hilton, said that the Everyman were both shocked and disappointed that Mr Nightly had chosen this moment to leave, at a point when a great opportunity had arisen. The Everyman have postponed their support slot at the Dorothy Ballroom this coming Friday but will go ahead with their audition in the studios of Dick James Music, the music publishers of the Beatles, in London next month.
'Around Cambridge' by John Forrester, entertainment reporter.

The *Cornishman*. Friday, 25 May 2006.

West Cornwall resident Mr John Nightly became the proud winner of the Carn Point Horticultural Society Gold Medal after showing what the judges described as 'world class' varieties of aeonium and canna at the village's annual horticultural show last Friday. Mr Nightly, of Trewin Farm, Carn Point, said that this was the first time he had ever won a competition in his life, and that the £1,000 prize money would come in 'very handy indeed'. Mr Nightly lives alone on the headland at Porthcreek, where he has built a special humidity-controlled greenhouse on reclaimed estuary land along this most beautiful and desolate stretch of West Cornwall.
'Gardening Week' by Jon Miller, gardening editor.

Who makes the Past, a patterne for next yeare
Turnes no new leafe but still the same things reads,
Seene things, he sees again, heard things doth hear,
And makes his life, but like a pare of beads

John Donne: Letter to Sir Henry Goodyere
Doctor of Divinity, Cambridge University, 31 March 1631

The offices of JC Enterprises, Carnaby Street, London W1. Monday, 12 January 1966. 10.30am.

Situated above *You Are Here!* – London's happeningest boutique – JC Enterprises is one of many young outfits on the capital's bright new music scene. Their biggest claim to fame being Stanmore act the Gloom, high in the charts with their debut 45, 'Bethnal Green', on EMI's new Mosaic imprint. The single, described by the group as 'a song about the area we grew up in, the East End of London', crashed into the Hit Parade at Number 39 this week after being played almost non-stop on the offshore pirate Radio Caroline.

In the narrow hallway, a young man with straw-blond hair, blue-and-white-striped scarf and brown leather sandals sits tight. He is about to be zoomed into space. Bolt upright, arms folded, foot tapping like a jackhammer, he appears anxious; like a school-leaver awaiting examination results. In the corner opposite, a young temp in a mad-patterned, sea-green mini dress taps away at one of the new *Memo* typewriters. Cornelia is employed to make tea, pretend she can type, and be decorative. In the other corner Sandra, or *Sand* as she is known at JCE, is nonchalantly re-pinking her nails.

'Bit like the dentist's, isn't it?'

The boy looked up.

'Had a cup of tea?'

'… oh… yes… yeh… thanks.'

'Well… would you like another?' Both girls had been briefed to take good care of the potential new client.

'… I'm alright… at the minute, thanks'. The boy uncrossed his legs and refolded his scarf.

This is London. And London is Swinging or *Swingeing*, depending on which way you look at it. If you're content to just look, that is. Because the only way you can get it really – really *get it*, London right now, right at this very moment – is to experience it for real. To be here. For to be here is to be happy. Happiness is all around. In the cobbled streets and courtyards, the *with-it* boutiques and *out-there* shopfronts. In the sunken velvet lounges of the new Chelsea nightclubs and the lime-washed white walls of Mayfair's smartest galleries. Even in old, antique places like the ancient Thames docks, the Port of London, Westminster, the City and the print centre itself, Fleet Street. The place that prints the newspapers that tell us every day what a fabulous town we live in. The people that wind the clocks and count the banknotes, the dockers, porters and drivers, the typesetters and hot-metal lappers in the Print – they're all part of the swinging city too.

But not only is London the commercial centre of the world; it's now also the most cultural. The happeningest, the grooviest. London is where it's at. *It* being 'the thing', the *zeitgeist*, the train of thought, the groove. The thing you have to have, or be 'with' or get 'in' or 'on'. To really get it. To *really* get it. To really get on.

All you have to do is tune in. And people are. Because at the moment it seems that everyone, the whole wide world, the universe, maybe even the cosmos itself, is on its way to Swinging London.

'Won't be much longer…'

Cornelia tapped away as she spoke, her eyes barely leaving the keys. The boy picked up a battered leather bag, ready to make his entrance.

'… okay…'

Nowadays, the capital's people are groovy, their clothes are groovy and their outlook is groovy. Even their streets are groovy, with groove-ridden names like Bond Street and Wardour,

Portobello and of course Carnaby Street, the grooviest of all. The magnificent *Carnaby* is probably the happeningest thoroughfare anywhere on the planet at this very moment. Doesn't that fact alone make you want to be here? With all these fabulous characters and streets and names and occurrences? It should do. If you have anything to offer, that is. Because what this all means is that London is suddenly a place of immense opportunity. A city of significance and enterprise. One great big Happy Cake you can all bite into.

Strolling along Carnaby Street or Ganton Street or Foubert's Place, right outside the window this very morning, you're more or less guaranteed to bump into someone particularly fabulous. Like Ray Davies or John Bratby, Terence Donovan or Celia Birtwell or Julie Christie or Peter Hall, milling around out there with all of the normal people just like you. There'll be Jeremy Sandford and Nell Dunn, Ron Kitaj, Rita Tushingham, Leonard of Mayfair, Murray Melvin, Andrew Oldham, Ronald Laing, Dr Roy Strong, Ms Penelope Tree or Robert Fraser or Hardy Krüger, just out and about down there, doing nothing much, 'cept millin'... and groovin' of course.

Any of these combinations of groovy types might pass you in the street and you'd never notice them. Because everyone you meet, literally everyone, looks different – *better* – now, don't they? Suddenly looks 'happening'. And just really, well... more alive than they did before. Even older groovers like Sir Malcolm Sargent and Sir Adrian Boult are part of it. There they are, decked out in their Regency cravats and Cuban heels just the same as the bright young things. And no, they don't look out of place at all, because nowadays you can all join in. So the Queen, the Queen Mother, Princess Margaret, Snowdon of course; all the royals, they're at it too. Completely affected by it. All groovy now. And, conveniently, regalia is in. Whether it's the Georgian gentleman's morning coat worn by Terence Stamp on the cover of today's *Daily Sketch*, the crimson military jackets they sell in Portobello Road, or the Queen's head in black silhouette on the new World Cup stamps. It's all 'in' and 'with-it' somehow.

'I can hear him finishing off...'

It's easy for things to be in because grooviness isn't exclusive; it's non-exclusive and non-class-based. That's the point of it. The reason being that for the first time ever, Britain is moving towards becoming a classless society. Well, that's what they say, isn't it? And it's true. Because grooviness is cheap or... well, it's actually free. And therefore immediately available to everyone. Anyone, anywhere, can be it. Groo-vy! All you have to do is get here and...

'Show you through in just a mo...'

It's a feeling, you see. It's a feeling, man... and everyone has to fit in and do their thing. In this rarefied, elevated atmosphere even the bird flying high and the breeze drifting by are *happening*. The narrow streets of Soho, with their Italian cafés and a newsagent or sweet shop on every corner, now so busy that their clientele are spilling out onto the pavement, are grooviness personified. Busy, busy, busy! Feeling Good! Feeling...

'He's ready!' The girl with fresh pink nails stared straight at the boy. 'Just through here...'

Cornelia walked over to the manager's office and held the door open. A tall, dandified young man with lightly waved hair waited in the doorway.

'John... Hey man... Come in.'

The potential manager extended his hand, visibly impressed by his first live sighting of the potential client.

'I'm John... John Pond.'

The man took a tin cigarette-lighter and motioned around the room.

'And this…' he offered, 'is my gaff.'

The boy, bag clutched tightly to his chest, crossed the threshold into the dismal office.

'… thanks a lot… it's… nice to meet you and… well… nice of you to…'

The boy was being especially nice today. Pond smiled accordingly.

'It's a… *John meet John* thing, then.'

The teenager and the dandy both smiled. The boy taking up the conversation as he loitered nervously, slightly intimidated by the manager's *swinging* appearance, the lush weave of his chalk-stripe 'grandad' suit; his perfectly knotted lemon cravat.

'… *Pond's* unusual…'

'Is it? My great, great… whatever it was, was *John Pond* also… quite famous a long… long time ago.' The manager spoke as if he were on television, picking up speed as he continued. 'No one's heard of him these days.' Pond turned his back on the visitor. 'An astronomer… "of some repute", as they say.' The boy brightened.

'… you're related to John Pond the astronomer?'

The manager looked round. 'Not heard of him, have you? 'Cause if you have…'

The boy seemed impressed. '…I know a lot about John Pond because, well… I do research… in my spare time… for pocket money really, on tidal patterns… the movement of tides… For the weather… shipping forecasts… things like that… in Cambridge.'

'Ships in Cambridge?'

Pond stared at the youth, who carried on without allowing for a response, in a misguided attempt to give the very best of first impressions.

'... I do a lot of things apart from music, you see... so I know exactly who your great, great, whatever it was... *is*...'

'Tidal patterns...' The manager had no interest whatsoever in family history. He sat down and lit a cigarette from a fancy box without offering one to the boy. Pond took a single, life-giving drag and indicated towards a bright-red piece of sculpture on the other side of the room.

'Come up from Cambridge today?'

The teenager moved around, eyed the appointed object suspiciously and sat down.

'... for the day, yeh. Jon Sands asked me to...'

'Right', the manager nodded. 'He told me about the contest thing'. Pond took another puff from the thin black stick and made something of an act of exhaling, turning his head away from the boy to release the putrid smoke. 'Said he thought you were the best... "most talented"...' The manager coughed and spluttered, 'of... *talents*...' *(cough)* '... he'd seen in a long...' *(splut)* '...time.'

'... well... that's...'

'Nice of him, yeah.' Pond coughed and rasped again. 'Wasn't so keen on the group...' He looked round for a glass. 'What he actually said was he thought they were a... *a right bunch of yokels*... I think was the actual...' – The manager cleared his throat and picked up a glass of caramel-brown liquid – '... *expression*'. The boy fixed on the ski-trails pattern of the carpet. He followed one broken drift as it divebombed into a tangle of jazzy hoops. Pond took a gulp.

'Not *so* nice of him, I guess. What are they called?'

'The Everyman' the boy jumped in, 'it's a…'

'Dreadful name, yeah. Whoever came up with it…'

'I came up with it actually.'

The new John Pond sat back, feigned boredom and plonked his heavy-booted feet up on the desk. He bent forward and carefully folded the slack of his worsted flannels. Abuzz with Dexedrine, a second glass of dead Coca-Cola at the ready, Pond's head twitched while his eyes flickered around the room, now and again fixing on something – a photograph, pin-up or a piece of 'art' – that would engage and detain him for a brief moment. The manager was at least as unsettled as his guest and his irritability and frustration with life in general showed itself in today's unnecessarily antagonistic, bordering-on-aggressive manner. The boy blabbed on.

'it's taken from a drawing, or a… a linocut – might be a woodcut, actually – by David Jones.'

'David Jones? *Lower Third* David Jones? Just saw them at the Marquee…'

'David Jones the artist. From Ditchling. He's…'

'Ah…' Pond looked away. 'Different guy…'

The provocateur trailed off, becoming momentarily distracted by Cornelia's impossibly long legs as she passed by the open doorway.

'What are you studying… at Cambridge?'

'I'm not studying there.' John switched his bag from one arm to the other. 'I'm not "at"… I'm… "in". I live there. Only just left school last term. I'm doing research… about the moon and the sun… at Cavendish… Cavendish Laboratory'. The youth, his confidence ebbing away, carried on uncertainly.

'… in a research group. We're looking into wave-power generation at the moment and… different things to do with sidereal time, which kind of leads on from, or you might say *to*… sort of…' The boy smiled apologetically. 'The tidal…'

'What is… *sidereal time?*'

'Star time. Time determined by the stars rather than solar time which is…'

'STAR TIME! Well, we're certainly that. Hope we are anyway!'

The manager could take no more. Totally derailed, he looked incredulously at John Nightly, wondering what the hell was wrong with him. This young, good-looking teenager, little more than a kid, comes into the office on the premise of playing a tape and suddenly he finds himself in the middle of a science lecture.

Having no clue at all about how to respond or stem the flow, Pond decided to leave the boy to his blabberings while he studied today's all-important chart position for the Gloom in the glossy magazine which Cornelia had just placed on his desk.

'it's all to do with energy… saving energy. *Fusion power* is what it is really, or what it's going to be called, or known as, in the future. That whole idea is going to be very important.' The explanation faded into the background as Pond lost focus and turned to this week's sales figures, his mind cancelling out the boy's mellifluous voice which became dull and distant. '… something we all need to… …pay attention to now… If we want to be able to… well… in the future…'

'RIGHT!' The manager tore himself away from the sales department. 'But in the *present*, man… what's the story? You've left the yokel people and you've got some songs of your own to play me, yes?'

The teenager fell silent and unbuckled his shoulder bag. He took a shiny 7-inch acetate from its sleeve and held it up at an angle to the light. Careful to keep his fingers away from the grooves, he began to inspect the impeccable surface for imperfections and scratches.

'I made this two days ago at Pye Studios. My father's an engineer there and...'

Pond didn't give a damn. He flung himself out of his chair, fag ablaze, and grabbed the disc from the boy's hands. Balancing the sharp edges of the record between his palms, he flipped the peach-coloured label, seeking a song title or group name.

'Just you on this?'

The boy nodded solemnly.

'Who does the backing?'

'I play everything.'

'Drums as well?'

'I'm afraid so... four tracks of, well... ...just me.'

John Nightly apologised for his own facility and backed away from the action as Pond squinted at the handwritten scrawl on the freshly cut demo.

'"Wave... Orange... *Love*"?'

The boy remained still.

Pond seemed to lighten. He lumbered over to the other side of the room and placed the record onto the turntable of a bottle-green Dansette lodged precariously on the window-sill. He checked the speed and positioned the arm above the outermost groove. As he hoisted himself up onto the ledge and hit *PLAY*, his clumpy heels dangling in space, he gazed down onto the busy thoroughfare below.

An innocent, childlike voice floated out of the room and into London's most happening high street, somehow sending instant calm into the Monday-morning rush. A guitar strummed softly against the low drone of a Hammond organ as a vibraphone threw sparks across the street. As the raga-like chorus built, a distorted, double-tracked voice delivered the song's non-message. After 30 seconds or so the lyrics developed into a kind of chant. Pond, expecting little, and piqued by the boy's uptight vibe, found it difficult to believe that this confident, laid-back performance belonged to the nervy school-leaver standing before him.

> *'I hear the Steeple bell*
> *Chime for you and chime for me,*
> *Telling us to be... together...'*

Pond turned back into the room. 'Like it...'

The boy looked immensely relieved.

> *'And I won't be late*
> *As long as my legs can carry me...*
> *All the way*
> *I know I won't be late for Steeple...'*

'Love it!'

The second half of the chorus was even catchier than the first. Very English. 'Churchy', 'village-y', 'countryside-ish' and... a little unsettling somehow. An image floated into the manager's altered mind. He saw windblown cliffs, a rough sea coast, a bleak headland. There was an old drystone farmhouse, an open door, a light-filled room at the top of a timber stair. Distant, almost strangulated music drifted along the corridor. Distorted and distressed, it was the same music that filled up the room right now but slightly out of sync with itself – uneasy with itself. Pond felt he was entering very private territory. Something very good – or perhaps not so good – was about to happen. The musical soundworld of the person delivering the message appeared sensitive, delicate, eloquent, but at the same time quite eerie, dissonant… ominous even. It was, Pond thought, also *very January '66*.

'This is… great,' the manager enthused. 'Great… … John.'

Suddenly Pond viewed the overactive, overanxious teenager in a different light. Quickly forgetting all about the Gloom – and tides – he appeared overcome by a kind of instant happiness as he leaped off the sill.

'Actually, I love it. It's… it's *weird* but… good. *Good weird*. Yeah!' The manager fixed on John Nightly as the boy allowed himself to sink back into the red chair. 'Catchy… weirdly catchy!'

Pond glanced back at the shellac circle spinning round on the deck.

'Great voice, man… weird… voice. Never heard anything quite like it before… to tell you the truth.'

'well… that's kind of… it's part of… I suppose.'

'But what's influencing you here?' The manager leaned forward. 'It's sort of…' Pond frowned – '*spindly* music?' – conscious of his own inadequacy.

There was no hesitation. 'Well… my biggest, or most recent, uh… influ—…' John Nightly replied, but the manager, now wising up, forged on.

'Kind of a *folk* thing about it…'

'*Folk?* Oh, I don't think so. I wouldn't say *folk* exactly…' The boy paused, not wanting to offend. 'And there's no… *spindle* to it either I don't think, unless…'

'I don't mean *Dylan* "spindle", I mean more…' The manager scratched his head, 'Phil Ochs…' He lifted the arm off the record.

'Same as he's doing now… but bit more… "ornate", you might say.' Pond looked at the boy, seeking confirmation. 'Yeah. That's it. Your voice… the tune itself, it's… dunno how you'd describe it exactly…'

'modal'

The manager looked blank.

'Modal. It's modal,' the boy repeated.

'What is?'

Pond twitched again as the boy relaxed a little more and perched on the edge of his chair.

'the tune… the way my tunes go. That's what you mean, isn't it?'

Not having a clue what he meant, Pond sat back down on the windowsill, ready to be enlightened.

'like him – Phil Ochs – I use different kinds of… "medieval" scales. That's what normal people would call them, anyway.'

'Normal…' The manager squinted and frowned again as the boy continued.

'so it's a bit *folky*, and a bit… I don't know… "jagged" you might say. Like what the folk singers do.'

Pond loosened up, appearing genuinely interested now as he took it all in. 'That probably is what I mean. Mixed up with a bit of a... a blues thing, maybe.' He searched his pocket for a cigarette. 'Seen Peter Green? Mayall's guitarist?'

But John Nightly wasn't listening.

'my big influence at the moment is Delius – Frederick Delius – the English composer. Well, he's a bit American, and... French, and German as well really.' Particularly his chords. A lot of Delius's music was based on folk songs, so there might be something there. And I've been listening to Bartok, things like that... Stravinsky. Well, he's definitely *modal*, isn't he?'

The manager couldn't say for certain whether Stravinsky was modal or not, but was becoming frustrated by the constant noise outside the open window. The busy comings and goings. Black cabs and delivery vans climbing the kerbs while trying to avoid dolly-bird shop girls and mouthy street vendors. The bleak reality of Monday-morning commerce as opposed to the walk through the mirror suggested by John Nightly's contemplative, almost sacred-sounding music. Pond flicked fag ash into Carnaby Street and swept his wavy fringe away from his face in an affected manner.

'Heavy stuff...'

It was a seemingly disinterested response. But only because the manager was now considering. The client zoomed once more.

'Heavy? It's not *heavy*... it's... well – it's not *light* either though.' The boy concentrated hard. 'It's very... *exciting* stuff, I think... Everything he – Stravinsky – does. And very easy to listen to. If you just kind of... accept it. Stockhausen as well – and Berio. All of them. Though there's a million miles between Stravinsky and Stockhausen, obviously...' The boy straightened himself up again. 'I did a course in contemporary music at Cambridge. A correspondence course, getting *homework* sent from America, even from people like John Cage. So that's what interests me more than anything right now. At the moment it is, anyway.'

By now, the manager, an instinctive recogniser of talent – and torment – when he came across it, was behaving in a much more measured and considerate manner.

'Heard the names, if not actually heard their stuff. But this track does sound very... different. In terms of the current *pop* scene I mean. It's unusual, John.' Pond calmed his bouffant with the flat of his hand and checked his profile in the mirror.

He turned full-on to the glass, running his index finger firmly along the line of his eyebrow to straighten it. 'Probably the most different-sounding thing I've heard for a long time. And your singing... your voice...' He continued to look while he adjusted his neckwear. 'It's... it's beautiful. Really clear and... *Clear as a bell* as they say in the trade. Would you be offended if I said it was a bit... bit...' – Pond paused for a second – '*choirboy-ish* or some-thing?'

The boy eased again. It was as if tiny, untold secrets were gradually being uncovered.

'Your influences are more "classical" than *pop*, aren't they?'

John Nightly considered for a moment, suddenly enjoying this first experience of someone actually asking him, honouring him, with questions about the origins of his creations. It's a privilege to be asked about your work – the very best kind of therapy – and something John Nightly had always dreamed of, fantasised about from the day he set his sights on earning a living by making music, using what talent had been bestowed upon him in order to become a bona fide (for want of a better term) pop star. In his own zoomy, hyperbolic head the journey he was about to embark upon would lead to him being regarded as perhaps *the* singer-songwriter and, if he could manage it, 'composer' of his generation.

'They are at the moment, I suppose. But on the other hand, I'm living in a "pop" time like everyone else. So it's... it's all mixed up with things I hear every day on the radio, away from more classical things…'

The enquirer, now listening intently, walked back across the room and pulled his chair up to his desk. Pond looked squarely at the boy before taking his seat.

'John… it's a good job you came in today. Fortuitous, you might say', Pond shuffled through a skyscraper of tapes and demos. 'I'm going over to meet George Martin this afternoon, to play him this group we've got – the Gloom.' He pulled out an acetate. 'Their follow-up record. Great little record. If anyone has the power to get things moving these days, I would've thought that this is just the sort of thing he might go for.'

'*George Martin*…' John Nightly found himself repeating the already oft-repeated name.

'Quick thought, though…"' The manager suddenly changed direction, looked the boy up and down then fixed on the magazine open before him.

'Ever done any *visual*… y'know… "acting" work at all?' Pond picked up the paper, 'Ever done any… modelling, John?'

'*Modelling?*' John Nightly looked up. 'You mean art?' Pond stared at him. 'Clay or…'

The manager wondered whether the new client might possibly be taking the Mickey. If so, it would not be appreciated.

'Not *clay* man. Don't be daft, John… I'm talking about *modelling*. Clothes modelling!' Pond waved the periodical in the air. 'Magazines and… models… *beautiful-women*-type modelling, John!'

Pond checked his watch and hastily adjusted the minute hand.

'I'm saying this because I've just had a guy drop out on a

session this afternoon. Seeing you standing there… I'm thinking you could… maybe… "fit the bill" as they say.' Pond scratched his head. *And* help us out of a spot at the same time.' He looked the boy up and down more critically. 'Reckon you could easily… *skim* through it, man.'

The boy broke into an immediate sweat. He got up from the red chair and began to gravitate slowly backwards towards the door. As he shook his head rather theatrically in disbelief, John Nightly's unruly blond hair fell over his eyes, making him look like a ten-year-old abandoned in a playground; the last man to be picked for the team. The boy's heart sank as he despaired of finding himself yet again in this all-too-familiar situation, even in this new, anonymous environment – the very same situation he seemed to have occupied too often in his life so far.

'… really… honestly… I… I don't think I'd be a good… *skimmer*…'

The manager got up from his desk, plunged his hands deep into his pockets, walked towards John Nightly and, at 6'3½" – several inches taller than the shrinking teenager – straightened himself up as he stared down.

'This is easy money, John. *Easy* money. For an hour's sitting around? You gotta be kidding. And JCE only take half…'

'Half?'

'Half of what you get paid…'

The boy looked completely taken aback. 'People get paid to do that?'

'Of course people get paid – *you* get paid, John. They're all making a fortune out there! Don't be so…' Pond searched for an appropriate condemnation before realising he might possibly be going just a little too far on what was, after all, just an initial, getting-to-know-you meet.

John Nightly also began to think. About the green Gibson Les Paul which only a few hours earlier had been eyeing him up from a shop window in Charing Cross Road. About the little second-hand turquoise moped he'd seen in the Meadowsweet Garage back in Cambridge. And about the possibility of being able to purchase an outfit like that of the potential manager. Pond noted the sea change and applied his most persuasive tone to the by now visibly fading teenager.

'In terms of helping us out… of a difficult corner, John.'

The boy seemed slightly dazed. '…it is… very nice of you… but I… I just don't think I could… well… that kind of…' John picked up his bag – 'I don't have any… training, for one thing…' – as he paused for a quick recce out into the corridor. 'Being photographed or anything, I mean. Nothing *at all* to do with anything like that.'

John Nightly turned up the collar of his windcheater, zipped it up to his chin and searched his bag for gloves. He made as if to leave, suddenly feeling uneasy and quite out of place.

'*Training?* That's a new one!' Pond grabbed another pack of Sobranie.

'Look. I'll get Sand to arrange a booker for you. See if we can't get you on something easy… something a bit classy. Bit of a try-out…" He slit open the pack and pulled out an elegant black cigarette. 'You've already got that classy thing going for you. *Cambridge* thing and all that. What they call the *English Boy* thing. They're all going on about that at the moment. Well, that's you – isn't it?'

For a moment, just for a moment, John Nightly seemed to be considering. Maybe, with a touch of application, there might be a slim possibility that he may actually find himself 'skimming'. The manager sensed progress being made.

'That's where it's at right now, John. *The Look*, as they say. In the papers all the time. *Swinging London*, yes? Heard of it? A cliché already, I know, but…'

Pond edged towards the door as if to prevent his captive escaping. 'They match you up with a fresh-faced, "innocent" chick – though that'd be difficult, come to think about it, and well…' Pond raised his perfectly straight eyebrows and gave the boy a knowing look. 'Got yourself a modelling assignment!'

'But I've already got a gir—'

'Got one of those already as well? All the better, then. You're well catered for in that area. Keeps you sane in times of trouble, I hear.' The manager lit up and took a puff before barking a question into the corridor.

'*Sand!*' Pond awaited an acknowledgement that didn't come. 'Who's the girl this afternoon?' There was a pause…

'*Iona*'

'Iona? *Well*… there's nothing innocent about that one!' Pond inhaled then appeared to reconsider as he stopped dead and stared into the distance. 'That's really, very… uncharacteristically uncharitable of me. There is… with that one, anyway. She's… well… she's nice… Iona.' The manager became uncharacteristically charitable for a moment.

'*Very* nice, that particular… Anyway! You should try it. You should definitely try it!' Pond moved away from the door. 'If we can get it for you…'

John Pond sat down at his desk, stretched his legs and lodged his Black Russian on the ashtray while strategically arranging his pens, pencils, paperweights, paperclips, address book, inkwell, blotter, calendar and telephone, as if about to do battle. He picked up the receiver and began to dial, then had second thoughts and put it down again. The manager swivelled round to face his charge.

'There's a feeling of something happening here, John. Sure you can feel it same as I can. London as a place I mean. But also JCE as a happening little… *cultural environment*… An "enclave", you might say. That's what we're trying to create, anyway. A place where things can happen.' Pond continued uncertainly, as he always would when he felt unqualified to speak about something, sensing his explanation might be a little *high falutin*, what he himself might have described as 'poncy', although he undoubtedly believed in what he was trying to say. 'A "well-vibey" place, is what I…' He laughed. 'Well-vibey…' Pond's piercing, almost hypnotic eyes were aimed straight at the boy as if to say, *You do understand me, don't you?*

'It's the kind of "vibey" you can feel in your bones, John.'

At that particular moment the boy was feeling a very definite vibrational quaking in his bones. With this bumpy, undulating vibe and the fast turnover of both mood and job opportunity from the potential employer, John Nightly wanted nothing more than to leave the vibey enclave as fast as possible. Pond began his round-up.

'We need to take advantage of that, John. The vibe, I mean. The reason I exist, in this place anyway, is to find hit acts. Maybe not just *hit* acts but *classy hit acts, career-type acts* – not just one-offs. Point being that one-offs do not make money. Your "one-hit-wonders" and all that'. He turned his nose up. 'They might bring in a bit of cash… or *cash flow*, but in the long term…'

The Swinging entrepreneur had become anything but laid-back. He was persuasive now, super-concentrated; and undeniably impressive. The impressive John Pond brought his pill-shattered mind back into focus. He sat up straight and flexed his fingers, ready to impart his own very particular philosophy. The guru of Carnaby Street, revealing all manner of previously un-thought ways and means.

'Let me put it this way… The owner of the company, John Carter; his background is not exactly in music. Not in music at all. It's in tin. As in *cans*. The tin can business. Baked beans, sardines… orange segments – all come in tins, don't they?' Pond got up and pushed away his seat, making unintentionally comical hand gestures as he expanded on his theme.

'He was in tin cans originally. Though that's been taken over by the Americans now. So at the moment he's into cars and ships… Ammunition as well, probably. Anything made of tin. Mining the stuff in Cornwall, which is where he spends most of his time, thank God; and not in here.'

Pond played with his fringe again, swishing it from side to side. He stared into space, posing self-consciously in front of a gold disc as he blew smoke rings out into the corridor, pausing to see whether Cornelia and Sandra were at all impressed by his *son et lumière* puffs. He leaned back on the office door, completely at ease with himself, his protégé, and the world at large.

'Ever been down there?'

'what?'

'Cornwall? Ever been there?'

The boy had also calmed down.

'no… no, I haven't. I did go once, actually, on a… family holiday… when I was a child…'

'The boss, John… John Carter I mean. Though he's a good guy and all that, doesn't really have much of a clue about the pop scene. Or music in general. Nobody does. It's a new thing, so *clues* don't really help. But I do… it's my business, obviously. My… *speciality* is what it is. It's what I know'. The manager walked back across the room, leaned over his desk and picked up the receiver again. 'Tell you what… If you wouldn't mind

just going out and sitting with Cornelia for a minute. Well...
who would, y'know!' He began dialling. 'Just give me a couple
of minutes of "phone time" man...'

In Cornwall, tin is a dying business. A century ago there were mines all over the county districts of Penwith and Pendeen. One hundred years earlier, John Wesley preached to vast outdoor congregations all the way from Quarry Bank to Carn Point. Tinners in Redruth and Morvah hung on his every word. Today, one thousand derelict sites lay abandoned across the rough coastal plains where once there were fifty thousand working pits.

Well, the tin has to come from somewhere now that everything is tinned and canned, doesn't it? Even laughter. And Tin Pan Alley itself, of course. It's more hygienic. It's more... what we come to expect from *Now!* But these days, all that tin is coming from America. So in Cornwall, and places like that, where the industrialisation of natural resources can no longer support the local community, people are looking for other ways to make a living. And this is where the new pop entrepreneurs come in, where they're emerging from – the most unlikely trades and industries. In the case of twenty-one-year-old John Pond at JCE, it's the TUC, the Trades Union Congress. The body that regulates fair wages and fair play for Britain's long-suffering workforce was the manager's previous paymaster, his 'alma mater', if you like.

When the position of Youth Employment Regulator turned out to be more of a desk job than anything else, the ambitious young graduate stayed for the statutory 12 months only before moving to the much groovier environs of Carnaby Street. Before the TUC, the precocious Pond had been the head of the Student Union at Bristol where he was studying for a degree in mining. And that... *little connection...* is how he came across John Aldebaran Carter. Mr Tin Mine himself. *Mr JCE.*

The universities and art schools of Britain are now breeding grounds for Pop, as people have quickly realised that it's a thriving new business, and that there's a penny or two in it. Again, it's the place to be. It's hard to see how a degree in quantum physics can lead to a dingy back room behind Oxford

Circus but that's how it is nowadays. Identify the zeitgeist and anyone can zoom.

Take Johnny Johnson, manager of the Witchdoctors. He came from Boxing, where he trained three Lonsdale Belt holders before using his contacts in the world of entertainment to secure the Canvey Island rockers slots on some of the biggest package tours of the day. Then there's Johnny Storm, who looks after new sensation Polly Pops (they used to be the old rock'n'roll band the Vampires); he still runs a string of hair salons and men's barber shops across the Midlands, which is where he started off. 'Stormy' Storm, so called because of his notorious black moods, was the first person anywhere to coin the phrase *Unisex*. And that is still his legend.

The fact is that today every opportunity is open. So if you have the will to make it and can get yourself down to London and get operating, well… It's all there for the taking, isn't it? The unlikeliest one of all being Johnny *'Dave'* Davison, currently proprietor of the new underground gossip mag *Grass*. Dave was originally in politics with the National Teenage Party[1], where he campaigned for a lower voting age and protecting the environment. One night on the campaign trail he came across Strawberry Quick in a pub in Mile End – they were called the Periwigs then – and took them to the top of the charts. The Periwigs needed money to record their debut single so Davison contacted old Johnny Carter, who he knew from the tinned-fruit world. And there you have it – Strawberry Quick became the first JCE success! In fact, their single 'Lovely Louvre' is about to be featured in the new John Schlesinger film and John Barry told someone he liked them a lot in an interview on the radio the other day.

Cornelia came back out of the manager's office and looked on the boy with new enthusiasm.

'John… do you think you could be at *GIRL* magazine at four this afternoon?'

'oh, but I… I mean, I don't… I… well… uh, no! Definitely not!' The boy sounded resolute. 'I'll be on the train back to Cambridge by then.'

'John wants you to see the picture editor there at four. They're doing a feature on stars who went to college. Graduates…'

Cornelia, suddenly finding the new recruit a deal more attractive personally, struck up a rather awkward model pose herself – a typical knock-kneed Twiggy – as if rehearsing for a potential future scenario. She held her file of *Young Possibles* away from her blouse, in order to show off her figure while balancing her statuesque, perfectly proportioned frame on her lacquered slingbacks.

'It's just *amazingly* perfect for you, John…' The girl put a small step forward to prevent herself from toppling over. 'They've got Jonathan Miller and Jonathan King[2]… but they want someone new as well. Brand new…', Cornelia raised her eyebrows provocatively at the awkward youth.

'but I… I mean I… I'm not a "pop star", am I? I'm not any kind of *star* at all…"

Cornelia leaned back and tapped suggestively on her clip-file, 'I think you'd enjoy it, John.'

'… I don't think I…'

'But what have you got to lose, darling?'

'… well… I… I don't know… I… I know I wouldn't…'

What the boy was saying sounded conclusive and final, but maybe he was really only waiting for an excuse to change his mind. On the one hand, John Nightly was thinking about the green guitar and the scooter, but he was also curious to discover how these fresh, innocent and most importantly 'foreign' model girls might appear in the flesh. The boy continued to playact with the decorative secretary. 'I don't even know where...' But Cornelia had to move on, get on with her arrangement-making. 'Wardour Street, John. You can walk there in two minutes...'

'... I've never done anything like that before...'

The boy sighed and played with his scarf. To turn down this out-of-the-blue assignment might discourage the vibey management from proceeding with the real business of the day, securing him that all-important gold-dusted recording contract.

'... I... uh... it might be alright, I suppose...' he mumbled to no one in particular as he turned to leave. 'Long as I can get back on the train to Cambridge...'

---

[1] The National Teenage Party, founded in 1963 by David 'Screaming Lord' Sutch, was the forerunner of the Monster Raving Looney Party.

[2] Jonathan King, formerly Kenneth King

Trewin House, Porthcreek, Cornwall. Saturday, 27 August 2006.

'I wonder if I could speak to Mr Nightly, please?'

'… who is this?'

'It's Neil… Neil Winters…'

'… this is Mr Nightly.'

'Ah… hullo… John… I'm really sorry to disturb you… and I… I hope I'm not disturbing you at a bad time, but… but what it is… I saw the article about you in the *Cornishman* yesterday…'

'… yes…'

'About your canna plants…'

'oh, yes…'

'The thing is… I'm actually a… a bit of a fan of yours from way back…'

Click.

John Nightly replaced the receiver, as he had done so many times over the years. Slowly and blankly. Then he went back to repotting and draining his collection of *Dorotheanthus bellidiflorus*, illegally imported from the Kirstenbosch National Botanical Garden in Cape Town, Southern Africa. Thousands of small green shoots were waiting to be done, and John couldn't wait to do them; the contraband packed onto the heaving shelves of his ever-expanding greenhouse encampment and his just installed E-Plasmic sunlounge extensions where his most expensive and treasured *Arborealis Expirus* were housed. DO NOT TOUCH FOLIAGE WITHOUT GLOVES. CAUSES BURNING IRRITATION TO THE SKIN.

John Nightly wouldn't normally have answered the phone anyway.

He didn't say a word to anyone for a whole nine years, except once during *Year 3*, when British Gas came to trace a leak after having to get a court order to advance just two feet inside the compound, and once in *Year 9*, when British Telecom needed access to the property to put in phone and fax lines, mainly for the use of Nightly's live-in male nurse, John RCN.

The man who had once been the very figurehead of pop, pin-up of every pretty young thing in the country – not to mention quite a few of their mothers – named by the *Sunday Times* colour section as 'the most beautiful man in England', whose music and lyrics and ideas and clothes and genteel behaviour and straw-blond hair and blue, blue eyes epitomised all that was youthful and happening but also somehow meaningful and sincere about *Swinging London*, as it was once called, wasn't in touch with the world at all anymore.

John Nightly wasn't even in touch with himself. John Nightly was just… hanging on. John hadn't put his hands on a musical instrument for thirty-four years. He hadn't flicked a switch to turn on an amplifier or an electronic keyboard, or to start up a tape-machine to record another of his spindly, modal compositions in all that time. The eras of audio cassettes and personal stereos had passed him by. He would have associated the word iPod with autumnal seed gathering, or visual injury. And John Nightly only opened his mouth to sing once every twelve months, on Christmas Eve, when he attended Midnight Mass in Porthcreek, at the little church of St Eina, always standing with John RCN in exactly the same spot – the back corner of the Lady Chapel by the old bell tower – in case a quick getaway was needed, as it had been on that fateful midnight eve of Christmas 1991.

Every year, John donated his very best *canna* 'Luxor', his own hybrid, always the deepest pinks, to the grateful churchwardens. He had even found a way of delaying the autumn flowering cycle of these South African queens so that they would synchronise and bloom at Michaelmas. Just in time for them to present their most magnificent flowers, the ones right at the top of the stem, and remain in perfect condition over the Christmas period. This and the Porthcreek annual horticultural show were the two big events in John Nightly's calendar. Well… they were the only events. And that's the way he liked it. That's the only way things were going to be. The only way it was ever really gonna 'happen'.

John hadn't put his hands anywhere near a woman either. Nothing in all that time. During the summer of 1971, the year of John and Iona's first break-up, John dated Donna Vost, Kassandra Parker-Pope, Myra Knoll, the Contessina Rafaella de Weyden, Flora Wood and Teri-Ann Christie. In other words, six of the most beautiful women in Christendom. John's problems were already coming on, but what set the torch alight was when Teri-Ann, not appreciating being jilted by the young blade, literally 'exposed' him in the *News of the World* with a photo essay detailing their exploits at the Savoy Hotel. It showed a depraved and decadent couple, a couple totally removed from reality. Naked, blurred, with John apparently mounting Teri-Ann in the marbled bathroom of the hotel's royal suite. That was the last off-duty photograph printed of John Nightly, until this week's feature in the *Cornishman*.

Although he never did officially release a single in England; in spring '68 John had the Number 1 disc in France and Germany, Holland, Belgium, Italy, Spain, Greece, Hungaria, Poland, Sweden, Norway, Denmark, South Africa, Madagascar, Australia and New Zealand. All at the same time. Touring was chaotic but lucrative. JCE hastily arranging extra live dates and TV appearances everywhere John Nightly performed. He'd been airlifted away from a snowbound Stockholm, suffered heat exhaustion in Canberra, been 'held hostage' by a group of hysterical fans in Munich, and in Johannesburg had refused to play to a segregated audience, creating a political uproar when he left the country without singing a note.

item: Monthly Cultural Notes: January.

At this time of year, much enjoyment can be derived from the greenhouse and from the cultivation of a number of different types of fruit and vegetables, but it's a slow start in January. If you have electricity, and therefore heating, use it sparingly. Keep an eye on the weather, using straw or old newspaper to protect from frost. Euphorbia, zygocacti, sedums, astrophytums and other succulents may be watered once a week if it is sunny. Do not overwater. Cannas and begonia tubers should be lifted and stored in peat for the spring. Ventilate and clean the greenhouse to prepare for the sowing of seeds.

GIRL magazine, issue #5. Friday, 30 January 1966.

GIRL is the magazine of the times. The magazine of the moment. This week Brian Jones is on the cover. Inside, Dennis Wilson of the Beach Boys talks about surfing the Californian waves and Mary Quant advises on how to wear the miniskirt in winter. Vidal Sassoon gives hairstyling tips on page 6 and the centrespread features the fabulous new holiday destination of Torremolinos, Spain: take part in our competition to sip sangria with Sandie and picnic on paella with Petula on its sun-kissed beaches. Lynn Redgrave and Hayley Mills both feature in our regular film round-up and on the back page here's Hardy Amies and 'Teasy-Weasy' Raymond with some hard-earned advice for the younger generation. Then of course our regular feature on the Beatles. Everyone is always talking about the Beatles. The Beatles are the reason we go on. The reason we're all here in the first place. If John has toothache, it's on the BBC teatime news!

Turn to page 21. Here's a new face! It's Cambridge graduate John Nightly in his purple John Smedley top and blue -and-white college scarf sitting in the offices of Southeran Books, Mayfair's famous olde-worlde bookseller, with Iona Sandstrand. Yes, *that* Iona Sandstrand! Danish fashion model and of course actor John Paul's most recent *ex.* Her long, tanned, over-insured legs are wrapped around Mr Nightly as they both recline in a large James St James gilt divan. In the background the art dealer John Kasmin has hung a painting of a solar eclipse and in the foreground the textile designer Celia Birtwell has arranged some cheesecloth-thin floral patterns to give this most traditional antiquarian bookstore an up-to-the-minute Moroccan look.

In the five-page centrespread these two *beautiful people*, seemingly unaware and therefore unaffected by their own extreme physical beauty, look each other up and down; they fool around and then feign disinterest in one another in John Christian's beautifully luminous photographs. In one picture, Iona is caught staring at John as if he's the most beautiful man she has ever set eyes on.

The most beautiful man alive. And that's because he is!

It's this same picture I'm looking at right now, reproduced on the cover of *Fashion USA*, April '66. *Fashion USA* is the American fashion industry bible. Reporting on and in some cases setting trends in youth and fashion across the United States. '*Fashion USA* comes to Swinging London' is the title of the feature. This is the photograph that John Farjeon, picture editor at *Fashion USA*, New York, has chosen to best illustrate the hope, the will, the desire to make progress, the ambition and the absolute optimism that has seized the country: England, Britain… London, Europe. A kingdom not hampered by Vietnam protests or race riots or presidential assassinations. This England. Our England. Our pendulum. England Swings – or they say it does. For the moment anyway. And now, everyone wants to swing along with it. With no thought for Air Traffic Control, it seems that the whole world is on its way to our very own tick-tocking capital.

Weekend World, 15 April 1966: 'London - The Swingers'
'London swings and you're hooked!'
Cover story by Sandro Timpani

Tomorrow magazine. 1 May 1966: 'London - a Swinging Scene'
'Okay, everyone, just get on a plane and go to London, do it right now!'
Special report by Marvin Sandberg

US News Today, June 1966: 'London - the City Swings'
'And so these are the Swinging Londoners, with their mix of Edwardian, Victorian and Regency outfits. They should look ridiculous but of course, being British, they don't. They look "fab", "groovy", "swinging"… '
A London diary by Sandy Weitzman

John JCE had done good. Just one phone call to an ex-girlfriend was all it had taken to secure this five-page spread in the fabbest magazine going. When John Nightly walked into Diana Waterbottom's office at the bottom of Wardour Street it took her approximately 2.5 seconds to figure out that standing right there before her this gawky, fidgety, clumsy, uncomfortable-looking, fresh-complexioned, moderate, self-deprecating, nervy boy; this potential employee – *Risk Factor 9* – with his straw hair and staring eyes and skeletal bone structure and very fine, very exaggerated, very old-fashioned manners, was going to be… the *Face of the Year.*

But John Nightly doesn't look like that anymore.

As John stands before me now, he is a very tired-looking sixty-year-old. A weary old fellow. A wobbly-necked, crusty-skinned, broken-lipped, wispy-haired, grey… old… git. John Nightly doesn't look sixty. He looks ninety. He looks like he hasn't seen an orange or a vitamin pill, a ray of sunshine or even a breath of fresh air for at least fifty summers. Though he has of course. John Nightly's poor old worn-out wreck of a body is the receptacle of the very best and most life-enhancing organic natural produce that record royalties can buy.

Heavy crates of the juiciest Tangier oranges, lemons and limes from Sicily and Sardinia, boxes of lush watercress and wheatgerm along with jars of vitamins and minerals and all manner of ludicrously expensive nutrients and supplements are delivered to Trewin Farm every month as part of a carefully controlled waste of money prescribed by John RCN. John Nightly walks five miles a day around the perimeter of his coastal plot – usually with his dog Alexandre. The old boy starts out and just keeps going. Round and round they go until somehow he knows when he's completed the course. And sometimes, nowadays with John RCN by his side, he'll venture out along the coast path itself, until – soaked in rain, mist and drizzle, and wary of their susceptibility to such as bronchitis and pneumonia – the pair of them decide to venture back.

But well, the beautiful face is gone. And as there has been no communication, no daily chats, no talking about the weather or pollution or how things are getting really bad in this country again, there is no longer any life in the face. No laughs, no agreement or disagreement, because there has been no one to agree or disagree with. No one to ask about anything and certainly no answers coming back. No one and no thing to get ready for. Nobody to either impress or account to.

All that shows in John Nightly's face is strain. Pure strain. The strain of life. Of existing. Of… being him. The strain of promise unfulfilled, of ability unrecognised, potential unrealised.

And, as the recipient of a truly divine gift, there is the immense underlying strain of not being able to do anything more with it. And of course the strain of not being in the same position, at the same elevated and revered level as his peers and rivals. His fellow travellers. Those who seem to spend their time bathed in eternal light. The strain of not being Michael Philip Jagger or Reginald Kenneth Dwight.

Over the years so many people had tried to contact John. To 'bring him back'. Even Iona. The ingénue who once arranged her long tanned legs around his in *GIRL*. And who, after their over-extended, sexually-dependent love affair had attempted suicide herself, and had been rescued and brought back to life by John, his fast-thinking actions saving her. Iona, now Lady St John Firmin, had visited John Nightly many times at Porthcreek. But she'd never seen him. Except one Friday morning, when he left the house to turn on the massive, electricity-guzzling winter heaters in the largest sunlounge, the one closest to the main road and therefore just about visible from the wire fence. But then, as she shouted out…

'John, it's… it's Iona… *Darling… … … …*'

All she'd gotten back was…

'No…'

Before John disappeared through a sliding glass door with his greenfly sprays, lime measurers and misters.

Even Eric, Eric Clapton − *God* − had come to Porthcreek, unannounced, probably at Iona's request, in the summer of

'85; and, because of who he was, John RCN (Royal College of Nursing) had let Eric in and sat him down. God sat in the old farmhouse kitchen with John and John and a cup of PG Tips and a biscuit and told the old git how much he missed his music and how much he admired him and the fact that he was now 'back'.

Eric said he wanted to take John Nightly into the studio to record a new album, believing that this would be the one thing that would really 'bring him back'. John listened patiently and even blinked his eyes and appeared to tap his foot when Eric said that Pete Townshend wanted to come and play on the sessions; but, after Eric had left, the old boy just turned to his nurse and said, 'what did he want?'

So many people had, over the years, in so many different ways, tried to bring John Nightly back. For very different reasons. Some wanted to bring him back so that they could sell his precious catalogue just one more time and use one of John's songs on a TV commercial for Orange or Apple, Motorola or Toyota. One of the 'good' ads. Others wanted to bring him back so they could hear all of the music he'd written in the intervening years. Would it be as weird and wonderful as his old albums? Would it have absorbed anything from the multitude of genres and subgenres that had come and gone since? A bit of New Age here, a bit of Techno there, subtle elements of Ambient, Rave, Grunge or Electronica. Would Hip-Hop loops and Nu-Folk musings be flavouring the mix? Or would it just be a '60s throwback?

Others wanted to bring him back so they could stare at him. At some highly touted VIP gig with full orchestra at the Royal Festival Hall or somewhere. *Invited audience only.* Barclaycard-sponsored, MTV-transmitted, digitally 'improved'. Somewhere they could get up close, have a good stare, and see just how bad he really looked.

John was afraid of all of them. John was more interested in

making the short journey from his bungalow outhouse to his washing line than he was in walking onstage again. That was a much more fulfilling journey for him. Although John did have all of the necessary equipment at his disposal, should he ever feel inclined to use it.

When he first moved to Porthcreek, Jo-Ann Locke, his most recent short-term *ex* now married to million-selling record producer Rik Locke, had had Rik come in with his people and install the latest easy-peasy-to-use, makes-everything-sound-great recording gear. Rik set it up all ready to go.

'There you are, John… It's all wired in and ready to go, man… You've got your screen and your monitors here… And your console and all your other bits and pieces over there'. The mixmeister of the West Coast power ballad stretched out his hands at least as wide as Malibu Beach. 'All you gotta do is turn it on…'

And when Eric came he brought John a present of the Martin D-45 acoustic John had always coveted, the one he'd borrowed from God to record 'Peachfruit Love Parchment #1', everyone's favourite song from the *Ape Box Metal* set. The seventh-biggest-selling record in North America in 1970, after *Abbey Road* and *Bridge Over Troubled Water.* John said it was the most beautiful-sounding guitar he'd ever held.

'It's yours, John.'

Eric opened the case and played an E major – 'Hey, look! It works!' -type chord – before almost forcing it into the hands of his old rival. 'Anyway… y'know… Get it out and play it – for God's sake…' Eric had said – 'It'll make you feel better…' – holding out the guitar for John for a second or two more before giving in and carefully placing it back in its purple, velvet-lined case.

'I'll phone ya…'

But the custom-built case would never be opened again. And Eric couldn't phone as John didn't have one. We weren't in *Year 9* yet and BT hadn't been.

'Easier said than done
Write your number on my doorstep
To take one more step
It's easier said than done'

Unfinished demo, 'Easier Said than Done', from
***Grantchester Love Chronicle*, summer 1965**

No one had any idea when John Nightly had last laughed. In a
normal way, that is. John RCN remembered reading his employer
his bank statement, all of the ins and outs, one evening sometime
around summer 1987 after Star Castle had covered 'Peachfruit
Love Parchment' on their *We Are Rock & Roll* multi-platinum
monster. The recording had delivered a total of $3,400,084 into
the account as the result of first-year sales, airplay and mechanical
royalties. This at least brought a faint smile to the face of the
legendary songwriter. But two weeks later, when Star Castle's
record label in Los Angeles sent John a gold disc in a frame and
RCN took it out and played it to him, John laughed.

He laughed and laughed. He rocked with laughter to the inner
depths of his despair. John Nightly never imagined that anyone
would ever be crass enough to turn his wistful teenage madrigal
into a bombastic rock'n'roll ballbreaker. Ever since then, if John
was away from his plants, which was rare, or was just very far gone
into his own inner gloom, RCN would get the record out and use
Star Castle's epic monstrosity to 'bring him back'. It always worked.

item: *'Dorotheanthus bellidiformis'*, Reader's Digest *Illustrated Encyclopaedia of
Garden Plants and Flowers, 1973.*
M. criniflorum, South Africa. Height 6 inches, planting distance 12 inches. A genus of
1,000 species of succulent plants. The colourful daisy-like flowers open only in bright
sunshine. Although usually grown as a half-hardy annual, this plant is quite hardy. It has
a low-spreading habit, with narrow, almost cylindrical, light-green leaves which have a
glistening, sugary appearance. Given adequate sunshine it carries a mass of brightly
coloured and zoned flowers, one inch across, from June to August. A wide colour range:
white, crimson to pink, and orange-gold to buff. Cultivation: these plants require a position
in full sun and thrive on light sandy soils. Propagation: sow the seeds under glass in
March at a temperature of 15°C (59°F). Prick out the seedlings into boxes and harden off
before planting out in May. Alternatively, sow directly in the flowering site in April, thinning
out the seedlings to the required distance.

Trinity College, Cambridge. Friday, 1 February 1782.
John Pond walked out of his rooms at Trinity College, gathered up his tailcoat, adjusted his bicorn hat to shield his eyes from the noonday sun and made his progress along Trinity Street towards King's Parade. His destination was the new observation platform constructed by John Carr of York, which he had been allowed to build on the vaulted roof of the stables behind the nearby Senate House. Walking through King's Arch and the huge Welsh-oak gate, the astronomer was greeted by Dr John Hilton, Keeper of the Keys of the Cambridge Astronomical Society, who, using a flickering lantern to light the way, led him up to the fourth landing and out onto the open deck, where he would spend the next eighteen hours writing in his journal and observing the trajectories of three fixed stars: Castor, Spica and Aldebaran.

Grantchester, Cambridge. Friday, 1 February 1966.
John was back in Meadow Road for the weekend. Back with his mother – the mercurial Frieda, a former university lab technician from Oslo who'd arrived in Cambridge as a war worker after the German occupation of her country – and his father – the impossibly tolerant John Snr, who put up with the volatile, fast-changing moods of his beautiful wife simply because she was so very beautiful and the intense near-autism of their only child, the first boy to be born in Meadow Road for more than a hundred years, because he was obviously so very gifted. Prodigiously gifted but uneasy with the world outside – because of his mother's overbearing love, the overprotection of her most treasured possession and their unnaturally close, almost telepathic relationship.

In the Nightly household it was always 'Frieda and John', 'John and Frieda', 'Frieda, John… and John' – meaning, generally, Frieda and the boy. The wife's relationship with John the father coming second to Frieda's altogether more spontaneous and somehow more absolute partnership with John the son.

Friday night, and the teenager had caught the bus up to Trumpington to pick up Jana, the 'love of his life' already immortalised by the fledgling songwriter in a handful of songs, particularly the little folk-song suite *Grantchester Love Chronicle**, most of which had been composed the previous summer.

John and Jana were off to see Wardour Street regulars, the Pretty Things, one of Jana's favourite groups, at the Dorothy Ballroom – the Dot – in Hobson Street in the centre of town. Jana couldn't wait to hear all about John's adventures in London. A three-day whirlwind during which he'd managed to get himself a manager and a major recording contract, sign a publishing agreement for all of the songs he would write over the next 25 years, and even appear as a male model in a five-page spread in *GIRL* – a publication that leaped off the shelves within minutes of its appearance on the university bookstands of King's Parade.

'But why are you letting her sit on your lap?' Jana asked, as John remained silent and a stray, unannounced tear fell onto the two Polaroids John JCE had given the boy as souvenirs.

'And the way she's looking at you in this one. She's got her hand on your knee... and you... you don't exactly look unhappy about it!'

'Don't be silly, Jan... that's just what happens', her boyfriend replied, 'or just... whatever happened on the day, that's all. It's not planned or anything. The photographer tells you where to sit, and positions you so you fit in with the overall picture. It's all... "Turn your head this way" or "Twist yourself that"... "Walk up and down on the ceiling". It's not serious or anything.'

The boy, seeking to allay the fears of his sweetheart, may have overdone it slightly. 'He shoots a couple. You take a look, he moves you around a bit and shoots a few more.' John threw his

*Though the complete set of (six ?) songs remains unreleased, one piece, 'Steeple Gate', the original demo recorded in Cambridge, late '65, turned up unlicensed on the bootleg *'All the Madmen, Vol. 4* (Tout EM341), which began to circulate among collectors and fans in the late '80s.

scarf across his shoulder and put on a dumb face. 'That's all it is,' he shrugged. 'All there is to it. No one takes it at all seriously.' He indicated they move on.

'He shoots a couple! Well, there we are then!' Jana's voice became unsteady as she thrust the photographs back into her boyfriend's hand. 'Suddenly you're all world-weary and nonchalant, John. You're a man of the world now...' The girl turned away and searched her purse for change for the bus.

'Jan... c'mon', the boy replied. 'The only reason they wanted me to do it in the first place is it gets publicity... which helps them get me a bigger contract so I can make an LP instead of just a single. *And* I got paid for it; four hundred pounds! You know how handy that comes in...' John plunged his hands deep into his pockets, not feeling it necessary to explain or justify himself any further. 'Doesn't mean anything at all... apart from that.'

But the convent girl was unconvinced. 'I don't like it, though, John. Don't you see? It doesn't make me feel right.' The injured party rubbed her eye with the back of her cuff, pretending not to brush away another unwelcome tear.

'No... well... Mother didn't like it either.'

The boy, having no experience whatsoever in dealing with the feelings of others, spoke abruptly as he pulled up his collar. A familiar back wind howled its way along the High Street.

'I shouldn't think she did', the girl sniffed. 'But John... these things are stupid. You know they are. These... *magazine* things are superficial things. You haven't even got started yet.' Jana reached for her handkerchief. 'You haven't even got your record out. So I'm... amazed that you let yourself be used like this.' Jana dried her eyes. 'You're an *artist*, John, a real artist. Sometimes I don't think you realise what you've actually got – your gift. You need to be serious about what you're doing. Not... *lolling* about in girls' magazines.'

'I'm certainly not "lolling about" – thanks very much.' The boy didn't deserve that. He rubbed hard on his forehead and wiped his hand backwards and forwards across his mouth, showing his frustration. 'I'm working… And anyway, surely I don't need to be serious all the time?' John tied his scarf tight around his neck, making a reasonable job of feigning injury. 'Surely once or twice, every now and then, once or twice a year maybe, if I'm lucky… I can have a little break from being *serious?*'

The boy walked out into the road and stared back at his girl-friend stranded on the pavement. 'I don't think… Stravinsky was serious all the time. Or… Schoenberg, was he? Not from what we know about them, I don't think. I don't get the impression that those people were always very "serious" – not about everything they did. In everyday life, surely not. Not from books, or from just… looking at them; their faces… their atmospheres. Not even from the things they created.'

John made his point as he balanced nervously on the edge of the kerb, bouncing up and down on his newly whitewashed plimsolls.

'I don't know about those people, John. To be honest, I don't give a damn what they get up to. But I do know that the people – composers – we both like; those people are… or were, very serious people. You know they were. You have to take yourself and your work – the things you create, as you say – completely seriously.'

Jana had pulled herself together and was now totally composed, able to present a clear case. 'Because you have this special gift – you know you do – a "knack" for music.' She stared at the defendant. 'I know that seems easy for you. Too easy probably. You probably don't even get it yourself. When people find out what a talent you have – and they will find out – they'll be envious. Envious… and jealous. And that envy might not be good for you. It might be bad… turn bad… might not do you a lot of good.' Jana looked up and down the road in both directions, hoping for a bus or at least for the wind and drizzle to abate for a moment. 'You even look happy in the pictures. Unusually happy, for you.'

The girl, by now frozen cold, though covered from head to toe in scarves and shawls aping the bohemian style of her mother, suggested they walk into town, forgetting the absent bus. She felt as if she'd said her piece. The boy looked exasperated.

'I'm sorry about that as well, but it… It was a nice day… that day… A great day. It's just that so many things happened in those few days.'

'So I gather…'

John continued. 'All the people I met were nice to me and they liked me. They didn't think I was… "weird" or anything. And they didn't look at me… suspiciously. Like they do in Cambridge.'

'You mean they liked you *because* you were weird? Or… because they just liked you?'

'I think they just really… It's not weird in London to be weird anyway. Even if I *was* weird, which I'm not saying I am, of course.' John raised his eyebrows and gave a little false laugh in an attempt to bring some lightness into the situation. 'There's nothing "weird" about me.'

'No, John.'

'What I mean is… I wouldn't be weird in London.' Again, he overdid it. 'That's what I like about it. Up there, they think I can do something… and leave it at that… Rather than thinking I'm a bit… *odd* because of it.'

Jana sighed. 'Well, they're right there, John. You are surely the cleverest person I have ever met – who I will ever meet.' She wrapped her headscarf tightly around her ears and, resigned to being unable to do anything more about it, took the arm of her beau as they hurried along. 'I know you are...'

'Fame and money are the temptations that gnaw my vitals without my being wholly aware of it'

Igor Stravinsky in a letter written from Ustilug, Ukraine, to his friend Maurice Delage, 14 October 1912

Monday morning John was booked into KCEMS (King's College Electronic Music Studios), a small, local facility housed in former artists' studios at number 34 Free School Lane. The control room of KCEMS boasted a Studer 4-track, Neve console, a GPO patchbay plugged up with red and green mini-jacks, an Ampex half-inch, a Revox and a pair of door-size Tannoy monitors. Next door, a handful of abandoned instruments lay scattered about the damp, soundproofed basement. A set of vibes, glockenspiels and chime bars, a single timpani drum and two over-strung pianos decorated the dead-as-a-doornail ex-storage unit. School-room instruments, probably left there by local rehearsal orchestras. An old Steck, newly converted to the status of tack piano by the addition of drawing pins in its hammers, lived in the hallway outside, while on the other side of a cracked glass partition stood a good Steinway upright, kindly donated by the Britten school – Benjamin Britten lived close by at Aldeburgh in Suffolk.

At the back of the premises was a further division, along a narrow, dusty corridor, where strips of sheet-metal, old wound piano strings, glass rods, wind chimes and lengths of clattery cheese wire hung suspended from the ceiling. This 5' x 2' cubby-hole, resembling a cartoon torture chamber more than anything else, was referred to as the *sound-effects suite* in the KCEMS brochure. The photographs showed the studio as it had been in the 1950s, complete with the old lever console, tongue-and-groove wall panelling and Festival of Britain carpet. In the far corner stood a Victorian school desk with an editing block, a wooden metronome, a set of Pyetone reference speakers, a Grundig 2-track and, best of all, a double-manual Hammond organ.

One of the signature sounds of jazz, as popularised by the likes of Jimmy Smith and Milt Buckner, the Hammond C3 and B3 models, used in an entirely different way than by their jazz exponents, often supply the magical 'coming and going' sound – *phasing* – on many classic pop recordings. A great asset in any studio set-up, the Hammond, along with timpani, vibraphone, glockenspiel and celeste, is often subliminally mixed in among the usual two guitars, bass and drums; adding scale and depth to even the most basic-sounding recordings. This nursery clutter provides the starlight, the flickering night sky of the soundworlds created by both Brian Wilson and his mentor Phil Spector.

KCEMS had been home to John Nightly on and off for the past six months or so, affording him a cheap, well-equipped facility in which to try out ideas and also discover how to use many of the techniques that would become commonplace in professional recording studios from the mid '60s onwards. At exam time particularly, the studio was often empty for long periods, being mainly used by the Cambridge Experimental Film Co-Op (CEFCO) – undergraduates from King's, John's and Trinity – to dub sound and record Foley work and sound effects on the many student films that were being made in the town at the time.

Today John was to be found in his usual position, hunched over the desk in the small back room with his best friend, guitarist and fellow stargazer Justin 'Just' Makepeace at his side – and at his beckoning. Having finished his course in electronic music at the end of December, John had made an arrangement with the bursar to carry on using the studio in any downtime. He'd also recently completed his correspondence course with Professor John Diamond at the Cornish School in Seattle, Washington, where he'd taken part in a 'mail art' musical chain letter initiated by John Cage. Because of his association with Cambridge University Music Society (CUMS), the enthusiastic teenager had corresponded with Cage a number of times and had even met up with the great man himself when the composer had stopped over in Cambridge on his way to the Aldeburgh Festival the previous summer, August 1965. Cage had encouraged the student in his experiments with random and 'chance' music and other non-formal structures. Ideas almost forced on John Nightly by the limitations of working in his father's garage on their own Grundig 2-track.

The problem being that on John Snr's simple domestic set-up there was no way to overdub – create 'sound-on-sound' – using the primitive stereo machine. John's solution had been to suspend a wafer-thin sheet of foil from his father's pack of Woodbines over the erasehead as the tape passed through. Thus blocking the previously recorded tracks from automatically being wiped as the new take was recorded, thereby converting the machine into a multitrack of sorts simply by never actually erasing anything.

The downside of this simple 'update' was that it was impossible to monitor and therefore play along with what had just been recorded. John would have to add each new part completely in the dark, humming to himself what he imagined was playing in the background while he performed or overdubbed the next layer. Hence the necessarily loose or 'chance' timing and the lack of any verse/chorus-based songwriting. By the time he reached even the first refrain or hook he'd almost definitely be out of sync with the other tracks. The only music it was possible to record in this situation was something that might charitably be called a 'sound collage'; in reality, a frustrating mess of ideas and parts.

John had managed to achieve some semblance of regular tempo by setting his metronome off at exactly the same point each time; the point at which he saw a chinagraph pencil mark pass through the record head just before the music began. But then the metronome itself was unstable, the metal rod having been bent through being thrown across the living room by Frieda during a particularly violent outburst at no one in particular.

At home, a constant beat would hold together for roughly fifteen seconds or so if you were lucky, so finding a base like KCEMS was like finding Lake Windermere in a desert. As John hummed along with himself and adjusted the EQ on the board it occurred to Justin that, although his friend was barely eighteen years old, John had been recording ever since they had known each other, a total of thirteen years. For John Nightly, composing music on tape was as natural as writing a postcard.

Sitting at the 4-track in the main room, chinagraph in hand, Justin began to build up a basic tempo by setting the pendulum to a regular 72 beats per minute. John tapped it out with his foot and played a kind of slow, irregular rhythm on the back of his acoustic guitar. After they'd recorded almost 60 seconds worth of the idea, the two of them listened back carefully, agreeing that the best section was from 41 to 49 seconds in. Justin marked the beginning and end of this 8-second space with the white crayon before John took the quarter-inch tape off the head, laid it on the edit block, making sure there was enough slack at both ends so it wouldn't crease, and made two diagonal cuts, one at each end, separating this 'good bit' from the rest. He then went next door, laid the extracted piece of tape on a second block and edited the section into a length of white 'leader', putting the gash onto the Revox so that he could transfer the chosen good bit via a tie line, before copying it back onto the Grundig ad infinitum. The boy would then painstakingly edit all of these identical extracts together.

Two hours later John had spliced enough of the repeated sections to cover three minutes' worth of music; a continuous looped beat. He then walked into the corridor, placed the newly compiled tape back on the Studer and checked it through, concentrating hard to make sure that all of the cross points were smooth and seamless. This little repeated collage was to be the backing track of a new song he'd been working on, 'Peachfruit Love Parchment #1.'

As the hypnotic, shifting rhythm played back through the tapeheads and Justin checked levels on the meters, John Nightly relaxed into his chair and began a winding arpeggiated figure on his Eko acoustic. The music immediately changed character and sounded exotic and mysterious; the new part being recorded by his friend on the second track of the four.

It was a time-consuming process that involved the making of

'reduction' tracks – sub-mixes – as you went along, before bouncing all of the separate elements into a single composite on the second machine. The process involving four interlocking parts being mixed down to one. The balance of the newly bounced track would then be checked, before erasing the original four on the other machine, giving four clean 'grids' on which to overdub and start all over again.

Simple really. But because there was only John involved creatively – the only way he would have it – the boy was having to do everything himself, both the compositional and practical work, with Justin lending an objective ear and helping out when more than two hands were needed. For John, this made the recording of music an all-encompassing and life-enhancing though sometimes repetitive process. It removed him to another world, a world away from the domestic dramas of Meadow Road and the drudgery of school. The recording studio transported John Nightly to a place where he was aware of neither time nor tide. A world of mechanical invention, 'make-do' technology. Experimenting and having fun with sped-up guitars and backwards pianos, overloading the audio signal with oceanic reverb or an infinity of repeated echoes. Making use of the strange-looking processing boxes designed for him by his father, filling wine glasses with different amounts of water to make a 'glass xylophone', singing through megaphones made out of toilet-roll tubes and tin cans. Investigating the particular dynamic of each instrument within its natural range or, even better, just outside of it. The pair of them viewed all of it as experimentation, as well as great fun. With little recording activity going on in the town John and Justin remained completely isolated, having no one with whom to compare notes or take their lead from. They must have sensed that what they were doing might be somehow new – 'groundbreaking', even, had that term been in common use at the time. They understood that it was at least 'different', but that it was still a process – a procedure. As it turned out, the very same procedure, albeit with slightly more facility, that the Beatles themselves were currently using in St John's Wood, sixty miles down the A10, at EMI's Abbey Road

Studios, to record their as-yet-untitled new LP*. But John Nightly didn't yet know that.

Back in the main room, John recorded some low-pitched guitar followed by a sequence of glockenspiel chords onto tracks one and two of the Studer. After that, he added two or three higher-voiced notes, modal and open-sounding, on the vibes. John loved the college's Musser vibraphone. It was an incredibly warm, dreamy sound that always inspired him. The instrument can often sound dark and gloomy; its expressive tremolando is used in films to denote moments of tension or impending doom. But John registered its vibrato as soft and soothing. A rich timbre that could be light and romantic but also ethereal and hypnotic. He'd been fascinated by the vibraphone since hearing the Modern Jazz Quartet's recording of Ornette Coleman's 'Lonely Woman' (Atlantic 8122-75361-2) again at Jana's. A synthesis of classical form and jazz attitude, the piece could almost have been composed by Poulenc or Hindemith.

As Justin added the spring reverb from the Hammond, 'Peachfruit' hit its fade section; a slowly reducing pattern with three beautiful though apparently unrelated chords building through each compositional block to an unresolved cadence. It wasn't really a song – not yet anyway. It was more of a... mood or 'feel', as John declared, sitting in front of the Neve making a mess with his jam doughnut while his friend attempted to achieve a rough balance with the faders.

The boy pressed *STOP* abruptly, leaning over to re-align the tape on the playback head in order to eliminate the 'cross talk' he could hear bleeding through from the other tracks. He hit *PLAY*, keeping his finger on the top edge of the reel to steady it as it picked up speed. Because the new composition was made up of twenty-four 8-second edits, a recurring 'pitch hit' happened at each edit point, acting like a percussive wood block

---

* Revolver (Parlophone PMC 7009) originally *Abracadabra*

note every time it came round. The pitch suggested two chords. Unluckily, these were E major and B-flat major, harmonically just about as bad as it gets and therefore for John all the more exciting. As Justin added compression to the guitar the music suddenly seemed to just 'sit' and come to life right in front of them.

John, excited about his new creation, began to improvise word ideas on top, asking his friend to stop the tape for a moment while he quickly made some notes on the back of the track sheet. *Flo-wer bond, flo-wer bond, Ba-sil-don Bond, flori-bund.* He repeated syllable by syllable, over and over, like a mantra.

The boy picked up his leather bag and pulled out a loose-leaf file. A few ruled pages fell to the floor. Typed words, evenly spaced, hopefully evocative of something, he wasn't sure quite what exactly, were arranged in columns down the page. John took a pair of scissors and cut them into small, single-word squares. He then asked Just to clear a space while he climbed onto a chair, held the word snow above his head and let it fall to the ground. As his friend rescued one piece of paper from his hair John stared down at the first word to catch his attention, it being closest to him and also face-up.

'*Smile*' he announced, attaching an almost mystical importance to the completely random syllable. Justin remained silent, giving John space to think, well aware that John Nightly himself was the only one able to make selections or decisions about anything regarding his own music. John moved towards the door and turned his head to a single scrap resting on a potted plant.

'*Prayer*' he whispered. Again, bestowing upon the word a meaning beyond the present, as if discovering the next important find in an archaeological dig. The third piece of paper had floated away from the others and landed on a painted wooden chair, as if it insisted on being treated differently from the rest.

'*Wish…*' John looked up at Justin. '*Smile, Prayer, Wish!*' He raised his eyebrows to the skies and his face lit up as if to say 'You see!' while his friend looked on reassuringly. John repeated the three single-syllable words several times over. *Smile… Prayer… Wish. Smile… Prayer… Wish… Wave… Orange… Love.* He mumbled to himself as he hummed a vague rhythm while his partner looked on, awaiting instructions from the boss.

In a situation such as this the boy was really concentrated. A different proposition altogether while he was actually 'doing' his thing. John always spoke about music as taking place in suspended time, as if there were no *actual* time moving along throughout the day. In an interview published much later he summed it up by saying that this was when he felt 'suspended on the vertical while the rest of the world was on the horizontal'. He described the making of music as a time when he needed neither food nor water, nor any kind of 'outside energy' to nourish and sustain him. No conversation, and no normal human contact. At KCEMS John could be lost in this state for days, or weeks… if the college authorities would allow it.

When Justin suggested a break, the two of them would repair to the Civic or the Whim for egg on toast and stewed tea, but on other occasions they'd remain in their dingy cell for twelve or fourteen hours on end, lost in their own little world, working up their sonic collages – or, as John would refer to them, 'curtains of sound' – using a layering process that George Martin would later call 'painting in sound.'

And so it was that in this tiny, padded room the basic ideas for the boy's debut, *Principal Fixed Stars*, would first take shape. Much later on it was widely acknowledged that *PFS* heralded the beginning of the whole 'symphonic rock' (for want of a much better term) phenomenon. The LP would go on to shift a total of nine million units in America alone, keeping John Nightly in ludicrously expensive hothouse installations for the rest of his life. Right now, the landmark recording amounted to little more than a sketch, a cardboard box full of tape reels, chord charts and paper cutouts based on the writings and the tidal correspondence – tidal-letters – of a *Boy's Own* hero of John Nightly's, the 18th-century Astronomer Royal, John Pond.

Despite being proficient on a number of instruments as well as being able to compose quite complex pieces at will with the benefit of a note-perfect 'sound memory', much the same as people have a photographic memory, John Nightly would never be able to actually read or write music – though from the work he created, 'proper', formal-sounding compositions, it would always be assumed that he could.

With his father to guide him, the young schoolboy had studied the orchestral score to Gustav Holst's *The Planets* at home late into the evening when he should have been concentrating on his history and geography homework. While Frieda waited closeby with her jigsaw puzzle, tut-tutting and questioning her husband about these unnecessary, time-consuming tuitions, John Snr would patiently go through each movement, each planet, one at a time, lining up the LP – the first recorded version, by Sir Adrian Boult – so that the two Nightlys could physically hear the dots they were staring at. The thunderous majesty of 'Mars' – John identified its sequential build as the ascending chords to 'Tonight' from *West Side Story* [1] – or the delicate floating woodwinds of 'Mercury' and 'Venus' would fill the room, entrancing and at times almost swallowing its inhabitants.

The young student would ask his father how these magical sounds were produced, so John Snr would pick out the inner harmonic parts – glockenspiel, flute and oboe – on the piano for him; in turn John, after seeing where his father's hands lay on the keyboard, would then slowly play back each solo line. But the boy never did learn to read or compose on paper himself.

The sheer beauty of Holst's masterwork, that of a Hammersmith schoolmaster, written at weekends in the composer's spare time away from the constant round of teaching, a piece more concerned with spirituality and theosophy rather than the assumed astronomy, affected the teenager deeply on both a musical and a philosophical level, having an almost overbearing influence on his own early work, which he jokingly described as being 'Stravinsky-ish, Tchaikovsky-esque… Holst-like!' Each time he played a figure on the chime-bars or a tremolando on the vibes, he'd announce to Justin, 'It's like in *The Planets*, the beginning of "Venus", the bit before the big chords… *Look! It's that sound!"*

Holst's grand suite was also influential in terms of format. Instead of following the usual theme and variation structure, *The Planets* were presented by their composer as 'globules' of music, with no repeat of thematic material from 'Mars' to 'Neptune'. The piece consisted of seven self-contained spheres of sound, the first real *space* music; an immense achievement for a part-time composer-teacher. It became one of John's ambitions to someday attempt a project of this magnitude. Even when he was working at KCEMS he fantasised about such a creation, a fully symphonic work – a real *Opus*. The inside covers of his schoolbooks contained endless lists of possible titles. He imagined the orchestra being conducted by Holst's daughter Imogen, who at that time still lived and taught with Britten at Aldeburgh. And as his father always explained to his young son, 'You don't need to write a lot of music, John… you just need that one really big thing. That one great thing. The thing you'll be remembered for. If you're lucky, it'll be a proper masterpiece… something that beats all of the competition, even Bach and Beethoven… Like 'Stranger in Paradise'[2], 'White Christmas'[3]… or *The Planets*[4]. Just that one big one, John. That's all.' What a pity the boy didn't listen to him.

[1] The melodic ascent also forms the basis of Andy Williams' Almost There (Keller/Shayne) (CBS 201803).

[2] Adapted from Alexander Borodin's opera *Prince Igor,* 'Stranger in Paradise' - a Number 1 hit in the UK for Tony Bennett, and John Nightly Snr's favourite song, was remade by song-writers Robert Wright and George Forrest. The opera, incomplete and unperformed after 28 years' work during the life of the composer, was assembled and completed following Borodin's sudden death by Rimsky-Korsakov and Borodin's flatmate Alexander Glazunov,

who knew the work intimately having heard his friend play it so often on the piano. The central aria, 'The Gliding Dance of the Maidens' from the *Polovtsian Dances,* became the evergreen hit 'Stranger in Paradise' (from the musical *Kismet).*

A solar eclipse features as a motif in *Prince Igor.* At the opening ceremony of the Winter Olympics in Sochi, Russia, February 2014, music from the opera was played while an eclipsed sun, crescent-shaped, drifted across the upper levels of the centre of the stadium, illustrating the importance of Russian history in the *Prince Igor* story.

'The episodes of the solar eclipse, of the parting from Yaroslavna, divide it into halves which fringe the entire prologue' Nikolai Rimsky-Korsakov, *Chronicle of My Musical Life* (1909)

[3] Frieda's favourite song – written in California in the heat of the summer.

[4] The Planets' original title was *Seven Large Pieces for Orchestra.* Theosophy, pioneered by Helena Blavatsky and with roots in Eastern philosophy, was popular in the early 20th century, influencing Holst's operatic works *Sita* (1899) and *Savitri* (1916) as well as his *Choral Hymns from the Rig Veda* (1908).

Shall I tell you about my life?
They say I'm a man of the world

Peter Green (b. 1946)

1 – 2 – 3 – 4 !

In the Nightly household Frieda ruled the roost, though it was John's father who had nurtured what both of his parents recognised, in the phrase of Dr Jani Feather, the boy's music teacher, as an 'ungodly ability' for music. While John Snr thought it important that his son learn to read and write the dots, believing that he had it in him to become a professional musician of the first rank, Frieda rejected this out of hand, convinced that the act of committing music to paper via an academic study of harmony and counterpoint would interrupt and disturb the flow that would naturally come down to John from... 'wherever it came down from'. As far as John's mother was concerned there existed a kind of magic seal between inspiration and execution – the arrival of inspiration into the mind of the creator and the execution or 're-playing' of it by him. Her argument being that too much study and knowledge, particularly dot-writing, might destroy this pure gold due to valuable 'receiving time' being wasted in transcription.

Frieda pictured her son poring over an orchestral manuscript, weighed down by his own facility, cantankerous and choleric, shock-haired, literally tearing his hair out, in the image of the great composers, as he feverishly attempted to commit gold dust to paper, as she imagined Mozart and Beethoven had done, while at the same time the actual logging of material blocked the channels of creation as a stream of top-quality content tried to force its way through. Her oft-quoted example was Irving Berlin, the writer of all of her favourite songs, from 'White Christmas' to 'Cheek to Cheek'. Berlin, untutored and untrained, but talented and tortured in equal amounts, both composer and lyricist, was a songwriter without peer as well as a canny operator and publisher of his own priceless catalogue. Lauded by even Gershwin and Cole Porter as 'the best', he never did learn to read a note. When John Snr pointed out that the reading and writing of music was crucial for their son so that he could at least remember what he had come up with and therefore be able to play it back, Frieda would just reply: 'But you can record it on one of your machines. At last there's a good reason for them to be sitting in the garage all this time, and his music can stay in his head.'

And, though John's father argued that understanding the transpositions, ranges and timbres, along with the individual characteristics of each instrument – in other words, a study of basic orchestration – would be of immense benefit to their son, Frieda would not hear of it, insisting that things must be kept 'pure' at all costs, and that (because she believed the boy could easily achieve anything he aspired to anyway) there was really no need for any kind of study or analysis of the subject whatsoever.

In the summer of 1952, the new Nightly family spent their holidays with Frieda's brothers, Sindre and Steinar, at their home in Trondheim on the west coast of Norway. Here, for the very first time, the painfully shy four-year-old set eyes on an inspirational arrangement of black and white; a repeated pattern of interlocking ebony and ivory ranged across a stained teak box. An early translation machine, capable of converting and transforming spirit into physical reality, the piano was an object that was to transform John Nightly's life.

When Sindre, sitting sideways on to the Bechstein upright, performed a rousing chorus of a Norwegian Christmas song while at the same time managing to have an argument with Frieda and also eat his Christmas dinner, the small child, fascinated by what he heard but also by the fact that his uncle, playing entirely by ear, seemed to be paying little attention to what his hands were actually doing, approached the keyboard and watched carefully for a moment in a kind of trance, before placing his right hand on the piano and literally copying, though very slowly at first, of course, the melody of the *julesang* emanating from Sindre's fingertips.

A few days earlier, at his grandmother Signhild's dinner table, John had been transfixed by the berry-red concertina that rested on her lap producing a happy little tune as the old lady eased the brown leather handles in and out. Seeing the child's amazement, Sindre had lifted up the boy and, holding the squeezebox in his own sausage-fingers, had given the boy a go. But the instrument was of course completely unfathomable and also much too heavy for him. John pressed the brass keys in anticipation, but nothing, except a couple of random splurts and squeaks, came out of the painted wooden box.

Next morning, John's grandmother sat patiently with him at the piano while he imitated the shapes her fingers made when they fell upon the keys as she played through what she imagined might be anything very easy for the child to master with just one finger. But by the end of the following afternoon he was somehow adding a corresponding bass note, the whole family becoming distracted by the astounding progress of the newly regarded musical genius. This two-week vacation was John Nightly's introduction to performing music himself instead of just listening and being entranced by it. On the morning the Nightlys were due to return to Cambridge, the boy walked up to the keyboard and began playing along, almost note-for-note, with the melody of the Grieg *Lyric Piece* that Sindre was listening to on the radiogram.

With the family back in Grantchester, John Nightly ceased all of the overactive behaviour with which he had terrorised both of his parents since he was born. All the tapping and beating on every available surface, the weird out-of-tune humming, the night-time whimpering due to the boy being terrified of the dark, and the low, morose drone he emitted whenever he was left alone, even for a second, without the company of either his mother, or Sandy, the filthy red mongrel John looked on as his partner in crime as they whimpered and moaned together from the safety of the cold, tiled floor beneath the kitchen table. Consequently, Frieda rarely left her son's side. With John stabbing constantly at the family's new second-hand upright, she would sit for hours gazing out of the garden window, particularly if it was a nice day, with her cup of tea and her magazine, a carton of her son's favourite Kia-Ora ready on the sideboard.

If it was a typical Cambridge rainy day John would sit glued to a radio broadcast from some far-off location – Hilversum or Antwerp, say. Or he might run around with his little tin watering can, putting much too much water on John Snr's potted cacti and chrysanthemums. Then, when Frieda got up to do the household chores, her son, like a little puppy dog, would cling on to his mother's skirts and coattails as he accompanied her on her tour of the house. If he was being particularly difficult she would snatch and tug at him, dragging him over the carpets and the shiny parquet floor, the pair of them laughing loudly at their own wild, unruly, most un-Nightly-ish behaviour.

Profile In Music, Yehudi Menuhin talking to John Freeman, BBC TV. Saturday, 1 March 1963.
That 'over-protection' too, erm, was mainly with the idea of preventing any, er… any, er, unnecessary, useless, intrusions into the life, which, er, would merely be… disturbing. There were various well-meaning friends who might want to… spend some time or tempt the children with sweets or games of one kind or another; and, after all, to achieve anything one has to be serious about it and give it a part of each day. You cannot build unless you build every day…

Two years later, when John was six, an interruption occurred in this intense, airtight relationship when Frieda suffered a miscarriage at home and had to be admitted to Addenbrooke's Hospital and kept in overnight. For the first time in his life John was without his mother for a whole day and night. Of course John Snr consoled his son and kept him occupied, but when it was decided that Frieda needed immediate treatment which necessitated her remaining in hospital for a further seven days, the boy soon became distraught. All the tapping and beating and whimpering returned, but much louder and weirder than before. John, now playing the piano for on average a total of four or five hours a day, was unable to understand where his mother had disappeared to, and he was not allowed to visit her. In an in-depth interview broadcast fifteen years later (*Six Composers*: BBC Third Programme, 3 June 1969), talking to the BBC's John Cherry, John Nightly, the by-now-established pop star-cum-avant-garde composer, described this week as 'one of the most traumatic of my life'.

When Frieda returned home from Addenbrooke's, she no longer seemed at all like the same person to her young son. What had happened to his fiery, short-tempered, beautiful young mother? And who was this dopey, dumb old aunt who had replaced her? The transformation had come about initially because of the effects of the pain-killing drugs administered to help ease the discomfort and the ensuing depression following the operation. As it turned out, the cause was Drinamyl – a compound of amphetamine and barbiturate, known also as *purple hearts* and used by prostitutes in the East End of London to help them stay awake. The tablets had initially made Frieda show such an improvement, controlling her moods so well, that her doctor had prescribed a second month's worth; but they had evened her out to such an extent that she literally wasn't herself anymore. Another month's prescription followed but, when Frieda asked for the medication to continue beyond that, Addenbrooke's pharmacy insisted that she take no more of the magic blue pills, it being apparent that an immediate addictive response had taken place. It was then that Frieda moved into a more or less continued dependence on tranquilisers and anti-depressants, then marketed as Valium and Librium, and thus set off on a course of prescription drugs to temper and balance her moods that would continue for the rest of her life, taking all of the life out of her while at the same time arguably making John the father's life much, much easier.

One thing that John Snr did manage to get past his wife was that their son, despite being unable to read or write music, should be encouraged to practise the piano every day – though it later became difficult to get John *off* the instrument following the sacrifice of the family bathroom, which was eventually soundproofed by John Snr using a combination of egg boxes and offcuts of carpets from Pye's soundproofed showrooms. Moving the big upright into the smallest room meant that the bath, the wash-basin and the lavatory had to be moved out, so John Snr had reconstructed the upstairs bathroom in the back-yard, on the plot where the garden shed had been. He had then cut a small connecting doorway through to the carless garage where he had his tape-machines and other audio equipment permanently installed. In essence, this was a very early 'recording-studio', with a separate booth made out of nailed-together flower boxes and pallets. Recording stopped when anyone needed to use the bathroom, but this small hideaway became somewhere John Nightly Snr could record his son's creations and even offer the possibility of overdubbing a countermelody or the odd bit of tambourine or tin whistle if required.

The result being that the already tiny back garden where John Snr propagated and tended rare cannas and aeoniums eventually disappeared beneath this ever-expanding construction, a shed-like observatory built to cater to the whims of his only child. There was even a quite good-sounding and rather eerie home-made echo chamber, which John Snr had managed to create by rigging up a microphone in an old water tank outside with a tarpaulin draped over the top. With only wax candles to light his way (part of the family's quest to save on electric power), his son would spend days on end sitting in this draughty shed slowing down 45rpm singles to 33 so that he could learn the guitar and piano solos in slow motion before transposing them back up and playing along with them in the original key. By the time John Nightly had turned twelve, in 1960, he had already composed and recorded several collections of piano pieces, noted down in *Happy* and *Sad* tunebooks along with various other birthday, Christmas and wedding songs for family and friends in this 6 x 5 shack, including a little minuet for Sindre's wedding the previous year to his childhood sweetheart, Ulli.

National Geographic magazine. 31 January 1961.
'Ham the Astrochimp'.

Three months before the first US astronaut blasted off, the 'chimponaut' Ham was strapped into a pressurised couch, locked into the Mercury capsule, and shot into the sky 156 miles above the earth on a 16.39-minute flight. Experiencing 17 times the normal force of gravity, but pronounced healthy after splashing down in the Atlantic, Ham* was given early retirement and spent the remainder of his days at the National Zoo in Washington, D.C. His legacy had been established as a true explorer, one of the first pioneers on the final frontier.

*On 3 November 1957, the Russians had launched their own *muttnik* – the space dog Laika – in Sputnik 2. She died from overheating and panic a few hours after lift-off.

item: *'Canna "Lucifer"'*, Reader's Digest *Illustrated Encyclopaedia of Garden Plants and Flowers,* 1971.

There are 55 species of these most attractive, tender herbaceous plants from tropical and subtropical America. Each flower is approx 3 inches long, with pale-red sepals, yellow petals and brick-red staminodes. The following varieties are recommended: orange-scarlet 'Evening Star', carmine-pink 'J.B. Vanderschoot', vivid scarlet and purple-leaved 'America', red with irregular yellow margins 'Wyoming' and deep-pink 'Lucifer'. Cultivation: plant the fleshy rhizomes in pots or boxes in February or March. Place in a greenhouse with a minimum temperature of 16°C (61°F). In April, move the growing plants to 6–7-inch pots or into tubs, and grow on at a temperature of 13–16°C (55–61°F). Propagation: divide the rhizomes when shoots are visible.

The next event to have a big effect on the young John Nightly was the adventures of Yuri Gagarin. On 12 April 1961 the Russian cosmonaut became the first man in space, completing one full orbit of the earth in his 4.5-tonne nosecone just 108 minutes after taking off.

One of the main preoccupations of the general public in the early 1960s was what was then known as the Space Race – the competition between the US and the USSR to achieve the historic feat of taking the first human into space, then establish dominance of the territory, neither side having any idea at all what they might do with it or even find along this new frontier. Russia was the victor, sending the twenty-six-year-old Gagarin into the earth's orbit, thus establishing the USSR as a superpower of the atomic era and capturing the imagination of school-children around the world.

Because of John Snr's employment at Pye, the Nightly family were one of the few locally to own a television set capable of producing a viewable picture. As a beaming Gagarin appeared on the BBC teatime news, newsreader Robert Dougall announcing the historic conquest, the boy rushed to the piano and produced a sequence of blurry clusters. These he repeated several times using his left hand as his right picked out a noble, angular melody based on the tritone motif from *West Side Story*, with which John was currently infatuated. In the next few months John Nightly created a whole book of ideas for Yuri, referred to as his *Yuri Tunes*; and two years later, when Russia blasted the female cosmonaut Valentina Tereshkova into space in *Vostok 6*, John reworked his tri-tonal Yuri theme producing a very poetic ballad in homage to *Valentina*.

This early composition, containing many of what would become known as Nightly musical signatures, was premiered at that year's end-of-term Summer Concert at St John's Secondary School with John performing on the piano and Jana Feather adding the simple yet undeniably moving theme on the cello.

Valentina won the school's annual award for Most Promising Musical Debut and earned its performers a guinea record token to be spent at Miller's music store. That same thematic idea, this time moving forwards and backwards simultaneously as part of an elaborate triple fugue, was to become the basis for the 'Vega Fluxus' movement of the *Mink Bungalow Requiem* some ten years later. But that is another story entirely.

After leaving St John's, John Nightly devoted most of each day to his instruments: the piano, from which of course he could never be separated, the Twinwood nylon guitar on which he was equally proficient, a rusty concertina, for playing what he called his 'stupid' music – songs in two keys at once with bizarre and constantly changing time signatures – and a saxophone presented to him by Jana on behalf of her father, Jani Feather.

Jana Feather was the perfect foil for John. Musically gifted herself, though possessing nothing like the ability of the object of her affection, Jana immediately recognised on meeting the young man that he was someone very special indeed. She had only to call out a tune or a pop song of the day and John would serenade her with it on the piano, laughing aloud at the extent of his own ability and amazing all of her friends as well as Jana's father, who saw even more evidence in private than at school that right before his eyes stood a bona fide 'musical genius'. This boy at twelve understood, without the benefit of any musical or cultural background whatsoever, a great deal more about the actual condition of music than his teacher – an accomplished musician himself – ever would.

John and Jana spent hour upon hour playing tennis at the local courts, reading poetry – Jana introducing her new boyfriend to the works of John Donne, John Keats' *A Song About Myself* and the war poems of Wilfred Owen – while at the same time systematically working their way through Jani's record collection. A particular turntable favourite was the Grieg *Piano Concerto* in a recording by Arturo Benedetti Michelangeli (Phillips BH4510), the second movement of which, in Jana's opinion, was one of the most utterly wonderful and perfect pieces that had ever been written. As her father had explained in his music-appreciation class the previous Friday: 'Every note, every phrase, every nuance means something… There is no waste. There is economy, but also elegance and romance. Lyricism. A thread, a through line, development… and what seems like a series of almost… inevitable resolves and conclusions. A balance of ideas and presentation which gives a serenity, a security, a… completeness, restfulness, a… naturalness… a true "humanity" to the piece. It is a gift of inspiration which must have arrived in the mind of its genius creator more or less fully formed.'

The other big favourite of Jana's was 'Apache' by the Shadows (Columbia 45-DB 4484), an exotic guitar-based track that they both loved. When the two young pop fans watched Hank Marvin perform with the group on ATV's *Sunday Night at the London Palladium* both became very excited indeed and started twisting and jiving around the room, rattling the dinner trolley and playing havoc with the already precarious TV reception while Dr Feather and his wife, the concert cellist Valerie Bloom, remained glued to the fuzzy black-and-white picture in disbelief. What exactly were these kids hearing?

Years later, when the Shadows had become the most unfashionable of groups, completely out of kilter with the post-*Swinging* world, John spotted his hero at the British Music Awards luncheon. Hank sat at a table at the back of the room with the other members of his new band Marvin, Welch and Farrar. His mastery of the guitar and his easy, melodic approach seemed like an echo from a bygone age, but John, thrilled at last to be in the presence of an early idol, rushed over and surprised the guitarist by telling him how much he admired his playing. Peter Green was a guest at the same event to pick up his award for 'Albatross'. Leaving the platform after receiving his statue, Green too went straight for Marvin's table to pay tribute to his first guitar hero, ignoring the judges and the audience applauding his own dazzling achievement.

But this period for John and Jana was not the heightened world of the '60s. The teenagers were at least a couple of gear shifts away from the fab, life-changing boom they were headed for. The seeds had been sown, and young people at least seemed to have been tipped off that a revolution was on its way, but March 1962 was still a pre-Beatle world. It was as if a huge convective tower of impenetrable black cloud needed to be dispersed before the new dawn could finally break.

It may be difficult now to imagine the lack of substance in the popular music promoted by record labels and endorsed by broadcasters in those early overcast days. The UK Hit Parade acted like a sedative on the hard-done-by British people. The adoption of the 45rpm format and the dependence on sponsored music broadcasting in the US may have been partly responsible for the never-ending diet of lightweight, moon-in-June confections, but even a casual glimpse at the new releases listed in *Melody Maker* any Friday revealed an appalling lack of much actual 'musical' music.

If there was a sound aimed more towards the youth of the day it would have been the machine-gun riffs and tribal rhythms of Dick Dale and other instrumental guitar groups like the Ventures and the Surfaris. Dale's 'Let's Go Trippin'' heralded a subgenre of releases by the Bel Airs, the Chantays and of course the Beach Boys, whose effervescent 'Surfin'' alerted the youngsters to the presence of a Californian chorister-voiced 'family' and their stripe-shirted harmonies. Although 'Surfin'' never hinted at the sophisticated grandeur of 'Surf's Up' just half a decade later, it was a phenomenally energetic and very raw-sounding record given the lack of fire in the popular music of the period.

Californian surf songs, their billboard titles telling of *rip curls, breakers* and *wipeouts*, along with homegrown singles like the Shadows' 'Wonderful Land', 'FBI' or 'Apache', and a handful of other instrumental TV-detective themes, were to be a big influence; John would later describe the main orchestral motif from the *Mink Bungalow Requiem* as being 'like a symphonic surf tune'.

In the spring of 1962, record shops in Britain still categorised their stock in easy-to-file compartments. The part-word *pop* had acquired neither the meaning nor the significance it was to have later; nor had it entered everyday vocabulary, except within a general association of the throwaway or temporary. In music, *pop* was used to describe a product which was lighthearted and therefore not particularly consequential – an inauspicious start for a term that would soon twist itself free from its beginnings in the broom cupboard of showbusiness to become shorthand for all things modern, a watchword for the times. Both the word and its sound were expressive, the very essence, or quintessence, of youthful purpose – the *mode* – the ultimate and much-required new state of being. The mode was a composite of various elements melted down into a single dimension; combining unity of purpose with purity of approach and popularity – often instant acceptance due to the era's inherent impatience and therefore apparent easy success. In the early 1960s, for young, half-alive adolescents and their sympathisers this state of mind – applied much like a clothes tag to every other branch of creative endeavour – was as fresh and liberated as the leaves of spring. An inexpensive, off-the-peg item in white PVC, chalk-stripe weave or silky Afghan that the acolyte would slip into in order to begin his or her own quest of self-discovery, the much-anticipated 'meta-journey'.

It seemed that those involved in music for the sake of profit had never considered that music for music's sake might actually turn out to be more profitable. So record retailers' stock consisted mainly of novelty. Jingly ditties performed by pony-tailed bobbysoxers or boy-next-door dreamboats. Music of spirit and adventure did exist but proved almost impossible to obtain, which is why fans in Liverpool and Newcastle became the first in Britain to purchase and become inspired by rock-'n'roll vinyl when limited-release imports were brought into British dock towns by merchant seamen.

Rifling through the alphabeticised JKL in Millers under *Popular Light Vocal*, the unsuspecting aficionado might encounter Teddy Johnson and Pearl Carr, Kathie Kay, Kathy Kirby, Cleo Laine or Frankie Laine or Evelyn Laye along with singing dogs, deceased music-hall comedians and seaside-cinema organists. Across the alphabet these extremely lightweight chart-bound sounds would be vying for space with curiosities like the Mousehole Male Voice Choir, the Red Army Choir, the Black and White Minstrels, the airmen of the Fleet Air Arm, the GUS footwear factory band or actors and personalities such as TV cowboy Ty 'Bronco' Hardin.

Along with other singing cowboys, Clint Eastwood or Roy Rogers, the racks were stuffed with yodelling shepherds, squawking chipmunks and even light operetta from the likes of Donald Peers and Mario Lanza. While next door in *Popular Light Instrumental* were to be found Kenny Ball, Chris Barber, Percy Faith, Geoff Love... and self-taught pianist Russ Conway – of whom the young Nightly took more notice, having watched him perform each week in his coy but appealing manner on BBC television's big Saturday-night 'light entertainment' staple, *The Billy Cotton Band Show*, the boy's favourite tune being the tinkly, self-composed 'Side Saddle'.

Pianists were popular in the era before guitars. Ferrante & Teicher and Rawicz & Landauer played film themes of the day, trying to compete with the life-enhancing smile of Winifred Atwell, the more refined touch of Semprini and the larger-than-life Liberace with his overwrought Chopin nocturnes. If the kids survived all that then in the *Rock'n'Roll & Beat Vocal* racks lurked the disparate jukebox talents of Cliff Richard, Jim Reeves, Johnnie Ray, Al Martino and Perry Como.

Spending every Saturday morning in the listening booths of Millers, the by now inseparable pair found at least some solace in the *Folk & Children's* section, which housed the more natural-sounding voices of Pete Seeger and Burl Ives, or in *Films & Shows*, where they would thumb through numerous different recordings of *The Sound of Music, My Fair Lady, Carousel* and Lionel Bart's *Oliver!* before trying them out in the booths with a good deal of incompetent kissing and cuddling thrown in. Eventually John and Jana would get round to the *Popular* racks, which occupied one whole side of the store and were home to such as Frankie Vaughan, Sarah Vaughan, the Beverley Sisters, Doris Day, Alma Cogan, Helen Shapiro and Elvis, along with the all-powerful Larry Parnes management stable: Adam Faith, Marty Wilde, Billy Fury, Vince Eager, Joe Brown and Tommy Steele. Soon, all of the above would form an orderly queue behind the Beatles.

John had first noted the name Lionel Bart on Justin's copy of Steele's 'Rock with the Cavemen'. Bart and his friend John Barry, familiar because of his credit on 'Walk Don't Run' – the theme tune to the BBC's *Juke Box Jury* – were two names John had already singled out as being on a level above the rest. The third was the cartoon-named Joe Meek, the producer of 'Telstar' by the Tornados, an otherworldly concoction that dropped on the Nightly household like a bomb in August '62. Cashing in on the popularity of the space satellite, the song's distinctive theme played on an unidentified instrument, the sound of which John tried his best to mimic as he made the daily two-mile trek back and forth between Grantchester and St John's Secondary. He also liked the fact that the Tornados, like the Shads, had their own stage-school dance routine, which they performed every week on *Thank Your Lucky Stars* as well as boasting a moody, peroxided pin-up in the shape of Heinz Burt.

Other favourite 45s of the day were the actor John Leyton's echo-laden 'Johnny Remember Me' (another Meek production), Bobby Darin's jaunty 'Things', Aussie singer Frank Ifield's hugely popular version of the standard 'I Remember You', which – probably because of its semi-yodelled vocal – seemed to be the record of the moment, and Acker Bilk's romantic 'Stranger on the Shore', the theme to Jana's favourite TV series.

Great Britain was indeed a tame land. And proud of it. Thankful for its very survival, while still being class-ridden and privileged, still a place of 'have and have-nots'. There was no precedent or appetite for dissent; most of the population would not have understood what the word meant. In the old terraces and the new cul-de-sacs the prevailing mood was one of *getting on with it* – the phrase drummed into every voter by their civic leaders in order to retain morale in the still recent war. In 1962, the British people never doubted the patronising hand of their decision-makers, their 'betters'. They welcomed it, for in those dull, drab days there remained an unhealthy respect for and polite toleration of those in authority. But while the population 'got on with it' it also thought itself lucky to be able to. This convenient equation became securely lodged within the psyche of the British workforce as it went about its business. You thought yourself lucky to have bread on the table and to have a job to go to. You thought yourself lucky to be alive. Hardly a notion likely to encourage ambition and enterprise or act as a basis for imagination and adventure in a recovering society.

It seemed like the nation was in a coma. In 1962, young people had no social voice. They were given no opportunity to disagree, which is why their voice was to find its true dimension within a format, the popular song, which their parents considered insignificant. Pre-Dylan and pre-Beatles, Britain was a tolerant society. It knew its place. But its recent history, its Victorian morals, its ambiguous and inconsistent laws, its corner-shop mentality, its excessive reserve and its undue respect for those in authority was turning it into a land of the past.

While the country's more serious artistic practitioners – its poets, playwrights and filmmakers – questioned the system, the caretakers of Britain's popular-music industry seemed content to churn out inoffensive tat. Pop music, by its label and much of its content, was transitory and cynical. Pop music was made to fit. Made easy to like and easy-going; a commodity like shoes or disinfectant. It didn't set out to challenge or change anything. It set out to please and to sell. To be literally 'popular'. With a cultural impact equal to that of cat food, this manufactured product was handed down to teenagers by *their* betters, the giant recording corporations. The product was not made by them but *for* them, and was thus viewed with suspicion, being mostly disregarded by the serious artist in every field. By the spring of 1962, *pop* had become its own dirty word.

A mere ten or so singles and a handful of LPs sustained John and Jana during the two-year period from early 1960 to late '62. But, in this safe and cosy pre-dawn, it mattered little what the records were, or even whether they liked them very much. The culture, or maybe just the 'procedure', the 'mode' – the act of discovery, trying and testing, approval or rejection – mattered, just as much as the content. Day after day, the teenagers piled up the *A's* and the *B's* on the autochanger of the Feathers' Dansette and (to the bewilderment of their guardians) set the machine to *infinite repeat.*

item: 'Pioneer Profile', *US Science Weekly* #591, May 1962.
In 1954, the American satellite pioneer and psycho-acoustic researcher John Robinson Pierce suggested that satellite communication would be possible by bouncing signals off of a passive, geostationary orbiting object. He was proven correct in 1960 with the launch of Echo, a giant balloon that bounced telephone calls coast-to-coast that were broadcast to it from the Bell Labs facility at Crawford Hill, New Jersey. The Bell System took the next step – a giant one – when it built Telstar, the world's first active communications satellite, and saw it successfully orbited and operational in 1962.

Several months later, Pye Radios was awarded the contract to supply speaker parts for the Tannoy Public Address system at the re-dedication of St Michael's Cathedral, Coventry. Long-term employee John Nightly Snr receiving complimentary invitations for himself and his family to attend.

Coventry Cathedral, reconstructed after the German bombing of 1940 by the architect Basil Spence, was to be the venue for the premiere of a new work by the English composer Benjamin Britten. Then forty-seven and with a number of major successes already behind him, Britten had been commissioned to write the music for the opening service and thus produced a massive choral symphony, the *War Requiem*, Op 66, a Requiem Mass set to words by anti-war poet Wilfred Owen, killed in action just a week before the end of WWI.

John had performed the composer's *A Ceremony of Carols* as a member of the St John's School choristers. But it was the sheer ambition of the large-scale Requiem that affected the impressionable teenager when he attended the opening with his parents on 30 May 1962. Importantly, it also made him aware of music being composed outside of the regular distribution channels serving radio and television; new 'classical' music which existed in a parallel world, a world removed from the commercial demands of pop.

As it turned out, John Nightly music, *real* John Nightly music, would always exist somewhere between the two. John had already begun to combine the sensation and instant commercial appeal of pop with the elegance and experimentation offered by an expanded format, thereby moving several steps closer to realising the sound he imagined in his head. Though it couldn't be said that classical music of this nature was *un*commercial; a Decca recording of the *War Requiem* made in 1963 with Peter Pears and Galina Vishnevskaya sold a quarter of a million copies in the first six months of its release.

Cambridge Evening News. **Friday, 15 January 1963.**
Cambridge schoolboy John Nightly, aged 14, has written to the Royal Greenwich Observatory in London to inform them of his findings regarding the relationship between the earth and the sun. The St John's Secondary pupil said, 'I've been studying the heat and the energy of the sun as part of a personal project and am also very interested in re-using sunshine and rainwater so it can be used again. I'm worried that in ten years' time we might have used up all of the sunshine in the world, which comes from the stars so I think it really important that we start thinking about this now before it's too late. My teacher thought that I should send my essay to the RGO.' John will be carrying on his investigation and hopes to win a place at King's College in order to continue his studies in this very specialist field.
'Spotlight on Schools', by John Miller, science editor.

In January 1963, Britain was enduring the coldest winter on record since 1741. The fenlands surrounding Cambridge were frozen hard; no fork or plough could break the ground. The land one huge blanket of snow as far as the eye could see. On Saturday the 12th, in the sitting room of the Feathers' detached house in Church Lane, John and Jana sat down in the cosy glow of the coal fire, steaming hot plates of cod and chips in front of them, and experienced a holy visitation in this suburban pocket of England's foremost university town. During *Thank Your Lucky Stars* the two ravenously hungry teenagers let their fish and chip tea go cold as they watched four lads from the North make their national TV debut to a record-breaking six million viewers, most of whom had chosen to stay indoors that night only because of the extreme weather conditions outside. There they were, the new messiahs, sending out the warmest of vibrations – human sunshine – in the form of electro-magnetic waves from small flickering screens up and down the country, as they came face to face with their future patrons and bobbed up and down doll-like in their Beno Dorn suits.

Instantly hypnotised, like all other teenagers in Britain tuning in that Saturday teatime, John and Jana moved closer to the high-contrast black-and-white image. Positioned just an inch away from the bright-eyed and slightly bemused faces, they studied intently what they could see of the four individuals through the combination of the 405 lines and permanent snowstorm that made up the early '60s TV picture. Hearing the Beatles perform their second single, 'Please Please Me' (Parlophone 45-R 4983), on its day of release and seeing the group 'for real' for the very first time had a devastating effect on both youngsters. As soon as John got home that night he marched straight into his father's garden shed and tuned to Radio Luxembourg. He waited patiently for the Beatles to come on. As it turned out, he didn't have to wait long as the group seemed to be played on rotation around every twenty minutes or so. As soon as John Lennon's blues harp kicked in, the young Nightly hit *Record* on his father's 2-track and logged the very first song on his *Album of Life* as it would come to be known. Side 1, Track 1 of endless reels of music copied over the years from any source his Fenman radio could tune into. Across the airwaves of the BBC Home Service, the Light Programme, Radio Caroline, the mysterious, intermittent FM, American Forces Network (AFN), Luxembourg, shortwave messages from the local Cambridge constabulary, and later, John's favourite of them all, the life-giving signal transmitted from the rusty North Sea *paquebot* known as *Radio London*.

From January 1963 to December '65, in the tool shed of the Nightly semi, John recorded anything that interested him long enough to remain for even a day or two in his own highly selective personal chart. Then, one night in November 1968, after taking 750 micrograms of lysergic acid diethylamide, he cut the compilation tapes into shreds, letting the quarter-inch ribbons fall to the floor of his newly purchased Marylebone apartment before he edited them together in whichever order they happened to land. This random tape assembly, compressed and distorted beyond recognition, became the basis for his transitional second LP, *Ape Box Metal*, dedicated to the American choreographer Donna Vost and released on Valentine's Day, 1970.

John and Jana spent their weekends in the junk shops along Mill Road, systematically trawling the racks for unusual discs. A samba LP by Reginald Dixon, T. S. Eliot's deadpan delivery of his own verse, live recordings of cup finals, criminal trials and medical lectures along with US presidential speeches, NASA's *The Pursuit of Space* and oddities such as the EP box of native birdsong recordings from the Royal Ornithological Society. Damaged stock and cut-outs, hi-fi demonstration discs, test records and acetates, flexi-discs given away with subscriptions to the Reader's Digest, like Transworld Airlines' *How to Navigate Our Globe* or the RAC's *Driving on Britain's New Motorways*. These and a mostly unfathomable double LP of shipping forecasts were all found on those magical afternoons and became part of John Nightly's never-ending tapestry of 'found sounds'.

Even at this point, the boy was considering his future. With an ability to concentrate on several different creative activities at once and even at this early age thinking both accumulatively and long term, John would mentally piece together the source material he had already collected. Just as he enjoyed cutting up photographs from his mother's magazines, sticking them together with paste made from flour and water to make bizarre-looking collages which alarmed his father, he approached the structuring of music in the same way.

John accepted that it was human nature to try to establish structure. Both the throwaway 45 and the most profound symphonic work existed within the same easy-to-deal-with formats; beginnings and endings consisting almost uniformly of *statement, repetition, development* and *variation*. But he imagined his own compositions having a continuous story-like quality. Not necessarily 'developing', but dealing with their material, their *fabric*, quickly, before moving on. The music appearing as a patchwork of fragments within an ongoing, ever-evolving roll. There would be no secondary material, no low points, no dips waiting for peaks; nor would there be any finite composition or 'definitive' recordings, either by himself or anyone else.

These intentions occupied John Nightly as he and Justin spent hour upon hour compiling tape reels from countless disparate sources, often using no more than a fill-in beat here or the odd empty bar there from the original before adding John's own ideas on top. New melodies criss-crossed old ones; chords were played in different keys and stacked up to create new extensions and polychords. Sections of cut-up backing tracks were either sped up or slowed down in order to link them harmonically or rhythmically into the next edit or 'sample'. John would then add tape delay, reverb and other effects before he distorted the result with his own homemade compressor, fuzzying up and fizzing up the signal when it came back out of the amplifier. The result was a dreamlike assemblage which through its constantly changing moods served as inspiration for John's always very autobiographical narrative – a day-to-day journal, real or imagined, of what might or might not be happening in his life. These spores of creation, combining backwards and forwards motion, flashback and premonition, conspired to create something new out of the entrails, the interior and the intimate, of the bits and pieces he'd investigated, filtered through the shifting sands of his imagination. Though he couldn't have known it then, John Nightly was already at least twenty years ahead of the times.

Jani Feather had promised to take his daughter and her by now very permanent young man to the Fab Four's live appearance at the Regal ABC cinema in March, but had underestimated Beatle appeal and lost out when every seat sold within ten minutes of going on sale. So, when NEMS announced a second visit by the group as part of their Autumn Tour, the open-minded music professor wasted no time in securing four tickets, two for Jana and John, and a pair for his wife and himself, for the group's performance there on Tuesday, 26 November 1963.

Having been unable to purchase four seats together, Jani and Valerie settled into the back stalls – giving John and Jana the benefit of two of the best seats in the house, JJ28 and JJ29 in the front circle (a bargain at 10/6 each for the first performance, at 6.15pm). The teenagers were so excited that they happily sat through Peter Jay and the Jaywalkers, the Vernons Girls and the Kestrels until a slight-looking foursome ran onstage with no announcement whatsoever. Even before the performers plugged in their guitars and waited for their bass player's 1-2-3-4 count, the fans had begun screaming. 'John! John!' 'Ringo! Ringo!' they hollered as the group launched into 'I Saw Her Standing There' and 'All My loving'. They shrieked along to 'From Me to You' and carried on in a more-or-less disordered state by the time of 'She Loves You', until they finally became hoarse and screeched to a halt during a manic 'Twist and Shout'.

Upfront in row JJ, two members of the audience sat absolutely still throughout the short 20-minute service. It was as if lightning had struck the old Regal, but only in John and Jana's seats. For God's sake, Jana thought, the Beatles were less than a hundred yards away. The girl felt her spiritual self rise up while her body remained in its seat as Paul and George beamed first at each other then out at the hysterical audience from the same microphone. The scene moved in slow motion as she furrowed and frowned trying to pick out John's choppy guitar and Ringo's clanky hi-hat. Disorientated and dizzy, tired of searching for sightlines through the screaming mob, Jana let go of the Here and Now and found herself zooming. Fast forwarding to a possible future scenario, she searched the new landscape for her beloved but he was nowhere to be seen. The girl took control again and began winding herself slowly back, seeing her own being, her own self, for the first time in her life, at the very centre of things; the old Regal on the one hand a sounding box for the coming revolution and on the other a rusty feast-day carousel grinding down on its own spindle. The mob swirling around her like a tidal surge; hysterical in the real sense of the word, an encircling force spinning freeform as the music boomed its way through the ancient plankboards of the pre-war stage and out into the newly velveted stalls of the Swinging era, a mass vibrational quaking in stalls and circle from A to Z; an awakened pulse suddenly bringing everything around it into existence.

In this moment Jana became whole, became herself – her new self – as she responded to the pull of the magnet. Finding in this coming together, this conjunction, this vanity, a glow which was to keep her, comfort and sustain her, for the rest of her days. Fast forward again into another gear and *Zap!* The girl was back. Properly back. Jana sat forward, leaned her elbows on her knees as if nothing had happened and gazed up at her blond-haired boy. Her companion was transfixed by what he saw. Like an expert marksman, his telescopic eyes held the group in their sights. His analytical mind tracked every chord change and bass note. His sensitive disposition was charmed by each loving nuance and expression of warmth. His manipulative nature was awed by the absolute power the magiciens were able to exert over their followers.

John Nightly had seen the future, and had understood it. He had also understood the magnitude of the task before him. The four young men onstage had already travelled a long road. Their tight-knit, brotherly groove, their infectious optimism and their sheer 'rightness' was the product of 1,000 pilled-up sessions at the Star Club in Hamburg and endless one-nighters in provincial Northern ballrooms. Behind it all was what seemed like a mercury gush of musical invention. John Nightly had yet to leave the starting blocks but he was confident he could travel faster having now finally set eyes on his teachers, his gurus, his healers, his yardstick and… what would come to be his great comfort in times of trouble.

But together these four spirits, holy men from the North, tour guides to the new cultural landscape, were also to be his nemesis; an impossibly high watermark by which all others would be measured and against which he would constantly measure his own achievement. Those who inspire can also force one to face up to one's own supposed potential, limitations, ability and inability, and this was certainly the case with the magical, mythical, Christ-like, four-headed omniscience that, in the early days at least, referred to itself using the collective term... Beatles.

Take my hand, I'm a stranger in paradise,
all lost in a wonderland

'Stranger in Paradise'
Robert Wright/George Forrest/Alexander Borodin

Carn Point, Porthcreek, Cornwall.
Photo: John Heath-Green Photographic (*Cornish Echo & Trades*)

Zennor Head, Penwith, Cornwall. Saturday, 5 April 1982.

A shiny black Jaguar XJS V12 drives westwards along the B3306, the coast road to St Just and Lands End. The car overtakes a holidaymaker's caravan before turning sharply onto a path beside a muddy compound. A close morning mist hangs over the land. Rabbits and hares scatter to take cover in the bracken and scrub. A dirt track leads to a freshly ploughed field where crows and gulls nervously pick over worms. The Jag bumps along this square acre, flattening out the turned earth until it comes to a field of native daffodils – *Narcissus pseudonarcissus*. Further up, beneath an old distressed oak, lies a patch of Himalayan poppies and a rusty water tank. The car arrives at the entrance to a small meadow. There is a fishpond filled with rubble and bricks. To the left, a path that drops away into marshland. To the right, a grassy bank with clumps of primula, gunnera and hosta. Beyond these little outposts and obstructions there is a clear view across the cliffs and out to the sea. Blue, blue sea. The deep turquoise-blue of the Atlantic. Five sky-tall Monterey cypresses stand guard over the ocean. The magnificent ocean. The sound of long, rolling waves and spring tides beckons the visitors on. Orange gorse has spread out to claim the driveway. The car ploughs through the dense thicket towards another clearing, until a curtain of trees leads into bramble and sea-heather. Suddenly there are fresh open skies and shimmering granite rock. Brilliant white light floods onto the steppes. Lilac and buddleja, lime and pear trees have arranged themselves around an open meadow as the Jag pulls to a halt beneath a huge overhanging oak. Up ahead, the remains of a shingle path and a five-bar gate.

A portly, middle-aged figure in a grey anorak gets out of the car and swings the gate open. It is incredibly hot this morning. The noonday sun beats down on the roof of the shiny black saloon. The man gets back in and the car starts up again. It continues along its way, mowing down thistle and mustard in the undergrowth. Half a mile further and we're almost on the water. Everything is blue now. A fine mist and drizzle blows in off the sea. White puffy clouds move fast across the headland. Stints and terns have come in off the cliffs. Looking east along the coast path three other farmhouses are visible towards Black Zawn. There are trails leading right up to the overhang of the cliffs. Purple schiff decorates the landscape, enticing the visitor towards the edge. It is a wild but idyllic scene. Crows and sparrowhawks bellow warnings from the cypress branches, alerting their many friends that they have company. The Jag pulls to a stop under a drip of trees. The driver gets out and walks purposefully towards a sign nailed to a broken piece of tin.

Legal Squatting
Do NOT come any further
No access

The man ignores this friendly advice and walks straight past the notice up towards a large stone building, a farmhouse in a seemingly dreadful state of repair. There are rotten card tables outside, and bunting from a long-gone feast day still adorns the guttering. On the front door a wreath from Christmas Past hangs on a nail. An old tied lavender lays abandoned on the doorstep. There is no one to be seen. Back in the car, a second man, the passenger in the front, opens the door slightly to alleviate the heat. He places one foot on the ground but remains in the vehicle. The place is overrun with birds. Ravens, jackdaws, black crows and owls. All of them blaring at the same time. The house is a mess. Chickens and guineafowl run for cover as the man approaches the front of the building, pauses briefly to kick away an old cardboard box on the ground in front of him, then disappears round the back for ten minutes or so. He reappears on the other side having inspected the total amount of space and acreage, which is considerable, and having taken a close look at five large plots out back. There are cutting beds, a rockery, a rose garden, the mature tea roses and the earth around them singed by a recent bonfire and large rectangular razed areas, two- and four-bay structures. Facing on to the sea are Victorian greenhouses with broken windows and timber joists more or less falling down. The man checks his watch, looks up at the sun, squints in disbelief at the atomic brightness, walks back up to the car and gets in.

'Lot of space back there.'

No response. The man wipes a bead of sweat from his brow with a dirty handkerchief. He turns to his companion.

'A *lot* of space…'

'do they face direct into the sun?'

'Straight on… full sunlight. 'Bout eight hours a day I reckon. Lovely view round the back…'

'let's get it.'

Pear's Auction Rooms, Penzance, Cornwall. Tuesday, 8 April 1982. Morning session.

At a property auction in Penzance the hammer falls on Lot 66. For the sum of £68,500 Mr John Daly has purchased a five-bedroom dwelling, the almost derelict Trewin Farm, at Carn Point, with a cottage, adjacent greenhouses and two further outbuildings in twelve acres of farmland along the coastal path at Porthcreek.

Trewin Farm, Carn Point, Porthcreek, nr Zennor Head, Cornwall. The Vigil of Candlemas, Sunday, 2 February, 1996.

Private Road
Beware of Guard Dog
No Public Access
No Cars. No Bicycles. No Walkers. No Ramblers.
This is NOT the Coastal Path

The dog wouldn't be a problem. Alexandre was a docile old Lurcher who had been with John Nightly coming up for eight years now. RCN had picked him up as a stray wandering along the sands at Zennor Head the week of Christmas 1988. A few months later, after no one claimed the pup he'd been welcomed permanently and lovingly into Trewin Farm by both Johns.

In terms of security there were no problems at all. Had anyone attempted to venture down the slippery towpath along this beautiful but bleak part of the headland, they would have found it extremely difficult to get anywhere near the house. For one thing, it was impossible to actually see the place until you were almost on top of it, and a copse of Monterey cypress and Claxus pines and their fallen spiky branches prevented any access being made either by foot or car.

Beyond that, there were layers of barbed wire and rusty ground spikes every few yards, with the meadow leading away from the coast path set with thick-branched gorse, the bramble so dense that it was more or less impossible to see the narrow, shingle pathway that once wound down to the side gate by the cold frames, the actual entrance, if you could call it that, to the Nightly property.

RCN had gone to great lengths to make it look as though there was nothing at all down there if anyone ever felt the need to venture on. But hardly anyone did; and when the burned out speed freak discovered the location, back in '82, as far as he and his handler were concerned they had happened upon the ultimate hideaway. The safe haven selected from Pear's Property catalogue after the very briefest of recces.

No visitors. No visitors at all. Unless in absolute emergency. No visitors under any 'normal' circumstances. It really was one of the most abandoned, out-of-the-way places in all England. Cornwall itself was not exactly the end of the world. Lots of celebrities resided here, in secret if they had any sense, and with its microclimate and full-on sunny days more or less all year round it was a natural resting place for someone whose only day-to-day interest was the cultivation and propagation of exotic plants, apart from John's only other interest which was occasional night-time stargazing activities; the pursuit of which was made easier by the lack of street lighting and the very low light pollution which rewarded the viewer with a blitz of galactic starlight unavailable in any other part of the country.

But today was a special day. Today Frieda was coming; mother and son not having set eyes on one another for fourteen years. Today was to be a very special day indeed. Both John Nightly and his nurse were looking forward to it immensely, albeit with some trepidation.

RCN had been instructed to gather up all of the potted mesembryanthemums and doroanthus to decorate both sides of the sunlounge in the main house with these African star daisies, turning the place into an overdressed panto set. The tallest and lushest aeoniums and phormiums had been placed all the way down the wide hallway so as to line the entrance for Frieda as if she were the Queen of Norway herself, in order that she for once might be able to compliment her son on something: his enormous achievement in being able to cultivate these most spectacular of tropical exotics so far from their natural climes.

RCN had been preparing the visit for weeks, ever since the news of the death of John Snr, from lung cancer – no doubt due to the forty or so Woodbines he had smoked every day since becoming engaged to his future wife. The male nurse had been up to the Tregan Nurseries, Penzance, to purchase much-needed equipment like the new Baronet weed-puller and a pair of Darlac DP400 lightweight shears, so that the violet-blue *Rhododendron cantabile* and the green-carpeter juniper which edged the new split-level lawn looked freshly pruned and nice and neat and tidy for Frieda. He had also been out on the recently purchased Easimow motor-mower after the early-morning dew, so that the boss would have no reason to fret about the state of the garden when the Queen arrived.

Trewin Farm wasn't a farm at all but an ex-vicarage. A large Victorian manor house of Cornish drystone facing onto the sea between Carn Point and Zawn Point, the folk-loric 'Savenheer' of mermaids, magiciens and Methodism. Comprising five bedrooms, a living room, kitchen, walk-in pantry, sunroom and four small bathrooms haphazardly arranged around a central hallway. There was also a separate utility room, outhouse, laundry room, office and even a small library. Outside stood a nondescript cottage, three adjoining long rectangular sunlounges, and a larger sun house that had once been the next-door garage. The additions which had so troubled the planners and surveyors at Penwith were the sixteen very large and very warm hothouses and the eight cold frames that played host to (at last count) more than 4,000 varieties of zygocacti, sedums and astrophytums along with countless succulents, alpines and other exotic species imported at great cost and with great persistence from the Northern Cape Province of South Africa, Brazil, Australia, New Zealand, the Cayman Islands, Japan, the People's Republic of China, Argentina, Peru, Chile and other far-off weird and wonderful lands.

The vicarage, as it was before, was one of the dwellings listed in the inventory on the death of the parson John Cardew, vicar of the little church of St Eina, the 'church on the beach', in the rural parish of Porthcreek 1789–1866. Cardew was most likely a relative of Cornelius Cardew, one-time headmaster of Truro School and dedicatee of the Cardew Memorial Roof Boss in Truro Cathedral (a special service took place in St Mary's Aisle in 1988). Like many preachers and ecclesiastical men in Cornwall at the time, John Cardew was probably using his various properties for smuggling. Although as a parson he would already have been receiving the usual tithes of fish, silk, wool and altarage, the alms given to the Church and its wardens, he would likely have been involved in the practice of using the church to store kegs of brandy, tea, post-office 'packets' and other fineries, which would then be transferred to various middlemen before entering the warehouses of wholesale merchants, where they would be sold to sailors, publicans and Cornish gentry. On his death the Reverend John Cardew left a sum of £30,000 – the equivalent of £2,000,000 today.

Another reason John RCN had recommended Trewin* Farm on John Nightly's release from SUMHA was that it had a secret passage via the old graveyard into the smugglers' caves directly onto the beach, some hundred feet below. More or less a private beach, as it turned out, there being no way into this particular cove from Zennor Head except perhaps by helicopter. RCN liked to entertain the idea that one day his charge might enjoy the exclusivity of his own sandy place, small though it was, and that he himself might like to take a swim every now and then or even do a spot of sunbathing in the long months of summer. But John Nightly had shown no interest whatsoever in private beaches or smugglers' caves. One morning in the very middle of midsummer, the boss had placed his trembling sandled foot onto the first couple of slimy steps that led down to the shore; but it looked most uninviting and, feeling the cold, wet stone on his bare skin, he quickly turned back again, asking RCN to close the door. This had been John Nightly's only encounter so far with a beach in Cornwall.

But the faithful nurse lived in hope, believing that one day in the not-too-distant future he and his friend might be able to walk along the coast path together. The boss had shown interest in seeing the various hybrid varieties of sea heather that lined the cliff edge and RCN knew that he would want to return once they had taken that first major step. It was a slow process, still a couple of years off, maybe, and John Nightly had already come a long way, but in his mind's eye RCN could see them both walking along the cliff path, the incredible blue vista of the bay laid out before them with only the bright sunshine, a light rain creating a soft rainbow, the distant wind and the sweet songs of the finches and robins to trouble them.

*Literal translation of Trewin: 'white farm' (parish of Porthcreeque 1303), tre + gwenn (feminine form of gwynn), with mutation of gw to w, or in Welsh *gwenn* 'smile, prayer, wish'. Also possible: 'windy farm' (Trewynt). Exact form uncertain.
(Settlements in Cornwall and their Origins, Cornish Record Office, book #9, Penwith District Council 1953)

It was unusual to find a beat group in Cambridge in May 1963. Jana could only think of two: the Golden Blades at Trinity and the Bridegrooms at King's. Then one Saturday, sitting with John in the corner of the Whim, she noticed what looked like a photograph of Pinky and Perky pinned to the café notice board. It wasn't the irritating TV piglets but the Tiddlywinks, a local group from Histon in need of a *fab* rhythm guitarist.

'Why don't you go and ring them up?' The girl put down her books and propped herself up on the counter. 'Find out what they're like?'

'I *know* what they're like. Tell that by the picture, and… well, I think I have to get my own musicians together…'

'But your "own musicians" won't ever actually *get together*, will they, John? Because no one will ever be good enough for you.' She sighed. 'You know they won't. Certainly not in Cambridge anyway. It'll take an age.' Jana was always lecturing the boy; pushing… pushing. 'And there's a readymade group right there… Ready and waiting.' She indicated towards the chubby foursome. 'Give them a ring, for God's sake. They look daft enough to… to do your bidding.'

John took a cursory look at the menu, pretending he was about to choose something he couldn't possibly afford.

'*John…*' The girl froze and stared impatiently at her boyfriend. '*Go and ring them up!*'

Jana got up from her seat, pressed two newly minted coppers into the boy's palm, put her hands on his shoulders and turned him around, laughing as she manoeuvred John's unwilling limbs, pointing him in the direction of the phone booth just inside the hallway of the busy tea bar.

'… hallo… uh… my name's John…' The caller paused for a

moment as if stopped in his tracks, 'ah… *well*… I've just seen your… your notice about a guitarist…' A further pause, 'ah… oh… uh. Well… I might do, I suppose. What? Uh… quite good I should think. Right then. I'll be there. Oh… are you? Prince Philip? Is that right? I do remember it, actually…' John glanced back and made a face at his girlfriend. 'I see… well… yeh, I'll be there… ask for *Vernon?* I will do… yep. Okay… well…'

The boy rejoined his promoter at the bench by the arched window.

'*Prince Philip?*' Jana sat with her chin resting on a large dictionary.

'… um… uh… They're called the Tiddlywinks 'cos…' John looked bored already. 'Remember when the Tiddlywinks Club was challenged to a match by Prince Philip?'

'*No…*'

He shovelled another sugar into his stale powdered coffee. 'Couple of years ago… He sent the Goons. To play for him… *represent* him instead. I remember it actually…'

'I don't.'

John sipped the opaque liquid. 'Ugh!' He frowned and pursed his lips, '*God!*'

'*And…*'

'And that's why they're called that…'

Jana lifted a napkin from its holder and began to pack away her papers. 'Don't understand… But it's a dreadful, dreadful name…'

Vernon Johnson and John Hilton, guitarist and drummer respectively with the Tiddlywinks beat group, were finding life busier than usual. Currently in the mid-term of a Natural Sciences Tripos* at Christ's, they found themselves consumed with college work while also sitting on the committee organising that year's social calendar. Having booked themselves into their own venue the Tiddlywinks were due to play Christ's May Ball in two weeks time. Christ's had a reputation as giver of the very best balls of the season. Always black tie, and usually with top-notch entertainment (the Who played there as late as 1967). After the main event, with food and drink circulating uneasily around young undergraduates systems and the promise of other varieties of recreation ahead, at around 4 or 5am, a small armada would head up the river to Grantchester for breakfast – maybe in Rupert Brooke's beloved orchard and the neighbouring meadows, where revellers would celebrate either by falling over and vomiting or by simply passing out just as the obligatory 'survivors' photograph was being taken.

May balls were crucial to the Cambridge music scene, supplying much-needed employment to classical bods, jazzers and rock-'n'rollers alike. Indeed, without the seasonal university events there was little going on anywhere else in the way of musical fixtures. On a typical damp Friday evening undergraduates congregated in cellars across the town, where various temporary clubs came and went. The Mouse, the Pink Scarf, the Zodiac, Brook's, Scales, the Carn, Ludo's, the Mill, Constable's, the Tin Mine, the Riverboat, Dolly's, the Alley Club in Falcon Yard and the Jazz Club at the Lion Hotel. There were one-nighters at the legendary Dorothy Ballroom and the Union Society, along with other regular well-known activities like the Corpus Chess Club, foreign-film screenings at the Kinema in Mill Road, the afore-mentioned Tiddlywinks Society and various private reading and study groups.

*Nearly all undergraduates take the Tripos (honours examinations) in their particular subject. The Tripos is divided into two parts, with Part II being (confusingly) known as the 'Finals' and taking place at the end of the third year. Results are classed into a First, a Second, or a Third.

Most other areas of social activity were of course to do with sport, particularly rowing and rugby. Life outside the colleges was unremittingly dull. For musicians, particularly jazz bands, 'trad' or 'modernist', and beat groups, there were very few venues in which to actually perform, although they were based in a supposedly youth-populated market town, which is why the nearby USAF bases at Lakenheath and Mildenhall, leaning more towards live entertainment, were a godsend to local groups and singers. With gigs almost every night of the week and fees of £40 or £50 for a couple of hours' work, they provided the means to learn the craft by hacking through the hits of the day, much like the Merseybeat groups had done at the Indra and the Star clubs in Hamburg.

But entertaining American forces wasn't easy, as GIs were much more in tune with current sounds than Cambridge undergrads were. On US Air Force territory, groups would be expected to perform all of that week's Top 10, along with a selection of rock'n'roll favourites, replicating them as close to the originals as possible. But the audience was appreciative and tips would be given for particular requests, especially end-of-the-night smooches and country ballads – the catechism song 'Deck of Cards'* concluded each Tiddlywinks performance – bringing back memories of home for stationed servicemen. Although it could be something of a slog, performers were at least on a stage, singing and playing live; playing music. US bases were useful for another reason: they were a reliable source of drugs.

Drugs featured regularly in the pages of *Varsity*, the university magazine. French blues, purple hearts, Dexies and Prellies, along with a vast array of uppers and downers, were readily available around the colleges. In February 1966, *Varsity* estimated that ten percent of students were regularly being 'enhanced' in some way or another. In November that same year the publication rocked the town when it claimed that there were forty

---

*'Deck of Cards' by T. Texas Tyler (Dot 45-15968), with its catechism-like list, was the scourge of every '60s 'function' band.

undergraduate heroin users and also regular LSD trippers in at least four colleges. Hard drugs came in from friends in London while others were homegrown. *Varsity* advised that local landladies look more carefully at what they were watering. In March '68, the magazine reported that cannabis resin was available at £10 an ounce – up from £4 in '65 – but that there was currently no grass (cannabis grain) available anywhere in the city. LSD however was doing a roaring trade, selling at thirty shillings a tab – double the London price. Mind expansion came directly from Holland, hallucinogenics being the new thing. But Pakistani green and black and Nepalese hash were also available. An article in *Granta* magazine in February '67 stated that LSD was being manufactured in the university chemical labs; the piece led to *Granta* editor Sean Hardie being reprimanded by the senior Proctor for failing to consult him before publication.

Later on, this would all be of great interest to John Nightly; but the following Saturday, as he walked into the Tiddlywinks' tiny rehearsal room, otherwise known as the Hilton family's lock-up, the only thing that concerned him was the group's physical appearance. The Bri-Nylon foursome, Vernon, Colin, Clem and John, on guitars, bass and drums respectively, were four of the most gormless-looking individuals he'd ever set eyes on.

The likely reason was that in real life the Tiddlywinks were actually a bunch of botanists. Spending their days propagating, feeding, clipping and planting out exotics at the Cambridge Botanic Gardens on Bateman Street. Only if you happened to come upon them when they were decked out in their peculiar tiddly-dotted stage outfits with their cheap second-hand instruments would you have any inkling at all that this was in fact a semi-pro beat combo. As it turned out, a pretty good one. A group that would give John Nightly his first helping hand on the ladder to fame and despair.

item: Monthly Cultural Notes: February

The month of February is taken up with preparation. Clean the greenhouse, especially the window panes, and label all seed trays carefully. Lithops, crassulas, saintpaulias and pelargoniums can be sown. Deadhead carnations and azaleas. Water plants in the mornings and from below where possible. Choose colours for mesembryanthemum and hand-pollinate flowers, transferring the pollen from head to head with a soft brush or a ball of cotton wool. Beware of frost.

'But they liked your songs?'

'yeh, but they looked terrible. Really, really awful. Can't describe it. Two fat ones – they weren't exactly "tiddly" – and the other one, *Clem* or *Clam*, whatever it was… a sort of… rugby type.'

'*God…*'

John and Jana adopted a superior posture and stirred their sixpenny teas.

'You should still do it, though.'

'dunno… they're… well, they're…' The boy puffed out his cheeks in an expression of disbelief. '*Completely clueless*… is the only way to…'

Jana continued to leaf through her textbooks. 'When's the next rehearsal?'

'Thursday. We're going to run through "Zigging & Zagging".'

'That's the one they liked?'

'they liked it. Kept saying it was a "hit" – whatever that means. But… same as always… people always like the ones that I don't like. The *normal* songs. They never like the unusual ones, the ones that are actually good, or "different" or *weird* or…' The boy picked up his cup, resigned to his art being misunderstood in the wider world. 'Whatever I do, they just like the normal stuff…'

Ludo's Cellar Club, Girton Road, Cambridge. Thursday, 17 May 1963.

Zigging and zagging and zigging and zagging and zigging
Zigging and zagging and zigging and zagging and zigging
Zigging and zagging and zigging and zagging and zigging
  Zigging and zagging and zigging and zagging and…

'Sorry, but… if we're going to play this song next week to anyone at all, we've got to get these harmonies right.'

An exasperated John Nightly backed away from the microphone, placed his hand over the neck of his guitar to dampen the sound and stared doomily at the floor.

'We will, John. It's a great song… really it is. We've just got to work on these parts. But it's so incredibly catchy… C'mon, us lot!' We'll get it!' Vernon continued to rehearse the 'difficult' chord changes.

'I want to make absolutely sure that we all know what each of these individual parts are actually supposed to be, before we start trying to sing them… Otherwise it's gonna sound… not right.' John walked over to his amp and adjusted the volume. 'Not right at all.' The boy drew a deep sigh and continued to tune his instrument as he spoke. 'Let's just do it again.'

Zigging and zagging and zigging and zagging and zigging……
Zigging and zagging and zigging and zagging and zigging……
Zigging and zagging and zigging and zagging and zigging……
Zigging and zagging and zigging and zagging and zigging……

The next day, John Nightly had a very different kind of musical engagement. The Cambridge Youth Music Society had commissioned his extended string piece *Six Second Echo* – named after the famously long sepulchral echo of King's College Chapel – as part of that year's King's Summer Concerts programme.

Six Second Echo, made up of repeated heavy strikes on the low end of the piano, played at random intervals against a long-bowed D minor9 chord, was premiered by a ninety-piece double string orchestra accompanied by two transistor radios. The short concert, given by the Cambridge Youth Symphonia, took place in King's Chapel itself before *Madrigals on the Backs* on the last Friday of term. In the audience were Frieda and John Snr, along with Jani, Valerie and Jana Feather and the Norwegian relatives, Signhild, Sindre and Steinar, who'd flown over specially for the big event. The highlight for John though was when the great David Willcocks,* the director of King's College Choir and the *über-führer* of choral music in Cambridge, wandered in without realising that there was a concert on. Willcocks stayed for fifteen minutes or so, listening intently to what he heard, asked something of one of the choirmasters then nodded appreciatively and walked out again, closely monitored by the schoolboy composer.

The piece itself was influenced by Michael Tippett's lush-sounding *Concerto For Double String Orchestra* (1939) a favourite of Jana's mother, and also by one of La Monte Young's *Compositions 1960* which required a single chord to be held 'for a very long time'. John had stolen the idea of including a tuned radio from Cage's *Imaginary Landscape #4* (1951), whose performers manipulated the dials and wavelengths of radio transmissions. At the King's concert, the transistors were 'played' by the Feathers' former lodger Daphne Mpanza, a Trinity music scholar from Johannesburg who would sometimes assist her landlord's most promising student by writing down the chords of his piano pieces so he could firstly remember and then (more often than not) forget them. *Six Second Echo* built not to a climax but to a gradual echoing infinity as the sound of the piano strikes ricocheted off the walls of the cavernous chapel. The piece really was a mish-mash of ideas John had picked up

*Willcocks conducted the Bach Choir for the Decca recording of Britten's War Requiem (Decca 4785433) 1963, as well as for the recording of The Rolling Stones 'You Can't Always Get What You Want' from 'Let It Bleed' (Decca Red Mono LK5025) 1969.

from his contemporary-music studies and was a good indication of where he was musically at that moment. There were probably snatches of *The Planets* in there too, a sprinkling of Delius and a helping of Stravinsky but, well… It was all a very long way from 'Zigging & Zagging'.

Town & Gown quarterly (May week offshoot of *Varsity*) reported in its issue 30 June 1963.
At the Cambridge Music Society's Summer Concert performance in King's College Chapel on June 18th there was a great deal of interest in a very modern avant-garde composition – 'Six Second Echo.' A "random serialist" piece by Mr John Nightly, a student at St. John's Secondary. Performed by the Cambridge Symphonia, the composition required the ninety-piece double orchestra to hold a single chord for almost forty minutes while members of the violin and viola sections struck harsh pizzicato chords every now and then, or whenever the mood took them, or so it seemed to quite a few of those present. Although quite a bit of murmuring was heard from some of the older members of the audience at the beginning, things soon settled down and Mr Nightly's seemingly random but most likely quite organised music created a rather hypnotic atmosphere as the long re-echoing waves of plucked strings reverberated around the chapel. What could have almost been an undergraduate's May Week jape turned out to be a rather relaxing, even quite spiritual "enlightenment". We'll look out for more experimentation from Mr Nightly in the future.
Cora Johnson: 'Music Notes', *Town & Gown* Quarterly.

I have a lot of ideas for so many different types of music. Sometimes I have to stop myself sitting down at the piano because I think I'm actually writing too much of it! Every time I sit down, I'll write something. There are boxes and boxes of tapes of all kinds. Short piano pieces, ideas and

---

*This piece contained detailed notes of what John imagined he would say in the event of being interviewed by the venerable music weekly. The book, along with other John Nightly schoolboy memorabilia, was sold at Sotheby's Film & Entertainment Auction, New Bond Street, London, on Tuesday, 17 September 1993 (Lot 143).

themes. Tunes I thought might be good for children's things or for end of term plays, even music for television programmes that I like, documentaries and animal programmes. Honestly, sometimes it can get quite ridiculous. Keeping track of all the tunes I've written in my tunebooks. Because I don't read music, you see, although I do have my own sort of... remembering system. Getting the ideas is never a problem, but carrying them out and 'realising' them is more difficult. Sometimes it's a kind of a... nightmare

Imaginary interview with the *Melody Maker*, notated in John's Modern Science exercise book, November 27th, 1962, St. John's school, Cambridge. Containing detailed notes of what he would say in case he ever was interviewed by the venerable music weekly. The book, along with other John Nightly schoolboy memorabilia, was sold at Sotheby's Film & Entertainment Auction, New Bond Street, London, Tuesday 17 September, 1993. Lot 143.

Benjamin Britten: 27 November 1963. BBC, The Light Programme: Talking to Douglas Brown.

I think one can say that the actual process of planning works comes to me fairly easily... the... That is before I get to the paper and start thinking about the notes. That is where the agony which Michael Tippett referred to in the *Observer* last Sunday begins...

It's a Caroline Sureshot! C-A-R-O-L-I-N-E and this is Simon Dee saying *Don't Touch That Dial !!!*
You're listening to All Day Music Radio on Radio Caroline on this very special, very sunny Bank Holiday Weekend and today, as if you didn't already know, it's official Caroline Merseybeat Day [sounds of hysterical screaming] *So here we go... And we're starting with one of the Liverpool originals themselves... It's the Fourmost!* [the group's 'Hello Little Girl' fades up in the background]

On Easter Saturday 1964, the pirate station Radio Caroline began transmitting on 199 metres with a power of 10 kilowatts off the coast of Felixstowe in Suffolk. In Cambridge and the surrounding area, due to the ship being so close, the reception was crystal clear. Teenagers in Cambridgeshire and the Isle of Ely, Suffolk, Norfolk and Essex tuned in and never touched their dials again. DJ Simon Dee launched the station and for the first time, 'all-day music radio' was brought to the UK, breaking the BBC monopoly. DJs included Tony Blackburn, Mike Ahern, Keith Skues, Emperor Rosko (Jana's favourite), Graham Webb and Norman St John. Many similar offshore radio stations were set up that same year, including Radio Atlanta, Radio City, Radio England, Radio London, Radio Britain, Britain Radio, Radio 390, Radio 270 and Radio Sutch.

John Nightly was tuning in. Having taken on weekend work at Addenbrooke's, he was beginning to develop an interest in music as a source of healing – spiritual health being a quality the young John Nightly had found severely lacking at home. That winter, while John had been concentrating on his music, Jana had been working her way through the bookshelves in her father's study, becoming interested in and drawing John's attention to the ideas of Eastern-styled philosophy concerned with spiritual health and healing via methods other than pharmaceutical prescription. Meher Hebera's *The Complete Principle of the Spirit* and *Music is a Healer,* a pamphlet by Vishnu Rabala (a.k.a. Cambridge don Professor John Toal), were tucked into the brown leather satchel John carried around with him wherever he went that summer. Psychological health in Cambridge wasn't good. By spring 1964, the Department of Psychiatry at Addenbrooke's was seeing almost two hundred students per year, with another thousand booked in for treatment at the Cambridge Student Mental Health Unit at Bene't Place. There were six suicides in the twelve months from January 1961 to January 1962 and seventeen up to January '64, with gas rings and fires in the college rooms providing a quick way out. John and Jana's solution was to arrange a series of lunchtime 'coffee' concerts in both facilities in order to try out ideas and also draw attention to the institutions themselves, which were invariably short of both funds and trained staff.

The other beneficiary of the performances was to be Christian Action. In April 1956, through the efforts of the international body, Jani Feather had been instrumental in organising the visit to Cambridge of Bishop Trevor Huddlestone from the Sophiatown slums in Johannesburg. Bishop Huddlestone addressed a crowd of thousands outside the Liberal Club in what turned out to be the largest ever public meeting to be held in the city. In an initiative set up by local action group Joint Action Group for Understanding (JAGUAR), a campaign was begun to enable South African students from British High Commission territories to attend the university on scholarships. One such student was Daphne Mpanza, who lodged with the Feathers from Lent '57 to Michaelmas '63, during which time she completed a PhD in music and became well known locally for her multipatterned garments and exotic headgear. By early 1962 anti-apartheid feeling in the university was so strong that students working at the railway-station buffet were reprimanded for discouraging customers from buying oranges and bananas that came from Swaziland and Rhodesia. Despite this continuing effort, visits to South Africa by the Cambridge Shakespeare Group and the Dryden Society (Trinity's Dramatic Society) went ahead.

Saturday, 18 June 1964: Jana's sixteenth birthday. Dutch fans trying to get closer to the Beatles threw themselves into a canal during the group's arrival in Amsterdam. In Cambridge, after taking Jana for her birthday treat – a punt along the Cam from the mooring at Grantchester to the pier at Jesus Lane – John Nightly and the Trinity New Music Group performed the premiere of his tone-poem *Silhouette* at the Student Mental Health Unit (ticket price: a two shilling optional donation) and then again that evening at the Student and University Mental Health Association, SUMHA (later renamed the SUMHA Centre then the *Summer* Centre). There was a further free performance the following night at St Andrews Church on the Market Place.

Silhouette would have been an ambitious piece even for a professional composer, let alone a (nearly) sixteen-year-old who could barely read his own score. It was an 'imagist' (John's word) interpretation of the eclipse-like after-effects John had registered from certain fixed stars he'd been tracking with his telescope when he should have been asleep. The work had been composed in an apparently 'revolutionary' way. *Silhouette* had come into existence by chance.

Taking his cue again from his long-distance tutor, Cage, John had tried to 'discover' the music as the result of dice throws, card shuffles and local telephone codes rather than create it through his own experience. The words, the rhythms and even the choreography, which John had worked out himself after consulting a book by Hermes Pan, had been put together so that there could exist random differences between each performance. The music being allowed to 'live' for itself without being directed and controlled by the composer. There was some composed music in the final section though, and this recalled the wide harmonic intervals of Tippett and Copland – John had seen the Cambridge University Opera Group's European premiere of the American composer's *The Tender Land* two years previously, and only last week he'd sat and listened intently to Tippett's *A Child of Our Time* on a BBC radio broadcast while John Snr installed a new 4-track board in the garage studio.

The two performances of *Silhouette* went down well, particularly with friends and family, confirming to Jani, Valerie, Jana and Daphne that John's future as a composer and musician was every bit as promising as they had imagined. While not quite understanding what they had heard, Frieda and John Snr were of course immensely proud of their industrious and talented son. On top of all this activity John had his new lunchtime piano spot in the Heffer Gallery in Sidney Street, where he would happily knock out anything from Chopin nocturnes to 'My Old Man's a Dustman' as long as they paid and fed him; and of course he continued to play and also play hell with the Tiddlywinks, now rechristened the Everyman, having been quickly transformed from happy-go-lucky amateurs into John Nightly's long-suffering backing group.

item: John Pond (1767–1836), Astronomer Royal, born London.
Aged 15, Pond detected errors in the Greenwich observations. At 16 he entered Trinity College, Cambridge, but was obliged to leave due to ill health. He went abroad, visiting Portugal, Malta, Constantinople and Egypt, making astronomical observations at his halting-places. Settling at Westbury in Somerset in 1798, he erected there an altazimuth instrument of 2 ½ feet in diameter which became known as the Westbury Circle (see Phil. Trans. xcvi. 424). In 1800–1801 his observations with it, *On the Declinations of Some of the Principal Fixed Stars,* communicated to the Royal Society on 26 June 1806 (ib. p420) gave decisive proof of deformation through age in the Greenwich quadrant and rendered inevitable a complete re-equipment of the Royal Observatory. Pond was elected a fellow of the Royal Society on 26 February 1807. He married in the same year and lived in London, occupying himself with practical astronomy. Dr Nevil Maskelyne, the fifth Astronomer Royal, recommended him as his successor to the council of the Royal Society and Sir Humphry Davy, from Penzance, who had visited him at Westbury in 1800, brought his merits to the notice of the Prince Regent. As a result, John Pond was appointed Astronomer Royal in February 1811 with an augmented salary of 600 guineas. In 1821 he substituted a mercury horizon for the plumbline and spirit level (ib. cxiii. 35) and in 1825 introduced the system of observing the same objects alternately by direct and reflected vision, which, improved by Airy, is still employed (Memoirs Roy. Astr. Society, ii. 499). He was a member of the board of longitude and attended diligently the sittings in 1829–30 of the Astronomical Society's committee on the Nautical Almanac of which publication he superintended the issues for 1832 and 1833. A translation by Pond of Laplace's *Système du monde* was published in 1809. He wrote one tidal letter.
Ref: 845 11 HOT LB3 (letter book #3) 74, Beaufort: Francis, Hydrographer for the Navy. Hydrographic Surveyors. Pond 22/12/1830.

Cambridge University Library (CUL): July 1964
Ref: Meteorological notes: letter research book 3869 ref: Tides.
St John's Secondary School pupil John Nightly has spent the past two
weeks in CUL trying to complete the first phase of his research on tidal
letters. Tidal letters were the means used by explorers, scientists and
astronomers in the 18th century to determine the movement of tides in
order to understand and help predict weather conditions. It is hoped that
he will eventually be able to turn his research into a more long-term
project and continue with his interest in his chosen career.
'Eye Around Cambridge', Cambridgeshire Schools Curriculum Notes,
end-of-year round-up. July 1964.

As if all of this activity wasn't enough, John had set himself the
task of writing a kind of dissertation on tides, waves and their
potential power using tidal letters and the notebooks and diaries
of the scientists and explorers who wrote them. John was in the
process of completing his research into the papers of two
astronomers: John Pond, Astronomer Royal and one-time fellow
of Trinity College Cambridge, and Francis Beaufort, hydrographer to the Navy. He would then turn his attention to Charles
Wheathouse, the scientist who had built wave machines to help
him understand the energy of waves and their rhythms in the
hope that this natural energy could be utilised for general power
consumption. John had been many times to see Wheathouse's
wave-machine models in the Whipple Museum in Cambridge
and had at one point made his own miniaturised versions by
cutting up the stiff white card packaging of his father's Rael
Brook shirts. Through his experiments in phase-shifting,
Wheathouse had happened to invent several important instruments; among these was the microphone, for which of course
John Nightly and many others would end up being very grateful
indeed.

'A Brief Explanation of Tides; Meteorological Effects on Tides',
UK Met Office Report. April 2004.
Weather conditions that differ from the average will have an effect on the
differences between predicted and actual tide times. Strong winds can hold
the tide in or push the tide out. Barometric pressure can cause fluctuations
in predicted levels. **Cause of tides:** The moon being nearer to the earth
than the sun is the principal cause of tides. Spring tides occur after a new
and full moonwhen the sun, moon and earth are directly in line and the solar

and lunar waves co-incide, as the moon exerts its powerful gravitational pull on the water which rises above its normal level. Water covering the earth furthest from the moon is also subject to this pull, so another distinct dome of water is formed on the farther side of the earth providing the basis for a second wave.

When the sun is at right angles to the moon, now in its first or third quarter, Neap tides are formed. Both the Springs and Neaps occur 48–60 hours after the corresponding phases of the moon. In most parts of the world there are two high and low tides every lunar day – which is 24 hours, 50 minutes and 28 seconds. **Her Majesty's Nautical Almanac Office: www.ukho.gov.co.uk**

On 10 September 1964, the Kinks' 'You Really Got Me' displaced 'Have I the Right?' by the Honeycombs – Joe Meek's final chart-topper – from the Number 1 spot. If this was, as rock'n'roll history books later claimed, the first official heavy rock, metal (or punk) record, it had little effect on the Everyman, who were advancing from strength to strength in another direction altogether. The group had a new rehearsal space, a former WWII shelter underneath St Edweard's churchyard, as well as a new lead singer, who, three times a week in this damp stone cellar, threw his weight around and repeatedly bullied the group into endless rehearsals of a suite of songs dedicated to his adorable girlfriend.

Grantchester Love Chronicle was a set of six ornate love poemes, in style somewhere between Martin Carthy, a regular at Cambridge Folk Club, and Richard Strauss, whose *Four Last Songs* were a recent discovery of John Nightly's. Performed by the Everyman as a kind of folk-song suite, what John Hilton insisted on referring to as 'mod-baroque' – John Nightly's set of four-minute ballads with connecting instrumental passages, including the standout 'Wave Orange Love', was a very early example of a sound that would emerge in records like 'I Got You Babe' and 'Mr. Tambourine Man' the following year, becoming fully formed with the eventual distillation of a variety of influences into the music of Pentangle, Fairport Convention and West Coast groups like the Left Banke and the Lovin' Spoonful. In a long-forgotten vault beneath the rainy pavements of Cambridge town centre, as lightly picked arpeggios collided with a Mersey backbeat, a movement that would come to be known as 'folk-rock' was a-coming.

O what a multitude they seemed, these flowers of London town!
Seated in companies they sit with radiance all their own
The hum of multitudes was there, but multitudes of lambs
Thousands of little boys and girls raising their innocent hands.
William Blake, 'Holy Thursday', 1789

The offices of John Carter Enterprises, Carnaby Street, London W1. Thursday, 5 March 1966. 11.00am.

'But we have to *promote* the record... even if we don't actually have the thing recorded yet. And you have to have some kind of... philosophy. Something they can write about. Everyone has a philosophy, man...'

The manager peered at the boy through a gap in the leaning tower. It was rare for Pond to consult with an artist regarding promotion, or anything else for that matter, and a mark of respect for this particular client that today he could be bothered enough to do so.

'What the hell they gonna write about, anyway? Those...' Pond spluttered before pausing for a moment, trying to summon up much more of an insult than the one which appeared. 'Pillocks!' he cried. 'Never met one yet capable of writing a word about anything at all... helpful – helpful to us, that is.' The manager seemed reasonably satisfied with his assessment. '*Personality* is the only thing those dolts understand. Telling you... *Per-son-a-li-ty!*'

Pond let the word slither out. He shot up from his desk and advanced, waltzed, towards the boy, as he enunciated Newley-like: 'Per-so-na-li-ty... *Hup!* Per-so-na-li-ty—' mimicking the popular entertainer's overenthusiastic delivery, firing off each tuneless syllable before breaking away. 'There needs to be some kind of... "thing". Protest... "political" thing. Something... *something...*' he paused for a second, 'with a point to it!' The manager broke off. 'They love "points". Love that kind of... thing. All the stuff you're actually interested in. *Anti-this* and *anti-that...*' Pond leaned back against the rubbish heap on his desk – 'Everyone has a *thing!*' – visibly frustrated at being unable to explain himself quite to his satisfaction. He leered at the boy and looked round for cigarettes, momentarily defeated.

John Nightly untied his scarf and smiled, trying to take it all in. Back in London, back in Carnaby Street, here he was, delivered into a family of… 'aliens' was the only way he could accurately describe his paymasters. JCE was an energetic, fast-changing environment. The pace of which was determined by the redoubtable Pond.

With the new employee a little under the weather due to a sleepless night at the Royal Lancaster, and with Cornelia supposedly taking notes, employer and employee were discussing an interview, John's first ever, to be given to the *Daily Telegraph's Young Idea* magazine. Almost a 'briefing' session, necessary because the concept of promotion was something the boy was obviously quite lost with.

'I don't understand why I can't just talk about my music?'

'You can talk about anything you wish. But chances are they won't be interested. They won't write about it and they won't print it, and therefore it won't actually do any good.' Pond pointed to the centre-spread open on his desk. December's *Record Scene* showed four new signings, the teen mag's own 'tips for the top': the Amazed, the Mike Kay Khorus, the Oliver Twists and new soul sensation Carl & Carla. 'Look at this lot!' he drooled, stabbing accusingly at the pages with a tatty fag end. 'They all talked about music.' He gurned and grimaced as he brushed his luxurious hair from his face. 'Where did it get 'em?' The manager rubbed his tired eyes and loosened his cravat. None of the acts' debut releases had achieved anything more than to be returned to the pressing plant from whence they came. 'Pillocks! Bloody pillocks! The lot of 'em,' Pond declared. 'Not the groups, but the so-called "managers" these *unfortunates* have the misfortune to associate with…'

He turned to Cornelia, *'Tea…'*

'What else *are* you interested in, John?' Pond looked up from his desk. 'What are your other "specialist areas"?' The manager was only half concentrating, as usual, as he picked through the morning's post.

'Other than …music?' John considered. 'Well… when you say *protest*… you've got things like *Ban the Bomb*…'

'Ban the Bomb?' Pond swept through the tapes and demos as if he were clearing a rainforest. 'No one's interested in *Ban the Bomb*. All that bomb-banning. *Folk* people got it covered from the start. Can't take anymore "banning of bombs",' he twitched. 'They're either gonna ban the things now or blow us all up! Have to come up with something a bit more interesting than that!' he concluded philosophically, before pausing suddenly, having realised what he'd just said. '"Better" than… y'know… "bigger"…' he sighed again. 'Something more… *unique*. More of a story… is what I'm…'

The boy summoned up the courage to respond.

'I don't know if anything could be much… *bigger?* Than, well… the *nuclear bomb!*' Cornelia turned to her boss, rooting for him while displaying a sneaking satisfaction at seeing him being made a fool of. The boy carried on: '…pretty big thing to… to ban…'

John…'

The teenager caught his breath. Sarcasm and a general air of superiority are not appealing personality traits. In John Nightly's case, whenever it seemed that he might be halted or slowed in his progress towards any goal he would always react badly. John Nightly's only wish in life was to be allowed to carry out his mission. At his own pace and with nil interference. No plan could be changed or decision revised, no matter how wrong-headed it seemed, once it had been decided upon. Not even by its instigator. It was almost as if he would still force himself to proceed in a chosen direction rather than reconsider, even while acknowledging that his own course may not be the best one.

In the corridor, Sand was attempting to deal with two unannounced visitors and a delivery; so Cornelia, who was about to pour fresh Earl Grey, left the room to answer the phone next door.

'Dave Davison on the line…'

'Call him later…' Pond shouted, pulling himself up from his desk.

'There's my astronomical things? Tidal things… uh… *thing* things? That's a good one, surely?' Suddenly John Nightly woke up, '*New Power… Wave Power…* all that kind of… power and… *Wave…* uh… interesting to everyone at the moment.'

'Never heard of it, and no one else will have either.' Pond made a dismissive gesture. 'Sounds like something to do with hairdressing! We need an angle… a good old… angle, like anything else.'

The manager sat down again. More post had arrived, and tea, hastily delivered by Cornelia between phone calls. A newer pile of tapes, contracts and begging letters awaited his attention. He pulled open the drawer of his desk and produced an ivory-handled cake knife. Selecting a large gold-trimmed envelope, he held it up, admired it briefly then slit it open. A gold-trimmed invitation – *New Musical Express* Poll Winners '66 – fell out. Pond threw the card up in the air and feigned a two-handed midfielder's catch.

'Come with me to that… Introduce you to some people.' He picked up a long-extinct cigarette and relit it.

Pond manoeuvred his head from side to side, as if he were slowly unscrewing it. The new employee was becoming frustrated. The new employer was becoming frustrated.

'John…'

But at least the boy was beginning to understand how to play the manager. He took a moment to catch his breath. What he was faced with on the other corner of the room was a conundrum. 'Irascible' was John Pond's natural state. Like his charge, Pond could operate effectively only if he had the full support of his co-workers. Could be successful only if someone let him.

John folded his arms, leaned back and stared straight at the opposing force.

'…I am only interested in music… you know I am. I only know about music. But I believe that I know… a lot… about it. I don't mean I'm… I'm boasting, or anything… I just do know. It is literally my *thing.*' The boy softened. 'And it's my only thing, so it's also my… my vocation. It is my life, or so far it is. My speciality, as you say, and therefore my… my "angle".' He stared directly at Pond. 'On everything. On… life itself.' John paused. 'So I can talk about it… till the cows come home if you want me to, and…'

'And… and… *and…*' the manager stirred from his chair.

John Nightly wasn't used to tension this early in the morning. A nervous Cornelia re-entered the office. She placed two tiny cubes wrapped in greaseproof paper on the manager's in-tray.

'Tell me what you'll say if you're going to talk about this!'

Pond, ever more irritated and fed up, had raised his voice to what he realised was an unacceptable level. This was a business discussion after all. He paused and searched his desk for a tea-cup, pen or cigarette-lighter, in need of a prop. He caught sight of the greasy cubes, picked one up and made as if to toss it over to the client.

'If you're going to talk about music as you describe, and promote yourself… *C'mon, then*… have a go. Try it out… and entertain *me*, the *dear* reader…' The boy sat up straight and allowed himself one more breath.

'I'll… uh… talk about how I make music, and what I… how I…'

'How can I say this, John?' Pond made a pillow shape with his hands and yawned. 'You're sending me off to the old Land of Nod a little too… prematurely…'

It really was extremely rude behaviour. Pond picked up the knife and sliced open another missive. A large, crown-size envelope with red sealing wax.

'Thing is… we're just starting a relationship here, so we… we need to be honest with each other.' There was no response. Pond pulled out another exclusive-looking card, raised his eyebrows and placed it to one side. 'Because… to be honest… if you don't me mind *me* being honest, for a minute… You can be a little… "innocent"…' The manager looked disappointed with himself. '"Inexperienced" is… yeah… a bit inexperienced about these things… about… the world in general maybe… If you don't mind me… saying so… *ISN'T THAT RIGHT, BABE?*'

Pond aimed the rhetorical blast directly at his secretary, who almost jumped out of her knee-length boots. He gathered the remaining pile of envelopes, straightened up and realigned the tower as best he could, edged it over to the corner of his desk, checked the wastepaper basket was positioned directly beneath, and tipped it in.

'You talking about *music* does not get us the coverage we need, that "good copy" everyone wants… and that… the journalists, those dopehead pillocks, are looking for. It doesn't.' Cornelia scribbled furiously, continuing to pretend to make notes.

'These days, when everybody and their grandads are making records, you do need an angle… a good one, as well… in terms of promo: *Pro-mo-tion*... harmless stuff, promotion... A crazy old inconvenience no doubt, designed by Stone Age managers probably, to promote things, so that people – general public, God bless 'em – realise that the damned record exists; so that in turn, knowing it exists, they can maybe even hear it once or twice on the radio... if we can get those pillock dopeheads to play the thing, the blessed public might even go out and *buy* it.' Pond took a breath. 'That in turn makes *you* very happy, gives *us* a chart position we can work with, and eventually, though it's only kind of a... by-product... in a way... of the whole... condition or "procedure"... *shebang*, perhaps...' he laughed. 'Anyway... eventually... hopefully... sooner or later, sometime in the not-too-distant future, it makes both of us, very... well, *happy*... "money-wise"... Rich!' He looked up at his audience – first at Cornelia, then the boy – before nodding conclusively in agreement with himself. 'Guess that is definitely the right word.' The manager seemed relieved. 'And that – not the *rich* bit, but the whole thing – the whole spaghetti... is the one and only reason I'm...'

'... I understand that. I really do. But the music I have is actually good...' The boy paused, 'so it doesn't really...'

Pond picked up his cube of fudge and took a bite while finishing off John Nightly's sentence for him. *'Doesn't need promoting!'* The manager whispered. 'I know, man... I know. *IT – DOESN'T – NEED – PROMOTING!* Because good stuff doesn't, does it?' He got up from his chair. 'It's that good! That powerful! Like the Queen doesn't need promoting. Mickey Mouse doesn't need promoting; the Pope doesn't need it. I do know what you mean. Coca-Cola doesn't. That's why they've all spent one hundred-odd years promoting these things, I guess? Heard that one before, y'see.'

The sticky stuff affixed itself to the manager's front tooth as he continued to proclaim. The scene having become farcical, Sand and a new visitor could be heard stifling laughter from the safety of the corridor.

'We know you're good at music, John.' Pond detached the piece of gunk from his mouth. 'That's why we've signed you... We think you're a genius at music. We hope you are, anyway. Bit of a mistake if you're not!' he laughed.

The boy gulped down his own sticky cube, more and more lost as he chewed and chewed.

Pond walked over to an empty wastepaper bin hidden under Cornelia's chair. The manager was nearing his limit. Today he had a million other things to worry about besides the interior musings of a schoolboy from Grantchester. One of which was the fact that the Gloom's follow-up, despite being played almost non-stop on Caroline the past fortnight, had only just made the tiniest of dents in that morning's Top 100. The Pond-sanctioned and heavily promoted 'Girl Tan' was a brand-new entry at Number 99! If the record didn't make it there would be no one to blame but himself – and the last thing JCE needed right now was a one-hit wonder on its books. Pond sat down, crumpled a cigarette packet in his hand, picked up today's *Record Scene* Souvenir Pull-Out Wall Chart and tossed it into the bin.

'*SAND!*'

The secretary appeared at the door, notepad and nail varnish at the ready.

'Look...' Pond lit another cigarette and sighed. '*Image...*' He got up from his chair ready to pace up and down, though there was nowhere really to pace to in the pokey room.

'*Beach Boys...*' he swallowed. '*Stripy shirts, surfboards...*' before pausing for a moment. 'They're kind of... all a bit... *Chubby...*' Pond looked up. 'That's a bit of a thing in itself maybe. *Fat boys...* yeah. Kind of trademark... "identifier".'

Cornelia, Sandra and John, now more or less in the swing of things, frowned in unison. Pond picked up speed. '*California... Sun* as well – that's a… a "signifier", sun is…' He paused again, for effect. 'See my point?' The audience nodded still more solemnly. '*Stones*… again… *Hairy bastards; unruly bastards.* Bastards in general, probably. *Mean-looking… rubber lips…*' He paused once more. '*Jerky dancing,* too…' then gave up. 'All this stuff is worked out, premeditated. They've got a manager who does know what he's doing.' Pond returned to his desk. 'I rest my case – as they say in the trade.'

The manager seemed wired as he resumed his position. Rather than giving the impression of someone who had just made his point, he fidgeted and twitched as if he had suddenly been injected with idea serum. He glared at a pile of Gloom promo discs, inspecting them with disdain, as if there were a sign hanging on them saying 'Extinct as a dinosaur'. He gazed out of the open window, picked up one of the 7" acetates and skimmed it through the narrow gap into Carnaby Street. The manager gazed down at the dingy thoroughfare, his own market square, his souk, a very un-square mile. Then, appearing extremely pleased with himself, turned to his audience once more.

'*Kinks*… They're *kinky,* for a start! *Riding outfits, toothy grins… apeshit singer… The Who…* very strong. Point being that all the big ones are.' Pond placed his thumbs in his pockets and paraded around his desk. '*Pop Art, mods, pills, speed, apeshit drummer…*' he stopped. 'I… I'm not trying to…' Cornelia fixed her hairband and wondered if she might be bold enough to ask teacher for a cigarette while the boy, visibly bored but unfazed by this kind of playacting, got up from his chair.

'I think we get it… uh… it's… well… you can break it down… like… theatrical costume…' John picked up his bag. 'But… getting back to music… and my own… the other stuff I like…' he paused. 'There are a couple of…'

John Nightly appealed directly to Cor and Sand, accepting that he was probably not going to be able to clinch it with the manager today. 'I could talk about poetry. He looked inside his bag. 'I read a lot of poetry…'

Pond walked back across the room, sat down behind his desk and grabbed the silver desk lighter. He appeared weary, as if he'd been standing up for all of his twenty-one years. He let out a huge exasperated howl…

'CORNELIA!'

But his secretary was a million miles away. Cornelia was snuggled up in her employer's bed, cruising along Carnaby Street in his Mini Cooper, inspecting the racks at Biba on a Saturday afternoon, awaiting her hair appointment at Rikki's while leafing through the pages of *GIRL* and about to repaint her pink index nail. She jumped as if suddenly electrified in her customised car seat.

John Nightly understood very well that today's had not exactly been what you might call a 'helpful' discussion. Pond answered a call as John moved towards the door. It was definitely time to leave.

'I do see what you mean…'

The boy didn't see what anyone meant, but when he left the offices of his patrons he began to consider what was going to be expected of him in this new environment. What exactly he'd gotten himself into. The reality of this whacked-out, supposedly swinging but precariously balanced, most superficial pendulum.

It was clear to John Nightly that the reality of the world he was about to inhabit was very different to the one he'd imagined. Though he didn't know it yet, John was about to be zoomed into space. The teenager that he was, the child he had been (so far) was going to change, be changed. The young man he was becoming was going to be diverted. John Nightly was going to become someone new, some*thing* new, on account of events that were about to take place and the circumstances in which he was going to find himself. If it worked out he would take on a kind of 'dual personality', able to turn 'the artist' *on*, and hopefully *off* again to become himself, or his old self, once more. If it got to the point where he couldn't manage to turn the persona off – or worse, was no longer aware that the artist needed to be turned off sometimes, like a clockwork toy does, like a lightbulb does, like a bright-eyed smile does – then we were in trouble.

It was true that newspapers and magazines did not write about music. They weren't qualified to do so. And the readers – teenage dollies, sixth-formers becoming aware of the new world, worried mums and dads – didn't want it anyway. So they concentrated on peripheral stuff. They wrote about people, per-son-a-li-ties, as the manager rightly pointed out. Any scandal that might lie beneath the surface. Rags-to-riches stories mainly, and… most wanted of all: failure. Preferably huge success closely followed by huge failure. The bigger the rise and fall, the better. And these days the *Daily Mail's* showbiz columnists seemed just as fascinated by the men behind the glamour, the new impresarios, as by the groups themselves. As the boy came to understand more about the manipulative and mercurial nature of his own 'boss', it was obvious that it was the combination of the appliance of ideas and sheer hard work on behalf of the managers with the raw talent of the artists that made the wheels go round and gave certain groups a significant advantage over others.

Artist and manager were co-dependent. The managers plotted and schemed, applying whatever was required to the product to make it 'happen'; a heavy lacquer polish or a quick shoeshine. They put the product through a filter, commercialising and standardising the material, in the process smoothing out the edges that had gotten the young innocents noticed in the first place. It was this optimum blend of the two elements, combined with co-ordinated promotion, everything going off at the same time, – the all-important week of release – that delivered the nervously awaited new-entry chart position and the hits. Closely followed by the royalties – and the writs.

The managers weren't equipped to do the job themselves, or they would've; and neither were the clients. Within the heavily competitive record business and all of its spin-offs, everything about the performers, their work and their lives, would be supervised and edited. Bits chopped off, new bits added, good bits repeated, the whole spaghetti carefully scrutinised, rearranged, taken apart and reassembled again, just like a record itself. The raw material put through a sieve, mashed up, regurgitated and then spat out by these tin-god Svengalis, Epstein, Meek, Larry Parnes or Andrew Loog Oldham.

John Nightly's approach to his chosen vocation so far had been from the point of view of a creator – of product or 'content'. Like all great creators he was both artist and appreciator – *fan*. But there was a whole other pay-off further down the line, and the boy began to see, if not quite understand, how that worked. The public personas of many of the better-known performers were often a fabrication. Their names and backgrounds, their hairstyles, the clothes they wore, the way they behaved on and off stage, all carefully considered before record company and management deemed it safe to put the concoction in front of the toughest audience in the world: an audience untried and untested; teenage record buyers with pocket money to spend.

There was a careful manipulation of this fan base. Wives and girlfriends being written out. Everything needing to appear fresh and modern. And *new. New* was the most important adjective of the era. *New* was the only thing 'fab', 'groovy'… 'happening' really had to say. *New* was the required meaning of everything. Every product, from soapsuds to real-live pop singers offered for sale to the general public, was required to be tantalisingly, heart-stoppingly *NEW!*

John Nightly understood from what he heard around JCE that a good deal of chart entries were 'bought in' to the Top 20. DJs and producers being paid or given incentives for airplay. The boy resolved never to allow anything of this nature to happen to any record released under his name. The only way John

Nightly wanted any kind of success at all was if people played and bought the music because they genuinely liked it. Liked what they heard. That was the only way he wanted the music issued in the first place. Otherwise, in the boy's simple little head, his work might be seen to be tarnished. That's how pathetic and stupid he was. John Nightly wanted everything to be clean. But his chosen profession was a dirty one. The records went up, the records went down; and how the manager's attitude changed when they went down. It seemed that things were about to become very gloomy indeed for the Gloom.

As he made his way along Regent Street, John began to think for the first time about these inner workings from the outside. About 'image signatures' and trademarks. That artists might end up being remembered solely for some non-musical stamp with which they were associated. The barefoot Sandie Shaw, Johnny Kidd's eye patch, P. J. Proby's 'pants episode'. Hardly a bunch of very dignified offerings. But the records themselves stood out, and that was the point. The point the manager was trying to make was that sometimes you have to use elements outside of the music, something seemingly unrelated and seemingly insignificant, in order to promote and therefore sell the music, the 'good' thing, the real, right stuff itself: the absolute *raison d'être*.

But now it was time to get back to the Royal Lancaster and continue working on song ideas. John had brought his Eko acoustic with him; and there was a piano in his room, courtesy of Jon at DJS. When the boy arrived in the smart Kensington lobby, the concierge approached as if he'd been expecting him.

'Extremely pretty young lady left this for you, sir.'

The man held out a folded note with a flower insignia, Mary Quant's poppy logo. Child's handwriting, left earlier that afternoon. It was from Iona. Remember?

'Hello! Remember me? I heard you back in London, JCE told me about

which hotel. I live in Knightsbridge too, not far, so if you have time... or you bored and like to ring me up... Iona... Ken 329.'

Suddenly the boy forgot all about promotion. Suddenly he was willing to do anything the manager asked. Suddenly he was malleable, all too happy to be manipulated in any direction whatsoever, and tremendously vibed-up. Although only last week John had read in his father's *Daily Express* that his photospread sweetheart was the on/off girlfriend of Jean-Luc Zeib, the French-Canadian Grand Prix driver, he rushed straight up to his room, turned on the radio and dialled the number.

'Radio London reminds you. Go to a church of your choice...'

'... oh... hallo... is... I mean... *could* I...'

'John! Hello John, it's Iona! *Darling*... don't you know my voice? How are you?' There was barely space for breath. *'Where* are you?'

'... I... well, I'm in my...'

'In your hotel?'

'well, yes... I've got to...'

'John, I tell you what you've got to do...' The voice on the other end trembled with excitement. 'You've got to come out and meet me at Kassandra's, that's what you've got to do. You know where? Old Brompton Road. Number... 93, I think? Just get a taxicab, it's not so far. I see you at 5.'

The boy was there early. A full ten minutes early. He really was clueless about matters such as whether to turn up early or late for girls. Ten minutes to five! No idea at all. Kassandra's was easier to find than he'd imagined. Along past the Science Museum, the only London landmark known to him, then over to South Kensington tube, a sharp right-hand turn and... All you had to do was to follow the parade of teenagers floating down Old Brompton Road.

It was easy to locate the tiny bistro – 'the scene' – from at least half a mile away. The convergence of beautiful people to this small, magnetised café was like flood water rushing to its conduit. It confirmed that the *youthquake* predicted by everyone – even the *Daily Express* and the *News of the World* – had definitely arrived.

Outside the French Lycée, amid the chaos of buses and taxis, two pretty ponytails posed in their satin hipsters. The redhead swished around in a purple cape, which became entangled in her friend's sleeves. The dark-haired one carried a bundle of heavy textbooks and waved her arms about in a very French manner. Both wore gypsy rings and bangles, with little velvet bags slung over their shoulders like ammunition.

Across the street, a girl in an impossibly tight skirt climbed out of a Mini Moke parked precariously on the kerb, oblivious to the black taxicabs speeding by within inches of her. She resembled a Jazz Age starlet in her pink bodice and crocheted hat. Her boyfriend, Stone Age hair blowing uncontrollably in the breeze, held onto his girl and his *John Stephen* shopping bag.

Only that morning John had been reading about John Stephen. The man who had revolutionised men's fashion, or so it said in *GIRL*. The *King of Carnaby* – Millionaire Mod – doing for men what Quant had done for women.

On the pavement outside Kassandra's a busker manhandled 'House of the Rising Sun' at twice its recommended speed while a petite blonde, arm in arm with a tight-suited mod, kept tugging at her white vinyl dress, embarrassed at the hardly-there hemline as she crossed the road to the bistro. On the opposite side of the street, in the direction of Chelsea, boys in parkas and green cords joshed each other while keenly eyeing up *the talent*.

The girls, who couldn't have been more than fourteen or fifteen years old, wore court-shoes or white plastic boots, while the boys wore Cuban heels like Billy Fury or shiny black brogues in more of a mod style, probably from *Gear* or the new *Trend* department at Simpsons. A girl on a scooter showed off her white PVC mac and her *Trend* carrier bag, which she held on to with both hands, guarding it as if it were the crown jewels.

This was all a bit like a street carnival to John Nightly. There were a few scensters in Cambridge, not in the university but in the town itself. You'd see mods at United matches looking for unchaperoned greasers to beat up with a few overgrown beatniks at the occasional CND rally or poetry reading at the Union Society, but that was pretty much it in terms of street cabaret.

The Royal London Borough of Kensington and Chelsea was another world entirely. The boy realised that each time he'd made the journey to the capital the whole scene had moved on, upped a gear or two, appearing to intensify with every trip. London seemed to be going hysterical. How to describe it? The way things appeared to John Nightly, everybody and everything was suddenly aglow. Glowing with confidence. As if a wave of energy had flooded the city, covering its shabby post-war emulsion in '60s glitter and in the process literally switching it on. Even the language had become more expressive. Caffs and cafés were now 'bistros'. Shops 'boutiques', clubs 'discotheques'; there was a zing about the streets. A rush. Adrenaline-fuelled, and – in terms of the hyperbolic Youthquake – amphetamine-boosted. To the recent arrival it seemed that everything was brighter, faster, louder, slicker, zippier and, well, 'groovier', if you *must*.

The new language already had its own clichés. *Fab, gear* and *groovy* were adjectives that would never pass the boy's lips, though they were an essential part of the new everyday-speak. It was an early indication that John Nightly – feeling the need to promote his music using his rather eccentric persona and his good looks, but hampered by an intense shyness and insecurity – was already in turmoil concerning his own integrity and the 'purity' of his mission. The interloper felt less than comfortable in this sped-up, souped-up world, but he was certainly entranced and enthralled by it. It seemed to him that not just South Kensington but the whole country, the Commonwealth, the new 'global village', everyone and everything you came across had suddenly blossomed, flourished, experienced a power surge; gone into Technicolor. Had gone a little haywire, suddenly gone... **POP!**

'Hello, fashion model!'

'oh...'

John got up to shake hands and make space on the bench for the Disney-faced girl.

'Where's your scarf?'

'... my scarf? But... it's not cold today, is it?'

'John... I'm joking! You seemed to be rather... attached to it last time I saw you.'

Iona made her way through the footstools and chairs. Her see-through, lightweight skirt swept after her, taking with it the eyes of every man in the crowded basement. She settled down a few inches away from her intended, though he no doubt wished she'd have come closer. 'They... really played that up, didn't they?' John immediately moved his bag, managing in the process to edge an inch or so nearer. 'Did you... like the pictures?'

'Like them? I loved them... and so did my girlfriends. Everybody wants to know... Who is that gorgeous man you are with, Iona?'

PROFILE: Iona Sandstrand. Born: Herning, Denmark, 5 May 1948 (age 18). Unmarried. Model, John Raymond Model Agency. Lives: South Kensington. Educated: Kongelige Academy, Copenhagen; Lucie Clayton's, London. Clubs: Dolly's, Sibylla's, Scotch of St James's. Restaurants: Bruno's, Chez Victor, The Spot, Alvaro's, Kassandra's, San Lorenzo. Clothes: Biba, Quant, John Bates, Cardin, Grade One. Shoes: Elliott's, Kurt Geiger. Hair: Rikki's. Drinks: whiskey and orange. Smokes: Sobranie (occasionally). Holidays: Denmark.

'Do you always drink orange juices?'

John stared into his glass apologetically.

'…well… I like it. *Them…* I mean.'

'But darling, it's five o'clock in the afternoon. It's time for alcohol!'

Iona playfully stamped her feet as she tried to attract the attention of one of the handsome young waiters.

'I don't mean… I "need the drink" or that kind of thing. Don't worry about this!' she giggled. 'It's not the alcohols-needing. Just that we always was used to have whiskey at around teatime in Denmark. My father always was used to…'

'Really?' John moved closer still. 'We never… well… *was used to…*' Iona perused the spirits list, a somewhat limited selection. 'Mm…' she mused. 'I'm going to have Chivas Regal.' The girl sounded like an expert. 'The old man's drink!'

The boy brightened again. 'I'll have a… I might as well have the same, I suppose…'

Kassandra's was full to the brim. John assumed every one of the shimmering clientele to be in the modelling or photography business. Maybe they were actors or playwrights, or some such occupation that he took to be London-ish and very un-Cambridge. The afternoon imbibers seemed incredibly young, probably no more than 17, 18 years old, like John and

Iona themselves. But the right age – the optimum age – for *Now*, this room of anointed people. Tamarisk was most definitely the 'in' place on this particular sun-drenched afternoon.

'How much do you go to London, John?'

'been down to the Science Museum a few times...'

'Ah, yes. Because you're scientific.'

The boy laughed, to the puzzlement of his companion. 'But I'm very busy in Cambridge, working on my music all the time.'

'You cannot work all the time, darling.' Iona shuffled around on her seat, crossing her legs and uncrossing them, trying to get comfortable. 'You mean "college" work, isn't it? Nevertheless... What about girlfriends and people like this?'

John noticed the parcel lying on the bench between them. A barely concealed paperback wrapped in a thin brown bag bearing the stamp *Better Books*.

'... what's this?'

'I just get it today. *Sexus*... from Henry Miller.'

The boy flipped the package over.

'Better Books. In Soho.' Iona continued. 'The only place that have this sort of things. My mother told me that I can get it there and that I could... I mean... *should* read it.'

'... your *mother?*'

Iona smiled sympathetically. 'It's a bit different in Denmark than it is in England, but he lives here now anyway.' She frowned as if disappointed with herself before her smile returned. 'My mother, I mean... not Henry!'

The girl sat back and laughed both to and at herself, having forgotten for a moment that she was now living in an atmosphere of post-war sexual mores. Her guest decided he may as well correct her.

'*She.*'

'*She*… that's right. *She* lives here.'

'you read a lot…'

'Quite, yeah. Nonetheless. Quite a lot.' She seemed to be considering. 'I do now, anyway. I'm going to America with some modelling so I'm buying books to take with me. Monika tells me which ones, because it's a lot of time sitting around in these situations.' Iona pulled herself up on her seat and pushed the table further away to get more space for her legs as the waiter finally appeared to take the couple's order.

'is it something nice to do, though? This "modelling"? Is it a… a nice job?'

'Oh, a very nice. Something very good, with very good designer. It's always nice with this,' she smiled. 'We have to do some catwalk… for American client, to promote new designs. And catalogues of course. Everything will be updated now. Very fast. Things are moving so fast now John. I will be very "jazzy" of course.' The girl laughed again. 'There'll be some dancing and…'

'… Jazzy?' John wasn't sure he liked the sound of it.

'All the models will be jazzy.' Iona's eyes sparkled with the thought of being jazzy. She pulled down her skirt and crossed her legs. 'I'm model for Quorum too, and this is good labels. How 'bout you? Will you stay in London now?'

'Hope so. I think my manager…'

'And your manager is John?'

The boy nodded. 'I forgot… you do know him, don't you?' He was careful not to seem too inquisitive.

'John Pond was boyfriend with Monika – my best friend Monika – and so she was girlfriend with him!' Iona sought to allay the boy's fears while sounding a little unconvincing. It was clear that this was the only explanation John could expect. 'Monika had the job with Marimekko,' she continued, changing the subject. 'You know this one?'

John looked blank.

'Very famous designer. I love this pretty name they make for their company. Meaning "a dress for Mary".' Iona smiled. 'I suppose a lot of people don't know this…'

John nodded again. He was very aware that he needed to stop gawking. The only thought going through his mind at that present moment was, 'There's nothing wrong with her… not a thing wrong with this girl at all'. At which point a waiter threaded through the tables with a tray of drinks, giving the boy a reason to stop staring for a moment.

'But now she is designing for herself.' Iona smiled at the attentive waiter as she addressed her date. 'Monika, anyway… just to start off .'

'and is she… is she good?'

'Good? Oh, she is good! Monika is half-Danish, half-Japanese… and this is very good… combi… *nation*. For business and… for looks. For style also.'

Iona gazed around the room, pretending to ignore John as she surveyed the sea of faces and returned some admiring glances. 'Her mother was – is, I mean – Japanese. Monika is a very good-looking and she can get a lots of men.' The girl stirred her drink, 'nonetheless, she lives in the flat just down from me.' Iona spoke matter-of-factly and nodded. 'Down the stairs from my home.'

An image interrupted John's already chaotic brain patterns. It was the 'home' itself. A two-up, two-down bedsit, TV sitcom layout, sliced in half like a Battenberg cake, so that the various activities in all four squares could be viewed simultaneously. A queue of rugged, good-for-nothing types lined the staircase between the girls' apartments. Although this was the first time John and Iona had ever really spoken, he was already extremely jealous.

Iona picked up her whiskey, took a sip and laughed out loud. 'I think you may be dark man really. Somewhere back in your mind!' She looked pleased with herself. 'Maybe because "night-time" name.' Iona sipped again from her sparkling glass.

'Did think about that... my name. Changing it. But I didn't think there was a lot of point to it. *Nightly* is neither here nor there. Not very ordinary and not very unusual. Sort of "in between"... and... I'm concentrating on trying to think of a name for the group at the moment.'

'Ah...' Iona sat up straight, ready to help. 'Perhaps I can think of one of these for you.'

'oh... that'd be... great.' John looked doubtful. 'But I'm... probably quite close to coming up with it myself.'

'Ha! Your ego so big you have to think everything yourself!' Iona laughed teasingly and plonked down her glass.

'Tell me then, clever ego man. What great names have got in your mind?'

John took a deep breath.

'well…' he said, rising to the challenge a little too seriously. 'I wanted to call the group John's Children.' The girl immediately cut in,

'I like this… but maybe I can think of something *good* for you…' She looked over towards the bar. 'Let me try!'

'the other one I like is the Sleepwalkers… like Koestler?'

A blank look from the centre of attention. John leaned back and kicked his heels. He was enjoying the company very much. He was also enjoying the fact that during the short time he'd been with her the eyes of every boy and man, and girl, on tables both nearby and faraway, had strayed over to the vision sitting beside him.

'… have to think about that one. Where exactly do you live when you're not in Denmark?'

'Exactly!' The girl stamped her feet again.

'pardon?'

'That's what I mean… *Exactly.*' Now both of them appeared defeated.

'I don't mean "exactly" as in… *exactly*. It's an expression… a turn of… well… it's what we call *a figure of speech.*' John suddenly seemed rather tired, 'what I actually mean is… *when you're not in Denmark.*'

Iona put aside her empty glass and picked up her cigarettes. 'I'm not in Denmark,' she replied as she slit open the plastic wrapping with her nail. 'I'm definitely in London. As a matter of fact, I live in that road. The one up there.' She gestured somewhere in the direction of the open door. 'Brompton Road. Not too long – "far", I mean. Opposite Bazaar shop. Famous, as well. The road *and* the shop, I think.'

John had been in the capital only two minutes but he had at least heard of Bazaar, been *pre-warned* about it, because Jana had always wanted him to take her there. 'I know about it but… I don't know where it is exactly…'

'Exactly! Exactly what I say! And you can find exactly where, when you come to our party.' Iona picked up a match, 'We're having birthday party for me – on my birthday!' The girl chuckled. 'Of course that is when it is!' she laughed self-mockingly again. 'Five… Five of May,' Iona continued, lighting up. 'This is big star-sign day, so don't forget to write this one in, John!'

The fifth day of May immediately engraved itself on the boy's psyche. Whatever else might be going on in the world at large on that particular stardate, he would certainly be back in London by then. 'I should definitely be back in London by then…'

Iona offered a cigarette. 'And where do you go now?'

'Right now?' John wasn't sure whether or not he was being propositioned. 'Right now… exactly now, anyway… I have to go to the hotel and try to write some songs,' he explained. 'John's got me… hired me… a piano up there. After that, I'll probably go back to Cambridge and try to record them. Unless they want me to record them here…' He looked around as he gathered his books and papers.

'But you do have the hit, don't you?' Iona finished off her second drink and peered into her empty glass. 'I maybe take that one again…' John laughed.

'I hope I have "the hit". Because that's, well… what the record companies are looking for, isn't it?'

'They're all looking for this one.' She looked him straight in the eye. 'And… and… and will this exact hit songs be about me?'

At this point the boy turned a blotchy purple and immediately faced away from Iona towards the other side of the room. A tableful of French students were arguing loudly in fashionable 'Frenglish'. A girl in gruyere sleeves leaned across the table in order to show off her cleavage as she stared intensely into the eyes of the young raver opposite and carefully divided a flapjack into six unequal pieces.

'I know this sound funny to you now, John. But as a matter of fact, you never know. One day they might be.'

John blushed again.

'And is Mr Sir Pond going to do the best job for you? A clever job?'

'Let's hope so,' John replied. 'He's a… a good… person I think. But he's also, well… He's what we might call a bit… *volatile* is the word really – what you would probably call "moody".'

'Ah… I didn't know this.' Iona looked worried. 'Is it like *violent?*'

John smiled. 'Not like violent at all, no…' He considered for a moment. There was a certain logic to it, he thought. 'He's sort of… well… "volatile" might sometimes be… the bit before "violent", in a way, I suppose.' He smiled and picked up his half-empty glass. 'He's instructed me to try to get my… my "image" worked out.'

'Ah… he gives *instructions.*'

'not exactly… I didn't mean…'

'And what "image" is this?' Iona played with the strap of her top and looked directly into John's evasive eyes. 'Because… darling…' she whispered, temporarily forgetting herself. 'I think you don't exactly need this "image" at all maybe.' The girl relit her cigarette. 'Not really, John… because… because that… This not having image…' Iona leaned forward across the table. 'This will be your charm… your luck, you see. You don't need image all the time, John.' She moved closer still and surprised the boy by suddenly taking his hand. 'I think you just be yourself, darling. Like you are, anyway. Not like other boys – *men* – I mean.' She let go of him. 'That is why you're so… so *charmant*, I think!'

John Nightly was struck dumb. He couldn't believe that any creature such as this wanted to take his sweaty, adolescent hand in hers. Iona elaborated.

'It's really… "old fashion", what you have, John. Really… *English*, isn't it? *N'est-ce pas?* And this is what all the girls – everyone… boys as well – is going to like about you. When you become very famous. And yes, of course… before you will become famous, surely. This will surely help.'

John cleared his throat. 'I don't think I'm going to get *very* famous… not *very* soon either, you know. And not *that* famous, anyway… probably, well… not ever…'

'But you are going to make some hit?'

'of course! Well, I hope I am…'

'Then you become famous!' She placed her hand on his arm. 'Or how they going to sell it?'

Iona forgot herself again. Completely entranced by her companion's good looks and his disarming naivety, she gazed into the crowd, consciously trying to avoid his searching eyes. Iona imagined running her fingers through John's thick head of straw, letting herself lapse into the state she hoped might one day exist, as both of them, a little embarrassed, but tingling with the excitement of this faint sexual moment, brushing against each other on the hardwood bench, pretended to appear serious, disinterested in one another, artificially un-sexual, unaffected by one another, as if this little get-together was somehow illicit and needed to be curtailed.

'Even I am become famous.'

'are you?' John was taken off guard. 'I mean... well, I know you are. Of course, I know that. Because I saw you in the paper, and you're already pretty... well, quite famous already.'

But Iona saw no humour in it. 'I am a bit, I suppose. But... it's not too much...'

She moved away from him slightly, so that they were no longer physically in contact. 'What does your manager say about this... this *image?*'

John looked embarrassed. 'He says it's about... "angles" and all that sort of thing. Ideas about what I should look like. I know that everyone does have an image, but... well... Benjamin Britten doesn't...'

Again, no reaction.

John decided to stop being light with Iona now. He actually wanted to talk about something. Anything. Properly talk. Not about himself, but talk normally. 'Can't think of one, anyway,' he said abruptly, trying to round off the conversation. 'Maybe his frizzy hair.' He laughed as he finger-combed his own lush head of non-frizz. 'Ludicrous as that might sound. And... Stravinsky... he doesn't have one either.'

'Stravinsky? *Russian* Stravinsky? But Stravinsky well, does have image.' Iona became suddenly very serious. 'My father said she had a really big nose...'

John couldn't help but be taken aback at the reduction of the great Master to his – or her – nose, but the girl would not be put off. 'And this is his image,' she continued. 'I still get these things mixed up.' She looked rather deflated. 'But I'm excellent on everything else... like... Mr General de Gaulle.'

'what?'

'*General de Gaulle*... my father said he has a big... *Versailles* of a nose.'

The boy gave up. 'Well, yeh... he... and thank God that you are...' John looked tenderly at her. 'You are really... *excellent* yourself... in that... exact... department.' The boy turned sideways on to Iona as he acted out a detailed investigation of her almost-perfect profile. 'Really excellent, actually.'

The boy checked his own side profile in the mirror opposite. He caught himself staring into Iona's dewey eyes. Eyes that twinkled with sensation, like those of a child collecting shells on a beach.

'but John Pond... he is a good guy, I think. Though what is bizarre is that he's a descendant of someone I've been researching – in a scientific way.'

'John is scientific?'

The boy laughed. 'That's not what I meant. But, yes... he himself is actually quite scientific. Got a degree in quantum physics.' The girl looked shocked.

'I didn't know this. No idea about it at all. Nothing to do with Mary Quant?'

Now they both laughed. 'Sorry, John... only things I know is these silly things. What time the shop opens and what time it closes. Don't know anything... anything "important".'

Iona patted John's knee as she picked up her scarf and gloves.

'Let's go to Science Museum!'

The boy got up too – excited and fired up, though slightly ill-at-ease with this level of familiarity.

'Got to go back. Get on with some work now. I have to finish these songs by tomorrow.'

'Have you eat some lunch?'

'I haven't, but…'

'So… I come with you to there and we make sure you have some good food tonight, while you use your mind…'

John Nightly had no experience of how to handle this kind of thing.

'that's… that would be… very nice, of course. But… I really don't think I can do that either. I've got to ring my girlfriend now and…'

'Ah! The real answer! So you do have one of these…' John cast his eyes to the ground. 'And I guess she is very… pretty girl-friend?'

John looked up. 'I'm sure you… well… that you have…'

'I don't as a matter of fact. I didn't, John. No girlfriend at all! Maybe a couple of boyfriends…'

It was obvious to John that with Iona he would have to get used to her quickly moving in this direction or that. One minute serious, the next playful. Perceptive and focussed one second, completely empty-headed the next.

'And will you be writing these songs tomorrow as well?'

'I'm writing songs all the time. In my head, of course. Then I'm recording all the ideas I have for the LP. Thirty-two songs so far, you see. At Regal, like I…'

'And where is your… *Reegal?* Regent Street?'

'… Denmark Street.'

'Ah… London confusion. It's never in the place it says? But I'm doing TV commercial tomorrow anyway, so…'

John smiled in agreement.

'For English milk… *Drinka Pinta Milka Day. Drinka witha Iona* you see. That's what they want, n'est-ce pas?'

The boy picked up his bag.

'And will you go to Marquee?' Iona twirled her hair around her finger, excited at the prospect of another 'date'. 'To see Who next week. Shall we go with us?'

'The Who? Well… that'd be…'

'Then you can meet Monika – she really like you – and you can meet some more friends people. Who always in Marquee Club Tuesday.'

'… think I do really have to go back…'

"John… You go back and do your music" Iona sparkled, "I'll go back and do my make-up!"

And with that she was gone. Red shawl tossed over her shoulder as she dashed past foppish Chelsea Cobbler types and chic French Lycée types whose eyes followed her out of the room, out of the bistro and out of the microcosmic 'happening' little bubble. Out of this world. John Nightly thought so anyway.

'I want to get some thigh-length boots while I'm here. No, better than that, waist-length. Just like Robin Hood!'
Bob Dylan. London, April 1965

PROFILE: Bazaar. 46 Brompton Road, London SW3; KNI 5300.
Tube: Knightsbridge for Brompton Road; Sloane Square for King's Road.
Opening hours: Mon–Fri 9.30–6pm (Thurs 1pm close); Sat 9–6pm.
Stocks: Mary Quant-designed clothes. Prices: 1s to £15.

BBC Radio 3, Broadcasting House, Portland Place, London W1. 'Music Live', John Nightly talking to Nicholas Campbell-Johns. Friday, 7 September 1970.

Along a narrow hallway, a young man in a bubblegum-pink cravat and goat-skin sandals sits tight. In the corner opposite, a researcher in a camel-coloured midi-dress is nonchalantly polishing her nails.

'Anything I can get you?'

The young man looks up as if slightly dazed, but says nothing.

'Have you had a cup of tea?'

No response.

'Well, would you like another?'

The young man stares into space.

'I can hear him finishing off...'

The girl smiles, gets up and gently pushes open a heavy soundproofed door into a small studio where a long-haired, middle-aged, side-parted presenter sits shuffling papers.

The young man takes his seat and shakes his head theatrically, trying to wake himself up. The presenter, winding up the previous item, motions for John to say something into the mike and test it for level.

Just a little test for level now... John Nightly... are you there?

... in a manner of speaking... yeh... [The presenter gives John a silent thumbs-up]

John Nightly, welcome to *Music Live* on Radio 3, our annual celebration of live music in and around the British Isles. And thank you for coming in on the eve of your tour; I'm sure you must be very busy at the moment.

[yawns]

Before we talk directly about your music I wanted to begin by asking you about your background – and specifically about the move from Cambridge, where you were born, to London. It is said that the spirit of the Swinging Sixties is long gone; and as we prepare for the challenges of a new decade I wonder if that period was an exciting time for you?

[twists on his chair, as if trying to get comfortable] uh... [clears his throat] hmm... well... [swallows] In... uh... Cambridge I was working so hard on music... had a head full of... plans... everything... [coughs] whole life – 'musical life' – mapped out... Where I saw myself [coughs] fitting in... [yawns again] p'haps I didn't... feel the need for normal things, friends and...

Was there a particular reason for that, do you think? Did you seek friends?

[fumbles around for a cigarette] ...don't suppose I... did... maybe. Didn't exactly 'seek them out', I guess. I wasn't... interested in things and I didn't know... cars... football... normal... those kinds of... Couldn't really go to the pub, you know? [laughs] But it changed when I got to be... 14, 15. My... musical mind... sort of... turned on... full on... I had these... 'classical' performances going on in Cambridge and my... music being played. Then people did take notice. [accepts a light from the studio engineer] People at school were... 'surprised' – I was gonna say *impressed!* – when I could just... sort of... pick out any old tune... That week's *Number 1* or... play it on the piano... while they were all struggling with their chord sheets... scales. Was a little bit of magic that I carried with me. Something I could do... that they couldn't... understand, earned me a bit of... 'status'... sort of important in a school... institution-type situation. But I knew I didn't fit in there, and they knew it as well.

This was partly because of you spending so much time alone on music?

[stares straight into space] I'd spent so much time away from school, at home a lot... playing music... I'd lost that school... *continuity*. Difficult not to be thought of as an... outsider when you go back after time away. But... I really didn't do well at it – 'academically' I mean. Only when we had *Music* or *Art* – not even that sometimes – that I showed any... *knowhow*. The music we had to learn at school was... basic... you know... 'Bobby Shaftoe'...

I remember it well. [presenter smiles]

[interviewee smiles] Yeh, there was all that kind of... y'know. You really couldn't get into it. What they should have been doing was getting us all together and playing through... 'Telstar' or something... [laughs] At the time I'm talking about anyway. Or a Shadows track, anything that was happening at the time. Something that the kids... we... were excited about. That would have been good... and... but at the time, in that atmosphere... it was folk songs about... ploughing... and all that. We were surrounded by it anyway – farming, I mean. Cambridge was surrounded by land. Fenland. All these little villages. We didn't need to be singing about the ploughboy as well! [smiles as though exasperated and gestures as if finally waking up]

Thing was that... there we were... living in a... the whole culture was... 'exploding', in a way. But the education authorities didn't want to... recognise it. You can understand that... in a way, as well. [clears his throat] But even conversation was discouraged. You weren't allowed to talk when you walked through the corridors of the school – the public areas – meant that in a school of, 500 boys, 500... manic people, the communal places; the corridors, quad, playing fields... they were completely silent. The school... as a place of learning – it was a silent place.

You didn't find school a particularly inspiring place?

It's the memory I have of it. The other thing was that in Grantchester everyone knew each other. They knew who I was and where I'd come from, descended from... So if I walked around with a bit longer hair than usual or... pink socks – something like that – one of the neighbours would... well, probably make a comment to my mother! It was tight, y'know – the local piano-teacher was also the winner of the local piano-smashing contest!* I'm sure it's changed now... guess everywhere has. But I always made sure I walked fast when I walked around Grantchester.

Your parents were very supportive of you, weren't they?

The people who saved me were my parents. Can hardly believe they let me get on with what I had to do... [pauses for a moment to consider]

The other people who made a lot of difference were my girlfriend's parents. So good to have them there. Really musical people... both so... uh... musical. Jani... Dr Feather... my music teacher at school, showed me... many things. But it's my mother who really has all of the music in her that I inherited. Not that she'd ever touched an instrument in her life or anything like that, but she had that dreamy, self-contained... that atmosphere about her. Thing that dreamers, music people, have. [stubs out his cigarette] My mother was a listener. You could feel a change come over her when she listened to music. That did affect me. Made me always listen very... seriously. Properly, I mean. My Dad, my father, could do it to some extent and we had all of the equipment and all that at home because of his work and all that.

He was a recording engineer, wasn't he?

He wasn't a recording engineer, no. He was... still is – though he's retired now – a radio engineer. 'Cos Pye – radios and record players; other things they made, TVs – were based in

* In the early 1960s piano-smashing contests were a fixture at every village show, fête and fayre.

Cambridge, we had this equipment, sort of 'on hand'... tape machines in the house; I used it all the time.

But she could really hear... and listen. She always turned to me when I played a good chord and she'd smile: 'that's a good one.' She'd always sing back, sometimes unconsciously, even the weirdest things I was coming up with.

Sometimes I'd be at the piano for hours... be in my kind of... 'trance'... [laughs] If you want to call it that. Got into this thing of trying to sort of *receive* music, rather than try to really write it... 'invent' it or anything. I waited for it to just come down to me... from, well, I don't know where it comes from... Somewhere, you know... [the interviewer smiles politely as the speaker carries on in earnest] That must have been pretty painful, in a way, for my parents to have to listen to, 'cos I was just... weirdly, horribly 'improvising'. Trying to keep myself away from the normal daytime and stay in my... 'dream'. They – my parents – understood that. So they didn't force me to do anything else, not even the household... chores... washing-up, mowing the lawn... Never had to waste my time on anything like that [from behind the glass the producer motions to wind-up the interview].

So in fact they rather... spoilt you?

[laughs wryly] Not really. If they did, they spoilt me for a reason. My parents weren't concerned with normal ideas, normal... social ideas... 'conditioning' or whatever you want to call it...

We are often led to believe that Cambridge was a... hotbed of talent in the early sixties. You don't seem to have been a part of that.

[pulls a face] I wasn't... but that's because it was all centred around the university. Like everything in the town. There wasn't much in Cambridge for the people... [scratches his head] It was all owned by the colleges anyway, even the housing.

You couldn't buy a nice house, not in the centre or anything, unless your family already owned one... all the property was owned by the colleges. The social life... it all took place in the colleges. Actually, there was always a lot of vandalism in Cambridge. [looks round for another cigarette]

What about the music scene in the town? Did you feel part of that at all?

Wasn't much of a scene there... in Cambridge... You had bands... 'groups'... doing things and gigs in pubs... but they were mainly playing other people's material... hits of the day... I never wanted to do that. Really would've been a waste of my time. [lights up and accidentally hits the microphone] *Oh... sorry...* [carefully moves the mike back to its original position] Sorry 'bout that... [laughs] People talk about Syd Barrett, I only remember him being in a band that used to play at a pub close to my parents' house. Pink Floyd hadn't got going then, and... well... Jonathan King, I s'pose... Though that was after I left. [picks up a glass of water, careful to avoid the microphone]

Pink Floyd were a band called Jokers Wild. There were others... The Original Sins... The Prowlers... The Quaynts – funny names. The Bridegrooms, that was an early one. The Soulbenders, the Free Winds. I had a friend in the Boston Crabs – from Boston – and then there was my friend John's band... The Huntsmen – from Huntingdon – well... [laughs][1] It was all a bit like that. [laughs again] The music thing in Cambridge really wasn't big at all.

You had already written a hit record for your group the Everyman?

[grimaces] I sat down for five minutes one afternoon and... knocked out... the kind of thing I thought the judges would want to hear. [sighs] Not putting it down or... I had no idea it could actually be... a... well, a 'hit'. [makes a face] And certainly not as... as big or... 'hitty'... as it eventually went...

Zigging & Zagging?

I know. [raises his eyebrows] Does sound incredibly… 'simplistic' now. But… [smiles] It was a… a kind of… a song for that year… thing of its time. ['Zigging & Zagging' by the Everyman fades up in the background]

And a huge hit around the world? [2] [track becomes louder…]

> *Zigging and zagging and zigging and zagging and zigging*
> *Zigging and zagging and zigging and zagging and zigging*
> *Zigging and zagging and zigging and zagging and zigging…*

[…before fading out]

Sounds weird to me now… Never do that again, obviously. Write something like that. Well… I really only write things for myself.

Doesn't that comment imply that you simply don't care about the audience?

Not at all. Not that you don't, or I don't, 'care' about them. It's that… you have to write things for yourself… *please* yourself. All artists know that. If you aren't true to yourself, then who are you true to? And if you do write some kind of… *thing*… and the people that you're writing it for don't actually like it. Well… where does that leave you… creatively? You're nowhere, you know? And also… you've… you've let yourself down, so… That kind of thing really does not… well…

You have an LP coming out to coincide with the tour, I believe?

It's called… yeh… *Ape Box Metal.*

And apparently this recording consists of more than 3,000 segments… sections… of cut-up music and speech'

[seems genuinely surprised] Makes it sound like a tin of oranges!

[looks sheepish] I suppose it… haven't actually counted them myself or… [deep intake of breath] Is that how many it is?

And the record, as I understand it, has taken… two whole years to make, which is quite a… a phenomenal amount of time. Mainly, I understand, because of all the copyright clearances necessary in order to get the permissions from the various… participants, to reuse and release their work.

… that's not something I personally… the record company… my managers and…

Let me ask you this, then. What do you say to people who say that – not to put too fine a point on it – this is by way of another term for… 'stealing'? As I say, for want of a better phrase. Because what people will say to you is that you are reusing other musicians' work. Their music and their words, and sometimes – as I understand it – this is completely 'intact'? So that this is a completely different approach to the one you described earlier, that of 'receiving inspiration' in the way in which you would refer to it?

[looks at the sound engineer for another cigarette] okay… Firstly… it is not 'completely intact', as you say. That gives a very… a… an incorrect impression. It's not… any of it, 'intact' at all, in fact. Not… no. Sometimes it's just a… sound… a 'fragment' of a sound. A syllable. Something… so small you wouldn't hear it – or you hardly would. But it is a completely… different approach… so… [reaches across the table for the cigarette and lighter]

I use something like a… a millisecond of something… a very small… 'sliver'. Then… then I… put together… all of these milliseconds and bits and… and make a… a cluster till that collective sound, repeated – or 'looped', if you like – becomes the start of a… a completely new rhythm track, which I can then improvise over. The method I've always used… sometimes mixed up with a level of… 'pure' composition. But apart from the time it takes to get the permission to use the copyrights – the bits of music – this is also in itself a very involved and detailed kind of... trial-and-error process. Laborious as well: we have to edit everything, all these... particles... and the larger sections... by hand. So, yeh... physically, it does take a long time.

What about the point that you're reusing other's ideas?

...the point is that... that this is the age of the 'cut-up', you know... well, it's supposed to be, anyway... the 'post-modern' period... 'era', isn't it? [looks for a glass of water] You take things from here and there... different times, different eras... You mix them up... turn it into a... a sort of 'tapestry' – or quilt. A new thing. Something completely new, out of them. You make them connect somehow. It's like a quilt or... [stubs out his cigarette] 'rearranging the stars in the sky'. [makes a mocking, grand gesture with his hands] And what I do as a... well... as a composer, is to try to present and represent my mind and my ideas... and... and... the age I'm living in.

[from behind the glass the producer motions to wind up the interview again]

And you think it important to be... of your era?

It's a... confused time we're living in now... an... age that seems to be... running out of... steam... Running out of time – everything else – in a way, as well. We've just come through an... optimistic period. Kind of revolutionary period. What the 'Swinging Sixties' were. It was optimism that was behind it. Well... there are... there's, about... 'the bomb'... all that stuff... still... and war... and everything... *still*. So many things going... that surely if we... all got together – all the countries and everything – we could... do something about it. That's what people don't understand. Why this never happened. Why we haven't all got together by now, you know? Because we've had long enough to think about it, I think. But governments don't actually want to do that, anyway – I don't think they do. Or it would have happened... by now. And there are new things to 'worry about', as well... Like, how we can keep ourselves... and the world... going... 'Cos if oil... the coal... runs out, which it will, then... well, what do we do after that? In terms of... carrying on?

And I hear that you already have another grand project in mind after this one?

[sniffs] I don't know... I... I don't know how these things work out really... [smiles]... I've been reading some John Donne poems again... who I was very... sort of keen on... when I was at school. And I'm thinking about doing something... on quite a big scale... [rubs his eyes furiously] Possibly using some of his poem-letters as lyrics. And multiplying everything, y'know... forwards... backwards... upside down... Well... every which way... In threes. Very 'numerological', I guess. To the power of three... The Father, the Son... the Holy Ghost. Kind of a... a... a... like a *Requiem*... maybe that sounds a bit...

A Requiem Mass?

No... well... No... don't think it'll be a... a 'Mass' exactly. It's just an *idea*. [stifles a long yawn] It'll be something on... maybe a bit of a... a grand scale.

I heard mention of an opera?

Opera? [laughs, and coughs] Don't think so. No, no. [looks surprised] Couple of years ago I was looking at... *Woman of the Dunes*... It's a Japanese film, by... [frowns] Just the sort of... really good... subject matter for an... you know. Sand every-where... [laughs]

Why is the number three so important to you? I understand that everything you've ever recorded has had a... three-word title?

[producer makes ever-more frantic hand signals, desperate to wind it up]

It's not... a 'gimmick' or anything. It's because I actually like it, the rhythm and everything, I mean. It gives balance... form... which feels natural to me. Makes everything... God the Father, God the Son – all that. Three primary chords, three secondary chords in music... verse, middle, chorus... and... sonata form... the spiritual triangle... Numerology works in threes as well – apparently. Three primary colours, three secondary... the family unit – it's all 'three', isn't it? Seems to be. Kind of balanced unit... Three notes in each triad... chord. *'Veni, vidi, vici!'* Everything! All in three. When you think about it. The whole world. *Principal Fixed Stars, Grantchester Love Chronicle, Ape Box Metal... Mink* whatever it is... whatever it's... gonna be. The... well, the perfect sort of... 'only child' family as well.

You were an only child yourself.

Yes I was.

And even in your Grantchester days all of your songs were in three time, weren't they?

[thinks] Pretty much. 'Peachfruit Love Parchment', 'Free School Lane'... 'Lavender Girl'... those too. All in 'three time' as well.

Waltzes?

Not waltzes! [laughs faintly now, becoming rather exhausted] Just divisions of three... 6/8... 7/8, a four bar, then a three bar. 'All You Need is Love' is in 7/4 – the time signature – you know... pretty weird for a big hit record. It's a little bit like... some of the Indian music. Ravi Shankar... Miles Davis uses it. They all have these endless... rhythms, ragas... talas... falling... tumbling rhythms, and if you... If you keep using these odder rhythms... like Dave Brubeck or something – he does it in a simple way – it literally becomes... well, a time signature.

I don't know if you are aware of this but we're going to be

hearing from Pink Floyd on the programme next week and their upcoming LP is apparently called *Atom Heart Mother*.

Heard about that! And it's obviously… 'another story entirely'… [blushes]

Well, it's been very interesting – and enjoyable – to speak with you, John Nightly, and I wish you all the very best of luck with the *Ape Box Metal* long-player and of course with your live concerts… John… Nightly… Thank you for coming in and speaking to BBC 'Music Live'.

[blank look]

[1] Other notable Cambridge groups of the period were the Utopians, the Redcaps, the Chequers, the Fen Four

[2] 'Zigging & Zagging' hit the Number 1 spot in the US Hot 100, March 1968, as performed by the Bellbottoms, an English 'Carnaby-style' quartet from Auburn, California (American Jukebox – Ultimate Record Index, 1979), which featured drummer/vocalist Dandy Rich (Daniel Groderich) later of Kiss followers Angels of Destruction (later still he was the drummer in thrash-metallists Black Oak Death). Groderich is currently CEO of the record industry's number-one metal merchandising online service: *mortenoir.com*

The one time John Nightly walked as slowly as he possibly could when he walked around Grantchester was when he made a detour past a house set back from the High Street. The sound of a piano trio – violin, cello, piano – could be heard from at least a hundred yards away.

The Feathers' modest semi phased in and out as the boy approached. The house had an aura; it beamed 'ahimsa' – sensation, vibration, 'creation', liberation . . . renunciation – and countless other 'ations' whatever they stood for or were meant to symbolise.

A zen arrow winged its way from the upstairs bedroom straight into John Nightly's indented forehead. Hearing the family accompany Yehudi Menuhin on the gramophone, the boy became a delinquent worshipper as he mooched past the front door several times that evening.

John Nightly could only guess at the cultural exchanges taking place at the home of the emigré maestro and his family. The recital over, the record and the players might break into self-deprecating applause and a silhouette holding a violin might appear at the window. In the cold city street that night John felt something he wasn't used to feeling, something warm and tender, cascading in and out. Vagrant comet, well-meaning, innocent, life-giving.

The teenager had been obsessed about finding a 'girlfriend' – someone musical, i.e. cultured, elevated, hopefully 'foreign' – as a concept, or more probably fantasy, long before he'd actually met or even set eyes on the pre-teen Jana; Cambridge schoolgirl swot, virtuosic violinist, chela and deshiki, the presence and counsel he would always refer to as "the violin girl".

Rosevean Beach, St Mary's, North Cornwall. Summer 1955.

1-2-3-4-5-6-7
1-2-3-4-5-6-7
1-2-3-4-5-6-7
1-2-3-4-
1-2-3-4-5-6-7
1-2-3-4-5-6-7
1-2-3-4-5-6-7
1-2-3-4-
1-2-3-4
1-2-3…

'John… what on earth are you doing?'

Frieda hated any interruption while she was sunbathing. 'Counting the… -1-2-… waves, Mummy… -3-4-…'

'But there are quite a lot of them, darling… are you going to count them all?'

'Timing them, Mummy… the frequency – 2 – 3 – the *regu*… – 4 –… *larity* of them.'

'Oh God…' Frieda lifted her sunhat from her face and propped herself up on the hard granite. 'And why is that, dear…?'

-2-3-4
1-2-3-4
1-2-3-4-5-6-7
1-2-3-4-5-6-7…

'There's definitely a… -1-2-… pattern, Daddy…'

The boy stood on the edge of a rock pool, school exercise-book held tightly in one hand, a dead starfish in the other. John noted down the sequences, as the waves lapped onto the sand and gulls picked over morsels in the foam.

'I'm doing important scientific research for the Queen, Mummy.'

'God...' Frieda sighed again.
-2-3-4...
1-2-3-4
1-2-3-4-5-6-7

'John... you sound 57, not seven. We're on holiday, darling...'

-2-3-4-5-6-7
1-2-3-4-5-6-7
1-2-3-4
1-2-3-4
1-2-3-4-5...

As the boy's father tried in vain to get comfortable in his deckchair, the pages of *Practical Wireless* shielding his forehead from the sun, Frieda turned over on her towel and applied another dollop of lotion to her pink Scandinavian arms. John Snr opened the magazine.

'There's an article here about Marconi, John. You know he made one of his first discoveries very close to this beach...' The news aggravated an already fidgety wife.

'You don't mean Cornwall?'

'Poldhu Cove, apparently... he sent a signal from there all the way to St Johns, Newfounland.' The news was too much for Frieda.

'Father, now you know that is nonsense. Marconi was Italian. He certainly did not do his discovering in Cornwall!'

It was obvious to Frieda that *Practical Wireless* was full of mistakes.

'He liked it because of the clear space out to the sea, Daddy... For the signals...'

...2-3-4
1-2-3-4
1-2-3-4-5-6-7...

Frieda huffed and puffed some more.

'Do you think you could count a little bit more... *silently*, darling?'

Golding Constable's Flower Garden
John Constable, oil on canvas, 1815, 13 x 20 ins
(Colchester and Ipswich Museum Service, Suffolk)

'When I look at a mill painted by John, I believe that it will go round'

Golding Constable, John Constable's elder brother, 1830

Listening to pop music can be bad for you...

The *Times*, London: 'Music and the Arts in Secondary Education', April 1966.

Councillor John Seaward, head of music at the St John Regis School, Huntingdon, and advisor to the school-curriculum board in the Cambridge and Isle of Ely area, has stated that listening to pop music and pop groups can be bad for young people. Speaking at a regional conference in St Neots at the weekend to discuss secondary teaching in the subjects of music and art, Cllr Seaward said he believed that youngsters who spent their time listening to pop music were depriving themselves of the deeper emotional experience that could be gained from a study of the classics. 'Beethoven, Mozart and Bach are the 3Rs because of the deep, emotional experience they can deliver to young people. The music and words of pop groups are simplistic, basic and often ugly. This music does not warrant repeated listening. In my opinion this music will not last and, indeed, I believe it can also be a disruptive influence in our schools. It is for this reason that I propose the banning of pop music and its related culture from secondary schools in the Cambridge area.'

Listening to pop music can be good for you...

Ekstra Bladet, Copenhagen: 'Pop! Today's Modern Language', April 1966.

Dr Johannes Drewaes, speaking at a symposium in Copenhagen last weekend on new methods of teaching, commented in his opening address that 'listening to pop music can be an excellent way for our young people to learn English. Particularly simple phrases and new, up-to-the-minute vocabulary. The music of the Beatles, for example, is very beautiful and modern. Its expression is heartfelt and simple, yet can be deeply emotional and profound. If you have a favourite pop song it is a very good way to learn English words, sentence structure and everyday modern usage and also to understand how the words are put together in a poetic form of expression.' Dr Drewaes quoted from songs by Bob Dylan and Simon and Garfunkel's 'Feelin' Groovy' as other examples.

The Post Office, Peneed, West Cornwall: Mrs Diana Kitty Cardew, sub-postmistress. Letters arrive from Truro RSO at 10.20am, dispatched at 2.15pm, weekdays only. Postal orders issued but not paid. Letters add RSO. Cornwall. Telegraph office. Postmark 18.5.1986

Dear Mr Daly,

Regarding your letter dated 15th May, which I hereby acknowledge, I'm afraid that I now have to give you formal notice that as of today's date this sub-Post Office will no longer accept or be able to store horticultural items and plants posted from abroad and addressed to yourself. I have discussed this matter with you at length before, and have done my utmost to be of assistance, but I hope you will understand that because of the nature of the potential problems I outlined on the telephone this morning, this is the Post Office's final notice to you that any further plant specimens received in the mail addressed to Trewin Farm shall be returned to sender without explanation or further notice to yourself. I hope that I may be of assistance with any other matters in the future.

Yours faithfully,
Diana Cardew, Postmistress

For the first four years, John didn't leave Porthcreek. He didn't leave the house. Having decided that Trewin was to be his haven, his *savenheer*, place of refuge from the outer world, he must have sensed that it would also be his salvation. As it was, it took this length of time for the vicarage to be adapted to the needs of not one but two dysfunctional travellers. To have papers drawn up and obtain planning permission for the solar houses took all of two and a half years alone, give or take a few weeks. It was a slow start. But after that, with the building reshaped and extended and all of the surrounding area cleared and the woodland replanted, things soon came together.

John Nightly knew damn all about gardening. Apart from a few visits to the local Botanic Gardens as a child with Frieda and John Snr and the botanical chit-chat of the Everyman, he had never shown any interest whatsoever in matters of horticulture. It was actually all RCN's idea. The nurse remembered his friend returning to Queen Square from the aborted South African tour, his tour bag stuffed with what he assumed was some kind of thick-stalked vegetable. But what John had in his bag were cannas, a subtropical hybrid brought to England from the West Indies and South America by Victorian plant hunters. With its tall stems and broad-leaved foliage, the canna behaves like an exotic princess from far-off parts. Its scarlet and yellow flowers and red-purple leaves immediately stand out in any garden. Starch is produced from its tuberous roots, which helps maintain an almost continuous flowering cycle. RCN recalled how careful John was with these awkward, sticking-out monsters. He'd never known John Nightly take care of anything like he did the tall-stemmed exotics; not his music or his instruments, certainly not his girlfriends nor even himself. But there he was each morning, gently cleaning their foliage with leaf wipes and gauze, feeding them liquid tomato food, carefully checking each stem for fly and disease.

John was forever rearranging the pots around the glass veranda of the rooftop apartment so that the plants would eventually find the perfect aspect and achieve what he liked to call 'plant happiness', and later on, when the stalks shot up and became tipped with intensely coloured bellflowers, John put the by now deliriously happy cannas on the inside of his balcony window with no one being allowed to go near. Not even Iona, the only person he trusted with anything.

The three specimens, now renamed 'Luxus', 'Lucifer' and 'Mortada', as he'd managed to quickly lose the original labels, were also the only things the whacked-out addict took with him when he was admitted to SUMHA.

In that six-year void the extinguished star managed to propagate thousands of the things. The tall, gladioli-like perennials adorned every room and unit in the centre, each corner of the continually extended common parts, every cubbyhole of each long, forbidding corridor; John being the only one allowed to water and care for them. An activity that would occupy most of his days in the sanatorium, this new horticultural interest a therapeutic and time-consuming substitute for the hours per day he'd previously spent creating music.

Each wing at SUMHA was canna colour co-ordinated. So, after the purchase of Trewin, the first thing RCN considered was the possibility of a nursery. The idea being to create a working garden – a big one; one that might even turn a profit someday – from scratch. His keeper knew full well from the way John Nightly's mind worked that 'big', no matter how big, would never be quite big enough for his boss. Any undertaking would have to be something huge, a project on a monumental scale, in order to feed the obsessive hunger his employer had for grand projects and bigness in general. So, when John St Just & Partners of St Austell, the architects commissioned to redesign the property, came up with the layout and plans for the general scheme, the old vicarage was reconstructed to accommodate the maximum number (meaning tens of thousands) of exotic plants. Maximum R'n'B. Or 'the undergrowth', as RCN referred to it. A mere 18 months later, with the help of St Just and a groundsman, Robert Kemp (a local man with his own small-holding at Twelveheads), where there had once been unfertile wasteland there were now agave and gunnera thickets, long swathes of voodoo lilies, a fairway of Magnolia stellata, slopes of nemesias and wide aisles of strelitzias setting off smaller beds of geraniums and cardoons.

Then the sunhouses went up, and Trewin Farm took on the look of a commercial nursery. The whole complex having been built for plants – their wellbeing, their habits and requirements – not people. It seemed wrong, indulgent even, to both Johns, that they should concern themselves or care very much about the needs of people. Their own needs.

Both realised that they were, in a sense, ruined men. But that nonetheless they had to continue; they had to exist. Maybe they felt happiest in the gully between the inner and outer worlds, the reason they focused on passive matters, i.e. plant life. Maybe they kidded themselves, but the propagation of tropical exotics became the main interest for Daly and Nightly. The main event. The Carn Point varieties were almost divine creatures: untouchable, all-encompassing, the beneficiaries of long-term accumulative investment. Affection, hard work and money aplenty had been lavished upon them. These adopted sons and daughters glowed with health – unlike their sponsors. The plants created their own community. To look down upon the paddocks and meadows from high above the sea wall, against the backdrop of the ocean's haze, was like attending a school or college Open Day as the community proudly displayed its annual and ongoing achievement. The pupils – the plants – were truly magnificent. It was just a shame that no one ever came to look at them.

At first, of course, neither John had the faintest clue how to go about it. Although a decision had been made to specialise in exotics, and in the most unusual, out-there varieties they could track down, all they really knew about was cannas; between them, they knew all there was to know about cannas. By the end of the second growing season the two Johns could grow cannas in their fingernails. So, for the first couple of months, RCN spent all of his time visiting local garden centres and horticultural shows, picking up information and buying slips and cuttings where he could find them.

It was important that both of them got round to some of the larger public gardens in the area – there were sixty-seven listed on the National Gardens Register – in order to get a general sense of things and discover how a large plot should be professionally laid out and worked. These trips would never be planned because it was impossible to know how 'confident' John would be feeling from one day to the next; and if he didn't feel confident, there was no way he was going anywhere. On a non-confident day John Nightly would walk straight out of his kitchen out-house into Sunhouse 5 – his favourite, as it had a panoramic view out onto the ocean. There he would remain the whole day long. With his cup of tea, and a sandwich prepared by Mrs Peed the night before, he'd sit gazing out at the waves, hypnotised by their swill and flow, their crescendos and cascades reminding him of a set of sea interludes, or a rolling Bach fugue, bothering to get up every now and then to open the skylight so that he could smell the salt and listen to the chafing gulls, until he would suddenly feel a draught and close it again. The only thing that would bring him back into the house was the creeping damp and, as darkness approached, the promise of Mrs Peed's hot cooked dinner.

John Nightly was always cold. No matter how much heating, natural or otherwise, was turned on in whatever room he happened to be. Ironic, of course, given that one of his schoolboy ambitions had been to develop the means to conserve and reuse heat and energy produced by natural resources – not to waste massive amounts of expensive manmade fuel on plants.

John insisted on the heating at Trewin being turned up full at all times. As with life in general, everything had to be *full on*. All his life he desired only intensity; the extremes of things – the rind of the cheese, the pith of the lemon, the spikiest cacti. The quadraphonic system he'd had at Queen Square produced ear-shattering volume that drove visitors away. In the brief period during which he used a car, he was stopped for speeding three times in twelve months and never sat behind the wheel (legally) again. He courted the most troubled and troublesome women and conceived of the most unrealistic, unreliable schemes, all the time popping pills as if they were Polo mints.

There was never anything at all subtle or moderate about the man or his actions. John would wander through the house accompanied by a small convector heater that he would plug in whenever he sat down, even for a moment or two, and angle directly towards his feet. Heating bills at Trewin were astronomical. £900 last quarter for the house and cottage alone, with a massive £2,200-odd every three months to heat the sunlounges and outhouses. The bill from South West Water was also exorbitant, around £3,000 to £5,000 a quarter. Watering the community properly was expensive. Financially it was daft, but ecologically it was completely immoral. Nothing less than a sin.

The industrial rearing of exotics, both specimen plants and difficult-to-look-after seedlings, isn't exactly a stand-alone activity. Apart from the problems of importing them in the first place – many require special licences and stamped government papers: 'plant visas' you might say – the massive amounts of soil, fertiliser, drainage material, fibre and compost and the endless pallets of food that must be regularly purchased in order for them to grow and thrive, there is endless administration and bureaucracy to be dealt with in registering each cutting and slip for National Plant Breeders' Rights (PBR).

In retrospect, this turned out to be a very good thing. It meant that every cutting propagated at Trewin Farm, mainly John's *Canna* 'Luxor', 'Lucifer' and 'Mortada' varieties, would be subject to a royalty when sold on, just like records, of around 15p per slip.

The payments soon accumulated and by the final accounts

quarter of 1994 songwriting income wasn't the only seasonal distribution to land on Trewin's welcome mat. The two Johns re-cultivated and highly improved strains of *Canna* 'Luxor', with their longer-lasting flowering cycle, strong colours and swan-like necks were suddenly in huge demand from the German and Dutch cut-flower importers.

Every night of the year, flowers from Zimbabwe, the Cayman Islands, Israel, Brazil, Chile and Cornwall are flown into Amsterdam and Rotterdam for the Dutch flower markets. During the twelve weeks of these floral superstars' continual flowering, John RCN would open the gates at the bottom meadow every evening, trampling the bindweed and twitch, to let in four noisy, articulated trucks. Just one hour later, variegated gold CL1 (PBR reg. 131190) – Trewin's best seller; their biggest hit – along with several other strains, would begin their journey back down the B3306 all the way up the A30 to the tiny airport at RAF St Mawgan near Newquay, where they would be quickly laid in ice caskets and shipped to the ex-army base at Hinszels or Aalsmeer* flower auctions in Holland for cleaning, stripping, trimming and spraying before being laid out in long white cardboard boxes. Here they would be carefully labelled and counted for British Association Representing Breeders (BARB), the whole operation taking less than 24 hours, before they appeared in the covered flower markets of Strasbourg or Stuttgart. Maybe one of Trewin's graceful stems of peach or gold would be trimmed and cut again before being placed on the conference tables of the European Parliament in Brussels or outside a hillside café in St Paul de Vence.

By June 2000, some 894,000 CL1, CL2 and CM1 stems had been dispatched. At 15p a head this amounted to a good profit. The agreement being that as John Nightly drew his income from songwriting and record royalties, John Daly would be able to take his not-inconsiderable salary from the sales of this now highly profitable enterprise.

* Aalsmeer flower market near Amsterdam is officially the largest room in the world.

But flowers and plants mean insects – and at any one time there would be hundreds of mites, motes, baby spiders and athletic daddy longlegs, some visible, some invisible, crawling over the Nightly property. Spiders were necessary, feeding as they do on tiny creatures you could easily live without as well as some you didn't even know existed. By the end of summer John Nightly's bedroom would be literally crawling with ming spiders, daddies and fireflies. When the situation got out of hand he would announce that a clear-out was due, at which point Mrs Peed, the housekeeper (now living at Trewin full time following the death of her sister), would come in and have a general clean and vacuum. Mrs Peed announced that her being able to identify more than one or two different species making their way across the boss's bedroom carpet meant that enough was most certainly enough and she would get out the Hoover and do her thing. But John himself didn't at all seem to mind sleeping in a room alive with, as Mawgan so characteristically put it, 'a bunch of gizzies and spids'.

Though there was no way John Nightly was ever going to bump off the native insect population, apart from those threatening the cultivated flowers, things did once or twice get out of hand.

Sitting in the kitchen one day, his head in the *Cornishman*, RCN noticed a small puddle of black flying ants in the scissor of light between the larder and the back door. Bending over nonchalantly to take a closer look, he was greeted by the sight of a festering, velvet-black wall, previously Dulux white, suddenly covered in a carpet of swarming ant. Somehow the heap had been disturbed, probably overnight by an inquisitive badger or fox, so that the whole family and their thousands of relatives were embarked on a mission to first camouflage then obliterate the house. Even Alexandre became anxious as he stood, back arched in defensive position, barking at the top of his lungs at the layers of reflective, scaly bodies until Robert calmed him and led him away to safety.

Although RCN and Mrs Peed made some headway with rose sprinklers, hosing down the creatures before stunning them with a sluice of water from the outdoor tap, an emergency call was put in to Penwith Pest Control, who responded immediately when their on-site infestation team dealt with the problem by administering Forax DDT in battery-operated sprayguns to the entire outer shell of the property. An hour later, the former vicarage was covered in a silvery glaze, organic household gloss, a mixture of aticexicide, quavaporous fluid and melted ant, which glistened in the harsh late-afternoon sun.

Next day the cement pathways, the steppes and rockeries surrounding the farmhouse were jet black and dripping with dead Antiphibus Anticus. Robert Kemp then disposed of the vanquished invaders by once again spraying down the whole surrounding area, flushing the goo along the concrete gutters until it filtered out into the wildflower meadows and beyond.

The two Johns next big thought was to finding some way of harnessing all this sun – which was full-on most of the day from March to October – and, if possible, in the process, the immense energy of the super-powerful, Atlantic-driven waves.

Ten years previously, they'd had Jean-Claude Marx from the Ondaaron Institute, the leading researchers into renewable natural resources, come over to take a look. JC and his team agreed that what the Johns were describing could be achieved but that it would indeed be a long job, involving taking re-plumbed seawater from the area beneath the inner coves so it could be re-piped and circulated around the house and outbuildings. Ideally, some kind of very large well, a huge underground vat, would need to be built beneath the heather fields, the midway point between the ocean and the farm; but, after reading the report, both RCN and Robert were convinced that Penwith would never give planning permission for something as disruptive as this.

Jean-Claude, the great solar-energy pioneer of the '70s and one-time lighting designer for the Pink Fairies and the Pretty Things, as well as of course the Nightly band, also suggested erecting wind-power mills that would build up and recycle the volume of energy they needed over the course of 24-hours. He produced a preliminary report in which he advised that, given a long-term period of careful management and investment – say fifteen to twenty summers – the project could achieve everything they had outlined to him. What's more, could become established as one of the most sustainable, renewable, solar/wind-based projects in the UK. A shining example to both local and national government as well as to public- and private-sector enterprises everywhere in showing how natural resources could be harnessed in order to generate a whole lot of recyclable power, particularly in such an idyllic setting. Trewin could be an example, a kind of paradigm, where others could come to learn about sustainable power, its very name a byword for carefully planned long-term energy renewal. A place of pilgrimage for those interested in ecology, regeneration, exotic plants, and, as JC added with a glint in his eye, dysfunctional ex-pop stars.

It was this last thought that persuaded the Johns to drop the project like a lead weight. That and the time factor: fifteen to twenty years? RCN doubted either of them had that much time left; and if not, well, what was the point? So, it was decided to dump the whole idea and instead use whatever means they already had at their disposal. With a bit of extra plumbing and pipe-laying they reckoned they could probably more or less achieve their aim. So the project, like so many others, was put on the back burner as something that would be 'nice to do at some point in the future'. A point both men knew would never come.

Speaker: Jean-Claude Marx, director, Ondaaron Institute (FRAS, SFS, GSR), at 'Renewable World': a conference on wave power and wind systems, Trinity College, Cambridge. 4–9 August 1984.
The future in terms of energy rests on going back rather than forward. Wave power and wind generation must take up at least 75 per cent of our energy systems rather than the 2 per cent they currently occupy if we are to be able to both renew and sustain. The work of John R. Pierce, and long before that of Charles Wheathouse, did much to show us the way, but modern man has forgotten to plug in his brain as far as this issue is concerned. Waves and wind are already with us. They're free, they cost us nothing and there also happens to be an inexhaustible supply of them. All we have to do is to figure out how to utilise their enormous power in a

much more ecological way than has been tried so far. To achieve that, we need governments to initiate and then co-ordinate it, and the public to embrace it. It is my belief that if we do not turn our attention to this concern immediately, then we are doomed.

The Who at Tiles Club, Oxford Street, London, W1.
Tuesday, 29 April 1966.

'But Monika goes to see them all the time, don't you, darling?'

'Ah yeah… I always goes there. Marquee, Tuesday night… Every people know that! Scene Crub last time… first time I come London. I go Jack of Crub, see *Davy Jones*, friendly man, very friendly man – very *like* man, this one – and his group *Buzz*, friendly group, good group, and good prace. Nice, good prace, Iona.'

Monika searched her bag for lipstick as she took a nostalgic look back at last year.

'But now they change name *Lower Third*… ah yeah! What your zodiac, John?'

The girl wittered away as she applied another layer of grease-paint to her candy-coated lips. 'I can go Ricky Tick… see *Who*… Guildford… Engrish countryside… nice prace.'

John thought he might make a stab at conversation. 'So you're… quite a… fan of… music, Monika…'

'Music? Ah yeah! Love music, John… every people know that. But love groups best. Noisy one best… *Artwoods, Georgie Fame* – see him Framingo crub. *Action*… this good one,' she sighed, as if remembering a very special occasion. *'Manfred Mann*… this very noisy mann. Very noisy! We very like singer…'

The girl tousled her hair as she peered into the club's filthy wall mirror and made the necessary adjustments. A bouffanted mod, his ensemble complemented by a pair of goat-skin gloves, came towards Monika; and throwing her a slightly menacing smile, placed a folded tissue in her hand. 'We very like Paul. And *Pretty Thing* – he's good! *"Hey, Rosalyn! Tell me where you bin!"'*

Monika zipped the lipstick into her bag, carefully removed

three tablets from the tissue pouch and looked around to see if she could spot anyone worth talking to.

'What your star, John?'

But John couldn't hear a thing above the cavernous echo of Phil Spector's soundwall. Every inch of the sprawling under-ground arcade rattled either in excitement or protest at Spector's tin-can symphony. The club was crawling with *Grade Ones:* teenage disciples confident about both their sartorial and musical requirements, as each attempted to out-cool the other. At the closed-off end of the ballroom narcissistic gangs fired requests at the hapless DJ – 'Get this crud *off* !!!' 'Play Otis, man!' *'Ska,* geeza!' – as the threesome found themselves surrounded by a coterie of worshippers.

The Japanese doll fixed on another two-toned mod holding court close by. She had no trouble at all attracting his eye as she smiled, feigned indifference, then began to twist and grind suggestively in the confines of the self-imposed anteroom while (amazingly to John) Iona began to join in.

'What about the other song, Monika? "Don't Bring Me Down"?'

'That good one, 'ona.'

John, a hopeless dancer and lip-reader, and therefore unable to make out very much at all, could respond only by using his eyes. Conversation was abandoned as the boy continued to try to adapt and fit in with his companions' state of mind in order to remain a part of the proceedings and not become separated from them.

"C'mon, little babee, don't bring me down…"

He cupped his hands to his mouth, as the girls sang along to the record, still trying to eliminate the thunderous racket drowning out the DJ's announcement about undercover police officers in the crowd.

'Thing is...' John shouted as loud as he possibly could. 'In Cambridge... you would never see these people...'

'What is it? Which people, 'ona?'

Monika was at best only half concentrating on the girls' new acquaintance.

'in Cambridge...'

'Ah yeah... very prace also... very old one. But now you come London, we take you, and your nice scarf, to see groups very soon now. C'mon, Iona!'

The girls grabbed hold of the ends of John's scarf as they pretended to strangle their guest.

'...uuuuuurrrh!' The boy struggled to disengage himself and, feeling rather out of place in his Cambridge togs – mail-order windcheater, cords and sandals – considered a future of being escorted around London's most happening nightspots by two of the best-looking girlfriends he could ever imagine having set eyes on, let alone actually being seen *with*.

'Tonight we go Poubelle after here prace... or Limbo crub, Wardour Mew, this one close here...'

Iona grabbed Monika's arm, struggling to make herself heard.

'Can't do that, darling. Got a shoot tomorrow... early morning, unfortunately.'

The news received her friend's full attention. 'Is it good clothes one, 'ona?'

Iona pulled the girl towards her and looked across at John, making sure not to exclude him. 'Biba!' she shouted with glee. 'Biba tomorrow...!'

'Ooo… can you get me some this clothes now time?' Monika placed a small blue tablet into the palm of Iona's hand.

'I'll try, darling, but… you know they always ask for them back.'

'You know I love Biba type, Iona. I have go there Saturday every time… You know I have. Saturday, every day… this my drug.'

'Maybe John can go with you next Saturday, darling – can't you, John? I do think you need to get some… some… *London-type* clothes…' Iona trod carefully. 'Maybe we ask your manager give you your "clothes money".' Monika nodded in agreement as both girls looked John up and down.

'Be difficult to get any kind of money out of him. At least till my record contract comes through. I shouldn't think my manager understands very much about… well, fashion and things like that. Don't think he does, anyway…'

Iona smiled and popped the blue tab, taking a sip of whiskey from Monika to swill it down.

'But he does, I think.' The girl swallowed. 'What he does understand much about these things is that they are expensive!'

Monika moved in on John, considering Iona's new friend up close, but decided not to offer him one of the little boosters – already suspecting the boy to be way too straight for comfort.

'And he understand the woman who wear this clothes, Iona!'

Both girls were quick on the uptake, surprising the boy a little, while Monika continued to serenade them as she dreamed about her *Biba* Saturday.

'Zoot Money group… he go Framingo… noisy, noisy group… Chris Farlowe… Yardbird one, Graham Bond one, ooo…

they good – good noisy, Iona.' The girl nodded her head enthusiastically, in total agreement with herself, as she continued to sing and dance, throwing up her arms and making twirly go-go shapes with her hands as if she were already in the audience on *Ready Steady Go!*

All in all, the boy had to admit to being thoroughly impressed and rather starstruck. By both Monika's appearance – her St Tropez look, her cartoon-like, dark-eyed mask – and her apparent insider knowledge of the Wardour Street scene.

'you're obviously very much up on it, Monika.'

'What is it?'

'you… you're obviously… uh… *Up on…*' He decided to revert to more standard vocabulary. 'You obviously *know* all of… the… well, you know, the *groups*,' he shouted, probably a little too emphatically.

'I do know them. Yeah, surely. Ah yeah!' Monika confirmed. 'I know groups many time.' She rearranged her top to show a little more of her newly tanned shoulder. 'Because they come my house…'

The girl threw back her head and held on to her bouffant as she launched into a variation on the Mashed Potato in response to a new DJ taking the floor. She waved enthusiastically to another Japanese mannequin on the other side of the room. The boy looked rather deflated as he attempted to communicate in the lull between record-spinner and live act.

'and… who would you say was your favourite of all these… groups?'

Monika and Iona, starting to become affected by the confectionary, seemed to half dance, half float now, as they somehow managed to cling on to the thread.

'Who? Ah, sure! Who is definitely fabourite one!' Iona nodded her agreement. 'And Kinks!' Monika cried. 'Kinks is best, Iona!' she said, before finding herself drowned out by the heavily distorted and very low-frequency floor hum brought about by the Who taking the stage. The drummer, at least as young as the audience, mop-haired, dressed in Hotpoint white from head to toe, jumped straight onto his riser and immediately served up a taste of what was to come. He grabbed his sticks and executed impossibly fast rolls around the kit, manically staring at and challenging the crowd after each one, as if to say *'C'mon, then!'* before proceeding to laugh his head off. The guitarist, back turned to the audience, repeatedly plugged and unplugged his guitar into his amp socket, purposely creating a series of sudden, un-earthed static charges, resulting in screeching feedback which echoed eerily around the packed basement. The audience, already over-excited by pills and shots, surged towards the stage. Iona turned to John and finished the story.

'I went their concert in Denmark and it was riot. Tivoli Garden, in Copenhagen. It was riot-ing, so they couldn't… they can't… play songs. But Kinks is, you are right… I mean, *are*… or… *she* – ah yeah… *She* is best!'

The Who cranked into action.

"I can go anyway, way I choose… I can live anyhow, win or lose…"

There was really nothing John could say except an overly polite and somewhat defeated 'Ah… yeah' as he turned away from his companions towards the stage.

John Pond had forewarned his charge that Monika was just as 'yum-yum' as Iona, and as far as the boy could see… on this one brief outing, it looked as though he might be… well, *almost* right.

PROFILE: Tiles. 79–89 Oxford Street, London W1; GER 2977. Tube: Tottenham Court Road. Mon–Sat 12am–2.30pm and 7.30pm–11pm. Admission: 1s for a mid-day session; varies for evenings. Coffee-bar and mini-Carnaby Street; live groups and discs.

Regal Recording Studios, Denmark Street, London WC1.
Monday, 12 June 1966.

John Nightly sat with his feet up on Regal's new leatherette couch, his head deep in the pages of *Disc*.

'Sounds good!' he shouted, half surprised at his own achievement as he leaped from the sofa and began to pack away his guitar.

The set-up at Regal was basic, though friendly and efficient. With the help of Lee Hide, the studio's teenage engineer and resident in-house mod, the boy had been able to record and track all of his instruments, impressing the soundman by playing the guitar, bass, drum and vibraphone parts himself in one short three-hour session.

As he puffed away at a hashish roll-up, the acne-ridden Lee was still fiddling with levels when the doorbell rang and Iona breezed in on a wave of patchouli. Today, her hair was tied in a loose pony-knot. Her little tulip cap, tangerine skirt and dazzlingly bright-orange kaftan were more suited to the Croisette in Cannes than dirty old Tin Pan Alley, her appearance bringing a whiff of exoticism to the damp, windowless cellar.

Distracted by the new arrival, the engineer continued to twiddle while quietly stealing glances from the corner of his eye. He raised the lever on the EMT plate, thereby lengthening the time of the echo, as John nodded approval and the new 'drenched in reverb' vocal swirled around the studio. A fraction more treble and the job was complete. 'Mu Mu Tea', 'Free School Lane' and the already epic-sounding 'Lavender Girl' were surely potential hits. An opinion shared by both Lee and Iona.

'This one is very beautiful, John... that part there...'

Iona was now installed on the couch. She lay back, kicked off her heels, crossed her legs and pointed a heavily ringed finger towards a corner of the darkened room, even though there was nothing at all up there to point at, except a pancake of mould slowly making its progress across the ceiling. No sound whatsoever came from that particular direction.

'...that bit... that *night-time* sound... many candles in the sky... camels walking across the sand...'

Iona seemed pleased with her poesy as her elegant digit changed its mind and indicated to a different area altogether, this time at the other end of the studio. The only thing John could make out in this dark recess were some broken cobwebs and a dislodged sound-absorption tile, with some exposed circuitry protruding from behind it. Iona smiled mischievously at Lee then playfully ripped the music weekly out of the hands of a rather flummoxed John.

'That's the vibraphone you're referring to.' John leaned over to explain. 'The... "candle" sound, as you put it. But as I said, they're only demos... to give an idea.' The boy paused for a response that didn't come. 'If John Pond likes them we'll go and record them for real, and at that point we'll fix it all up and get the orchestra and all the other stuff in.' Once again, John found himself justifying something that didn't need defending. Again, there was no response. To Iona, things sounded perfect already. 'I've got the arrangements all worked out in my head, so I know exactly how it's going to sound – and it'll be a lot bigger than this!'

'Sounds pretty big already, man,' chipped in the seventeen year-old Lee as he casually puffed away and directed all of his wiry charm towards Iona.

'Try this, babe?' Lee spun round on his chair to offer up the joint. To John's surprise, the girl leaned over enthusiastically to accept it.

The soundman was obviously smitten. He challenged his client by continuing to refer to Iona variously as 'babe' or 'doll'.

'There you go, doll.' Lee croaked, as he passed the limp roll-up and Iona took her first drag. 'You can invest in a block, if the mood takes ya ...' Lee turned back to John as the girl settled down with the spliff and gazed up at her beau.

The client's reaction was, as so often was to be the case, misjudged. John came over all uptight and threatened as he uttered a very non-committal, 'uh, no... thanks...' while Iona lifted herself out of the sofa, tossed her cap onto the mixing desk and blew the luxurious smoke straight into the face of the object of her affection.

'Ooo... this is good one,' she puffed. 'Ve-ry good...'

As John began to huff and puff, Iona – slightly put out by her intended not joining in – mused over a little philosophy of her own.

'Nonetheless, John, the thing is, you are probably too clever...' she opined hazily, 'too, too clever... *Too Clever to be Good!'* Iona sat down again as her companions exchanged quizzical glances. 'You know this thing they say?' She revised her wisdom: 'No... that is not... exactly anyway... just what I mean... *meaned.'* Iona was, as ever, frustrated at not being able to communicate in the way she would've wished, 'for your... *for your good,* I mean... *for your "own" good* – that's it!' She raised her eyebrows. *'Too Clever For Your Own Good...* or what it is they do say...?'

John shifted uncomfortably again. The boy wasn't sure whether or not to appear grateful. Iona continued to put her foot deeper in.

'That's what I mean – and too clever to ever be very, very happy either... if you ask me... and... as I keep want to ask *you.'* She slid further down the couch and took another drag before provocatively passing the spliff to John. 'What *is* your star, John?'

'Star?' the boy replied, irritated, though for absolutely no reason. 'I told you. Look... there's nothing clever about something like this. It's just... it's a process, that's all. Recording songs is... well, it's "reproduction" more than anything,' he continued, completely ingenuously, as Lee raised his eyebrows and admired the view.

'Trying to create a sound you already have in your head, trying to capture a moment or… not trying to "create" it exactly, but trying to reproduce it. That's what *I* mean. So that everyone else can hear what you hear, or what you think you hear.' He sighed heavily. 'The real work has been done, though – the "imagining" of it.' He thought again. 'Of course, it's not… I don't mean "work" either exactly… but you understand what I mean…' The audience listened intently. 'That's why it's so frustrating. Because it never does turn out sounding the way you imagined it. The "imagining" is always better! But… it's something that, well, I can do quite easily – the process, I mean – something that I just happen to be able to do – fairly easily, anyway.' He paused… 'Doing this, all this stuff, it's, well… it's no amazing thing.'

John took the remains of the joint and lodged it on the rim of an ashtray beside him, careful not to show his disapproval. 'And don't *you* be facetious either…' he smiled, half-jokingly, as Lee looked on intrigued by the antagonism developing between the two characters.

'But this is things that normal people cannot do at all, John, anyway – writing this songs and everything,' Iona replied. 'I think you don't… almost understand…' she appealed tenderly to a most unconfident looking John. The boy sighed.

'I'm honestly not so sure about that… I should think most people probably… to some extent, anyway. If they got half the chance…'

John was already impatient. Lee watched the interplay between them, trying to figure out the status of the couple. Were they actually together or could it be the case that the lightheaded girl opposite might possibly be available? If not right now, then maybe later on that evening? He turned to the client.

'Wish I could do it, man. Come in handy in this job, tell ya. All the stuff I have to deal with "in a day's work", as they say.'

Lee Hide was the archetypal London 'face' of the period. Sharp and fast, literally a whizz-kid. Lee began each session by asking the client whether they needed a 'top-up'... *Blues* or *Bennies*... always preceded by a nervous cough and an overtly casual 'by the way...'

'Sixpence each, but if you wanted ten... fifty even?'

The teenager was also an 'associate', as he put it, of Peter Meaden, the Who's publicity agent, image adviser and guru. Meaden, an amphetamine-head who more or less lived on purple hearts, was an obvious hero figure, 'face of faces', and Lee relayed how Meaden had recently attempted to change the group's name, then had second thoughts and changed it back again. The self-confessed Who's Greatest Fan was anxious for today's session to end, as he wanted to get along to the Scene Club in Ham Yard, via Wardour Mews, just around the corner, where he and his friends would regularly get pilled up for the weekend. The names of Meaden, Kit Lambert and Chris Stamp, the Who's razor-sharp management, cropped up every few minutes as the cocksure and ultra-confident soundman tried his best to set the controls for the heart of chart success. Same as he did every morning in this sweaty underground bunker, sporting his best Italian slacks and brogues, just in case Meaden or his associates came in, which apparently they did from time to time. The Who themselves had dropped by the studio socially, though they hadn't actually recorded there yet. Lee's fave session to date had been with the Action, local heroes from Kentish Town, his own North London birthplace.

'Do you make sounds for famous groups?'

Iona wasn't really interested but felt she should make some attempt at conversation with the provider of her relaxant, particularly as he had been too obviously impressed and entranced by her presence to bother to ask for it back. In the meantime, Lee lit a regular smoke and offered her one as he responded.

'Not that famous… not yet anyway. Y' get a lot of stuff comes through. Some of it's great and some of it… it ain't that great, y'know?' Lee appeared uncharacteristically philosophical. 'But it's a stepping stone, babe… Stepping stone; 'swhat I been told, anyway!'

The engineer flicked ash from his shirt seam onto the sodden carpet. John busied himself by making mental notes. He often became uneasy if there was a pause in any conversation. The boy picked up his acoustic guitar and began to strum.

'Anyone wonderful been in recently?'

Lee finished logging the session and swivelled round.

'Shadows of Night… they were good… did their demos, and some stuff with the boys from the Action, who are just, like… they're a fabulous group, man… really fabulous.'

John pretended to be listening.

'Last week the Beefeaters… and Cat Stevens – great guy, the real deal. But it's so busy at the moment. Usually we get through three sessions a day, strict three hours. Last couple of months it's like four. Suddenly everybody's recording…'

Lee began to brush his trousers with a stiff piece of card, wiping dust from his brogues using the studio's tape-cleaning cloth. 'All making records 'cos it's the thing to do. Y' grandad's makin' records, man…' Lee shook his head in disbelief as he slid the plastic reel back into its carton.

'…Marc – know him from the market – he come in… and 'smornin', Schonfeld played me some 'mazin' tracks. Know Victor? Runs these gigs at the Marquee… Sunday afternoon, when there's nowhere else to go… 'cept sit at home and argue with your old man! Perfect time to get out of the 'ouse! Who else?… Guy… Guy Stevens… at the Scene. Good mate of mine.

Come in to have a chat 'bout… life.' Lee sat back and ogled Iona, more relaxed now, having reached the end of another long, concentrated day. 'Andrew Oldham… not with the Stones, but his label… 'mazin' acts on there. Down here all the time, they are, the "real people", I mean.'

Lee unplugged the leads on the patchbay and sprayed solvent onto the faders to rub off that day's pencil marks, as he got things back to normal for tomorrow's session. He carried on talking as he wiped and cleaned. 'Been workin' on stuff with Marko Markovitch, but he can make a load more money floggin' pinks than he can from music. Actually… if we're done…' The soundman leaned across to close down the mains power, 'Need to make a bit of a detour down to the old cul-de-sac meself fairly soon. Wanna come with?'

With that, the engineer got up, straightened out the creases in his immaculate slacks and flattened out the hair on his immaculate head. He checked his parting in the mirror, momentarily alarmed by the untimely appearance of a blackhead on his left nostril. Lee was to chaperone his clients as they exited Regal Sound to walk giddily up Denmark Street, where, once above ground, music could be heard seeping from every doorway.

Soho was certainly the place to be in that early summer of '66. The true centre of things. Tonight boasted Tubby Hayes at the Flamingo and Brian Auger at the Limbo. From makeshift studios and backroom bars across Soho's square mile, R'n'B, bebop, straight rock'n'roll, trad jazz, skiffle, blues and bossa nova echoed around the streets, a cacophony of familiar songs and scattered, ancient riffs. Snatched conversations, fumbled sexual encounters and poisonous old arguments still lingered in the alleyways and doorways of basement clubs and unlicensed all-night coffee bars all over the area.

Emerging into the glaring neon of night-time Soho the trio hurried along. Past the in-crowd at the Giaconda, in and out of the scooters and double-deckers careering along Charing Cross

Road. They crossed Greek Street and Frith Street before they hit the smoke and gas of Wardour and the massed ranks of pillheads, pushers, rent boys, strippers and all the other shift-workers who flowed in and out of Soho's nocturnal maze of small family restaurants, strip clubs and peek-a-boo cubicles.

Mods would regularly make the pilgrimage between Le Kilt or La Poubelle and the secluded environs of Wardour Mews, just off D'Arblay Street. Here was the pill factory itself. The local village store, late-nite chemist, Soho's very own souk – except that the only thing for sale was drugs. Against the backdrop of the amphetamine clubs actually in Wardour Mews – the Limbo, the Granada and the Take Five – teenage speed dealers, often no more than fourteen or fifteen years old, would position themselves in each of the four corners of the stable yard where customers would form an orderly queue for weekend supplies of Mandies, SKF Dexies, reds, pinks, 'ludes and French blues.

Lee introduced John and Iona to the regulars. There was Velda – '*another* model acquaintance', Lee announced as he presented Iona – and Velda's friend, Gert, an olive-skinned youth with Cary Grant shades, decked out in his uniform of white cotton shirt and white pressed Levi's. Gert was, Lee explained, 'friendly with a lot of politicians and business people…'

In the Berwick Street corner stood Marko, the former St Martin's graduate who by day worked on the market alongside Lee's other 'best mates', Peter (Grant) and Marc (Feld). Opposite Marko was Cherry, who had another related business operating out of the one-at-a-time passage between Berwick Street market and Wardour Street itself.

In the opposite corner across the cobbles stood 'Fruity' Fritz and his dog Larry who was fond of sniffing excitedly at fur-lined parkas and go-go boots. Fruity would not only sell you the biggest variety of poppers on the market but was also happy to put you in contact with other branches of his business in Curzon Street and Lancashire Court.

''Mazin',' said Lee.

Wardour Mews was a hive of activity. With art students, actors, designers, waiters and waitresses, journalists and every type of musician or 'head' joining the lowlife to buy a high life, sometimes in bulk, from these reliable unreliables. Most would then head off to the Marquee or the Flamingo, or for the more jazz-orientated Ronnie Scott's or Dinky's, to mingle with other faces and catch up on the latest sounds. Later on there'd be queues at Dolly's, Sybilla's and the Bag O'Nails in Kingly Street, where more of a model/photographer/film-star clientele would assemble, and there was the possibility of the occasional visitation by a Beatle or Stone.

Iona and Monika's regular night-time supplier was the gruffly-spoken but sweet-hearted Lenny, known to all and sundry as The Bear because of his hairy neck and extreme barrel chest. Lenny's usual attire was a mechanic's one-piece boiler suit unzipped to the waist. He carried his wares in a small metal toolbox with a leather tool belt strapped to his belly. But the usual screwdrivers, spanners and carpet tacks had had to make way for a variety of pastel-coloured pep pills and the new big thing, LSD – sheets of it.

It was a frantic market. The mods would ''lude out' on Mandrax or Quaaludes and other painkillers, sedatives and tranquilisers; then, later on, get trippy with the new product, little gelatine squares, sheets or 'windowpanes', as they were known – 1,000 micrograms, usually referred to by the customers as White Lightning or Purple Haze.

John and Iona bade farewell to a disappointed Lee at Beak Street and Golden Square, deciding to walk through the park so as to come down from the exhilarating rush surrounding the speed freaks – or 'motorheads', as they became known – of Soho. The pair was headed back to Iona's flat in deepest Fulham, a world away from the quick hit of the West End, though likely just as drug-oriented.

On the doorstep of 45 Old Brompton Road they encountered a lonely soul. Huddled together with a small white dog inside a caravan blanket sat Alice, Iona's flatmate and local 'slumming it' debutante who had managed to lock herself out after taking Koko, the girls' attention-seeking fox terrier, for a midnight stroll. Alice's unforeseen presence immediately removed any possibility John may have been hoping for in terms of a sexual liason that evening and with Koko deliriously happy to see Iona and therefore barking non-stop without letting go of her coat, they opened the door and entered the laboratory-warm five-roomed conversion.

Iona and Alice's whitewashed living space was adorned with shawls and textiles, posters, rush mats, beads, coloured glass and abstract canvases. It was the first time John had been into a home with anything like what he might have identified as real modern art. In Iona's Danish kitchenette hung a large oil by the CoBrA artist Asger Jorn, all green squirls and messy red knots, while in the hallway was a set of three gouaches by Corneille, given to Iona by her father, the art collector Dr Jonas Sandstrand, on the occasion of her eighteenth birthday. John admired the paintings and made a promise to himself to invest in some art as real as this as soon as John Pond had gotten his contract through and found him a place to stay.

This twilight ending to an eventful and productive day was to be an important one for John Nightly for another reason. As they decamped to the kitchen, where Alice made mu tea and brought flapjacks followed by Iona's homemade hash cake from the fridge, Iona, perched high on a stepladder, lifted the latch on the roof light, sat down and began to roll one.

John turned off the flickering, crackling television, left on for the past five hours while Alice had stepped out for five minutes. He picked up one of the copies of *Vogue* and *Queen* from the piles strewn haphazardly across the floor. The corners of the pages featuring Iona had been neatly folded down, with Alice herself having put in an appearance, in *Country Life*, as the about-to-come-out debutante daughter of Isabella, ex-deb and now wife of Colonel Jonty Latimer, of Venn House, Nineveh, Cornwall.

'Alice hunts and events and will read philosophy and art history at Oxford after travelling to India as a volunteer with the Sri Bhagwan Foundation', announced page 161. Alice's mother, the former Bella Kaminsky, was from Lithuanian stock, which is where Alice had gotten her peasant-girl looks – as confirmed by John from the picture on the mantelpiece, Mama Bella at the Berkeley Square Ball, spring 1948.

As Donovan's LP played on the stereo and Alice served more tea for three, Iona selected six sugar lumps from a wooden bowl and laid them out in a perfect semicircle. She opened a small box, from which she took out a phial and casually dripped two drops of lysergic acid diethylamide onto each one, saturating the sugar until it began to crumble; then took a small teaspoon and placed a cube on her tongue before asking John and Alice to 'Open up'.

And so it was that in the early hours of 13 June 1966, the same night that the giant star Zuse exploded in a supernova, seeding the universe with tangles of gas and dust that would later create new stars, John Nightly blasted into his own Space, his own celestial oblivion, when he embarked upon his first LSD expedition, his orange-sunshine voyage of discovery, in a Scandinavian cabin kitchen in South Kensington courtesy of Miss I. Sandstrand and an ex-heating engineer known as Lenny the Bear.

Derived from a parasitic fungus that grows on rye, lysergic acid diethylamide is mixed with volatile diethylamide (used in vulcanising rubber), then frozen. The LSD is extracted by using chloroform or benzene for fractional distillation, or else by means of a simple vacuum evaporator. Available in pill form or else as a soluble crystalline powder (the liquid-dunked sugar cubes of yesteryear are out), LSD produces an 8-to-12-hour trip highlighted by profound changes in thought, mood and activity. Colours become heightened, sounds take on preternatural shades of meaning or unmeaning; the trip passenger feels that he can see into his very brain cells, hear and feel his blood and lymph coursing through their channels. It is this sense of intense perception that stays with most hippies and, in part, sustains their fondness for bright colours, flowers and bells. Yet, for all its reputed ability to make a man aware of his true 'nature', LSD has demonstrably damaging qualities as well. Mood changes can range from tears to laughter to intense anxiety, panic, and a psychedelic paranoia that duplicates psychosis to the last dotted shriek – and can go on indefinitely.

'The Flower Children', The Hippies. Times Inc. New York, 1967.

Sweet silver angels over the sea
Please come down flyin' low for me

'Jesus Was a Cross Maker', Judee Sill, 1972
(Asylum AYM502)

September tides. A regular seven-second breaker rolled into the bay at Carn Point as a handful of surfer kids bobbed up and down in the foam, trying to stay vertical if only for a few seconds. September tides are supposed to be calm. John Nightly ought to know. He's been studying them long enough, using the same stopwatch and sliderule bought for him by his father while he was still at St John's Secondary. Way back, in another world, another time. Back before everything went haywire, bonkers, completely nuts. Way, way back, before all the zigging and zagging and swinging and swaying led to, well… it led to oblivion.

John often sat up here, high above the white-water, the highest point of the Nightly property, on this same, familiar patch of flattened grass. Windcheater zipped right up to his chin, cap and goggles wrapped tight around his skull, as he monitored the movements of neaps and springs comforted by the warmth of the sun but irritated by the swirling sand that every now and then would suddenly stir up around him, graze his face, and sweep into his nose and ears.

John had once remained on this spot for six whole days as he listened to the lapping waves and the surfer's distant cries, meticulously timing each ebb and flow, checking the accuracy of the predictions in *Her Majesty's Tide Tables HMSO0296*. They were close enough, but he knew that he could have done a better job for her. Today, he compiled his findings, drawing out a few basic charts before RCN appeared with coffee, Club biscuits and Jaffa cakes – the Johns' preferred mid-afternoon combination. Mostly there'd be little said, but every now and then RCN would stay awhile and sit down if there was something special to look at – ghostly shapes in the clouds, a horsehead nebula; a double or even triple rainbow, a truly spectacular sight and on these occasions they'd maybe chew the breeze, and the sand (literally), and chat about the view, the weather, the rain, tides, post from abroad, irrigation systems, insecticides, plant catalogues... The usual things. Never anything important. And never anything to do with the old days. God no, not that. Never that. Nobody wanted to hear about the old days anymore; not those kinds of days, whichever ones they were or might happen to have been – neither the good nor the bad.

One morning (it was a Monday, because RCN had gone to St Just to do the week's errands) Carn Point was enduring the third week of an almost continuous sandstorm. Everyone thought of this part of the South West as a sunny place, and it was, but when the bad weather arrived it was not only extremely wet, with the rain coming down in huge globules without leaving any gaps for running across roads or under trees, but the enormous storm power of the gales meant that it was also very dangerous. Local-radio reports told of giant conifers uprooting themselves on the spur of the moment and of houses giving up the ghost and falling down on people. The wildflower meadows surrounding Trewin Farm had been transformed into treacherous mud rinks and you wouldn't want to be up on the coastal path in a million years, not even in the most sheltered of spots. No structure was safe from the relentless, uncompromising wind. It wasn't for nothing that the district of Pendeen, one of the original tithed 'Hundreds', as they used to be known, directly translated from the Cornish as the 'Headland of Slaughter'.

For this reason John Nightly was having a day in. We find him hunched over his new aluminium PowerBook G7 running Pro Tools, Version 2.4 MasterCode, with Bluetooth, Vision, Cyberex and Notator. That's right. This is probably going to come as something of a shock, but from sometime around April 2002 John Nightly spent quite a lot of his waking hours actually doing music. Or, rather, redoing it. Specifically, he was reassembling *MBR*, his very own 'lost masterpiece': the *Mink Bungalow Requiem*. The sequence of events that brought us to this wholly unexpected scenario went something like this...

In December 2001, during that dead spot between Christmas and New Year, both Johns were paying a seasonal visit to the Tregan Garden Centre just outside Penzance. No one ever went to garden centres in these few dead days. That's why they were there.

While waiting for a trailer to be loaded with industrial amounts of cactus grit, loam and potash, the odd couple were approached by the owner's son, Julian Tregan – university dropout, champion surfer, local male model and trainee customer-services assistant. The young man explained to RCN that his surfer-dude compadre, Mawgan, a huge fan of the man loitering over there near the children's cacti garden, was currently employed as trainee recording engineer at Sandy Sound, a small residential music studio at Sandy in Bedfordshire. Sorting through the tape store one day, with a view to having a clear-out, Mawgan had come upon six or seven boxes of old multitrack reels.

On the labels there was little to identify the artist or the sessions, though a list of studios including Trident, Regal Sound, Sound Techniques, Kingsway Hall and St John's Smith Square identified whatever was inside as a late '60s/early '70s recording. More importantly, the engineer recognised these five facilities as the locations used to record one of his favourite, most sought-after and impossible to get hold of pieces of music – 'Adagio Mortada' – the slower-than-slow *Remembrance* section from the Requiem. But what really set him buzzing was Box 4.

Inside the torn cotton slipcase between the mouldy inner sleeve and the tapereel itself sat a grubby scrap of paper: *Free Expression and Tin Mine Presents… The Gliderdrome Amphitheater, SmokeStack Entertainments, Inc., San Francisco, Calif. 10909. Tourdate, May 28 1972 Symphonia da Requiem for Group, Orchestra and Choir*

Jotted down on the yellowed page in blunt pencil was a list of timings: 'Allegro: T1 00: T2-03+T3-019' and so on. Sync points. The count-ins of each movement, directions for keeping the onstage performers – three orchestras, five choirs and various groups of rock, jazz and folk ensembles – in sync throughout the event using the recorded rhythm tracks as a backdrop to what was being played live. Without this, 'Allegro Castor', 'Adagio Mortada' and 'Fantasia Capella' would be even more 'all over the place' than they were already on the momentous, historic day of that final, seven-hour performance inside a scorching-hot baseball stadium in downtown San Francisco.

But it meant nothing unless you knew something and Mawgan Hall, collector of weird and wonderful audio product: shaped-discs, 8-track cassettes, acetates, scratch 'n' smell sleeves, triple-LP boxed sets and quadraphonic bootlegs, knew quite a lot. There, inside the fourth box, chinagraph-marked and edited to red leader, were the original 2ins rhythm tracks, along with crumpled track sheets for the live recordings and the 2-track stereo master of collage FX for the live concerts. There were even two lighting-cue sheets, one for the Royal Albert Hall and one for the Shrine Auditorium, Santa Monica. The music inside wasn't the 'final' mixes that John Nightly had spent every waking moment of the last three years of his career getting nowhere at all with; but the raw tracks, the rough material, the unmixed fabric. Amazingly, all more or less intact, apart from one seven-minute interlude recorded with the London Symphony Orchestra at St John's Church, a classical-music venue in Smith Square, Chelsea, which had served as a basic 2-track master on which to overdub an audience in Atlanta, Georgia, four months later. The label stated that it was inside, but no... £60,000 worth of expensive orchestral recording had gone astray.

Here then was the much-talked-about lost masterpiece. Staple of every self-respecting music lover's search list. Subject of endless mentions in broadsheet know-it-all rock'n'roll supplements and Dadrock music mags, with hundreds of listings on record collectors' want lists, track-finder websites, eBay and all the rest. Wow... was this really it? Was this the gold that had contributed to the demise of at least four characters in the Nightly tale? As well as the withdrawal from the real world of its very creator...

The train of events leading up to the discovery wasn't unusual. Following the untimely death of John Pond, Nightly's legal representatives had tried in vain to secure the whereabouts and ownership of said multitracks; but, with the liquidation of the former management and the scattering of those in its employ, John Nightly had either more or less given up or was so far out of it himself by that point that he could never imagine wanting to hear one note of his beloved *magnum opus* again.

Could what this loopy kid was saying be true? Thirty years on? Probably not, thought RCN, though the faithful nurse asked for the dude's telephone number and said they'd be in touch. Three weeks later an apprehensive-looking Mawgan Hall accompanied by six heavy 2-inch boxes of multitrack tape arrived at Trewin Farm. On this occasion the dude still did not meet with his idol, who had decided to spend the day up on the coastal path rather than confront the possibility of his monstrous past coming back to haunt him, but Mawgan did meet with RCN, who, during an extended debriefing session, managed to extract the remainder of the story before the both of them carefully examined each reel of tape, checking for corrosion, rust, mildew and other damage to the outer layers of the ionised masters.

'Hello, Mawgan… John Daly…' The nurse paused for a second. 'How are you?'

'Oh hi… Yeah. I'm good thanks… Thanks, man.' The voice on the other end sounded somewhat relieved. 'I was gonna phone you anyway,' it continued, 'just to say it was amazing to meet you and to see your place… Awesome place, by the way… Thanks so much for letting me see everything… really… an amazing day.'

RCN put the handset closer to his ear; the kid's voice sounded lazy, half-asleep. 'Mawgan… It was a pleasure to meet you and I just wanted to say that John was so grateful to you for finding these recordings in the first place… then of course for taking the trouble to come all the way down here. As you know, he was sorry that he wasn't able to meet with you himself that day, it's just that... Well, he just happened to be particularly busy on that... particular day, mainly because he...' again RCN paused. 'He does a lot of gardening, as you know... hell of a lot... and... well, as you also know... it's a time-consuming business.' RCN popped a cough candy into his mouth and lodged it in his cheek.

'I know it is, man... my Mum's a big gardener and... she's doing it all the time. So... I can see you got a lot of flowers in your place... lot of garden there, a real lot... foliage as well...'

'The thing is, Mawgan...' RCN pulled the kitchen chair towards the telephone. 'Now I've had a chance to go through everything... it does seem that there's a lot of material which... does seem to be, as far as we, or I... can see...' He paused once more, to swallow a mouthful of glucose and tincture, 'pretty much complete, which is... given that amount of time, for it to just... turn up like this...'

'I brought everything out to you that was there, man,' the dude jumped in. 'It's like, as I say... I don't know who it actually belongs to legally or anything... guess it was brought by the studio as tape to be reused. For budget sessions... But that was a long time ago now... don't know how playable those reels are. I did put the beginning – the "Allegro" – on to the machine and it actually sounded great, y'know?' Mawgan stared up at a CCTV monitor showing a band arriving outside the studio for today's session. 'Needed a bit of lining up and stuff, 'cos after 30 years... But apart from a couple of little creases in the first section... it all sounded fine. It's dirty and all that, physically dirty, needs a good clean and stuff.'

'Mawgan... let me ask you something...' RCN crunched matter-of-factly into his diminishing cough sweet, 'Do you know the project fairly well? I mean, at all well? It's a big project, and... I wouldn't expect you to know all seven hours of...'

'I know every second of it, John.'

RCN nodded to Mrs Peed as she placed a steaming hot mug of tea in front of him. A sandwich stacked high with ham and his favourite cheap pickle lay waiting by the sink. 'In that case… let me ask you if you have the facility down there… to make copies… in the studio where you are now?'

'Course I do. I've already made, I mean…'

'…Right …so would you be interested, if we paid you to work on it a little bit? Do you think you'd be able to get the thing in some kind of… order? So we could maybe listen to it properly down here… and see just exactly what we've got?'

'Could I? Absolutely I could!' The kid livened up and was suddenly all action. 'Course I could… the *Requiem* is one of *the* lost albums… it's the only lost album that is still like… "lost".' Mawgan spoke faster. 'The one that everybody talks about anyway. You can get bits of it on bootlegs and that… I've got a few myself, or, well… I was given them, y'know… Except for the one I got at… wherever it was…' Mawg stalled for a second, unsure what the copyright owner's attitude towards piracy might be, even on a very miniature scale. 'But they're just like… bits, yeah… from live gigs mainly, probably taken from the desk.' Mawgan got up from his seat and hit the buzzer to let the band in, elated about the offer of work on this potential 'dream job'. 'The recorded bits are just slotted in really, 'cos the music itself is…'

'Mawgan, I'm going to ask you if you'd be able to come down and speak to us about this one day.'

Jonathan Foxley (RCM, FRAS, MBE), music supervisor and conductor and MD of the *MBR* 39-city US Tour, 1972, talking to *Record Collector's* Lost Masterpieces special issue. May 1996.

It was a very interesting and in some ways overwhelmingly inventive piece, but those days were so incredibly inventive anyway... and chaotic. It did seem that, in a way, 'invention' was the norm. My job – such as it was – was an impossible one. To co-ordinate all of that; John not being able to read music... then having to deal with all his other 'problems', and just that amount of physical people... [blows his nose] It was exciting, though. Tremendously exciting. But then again, really completely... quite nuts. Very under control and out of control at the same time.

[Jonathan becomes distracted by the interviewer's tape-player]

If I had to describe it musically I'd say that overall it was an... *impressionistic* piece – I don't mean that pretentiously, or in terms of paintings or anything like that – I mean it more... more physically than anything, because it... In its presentation of sound anyway... It wasn't... it didn't... wasn't at all 'centred' musically, is what I mean. And very loose, non-logical... and 'non-formal', in the way it... in its use of... in its *handling*, I should say... of rather complex musical language. Because he was, at that point, more interested in cutting up pieces of this and that, just going with it, rather than pure composition. Though he could do that as well, of course... could do anything really... so damned... accomplished... I'd think that, at that time, the piece was the purest example, the ultimate example maybe, of a cut-up or whatever you want to call the idea – 'randomness' – in terms of music. You get that all the time now, don't you? With dance records... club records... sampling... But, randomness on a massive sort of... 'oceanic' scale... which was exactly what he was aiming for.

[Jonathan frowns at the cassette going round] We had the John Donne text, which he used in the 'Letters' section – from the

Donne verse-letters – all these actors reading out letters that Donne had written sort of 'in verse' – very moving – which was organised by Donna [Vost], beautifully I might add… and then the *Holy Sonnets,* and I think he was very interested in the… metaphysical aspect of it – or however you want to refer to it – because he had his imagery in there, and his musical references as ever, but he knew he had to do something else with it as well. He was interested in Donne's subject matter and of course it also related to what he himself was going through at the time. [looks at the cassette-recorder again] I think that thing's stopped, you know…

It's alright. It'll turn itself over

Will it? Okay… [interviewer motions for Jonathan to carry on] John could see that there were technical problems in setting the poetry… Sometimes the words weren't really weighted towards being musicalised and they weren't really very regular either. Donne himself said that what he was about was passion, rather than 'syllables' anyway. So John thought that the cut-up thing would work, obviously keeping the main body of the idea together if he could. What he ended up creating weren't songs anymore, and they weren't… expanded songs or structured movements or even building blocks. They were more… 'blobs' of something… globules… blobs of music. What he called 'formants', when he did these interviews with journos who obviously didn't understand a bloody… oh, eh…

[interviewer smiles, noting the word 'formants' in a glossary of terms]

Boulez's description, obviously. I remember John said in some magazine, where they were talking about… these other things, getting it all wrong as usual… *Hair… Tommy… Arthur* – the Kinks' one – and the other one – the Pretty Things' one – *Sorrow**… so-called 'rock operas'. Basically just a collection of songs. [*Sunday Times colour supplement. 'Pop Goes Legit'. Special feature by Joni Beech, 9 May 1969*]. Nothing at all to do with what we were doing, and also John said the work would be 'imagist', meaning like Imagist Poetry; said something… something ludicrous… [clears his throat] 'A compendium of musical fragments and activities in different media' or some such thing. Must have gotten that from somewhere because he actually didn't talk like that at all. Thank God. Not in real life… John was really… a very simple person. Simple soul. Simple guy. [turns away from the interviewer]

How much more are you going to need of me? [interviewer indicates for Jonathan to continue]

The *Mink Bungalow Requiem* had everything, literally everything thrown into it… Freeform dance, the element that Donna put in, some tremendous things, really… beautiful and moving. At the time I would guess she was probably the leading person of that period, at that point, so we were lucky, because… she was doing this kind of… rock'n'roll tour thing with us, very tiring and… and… giving us her best dancers… And there were some… some quite stunning, really quite stunning set designs… Incense, perfume… the fragrance of it… and hundreds and thousands of candles of course – all the lighting was candles, as you know… which was… just stunning. Obviously before the days of 'health and safety'. [raises his eyebrows] Because we, as you know – John – he refused to use electric power. Wanted to show how beautiful candle power, candlelight, natural light… can be. That was very difficult… as lots of things got burned, some of the musician's scores got burned… Oh God! [Jonathan laughs and takes a sip of water] And some of the musicians themselves got burned – in more ways than one, I expect!

* *S. F. Sorrow* by the Pretty Things (Columbia SCX6303), 1968. The story of Sebastian Sorrow and his encounters with Baron Saturday.

Faber Guide to Contemporary Classical, March 2005 (Faber)
'*The Mink Bungalow Requiem, a piece for Singers, Players, Dancers* pre-dated other contenders such as *Roger Smalley's Beat Music '71, for Orchestra and Four Soloists* (1971) and *Stars End, for Two Rock Guitarists and Orchestra* by David Bedford (Virgin V2020), 1974. John Tavener's *The Whale*, issued on Apple (Sapcor 15) was a direct if safer contemporary competitor.

'To achieve great things, two things are needed: a plan and not quite enough time'

Leonard Bernstein

Mawgan Hall's Hash Browns

Take 2lbs potatoes (King Edward or Majestic), half a bar of butter, 1 teaspoonful of olive oil, 1 large onion, a teaspoonful of 'flavouring'. Salt (sea) and pepper (black) to taste.

Wash the potatoes with a scourer - do not peel. Blanch in boiling water for 3 to 4 minutes. Slice the potatoes thinly or put through slicer. Add the flavouring, and lightly dust with flour.

Take a small frying pan and melt the butter then add the potatoes. Toss when the panside is golden, then turn over. Continue until both sides are cooked. Eat with heaps of ketchup – before everyone else does!

Trewin Farm, Porthcreek, Carn Point, Cornwall. Monday, 11 March 2002.
'When John comes in you might find him a little… "detached", is the word I'd probably use.'

The kid continued to play with his dreads.

'Sometimes it seems like he's bored. But he's not… so…'

RCN smiled and cupped his hands around a fresh mug of tea.

Mawgan took a breath as he checked the condensation-heavy room and tried to fathom from which of the three possible entrances the Master might appear when he did finally choose to appear.

'I say this because… it's just that he is always… thinking about a lot of… things… *stuff*… at the same time.'

'Yeah… well, he's… y'know… thinking about stuff, I s'pose…'

'So his mind is... it... flits between these various things.'

The kid ran his hand around the neck of his collar. It was unusually hot in the hothouse today.

'I'm saying this, Mawgan... just in case...'

'No worries, man. As I say.'

'Obviously John is grateful to you... for your "discovery".' RCN coughed his familiar single-barrel cough. 'We all are.'

The kid remained immobile. 'Anyway... my idea was...'

'Wicked, man... as I say, it's...'

'And talk about... whether we can...' The male nurse rose stiffly, placed both hands on his lower back and took a deep inner breath, as if he were in some pain. He yawned, picked up a cushion, placed it on the old farmhouse chair and flopped down again. 'Try to... see if we can't... get to the next stage with this.'

'But...' Mawgan sat back and twirled his spiky dreads around his fingers, 'he is sort of... like, a... a *nice* guy and all that?'

Mawgan sought reassurance that in normal everyday life his idol, musical guru #1, 'disappearing man' and absolute Godlike genius, now almost within his reach, was – despite all that the guru had been through; all he'd given; the road he'd travelled; all he'd surrendered of himself – still a 'nice' fairly regular man, rather than the burned-out shipwreck the kid half expected to sail through one of the three doors that served the old vicarage kitchen. RCN rubbed his bloodshot eyes and, obviously restless, got up again to walk over to the garden window, turning away from the kid in order to avoid answering the question.

'Only thing... Sometimes he stares at you – "looks at you", I mean – in quite an odd way… Maybe not *at* exactly, but sort of… *through*…' RCN raised his eyebrows. 'Straight through. Then again, when he does that he's just… thinking. About something, so… don't be put off by it.' RCN scratched his head and cleared his throat, trying his best to sound reassuring. Mawgan nodded.

'All sweet, man. But like I say… the guy is like, a nice guy, uh… easy to get on with, and all that…' Mawgan upped his dynamic a little. 'Isn't he?'

'He's a… he's a "good guy", Mawgan.' RCN turned back to the kid. 'John's a good guy and he always has been. One of the *good ones.*'

The kid seemed to go slightly wobbly. 'Good guy…'

Mawgan appeared more anxious than ever as he picked up his notebook, ready for action. The thick, foliate lettering of an artistically scribbled R-E-Q-U-I-E-M had been scanned across a cover decorated with psychedelic ornamentation in late '60s style.

'I reckon that only someone… really "nice". Real cool person and all that… coulda written… come up with… all that amazing stuff anyway… couldn't they?'

'As I say, Mawgan… John is…'

"BLAM !"

As RCN spoke, the kitchen door of the old farmhouse flew open, black crows squawked in the cypresses above, a chill breeze rustled through the japonica and a dense curtain of impenetrable thundercloud momentarily blacked out the house, the grounds and the surrounding woodland, maybe even the whole village, and all of the headland from the white farm up as far as Black Zawn. It was as if the National Grid had suddenly collapsed. A sand-dry stillness came upon the place…

'Hallo……………… you must be Mawgan.'

The kid almost jumped out of his trainers before he stood up and sort of… dawdled to attention for the Master. 'And… you must be… John.'

'I suppose I was…'

The Master shuffled slowly and ever so unsurely into the kitchen in his ill-fitting dark-brown cords and green leather sandals. As if he expected to enter the room without being noticed. His bone-china fingers, singed by decades of tobacco, fingernails black with peat, clamped themselves tightly onto the sleeve ends of his fraying, nondescript cardigan. Proceeding in slow motion, creaking like floorboards, the old boy made himself comfortable next to the male nurse without acknowledging him. A scruffy mongrel ambled in and stretched himself out across his master's feet.

The Master's hair was unusually coiffed today. Forward-combed, fluffed and teased – almost Mr Teasy-Weasy teased. Someone, somewhere, had spent time on it. Wispy and colourless, like the roots of a dry spider plant, it framed a flat, droll face upon which the Master had today put his dumbest, most bimbo smile; as if he were already in a much too receptive, 'surrendering' mode. As if he instinctively realised that he might be in the presence of a kindred spirit. A like-minded soul. Possibly more than that. A potential 'friend', from what his faithful nurse and companion had told him. Well, it was someone who liked him, anyway. Liked what he did. That was the thing. The most important thing. Probably 'good shit', in the confusing modern parlance of last night's PayPal movie. The same phrase that the fish man's son had used yesterday, referring to the two huge spliffs RCN had laid out on the kitchen table. The Master didn't seem at all apprehensive, but then neither did the kid. Alexandre was relaxed too. He sniffed inquisitively at Mawgan's muddy flats before he wandered off in the direction of the pantry to search for crumbs.

'Do you come from a musical family, Mawgan?'

Oh no. It was a kind of 'hairdresser's question', wasn't it? Not the brilliant opening gambit the kid had expected from the Master, the Wizard, the Magicien, *God* himself and Lost Genius of all lost geniuses.

'In a way, I do… s'pose.' Mawgan attempted to connect with his potential employer for the first time. 'My dad was called, is called, Mark Hall?'

No response. The Master's bimbo smile was set in stone.

'You probably won't have heard of him, but he's… *sort of* famous – locally, if you know what I mean – in Sandy, where we come from…' The kid, suddenly unsure of himself due to the lack of exchange, looked down at the floor and addressed the ancient flagstones rather than the Genius himself, 'round where we live… in… Bedfordshire,' he continued, 'my dad had a band… a group, anyway… his own group.' Mawgan looked up again. 'Mark Hall & the Hallmarks.'

No response. Mawgan floundered. At the very least he might have expected the odd 'ah…', a half-interested 'I see…', or some such similar, reasonably humane nicety. What he failed to realise was that John Nightly's sensitivity as a human being when engaging with fellow human beings, his ability to relate to people, their social needs and responses, along with their expectations, no longer existed. Normal human relations having been knocked sideways, first by the recreational toxins he'd seen fit to shovel into his vessel and then by the process of extracting that poison from him so that he might survive – taking with it most of his personality.

'Changed their name to… just… the Hallmarks… Long time ago now… I s'pose.' Mawgan could feel himself sinking. Today was turning out to be much more difficult than he had imagined. 'Sometime around…'76… sometime round uh… *punk*, I guess…'

John Nightly wasn't the least bit interested in Mark Hall & the Hallmarks. John Nightly had been on another planet altogether during *punk*. He knew that the phenomenon had existed sometime during the seventies and that, as John understood it, it was based on rock'n'roll, or Teddy Boys – 'greaser' music – but that was about it. All John Nightly wanted to do was to get on with it. Having made the decision that he would get into the excavation business, he was impatient to discover what he'd been up to all that time ago – thirty years past. What exactly had possessed him to work that hard? To come up with that much stuff? To drive himself, and everyone close to him, to the limits, then… tip the whole thing over the edge? John Nightly was, as ever, wary, weary, and at the same time anxious, but remained self-absorbed and therefore newly motivated, keen to make the first deep gouge in the ground.

The kid sensed his potential boss's unease, smiled and kicked his heels.

'Small world down there…' RCN smiled benignly.

'Where is it you… come from?' Nightly let go of his cuffs, leaned forward and clasped his hands around his knees; a sign of closer engagement. He sat back, unscrewed a bottle of homemade lemonade sitting on the table beside him, and poured himself a neat half glass.

'Bedfordshire. Twinwood… that's the name of the village, anyway.'

A look of recognition. The Master sat up straight. 'Twinwood? I've… heard of that…'

'It's famous as the place Glenn Miller left from – flew out from. The airfield… when he went to France? When he disappeared in like… the war.'

The Master's eyes lit up. Mawgan continued.

'Twinwood Farm, it was then. Still is. 'Cos it's still there, sort of intact and everything.' Mawgan brightened too, delighted to have finally engaged his adjudicator. He flicked open his notebook and bent back the spine, ready to take instruction.

'What was it that really happened to him?'

'Nobody really knows, do they? People round there still talk about it, though.' Mawgan stared into his empty lemonade glass.

'I should think they do…'

Both Johns, by way of a mess of nods, grunts, general shuffling and eyebrow raising, indicated something of a genuine interest in all things Glenn Miller.

'Happened on my dad's birth date – the 15th of December 1944 – the actual day my dad was born. That's why it always comes up… in our house.'

John Nightly lifted himself from his chair, took a breath and patted Alexandre on his soft old head. The dog, immediately at home with Mawgan, gazed longingly at his master, who mooched over to the window and looked out at the brilliantly sunlit rose garden.

The kid put down his book and became visibly calmer.

Although Mawgan hadn't meant to, even promising himself that he wouldn't, he rashly took the opportunity, while there was a relaxed moment, to slip in one or two of the 3 million questions he had saved up for this much-longed-for day.

'John. Can I just ask you… uh… ? Do you know *American Crucifixion Resurrection?*'

Nightly turned back to face the room and propped himself up on the kitchen sink, one hand flat behind his back.

'don't think… I do…'

'Four Seasons?'

The Master shook his head. 'The band, you mean?' Mawgan nodded.

'Sounds like one of my "things", though.'

'It's something really good, y'know? Like your… things… *Really* good. It was their version of a concept album, I think; 1968… something like that.'

'The right year for it…'

'Really good record as well, though. *Awesome*… I mean, *seriously* awesome… completely different to their other stuff.'

John smiled and warded off a yawn. 'I'll have to… hear it.'

'Guess you know the *Five Bridges Suite?*'

The Master turned round again and stared out at the majestic Queen Elizabeth blooms. As Alexandre continued to scratch away at the patio window and yelp at his master, John lifted the latch and slid open the heavy door, letting the dog escape. RCN, silent… still, but watching like a hawk all this time, got up and walked over to the pantry to bring biscuits for the hound.

'Remember that one… because I, umm… went to the recording of it… Fairfield Hall, I think?'

Mawgan got up from his chair, looked around and attempted to lean as nonchalantly as he could manage on the Aga, though it was scaldingly, boiling hot, now that everyone else was suddenly up and mobile.

'Haven't heard that for a long time… the record anyway.

Good many years. Not since it came out I should think.' John continued talking with his back to the kid.

'Just came out on CD.' Mawgan smiled. 'At last, y'know!' The kid was certainly feeling more confident, 'What a great bit of music. It's just so…'

The Master slammed the door closed.

'Then there's the Sinatra one…'

But John Nightly had had enough.

'*Watertown*. About the imaginary town? Sort of… "*Everytown USA*"-type of thing? Something to do with the Four Seasons as well – bizarrely enough.'

John Nightly twisted himself around and stood up straight. A slither of yellow sunlight beamed through the glass and backlit the Magicien against the wide, double-glazed patio window. John Nightly's whole body suddenly seemed possessed with new energy; his limp, droopy head sat proud on upright shoulders. His dry, succulent hair had become lush and verdant. His whole being was aglow, vibrant, intelligent. The Master was suddenly adorned with the most shimmering, most sparkling halo, which transformed him into a figure from an Adoration of the Magi scene. Suddenly he was upstanding and erect. As if he'd been watered after long years of drought and the water had already seeped into his thirsty roots. Replenishing and nourishing. Oiling and energising him. John Nightly wasn't frail or dim anymore. For the first time in years the Master actually seemed masterful. John Nightly looked his new friend in the eye, confident enough to say, 'Let's get on with it.'

He was now also bothered enough to deliver an explanation.

'You see, Mawgan… you probably know… a lot more than I do, even about those days. Sometimes when you're actually making music, like I was… I was young… and industrious, during that period… you… you don't always listen to a lot of things. When you're working on your own thing. Don't have the time… more than anything else. Sometimes… if you're in a period of… change… which we were, more or less… constantly… it being the end of that… period… you're a little… scared also… in a way… to actually listen. In case you might copy, or be just a little too influenced by something.' John gazed out at Alexandre, now engaged in chasing squirrels across the grass. 'You understand what I… ?'

The kid looked both relieved and also rather amazed to be getting this, reasonably detailed, seemingly 'personal' viewpoint, from the horse's mouth, so to speak.

The old boy continued.

'Like someone said at the time… "pollen coming off a dandelion".' John scratched his forehead. 'Must've been a… a "golden" thing – golden moment. The "novels of our era", as they say. Lot of those songwriters seemed… "hit by a comet".' The Master sighed. 'Whatever it was people said…'

Outside, Alexandre once again scratched at the glass. The boss turned and pulled the door open for him to come inside, but the dog loped off teasingly. 'If you listened to a lot of that music, took too much notice of it… you'd be worried that you might try to copy it. Sometimes just… subconsciously. So I was safe in a way, because I was in a different field, but I know that some people, people I knew at the time, people around me… were… overwhelmed by what was going on. Completely taken in… and it just seemed to take them over. Because… well… the Who… Dylan… and that other lot! They went and spoiled it all for everybody!'

The sound of John Nightly laughing, which RCN could hear from the pantry through the thin kitchen wall, was a very unusual sound indeed. A sound not heard at the white farm for many a year. The way he laughed, or 'cackled', John RCN hadn't heard that particular cackle since the late '60s. That rat-a-tat, sand-paper, back-of-the-throat repeat. Almost as if the Master needed a little bit of practise at laughing – or chuckling – again, not having responded conversationally in that way for 30 or so years. No one knew for sure exactly how many years it was or might have been.

What it meant was that the boss appeared to be completely at ease with this wide-eyed, fazed-out, dimly shining, seemingly quite untogether skater dude. The link between ancient and modern. The missionary who was somehow going to make everything okay again. Solve problems and at last bring some kind of resolution, what they now – on CNN, and in RCN's beloved US primetime series' – refer to as 'closure', to this particular lost genius's lifetime's work.

Next door, RCN quietly closed the refrigerator. The fat man's heart beat slower. He put his hands in his pockets and breathed again, confident that everything was surely going to be alright, must be… alright, now. If young Mawgan Hall could put the Wizard at ease like this, this easily… the very first getting-to-know-you meet, without a note of music passing between them, then the nurse had great hopes for what lay ahead. He wandered out onto the back lawn to round up Alexandre.

Trewin Farm, Porthcreek, Carn Point. Monday 25 March, 2002.
The dog loped in, nose to the ground, hot on Mawgan's trail. A familiar scent but a new pair of trainers, with brand new shit on them.

Alexandre settled down in a corner of the room guided by the dog-specific attraction. He lay himself out on all fours at Mawgan's feet, lifted his head up to confirm the identity of the owner, then proceeded to make short, excited intakes and outtakes of breath, presumably overwhelmed by the sheer seductive beauty of Mawgan's shitty pumps, before he carefully sniffed and worked his way up the outside seam of Mawg's jeans, leaving a soft moist snail trail with his dribbly lurcher nose.

'He likes you,' said the Wizard.

'Probably smell my dog, Fred — named after Freddie Mercury, by the way.' Mawg turned to the Master for approval.

'Well, that was a feat... of recording... the work that went into it. What was the one I liked?'

'... early stuff's best.' Mawgan was eager to assure his employer that he undoubtedly knew his stuff.

' "Seven Seas of Rhye".' The Wizard seemed amazed at his own ability. 'The one I liked and... the other big one... when it came out. That guitar solo...'

Alexandre began circuiting the edge of the room, huffing and puffing, invigorated to see a new face for once. A young, new face.

'He likes you...'

The Master seemed genuinely excited by the dog's endorsement of the potential saviour.

'Where'd you get him, John?'

'Alexandre? John found him on the beach – the other John, I mean. Confusing, yeh. People find it confusing. We don't, of course.' He half laughed. 'There's only two people live at this address... and they're both called John, it's that simple.' Nightly looked around for a cigarette, 'few years ago now... several years... eleven... twelve maybe... maybe longer...'

'Doesn't look that old'

'John... or the dog?' The Wizard cackled again. 'It's all those flowers he eats!' The boss looked upon Alexandre in a fatherly way. 'He's not young either, though – in dog years. We found him out in the dunes somewhere; he was probably a Christmas present that got... well, thrown away.'

'Sucks...'

'How anyone could do it? Yeh.' John sighed. 'We did a bit of... asking, locally, or RCN did, when he first found him. Didn't want to get... too attached to it. In case somebody did show up. First couple of weeks we... kept an eye on him... and fed him... and well...' He lit up and took a drag. 'But they... luckily, they...' The boss sat back and released the mentholated haze.

'Heard a wicked solo the other day, '25 or 6 to 4'... Chicago...'

'That is a good one... Terry Kath.'

'Sweet...'

'Yeh. Wonderful player... but it was an era of wonderful players...' John cleared his throat. 'Why are you listening to all these old records?' He thought for a moment. 'Terry shot himself... by accident. When I was in LA, when I was... "incommunicado", you might say.' John rolled his eyes and chuckled again, behaving quite playfully for once. 'Other one was... "Whiskey in the Jar".'

Mawg felt suddenly out of his depth. For the first time ever in his life being confronted with 'a person who was really there'.

'Eric Bell... the first Lizzy record. Don't know what happened to him, or anything else about him.' The Wizard seemed surprised that he knew that much. 'But that was his name, and that was very, very good – inspirational – guitar playing. And that was also... well... it was a very, very long time ago...'

Trewin Farm, Porthcreek, Cornwall. Tuesday, 17 April 2002.
Alexandre wandered out of the kid's bedroom. The hallway was strewn with clothes: handpainted Carhartt jeans, Twister T-shirt, neoprene surfer-boots, fluorescent wet-socks and two pairs of trainers with CND badges safety-pinned to the flaps. At Trewin, everyone went barefoot almost all year round. It was so incredibly humid indoors because of the non-human residents that socks and shoes, particularly trainers, would've been unbearable. A trail of white Apple leads, green jack-to-jacks and a Pro Tools manual acted as clues to lead Alexandre into the hastily set-up music room.

'...this is the connecting passage?'

'Think so...' Mawg stared deep into the monitor. 'Just before you hear the first E flat. 'cause you were in E flat before.'

'...was I?' The Wizard had no idea what country he'd been in, let alone what key.

'You were bitonal... technically... But this bit's definitely in F.'

Mawgan placed his hands on the keyboard and played along with John Nightly's own piano part. Same chords, same sound, as on the thirty-year-old recording.

'you're right. Obviously.' John watched Mawg's hands on the restored electric piano. 'Difficult to be sure, though, without hearing the other… "possibilities".'

By now, Mawgan Hall knew at least a little bit about John Nightly. The way he registered music, related to it, remembered or didn't remember it. What he was likely to do with it – in terms of repeating, expanding, developing or treating it in some other, usually highly idiosyncratic or imaginative way. Mawg understood that his employer heard music more deeply and in a more knowing way than most people on the planet. Having said that, the kid had yet to formulate any real understanding about the way the boss connected say, one thirty seconds' worth of sound to another. 'I'm sure you're right. You usually are…' whispered the Master as he sat down again and scratched his head. Feeling a slight chill, he zipped his cardigan up to his chin and picked up a blanket lying on the chair opposite. John switched on his foot heater. Mawgan focussed his attention back to the screen.

'See this bit here…' Mawg pointed to the centre of the virtual track sheet. 'Tells me there's thirteen seconds' worth, before it changes again…'

The kid angled the lid of his heavily customised laptop towards the boss. In the top left-hand corner of the display a virtual counter timed each flicker, each frame of activity. An imaginary tick beat through each pink block or 'verse' as three chords, purple, lime and blue-black (or F-C-D), highlighted a transposition from E flat to G minor underscored by heavy brass – trumpets, trombones, tubas and timpani – together with long-bowed cellos and violas.

'How much more should there be of it?' Mawg addressed the boss without looking at him.

'… …I …really don't know. It's… it's a million miles… years ago… literally a million years ago.'

The sonic-architect dude stayed focussed on the construction of the saturated cityscape laid out across the screen. 'You think there was more to it than this?'

'... there was probably three or four minutes... because I don't think I would've gone straight to G minor there.' The Master looked round for Alexandre. 'Sounds too... crude...' John edged himself out of his chair. 'Doing it that way. Don't think I would have.'

'No worries, man...' Mawgan furiously rubbed across the trackpad, trying to summon up the other link passages he'd filed away in case they might be needed. The kid took a sip of carob cappuccino from a mug balanced just a little too precariously on his guitar amp and glanced at a plate of toast he'd last looked at an hour before. Mrs Peed's local-farm lard had now had the opportunity to congeal and coagulate with her homemade farmberry jam to create a series of tiny gum-coloured tributaries, veins running through the buttery surface liable to cause extreme discomfort once the toast had made its way down into your stomach.

John Nightly was sprightly today. John Nightly was sprightlier generally. Physically moving a lot sprightlier than usual, or so everyone, i.e., the inhabitants of Trewin, was fond of saying. Not just big movements like walking, sitting down or getting up from his smelly chair, but small things... Scratching his back, adjusting his glasses or demonstratively sweeping what hair he had remaining on his head away from those glasses. An empty gesture these days, signifying nothing but desperation in the hair department, but nonetheless one of the few remaining recognisable John Nightly mannerisms from the old days.

Days of much lusher hair and more graceful, almost cat-like gestures characterised another John Nightly. The John Nightly who was, for a short time, master of his own destiny. One who had conceived, imagined and almost realised the immensely ambitious orchestral passage now converted to digital tundra across the kid's screen. The Trewin family put this sprightliness down to the freak spending so much of his time with such an inspiring dude.

'Wait...' John leaned across to peer over Mawgan's shoulder, 'because, Donna... I remember now... She had to get the dancers in somewhere around here...'

'But the next bit's in E...'

'yeh...'

'So that's not gonna fit at all...' The kid rubbed his screen-tired eyes and looked to the boss for instruction.

Mawgan adjusted the lid of his machine in order to angle it away from the sun streaming through the huge patio window – 'Difficult to see...' He picked up a dirty T-shirt from a pile on the floor and draped it over the top of the display. 'That's better.'

The kid opened up an audio file labelled *Connecting Bitz* and hit *PLAY* on track 16. 'Then there's this...' Another section began... Syrupy cellos rising in thirds, reminiscent of John Ireland or Bax. Pastoral chords. The composer immediately recognised the passage and identified the new key.

'That's G... G minor.'

'E flat... Awesome... so that might work?'

'I think that is it, actually.' John squinted in the direction of the screen. Though he could make out very little and wouldn't have understood it if he could, he thought it polite to show interest in what seemed to him to be a hugely skilled aspect of what the kid was doing. The digital representation of dots, the gravel of highlighted dips and recesses, resembled nothing more closely than a craggy Flintstones-like map of ancient Cornwall.

'That's the… crossover point, Mawgan… right there…'

Mawgan stared further into the infinity of the music. A jumble of overlapping windows; instrument lists, cue points, ticks, short scores and all of the multifarious combinations of cadence bars, beginnings and ends of phrases, sections that might join up and connect to others, and some that definitely would not – twenty or thirty possible score sheets, all notated and active, which might just make the whole thing come to life… live again. Right now, it looked more like Microsoft Corp's cash-flow projection than the retrospective assemblage of a late-20th-century cultural landmark.

'That's it. I'm sure that's it!'

'Just… there!' John cried. Mawgan highlighted the new, right-sounding passage and hit *SAVE*.

Far away in the past
In a far distant time
A more distant, benign time
Long time ago
Generations and philosophies ago
An oft-remembered time that many new philosophers still find magical
But always get completely the wrong idea about
The music swelled up.

On the stage of the Lyceum Ballroom
In the nave of St John's, Smith Square
In the backstage bar at the Reading Jazz and Blues Festival
At Friar's Club, Aylesbury
Manchester Free Trade Hall
Regal Recording Studios
And the vast sunken auditorium of
the Gliderdrome, San Francisco, California
The music swelled up.

In the blue-green lagoons of the white-sanded coves and on the cheap

*transistor radios playing in all the little fish vans travelling up and down
the B3306 coast road, along the carns and zawns of the headlands of
West Penwith. The music swelled…*

'Can you turn it up a bit more, Mawgan?'

The kid leaned over and wound the volume through another
three or four notches. The increased surroundsound coincided
with a visible crescendo in the 'Star Mink Interlude', one of the
most thrilling and deeply moving sections of the Requiem.
John Nightly relaxed back into his filthy old chair, the over-
sprung back and arms soiled with grit, compost, Miracle-Gro
and other plant feed, the residue of twenty years' worth of really
'bringing the outdoors in', and bringing Alexandre in. Years of
slop and sweat had made the once-valuable spoon-back
parlour seat quite a disgrace. But that had never bothered John
Nightly. He quite liked the smell of decomposition.

'Bit more, Mawgan… bit more…' The Master turned to
Mawg and smiled, 'sorry… just a bit, though…'

The track was already loud. And now louder. Over-loud.
More bass. More treble. More overall punch and boom. More
compression. More middle. More meat, more thump. Just more
of everything. The loose bottom end crunched and distorted
the speaker's bass cones, rattling the racks of vintage processors
and effects the kid had painstakingly assembled in order to do
justice to his master's original vision. The dude winced. His
young, forensic ears resisted distortion (falseness) of any kind,
but on the other side of the room the boss's eyes lit up and a
broad, transforming smile appeared on his lips. John Nightly
just loved that blown-out, bombed-out sound. Reminding him
of all those '60s PA systems, speaker stacks either too big for
the local dancehalls and university common rooms they were
supposed to serve, or laughably small for the huge stadiums of
zonked out 'heads' and screaming teens.

The music quickly gained momentum and swelled like a wave.

A real six-footer. A long polytonal chord piled high with triads of G minor, B flat major 7th and a low-voiced inversion of D spread out against the headland like a convective stormcloud.

When he'd conceived the piece, Cornwall didn't exist. Not in the Master's private thought world. John had no idea about its sea-polished rocks, its sandbars, squills, zawns, coastal paths or quoits. But now the originator imagined a huge breaker crashing against the rocks, sweeping all manner of small sea creatures and other indigenous marine life before it. That was what the music was telling its maker *now*. This monster would hit the shore, break and shatter, ending up as a shallow layer of sparkingly clean transparent saltwater stroking the coastline, before it receded back into the ocean, and back into John Nightly's vast, oceanic imagination. The master closed his eyes. A hand pushed up the faders on the lighting console and the auditorium, the people, the music; *the* music; nature itself, was right there before him. The curtain opened. Dawn's morning light appeared along the headland. A soft crescendo from one scene into the next.

The percussion rattled and roared. Heavy timpani rolls, a bank of kettle-drums performed by two Zen masters John had picked up in Las Vegas, of all places. High on a riser towards the left of the stage these two unnamed, unremembered virtuosos attended to a large gamelan. There were tubular bells and mark-trees, two or three vibraphones, crash and ride cymbals, a series of small gongs and a tam-tam. John didn't remember how many instruments exactly. But he did recall a whole bank of marimbas and metallophones put there just for show. The Nightly band had never managed to find anyone to actually play the things but John insisted on having them onstage anyway, so there they were. A sinful waste of musical instrumentation, treated disrespectfully by one of the most talented *talents* of his era. Set above that was a massive multi-timbral selection of chime-bars, glocks and celestas. The Nightly stage set resembled nothing more than a percussion factory at night-time – empty of workers and players. There was the swirling double-manual Hammond played by Jonathan Foxley, the sonorous echoes of four nine-foot

Steinways, hired in at ridiculous and quite unnecessary expense to be played in unison by Justin and Ron to emulate the submerged drones John had first heard in Debussy's *La Cathédrale engloutie.* Suddenly he saw it all in his head, the soft and the loud, piano and forte, the formally composed music and the hysteria. Seeing within this remembrance and flashback, both the night dream itself and the eventual realisation of the dream; the ensuing, seemingly never-ending night-mare.

More. Just a bit more. John asked of his friend, until it became just a bit too much. Although, in terms of physical volume it didn't matter. Apart from the hound slinking away into the next room, there were no other humans or animals for at least eight or nine miles. No one within earshot at all. The two Johns, if they so desired, could have put on discos, 'raves', or whatever they called them nowadays, in the outhouses and barns; free concerts in the flower meadows. Even outside, with all that noise, the music would still be up against much louder stuff: the elements, the wind, the hail squalls, the sand whirls, the almost constant blow. And the birds.

The birds were actually really noisy. Mawgan thought so anyway. Ridiculously loud. And more or less continuous. The thing that most surprised him about coming to work, and live, at Trewin. It really was a racket out there. Though naturally noisy, at least. The music would still have to compete with the elements. As the group themselves had to, day to day. Compete with life itself.

The usually tolerant speakers began to protest. The massed ranks at the dawn of 'Mink Lux Eterna' blared out, creating an enormous blubber; exploding, lurching mass. Both the Wizard and the kid became fixed and concentrated on this new idea. Long, ambiguous, two-keyed tritones, toboggans running parallel with each other along a two-lane track. The sleds kept converging then gradually moved away again. Two streams, two passenger jets, cruising side by side. The sound of three hundred and eighty orchestral players and six jazz stickmen made the grade-A sound system play safe. The tweeters began to woof as the woofers began to tweet. Somehow the system managed to keep up with the music.

'Mazin' would've been the word. It certainly was a magnificent thing. Speedy, yet graceful. Carefree and loose, a celebration of life itself, though still elegant, literally 'composed' – worked out – as if Mingus had stood in with Stravinsky. The *Mink Bungalow Requiem* was a symphonic mash, truly a graveyard smash. Scandinavian, due to the scale of the thing. Wardour Street, because of the pulsating energy. Grantchester, in the delicacy of touch, the village stillness, and the familial human nature, the true spirituality, of the original concept itself.

Iona, Frieda, Jana, Monika, Myra and Donna. All in there somewhere. In the music's very humanity, its grace – and its disgrace. Its fiery intelligence, its innocence, invention – and reckless ambition. The lives and times of these heroines entangled within its harmonic ambiguity. In the layers and textures and various multi-personalities and approaches configured and reconfigured in each inspirational blob, along each polytonal corridor, on each heavily layered plateau, inside each wholly unanswered question within John Nightly's psychological melting pot.

Even presented this way, the music coming from Mawgan Hall's 'crappy lappy' – unmixed, un-finessed, unfinished... the almost lost, almost re-assembled, chucked together *Mink Bungalow Requiem* sounded mesmerising.

RCN appeared at the door. A hesitant smile. Careful not to appear to want to turn it down, he moved casually towards the amp, bent down and notched it up one dB more; the slightly increased volume gave the track still more definition. Now there was all manner of exotic percussion being highlighted – triangles, skulls, shakers – and all manner of God-knows-who playing the bell trees, cabasas... rainsticks and cimbaloms. High-tone instruments. It moved into freeform – *'Free Music, man!'* shouted the Wizard at the top of his voice; *'Free Music!!'* – the scene all too familiar to RCN. *Very* 1972. A long fragmented passage unwound as the choir began a gradual descent, a slide, in fifths and sixths, pagan and bleak, but because of the lush orchestration supporting it, crisp and even… Warm, kindly, benign.

RCN moved to a point midway between the two monitors, listening in detail to the stereo picture, its wide double-rainbow of sound. Three primary sonic colours. Three secondary ones. The speakers delivered a faithful reproduction, perfect indexing and imaging. All of the complex detail, the subsonic low bass 'shelf', the supersonic highs, using the jargon salesmen at the Hi-Fi Center in Penzance liked to dazzle with. The nurse turned to the others, smiled, fixed on the boss and nodded his approval.

Then it stopped. The new slab of sound, all four minutes of it, decided to cut loose. As if a page had been ripped from its binding to prevent it being read. This abrupt stop was followed by a loud static click, gashed on to a ticking, mechanical pulse. Sync points. Next came a massed shuffling of feet and for the first time it was possible to hear the ambience of the auditorium itself.

Suddenly there was no music at all. Not a whisper… from any of the 400 or so participants gathered together by the Santa Monica Freeway… suddenly it was just the sound of the *place*. A sensuous, panoramic nothing. Except for the sense of being in a very large space, an auditorium or mausoleum, of vast proportions. The ambience so real that it seemed that John, John and Mawg, unwitting time travellers, really were back there. *Then*. Not stuck in a drystone-wall ex-vicarage in West Cornwall in the present tense… Not in these 'nothing' times, but back in the sold-out concert hall, the twenty-eighth day of May, 1972. West Coast grandeur. Proper 'something' time. Here it was at last, then; reconfigured and re-ordered. Reheated. Right here before them, the absolute zenith of rock-'n'roll over-the-top-ness. All the seething, creeping, cloying, mess of creation. The *Mink Bungalow Requiem* was back. The *Mink Bungalow Requiem* was reborn. The *Mink Bungalow Requiem* really was the ultimate in counter-cultural, eco-revolutionary, fusion-powered, psycho-dependent musical calamity.

An expectant nothingness fell over 41,428 Californian hippies and dropouts. Paying customers and willing victims. The abrupt tacit in the music revealing the distant drone of wave generators parked out in the ocean. The hums and whispers of the over-excited performers, cola vendors, ticket-tearers, front-of-house security, police, journalists from around the globe and thousands of West Coast VIPs – oil men, land men, fund managers and corporate whizz-kids. All there to grab a piece of future memory. A token of the Wizard himself. With his attendant band members and roadies, dancers, orchestras, choirs, music copyists, groupies, drivers and candle lighters. This unexpected and quite hypnotising environmental nothingness, in its way, just as revealing as the music which came before it.

Then, from a corner of the room, extreme stage right, someone spoke… was it… Josh? – choirmaster extraordinaire, tireless campaigner for gay lib, trusted member of the Nightly inner circle – instructing the children's choir not to hold back.

'C'mon now, kids… Shhhh!!! Your teachers have paid a lot of money for you to be here!' Josh laughed, though the kids didn't. 'So make sure you sing up next time! And for God's sake people… *enjoy yourselves!*'

This rather anxious voice, encouraging the local pick-up choirs, was followed by a woman's softer tones, so focused you could almost hear her heart ticking, her mental organisation… Thinking… counting… and tapping. An intense inner concentration; a precise, commanding delivery earnestly counting out the steps.

2-3-4-5-6-7
2-3-4-5-6-7,
2-3-4, start a-gain…

'…Donna…'

John Nightly got up from his chair. He stood unsteadily again, suddenly old, suddenly 'wrong', as if he might fall down at any moment. He spoke softly... tenderly... and privately.

'Donna...'

The voice on tape was now dissolving beneath the sound of tapsteps on floorboards as the count-in continued and someone dragged the mike away from the counting voice across to the other side of that stage.

2-3-4-5-6-7
2-3-4-5-6-7
start a-gain, 2-3-4-5-6-7,
start a-gain...

The counting voice eventually disappeared. Drowned out by a very low modular sinewave and with it a roar of applause as whatever happened live in the stadium that night – so long ago now, that none of those gathered could possibly hope to remember – happened.

'it's Donna... it's Donna...'

John Nightly stared straight up at the ceiling, straight into space, away from the room, away from people, exactly as his nurse and companion said he would. He turned to the kid.

'thanks... Mawgan... really... good. It does sound really good, man...'

The Wizard gathered up his blanket, gave another little turn of the head towards the kid, a quiet acknowledgement of all of the boy's tremendous hard work, then... grey-faced and with all the colour of everyday suddenly sucked out of him, he swallowed, took a resigned half-breath, stared blankly at RCN, and shuffled out of the room.

item: *Record Retailer Audio Guide,* (37th Edition). 2006–2007.

John Nightly: b. Grantchester, England, 1948. One of the forgotten men of popular music. Nightly began his career in Cambridge beat group the Everyman in the mid-sixties. He was the first to fuse developments in 'contemporary-classical' via the London avant-garde of Cornelius Cardew and Harrison Birtwistle with the forward-looking, more adventurous pop music of the day. Influenced lyrically by modern poetry, his pseudo-classical debut, *Principal Fixed Stars* (for rock band, tape, electronics and double string orchestra) bears comparison with both Deep Purple and the Nice. His first two albums proper, *Ape Box Metal* (AIC JCE7036) and *Quiz Axe Queen* (AIC JCE7039) with their postmodern pick-'n'mix approach, are now acknowledged as an influence on the progressive era that came after – as well as, perversely, the sunshine-pop revival of the mid-1990s.

The multimedia performance triple-set *Mink Bungalow Requiem* still ranks as the most overblown concept of the era. Yet in revisionary thought it is a sort of masterpiece. A visionary work, essential to an understanding of the development of the pop song from three-minute wonder to quasi-symphonic tone-poem.

Nightly's period of activity was short – by late 1972 he was finished. Addled by hallucinogens and bankrupted by the cost of an ambitious world tour played out as a 'multimedia eco-event'. Nightly played his last note live, for Christian Action, from under a circus top courtesy of Billy Smart in Regent's Park, London. He moved to California in the 1980s.

Won-Der-ful Ra-di-o 1! Steve Rich on Sunday Morning, BBC Radio 1. Sunday. 17 January 2006.

[Lionel Ritchie's 'Hello' fades into the background]

Now... a very special request this Sunday morning for Mr and Mrs John and Edie Hope from Ely, in Cambridgeshire... went there once I think, didn't I? [speaks off mike to imaginary 'gang'] Think I did, anyway. That is a beautiful town, isn't it? Ely? In... Cambs, was it? Now... John and Edie, *Edie from Ely!* Right! Your son John – oh, he's called John as well is he? Run out of names down there in Ely have you, guys? [the intro to an '80s *Hit-pick* bubbles in the background] Your... y'son says you'll be celebrating your sixtieth – yes, that's 60 times 365 days together, everyone – *wow*... So that'll be your... [listens to the feed in his ear] Diamond wedding anniversary today then, my darling! [cue canned cheering] This is a request from your son John... who wants to say *thank you* for being such a great mum and dad... [canned audience: 'aaaaaahhhh...'] And also for never asking him to turn the radio down, ha, ha... [cue massed canned laugh] Well, that's always a good thing, isn't it, Mum? 'Specially when you're tuned to good old Radio 1! [cue 'Ra-di-o Won-der-ful' jingle for the fifth time] So... let's not get started. Now, John – 'Dad', that is – your son says that you will be 89 on um... Monday, so... er, well done, mate! Apart from anything else! Shall we have a round of applause in the studio for John? [four people clap] And Edie, who is... Well, you'll be 87 in February! I hope you don't mind me revealing your age, my darling! [cue football-crowd sound effect, followed by extremely distorted fuzz-guitar riff] And here's a record... chosen by your son, 'specially for you both... with memories of a very happy childhood in the sixties... It's the... the Jimi Hendrix Experience and 'Purple Haze'!

Trewin Farm, Porthcreek, Carn Point, Cornwall. Friday, 17 September 2002.

RCN came into the music room with Alexandre trailing after him. A sacred intermezzo, more suited to the atmosphere of a chapel or cathedral, lay interred on Mawgan's desktop. 'Adagio Mortada' was being burned into eternity. The bleak, angular trajectory of John Nightly's elegiac ribbon stopped and started repeatedly as Mawgan hit *PLAY* and *PAUSE* while carefully adjusting gain and level on his virtual input. The Wizard was deep in thought.

'Christ's life.'

RCN looked blank.

'Christ's life…'

The nurse placed two coffee mugs on the console and handed a mu tea to the Wizard. The Wizard took the cup and stared down into the dark, creosote pool. It appeared lukewarm… medicinal; most uninviting. He turned to RCN. 'John… I've not actually heard this sound for thirty years.' It was the only time the kid ever heard the Wizard address his friend and nurse using his Christian name.

'Christ's life… his age…'

RCN moved Alexandre's blanket and sat down on the hard oak chair.

'The duration of Christ's life… it's that long since I heard this piece of my own music…'

With their hot drinks, Jaffa cakes and roll-ups, radiators and amplifiers, the Johns and their accomplice sat in reverential silence, wholly concentrated on the 30-year vintage offering that now filled the room.

Minutes or so later they were more or less zomboid. The

Master's vision had transformed and transported them. They had all zoomed. So zonked were they – conscious, but only just – that the three of them let their facial muscles relax and droop. Their arms hung limply at their sides, their legs appeared disabled and defeated. If intruders from another world had happened to enter this airless cabinet they would've come not upon three hippies but three hippos, jowly and flabby, thoroughly at ease with themselves and the world as they lay beached in a hot summer brook beside a jungle clearing in this most careworn of care homes.

The stooges lazed and slouched, totally de-concentrated and open to the vibe, or 'flow', as if sedated by what came streaming out of the speakers. Unwound and unbent they received and absorbed the music, listening in a way that people don't listen anymore. Truly listening. The Kid, comatose under the desk; the Nurse, fat-bellied and fulfilled, a wide grin across his face; the Wizard, empty-eyed, castaway, tired of the wheel of life itself. Mawgan dragged himself upright, rubbed across the trackpad on his keyboard, lined up another edited segment, picked up his spliff and hit *PLAY* once again.

In these *nothing* days, we don't treat music very well. It's not such an important part of our lives. No longer a stand-alone recreational activity in its own right; we tend to think of it as more of an add-on, often to another quite unrelated activity. For John and John, and a thousand other Johns, this invisible stuff, which only becomes visible, and physical, when you take spliff and hit *PLAY*, is life itself. To this thousand there is nothing more important, either emotionally or spiritually, than to experience that mercury flow, nothing more rewarding than the magic spell cast by the few very truly great listening experiences.

In *nothing* times we listen while we're already otherwise occupied. Making calls, paying bills, hoovering, surfing the net or exercising, getting the kids off to school or fiddling our tax returns. Self-proclaimed 'music lovers' listen to a recorded work with the radio or TV on in the background. We do other strange things. We buy music which we will never listen to. We flip from track to track on our pods, reducing our greatest performers to digital sludge to be sampled for a few moments only, like a taster plate, or children's menu. There is nothing at all grown up or sophisticated about this low-grade, low-concentration experience. If we ourselves are creators, we are the victims of this approach; if we are receivers, we go along with it – for the sake of convenience. That couldn't be said of the Kid, the Wizard or the Nurse.

The tight little threesome, united in trying to rebuild this unwieldy and impossible-to-categorise conceptual work, listened like people used to listen. In the sixties and seventies. Good ol' 'something' days. Deeply, profoundly, attentively – properly. Wanting and needing to listen. Truly receiving. Eyes closed, heads angled towards the source like ravens on a BT cable. Volume turned *Up*. A concentration on receiving but not on analysing. 'Don't analyse!' It was one of the Master's absolute dictats. Don't think, whatever you do; don't think as you receive. Just let it come... let it flow... let it come down... come like a wave... Let that gold dust, someone's life's work, their essence, that ribbon of a million carats, a million days, come through; respect it and pay absolute attention to it when it arrives. Let it wash, rush, rinse and wash and wash and wash over you – until you drown in it.

In John Nightly's experience sometimes stuff came and sometimes it didn't. Then nothing came. But one thing John was convinced of was that some very precious golden thread had been delivered to him in that period of peaking creativity and personal crisis, January '70 to January '71, the gestation time for this final devastating work, and now, with the imminent release, in all of its 3 x 3 x 3 Gertrude Stein-like majesty, it would be for others, critics and audiences, and the mass of receivers out there in space, those thousands and thousands of Johns in bleak suburban cul-de-sacs from Redruth and Redcar to Far Rockaway and Venice Beach, those in small back rooms along the headland, school dorms and student bedsits, to decide whether or not the Wizard's judgement of what to take and what to leave was still to be trusted and whether the really good stuff, God's grade-A transcendent slub, had indeed been offered.

'This is the CBS Nine O'Clock News,' Dan Montgomery and James Hills reporting. 'Entertainment News' CBS Television, New York. 5.5.72
' *John Nightly is Johann Sebastian Bach, George Frideric Handel, Igor… Stravinsky, Al Jolson, William Blake, Leonard Bernstein, Brian Wilson…* That's the Beach Boys' Brian Wilson, right, Jim?'

'That's right, Dan.' [second anchorman nods and raises his eyebrows]

'… *Oscar Wilde, Rudolph Nu-ri-yev, William Burroughs and Rodgers and Hammerstein all rolled into one!* That's ahm… quite a line-up!'

'Now *tonight, as part of the multi-platinum rock star's New World Tour, the English rock singer John Nightly will present his seven-hour, three-part, 'triple-screen' mul-ti-media 'random' performance work, the ahm… Milk Bungalow Requiem. Not in a church, but in front of the largest crowd ever gathered together anywhere on the globe for a live rock-music concert. A world-record 300,000 people will pack into the specially constructed On-ga-ku Stadium just outside of Kyoto, Japan, this evening… to hear and see this pop, classical, jazz, film, ballet, choral, symphonic extravaganza, which features 400-plus performers and at least another 100 technical support staff and crew.* Phewee!'

The newscaster wipes an imaginary bead of sweat from his brow, mocking the ambition of a rock'n'roll eco-messiah.

'*One of the features of this… 'bigger than previously' rock-music tour is that the whole event will be powered by… re-cy-clable wave-power energy, which utilises seawater. That is, there is no mains or grid-supplied electricity used. The only lighting will be… ahm… candlelight. The performance gets through approximately 18,000 candles during its seven-hour duration*'.

The veteran newsman turns to his partner, '*That's a lot of candles, Jim*', before his round up'

Jim raises his eyebrows and nods dimwittedly.

John Nightly comes to the US in two weeks' time, when the Mink...
Milk... [news anchor stops] 'is it *Milk* or is it *Mink*, Jim?'

'It's 'Milk', Dan.'

'... ...*The Milk Bungalow Requiem premieres at a specially constructed*
auditorium on West Jefferson Boulevard, Los Angeles'.

'What do you think about that, Jim? Are you planning to go to
the concert?' Dan shuffled the papers on his desk, impatient to
move on to the next item.

'I am planning to go, Dan. [nods sheepishly]... my wife has
bought tickets and we're hoping to attend the LA date.'

'And she is a fan?'

'She is a fan, Dan.'

'Well, it's a long... eh... show ahm... Jim. Let's hope they got
enough bathrooms in there!'

'Let's hope so, Dan!'

NBC News: Ten O'Clock Bulletin, 12 May 1972. Read by Joan Traddorvelis.

Mr Bill Knoll, the oil and electricity industrialist and father of tragic heiress Myra Knoll, has said that he will serve a Federal restriction order on British pop singer John Nightly if he… 'so much as sets foot' on United States soil for the US leg of his upcoming world tour. Mr Nightly, whose group is due to play in Los Angeles next week, was driving the car in London, England, on the night on which Miss Knoll was tragically killed while a passenger.'

'This was the work of an old young man.
If I am older, I am now also younger.'

R. D. Laing, *The Divided Self – An Existential Study in Sanity and Madness***, 1964 (preface to the Pelican edition)**

Who will buy my bright purple?
My clump of sweet lilac
Sweet, fragrant posy
My Lavender Girl

'Lavender Girl', Cambridge street cry, notated by Percy North, chiropodist, Newmarket Road, Cambridge (courtesy The Cambridge Collection)

John Daly began his musical career as rhythm guitarist in Huntingdon band the Huntsmen. With a Sunday-night residency at the Railway Tavern, Bishop's Stortford, the Huntsmen seemed to be going places until they decided to transform themselves from lounge-suited modernists into a freakbeat outfit, briefly becoming the Ravens before a final line-up and name change to the Sky-Rays, after the popular Wall's ice lolly. The group then won themselves a place in the final of the *Melody Maker's* National Beat Contest, held at the Eagle Public House in Cambridge on the night of 2 January 1966.

It didn't look good for the Sky-Rays. Any group comprising two mods and three rockers was hardly a recipe for success in January '66, and the song they performed, the 'self-penned' 'Saturday Girl', a tale of the drummer's fiancée, a Saturday girl in the record department at Miller's, lifted the stomping battle-cry of the Dave Clark Five's 'Glad All Over' and grafted it, completely against its wishes, onto the chord pattern of 'Tell Me When' by the Applejacks.

The Sky-Rays' masterplan had been hastily assembled with the help of two manuals their vocalist had received that Christmas from his mother, Babs: *How to Write a Hit Song* by the hit-song-writer Mitch Murray and *How to Run a Beat Group* – a 'day-to-day handbook for guaranteed chart success' produced by the Hollies. Despite a scorching version of the Fentones' 'I'm a Moody Guy', the Sky-Rays came last out of eight hopefuls in the competition (which the Everyman won), with just two votes of a possible forty-five cast in the group's favour.

After all the excitement of the day, as the members packed away their equipment and licked their wounds, Huntingdon boy Daly wandered over to congratulate the young Nightly and his rather eccentric group on their winning turn.

'Just wanted to come over and say congratulations!' John Nightly stopped what he was doing and looked up, 'oh... thanks very much... thank you...'

The boy turned away and attended to his guitar. John Nightly hadn't been at all happy with his group's performance, even though they'd won hands-down. As far as he was concerned the Everyman had underperformed and he was in no mood for taking compliments. Daly persevered.

'I mean it. You were really... really good. You deserved to win it, you were... *different*.'

'Right... well... uh...' John Nightly paused for a second. 'We thought you were... really good too.' The boy spoke matter-of-factly without facing his advocate.

'Thanks, mate. You're obviously a bloody good liar as well!' The underdog began to back away as he spoke.

'If you ever needed a hand with anything, carrying stuff and that... I'm only at Huntingdon. Got a van and everything. Got a phone number if you want it...' Daly reached into his pocket. 'It's my dad's... it's on the van there... phone me up if you...'

The boy stared out at the bottle-green Transit backed up to the pub doorway – *J. P. Daly & Son. Builder's Merchant & General House Repairs, Huntingdon 535* painted in yellow and black on the recessed side panel. John Nightly, thinking that he might well need some practical assistance in the near future, became more welcoming.

'I might do that. Might need some help. I don't have a… a car or anything… so… well… good luck with your… *career* and all that.' The boy got up and smiled, picking up his guitar and amp ready to make a move, 'obviously…'

And so took place the first meeting of the happy-go-lucky loser and the polite but miserable winner. A few months later, when John Nightly took him up on his offer, the ex-Sky-Rays guitarist had just begun his training at the Royal College of Nursing in London. So proud was he to have gotten through the notoriously difficult exams that he never let his friends, or himself, forget the fact, adding the letters RCN, like OBE or MBE – only partly in jest – every time he wrote down his name.

Daly was also road managing a group from London, the Gloom, to help pay the bills while at college. The Gloom had been taken on by Carnaby Street management John Carter Enterprises, and so the two Johns' paths crossed again when Daly organised a special London gig for his Cambridge contact. Proving his worth, particularly his ability as a problem-solver, the Huntingdon man quickly found himself engaged as the boy's personal day-to-day nursemaid, eventually being offered a permanent job by John Pond.

All went swimmingly well until one night at the Railway Hotel on Eel Pie Island, when the newly qualified male nurse flipped over a blonde female nurse, the too-good-to-be-true Hannah from Kiwi-land. In November 1967, during another extremely harsh winter, the pair of them left England 'for good', for New Zealand, where they worked as team managers in a care home in Porangahau and swam in the blue coral sea, until a long, unrewarding stint as day nurse in a primary school on the South Island and a wife gone AWOL made the Huntingdon man long for his fish-and-chip suppers and rainy days. John Daly remained in the Antipodean sunshine for exactly ten years.

Daly wrote his former boss a spoof tidal letter from Queenstown and mailed it back to Grantchester. In the blazing-hot summer of

'77 this rather unfathomable 17th-century airmail was opened by Frieda, who, having no idea about the identity of the tidal correspondent, misread the sender's name, referring to him as 'John RCN' when she forwarded the letter on to Iona, who in turn responded with a telegram to Daly asking him to return to Britain with a permanent job offer – that of keeping John Nightly on a straight and secure path after his release from SUMHA.

Four years later, on 17 October 1981, a very tanned, very healthy-looking Huntingdon man met a deathly white, clapped-out clinically paranoid schizoid man in the reception hall of the Summer Centre outside Brampton, Hunts. John Daly drove his new/old boss the few miles back in time to Grantchester and Frieda, then booked himself into a room at the University Arms Hotel while they bided their time. Songwriting royalties, delayed due to legal disputes with John Pond's estate, came through a few weeks later from Pacific Music in Los Angeles. In April 1982, after the purchase of Trewin Farm, both Johns made the move to Porthcreek.

item: Monthly Cultural Notes: March

The days move fast in March. There's the familiar sight of daffodils, scented narcissi, cyclamen and of course tulips. Secateurs, shears and cutters should be sharpened. Half-hardy annuals can be sown in the greenhouse or on a windowsill. Take care with draughts and also night frosts. Keep an eye out for shoots of canna and gloxinia, and of course for those notorious insects.

I am under the direction of Messengers from heaven, daily and nightly
William Blake, (letter to Thomas Butts, 10 January 1802)

London, 26 June 1806. The Royal Society, Carlton House Terrace, London SW1.

John Pond drew shut the front door to his temporary lodging at 77 Beak Street, next door to John Wilkes the rifle maker, and set the buckle of his brunette periwig, clipping it tightly onto the one remaining clump of hair still actually attached to his head. The sun beat down on the filthy thoroughfare, a hurry-scurry of coachmen, reeves, herbalists and housemaids, all at the service of the fine families of Golden Square Villas, the most exclusive corner of the St Anne's Parish. Pond put on his pitch-black hat, newly adorned with gold-wire trim and Royal Household button, while managing to narrowly avoid a splash of slop from a nearby window. He fastened the paste-encrusted bands of his velvet tailcoat and fastidiously turned down the fine embroidered edgings of his silk blouson, then tightened up his matching breeches, glancing over to the young mistresses gossiping on the corner of the square to make sure they had not noticed him.

The Astronomer Royal was getting fat. He coughed a croaky cough and wiped a bead of sweat from his brow as he made his way up Spring Street until he hit the smoke and gas of Regent Street and Piccadilly. He quickly crossed over, ignoring the stinking death wagons and horses, the herb simplers and lavender girls, before turning left into Sackville Street, where he momentarily paused to look into the fashionable shop window of Southeran Books before continuing on his way. Pond was headed towards the Royal Society in Carlton House Terrace, where he was due to deliver his lecture *On the Declinations of Principal Fixed Stars* to its honourable members.

At the entrance to the Society he greeted the Misses Brook and Glade, daughters of his good friends and fellow members Ian and Jann. The ladies enjoyed the early morning sun and exchanged gossip by the door. He complimented both on their straw spoon bonnets, Miss Brook on her Spitalfields brocaded gown and Miss Glade on her dark-brown orphanage uniform with its white-linen detail.

The Royal Society, Carlton House Terrace, London SW1.
26 October 1966.

John Pond, manager-about-town, slammed the front door of his new pad at 77 Beak Street, next door to John Wilkes the rifle maker, and adjusted the buckle of his pink leather belt, a present from his new girlfriend Vanessa. (Vanessa Frye, a 16-year-old schoolgirl from Penzance, hit the charts with 'Mu Mu Tea', a Millie-inspired cover of the John Nightly song, in December that year. She was never heard of again.) Encountering a typically damp London morn, and late as usual, he put on his new pitch-black corduroy cap, narrowly avoiding a splash of mud from a green Mini Cooper. As he skipped between kerb and tarmac he fastened the pinked bands of his jacket, turned down the embroidered edgings of his Mr Fish silk shirt and tightened the belt of his matching cords. The young entrepreneur then made his way across the smoke and gas of Regent Street, where pick-up shots for Dick Lester's new movie and a photo shoot for *Trend* magazine were adding to the mayhem.

'Charlie!' Pond yelled to Charles Wheatstone, former variety agent, now manager of the Kyst, without bothering to wait for a response before he turned into Sackville Street, pausing momentarily to look into the old-fashioned chocolate-box window of Southeran Books then continuing on his way towards the Royal Society. Pond had been due to arrive there an hour earlier to check on the preparations for that night's launch of his protégé's debut LP, *Principal Fixed Stars.*

At the entrance to the Society he came upon fashion model Bambi Brook – a recent ex – chatting to his own former secretary, the TV presenter Cornelia Cassell. Pond complimented the girls on their see-through minis and Cornelia on being on the cover of this week's *Fab Girl* (the series *Cor, it's Cornelia!* ran on Children's Rediffusion TV every Friday teatime from

September '66 right up to December '77, achieving a record of re-commissioning in children's television beaten only by *Blue Peter*).

The manager passed the MoD building, allied flags asail in the breeze, and held on to his cap as a keen wind began to whip along the Mall. Pond felt good. He should; he had everything going for him. He felt bolted to the zeitgeist. He heard voices, the usual ones, advising him to follow his instincts, and he felt vibrations, unusual vibrations, a distant guitar riff that rattled the white-columned facades all around him representing what would become one of the most valuable assets of all in terms of England's future wealth. Homegrown rock'n'roll, the new currency, rang out across Horseguards and Trafalgar Gates from a distorted PA system somewhere close by. It rumbled the dustbins lining the alleyways behind Buck Pal and it rattled the pockets of the labels that released and manufactured the product. The record-pressing plants of England were the new tin mines, the new steelworks, and vinyl, a composite of crude oil and acetate, would soon make the brand names Parlophone and Decca as world famous as Wedgwood or Chippendale.

Pond tripped down the steps from St James's. Inside the venue, the smoke-stained walls were awash with condensation. The place buzzed with *It People* – tastemakers and scenesters the manager had papered in order to initiate a sense of excitement about his charge's London debut. At the end of the narrow hallway the first person he encountered was the last person he expected, John Nightly himself, undergoing counselling by his newly appointed road manager.

'What 'y' doing out here, man? You shouldn't be out here in the public... *bit*. You should be backstage, John... stay back there... Away from this...' Pond looked around disparagingly. 'This... *lot*...'

Dispensing with any greeting whatsoever, the manager attempted to lead the boy to safety. 'It's no good if the audience sees the star trying to sort out the practicals, man.' Pond directed his star towards a narrow corridor. 'That's what we've employed your trusty road manager here to do...'

'but there's a problem with the dancers and... a bit of a problem with the piano and... and the orchestra... and...'

John Nightly furiously rubbed his forehead, attempting to rub away the splitting headache that had descended on him three days earlier. Pond held onto the boy's arm in the manner of someone helping an elderly lady across the road. He spoke reassuringly.

'We'll sort the dancers, man... and all the other stuff... Let's just get you back in the dressing room and out of this public... *bit.*'

'but no one actually knows who I am anyway,' the boy protested.

'The ones in the know do,' Pond replied without listening.

'"...in the know"?'

'*In the know!* The ones who know their stuff! And everyone will be in the know soon. Don't worry about that...' The manager urged on again: 'C'mon... this is not good.'

Pond put his arm around the client, sheltering him, taking him literally under his wing. Like boxer and trainer, they hurried back along the corridor. With its linen-fold panelling and fixed glass lanterns it was like walking down a tunnel into the past.

'I just want to be told what is actually happening, *when* it is happening...'

John Nightly stumbled on, visibly unsettled by what seemed like the amount of 'practicals' that had not actually been attended to. Pond continued.

'That's great, John. But as I say, that is your road manager's job, and I completely trust him to be able to do it. Part of that job is to not actually burden you, or me, with literally every little thing that might crop up. To keep the practicals – the actual "practical"… practicals – well out of it.'

The manager employed his usual flamboyant hand gestures to make the point. 'Practicals are boring, man… All that bad old boring old stuff, bad, bad, bad… boring, boring, bor-ing!' He emitted a huge mock sigh of relief, in the manner of someone who had just climbed a mountain or completed a marathon. Sometimes the manager came across more like a music-hall entertainer than the intelligent strategist his client understood him to be. 'Not that there is any bad stuff or anything… Not yet, anyway… but there will be!' Pond assured his client as he raised his eyebrows. 'In the future.' He smiled. 'Sometime in the not-so-distant…'

But Pond's reassurance had the reverse effect of that intended. The more his manager reassured the more John Nightly became alarmed. Pond turned to his road manager.

'I assume everything *is* alright?'

RCN nodded matter-of-factly as he led the way, John Nightly's old Eko guitar in one hand and a new attaché-case in the other.

'There you are then. All is fine, all is…' Pond looked around and smiled at both Johns. 'Both of you… everything is really fine.' He checked his watch. 'Still two hours, for God's sake! Loads of time yet, people…'

Pond repeated the phrase under his breath one more time as if to convince himself.

'Where's this other lot… *orchestras*… coming from, exactly?' Nightly answered before his road manager could.

'Cambridge Music Society, but there was a sit-in this morning and that's made them late.'

The manager continued on, falling into Daly's slipstream, as both of them led the boy through a side door into the east wing of the building. As it opened out onto a small bar with a drinking room beyond, they could see that the auditorium itself was packed. Wardour Street regulars and Chelsea Set hangers-on, bright, shiny new beings – 'freaky beaks', as they would come to be known – had all turned out, tipped off by Pond's on-the-ground public-relations offensive that this was going to be an evening to see and be seen, an event to have been at.

In the far-end corner, the Cambridge Student Orchestra lugged bulky instrument cases down two flights of steps into an adjacent dressing-room while the ballet school's humpers pushed large portable wardrobes through a channel in the crowd. In the main lecture-room itself, a loud slab of mutated rock'n'roll added to the excitement. Pond nodded to the beat like a cockerel parading around its coop.

'What's this?' he asked of the track, a segment from one of John's new songs, as an ashen-faced piano-tuner came towards them. The boy approached him cautiously.

'is it okay now?'

'What?'

'the piano...'

'It's better than it was, son.'

'and the middle area?'

'No idea, my friend... Had to stop when they put this horrible racket on.'

''Mazin'... 'ma-zin'...'

The sharply attired figure of Lee Hide blocked the doorway.

'Looks like a opera or suffink in 'ere…' All of the Johns seemed relieved to see him.

'John, John, I love your coat!' Daphne ran after the manager and his contender as they progressed further towards John Nightly's own cubbyhole. 'Where did you get it?'

'this? Oh… don't know. I… well… John here chose it for me,' a quietly decomposing Nightly mumbled as he indicated towards his road manager. 'Somewhere in London…' But the coat, a one-off sample from Ossie Clark's Quorum label, was special in more ways than one. It was a present from Iona, having been chosen by Monika. Daly only ever shopped at Mr Byrite.

'It looks fabulous on you, John,' Daphne gushed attentively. 'Makes you look a… a… a… film star.' The student took it all in, amazed and impressed by the frantic activity in aid of her friend from Cambridge. 'Is Jana here?'

'Really don't know, Daph… she's definitely on her way… I know she started off at lunchtime.' The boy looked pained. 'sorry… finding it a bit difficult at the moment.' Daphne beamed a good-luck smile and detached herself from John's sleeve.

As Cornelia and Bambi appeared at the door behind Sandra, Daly and Nightly surveyed the mayhem around them – an ant-like degree of activity in the small back kitchen-cum-dressing-room. The vestibule reeked of stale incense, joss sticks and cheap Communion candles. Baskets of lavender from a previous function lay stacked against a wall. The familiar riff from 'Lavender Girl' leaked from a corner speaker as an orchestra of sorts attempted to tune their instruments, hindered and distracted by some sixty dancers in varying states of undress. Leotards, tights, shawls, curtain-lace suits and ostrich feathers lay draped over every surface.

On the other side of the room John Vost, the Rambert

choreographer, assisted by his younger sister Donna, balanced precariously on wobbly flight-cases as they shouted out beats in the bar, for anyone who wanted them…

2-3-4
…2-3-4-5-6-7
…1-2
…1-2
…2-3-4
…2-3-4-5-6-7…

'It's a pattern, darling… *Lord Jesus Christ!*'

'Shout where the beat is, will you?'

'As I say, girls… it's a pattern. You're supposed to follow it!' The choreographer barked his instructions:

'2-3-4, 2-3-4, 1-2, 1-2, 2-3-4-5-6-7, start a-gain!'

Pond gazed in dismay at what seemed to be utter chaos in the choreography department.

'Start a-gain, start a-gain, 2-3-4-5…'

But Lee, far from being at all dismayed, remained thoroughly impressed. By the sight of 20 or so young *dolls* stretched out in front of him wearing barely any costume. The seemingly possessed Donna, consumed by the encircling tempo, climbed onto a chair while a line of impossibly pretty girls copied her movements. Their supple bodies writhing around one another, like the themes of the music itself, as they tried to make sense of the ever-shifting rhythms.

'That's it! That's seven beats, girls!'

Pond looked on suspiciously. 'What's he doing?'

'He's getting them through the difficult timings. There's a couple of bars of seven in there… and a couple of three. You just have to count it, though.' John acknowledged Donna, no doubt appreciative of what she was trying to achieve. 'I'm not sure how they count it like that; they go into weird numbers like 9 and 15, though there's nothing in 9 in there!' The boy surmised, 'I suppose they have only been working on it for a week…'

Carnaby Street and Foubert's Place, 1967
Photo: Eric Wadsworth, courtesy the *Guardian*

The offices of JCE, Carnaby Street, London W1. Friday, 21 November 1966
' "Lavender Girl" is the one, John. We've got to go with it.'

'You're sure it's not too similar to the other one?'

Pond shook his head. 'It's right in the pocket, man. *Right there in the pocket.*' The manager spoke decisively, as always.

'Because I don't want to… repeat myself…'

'Then why did you write it, man?' Pond retaliated, not a bit light-heartedly.

It hadn't taken long for John Pond to identify a self-destructive streak in the client. Most likely a deeply embedded geological strain. Not an unusual thing to find among the prodigiously talented, but an aberration that had to be dealt with. The manager understood that. Pond wasn't averse to game play, but a serving of doubt or self-questioning, often existing just for the hell of it, had to be volleyed straight back at the doubter.

'You mean I am repeating myself?'

The manager picked up a pack of ciggies.

'John…' Pond slit the pack open. 'What I'm saying is that the track is a hit.' He looked around for a light. 'What you got there is a slab of… *maximum R'n'B*, as they say in the trade. It's a *smash*, man – a *cutie*, a *butie*, a *right rooti-tooti*, my friend…' Pond made his point by *dum-te-dumming* the words. 'Gotta get it out there right away. Before everyone else gets on this… *folky-rocky* thing you got going there…' He looked across to check the reaction of his client, having gently eased the 'branded' phrase into the sentence. 'Might be big… that *folky-rocky*… whatever. Tell ya. It's gonna happen… And we don't want it to happen without you…'

The boy slid a box of matches across the table. 'As I keep saying... it's not a *rocky-folky* or 'rock-folk' anything, or whatever it is you want it to be. Because that's so... *limiting*. Better if we don't actually call it that.' John shuffled around in his chair. 'Better if we don't call it anything at all.'

Pond lit up, took a drag and gazed out of the window, already gone, already at least a million miles away. The boy carried on – 'I do not want my music to be...' – before making an unflattering and quite disrespectful facial expression as he tied and untied his cravat. Pond cleared his throat and turned round. 'Whatever we end up calling it won't matter a damn in the long run. The reviewers and the... the marketeers will call it whatever the hell they want. We can try to influence that... a bit, but at the end of the day, we can't write the reviews for them, can we?' He walked back to his desk and sat down. 'Wish we could!'

Because you're the "new guy", man – or you will be. "Let's get the new guy!" and all that kind of...' Pond looked at the boy. 'Very often there is only one "new guy" – the one who everyone wants – at that moment. Who's... uh... well... *newer*... than anyone else. You're gonna be that guy, man. Gonna make sure you are.' Pond gurned his mouth and twitched excitedly.

' 'cause one day, John... you're gonna be... "the old guy"... if you... get my... uh... and that day *will* come – but hopefully not anytime soon. It's my responsibility, my *duty*... as your... y'know... as your "guide" to the new... apart from anything else, to delay that day for as long as I can – *distant as the stars*... as they say.'

Pond appealed to the client. 'Now, if you maybe... just let me get on with my part of the... creative endeavour?

The manager sat back, spread his legs, unzipped his boots and attended to his desk.

Nightly took a scuffed notebook from his bag. 'As long as you think this song is definitely the right song to release. Because, the other thing that's worrying me is that it… Well, it doesn't have any cut-ups in it for a start.'

'Any?'

'Cut-ups.'

'No idea what you mean…'

'Cut-up writing? Random writing? *Cut-ups*. We said we were going to do something on that. As in your "trademarks".' The boy opened his book. 'And that *is* kind of my trademark, I think.' He appeared unsure again. 'Or at least it's one of them.' Nightly didn't bother pausing for breath. 'Iona always says my style is… Well, what she means is… it… It's against all the other stuff. Is what she means… I think.'

'Against?' The manager furrowed and twitched. 'Opposite of… what exactly? Sorry, man, but…'

'the opposite of… well, *pop music*, I suppose. *Normal Pop Music*. The stuff that's going around. Other people's stuff. You said so yourself…'

'*Normal?*' Pond raised his eyebrows. 'Long as it's not the opposite of *hits*, man! 'Cause that'll be a pretty unhelpful *opposite* – for all of us.' The manager picked up a pen and put his signature to an extremely long-form document without bothering to read it. 'I'm really not absolutely sure where we're off to today…'

'we could call it… "anti-pop" …or something,' the boy mused.

'Anti-pop?' Pond repeated the words as if they'd been issued by an undertaker. His complexion turned waxy. 'Good *term*, good… eh.' The manager didn't like the term at all.

John Nightly considered for a moment. 'We could say that what

I'm doing is actually… *deconstructing* pop music… Because I am, actually sort of, you know… *cutting it up.*' He leafed through his notebook. 'Taking it apart, and then… well, putting it back together again, in a way…' John looked up hopefully.

Pond felt that he had done his duty for today. He pulled his boots back on and yawned. 'Look, man… "cut-ups", "cut-downs", "cut-outs", whatever the hell they are. The record company's convinced that this track of yours is a hit and I'm not about to inject anything into the equation that might upset the boat. That's not what I'm here for. I'm here to get the boat to sail!' The manager stubbed out his ciggie and took another breath. 'Fact of the matter is they don't need your permission, my permission or anybody else's permission to release the thing anyway, and I'm not about to put Stonehenge in the way of what they wanna do. If we kick up a fuss and get all awkward now and they get fed up with us and they pull the promotion and that whole… It ain't gonna happen anyway.' He twitched repeatedly. 'Whatever we… call it…'

The boy was going to have to concede the psychological argument. Even he could see that things needed brightening up.

'I like the song, of course. That is why I recorded it in the first place… as you say. I guess I'm thinking more about the album. Want to make sure that it, the single, does actually "represent" the album. I want to keep developing… evolving, releasing different kinds of songs…' John Nightly closed his book and dropped it back inside his bag. 'What about 'Lavender Girl'? Did you play that to them?'

'Didn't like it… and I can see why. Second or third single, that one – not a first.'

'It's the only other one I'd want released, though. "Mu Mu Tea" is much too… *commercial* somehow…' The boy broke off. 'It sounds too much like… well, a "hit" already, an "instant hit" or something…"

'Well, we wouldn't want that! Christ Almighty!' Pond thundered his heavy boots on the carpet in a fit of mock incomprehension.

John...' The manager leaned across his desk at his beleaguered friend. 'The one thing we can do that'd probably please you no end would be not to put out a single at all! Why don't we try that? Release the album and forget the single! No one's ever come up with that masterstroke before!' The manager made the suggestion in order to scare.

'Could we?'

But it didn't.

'Godsake, John!' Pond wiped his brow. 'People do have to release singles — unless they're bloody bonkers. To have one little hope in hell of selling any albums whatsoever.' He looked round for his secretary. 'And... before I forget... I'm setting you up in a meeting. Film producer who sent this over for you. Name mean anything?'

The boy stared blankly into space. Pond continued.

'Myra Knoll... she was in the paper yesterday.' Pond gave a cursory look back to his desk. The feature he wanted lay interred there. 'Well, you *should* know, man. You should read the stuff we send you.' He looked exasperated. 'That's why we send it to you, John.' The manager checked underneath the protruding envelopes and contracts. 'The film, *Tsunami*... the surf film?'

'...I think Iona saw that...'

'She would've. At least your... your woman is up on... *life*...' Pond made his point and pursed his lips. 'Anyway... this is a new one.' He located the script in his in-tray. '*London thriller... one of three new projects... Pitfall...*'

Nightly listened attentively. 'As in... *falling from a pit?*' Both of them grinned.

'Don't think so, man.'

'it's a nice title…'

'Yeah?' The manager perused the topsheet. 'Says it's… *like a Dirk Bogarde movie* – but *with sex!*' The manager twitched… 'Looking for someone from England to compose a sound-track… wants the music to be…' Pond squinted at his own scribble. *'Particularly English*, it says. So there you are! There's no one more "particularly English" than you, man.' He carried on: *'Shot in London… Psychological thriller.* Right up your street, surely! You're quite… "psychological".' The two of them smiled knowingly. The manager unrolled the palms of his hands as if he were unwinding yarn, which he undoubtedly was. The gesture denoting a fait accompli. *'Hello, Mr Film Composer!'*

Pond tossed the heavily bound script over to the boy, challenging him to catch it before it fell apart, certain that he'd delivered something of real worth to his client. The irony of their partnership being that in reality both players were as ambitious as each other. In Pond's mind, they were already winners of the Academy Award for Best Soundtrack. Manager and client were ensconced in adjacent cabanas at the Beverly Hills Hotel. Pond had already half-written John Nightly's acceptance speech in order to get maximum exposure in every conceivable direction for this most 'happening' of talents. The manager drifted haplessly away, fantasising about which Hollywood legend would read out the nominations and how he would then be able to further exploit the historic moment the following year when they would both show up at the Oscar ceremony as special guests of the Academy – 'previous winners' and all that – and then… of course… most important of all, the parties afterwards. He looked to John Nightly for a response. The client liked both the sound of the project and the idea of writing for films, but was too set in his act to suddenly come over too enthusiastic. John looked down at the title page: *Pitfall, Knoll Film Company, 72 Berwick Street, London W1.* Let's hope it won't be, he thought. There was a note scribbled in red pen and circled:

'*John Knightley*... K-N-I-G-H-T-L-E-Y... *English music*', it read, suggesting that the scribbler had actually never heard of him.

'You said you wanted to do a film score...'

The boy remained silent.

'I've set you up for lunch... Kettner's, next week.' The manager waited for approval. There was no hesitation.

'Of course it sounds... interesting, but what's it going to be like, this *Pitfall?* It's not a... a... a corny thing, is it?'

The boy's naivety still came as something of a surprise. '*John... man...* I wonder how I, or anyone else, would know that given that I haven't seen the damned thing and presumably no one else has either, as the film company haven't actually made it yet!'

The manager's words ricocheted along the corridor. Pond really needed to get on this morning. A potentially very stormy day loomed. A damaging hyping scandal with another of JCE's acts entailed allegations of records being illegally 'bought in' to the chart; and today people needed to be calmed down, backed off a little. There were a lot of 'persuading' calls to be made. He picked up a rather worrying note from Cornelia as his mind moved on to other things. Pond turned to the boy.

'...Big American company... previous film did well... You keep telling me you want to do a film score. The project's loaded... the girl's loaded, I think... *Daddy is an oil guy.*' A Big American oil guy. Pond picked up the receiver, ready to dial. 'The one thing I can't tell you is whether or not she's pretty,' he put his hand over the receiver. 'But I can tell you she's rich...'

The boy smiled, acknowledging that the manager probably did have his best interests at heart.

'I'll tell you if she's pretty...'

Kettners restaurant. Romilly Street, Soho, London W1. 8 December 1966.

'… hallo…'

'Morning, sir.'

'Hallo… nice day, isn't it…'

'Always a fine day at Kettner's, sir.'

'…okay… well, I'm… let me see now…'

'Trying to remember who you are, sir?'

'No, no – very funny, though – who… I'm…'

'Who you're meeting?'

'…that's… Yeh.'

John put down his guitar-case and fumbled in his pocket for the slip of paper containing his dining companion's name. Kettner's was a regular lunch spot for music-business types, with several faces already scattered around the restaurant's champagne bar. Characters John now recognised. Most of them cropping up in conversation with his manager as examples of how or how not to do things. 'That's what Andrew Oldham would've done…' or 'I can't see Mim Scala doing that!' was a regular tack. He recognised two very pretty girls sipping sangria at a table by the door, their eyes flitting around the cherry-pink room; they were friends of Iona's, and they recognised him, but each without really knowing who either party was. The boy fumbled and fidgeted, while right at the end of the square room, waiting patiently, and sitting pretty, was the reason for his visit. With her hair in a tight ponytail, hazel eyes, orange-lipsticked lips, silver chain-dress and silver Bentley waiting patiently outside, sat Miss Myra

Knoll: heiress, oil daughter, film-maker, troublemaker.

'Hallo… I'm… very sorry… I think I'm very late…'

'By American standards yes. By English standards… maybe not.'

The unusually well-groomed Miss Knoll did not trouble herself to get up.

'Really am sorry. I… I didn't realise… the time…' John tidied his hair as he knocked into the adjacent table with his guitar case. 'Really rushing today.'

'Yellow pills or blue ones?'

'Right…! No, what I meant was, I've got a lot to do and…'

'So have I!' Myra snapped back. 'One of the things I was planning on doing was having lunch with someone, music guy, at… one o'clock, I believe it was…'

The boy couldn't apologise anymore. He was still coming down from last night after a weekend of rehearsals that had made him slightly deaf – temporarily, he hoped. His luncheon companion softened. Warming to his overtures and his seemingly out-there, thoroughly English manner, she smiled as she finally got up to shake hands.

'I was about to leave… But I'm practising getting used to London's more relaxed attitude to timekeeping.'

John smiled and looked for somewhere to put his guitar as the waiter swiftly pulled out a chair. 'There you are, sir – and I'll take that for you.' The boy honed in on the music coming from the bar.

'…know this one?'

'Excuse me?'

'Do you know this song? The one that's playing…'

The young woman, not having registered any music at all, sat down again.

'Something of yours?'

Myra took the wine list and gestured for John to sit, for God's sake. He picked up his folded napkin and… folded it over again.

'My Funny Valentine' faded in and out of the scene.

Exactly sixty minutes later the pair marched out of the restaurant. The fledgling film producer having found herself a composer, the novice soundtrack composer having found himself a patron. So absorbed in their own pitfall were they after this short but revealing hour that they completely ignored the waiter, who had a message for Ms Knoll, a guitar-case and a bill for Mr Nightly.

SOUNDTRACK – a Music and Cinema special supplement. November 1970. Live broadcast by Jan Browntree. The LFF (London Film Festival) brochure, featured five contemporary musicians considering the influence of music on cinema.

John Nightly: composer. Age 22; b. Cambridge, England.
John Nightly's Ape Box Metal has been in the upper reaches of the LP charts since its release in February. I spoke with him as he was completing work on his first film score – the soon-to-be-released Pitfall *by the Polish director Joseph Karmov.*

Would it be true to say that your music has a strong visual element?

[sniffs] Music is the root of... everything... of all art... in a way... isn't it? I don't think anybody can direct or... edit a film or write a book, a poem... a play... without being musical. I don't think so anyway. Not properly... [sniffs again] The musical... instinct you need for composition... it's the basis of everything anyway. How often events and characters appear in a book... novel... the rhythm of a sentence... and dynamics. A musical person will be a 'natural' at these...skills. [wipes his nose]

Is there anyone you particularly admire in terms of directors? Someone with whom you might like to work in the future?

Ken Russell is... really good. The... Delius and the... Elgar film[1]. The guy who is the... (amanuensis, Eric Fenby *ed.*)... the bit where Jelka throws the rose petals (magnolia, *ed.)* over Delius' dead body. I love the new one[2]... saw it, the other day. The bit with the boy running through the forest, Glenda... Jackson blown away by the strong winds. Like Michael Powell or... it's really... It's really good.

And which, if any, film composers do you particularly admire?

the people who do the cartoons... animation composers... The ones who do *Tom & Jerry*. Bernard Hermann I like a lot, the music for *Vertigo* – but it's like *Tristan & Isolde*... isn't it? The... *love music* from that. [sings] All Hitchcock's films have great music. Hitchcock isn't afraid of music, like a lot of directors seem to be. He really... gets... gets into it. Lets the music completely take over the film. [thinks] Alfred Newman, Randy Newman's uncle, isn't it? The music to *Wuthering Heights.* You know... because it could not be more... perfect, without being sort of...intrusive – or even very noticeable. John Barry... I love *On Her Majesty's Secret Service*... *Daa, da, daaaaa*... [begins to hum the theme] Can't get it out of my... [laughs] It's just so... It just doesn't muck about.

Butch Cassidy[3] – the music was really good. [looks for coffee] Truffaut films have... great music. People driving around in cars with nothing going on except music playing all over the... scene. In English films they'd be talking all the time. [takes a sip of coffee]

There's French... *Un Homme et une Femme* and Johnny Dankworth's films... Sonny Rollins and *Alfie*... with Tubby Hayes... There's a lot of beautiful film music... uh... in films...

[Rollins' theme ushers John Nightly out and the next composer in]

John Nightly's LP *Ape Box Metal* is released on the Mosaic label. The live tour: Bristol, Colston Hall, Friday, 7 November. Tickets: 31/6, 21/6 and 17/6.

[1] *'Delius – Song of Summer* (1968), d. Ken Russell (produced for the BBC's *Monitor* series). *Elgar* (1962), d. Ken Russell (BBC *Monitor*).

[2] *'The Music Lovers'* 1970. d. Ken Russell

[3] Burt Bacharach 1967

'I became conscious of an incredible kind of beauty, the existence of which I had never dreamed. Even the bees stopped to listen and became as entranced as I. I wished the music would never end. When it did I was weeping. The announcer gave the particulars of the recording. I got up. I pumped up the tyres of my old Hercules, cycled to the nearest record shop and bought *Tchaikovsky's Piano Concerto in B flat minor* played by Solomon and the London Philharmonic. From that moment on I was imbued with magical powers.'
Ken Russell discovers the magic power of Pyotr Ilyich Tchaikovsky in *A Very British Picture* (William Heinnemann) 1989.

Jonathan Foxley interviewed by _The New Underground_, June 1987, speaks about the beginnings of avant-garde pop music in Britain. Interview by the late John-Julius Bowman. © Transcom Publishing Company Ltd.

Monika was friendly with one of the tutors at the Royal College [of Art] and we all went. Probably me, Pond, Iona, John, a few others, Daly… we used to go around in a bunch in those days. The concert was like a sound-workshop thing in a basement room at the college. One of those 'happenings' or, you know… things of those days, organised by Victor Schonfeld I should think… Great fun − or I remember it as being fun, anyway − perhaps it wasn't so much fun when we were actually there! We were probably all a little 'under the weather', I should imagine, as usual for those days… The audience sat on the floor for, a hell of a… couple of hours probably, of this… 'musical experimentation' by the AMM. I can't remember what it stood for − it's not… you wouldn't know it now, but it was a known thing then, something that people respected. A good thing… as they were a freeform group, four of them, led by Cornelius Cardew, who was coming up then, although he was already big… in that area − had been Stockhausen's assistant − which is… it's fairly big, you know. [nods to himself] It was quite whacky… they all wore… white lab coats. Very… 'laborious' they were, or… hah! [chuckles] Whatever, however, you would say − sorry… I mean, 'laboratory-like', don't I? Yes, _laboratory-like_…

Cardew was Professor of Composition at the Royal College [of Music] anyway, so… it would've been quite a thing… But we all sat there while he sort of… tapped on the leg of this piano for ages, or… what seemed like ages, with a piece of wood, and that was about it. They had… he had… these children's toys… electric toys… on a steel tray… They were vibrating them on this tray. Wind-up toys… and they were letting off sirens… It was all this kind of thing…

[Jonathan raises his eyes at least as high as the sky and slips off his watch; he uncrosses and then re-crosses his legs].

John was really quite taken by this kind of thing. I think he was immediately intrigued by it and really... You know, to have that kind of thing... experimentation going on and you could actually pull in some kind of audience. It wouldn't happen now. Wouldn't be anyone there! Ha, ha! [Almost doubles up with laughter] John did become a big... supporter of Cardew after that and I think it inspired him to be as adventurous as he could with his own music and not to pull any punches. Showed it could be done. Showed you there was 'another' world. I remember them at Spontaneous Underground... that was at the Marquee – the Floyd used to do it – and all sorts of weird and wonderful things. Oh... it was a really *real* time... mad time... mad... Fantastic, crazy time. *Really real*, as they say now...

Trewin Farm, Porthcreek, Carn Point, Cornwall. Thursday, 2 June 2002.
'… how can you see all that, Mawgan?'

'It tells me what the chords are as they come up. As they get printed underneath the stave.' Mawg tapped his foot mindlessly to the computer's mindless click.

'E minor, F minor 9, D over C…' The Wizard squinted as he peered into the screen, doubting that his complex harmonies and polyrhythms might ever be properly deciphered by a 'typewriter'.

Mawg reached for a piece of chewy and sunk back into his swivel chair. He balanced the thing on its back legs, his favourite, most precarious position, kicked his feet into the air and turned to the boss.

'There you go, John… you don't have to be musical anymore!'

'… well… I don't know about that Mawgan! You have to be musical to think of it!' The Wizard cackled as he gazed out of the window, then quickly turned back to the kid. *'That's it!'*

'What?'

'the bit… that's it! The bit you just played. Wind it back!'

'I can't *wind it back*, John. It's digital, man,' Mawg laughed. 'There's nothing to wind back.'

John stroked his chin. '"Di-gi-tal, di-gi-talis", as they say in Latin countries…'

The kid hit *REPEAT* on his sequencer. 'Here it comes again…'

Mawg dragged the cursor back across the digital terrain. The once-grandiose 'Fantasia Capella' had been reduced to a pile of oscillating stalacmites and stalactites, the cyber-visual representation of the tonal dynamics of John Nightly's most profound thoughts of thirty years back. Not the musings of a prematurely aged, bad-tempered old codger, but the considered wisdom of one who, besides his standing as a sage or a seer, had been a consummate strategist in the promotion of both his music and his own myth. A sheik of the musical desert. A well-tempered Kapellmeister, pitch-shifter to his hundreds and thousands of fellow travellers.

As if in an act of defiance, from underneath the rugged lime-green shoreline, there appeared a more recognisable musical representation. Crotchets and quavers from a previous era suddenly coming back to life for the fast, percussive interlude.

'That's the… *guide track*… for the next interlude,' announced the kid, as he turned up the fader on a wooden metronome.

'Hm,' replied John. 'The bit where all the candles go out.' He arched his neck and pointed his chin in the air. '*A patterne for next yeare…*' he said, as his head rocked from side to side, gently rotating on its neck socket, and he attempted to home in on all of the detail emanating from the tiny, takeaway speakers. 'Play it again, can you?'

'…eleven beats… eleven chords,' murmured the Wizard. '*That's the bit, Mawgan!* They go round the clock on twelve.' John turned to his pardner. 'Where the last candle goes out… That's definitely it!' The Master rubbed his eyes. 'Extremely difficult thing for them to do…'

The kid followed the cursor as it made its way through the Alps. 'That bit, John… what are the chords there?'

John Nightly hoisted himself up on his chair and stared mysteriously into the screen. 'Can you get it any bigger?' he asked as Mawg dragged the window wide open on the desktop, 'can't see a thing…'

'Can't get it any bigger, John. Too much stuff going on.' Mawg tapped away furiously as he tried another route. 'It's telling me… *C minor 9*, then add *D*, then… *A+*… Yeah… *augmented*.' The kid wrote in felt-tip on a scrap of paper.

'What I've got next is the… *Chaconne*, that's the next dance movement…'

'well, that's not right, then… we must have gone away from it somewhere… or lost something along the way.' The boss breathed in and out repeatedly as if trying to fill himself up with air; an ancient mannerism that could be alarming unless you knew him. 'So annoying, this…' John Nightly tugged at the sleeve of his cardigan and sat down again as Alexandre entered the room, sensed his master's frustration and lay down across his feet seeking attention. 'I just literally can't… remember.'

'But John… *man*…' Mawgan appealed. 'We've got seven hours' worth here. It's in Quad as well, and 5.1 and all these other things. I don't think we're doing so badly with what we have…' Mawg dragged open a new folder. 'If I time it all up… add it up… we're up to almost four and a half hours already.' Mawgan's hands scattered around the keyboard at incredible speed. The kid knew his shortcuts and alts so well that sometimes when they'd work through the night, as they had on numerous occasions, he'd turn off all of the lights and work blind. 'We're quite a bit further than, well… we're at least halfway there…'

'I know we are – and I know that's because you've put in a lot of hours, Mawgan – and I'm very grateful to you for it.'

'I didn't mean that, John… it's not a case of…'

'I know, I know…' the Wizard nodded. 'but really…'

To save them both embarrassment, the kid turned his attention to Alexandre.

'The next bit is where the violins play with the back of the bows… bit you marked as *Britten.*'

'…the bit I took from the *Spring Symphony*… A great bit, I thought… just…' The boss leaned forward again. 'You know that symphony?'

The kid shook his head.

'Well, that's what he does there, with the violins… it's a… cold sound, but warm at the same time – you get it in *The Planets* as well.' John scratched his head. 'I suppose it's… how long is that bit?' The kid checked his digital read-out.

'Two minutes, forty-two seconds; three frames. I can give it to you in milliseconds if you like…'

item: Monthly Cultural Notes: April

Days become suddenly warmer in April. 'Seeds to sow and lawns to mow!' goes the saying. Set the blades on the mower high and follow up with a nitrogen-based Weed and Feed. Cover seedlings in straw or waste paper to protect from cold nights. Thin out herbaceous borders and trim camellias and rhododendron. Pelargoniums, lantana, pinks and early roses should be in full bloom. Check your climbers and creepers and their ties, canes and supports. Roots of mint and sage can be planted out. Look for shoots of canna and montbretia. Remember: April showers bring May flowers.

If they happened to be in London, John and Iona would be out exploring five or six nights a week, often to several gatherings a night, after which they'd end up at the Ad Lib or Sibylla's, the Scotch or any one of that week's places, along with everyone else. The London in-crowd was small and self-contained, more or less the same faces each evening, with the addition of visiting film or fashion types and the odd philosopher, activist or evangelist who might be in town. A convergence of like-minds generally occurred by word of mouth, getting together to check out the latest thing, whether it be a concert, art opening or 'benefit'.

Sometimes the group would come together to check out itself, narcissism being a major preoccupation of a scene that consisted of re-made mods and rockers, converted Teds and greasers, scruffy Cambridge grads and Oxford 'letchers' along with the first hippie capitalists; the architects of the new society – a group specialising in the creative sciences of independent film production, pop-star mismanagement, performance-based art, book publishing and people's theatre. Like all social movements and trends, the new establishment was launched on a wave of ambition, adventure, creativity and commerce – just like the old one.

If Iona was modelling and John recording she'd show up at Regal, Sound Techniques or Levy's, where they'd smoke a joint or two and generally be 'together' – often to the embarrassment of their co-workers. Hashish and pot were an integral part of the couple's carefully controlled diet. John and Iona would get through a couple of spliffs over breakfast with perhaps another one or two mid-morning. Afternoon 'snacks' would be followed by the new 'family entertainment'. Getting high on acid was, more often than not, a communal event organised within a familiar domestic circle.

At the end of the evening most people expected to have some kind of out-of-body experience; finding themselves in a semi-comatose state and behaving in a very silly manner. The fact that everyone around them was joining in, usually in the confines of someone's home or within the locked-away, sheltered world of the recording-studio, meant that it mattered very little how much of a fool they made of themselves. Though there were few musicians who could afford to waste very much studio time on anything but the job in hand, with Central London facilities coming in at a rate of around £200–£300 for a 12-hour day.

In 1966, the recording industry still operated on a basis of strict three-hourly sessions, carefully regulated by the Musician's Union, whose rules stated that all players booked to perform in Britain's sound factories must be MU members, adhering to an MU contract of employment and booked by a certified MU contractor, or 'fixer'.

If a group or band had an orchestral session in progress, or if any contracted musicians had been booked to perform solo or as part of an ensemble playing along with the group – the 'artists' themselves – the rules would have to be strictly observed, with an MU rep – a kind of sonic shop steward – in attendance at all times. When a three-hour stint was up there would be no possibility (even when players were available and willing) of going even a few seconds over without consultation – closely followed by remuneration.

Jonathan Foxley talking to DJ John Oakes for the Radio 1 series, *The Record Makers,* BBC Enterprises. 1977.

One time, at Levy's, the old CBS studio in Bond Street, we had five minutes to go to the end of recording some strings. The violinists put down their bows and started to put on their crash helmets – wanting to get off to the next session. John took offence and asked them how they imagined they were going to be able to put their headphones around their heads to do the next take on top of these helmets. He managed to make them feel pretty stupid and rather… ashamed of themselves… Amazingly, they agreed to stay on to make up the extra ten minutes.

Recording schedules… studio time, and money, were very tight in those days, which was why, for example… [smiles as though about to reveal a secret] The French horn that you hear at the start of 'Dead End Street' [the Kinks – Pye 7N17222] is actually a trombone. The story being that the producer, Shel Talmy, not wanting to… I was going to say 'shell out', on a horn player… [chuckles] Nor having either the time or inclination to book one, had come across a trombonist in a trad-jazz band at the local pub during a break in recording and asked him to come round to the studio. They got the guy to play in a kind of 'muted' French-horn style – putting his hand inside the bell, I assume… [puts his hands together in the shape of a brass horn] Like a horn player would. And that's what you hear on the record. [smiles again, pleased with his recollection]

Most sessions, except in the case of the Stones, who became… renowned for doing things over and over and over again, were actually very organised in terms of a… normal… 'un-experimental' situation, you might say. [takes a sip from a glass of beer]

We weren't at all in the era of silliness that we got into in the '70s. [feigns exhaustion] Endless amounts of studio time wasted 'experimenting' with sounds and long hours and… All sorts of craziness and God knows what. In the mid '60s the engineers still looked, and behaved, like technicians. They wore white coats. And though that kind of… 'getting it together in the country'

thing, a much looser – Traffic, Led Zep... kind of approach...
[mimics people with lots of hair... thinking himself hilarious]
Was sort of becoming *the thing*, in summer '66 there was a lot of
exciting recording... Orchestral sessions, recording controlled by
the producers and arrangers, all the musicians playing together
at the same time, actually doing 'takes' – like on a film. A lot of
discipline... *real* excitement. And a lot of very... structured songwriting going on. We were still a long way from those crazy...
ludicrous...

item: The Weekend Book: *'Children's Stories from Cornwall'*, John and Joanna Gingold (Very Small Books). 1954.

The sand whipped itself up into a swinging, swirling mass. Farmsteads were overwhelmed and lay buried, leaving wastelands of sedge, sea-rush and bog. Stiff-stemmed reeds were planted by the locals to stay the driving sand. Then one morning, all was calm.

The cliff edge now lies silent. Rain falls in a mizzle, the tide ebbs, birds swoop to the mudbanks, the tide slackens and the birds are hushed. Porthcreek, near Morvah, beyond St Agnes Head, sits high on the moors of West Penwith, near the quoits and tombs of the burial places of the Spanish settlers and invaders.

item: John Calve. *A Survey of Kernow (Cornwall)*, 1666.

There was somtyme a haven towne at Porcreeque decayed by reason of sand which hath choked the lande and buried the church and houses. Manie devises they use to prevent absorpation of the churchyarde upon the cliffe.

item: Baptism Register, No 9, 1816/1856, ref. Carn Point, meteorological data, p118 hurricanes/sand. In 1607, in the reign of James I, a dredful hurricane occurred. An influx of sand gorged the coastline, shocking churches on the coast at Gwithian, Perranzabuloe, St Dinesor, Black Cliff, Porthlee, Peneed, Zawn Moor and Carn Point producing massive sand dunes (towans) and… [remainder illegible]

The sand invasion of 1607 created enormous problems for John Nightly. On the one hand, in terms of drainage for exotics, it was a godsend, but when the two Johns first began planting at Trewin, in the summer of 1983, they hit sand just a foot beneath the peaty earth. Wherever they dug in any part of the property they found pockets of the stuff just under the topsoil. There were ledges of impenetrable granite, knots of ancient cedar root, then… a good deal more sand. When BT came to install phone lines they found furrows of sand under the kitchen floorboards and behind the lime-plastered walls. The Johns had to get sixty-two tonnes of peat put down beneath the cold frames and along the cliff edge to stop any subsidence of the new structures. Sometimes John Nightly would be walking up to Hothouse 5, the agapanthus house, and be literally blasted and almost knocked over by sand blowing up off the cliffs.

Although he and John RCN had tried to establish a proper shelter belt, with fast-growing and salt-resistant shrubs, copying the example of St Michael's Mount, the sand would still swirl up and beat at the windows of the hothouses closest to the sea, numbers 6 and 7, in the process frightening to death Chilean bromeliads, *Fascicularia bicolor* and A. arboreum 'Atropurpurea'.

The answer was to build a walled garden, which they had begun to do the following year, establishing *Sparrmannia africana* (African hemp) along with strelitzias (birds-of-paradise), escallonias, opuntias and healing aloes. If you positioned yourself on the perimeter of this semi-circular sunspot in calm weather the garden unfolded in a mosaic of colour trailing down over the rocks all the way out to the water and the vast horizon of the bay. Such was the extraordinary confluence of light that quite often, with just a couple of minutes' worth of drizzle, a double-rainbow would form, the outer circles framing the edge of the coast as far as the eye could see, the inner forming a multicoloured bridge from the corner of the north cove, the extreme edge of Trewin, as far as the old churchyard at Black Zawn, some three miles further up.

In terms of being able to carry out physical work or even just looking after himself, it wasn't that John Nightly was incapacitated in any way. He wasn't. Mentally (apart from his brains being fried like onions on a burger stand) he was fine. Physically he was in good shape too, or at least 'okay' shape, and so when RCN had to go into hospital himself – three days of tests on what turned out to be nothing more than a minor but still painful stomach ulcer – John Nightly was actually fine. He could probably have coped by himself. But of course a replacement was laid on. A Cornishwoman from Verdah Care in Truro, the place with the best reputation locally, as far as RCN's research could make out.

Mrs Peed came and stayed over at Porthcreek for three days, getting John Nightly his dinner and tea and generally keeping the place clean and tidy. In fact, RCN thought that his old friend had enjoyed the company, and the change.

The elderly former staff nurse had visited Trewin before, of course, for the 'audition', prior to which RCN had had her checked out separately as well. Two brief visits to meet both Johns and to quickly go through what the day-to-day requirements might be.

Like everyone else, the housekeeper had been enchanted by the ex-heart-throb, and fascinated by the strange, otherworldly atmosphere surrounding the white farm, its weird and wonderful vegetation and even weirder (though slightly less wonderful) Homo sapiens. When it came time for Mrs Peed to leave, John presented her with a giant *Canna* 'Lucifer', carmine-pink, three stems already in flower, cultivated from one of his very best rhizomes. It was a magnificent specimen, a show plant, and he explained to her how it should be looked after before being divided up and re-potted next spring – not into a very large pot but just one stage up at a time: a 7-inch up to a 9 before being put into a deeper, more protective 12-inch container a few months later, ensuring that the roots had good drainage of course, as cannas, like so many other rhizome-derived varieties, do not like to sit around in the wet. As RCN looked on, he could see that his temporary hospitalisation may well have turned out to have been a very good thing. His employer had been forced to communicate with someone else for a change – the eventuality being that this episode would turn out to be the beginning of some kind of 'comeback'.

Trewin House, Porthcreek, Carn Point, Cornwall, Saturday, 26 August 2002.

'What happens if you toast cake?'

'Toast cake? Why would you want to do that?'

John Nightly put down his chunk of Endycake and picked up his guitar.

'I like toast... and I like cake. Just wondered...' The boss played a shimmeringly unresolved chord as Mawgan knelt before one of Trewin's most valuable 'antiques' – RCN's treasured Zorbot stereo-replicator, circa 1971.

'Ancient!' cried the dude. 'We can do a load with this!' as he flipped the toggle-switch marked 'triple-stereo'. 'Can't really use it like normal 'cos it's, like, ancient and stuff. But we can link it up to my lappy and...' Mawgan stopped abruptly, noticing a pre-war (Falklands) Atari. 'Woah... this is some shit!' he whooped as he picked up the clunky keyboard and turned it over. 'Does it still work?'

'Course it *still* works!' cried RCN as he peeled off a couple of slices of cheese. 'It's all brand new – it's just old... like me!' RCN spoke with difficulty, a doorstep of toast wedged between his teeth. 'Literally never been turned on. Think we turned it on when the guy came to install it, but that was...' he thought hard, 'back in... 1982 or...'

'Ancient!'

'I suppose so...' The nurse scratched his head. 1982 didn't seem all that long ago at all to RCN.

It wasn't every day that Mawgan walked into a wax museum of '70s recording equipment. He picked up an automatic *Harmonizer*, an effect developed to provide an electronic 'harmony' to whatever was fed into it. The matt-black box looked like it could do with a session with Endy, her scourer and a tin of lint. Another unit, a 'compressor' – complete with valves and levers – a machine that squeezes the highs and lows of a signal into the middle area, making a track sound harder, tighter and more dynamic, lay beached in its rack, road-weathered and rusty. A BBC Commodore computer – the very latest thing in 1982 – corpsed in its corner, exactly where Ric Locke had installed it all of twenty years ago now. Well, twenty years was a good few years, though still firmly in the era of 'modernity', the way RCN looked at it.

*Yes, I went to school when I was a youngster but
you can keep your maths and GCEs.
Now the only thing that makes me feel better
is the London Social Degree*

**'London Social Degree', Billy Nicholls, 1968
(Immediate 009)**

Without his model girlfriend, John Nightly would have been little more than an outsider in London. But with Iona he zoomed. The shy, unsure-of-himself Nightly became sociable; joining the swinging elite at the highest level. And because the in-people desired the company of Iona – starchild, note-perfect hippie; 'girl of the moment' (Trend); 'She's the ultimate Face, the one we all copy' (Harpers & Queen); Model of the Year '68 (Great British Fashion Awards) – a face which lit up every room, entrancing both young men and old, and setting fire to quite a few... Because people wanted all that, they got the company of John.

On the loose, Iona would have been pursued by every eligible young bachelor of the parish. Fey dandy types, actors and speed-obsessed racing-drivers chased after her. Car mechanics taped her photograph to their toilet doors, pop stars and play-boys sent flowers to fashion-shoots, employed ex-policemen to obtain her phone number, invited her for weekends in Biarritz and Barbados. But Iona wasn't on the loose and never would be. The girl was already tied up. Iona had made a commitment to something early on and that thing, that one crazy thing, the only object she herself ever truly desired, longed for, but most certainly did not need, and never should have bothered herself with IN THE FIRST PLACE, was John Nightly.

The love of John Nightly was all that she craved. The want of John Nightly. Iona never did consider anyone else romantically, almost from the moment they met. And so, with such a desirable prize on his arm, this particular parish boy was able to gain entry to the kind of society that included great names and – as always in England – their willing, clinging patrons; privileged hangers-on. With Iona, John Nightly went straight to the heart of the old, existing establishment. He made himself comfortable there, which in turn made things more comfortable for him. One evening John found himself mixing with acid freaks from San Francisco or working-class, underprivileged kids from Newcastle or Manchester – they just happened to be world-famous musicians. There he was, the still nervy youth, lounging in the corner with his whiskey and smokes, deep in conversation with fellow royalty.

John had on what he called his 'Mr Zen' gear while Iona paraded her own homemade yarns entwined with ribbons and small bells. Viewed objectively they wore fancy dress; subjectively they were no doubt satisfied that they appeared 'newfangled' – somehow.

Introduced by Iona, half-jokingly, as 'My… bohemian boyfriend'; the boy did look a little ruffled, with his unruly hair and mismatched togs, whereas in reality nothing could've been further from the truth. There was nothing at all bohemian about John Nightly. John was a typical village boy; socially inept, naive and unworldly, not in any way a 'people person'. Although his thrown-together appearance and eccentric manner didn't do him any harm, because Society… polite, English Society, loves a bohemian – particularly a fake one.

The door to these worlds was opened because of his beloved partner. It was obvious to those who knew the couple that 'Free School Lane', the song he'd written just after meeting Iona, was actually about the Danish model and not a 17th century Cambridge free school, as John stated in interviews. The lyrics forewarned of his own later circumstances while telling of being so suddenly, unaccountably in love after meeting someone for the very first time. John Nightly had knowingly put himself in a vulnerable place while tragically, this new, earth-shattering romance was being played out, in the early days at least, while he was supposedly still committed to his childhood sweetheart Jana, the 'love of his life', left abandoned in Cambridge during the first year of her Architecture degree. As with Picasso's discarded lovers, those who live on in his paintings, frozen in the Master's loving embrace, Jana's place in the annals of popular music was assured because of the songs John had composed about her before meeting Iona.

How on earth did John intend to deal with this impossible state? The situation lingered on, with John's inability to cope with either 'practicals' or 'personals' coming to bear on his attitude to his own morals each time a new temptation came along, which, given his occupation and his status within it, was often.

John Nightly did not score many points in this respect. For, as Lee Hide pointed out, if John had spent as much time on his music as he did in keeping up with various females wants' and desires, he'd have been 'bleedin' Beethoven by now' – or at least Bob Dylan. A cursory look at Dylan's workload during this period, an inhuman amount of hours taken up by writing, recording, filming, touring, promoting, plotting and generally creating, gives some idea of the amount of hours one needs to put in in order to continue to dominate the market. John Nightly put in a tenth of these hours – but talent is an elemental force; and therefore, it has to be said, he didn't do at all badly.

During the next few months John and Iona became a very visible couple at every pop-historical event of the period: the Stones at the Albert Hall in September, the launch of *International Times* in October and Hendrix at the Bag O'Nails in November – the night that Jimi, his guitar swooping through a particularly trippy 'Hey Joe', fixed Iona in his sights, glaring at her from the stage in front of a visibly unsettled John. Luckily for the boy, there were already a handful of willing hopefuls waiting in the wings – and in the dressing room – for the 'black Elvis'.

December saw the Psychedelia versus Ian Smith concert at the Roundhouse, a cause John later became involved with, and by the time January came around again, bringing with it further social developments, they were an inseparable pair. The Age of

Aquarius, full-on Flower Power and the era of protest and disillusionment were about to dawn, but the happy couple were more or less oblivious to it all, lost as they were in their own little capsule. John had great success with *Principal Fixed Stars*. The album was unanimously well received, with features in the *Sunday Times'* colour section, the *Telegraph, Times, Listener, Melody Maker, Disc & Music Echo, New Musical Express* and others as well as the underground press, where he was interviewed by *IT* and *Grass* and in the US by the *Village Voice* and the *East Village Other* along with *Cashbox, Variety* and the *Los Angeles Times*.

As things worked out, Mosaic/EMI never did release either 'Free School Lane' or 'Lavender Girl' as a single in the UK. They didn't need to, for events had overtaken them. Behind his back, John's former associates, the Everyman, had gone ahead and recorded their own version of 'Zigging & Zagging' with producer and *Ready Steady Go!* stalwart Johnny Johnson, scoring a Top 5 hit with a track that anticipated the bubblegum explosion on its way from America courtesy of records such as 'Mony Mony'[1] and 'Simon Says'[2]. The disc, licensed around the world by Decca, became a Stateside smash, giving the Cambridge botanists a whiff of temporary celebrity while assuring their place in the history books but (because they hadn't written it) very little in the way of cash remuneration – the real money went straight to JCE and John Nightly. Just twelve months on, Vernon, Colin, John and Clem were back in Bateman Street re-potting, re-planting and fretting about the weather.

Another reason the idea of a single had been ditched was Vanessa Frye. The one-time (underage) girlfriend of John Pond, sixteen-year-old Vanessa hit the Number 1 spot with a bullet – a ska-inspired, impossible-to-dislike cover of 'Mu Mu Tea' – and stayed there for four weeks. John Nightly disliked it, of course, and donated the first batch of 'Mu Mu' royalties to anti-apartheid groups in South Africa via his local North London ANC group.

[1] Tommy James and the Shondells (Roulette A7103)
[2] The 1910 Fruitgum Company (Buddah A24)

In Sweden and Denmark, the Nightly version of the song – different chords, more modal tune – remained in the Top Ten for twelve weeks, spurring a craze for the muddy beverage in Scandinavia.

By Christmas, the Nightly band was busy preparing for its first live dates in Europe. Concerts in Paris and Brussels before going on to play Munich, Amsterdam, Rotterdam – the circuit – with one-off dates in Italy, Spain and Greece. John had a new band (for whom no one could be bothered to think of a *good* name) and a simple business set-up run by his now close friend and constant advocate John Pond, with John Daly always there in the background to watch over the boy's day-to-day affairs.

After that, John Nightly planned a return to Cambridge, which would turn out to be the last for another fifteen Christmases, in order to spend a few days at home with John Snr and Frieda. This time the vacation would be a rare solo trip as Iona was off to spend the holidays with her father in Denmark.

John Nightly had done good. He had succeeded in building on an early, more or less immediate acceptance of his music while maintaining a sense of his own musical identity. He understood the course he had embarked upon and his group had a growing reputation for their live performances. John Nightly was an artist very much of the moment, but with a good deal more integrity attached to him than was the case with many of the era's common-or-garden performers. With the fashion already moving from a singles-dominated sales format towards a more album-orientated market, the non-appearance of any kind of single release didn't appear to have done him any harm.

PROFILE: *John Pond. Born: Keynsham, Bristol, 14 June 1945 (age 21). Unmarried. Music executive, JC Enterprises. Lives: Soho, London. Educated: Bristol University. Clubs: Scotch of St James's, Bag O'Nails, Dolly's. Restaurants: Rules, the Chanterelle. Clothes: Mr Fish, Simpson's, Charles Stevens (tailor). Hair: Vidal Sassoon. Drinks: Smirnoff vodka with lemonade. Smokes: Sobranies, Rothman's. Holidays: Greece, Turkey. Photo: Syndication International/London Features*

Sales of *Principal Fixed Stars* to Christmas 1966 stood at 181,000 copies in Great Britain alone. In twelve months time, after the royalties had come in, John Nightly was going to be a wealthy young man. He wasn't the only one. Iona's earnings soon became supplemented by her appearances in several high-profile television commercials, most notably, *Vosene*, *Knight's Castile* soap, and *Kit-Kat*. Her impact on the, mainly children's TV audience, for Cadbury's cheap chocolate wafer meant that by the third nationwide campaign she was well known to schoolchildren everywhere - as well as being fancied by Dads in every household up and down the country – as 'the *Kit-Kat* girl'. A too frivolous title for the outwardly sophisticated young woman, but an epithet which she would never quite manage to live down. It was said that families would switch to ITV in the middle of a BBC serial "in case the *Kit-Kat* girl comes on". Even in *the Times* obituary for her husband, landowner and philanthropist Gerald St. John Firmin (June 2005), his wife was still referred to as '*sixties fashion model and Kit-Kat girl, Iona Sandstrand*'. If John wanted to annoy her, which he often did, all he had to do was to call her '*Kit-Kat*'.

The couple's combined income meant that they could easily afford the four-bedroom, two-reception fifth-floor mansion flat in Queen Square that became, over the next twelve months, the happiest of happy homes. A Georgian terrace adjacent to Regent's Park, Queen Square was one of those tree-lined London enclaves deserted for most of the year due to the fact that almost all of its inhabitants were gentrified seasonal folk who lived outside of the capital, most likely in the home counties, keeping one of the luxurious townhouses or apartments lining the square as their London base. Here the couple would spend much of their time staying in bed all day, billing and cooing, or generally mooching about the flat, floating, drifting, dreaming; just being hopelessly in love with each other and themselves.

Sometime around mid-afternoon, as the sun moved in slow motion across the panorama of church spires and construction cranes, John would 'swing into action' as he termed it; locking himself in the boxroom and getting down to some serious writing and composing. As well as assembling tape collages and over-dubbing on his 4-track, he'd spend a good deal of time staring into his new obsession: a prototype *dream-machine*, the flicker-lantern presented to him by cut-up pioneer Brion Gysin, which John claimed relaxed his mind, making it possible for him to 'get psychedelic' without drugs and therefore able to stay completely focused on his composing. He also used his new six inch solid-tube reflector telescope, a Christmas present from John Snr, in order to keep up to date with the ever-changing, ever more light-polluted (and therefore difficult to see) London night sky.

When she wasn't being paid a fortune to eat chocolate biscuit on TV, Iona would spend her afternoons at the Earth Centre in Portobello and her evenings at Shiatsu classes in Belsize Park. She began consulting sessions with pop psychiatrist Ronald Laing and spent her free weekends learning all about macrobiotic cookery. If she were at home, Iona would either be sunbathing on the balcony or exercising on her Japanese prayer mat in order to keep herself in tip-top condition so that the lucrative high-profile work would keep coming in.

Both kept themselves individually busy. The boy was constantly motivated, on a kind of quest it seemed, while Iona stayed more occupied than she ever needed to be as a way of dealing with her partner's apparently limitless ambition. They also took a lot of drugs.

'Cut up everything in sight. Make your whole life a poem. you can't lose, man. You can't lose because you've got nothing to lose but that worthless junk you're sitting on. Get out of that blue Frigidaire and live. You'll know everything. You'll hear everything. And you'll see everything that's going on. Really make the entire scene. Not many chicks will. Say they know plenty already. They do. Try it. Be a Poet. Be a Man.' **Brion Gysin**

In terms of Society, January 1967 brought an ending and also a beginning. Firstly, the premature death of Swinging London, now established worldwide via its mass-produced Union Jacks, Mini Coopers, RAF targets and reproductions of Lord Kitchener and Queen Victoria. Originally fuelled by the consumer boom and in reality shortlived and centralised on the capital; by summer '66 most of Swinging London's leading lights were upgrading or dropping out, slowing down the communal pendulum as they morphed into flower people and hippies.

Over-commercialisation, a saturated aesthetic which had become a cliché in itself, and the dawn of a supposedly more ideological society had made the Swinging London scorch mark almost a liability. The *counter-culture* was gearing up and in just a few months would be in full swing. John Nightly was again lucky professionally in that the combination of his 'acid-pop' mini-masterpieces mixed with more avant-garde musical meanderings, hippie wallowings and very non-commercial, 'experimental' nothings would prove to be the perfect soundtrack for what lay ahead.

Musically, the Beatles were the catalysts. In their early recordings, up to and including *A Hard Day's Night* and *Help!*, a batch of simple but inventive songs were presented and packaged as Pop Product. In this first flush the Beatles were apparently as disposable as Bobby Vee or Russ Conway. Then, without the group themselves attempting to promote it as such, the product, perhaps the best example of the demon *Art* in any medium representative of the period, quickly transformed into *Pop Art;* each new release was eagerly awaited, pre-ordered and purchased unheard by massed consumers worldwide. The disciples were fiercely loyal, confident that with each new recording their idols would come up with something extraordinary. The Beatles would never disappoint. But the doubt, introspection and questioning which surfaced on *Rubber Soul* and continued into *Revolver* and *Sgt Pepper* meant that as the Beatles themselves grew up, their music becoming more profound, and they themselves becoming more cynical, their audience did too. There were no more clicky off-the-cuff quips, fewer fast-volleyed witticisms. The Beatles, searching like young people everywhere for meaning and direction, were thinking from the outside, about the world and their position in it, not just about themselves at the centre of things. Because of their all-pervading influence the group lent their collective voice to any cause that happened to float by, from Vietnam to Oxfam. While Flower Children placed long-stemmed African marigolds into the rifle-barrels of the US Marine Corps and Dylan criticised everything under the sun before withdrawing from public view, the Beatles, because of their responsibility to their audience, maybe the world itself, were forced to carry on, but tried to find their collective soul away from the spotlight.

Summer 1967 saw a bearded and stoned fab four in Rishikesh dressed in what the British newspapers of the day referred to as 'rags', along with their associates the Beach Boys, Donovan, Marianne Faithful and Mia Farrow. John and Iona spent the Summer of Love in Marylebone. John working on a dance piece for the London Contemporary Dance Theatre that would debut at the Roundhouse in October, and Iona on designs for her own 'ethnical' fashion line.

The rise of CND, anti-Vietnam movements, Women's Liberation, Gay Liberation and anti-racist organisations in South Africa and the US, along with enterprises such as Shelter, Release, BIT, Greenpeace, Friends of the Earth and Amnesty, pointed towards the new cosmos. A peaceful, free-thinking, free-loving adventure playground. A reality concerned with artistic and spiritual expression and the distribution of that expression. The New Age was still about commerce, though structured towards artistic freedom rather than profit. The message was to stay clear of corporations and governments – the answer being entrepreneurial DIY, a visionary mix of artist-controlled endeavour. Record labels owned or part-owned by the artists, free live gigs and open-air concerts, book publishing using small presses to produce pamphlets and limited editions, director-led film and theatre projects and the growth of experimental film-making with student unions staging almost weekly events and rallies to promote 'the message'. With boutique and specialist cinemas and, in the print media, alternative bookshops selling censorship-free magazines like *Frendz*, *Oz*, *Ink* and *IT*, this ship of hope seemed to be coming ashore on one big frontline breaker to represent the beginnings of what most people seemed convinced would become the new highway; truly a new, New Alternative.

In the capital there were establishments such as Indica, the art gallery and bookshop evolving from Better Books, which became one of the meeting places for the counter-culture, along with Jim Haynes' Arts Lab in Drury Lane, which presented films, plays, music and various happenings. There were other enterprises: project spaces, vegetarian restaurants, alternative-medicine and counselling centres pointing away from the frivolity and instant hit of pills and alcohol towards the new consciousness. But this new 'soul' had its own sedatives.

The daily consumption of drugs – cannabis, hash, pot, grass, LSD and other psychedelics – would sometimes become the whole raison d'être itself. For many in the higher echelons (those who could afford it) heroin and cocaine in the form of speedballs and mescaline, codeine and other Class A mind-altering substances became the day-to-day solution.

John and Iona were a couple typical of the late sixties. Beautiful People thinking themselves far more radical and effective – and beautiful – than they actually were. The pair adopted a vegetarian, vegan, fruitarian and finally an uncompromising macrobiotic diet of miso, soya, seaweed and little else, which kept their hair shiny and their complexions clear, while at the same time throttling themselves silly with grass, weed, mushrooms and other hallucinogens obtained from contacts at the short-lived World Psychedelic Centre (WPC) in Belgravia, if not in bulk from JCE.

Somehow they managed to survive the physical assault on their systems and still maintain a level of creativity. But then, they were young: both just nineteen years during the Summer of Love and John barely so. The reason John was able to do as he pleased and behave in such a manner was because he had been so fortunate in terms of the business planning of his chosen profession. John Nightly had never had to pay his dues. He had never bumped up and down the M1 in a transit van like most of his contemporaries nor had he been ripped off by Tin Pan Alley.

In the faithful and constant John Pond, from the first day of their meeting, John Nightly had benefitted from the professional services of a creative collaborator who believed in his client beyond the need to make money and, most importantly, cared about his wellbeing. John Nightly would never be forced to record anything he didn't want to, or perform in venues he didn't wish to. With the help of the now permanent Lee Hide, John was able to self-produce his own recordings, having the pick of London's top session men and world-class orchestras if he so desired. Almost uniquely, the boy did have absolute artistic freedom, which he continued to enjoy, and take for granted, during the whole of his six active years, simply because he actually shifted units.

Touring was extremely comfortable. Even in America, John never had to endure the ignominy of UK package tours with journeymen like Herman's Hermits or Freddie & the Dreamers. John Nightly recorded what he wanted, where he wanted. His product was designed, packaged and marketed exactly how he envisaged.

Apart from the sleeve to *Principal Fixed Stars*, which would have benefitted from proposed designs (by John Latham then David Hockney blocked by both Pond and EMI), John had more or less conceived all of his album artwork himself. Each of his three LPs featured facsimiles of 17th-century volvelles, the lunar-clock and astronomical problem-solvers, drawn by his guitarist and stargazing chum Justin. A legacy of the both of them spending long hours with Jana in the library of Trinity Hall, Cambridge.

Justin, who had always displayed more visual artistic prowess than John, acted as art director and illustrator. The three albums they created covers for are now considered high points of late-sixties graphic design: a 17th-century astronomical template serving as a blank canvas for colourful, acid-inspired ornamentation and lettering. Like his heroes, John Nightly never went for what was going; he went for what wasn't going. John Nightly was always thinking long term. And so, when neo-hippie kids and grunge dudes like Mawgan Hall and Julian Tregan began to trawl the Nightly catalogue in the mid '90s, the recordings themselves appeared neither ' '60s' nor retro in any way and neither did the sleeve designs. If the covers resembled anything at all it would have been a psychedelicised local-parish record; a tripped-out churchwarden's journal. The volvelles were handmade, cut up from medieval sources but overlaid with colour ways that didn't exist in 1650, the modern design update being a cleanliness of line far removed from the elaborate decoration from the time of Galileo or Newton, giving the circles a freshness and instant 'branded' appeal loved by students and record collectors up and down the country whose walls they adorned.

The Nightly albums, their covers produced in limited editions of 10,000 before reverting to the standard printed sleeve, soon became collector's items. Physically, the jackets consisted of two boxboard circles mounted on a central spindle so that they could be rotated and the colours and type matched or mismatched. The cartons resembled little pop-up cakes. There was certainly nothing like them in terms of album artwork, one reason being the enormous cost incurred in printing the things. John Nightly, being the fool that he was, probably at some time in the past, had put his name to some hidden, bottom-of-the-page, record-company sub-clause agreeing to absorb such expenses. He was paying for it now. Although never expecting to make money from his music, the one thing he truly loved in the first place, the boy reasoned that he might as well end up with the package he wanted, exactly as he'd imagined it – if only to have a copy for himself.

Of course, what happened was the reverse. Like so many ephemeral items of the times, most of the original volvelles were destroyed, or at best survived in tatty, worn-out condition; a little like their perpetrator. But those wily types who purchased multiple copies, in order to hive away four or five in mint condition, were able to capitalise on their investment twenty five years later when copies of *Principal Fixed Stars* and *Quiz Axe Queen*, lovingly preserved in acid-free tissue by fan-club members, still folded in their red and white HMV record bags – and signed by the artist – were sold at Christie's, South Kensington, for £42,000 each.

item: 'Pond Life – Today's Young Entrepreneurs', the *Daily Telegraph*. Monday, 6 March 1969.
It would be hard to imagine a more successful or flamboyant young entrepreneur than 23- year-old John Pond. The Bristol-born graduate has quickly established himself at the forefront of today's burgeoning pop-music scene – now one of our biggest exports – almost equalling Britain's annual revenue from tin and steel. With the loss of Mr Brian Epstein, and with a question mark hanging over the business empires of both Mr Andrew Loog Oldham and Mr Larry Parnes, it seems that Mr Pond, who heads the JCE music-management team, is currently the most visible and visibly successful of the pop scene's 'young meteors' of a few years back.

'It's not as if Benjamin Britten has groupies…' John reasoned during a 4am bout of general malaise.

'And how do you know this?' asked Iona, taking another puff from her herb pipe. 'Me and you don't know enough about Benjamin Britain to know…'

This was of course true. But it was also true that the more you knew about John Nightly, the more you realised there was very little to him. Little of anything left within the bones and sheckles after the music had been carefully extracted. No accompaniment or background noise. Certainly nothing that might interfere with his ambition, the purity of his mission. Throughout this journey, the boy remained magnificently empty. His vessel echoed with a vast nothingness, except for his magnificent gift. A gift nonetheless appreciated by many. As John Nightly's fame spread, there grew up several armies of followers, disciples, acolytes, hangers-on and groupies ready to sacrifice themselves at the altar of Nightly. This prospect, which had alarmed the boy early on, was now a reality. Whatever amount of time John Nightly deemed reasonable to allocate to his fans would never be enough. The fans gave their money, but John Nightly gave his nervous system*.

John was hunted and haunted by his followers; the extreme fan worship existing because of the very nature of the Nightly oeuvre. Conceptual, pseudo-philosophical and, in the later years, more and more pretentious lyrically and therefore appealing to the intellectual, most likely gifted and impressionable listener. Although he hated it to be described as such, John Nightly's music somehow also managed to have an 'instant commercial appeal', inviting the listener to enter a special world, or to view the existing world from a secret vantage point, down a long corridor, through a clearing in the wood – much like Charles Dodgson, Sam Clemens or James Hilton invited their readers to peek into their very particular flights of fancy so that after

* A quote by George Harrison referring to his group's mass popularity.

the temptation of a sandalled toe on a stepping-stone, the reader would be captured and held hostage. This creation of an evocative, private and generally nostalgic world attracted the kind of... obsessive individual who might be apt to take things just a little too seriously.

To the John Nightly fan club, they were known as 'Johnnies'. John Pond referred to them as 'nutters'. Or was that just the record-buying public? Inventing and inverting, finding meaning in everything and nothing. Reading lyrics and liner notes upside down, adding and subtracting release dates, track listings and catalogue numbers. Hand-winding whole LPs backwards from beginning to end, in order to discover what may be 'revealed' within. What hidden meanings and messages might come out of this pointless exercise. The Nightly albums invited that sort of involvement. John Nightly asked you to 'Step right this way'. He held the curtain open. His records spoke to their audience: 'This is the way I see things... This is what I believe in. This... is who I am.'

In the early days, the adulation took the form of everyday fandom. The immediate popularity of 'Free School Lane' and 'Lavender Girl' (or, 'Lavatory Girl', as the band performed it live) resulted in massive album sales and a rush on brightly coloured neckwear from Ryder & Amies, the supplier of Saxony wool scarves to the inmates of Cambridge University.

Carnaby Street was awash with teenagers proud of the fact that they were Fellows of Trinity Hall or Magdalene, Rugby 'blues' or coxswains in the St John's boat-race team without actually realising it. It didn't take long for Lord John, Mr Pimpernel, Miss Scarlett, Gear, Lady Faye and all the other high-street purveyors of Swinging tat to jump on the band-wagon. John Pond always said that it was entirely possible that his client could have made more income from scarf merchandising than he ever would from sales of records. But this essential item of neckwear during the long fenland winter did become characterised as something of a Nightly signature and therefore his followers took it up – along with most of London's narcissistic mod population to whom the 'college-scarf' became, and remains, a staple of the uniform.

It was ironic, of course, because John himself never did have the faintest clue about style and he certainly knew nothing of fashion. As so often happened in John Nightly's career, the boy hit upon something at random; he caught a spark and the audience blew it up into a forest fire.

Queen Square, Regent's Park, London NW1. Sunday, 1 May 1967.

The noonday sun seeped into the room like thermal plasma. A saucerful of mellow yellow. The air was completely 'stuck', as Iona would say, the bedroom a hothouse. Through the balcony window, tubes of smoke billowed from the chimneys of Euston and King's Cross as LEB power cables and TV antenna emerged like steel ferns in the huge craterful of sky. The blue, blue sky. Boeing 707s trailed pink ribbons across it as they encircled Central London in a vertical stack that Air Traffic Control could barely control. Even now, with the swinging about to stop, it appeared that just about everyone was making their way to the city.

It was a perfect morning any way you cared to look at it. The teenager squinted in the sunlight, threw off the kimono-silk covers of his king-size divan and stumbled zombie-like over to the wall-length window into the panoramic view. From inside his Sunday-morning fug he felt an overwhelming and quite unexpected sense of bliss. The distant murmur of the capital going about its business was put into strict tempo by the repeated scratch of an LP stuck in last night's grooves. The boy pulled back the heavy sliding doors in order to un-stick the air as quietly as possible, then stepped out onto the crumbling masonry and a mess of raffia mats, chawans, sandals, pamphlets, tarot cards, star charts, Shiva beads and joss sticks scattered among the fashion magazines and drug paraphernalia. Beyond this domestic junk the tin-blue haze rising from traffic exhausts and factory emissions slowly cleared to reveal the arc of the city's most heavily manicured green space. The sight that greeted John Nightly on this chill, bright morning resembled nothing more than a Disneyfied recreation of the properly royal Regent's Park.

The white terraces of John Nash's York Gate formed a perfect picture-book vista with the Corinthian portico of Marylebone Church. John and Iona looked forward to the peal of its communion bell. The image on the box top of John's *Mattel* London jigsaw, a birthday present from Sindre and Steinar still packed away somewhere in his studio room. From this elevated POV John Nightly's 'second state' tuned in to the traffic's hum, the sonic *floor* of the locale, until the spell was broken by a workman's transistor in the next-door flat. The BBC lunchtime news reported a disaster at Land's End in Cornwall involving the *Torrey Canyon* oil tanker. An environmental catastrophe which was to dominate the headlines for months, bringing home the reality of industrial destruction on Britain's supposedly protected coastline.

On the adjoining balcony two jackdaws fought it out over the remains of Iona's hash cake; on the ground below, the citizens of Regent's Park walked their dogs up and down, admiring the fragrant Queen Elizabeth roses and the freshly mowed lawns, while dedicated royal groundsmen tended the beds and dealt with aphids, thrips and blackspot armed with knapsack hand sprayers dispatching Karathane and DDT. The boy gazed back into the bedroom, finger-combed his hair with his anaemic digits and shook the sleep from his limbs. While one of the world's most desired women slept soundly in his bed, he stopped for a moment to consider his situation, the condition of his inner and outer worlds, a regular flash back and forwards he often succumbed to, fading slowly in and out of his perceived and seemingly on-course lifetime trajectory.

John Nightly felt good. He should. Apart from all that he surveyed, the material rewards of his achievements to date and all that he had been informed was likely to come his way in the near future, he was in great shape artistically and creatively too. He was in amazing shape. The everyday money worries that had dogged his parents, influencing their every move, would never trouble him. The conventions of financial and social status, possessions, the search for a mate, family life, the nine to five and seven-days-a-week drag were of no concern. That 'conditioning' which, he reasoned, placed individuals within a foldaway, common-life structure, a structure which soon became a trap, one within which they could more easily be controlled by the system. John Nightly wasn't seeking or expecting anything at all within the safety net that his fellow travellers – those 'un-weird' people he often referred to – seemed to crave.

Taking a look around him, and taking a deep breath in – as deep as his smoke-filled lungs would allow – while looking out as far as he could see, then maybe just that little bit further, as if he were riding on the milkiest of milky ways, the boy surely had it made. His accountants and lawyers told him so. John Nightly was extremely comfortable, and conventional, in his non-conformity. Here he was, still only nineteen summers, named as 'one of the songwriters of his generation' by the venerable *Melody Maker.* The *Times*' review of *Principal Fixed Stars* stated that as a vocalist he was 'gifted beyond compare'. His *Silhouette for Double String Orchestra* had been premiered on the BBC Third Programme, *Six Second Echo* was being performed next week at St John's, Smith Square, while the current LP was a heavily rotated *powerplay* on pirate radio weeks before its release.

And that was just the records. Yesterday, John's manager had taken a call from Jean-Luc Godard's production company about a potential film, and earlier in the week Pond had waved a telex in front of the boy's eyes from Robert Evans in Los Angeles. John Nightly was undoubtedly golden. In addition, the BBC was in production with a profile piece around the *Quiz Axe Queen* LP, Pond having received news from America that advance orders there were approaching 100,000 copies – a previously unheard of figure for a new act from Britain. The boy was truly sensational. A sensation indeed. John Nightly really had zoomed this time.

Twelve months was all it had taken. Twelve 'mazin' months, since he and Pondy had set to work.

Then there was Iona.

The Danish model was now one of the most sought-after faces. On call for Thea Porter, Jean Muir, Mr Fish and Ossie Clark as well as the TV companies and ad agencies. Now that she was pregnant the couple were making plans to look for somewhere outside London, to escape the treadmill of this place, maybe with Iona's aunt who lived on an abandoned stretch of beach in Cornwall, where she said it was always warm and sunny. The pair were off to investigate this far-off spot next week, their first trip together outside the capital. But this morning the priority was to meet with management and record label about John's new album sleeve. A plan had been hatched for John and Justin to deliver a cover based on a medieval clock face. There would be no 'pop-star pix' of John or his group, the design concept being as far as could be imagined from the vogue for distorted visuals and bubbly typefaces. Although both Pond and EMI worried about what they might be getting into if John Nightly's 'anti-promotion-al' ideas came within breathing distance of a commercial record.

In his own mind John wasn't any kind of a control freak or anything like it. But when he had an idea for something, well… He wanted to be allowed to do it. John didn't want to have to explain or discuss the ins and outs, justify or defend it. This very single-mindedness, a refusal to be stopped or diverted, backed up by a stream of consistently imaginative ideas – not just for the music itself, but also for alternative ways of doing things; presentation and promotion – would drive the boy's charmed career. The need to get something done the way he saw it, and an appalling lack of interest in the financial consequences, would lead John Nightly to sign away amounts of recoupable costs that would usually be taken care of by a record or management company. A resounding 'No' from the record bosses was always met with, 'Well, I want to do it anyway, so I'll pay for it myself!' Thereby halting further discussion and leaving the way open for the label to save on even the most basic packaging costs – printed sleeves, labels and inserts – that they would normally expect to absorb.

In the visual arts there was still a line drawn between the graphic artist – the craftsman who would design layout and type for book covers, posters and record sleeves – and the more elevated 'fine artist', more likely to be found in a gallery setting, raising his work above the level of commerce, seldom allowing it to be used to promote or sell a commercial product. To John's way of thinking this was absurd. It created a prejudicial chasm between the talents of, say, Eric Gill and Jackson Pollock or between William Morris and Francis Bacon, though there were signs that attitudes were beginning to change since the appearance of Warhol and Lichtenstein in the US and Bridget Riley and Peter Blake in Britain. The argument was less clear cut. Was Andy Warhol more artist or graphic designer? For although this definitive Pop Art practitioner had the nous to actually call himself 'artist' there was no doubt little difference between the set up at Warhol's Factory, Morris's Merton Abbey Works or Gill's Ditchling 'community'. So the idea of the artist-craftsman had begun to make some progress by 1967; and John, who had begun to purchase real art for his walls, was determined to get the design he wanted for his sleeve.

John Nightly picked up his sandals, pulled the door closed, wandered into the bathroom and turned on the shower with his left hand while simultaneously turning on the radio with his right, as he did every morning, or afternoon.

Da, da, da, dah… da, da, da, dah… da, da, da, dah…

The staccato intro to Cat Stevens' 'Matthew & Son' seemed to be everywhere that week. The song's lyrics, if John understood them correctly, related the tale of a London apprentice whose 'work was never done', the track being set firmly within the idea of the pop-song vignette, clothed in images from childhood and our literary past, as in 'See Emily Play' or 'Lady Jane', a trend ignited by 'Eleanor Rigby' – suddenly there were herds of Emilys, Eleanors, Lucys and Samanthas running around the record stores[1]. While, as if to counter this whimsy, the Top 20 was filling up with disillusionment and cynicism – the impact of Dylan, Joan Baez, Phil Ochs and the other, mainly American, folk singer-songwriters – as night-time current affairs programmes in Britain began to include a singer-songwriter slot, giving a voice to Julie Felix, Tom Paxton, Cy Grant and Lance Percival and their topical, socially aware ditties.

The boy sang along with Cat until the shower head clogged and began to spit scalding hot water, causing John to miss the rest of the track while he fumbled around willing the spray to come through again. It cleared as the music segued into 'Purple Haze'. The opening riff sounded like it came from another world and John, mesmerised by the sponge-like guitar celebrating the power of LSD, marvelled at Hendrix's sound – how exactly did he do that? – before he flipped to the next-door station. There he found a competition between two popular young ladies, 'Eleanor Rigby' and 'Ruby Tuesday' – the latest off-spring of two pop religions constantly challenging and routing each other.

Spring 1967 was a golden season for music. The Stones' madrigal faded as Manfred Mann's 'Semi-Detached Suburban Mr James' took over. Another timely disc which contained all of the elements John loved about pop music at that moment. The boy turned off the shower, grabbed a towel and held his breath. For a start, there was the title itself, which fine-tuned into the social clichés of the times, the lyrics a teaspoonful of pop philosophy railing against middle-class conformity. Then the voice of Mike d'Abo, who John admired as the writer of 'Handbags & Gladrags' for Rod Stewart, a favourite song of Monika's. The record featured a chorus of wooden recorders, instruments *du jour* – the one musical sound in every schoolchild's satchel. Double-tracked descants played a neat turnaround before each verse. In John's opinion, 'Mr James' had the best fade out – and fade back – of any record he'd heard to date. The Manfreds even beat 'God Only Knows' on the fade.

And tonight, don't forget the Radio London promotion at the Scotch of St James, where we'll be giving away ten copies of the Kinks' new one due for release next week… All you have to do is call the number coming up in a minute, so just stay tuned to Radio London and Emperor Rosko!

Rosko's snakeskin drawl announced 'Dead End Street', a standout from the year before. The boy grabbed for the volume as a downbeat French horn segued into the vaudeville rhythm of the verse, Ray Davies' deadpan voice giving form to the brass-band chords which accompanied it.

A culture which delivered the Kinks, Rolling Stones, Beatles, Who, Cat Stevens, the Beach Boys, Phil Spector, Burt Bacharach, the Mamas & the Papas, Lovin' Spoonful and many of the records of so-called 'second division' acts – Manfred, Herman, Dave Dee, the Hollies, Herd, Mindbenders, Tremeloes, the Move and Amen Corner on a weekly basis – was a very rich culture indeed. Ten years previously, these messengers would have been angry young novelists; ten years before that they'd have been poets, playwrights or abstract painters. And now, with the rotation of single releases per group at roughly four per year, each Friday brought not just one but several trailblazing new items, all eagerly awaited by musicians and fans alike who would form a queue at start of business each Saturday morning outside the many family-run record emporia dotted around England's towns and villages in order to make their purchases and seal the fate of hundreds of pop hopefuls from London, Manchester, Liverpool and Newcastle.

Within their compressed lyrical forms all these little slabs of art contained ideas that society at large seemed to find it easy to relate to and quickly took up, some of which supplied the rocket fuel for cultural change in the so-called 'new age'. Importantly, though the songs themselves commented on and questioned the status quo, the tone and the performances of those delivering them sounded ever optimistic, rather than cynical. The musical and lyrical content of many of these three-minute epics seemed to draw a line beneath post-war despair, the old black-and-white world, and the new age of possibility. The sun shone on Britain through the storm clouds of the previous era and a wide, psychedelic double-, maybe even triple-rainbow appeared.

Pop – no longer just a word or a descriptive term but a new state of mind – now earned itself a different reputation. It had earned respect, to whichever format it was applied. Pop content and philosophy, not just as a bolt-on style but as an attitude or as an insight, a different way of looking at things, occurred in literature, film and visual art too of course, but seemed to find its perfect expression in music, particularly in the newly liberated popular song. In another age, John Nightly might well have been a novelist, poet or a scientist of some kind. But in his own era he could not have been anything other than a popular songwriter. Ideas were his stock in trade, and he was able to express them in this new medium, which was forever evolving, almost weekly it seemed, from hastily thrown together product with a lifespan of three weeks to a more elevated, enduring, more expressive, more 'profound', maybe even revolutionary 'fine art' form.

Like artists and writers before them, each of the groups and solo acts of the mid '60s cultivated their own defined musical vocabulary and language... and image. Their records, singles particularly, little globules of sound, contained all of the trade-marks they and their producers invented to identify themselves and adorn each recording. The Who's amphetamine blast, the Kinks' music-hall vamp, the Hollies' thrilling vocal harmonies. The more classical, Zen-like perfection of the brothers Wilson, the sweetest-sounding voice of them all in Mama Cass, the nursery freakbeat of Pink Floyd and the Move. You would never confuse the Yardbirds with the Hollies or the Move with Manfred. This spirit of revolution pushed each group to its limit, forcing ambition on all-comers, so that each would aim higher. And, for the first time in history, sound itself – electrified sound, combining sonic colour with increased hi-fidelity showcased in mono, mock-stereo, true stereo and then Quad – was now a conceptual, almost philosophical component of the popular song. It was no longer just about chords, melody and lyrics. Pop, developed from humble and unpromising beginnings, had broken out, become a kind of self-made phenomenon. Backward loops, feedback, varispeed, compression and signal distortion were now compositional features of each new release. The innovations motivating artists to outdo their peers, move forward, achieve bigger hits than their rivals – to ensure they got there before anyone else did, wherever 'there' might be.

John Nightly realised that invention within the confines of the three-minute opus was reaching saturation point. He himself was already expanding both the structure and fabric of the format. There were no real 'verses' or 'choruses' in Nightly recordings anymore. The standard model was about to be increased to six, seven, eight minutes and beyond. The sluice gates were about to open, leading to an oceanic swell with Yes and ELP on the one hand and Led Zep, Deep Purple and Black Sabbath on the other. Although at this point 'MacArthur Park'*, 'Eloise' and 'Excerpt from a Teenage Opera' – the longest pop songs in history – were still to happen, in May '67, neither these over-imagined epics nor the northern light of *Sgt Pepper* existed except in the minds of their creators.

Of course, any middle-of-the-night, worse-for-wear discussion of the above would automatically exclude both the Beatles and the Rolling Stones. It was impossible to consider the merits of these elemental spirits in the same breath as the other contenders, even John's beloved Who – though the Who were certainly the most exciting live act John Nightly had ever witnessed; he was forever urging his group to 'play it like the Who!' or 'make it like the Who!'.

As for the Stones, the last two years' worth of successive, quick-fire hits, showcasing their unique approach to both the 'rock' and the 'roll', meant that they existed on a level above the other groups of the period. They behaved like it, too, lording it round the London clubs where they held court like rock'n'roll princes with an unshakable belief in their own myth. It was impossible to quantify what was going on with the Beatles. The group had long since ceased to be anything to do with mere entertainment. The Beatles recorded output,

*'MacArthur Park', as performed by Richard Harris, written and produced by Jimmy Webb, was part of an intended cantata.

viewed within the history of creative art in Britain, widely seen as being 'radical' and against the mainstream, was now as popular, and quintessential, as the contributions of William Shakespeare or Lewis Carroll. When visitors from abroad thought of Britain now, they thought about the Beatles and Liverpool, the industrial seam from which the gold had been mined.

While the Rolling Stones live show represented the zenith of rock'n'roll performance, heavily premeditated 'performance art' as opposed to the empty sensationalism of the Who and other groups, the Beatles never bothered with a live act. In their recent shows the four of them appeared marooned onstage, bemused at the ongoing chaos out front while they rattled through their short 30-minute set. The group never seemed particularly eager to actually 'perform'. They didn't need to. Their very presence, like that of all holy men, was enough. They would turn up as booked, stare out at the abyss and go through the motions like they used to at the Star Club or the Indra, full of Percodan and Preludin. Except now they too were full of disillusionment.

The news was that the group was never to play live again, preferring to spend their time in the recording-studio where they felt they could realise their potential as well as on their arts-lab project, Apple. Well, the Beatles did whatever took their fancy. They were in the pre-eminent position everyone else wished to be in but never could be. The group seemed to be able to operate at a supernatural level. Cultural commentators everywhere were saying crazy stuff, insisting that the Beatles' output could be up there with *Alice in Wonderland* or *David Copperfield*. At the entrance to the British Museum, turn left for William Shakespeare first-edition folios, turn right for Beatles handwritten lyrics. As Iona said to John, 'My religion is clothes, yours is Beatles.' They were indeed the perfect 'control group', literally what they were: an index against which everything else must be measured. And as for social influence, Harold Wilson might have thought that he was the prime minister of Britain but every British teenager knew the Beatles were really. The group itself was the prime minister of England, Britain, the

Commonwealth, probably the world. The Fabulous Four still led the way, whatever anyone thought, and that's all there was to it.

'John… John… please turn it down a little bit, darling… not 'off', just 'down', we'll get the compliments again…'

'Complaints! For God's sake…'

'It is early, John… it is…'

'Yes… I know it is…'

'Are we going to the beachside, darling?'

'No… we're not going to "the beachside".' John slowly wound the amplifier down. 'You know I have to go and meet these people.' He stopped the tape. 'Go back to sleep, my darling. I'll be at the Kardomah… back as soon as I can…'

Other titled 'ladies' included 'Lady Jane' (the Rolling Stones), 'Lady Samantha' (Elton John), 'Lady Godiva' (Peter & Gordon – formerly *Gordon & Peter*), 'Lady d'Arbanville' (Cat Stevens) and 'Lady Madonna' (the Beatles). 'Titles' songs included 'Mr Second Class' (Spencer Davis), 'Mr Pleasant' (the Kinks), 'Semi-Detached Surburban Mr James' (Manfred Mann), 'Mrs Brown You've Got a Lovely Daughter' (Herman's Hermits). Some weekday songs: 'Monday Monday' (the Mamas & the Papas), 'Ruby Tuesday' (the Rolling Stones), 'Wednesday's Child' (Matt Monro), 'Jersey Thursday' (Donovan), 'Friday on My Mind' (the Easybeats), 'Come Saturday Morning' (the Sandpipers), 'Lazy Sunday' (Small Faces) and 'Pleasant Valley Sunday' (the Monkees).

There were plenty of 'colour' songs: 'Mellow Yellow' (Donovan), 'The Red Balloon' (Dave Clark Five), 'My Little Red Book' (Manfred), 'Little Red Rooster' (the Rolling Stones), 'My White Bicycle' (Tomorrow), 'A Whiter Shade of Pale' (Procul Harum), 'Love is Blue' (Paul Mauriat), 'Black Night' (Deep Purple), 'Paint it Black' (the Rolling Stones), 'Green Tambourine' (the Lemon Pipers), 'Yellow Submarine' (the Beatles). And a bouquet of Brontë-ish, fairy-tale inspired girl's names: Eleanor, Prudence, Dandelion, Delilah, Eloise, Jennifer Juniper, Jesamine, Samantha, Martha et al.

Drug references abounded in the obvious places: ' Mr Tambourine Man' (the Byrds) and 'Purple Haze' (Hendrix); but also in records where maybe even their makers were unaware of the connotations, as in 'Along Comes Mary' (the Association – 'Mary' being the syllable slang for marijuana), or 'What's the New Mary Jane?'*

Even 'Yellow Submarine' was suspect — who knows what damage use of the bright-yellow capsules might have done their huge audience of children? But drug references went back as far as Irving Caesar's 'Tea for Two', which celebrated the tea or 'gage' beloved of Louis Armstrong, as well as the more current 'Walk Right In' by the homely, folksy Rooftop Singers. What other explanation could there be for a 'new way of walking' or 'letting your mind roll on' in 1963?

*Still unissued but to be found on any number of bootlegs — e.g. *Supertracks, Vol. 1*, (CBM WEC 3922).

item: Monthly Cultural Notes: May.

Sharpen your tools – you're going to need them! The garden is growing faster than you think. Take cuttings and weed out the garden and the greenhouse. Boiling water may be used to kill weed seeds before planting out your seedlings and drilling. Cover strawberry runners and harvest fruit only when in full colour. Regular watering is essential – plants may need daily attention. Night frosts are still a hazard but remember also to damp down the greenhouse or outhouse temperature during prolonged sunny spells.

BBC Six O'Clock News, BBC Television. 18 March 1967, read by Richard Baker.

The oil tanker Torrey Canyon has run aground off the coast of Cornwall while carrying 120,000 tonnes of crude oil. The supertanker is said to have broken up on the Seven Stones reef off Land's End. Severe pollution has affected the whole of South West Cornwall; some beaches are 18 inches deep in oil. The tanker broke into three pieces and has been bombed by order of the government to try to set the oil on fire in order to disperse it.

By autumn 1968, John Nightly had spruced up his act, sartorially at least. Dispensing with his teenage windcheaters and cords, John had taken to wearing suits. Partly because the midsummer of that year merged into one continuous blur of heat and partly because it made it easier for a lazy bastard like him to get out of bed and into clothing to fit his daytime and evening needs.

John Nightly's choice of attire wasn't the demob two-piece favoured by his manager, but fine tailoring from a previous swinging decade – 1920s America. A natty, Jazz Age outfit that might have been worn by a Duke or a Cab or one of Tennessee Williams' grandees. Soon, John had a wardrobe of white cotton. *Gatsby* suits, he called them – and indeed he was becoming something of a Gatsby character himself.

After John Nightly appeared in public in his new persona for the first time, at the October premiere of *Pitfall*, with his sun-bleached hair and other accessories – St Tropez tan, suede crocodile belt, orange string bracelet and his ever-present draw bag – the 'look' quickly caught on. Lightweight cotton and silk jackets featured in the catwalk shows of every French and Italian designer eager to capitalise on an elegant town-wear style they'd been promoting for years.

It wasn't easy for the average Nightly fan to contemplate a Paris- or Milan-designed man's suit but British street style once again came to the rescue. A month after John was photographed for *Rave*, his ensemble topped off by a wide-brimmed fedora borrowed from Iona, the lords and ladies of Carnaby Street were in production with their £19/11d, drip-dry alternatives. Most London mods were growing out their helmet cuts and adopting Nightly's English Boy look – a two-piece day suit with finely-creased slacks, no turn-ups, three-button jacket, wide lapels and narrow cuffs. Longer hair, a round-collared, patterned shirt, knotted silk neckerchief or cravat, with white tennis-socks and Derby shoes or brown leather sandals with no socks, completed the look. The above combination, give or take a shampoo or two, became accepted post-hippie daywear for creative London 'heads' from autumn '68 through the next couple of summers.

Everyone was smartening up, as physical appearance reflected mental attitude. Fashion-wise, perhaps in a reaction to the San Francisco 'Hashbury' look, too unkempt and filthy for the English, there began a definite move towards smartness; probable influences being the films of Fellini and Antonioni or Sunday supplement shoots in Tangiers and the Cote d'Azur. Magazine design and content was polarised between the chic, minimalist spreads of David Hillman's *Nova*, the layout of which looked forward to the next decade, and the more traditional *City Gent/Man About Town* conservatism still with its base in Savile Row.

By the time Jack Clayton's adaptation of the F. Scott Fitzgerald classic opened in cinemas across America (spring 1974), John Nightly was already in aspic but to latent mods and the well-to-do hippie set it must have seemed like this new, or 'next look' was already a revival. Three of the Beatles wore tailored suits on the cover of *Abbey Road*. The film of *Bonnie and Clyde*, re-runs of *Casablanca*, the craze for vintage fashion and the vogue for 1930s Noir had been an influence in dragging hippie kids out of their cheesecloth and into second-hand tat.

This carefree, wind-in-your-hair, Rive Gauche extravagance would mutate into hard-lacquered glam as peddled by Roxy Music, Sparks, the New York Dolls and Jobriath, which faded badly in the light. Its spiritual home being the new Biba department store in Kensington High Street, the Sistine Chapel of re-made neo-thirties décor. Art Nouveau and particularly Art Deco were given some oxygen and quickly revived, immediately moving things on from Victorian and Edwardian influences. The trend for Astaire and Rogers-era Hollywood dragged on for one more year at least, becoming sleazier and obvious, until leopardskin prints, fake leather, Oxford bags, and 'boudoir chic' sent a '50s rock'n'roll revival crashing head-on into the punk explosion of 1976.

Through 1967 and '68 John Nightly continued his rise and rise while he improved his credit status supported by royalty income from worldwide sales. Almost a million albums in 1967, a million and a half in '68 and two million in '69. Then, after this series of forward-looking recordings, applauded by critics and public, he too lapsed into another world. Had certain events not turned out well, and had he not been fortunate enough to have surrounded himself with those who had a concern for his welfare and respect for his talent, then John Nightly would not have survived either and his story would never have had an Act Two. Progress through life is nothing more or less that a haphazard mixture of fortune and judgement. In John Nightly's case the scales were always balanced in favour of luck and that in itself was fortunate for him; for, as we shall soon see, his own judgement remained severely faulty.

'I was going at a tremendous speed... at the time of my *Blonde On Blonde* album, I was going at a tremendous speed'

Bob Dylan, New York City, October 1969

How to buy the Summer Centre double LP

By Post

Simply send your contact information with a cheque for £38.00 to the following address – we suggest that you print and complete the form in Option 4 below:
The Summer Centre, Addiction Recovery, Well House, Vinecose, Brampton, Huntingdonshire, England.
Cheques should be made payable to **Summer Centre** only.

'The best conference weekend I have ever attended.' **Dr Jon Sandiland**

The Summer Centre's recent **UK Symposium** on **Addictive Disorders** was widely recognised as the most innovative and wide-ranging therapy-led debate ever to be held in the UK. To enable absentees to experience this event, the Summer Foundation has teamed up with **Recover** to produce a double-LP recording of the symposium in both standard stereo and/or Quad audio format in order to celebrate the collaborative nature of the weekend along with synchronised slide-projections and transcriptions. The various components of the conference can therefore be recreated locally exactly as they were presented on the day.

For the discounted price of £38.00 (including VAT), you will receive a double-vinyl package including the following presentations:

Opening address – Lord Sanderson, Baroness Romney-Johns and former addict (now property developer and activist) Iain Grey
* **Reality: Building Relationships with the Chemically Dependent** – Joan Green
* **Relapse/Regress** – John Kemp
Dual Diagnosis/Co-morbidity and Risk Assessment – Dr Joanne Mendelssohn and Jo Weeks
Treatment: Counselling, Drugs and Therapy – Joan Weinrich (the Weinrich Centre)
* **The Art and Science of Treatment** – Carter Piner and Jojo Redman

* **Condition,** *not* **Disease** – Johanna Zorn
* **Diagnosis and Treatment of Sex Addiction** –
Johannes Holmes and Dr John Hart
* **Burnout and Compassion Fatigue** – Dr Joe McKay
* **'Going Back' – and finding the child within** – Dr Jan Snow
* **Dependency and Comeback** – Dr Jonathan Ruthman
The Return – Dr Joanne Mendelsohn and Nick Black

If you live in England, Scotland, Wales or Ireland and have a family member or friend in need of treatment for alcoholism, addiction from drugs such as cocaine or heroin, inhalants, substance abuse, or perhaps an eating disorder such as bulimia or anorexia then an innovative residential treatment centre that is quiet, private, reflective and introspective may be the appropriate place for your loved one. Feel free to call us at 1-0140-809-0250 (UK freephone) or at 1-0140-909-9198 (Ireland freephone) or e-mail us for a free information pack and video (state format).

One of the most beautiful residential locations in Southern California, *Summer by the Sea* was established to provide hope and treatment to those in need of assistance for alcoholism, chemical dependency and other harmful addictions, including prescription medications.

SBTS offers clients a formal 90-day residential treatment programme, with the option of several complementary courses while in treatment. Other linked facilities include *Winter By The Sea*, our new facility close by the resort of Aspen, Colorado, with its 28-day detox and macrobiotic programmes within our centre for eating disorders also housed on the premises. All of our facilities are residential – there is no need to venture out! However, residents are encouraged to do so and to mix with the local community while benefiting from the comprehensive care programme, which we offer in locations with ocean and private beach facilities and forest walks.

Home – Programmes – Activities – History – Links – Events – Contact

Trewin Farm, Porthcreek, Carn Point, Cornwall. The very middle of midsummer 2006.

'Sand! Bloody sand! Just damned bloody sand... all the way down!'

Robert Kemp – nurseryman, smallholder, plant expert and CEO of Trewin Exotics – stood upright in the middle of the damp, peaty plot, digging in a large *Magnolia stellata* in the shadow of a full-flowering buddleja, taking extra care not to damage new roots.

'Only thing you ever get here is bloody –' the digger wiped his brow – 'buggerin' – before taking one more jab at the earth – '*sand!*'

Mrs Peed threw a pail of washing-up water onto the roses, keeping one hand on her bonnet to prevent it from falling onto the thorns. She chuckled, clucking like a farm hen at her colleague's obvious frustration.

'Can't you get a grip, lad?'

'No, I can't get a bloody grip... that's the point!'

Robert huffed and puffed as he dug deeper, switching to the large foot spade in the hope of finding clay or some other more helpful organic material underneath. But it was all sand, the whole plot; everything 'bloody' sand. The only other thing he came across, about a foot further down, being a blue and white Tesco bag.

'Thing is...' Robert sank his fork into the ground so he could lean on it. 'I'm going to have to put down some clay or something... or somebody is. Nothing'll ever take otherwise.'

"Always been a problem round here, that... sand..."

The housekeeper chuckled and clucked some more as she bent

down to pick up the hat, which had been lifted off by the breeze and carried onto the small bonfire being prepared by RCN over by the washing line.

'Ever since that sand invasion...' Endy fell silent, seeking a response that wasn't forthcoming. 'Few year ago now...'

'1607 was the big one, I believe...' Robert looked around to see if there was another, sharper tool.

'My father remembered that one. Oh, he knew a lot about a lot of things, my father did...'

'Your father remembered quite a way back then!'

Endy did not appreciate the attempt at humour. 'My father remembered quite a few sand invasions, I can tell you.'

But Kemp had more or less given up. 'The bush is too big for this space, anyway... I did say that to John...'

'If that's what he wants... you'll have to do it, won't you? Won't hurt anyone, I'm sure.'

'He never thinks about how big these things are going to grow,' the groundsman huffed.

Mrs Peed turned her hat inside out and placed it back on her head, giving it a pat or two to make it sit snugly on top of her new perm. She pulled down the brim to shield her eyes from the sun, which even at 8.30am was dazzlingly bright. The nurseryman was bent double on the lawn frantically de-sanding his clothes.

'Won't hurt anyone...'

Endy twisted the bonnet round and gave it another tap. Robert looked up at her protectively.

'That's the main thing, then, Endy.'

It was already a warm, hazy midsummer morning. A normal day in West Cornwall for mid-August. The busiest time of the year for the local tourist industry and the busiest and best time of the year in the garden.

Had any visitor made it up the overgrown path and suddenly come upon the flower meadows at Trewin they might well have gotten the impression that a supernova had exploded on the spot before suddenly freezing, petrified and stranded, mid-explosion. Its spores were light-blue agapanthus, their tall reclining stalks supporting bright star-headed lanterns. Its dust was huge clumps of dahlias, aquilegias and lamiums. Plants and vegetables appeared lush and hardy and no doubt very, very happy as they benefitted from hours of endless sunshine followed by regular watering and mild, airy nights.

But so did the weeds! A carpet of horsetail and dandelion was attempting to conquer the entire back lawn. There they were, poking their horrible frizzy heads up between the flagstones as they checked for buttercup competitors before quietly slipping through. An invasion indeed. Mrs Peed had noticed them last week while picking wild strawberries growing along the back path. But RCN hadn't bothered to do anything about it and now these tight bundles of nothing with their scrawny white necks, a weak attempt at some kind of flowering, were all over the place, literally all over. A plague of unwanted vegetation, sown by the sparrows and fed by the light, morning dew.

As usual, it would be up to Robert to deal with the problem, although of course no weedkiller or commercial destruction kits were to be used. No DDT, paraquat or toxins of any kind had ever been employed at Trewin Farm, not in the twenty odd years the Johns had been resident. It's now a well-known fact that it can take at least fifteen summers for man-made weed-killer to be erased from the topsoil; so it was likely that, at the present time, the wind and the elements permitting, Trewin was already nearing organic status. Certainly both Johns had done everything they could to make that intention a reality – so digging the damned things up, one by one, was the only allowable solution. Each steadfast root and tuber would have to be levered out with a fork, turned, allowed to dry and then gathered up and chucked in a bag. No weedkiller? It was the bane of Kemp's life.

'Think I'll have to get on and do these weeds tomorrow instead of right now. Looks like it might rain. Be easier to get 'em out after a rain.'

'You do that…'

Mrs Peed, christened Endymion, but known to her friends as Endy, having no time for complaint of any kind and certainly not for idleness, a trait which, along with a person's zodiac, told her all she needed to know about their inherent character, had a few jobs to attend to herself. RCN had asked her to go round and change the batteries in every appliance in the house 'when she got a minute'. He said he was fed up with turning things on and them either not working or running at 'half-tilt'.

'When she got a minute?' That was a good one! What minute did she ever get? she had to ask herself. Apart from anything else, the put-upon housekeeper had absolutely no idea how many handsets, remotes and other gadgets this related to, but she knew there were a fair few.

Trewin Farm boasted at least thirty or forty radios, for a start, ranging from the post-war transistor to the bleeping space-age pod – the old wireless to the new wireless. Both Johns liked to have one in each room, the small pocket-type with round-dial tuning if possible. Tin or wood – not the new plastic rubbish. Unless, of course, it happened to be '60s plastic, in which case it was okay. Particularly with a Rexine finish, to make everyone feel completely at home. That was acceptable. Otherwise, they preferred something chunkier and a bit more, well, 'radio-looking'. Although recently, since the arrival of Mawgan, things had gone rather 'apeshit crazy', you might say. There were now at least another thirty more chargers, convertors, channel-changers, players and plug-ins strewn all over the property.

The new additions were something of a bafflement to both Johns, who every now and again would happen upon one of the things – a slimline pod the size of a fag packet, say, absent-mindedly left by Mawgan on the back porch or on the chair where RCN read his newspaper in the mornings. They'd pick it up, fail to recognise anything resembling a knob or control of any kind, turn the thing over in their hands, run their thumb across it, press on anything that looked pressable, raise their eyebrows, frown, and put it down again.

There was at least one transistor in each of the sunlounges and probably a couple in the garage... Mrs Peed thought she remembered seeing one outside on the old wooden shaft near the rubbish dump, another strung up to the front gate, a bulky old thing over near the compost heaps and one or two more little boxes up there in the side meadow as Robert liked to check the weather forecast late at night when the trucks were loading up.

Changing the batteries wasn't exactly something that could be done in your tea break. Not that Mrs Peed ever had one of those either! And although Mawgan had said not to worry, that he would do it for her – when *he* 'got a minute' – she wasn't banking on it, as laziness, the laziness of youth, or at least a talent for doing things when he got a minute, was one of the kid's most noticeable character traits. Though there was no way Endy would ever say a word against Mawgan. They had quickly grown as close as grandmother and grandson. If Endy needed something lifting or fetching she'd immediately shout for Mawg, not RCN or Robert. Sometimes just as an excuse to see him, and ask if he'd like a Coke, juice drink or one of those packet cappuccinos he seemed addicted to. And if Endy called then Mawgan would abandon the job at hand, a complex remixing of four hundred musicians from thirty odd years ago, maybe a balance that he'd been perfecting and finessing for hours... days even, and come running.

'Darling…'

With this expanded family consisting of Mawg, Mrs Peed and Robert now being a more or less permanently settled group, summer days at Trewin were very happy. Neither John could remember a happier time. The early mornings, with the sun flooding onto the steppes and into the large TV lounge, giving the whole house a warm, yellow glow; the smell of Endy's burning toast drifting through each room in turn; the constant chee-aaw, chee-aaw of the gulls; the dappled light falling from the cypress trees; the fragrance of expensive patio roses; and Alexandre running around like a peripatetic donkey as he chased after giant spiders all contributed to the happy scene.

'Darling…'

It was certainly a whole lot happier than the apeshit-crazy times of the past. *Swinging London* and the self-inflicted solitary confinement of recording-studios, tour buses, anonymous motel rooms and baseball stadia. The day-to-day affairs of Trewin Exotics were so much easier to deal with than the logistics of trying to record and tour 'difficult to categorise' long-form masterworks to 20,000 worshippers up and down the West Coast of America, while at the same time drugging yourself silly just to get through it all and somehow emerge in one piece at the other end. Well… the two Johns might not actually be in one piece – they weren't exactly sure themselves – but they had gotten out alive… just. So, the current situation was a lot better than that, they thought to themselves. One hell of a lot better.

'Darling!' Iona's voice became louder.

Though Daly and Nightly might sometimes have doubted the reality of what they'd created at Trewin – the two-syllable assonance worryingly containing another – 'ruin' (something the superstitious Iona and Monika would have noted immediately) they weren't about to lose sleep over it. If John Nightly had given it more than a moment's thought, he may have concluded that he'd replaced one dysfunctional family – his Cambridge birth group – with another, his music group, a quintet as dysfunctional and depersonalised as families come, only to end up as part of a third: the 'family' at Trewin, the white farm. The *house on the hill*. The asylum. Literally 'funny farm', as some locals no doubt referred to it. If John had thought about stuff like that, difficult stuff, with possible indications of little progress regarding his personal situation, he would've gotten very depressed indeed. Regressively depressed. The old codger would've slunk off to his room at the end of the long corridor and put on one of his all-time favourite masterpieces; a Rachmaninov piano concerto performed by Horowitz, Howard Hanson, the *White Album* (the chosen side would depend on the blackness of his mood), Prokofiev, Fauré, Ravel, Poulenc, Sibelius, Delius, Todd Rundgren, the Who – they all fitted the bill. John would have turned the volume up loud: real loud, distorted and crazy – blow-out loud! Deafening to most ears, and… Well, it would have been completely, completely…

'Darling… can you please turn it down! I hate to ask… You know I do, but…'

Iona was trying to speak on the telephone. The regular mid-afternoon update from her agent. In the boxroom next door, John had this thumping rhythm turned up so damned loud. Even Lee had retreated to the relative safety of the balcony.

Tomorrow was the big day. The day they were due to start sessions proper for *Pitfall*. Track-laying should have begun a week before, but the edit had been changed yet again by the director, which meant that the composer was having to reorganise and rearrange once more, for the hundredth time it seemed, all of the music he'd prepared 'to picture' so far.

An arduous job, having to add half a second of suspense when a shot lingered too long on an abandoned farmhouse or interrupting a theme just when it had got going because of the need to speed up the action – which for purely musical reasons, John Nightly hated doing. At yesterday's production meeting, Myra had made it clear that it could all well change again. That it was, at the end of the day 'all up to the director', she said; and after that, 'the money people'.

Since lunchtime, John had been working on a meticulously timed and quite harrowing sequence where the young female lead, played by newcomer Teri-Ann Christie, is taunted by a farm labourer – Bruno John in his first role – having to hide from him by submerging herself in a stinking mud pond. The boy had done a commendable job, heightening the tension in Karmov's close-ups without being overly musical or too dramatic.

John was now on his second task: smoothing over queasy edits in the next scene, in which Bruno and Teri-Ann were driving at speed along Old Bond Street while being pursued by Teri-Ann's guardian, the character-actor John Sanderson, trying his best to keep up with them in a delivery van. The action occurred at a point in the story where it dawned on Teri-Ann that Bruno may not in fact be the person he claimed to be. Since the timing of this dawning had been left visually unmarked by the director, for post-production reasons, it was up to the composer to construct a clear narrative. But, after having heard and watched each scene at least a couple of hundred times, as Iona and Lee had over the past few days, well… there was a limit.

'You know I hate asking you, darling, but…'

'I know, I know, darling… and it's no problem at all… I told you… I know it's ridiculous… *horrible*… literally horrible for you… for *anyone*… to have to listen to this rubbish – or, well, anything, come to that – this many times.' John furiously rubbed his tired old eyes. 'No different from torture…'

He adjusted the sync on the Steinbeck while at the same time winding the volume up one more notch.

'It's not "horrible" darling – that's not what I mean,' replied Iona as she prepared for another day-long tanning session on the balcony. 'Or *torture!*' she shouted from the bedroom. 'Your music – something that came from you, came out of my own very sweet darling – could never be… "horrible". "Horrible" is not the word I mean today.'

'Well… I'm sorry, anyway,' the composer replied, 'really I am.' John looked up, missing his soundman. 'Lee? You ready? We can do a bit more now, I think.'

'Ready for anythin', man.'

Lee took a final puff before he carefully balanced his joint on the iron balcony rail and wandered back into the room.

May 1968 seemed like a golden time. A blessed time. Everything was looser now. People really seemed to be flowing, reaching out for something, following their own path. It sounds idealistic in terms of the complex man-made terror society now finds itself engulfed in, but that's how it appeared to John Nightly as he gazed out over the rusty balcony at Her Majesty's sea-pink roses and forced himself to watch the scene play out on the editing machine just one more time.

John, why we have to have so many radios all over the house?'

'It's not a "house", darling.'

The boy turned back into the room, squinting in the yellow sunlight.

'Don't be funny with it, John. Why *do* we have so many? How many we have? Maybe *one hundred…*'

John and Lee both laughed out loud.

'It's so 'e can hear all 'is 'its, innit, John? So he can count his cash,

384

man,' countered Lee as he lit a regular smoke and managed to sneak a glimpse at Iona, loosely wrapped in her bikini, a see-through cheesecloth skirt and John's kimono. The girl beamed at the soundman's obvious delight.

'You are surely right, Lee… that is the reason we have it!' Iona laughed along with them both.

John closed the balcony window and automatically nodded his agreement, without taking the slightest notice of what was being said.

Iona leaned back against the living-room door. She forgot herself, and let the robe fall away, in the process showing off very nearly all of her exquisite and heavily insured body. Lee could hardly help himself as he proceeded to stare full-on at this unexpected and quite magnificent display. It was worth the embarrassment of Iona seeing him drool to catch a glimpse for a few seconds. He looked hard, imprinting the image into his visual deep-storage. Iona pulled on the sash of the kimono, literally pulling herself together as she held out three very small Japanese transistors.

'Can't we… des-*troy* some of these? You know half of this things is not functioning.'

John turned around again, his head still stuck in the complexities of the dramatic scene.

'We can't "des-troy" them, no.' He looked back to check on his cue point. 'We can "chuck-them-out", if you want. It's… the Daleks that "des-troy" things.'

Lee sniggered nervously at the ridiculousness of it. John continued.

'It's the batteries that don't work – or *function*… not the actual radios themselves, y'see.'

'So can we do that?'

'What?'

'Put the new batteries?'

As usual, John found himself trying to concentrate on at least three important things at once.

'Of course we can change... or... *put* the batteries, darling... You just go down to the shop and buy new ones. Surely you're as capable of doing that as anyone else?'

John!'

'Or is that something I have to do personally for you?'

Whoa! Whoa... Dear God Almighty! At once an eerie silence fell upon the place. An acreage of uncertainty appearing from nowhere, as the four walls of the tiny brick-shaped room expanded and a swathe, a whole swampland of lush white Axminster rolled out before the players, the silken fibres glistening as if after a heavy snowfall. A vast runway of the stuff; a shimmering, white cultivation stretching out into infinity. There was a quaking. Vibrations – bad ones – echoed around the chamber; an impenetrable, cubed void suddenly existing between king and queen, genius and muse. As if a giant iceberg, an opaque drystone bloc, had been dropped from a great height. The overwhelming feeling inside the penthouse being one of detachment, disenchantment, estrangement, unknowing-ness, un-love. For an event had just occurred between the two protagonists that had never occurred before.

John!'

Only a few short months ago it would have been inconceivable for John Nightly to speak to his one and only inspiration like this. This sarcastic, disengaged manner. A shock, for as far as the awakened Lee was concerned – as far as everyone was concerned – John worshipped his muse. A worship that was reciprocated, frame by frame, moment for moment, completely and utterly in sync; locked, immoveable. And importantly, Iona was the prize; of that there could be no doubt. Her boyfriend's every gesture and response being polite and affectionate, understanding, allowing – reverential even.

In company sometimes, Iona would coquettishly ask John for confirmation of his affection – 'Darling… you do still love me, don't you?' – a routine usually played out at the dinner table in front of close friends and attentive would-be suitors. Without fail John's response would be, 'Darling, as I have always said… the thing is… I don't… *love* you as such… in the sense that… it's gone much, much further than that, I'm afraid!' as he looked around the table for approval. 'I *worship* you, you know I do. You know that…' Comedically timed and resulting in cheers all round.

Today the question was not coquettish and the declaration did doing nothing to satisfy Iona. 'But I don't want you to *worship* me, John. Don't you understand, my sweet thing? I want you to *love* me…' was the girl's all-too-confused and, of course, to John, ungrateful response.

'But… but… this is what I mean – oh *God*…' The boy switched to his most charming and beguiling self as he attempted an explanation. 'Surely "worshipping" is better than… *loving* ? It's bigger… *deeper*, for a start. Much deeper… and more intense, more… *valuable* in a way. Better all round, surely?'

He really was a complete pillock.

'I think you *do not* understand, John,' his lover replied. 'I don't want *worshipping!* It's *loving* I want. What I mean… *loving.*' The girl's face turned pink. 'I definitely want loving!' She slapped her hands on the table. 'What is this *worshipping?* Something to do with God… or… Tutankhamen!' Iona clasped her hands to her head in exasperation. 'But not woman… this is definitely not for man and woman!'

The tension between John Nightly and his muse had existed since February, when, at a fashion event for Quorum, John had been paying attention just long enough to catch the light of a smile between the object of that misunderstood worship and Mr Antony Spring, a being John Nightly believed to be no more than an acquaintance of his wife. The look that passed between Mr Spring and Iona, little more than a slightly-too-familiar acknowledgement, signalled to John Nightly that things were somehow not quite level anymore; at least not as completely, perfectly, level as John had understood them to be.

John and Iona's thing, their unique, all-encompassing, taken-for-granted partnership, would never be the same again, after this one fleeting frame. For the first time ever in the relationship, the boy fancied, not too seriously at first, then suspected, quite seriously – the pain of suspicion hitting him like a death in the family – that something was going on and was ongoing. The exchange of absolute understanding John witnessed between his personal property and a third party seemed far too intimate and knowing to actually be any good.

The smile that passed was a smile that should only have been possible between intimates – lovers; between Iona and John. It wasn't a smile between friends, because it wasn't friendly. But here it was, this upsetter of a thing, being flashed around the Revolution Club in front of Justin, Monika, Connie and Alice, Lucy and the others. What John Nightly recognised in that fugitive exchange made him feel firstly incredibly uncomfortable and unsettled, and then very, very frightened.

The truth was that Iona had been regularly escorted by the Cork Street art dealer while John had been away touring. John was aware of it, and hadn't given it a second thought, but now it seemed possible, plausible, then probable, that some extra-curricular activity had taken place.

The boy decided not to challenge Iona that night, believing there to be a possibility that he had made a mistake and that everything would be the right way round again the next day. But each time the phone rang over the next few days it was Tony. Getting straight through to Iona – because John, like his mother before him, refused to have anything to do with the telephone himself, both of them declaring themselves 'allergic' – and if the young woman wasn't there a too-stuttery message would be left concerning some new exhibition or other that Mr Spring wondered if the newlyweds might be interested in seeing.

Someone like Tony Spring, an established man-about-town sort of man, was the only kind of suitor who could possibly upstage John Nightly (excepting another pop star or actor – and then it would have to be someone of a similar or higher stature than the boy himself). Although, as John always reasoned, Iona must have had enough opportunities with actors, photographers and racing drivers as well as the 'physically perfect' male models she spent her working days with way before John himself came along. Tony Spring certainly had what it took to be a worrying competitor. One of the *Daily Telegraph*'s Men to Watch at just twenty-three, he too was a Cambridge man, former King's chorister and rowing blue, with the looks, grooming and easy charm to complement his well-ordered intellect and social standing.

It would have been too naive, and far-fetched, for John Nightly to imagine Iona sitting at home with her knitting during the long weeks he spent away from her. They did speak by telephone every night – sometimes several times; often backed up by further calls during the day – but John still found it difficult to believe that the girl, innocent as a peach, open as a spring bulb, would ever betray him.

Eight weeks after that shook up May afternoon, on the warmest night of the year, couched in a booth at the Beachcomber, too many whiskeys and too many spliffs having passed between them, an emotionally fragile evening ended with both Iona and John in convulsive tears. Tears which opened up a seam that continued to appear without warning over the coming months. Snuggled up to her boyfriend, arms tight around his waist as if she were trying to prevent him from falling halfway down a mountain (which she was), clutching his thin fingers as if her life depended on it, Iona confessed that she and the man to watch had become lovers; although, like a hoary old typescript, the episode was now of course all played out – 'Over and done for', as she announced. The only thing Iona knew for certain right now – the thing that mattered to her more than anything in the world, in her life, and all that would ever matter, she insisted and implored – was the person she was holding on to as if her sanity depended on it (which it did); the unique bond that existed between them, and the importance of getting back to where they once had been.

In the ensuing drawn-out decades, preoccupied with that constant flashing back, and in a permanent state of limbo, Iona made it impossible for anyone travelling with her, particularly her new but old, conventionally minded husband/companion, to 'move on' in any way whatsoever.

While Iona mourned her loss there was also, if she were honest, some strange comfort in it. Going over what had occurred, again and again, in terms of real life, the thought of getting back ran like an underground stream, a slipstream or leat, alongside the practical reality of her married routine, and her routine marriage, full of all the regular conventions and commitments, social and seasonal, family-orientated and festive.

Deluded and alienated and so very, very sorry, the abandoned Iona proceeded along an ever-narrowing pathway that transformed her mortal taste, as a cotton-wool John Nightly began to appear in the blackened windows of her Cornish estate house. His image stamped like a footprint in the snow, blanketing the sandstone rocks and shingle banks separating her own fragile state of mind from the ocean, making them slippery and treacherous and hidden from view until the sun came out to melt the snow and they reappeared to reflect the light of hope rather than hopelessness. *Getting back.* Iona was most certainly honest about that bit. In all her life nothing ever mattered to her as much as John Nightly, and getting back to and with him. Over the next thirty years, a midlife in which an incandescently bright future turned into a cascading nothingness, a kind of perpetual shock and solitude, Iona Sandstrand would think about no individual and no presence – or absence – as often as her once-betrayed boy genius. Her *spirit wind*, her forever 'bright starre'.

John's sapphire eyes caught the light in the thread of the twill silk scarves that Iona hand wove as samples to be sent to Pakistan for mass-production. His lantern skull strobed in and out of the spokes of the old water wheel that struggled to produce just enough energy to run the small loom she'd installed in the outhouse, the lo-tech centre of her burgeoning retail empire. On her morning drives Iona even saw John's bimbo smile in the radial field pattern surrounding her property; and during her therapeutic afternoon strolls in the whorls and lobes of the wood anemones along the rocks and blasted trees that protected her expensive face from the unrelenting sea wind.

But the Nightly face Iona imagined was a young face, *Face of Faces* circa '67/'68. A face of promise and enlightenment, still possessed of all its natural flow; a face of clarity and intelligence, before the river was tapped. An image captured in one of the Polaroids Iona took of John walking in Regent's Park with their golden labrador, Sable, chasing around like a madman as he tried to stop the young pup terrorising the Queen's squirrels. The photograph, faded in reality but not in memory, was still pinned inside the wardrobe that held all of her most treasured possessions – clothes mainly, and jewellery from her father, her brothers and sisters, and of course her new husband. Maybe it was a photograph of John on the balcony at Queen Square watering his plants. An activity she'd had plenty of opportunity to capture, since it occupied almost one full hour of each waking day.

What it all meant was that Iona herself was intent not on

keeping things real but in keeping them as unreal as possible. Like Donne's transitory comets, Iona and John floated in and out of each other's orbit and universe for the next thirty summers. As we already understand, they never did actually meet again. Maybe they almost did, though. Maybe they drove past each other on the B3306, on one of the rare occasions that the two Johns might have been off on a daytime gardening recce or Sunday driving on a frosty Monday morning.

Iona would have had no trouble in recognising the old black Jag. An unusually class vehicle for West Cornwall, an unmistakeable 'pop-star drive', and therefore suspiciously easy to tail around the winding back streets of Penzance or Truro.

With echoes of Reality TV or a very bleak Wednesday Play, in those few black days the couple went through emotions easy living had not prepared them for. Feelings neither had ever had to deal with, separately or together, and which John in particular was incapable of either confronting or finding any solution to. The unreality of this chaotic state quickly reduced these two golden beings to the emotional level of young children – which in terms of experience is exactly what they were. Neither having had any taste of betrayal or loss nor any psychologically balanced domestic background in which they could find comfort.

So... the first thing the injured party did, instead of considering things practically, or at least letting the situation calm down for twenty-four hours, was to move out of Queen Square and move in to the Savoy Hotel – with the nineteen-year-old Teri-Ann.

The debutant film composer was photographed tearing along Portobello in his green Mini Cooper. He chased round Sybilla's, the Savoy Grill, the Ad Lib, Dolly's and other safe houses with the American actress hanging on to his arm. John Nightly wanted to be as visible as possible, in the hope that Iona would see them together: this was the sole reason he frequented places that usually held no interest for him. Suddenly, 'being seen' was the only thing John gave a damn about. Once production on

Pitfall was completed Teri-Ann left for a new city, Rome, a new film directed by Tito Rosso, and the arms of a new leading man, the redoubtable Lino Trevari.

For John and Iona, what had occurred was unfixable damage. A single event sparked by the underlying gaps in the waves and curves of their life together.

But why Iona had done it no one could figure. Not her friends, who had always seen in her the innocent she now more visibly became, or her enemies, model friends, envious of the easy ride she appeared to have been given, with the best bookings, the most exotic locations, the highest earnings. It was easy to be jealous of such fortune. More unfathomable was the fact that John had remained faithful to Iona in so many opportunistic situations. Completely, absolutely. Even in the Summer of Love! All those wasted opportunities. The things he could have done, the beautiful women he could have had. Passing him their numbers in restaurants and booths, slipping notes under his hotel-room door, grabbing hold of him in corridors and lifts. Delivering love poems... chatting him up... showering him with compliments about his music... throwing him kisses in the street and putting their arms around him for photos. 'Do whatever you want with me,' they'd say. 'Use me... enjoy me... anything you want... however you want.' All the standard lines.

No doubt John would have liked to experience them. He was a young man, just twenty years young. But the boy hadn't done that. Hadn't done anything. Nothing wrong or regrettable. He hadn't taken advantage. The young John Nightly had kept himself to himself. Unbelievable as it may sound; that's how damned stupid he was. And now, thirty-five years on, with all the pop-star confessionals and scandal biogs having come and gone, revealing the orgy-tastic antics of rock'n'roll provincials working abroad during the cultural maelstrom of the '60s and '70s, lost without their pints and butties and other comfort zones, it can be recorded that, at the outset of his career at least, John Nightly had not behaved like everyone else.

John Nightly had, for some odd, misguided reason, stayed completely faithful to his muse. As to why she had strayed, he had no answer. And neither did Iona.

Maybe the girl wanted to wound; maybe her boyfriend had let her down in some other way we are unaware of. Committed some awful, emotional crime. Something of which to be ashamed. Maybe Iona was jealous. But that wouldn't just be it. For, although she was young, Iona was in some ways a grown woman. Psychologically she was more mature than most English girls of her age. Perhaps mentally, emotionally and sexually, too... Certainly more mature than John, who, well... John wasn't mature at all. Obviously not. Emotionally the boy was a mess. John *was* creative, purely creative. John was imaginative. John *was* a genius. Everyone said so. And, contrary to longstanding beliefs in terms of a link existing between creative gift and depression – or, as in so many cases, self-destruction – John Nightly was far from depressed. John Nightly was energised. John was always zooming. John was bubbling over. John was on fire. Everyone who worked with him even for a short while understood that. Iona was the more steadfast, feet-on-the-ground earth daughter. John was the nutty professor, the analyser, the information sponge. The Moonie kid who, as God would have it, just happened to be the best-looking guy anyone'd ever set eyes on.

There it is, then, to finally use the word... John Nightly did most likely qualify as some kind of *genius*, as one and all later acknowledged. With darling Iona being the conjuror's perfect accomplice – had she not been so successful in her own right – to look after and care for him. Provide stability. Which is what she was doing, so perfectly... before it all disintegrated so suddenly.

It may have been that Iona was out on the town, alone and most likely stoned, which she often was, or perhaps at home, experimenting with other tinctures. Maybe the girl was just... bored. But with him? How could any woman be bored with John? It was difficult for Iona's girlfriends to fathom. With his star-bright demeanour and voodooistic charm, his slight, feline elegance so appealing to women, his straw hair, newly lemon-bleached by the sun after their holiday in Morocco, John Nightly was a mess of frustration and longing. Every one of Iona's friends agreed, and that's because it was true.

Using his bony fingers as a comb, in a familiar trademark gesture, the boy dragged his flaxen locks back over his tawny features. In his white cotton jacket and brown leather sandals, legs splayed, taking a slow drag from a cigarette while nonchalantly gazing out into space, quite unaware of his immense sexual charge, John's appearance was more akin to that of a movie star, a real one, from the old days – John Barrymore, Ronald Colman or Douglas Fairbanks – than a tupenny-ha'penny pop sensation. Whether you were a woman or a man, it would've been impossible to be unimpressed with that.

Whatever the reason, this was the single event that changed things. Stopped everything. Removed trust, tore up unwritten rules and dropped a bomb on Queen Square – on the perfect loving cup shared between the enchanted boy and the cutest bride-to-be. So, although the thing had been initiated by Iona, as soon as John himself began to transgress, he didn't mess around… that is, in terms of 'messing around'. John really messed around. John Nightly actually went apeshit fucking crazy.

The boy started on a whole stream of affairs, a sequence of short-term trips in and out of bed with the most beautiful women available to him, in other words… those every other man desired.

John never set eyes on Teri-Ann again, except on film, which was no bad thing – particularly after the Savoy incident, which had a damaging effect on him personally (although career-wise he quickly recovered from the adverse publicity and almost benefitted from the glow of Stones-level decadence, which was of course exploited by his grateful manager).

The actress made three more movies before a change of career led to her becoming one of television's most in-demand script editors, and the consultant behind some of the most successful US TV soap operas of the '80s. Their paths were unlikely to cross again*.

Over the next twelve months John Nightly conducted flings and various unstructured relationships with the art collector Jane Cone, children's television presenter Jeni Speed and actresses Phoebe Rothwell and Frances Geer as well as just about every model on the circuit. It seemed like that anyway, until John got together with Myra Knoll – the woman for whom he eventually left Iona. The self-dependent, all-too-sane film producer was to leave her young husband of just three years because of the idiot Nightly, creating a cavern of disbelief in the staid old-moneyed world of the Knoll oil family, tarnishing its business image around the globe and even leading to a fall in the company's quoted share price. The result being that Myra's father never spoke to his beloved daughter again.

John Nightly was beginning to cause chaos. Chaos that would lead to his undoing. He would literally unravel, and be dragged into a life of addictive pursuits that would lead to his eventual collapse. The fact that Iona Sandstrand had been unfaithful first was something the girl never forgave herself for. Iona wasn't stupid. She accepted she'd been charmed to begin with: meeting the 'love of her life' early on, realising it from the moment she set eyes on him.

One of the things about being a couple in London 1968 was to be seen to be totally involved in its culture as well as in each other. A culture built on a misguided sense of exactly what so-called real life was about. The *London Social Degree* proving to be an impossible backdrop for any kind of lasting romance that might benefit both parties. If the couple concerned were reasonably mature in terms of both their experience and temperament, then maybe they had a chance. If they were as unwitting and light-headed as Iona and John…

*At the1998 Golden Globe Awards in Los Angeles, the Teri-Ann Christie-scripted docu-cop series Speed of Angels won the award for Best Original Teleplay.

What happened next was that John Nightly put the whole of himself, his every spark and breath, into an enterprise that would only see the light of day some thirty years later, and then with the assistance of someone who wasn't born the last time John cast his ear over it. A kid as ambitious as John Nightly himself, maybe even with the same degree of talent as the Master he served. No one knew for sure, but in John Nightly's own mind this someone was really very like himself. Almost a… a 'reincarnation' as he put it. He and Mawgan Hall worked side by side, eye to eye, ear to ear. As if they were 'brothers', close collaborators – 'compatriots'. That's how it felt to the Master, recently returned from Limboland. Everything felt the right way up again. *Alright.* The Project was nearing its natural conclusion, the Requiem Mass finally being laid to rest itself, after all these years; the results about to be issued to anyone who wanted to hear them.

As for his muse, Iona, having 'fucked up big time' as Mawgan would've put it, spent the rest of her life with a landowner, dairy farmer and judiciary in the South West of the country. She lived out her days designing her rather too whacky woollen outfits for women of slightly more mature years, a successful operation that led her to travel regularly to India, Pakistan and Afghanistan to source materials and meet with manufacturers, and to the Far East every now and again to launch yet another of her chain of franchised retail outlets (twenty or so *Iona* shops opened in Japan between 1982 and 2000).

Before all was officially recognised as lost, the lovers made several further attempts at reconciliation – though it must have been obvious to both that whatever they had once shared was gone. Maybe all they needed was company. To help each other out emotionally more than anything else. Trying to 'help someone out' was the reason Iona had put RCN back in contact with John Nightly in the first place; and the reason she was still eager to see and speak to her former lover and partner – her 'main man' in every sense – after all this time: thirty-six years after their first meeting. Just one more look. One more 'hello' and... 'goodbye'. One more sapphire sparkle.

item: The New York Times. 'Weddings, Celebrations', Sunday, 12 May 1967. Myra Whitney Elizabeth Knoll, the daughter of Elizabeth Isola Knoll and William Emerson Knoll III of Pacific Palisades, California, was married yesterday evening to Jay Merrick Blom Jnr, the son of Dr Jay and Samantha Blom of Inglewood. The Reverend Jonathan David Speed, an Episcopal priest, officiated at a ceremony at the home of the bride's parents. The bride and bridegroom both graduated from Harvard, she *summa cum laude*, he *magna cum laude*. They met at a programme of the Academy of Motion Picture Arts & Sciences in Hollywood, where both bride and groom studied film finance.

The bride will keep her name. She is CEO of the film-production company Knoll Entertainment Moving Picture, Inc. (KEMP) and a partner in the associated business the Someday Umbrella Marzipan Mutual Electric Record Corps. She worked as an administrative assistant in the New York and London offices of Knoll New Energy, Inc., a division of her father's company, along with her two brothers, John Knoll and William Knoll IV. The bride's mother recently retired as costume designer for the Sunset Community Players, a local charitable dramatic society in West Hollywood, and is also a set designer for film and television. The bride's father, Bill, is chief executive operating officer of Knoll Oil and Energy, Inc. Previously, along with his own father, William Knoll II, he ran the private-investment and fixed-income securities division of Knoll Isaacs Standing. The bride and groom will live in Westwood Village, Los Angeles, and also in London, England.

Alice B. Toklas' Hashish Fudge
The Alice B. Toklas Cookbook (Garden City, New York 1960)
*Take 1 teaspoon black peppercorns, 1 whole nutmeg, 4 average sticks of cinnamon,
1 teaspoon coriander. These should all be pulverised in a mortar. Take about a
handful each of stoned dates, dried figs, shelled almonds and peanuts: chop these and
mix them together. A bunch of Cannabis sativa can be pulverised. This, along with
the spices, should be dusted over the mixed fruit and nuts, kneaded together. Almost a
cup of sugar should be dissolved into a big pat of butter. This should be rolled into a
cake and cut into pieces made into balls about the size of a walnut. It should be
eaten with care. Two pieces are quite sufficient.*

When Brion Gysin gave Alice B. Toklas her famous recipe for
hash fudge, he started a hash-cake chain letter from Gertrude
Stein's lover and biographer to everyone's favourite '60s model.
Brion Gysin's *hash cakes* became Alice B. Toklas' *hashish fudge*
became Iona Sandstrand's *hashcake*. And one day in midsummer
1979 a cake fitting that exact description arrived from Alice B.
Toklas herself for the sole resident of Wing 3U.

The SUMHA Centre, in the pretty village of Spoed near
Brampton, Hunts, is one of the leading independently funded
programmes in the UK for the treatment of paranoid schizophrenia and other emotional disorders. It also treats addictions
arising from the abuse of alcohol and both illegal and prescription
drugs. Founded in 1957 by the 'anti-psychiatrist' John Bedding
and his wife Dr Peta John Hardy, Compton Fellow of St John's
College, Cambridge, SUMHA also pioneered research into
genetic links for addictive personalities and has published
results via its *Seasons* imprint of booklets and pamphlets (now
available via the centre's website).

*The discovery of a gene called mu-opioid confirmed suspicions researched by scientists
at the University of South Florida and James A. Haley of VA Medical Center in
Tampa that drug and alcohol abuse may be linked to a common genetic trait.
Almost all of the study participants who were alcohol abusers or who smoked and
used drugs shared a specific variation of the mu-opioid gene. About half a person's
likelihood of developing an addiction is based on genetics. Dr John Schiona, director
of the neuropsychology clinic at James A. Haley and the study's lead author, states
that 10 to 20 genes might be involved, but only mu-opioid has been confirmed.*
'California Health Today': bulletin, June 2003.

Spoed Lodge, originally a racing stable and stud for National Hunt trainer John 'Jonno' Sander, began as a U-shaped configuration of detached chalets designed by modernist architect Sir John Vasten (RIBA, FRMS), best known for his post-war rebuilding of Watford Town Centre and other overspill areas north of London. In May 1967, five years after it opened, because of the success of the centre as a one-stop treatment shop, and also because of the place bursting at the seams with acid casualties, a second U-block was added which adjoined the foot of the original 'U' creating a large 'S' configuration with six separate single-roomed annexes or 'private wings'. A number of its inhabitants would arrive at the centre by helicopter, remarking that the view from the air was rather like landing on top of a giant serpent; the original layout of the building being based on the contours of a tuliphead. One of Spoed's ancestors founded the Dutch flower-import business Spoed Vasten Bloem (Uitvoeren AA).

Set in thirteen acres of dense woodland, *SUMHA* suited John Nightly down to the ground. He spent six years there on and off, mostly on, until the centre officially changed its name to *SUMMER*, at which point he was referred to its newly opened residential compound in Los Angeles.

Summer By The Sea, one of many drug-help facilities for musicians – others in the Los Angeles area included the *Exodus Program*, the *STEP* clinic and *MAP*, the *Musicians Assistance Program* – was where patients who could afford it would transfer to be able to complete their treatment, however long it took, and move to the final stages of recovery before they could be released back into the wild.

John Nightly could afford it, which was a good thing because during his second month in California he suffered a major relapse and spent most of the next three years in bed. At $300 per day 'celebrity discount' (special monthly rate), he was certainly getting the star treatment. Death would have been cheaper.

'Hi…' The visitor smiled politely. 'And how are we…?'

The visitor angled her head towards the patient the way one might with an infant or dog. The patient rotated his index finger around the socket of his eye. The patient sniffled.

'Maybe not quite so… "wonderful" this morning?' the visitor continued.

'… well… there isn't… there's nothing I can really put my finger on…'

The visitor pulled up a chair.

'… obviously I'm not very, very well…' The patient inhaled. 'Or so they tell me. If I was… I wouldn't be, "residing" here, would I?'

He massaged the bristle on his chin, … 'don't think I am really…' He sniffed again. 'I keep it in, though – probably. Not usually a very… "emotional" person.' John smiled one of his half-assed smiles, 'not given to… large or… *demonstrative emotional displays*, so they tell me. Even when…'

A longer-than-usual silence followed. The visitor leaned forward. 'Excuse me?'

The patient looked blank. Johanna continued: 'Even when… *what?*'

'… even when… what… *what?*' John sat up. 'Oh, I see… Even when I am… "alright".' He bent down to slip off his sandals, took aim and slung them across the finely polished floor as if he were skimming pebbles. The visitor sat down, opened her casebook and positioned her Dictaphone.

'You mean you don't usually "feel" emotion, even when you're feeling "reasonably" or – "averagely" well?'

'Not "well". I never said I was "well",' he replied, moving sideways on to Johanna as he eyed her up. 'I said I was… *alright*.'

As he spoke, the patient turned away towards the long double-glazed window and the picture-perfect backlot masquerading as a cottage garden.

A pool guy was threading heavy power cables, cleaning up after the weekend, while a blue-aproned, suspiciously English-looking gardener crouched down in the winter rose garden, deadheading what looked like magnificent Queen Elizabeth roses, some still in healthy bloom. Two other men clipped parterre boxes on the lawn. Then the rainbirds came on, the men ducking and dodging the spray as they transported the fake Victorian planters across the tennis courts. A hippie girl, long-term patient – or 'resident', as she most likely preferred – sat cross-legged on the edge of the baseline, catching the odd wave of mist from the sprinklers.

John often sat on this exact same spot himself, hypnotised by the water cascading out of the rotary hoses. He would angle his chair so that he was positioned directly behind them, the warm California rays creating mimetic patterns on the grass. If he fixed on the cypress trees in the distance, then let his focus go, the water created a spinning, swirling, liquid light-show far better than any Sunday-afternoon UFO Club special.

A trippy but totally harmless animation danced and hovered across pools of blue and green in shades of medieval stained glass. If he allowed his mind to travel, and concentrated on the middle distance, the boy could be lost out there for hours, in nature's own Dream Machine. Some afternoons he'd be completely 'gone with it', as he liked to say, as he often had been at Queen Square. John's head would drop like an oldster dozing on a park bench. He'd be transported back to a dingy dressing room in the north of England, or worse still, an open-air stadium on some forgotten tour date full of people he didn't recognise – onstage and off. He'd then suddenly feel himself drowning, falling, rapidly losing height, suffocating, a blue-and-white Tesco bag pulled tight over his head. He would struggle to get free of the thing but there was no escape – and also, in a way, no point in escaping. Outside of the bag, there was nothing but a deafening, distorted din. Inside, only 'flashbacks'. Same bad old dream. Replayed and re-edited. Scenes that would never let him go. Then John would be awakened by the harsh whirr of a 'copter – emergency landing probably – or by a familiar voice, that of a nurse, intern or other patient, enquiring whether the old boy was okay.

'You okay?'

'… what? Oh… yes I am.'

'We were talking about… anger, weren't we?'

'… were we? When?'

'Just a moment ago…'

'I don't know.' The man came round a little. 'You're the one supposed to be taking notes.'

Johanna slowly turned the pages.

John Nightly rubbed his tired old eyes again, '… it's certainly an interesting object… *subject*… my…'

The consultant psychiatrist remained silent.

John lifted his head. He bit into his forefinger, making little nicks in each finger in turn as he progressed one by one along the worse-for-wear digits. He straightened himself out and cleared his throat. 'Okay…' he said dramatically. 'Let's do it… …' The CP sat up in anticipation.

'… I wasn't "angry", until… that is an emotion, isn't it? So yeh. You've got it right again, hit the nail on my head, and all that. You keep doing that…' he whispered. 'And… now that you are here… I've decided I am actually a bit… *angry*… frustrated… today.'

Johanna sat still and waited. A full sixty seconds passed.

John Nightly leaned towards her. 'The fact of the matter is that I'm not really *angry*, Johanna… I'm…' He faltered. 'That's the point. I'm just… I'm… I'm obviously just… bloody bored.'

The man treated his audience to a beautiful (and nowadays extremely rare) wider-than-wide, really-most-charming *John* smile.

'Just joking… I'm joking with you… I'm playacting.' He bit on his other hand.

'Christ, I'm bored!' he snapped. '*BORED!* Can't y' see? Bloody bored, I am. Until you leave that is, then I'll be really…'

Johanna Zorn was one of the best-paid psychiatric consultants in the system. As well as her private practice, which for two days' work per week brought in a pre-tax gross of more than $1.5 million per annum, she had her books, research programmes and lucrative advertorial promotions, which were worth five times that. And, though she would sometimes admit that she had once or twice in the past become a little star struck, given the sheer celebrity status of some of her 'priority' clients, Johanna hadn't really taken to John Nightly at all. She never would. The calmly beautiful mother of two hadn't at all fallen under his spell.

But Ms Zorn did not object to coming to the Center two afternoons a week in order to sit down on a comfortable chair and help drain John of his record royalties. Johanna took up her pen to write today's page of her daybook – what she liked to refer to as her 'daily Nightly notes'.

'That's fine,' she comforted, as she prepared to commit her thoughts. 'Did you feel anger when you woke up this morning?'

'don't actually 'member.'

'Feeling angry or waking up?'

'yeh... don't remember it.'

Johanna stared at the notebook, flustered at not being able to write down anything of substance. 'Do you have any idea at all why you're feeling so upset, or unsettled, today?'

Johanna relaxed her pen hand, folded both palms onto the open book and let them rest on the pages. John trained his sights on her again.

'you know that if you split... separate... the word "therapist", you get "the rapist", don't you?'

Joanna looked away. Johanna adjusted a hairpin.

The man relaxed back on his cushion, satisfied that his arrow had hit wood.

'Can I say – and record, if you don't mind – that you do appear to me to be in a state of... mild...'

'you can record anything you like, darlin'.' The patient rotated his eyes from side to side. 'You have complete "artistic control" – just like me!'

'A little more... unsettled than usual, maybe?' Johanna took up her pen. 'Has something... happened? Taken place?' The patient looked indignant.

'How on earth can anything "happen" in here?' He gnawed at his fingers. 'What the hell *could* happen, anyway – if it did happen?' raising his voice again. 'Nothing happens in this place. That's the whole idea, surely? And anyway... everyone tells me I'm actually a very happy person. I bring "sunshine" into their lives… apparently.'

'I'm sure that has always been the case.'

John put on a mock-Southern voice, aping Johanna's pronounced South Carolina drawl. *'Long as I can 'member, darlin',*' he said.

'And who is… "everyone", John?'

'The usuals, my dear, *mah darlin'.*' He spoke faster, 'all my friends, mah 'ssociates, ah guess…'

John's manner, his demeanour, his accent, vocabulary, his whole manifestation, had changed at least four or five times during the past fifteen minutes. Johanna found it unsettling… spooky.

'That being the case… what exactly are your thoughts… your feelings towards your friends, John?'

'my *friends?*' He smiled, 'I was thinking about them this morning – or was it yesterday? And… what I'm wondering…' John looked through the swing door into the corridor, 'the main thing… what *I* wonder – when I have time to wonder…' He stared directly at her, 'Where are they?' The patient wasn't playacting anymore. 'Where the hell is everybody?'

Johanna let herself be distracted too, most unprofessionally, and found herself gazing out of the window on the opposite side of the room. In the far distance the permanent taken-for-granted idyllic backdrop. All was blue. The sound of long, rolling waves and spring tides beckoned. She looked forward to a swimming session with her five-year-old later that afternoon. Cocooned inside the 26-foot glass wall of John Nightly's garden penthouse Johanna watched silently as a gas-jet blue coupé made its way up the shingle path. A slim, unusually well-dressed middle-aged woman got out as two porters rushed to help with her bags.

'What would you like to do most in the world right now, John?'

'that's easy!' He looked the consultant psychiatrist up and down. Starting from her blue, blue eyes and her bridged nose and her dark Spanish skin, before moving on to her curvaceous curves, her surfer's waist and her long, fake-tanned legs – particularly the bit from the knee to the foot. That bit was a truly spectacular bit of leg, he thought, as he lay back on his daybed and raised his eyebrows to the moon. 'What I would like to do, most in the world, right now is… to stay in this room right here with you… right where I am… obviously, Johanna…'

John's laugh was hearty. It suggested confidence.

'nice and safe and warm. That's what I want most… *in the world*, he continued. 'It's my life's work, that… and well, it's cold out there.' John gave a little mock shiver. '*Freezing*. When I was last out, anyway.'

'This morning, you mean?'

'not this morning… no. A long… quite a long time. Few years now… when I was last out there… would have been when I was at… Regal…'

Johanna sat back. 'And where is that exactly?'

John's voice became hushed, as if he were about to reveal a life-long secret.

'in Denmark Street… Yeh. Always been there. Same place. That's in…'

'Denmark?' Johanna conceded a cute half-smile as the boy returned the volume back to normal.

'Not Denmark…' John lifted his hand. 'It's not in Denmark – Denmark Street. It's… well… *London confusion!* as they say! It's never in the place it says.' He sounded exasperated and suddenly exhausted.

Johanna gazed out into the sunshine. The oldster continued in more contemplative mood.

'don't matter where these places are. They're in the background. Where everything is. Somewhere in the background out there… all the time.'

'And your wife was from Denmark… Wasn't she, John?'

'Deferately not… no… she was… I don't know… somewhere round… there. Lost track of her really. No idea where she's at anymore.'

John twisted round and sat up. A quite delighted expression came upon his face.

'there are just so *many* people, though. People around at the moment.'

'There are quite a lot of… *staff* this week, if that's what you mean. And it appears there are a lot of visitors as well.' Johanna looked back along the wide corridor. John yawned.

'Is there anyone in particular you'd like to see maybe…? *Coming up*, in the… in the coming future?'

'the "coming future"? Hilarious, darlin'. When is that future coming, exactly? Is it when you "come"?' He chuckled, without embarrassment, at his own, awful response, 'cos, well… suddenly I've got a future – if it is.'

The patient laughed again at his own terribleness. 'Didn't think I had, Johanna. I thought you'd got that one expedited in the old filing cabinet somewhere.' He grinned, 'was under that impression, anyway.' John became suddenly animated. 'Like it!

Love it! So let's do it! Let's *go* with it… as my old Master, my *guru* – used to say, 'cos now, suddenly, I've – *we've*, rather – me and you, I mean – *we've*… got a future… *together maybe!* He rattled his throat. 'Together at last! Like Sinatra and Sammy Davis. Ella and Louis… Ravi and Yehudi! And that – is progress! Wouldn't you say?'

The man really was getting so much better. A whole lot better. The improvement in his general mental state now visible in his physical self. There was colour in John Nightly's face; in his cheeks and lips, on the tip of his recently broken nose. For the first time in so many years there was colour. John's white London pasty-face had vanished. Replaced by a soft San Fran tan, no doubt from the long afternoon lawn meditations, the outdoor waterings, the corridor tending. A scarlet hue, almost a halo, about the head. Like that of an old Cornish labourer with too many miles against the wind. The blood rushing in to guard and protect him. Blood colour. The colour of life itself. Ruddy colour. Blue colour. Together they make blood. Somehow, some way… John Nightly was bloody well coming back to life. John Nightly, like other famous comebacks: James Bond 007, he's always back! 'Ol' Blue Eyes' Francis Albert, the …unfathomable Evel Knievel – even bloody Vladimir Horowitz – along with almost every artist of any consequence who came before, started small, made it big, bowed out and then was 'back'. Weren't they?

When the unlikely Ms Zorn had started with John, an unbelievable five and a half winters past, the most she could get out of him had been the odd 'yeh' or 'no' with the occasional 'so what's the point, then?' After that inauspicious beginning, John Nightly fell into a 'meek and mild' phase, lasting approximately another two winters. A period of strict non-commitment. No opinions, no preferences, no requirements. As if he were turning into a kind of lone being, a lone star, apart from the world and its choices. More isolated and remote than before. Ascetic and self-contained throughout this era, as long as John Nightly got the 'bare ne-ces-si-ties', as he happily musicalised them, he appeared to be content. The patient, after that prolonged spell, was at least stable. Following that, John entered his freefall period. Paragliding, you might say, between good recall and bad. A typical 'reclamation' phase, which Johanna had not found easy, wherein John really did have to relive certain situations, particularly 'wrongdoings' – some personal, some professional – in order to progress to the next and hopefully final stage of recovery.

But now… now we were talking. In sentences. Mocking the CP, irritated by her, angry with the institution, with the world, with the act of living itself. Showing much more confidence now. To actually be someone again. Today the patient was insufferable, rude – horribly unpleasant. *Good…* she thought; very, very good.

'Who would you like to see in the next… Perhaps tomorrow, for instance?'

'tomorrow I'd like to see Iona.'

'That's what I meant.' Johanna was relieved to have the patient back on track. 'And if Iona is… not available?'

'my mother, of course… but you'd have to be extremely clever to sort that one out… dig all that up again.'

John took a blanket and pulled it up to his neck.

'even before I went daft in the head. I'm not… very good with people. Not good at all,' he concluded, 'you said so yourself.'

'Did I?'

'saw you talking to Hank about it.'

Dick Marvin – Dr Marvin – the chief consultant psychiatrist in charge of John Nightly's annexe, had always been referred to by the patient as 'Hank'. Even to his face John would say 'Now look, Hank, the thing is…' when complaining about a consultation being rescheduled, or 'What exactly are you gonna do about it, Hank?' if one of John's cannas had been tended by another patient, and while chuckling to himself as everyone around appeared puzzled.

John was tickled pink when he discovered that the chief consultant, the guy who actually ran the joint, had the same surname as the famed guitarist.

Johanna was flummoxed. She *had* had a conversation with her boss, but there was no way John could have possibly overheard what had been said. She remained silent, and tracked back, trying to recall exactly where she and Dr Marvin had been positioned while discussing the patient's complete inability to relate to anyone from the 'new days'. They'd actually been standing on the other side of the glass. No more than a few inches away from where they were right now. But that glass was at least an inch thick. There was no way the boy could've overheard anything.

'read your lips!'

The CP squinted.

'You read my lips?' Johanna lost her cool. 'I guess you're well-versed in that activity, aren't you?'

'I am, yeh! Well "well-versed"!' he smiled. 'When you've watched as many film edits as I have. The thing with it is… in terms of… actually "seeing people",' he proceeded, 'it's okay for me to… "imagine" I'm going to see someone. I'm fine at that stage, but when that… *possi-bi-li-ty*…' He coughed and spluttered, 'actually looks like it might turn into *re-a-li-ty*…'

John stretched both words out of shape, the way a modern-day BBC newsreader might.

'then… "when tomorrow comes", as they say… I won't be on

it.' He took a deep breath. 'Won't actually want to see or meet anyone at all!'

Johanna was coming towards the end of her allocated session.

'If we can get someone important from here, the Center, to see you... move things on. Will you actually... see them this time? Instead of turning them away?'

'*Important?* Who is this "important" person? I was under the impression *you* were the important one, my dear? Surely you're the boss?' He shuffled on his couch. 'I told them, or somebody did – *they* told them – I know they did... it was John wasn't it? RCN... John Daly? That I had to have the most important, the very best, *bestest* "boss"-type person to look after my... mental "wellbeing", and my subsequent recover me...' the boy laughed. '*Recovery.* And... *guide* me, guide me back to... the place I need to be guided back to.' Johanna looked apprehensive as a car came to a halt outside and a casually dressed pudgy man with shoulder-length hair alighted.

'you *are* that person, aren't you, Johanna?'

John Nightly got up from his couch and stood before her. Something he had never done previously. Stood in the CP's presence.

'*Tell me you are!*' John put his hands deep in both pockets, not knowing at all what to do with them. '*Tell me that you are!*'

As someone in charge, as a woman and as a doctor, Johanna Zorn was offending the patient on every level.

The boy was in a horrible mood now; a stinking mood. As if he were berating John Pond, one of the members of his long-suffering band or road crew. The psychiatrist stared straight into him.

'Will you see someone who can make a decision about what's going to happen to you? If I bring them....?'

The patient had no idea that he might have actually reached this stage in his recovery. He remained silent. Not because he didn't want to take the proposal seriously, but because he couldn't take the risk of letting himself believe that things had actually improved to a degree where he and Johanna could even be having this conversation, and he did not want to be... couldn't be, disappointed. Disappointment was a hallmark of John Nightly's old career. Disappointment, its seeming inevitability, and how to deal with it when it showed up.

'If I set it up,' she breathed.

John lifted himself back onto the lounger, lay sideways-on to her and dragged his hair away from his eyes. The boy looked quite ashamed. And so... very, very tired. Like he hadn't slept a wink for five-and-a-bit years.

'I can do it, yeh... at the moment I can. I actually can.' John heaved and sank back into his couch. He reorganised his long limbs and began to sniffle as he wiped his eye with the back of his hand. 'I'll see them... whatever you want. Because I am... capable of it. I am... a genius! Like they say!'

John Nightly sniggered embarrassedly as a horrible smell suddenly terrorised the room.

'God...'

'no, I'm not God, my dear...'

Johanna got up, pushed her chair away and stormed back through the double doors.

'Hi! Hello! Excuse me! Um – pardon me... Someone, sorry... somebody, please... can you...?'

She lowered her voice, realising that she was now out in the communal area.

'Can someone come and... You'll need a...'

The work's never done, there's always something new

**'Matthew & Son', Cat Stevens, 1966
(Deram 45 DM110)**

Göteborg Cirkus, 'Kettering–Granada', Crawley Starlite Ballroom, 'Musicians Union Member', 'Marshall Amplification', 'Swansea – Top Rank', Berlin, Bremen, 'The Jupiter Klub, Kassel', 'It's a Fender!', 'Oslo Njårdhallen', 'Air Freight Only – DO NOT STACK!', 'Musicians' Union Live', Welcome to the Republic of Eire, 'Be Sure of Shure Microphones!', Business Traveller, The New Santa Monica Hotel, Bruges, VERY FRAGILE, 'Freight: Waterloo, London', 'Keep Music Live', 'Hungaria Kustom', 'Electrical Goods', 'Picato Strings – the Professional string!', 'Paris: Le TeePee', 'Electrical – DO NOT STACK!', 'WEM – the Professionals', 'Sunbeats', Manchester Free Trade Hall – Stage Door, 'Duty Exempt – DO NOT STACK!'

The Fender guitar strapped tightly across his back weighed heavily as John Nightly covered the half-mile through Regent's Park. The collection of labels affixed to its case was an indication of his movements over the past few months. Musicians invariably defaced their instrument cases with stickers promoting concerts and music products; tools of the trade – guitars, amps, microphones, drumsticks, strings.

As evidence of gainful employment it became a sandwich board of sorts, advertising the wares of various equipment manufacturers from whom a discount might be negotiated in exchange for promotion of the much-discussed 'gear'. As if plumbers walked around flagging motorised flushing systems on their toolboxes, or the GPO delivered to you from a sack proclaiming the benefits of postage.

The last six months had been non-stop. A whirlwind of airports, hotels, dressing-rooms and soundchecks during a recently-completed promotional tour of seventeen countries – forty dates in all, accompanied by roadies and the usual close circle of friends. As it does for all groups, professional employment had already taken on the emotional weight of family commitment. The Nightly band never actually appeared under a regular title[1] but if a promoter insisted then the *Sleepwalkers* seemed as good as any. And this morning that's exactly what they were, having returned home just a few hours earlier.

The now permanent line-up consisted of Justin Makepeace, John's childhood sidekick from Cambridge, on lead guitar; Ron Bloom, late of the Gloom, on organ and Mellotron; new recruit Ashley Root on drums; with Jonathan Foxley filling in on bass. While Lee Hide manned the sound desk as usual – late today, as usual – Jean-Claude got paid more than any individual band member to create a trippy, spaced-out atmos using a flicker machine, a Death Kit smokehead, a picnic grill on which he burned coloured gelatine, and a cardboard stroboscope.

John himself played as much rhythm guitar and piano as he could manage while at the same time trying to remember the lyrics to his own songs.

So the gathering this Sunday morning at the old Diorama behind Regent's Park was, give or take the odd guest appearance, the complete Nightly line-up. A tight little unit that could happily motor along all night, no matter how many orchestras, choirs and ballet companies might be bolted onto it.

'What happened to the Syndicats?'

Justin was fixed on the back page of *Melody Maker*, while Ash made tea for everyone – the cable to the electric kettle plugged in (a little perilously) to the back of Justin's amplifier.

'That was Steve Howe's band. Sugar?'

'Three, thanks. What about the Midnites?'

'That was Andy Pyle. Somebody else good in them…' Justin poured a cup of mu tea for the boss.

'John… no sugar still?'

No response.

'Dunno how you drink this stuff, man.' Justin gazed down into the murky pool.

Again no response. Justin gave the goo a stir and handed it to his employer.

'Ash… you'll know this one…' Justin brought the damp newspaper closer to his eyes.

'Why was the 2i's called… the 2i's?'

'The coffee bar?' Jonathan chipped in. 'I actually know that, Justin. It's… it's because the two brothers who owned it were the *Irani brothers:* the 2i's. Isn't that right?'

Justin seemed impressed. 'Got to hand it to you there, Jon… *Absolutely right, Jonathan!'* he announced in the manner of a TV quizmaster.

'Howd'ya know that, Jon?' Justin put a crease along the page as he tore out the article for future use.

'Cliff Richard Story… the book. Something I was reading very recently.' Laughter all round as Jonathan admitted the extent of his literary excursions.

On the other side of the room, the boss fiddled with his echo box and took a sip of tea. He invariably seemed to invest in equipment that broke down the minute it left the shop, or else on the first night of a tour. As he hit the selector switch on the tin box a sound like the end of the world, or at least the end of Regent's Park, filled up the old observatory, rattling the leaded glass in its domed roof and bringing bits of lead, rust and ancient cobwebs raining down on the Sleepwalkers.

'Chrissakes, John!'

'Sorry everyone… but can you… can somebody… just come and have a quick look at this damned…'

The lead guitarist and question master – who was also the group's self-appointed chief electrician, mechanic and plumber – left the tea-making to Ashley and walked over to help.

The boss had unscrewed the lid of the Fablon-covered unit and was peering inside in search of a disconnected wire, dislodged fuse or valve. The Watkins *Copicat*, a must-have piece of kit of the day, was in essence a mini tape-recorder with one extra record head. The box, dropped in transit the previous evening, now emitted a stream of electronic crackle instead of its usual spectral echo.

Ashley put down his sticks and picked up his diary. 'Can I ask about what's coming up? For a minute?'

Justin, one hand holding a soldering iron and the other a half-eaten biscuit, was still listening.

'What's coming up? What do you mean, what's coming up? What is coming up?'

'Gigs… what's happening with gigs?'

Ron rounded off a rousing pub-piano rendition of 'Abide with Me'. He rubbed his hands together for warmth and picked up his over-sugared tea.

'What is happening, Ash? Apart from the usual… *complete chaos, lack of sleep, freezing bedrooms, sore throats, damage to the eardrums, late payments and… general disillusionment?*'

Ron was undoubtedly the cynic of the group. Ashley ploughed on. 'What I mean is – when we get to South Africa…'

The players stopped fiddling and fell silent as they gave their collective attention to the drummer, for the first time ever.

'In terms of what we do if we get stuck with – I dunno – "problems". Protesters and all that?' Ashley directed the question straight at John, now balanced on his AC30, rocking gently to and fro against the wall, beverage cupped in both hands, quite obviously the worse for wear.

'No doubt John Daly or... Pondy'll be able to tell you more about that than I can...'

The boss had been briefed by his manager never to enter into discussion with the group concerning any kind of organisational or philosophical day-to-day business.

'Janice said about the Dusty Springfield thing... you know she was supposed to go with her... *hair and make-up*,' replied Ash.

The boss rocked back and forth a little faster.

'Didn't know *Janice* had anything to do with Dusty Springfield.' John Nightly could barely remember who Janice, Ashley's new acquisition, was. Some nights, when the boss introduced the group at the end of a gig, he had trouble remembering their names.

Now everyone was listening. A rare moment of group communion. The drummer continued.

'Janice got scared in the end. Don't like flying much either. Physically I mean – seems okay with the other sort!'

The boss stopped rocking and disconnected his guitar from the cackling box so that Justin could get the screwdriver to it. In the absence of John Pond, it seemed John Nightly was going to have to respond to and deal with the question decisively in order to deliver some semblance of leadership to this faithful few.

Something John was very unused to doing.

'Dusty wasn't scared, though, was she? So I think we'll be alright – all of us. Five big grown-up guys'. John put down his guitar. 'And… well… we are definitely playing to a non-segregated audience. I mean, it *will* be… but if it turns out that it's not, then we just won't play.' He shrugged. 'We'll… down tools, and come home.' The boss looked around at everyone in turn. 'Simple as that.'

It was amazingly silent in the old observatory, the players having stopped making the usual racket that ensues whenever a musician comes into contact with an instrument. The Sleepwalkers put down their guitars and perched on their amps, quietly sipping tea as they considered the possibilities of the coming tour. Ashley had more.

'Went down the *Limbo* last night.'

'I was gonna do that.'

'*Bluebeat Nite.* There was an African – South African – group on. Went up and had a bit of a jam. So I was talking to the guys after…'

The drummer stopped mid-sentence and released a long, slow breath that seemed somehow to deflate his whole body. Realising that he had the band's full attention, he shook out his unusually long arms and slowly rotated his neck, as stickmen do, pausing a moment for dramatic effect. Ash lodged his drumsticks in the waistband of his loon pants, picked up the set list and tightened the nut on his crash cymbal. Justin looked down into his teacup, noticed the spoon standing upright in sugar and gave it a stir. Knowing Ashley would go round the houses, just as he did with his playing, the others waited patiently for the punchline.

'And… *what did he say*, Ash?' enquired Ron, switching off his Hammond.

'Basically, what he said was... Don't go over there, man. That's what he actually said.' Ashley spun his cymbal around and gave it a little 'ting' with his finger. 'Seems like a... a pretty dangerous situation. The protests and everything, the atmosphere. They said it's very different to what it is here... and Europe. Really very different over there... all... coming to a head...'

Suddenly the hall filled up with spooky seagull wails. Whoops and yowls rose up from the boss's echo box into the lenticular roof, making the open-mouthed congregation jump.

'There you go, man... Echo-oo-oo-oo-oo! That's what you want! Proper echo!'

Justin, oblivious to what was being discussed, unplugged his own Strat. He took John's guitar-lead from his sweaty hand and plugged the boss back into his own effects unit. John leaped from his amplifier, strapped his guitar on and turned up the volume control.

'Exactly the reason we gotta go!'

John Nightly wanted to get right off the subject as soon as possible and back to the usual mellow vibes that existed between the group members.

'Because if nobody goes there and everyone stays away and nobody does anything about the... Then nothing'll ever change... will it?'

The group, inspired by this imperative, picked up their instruments and assumed playing positions. Justin went to the console to check everyone's faders. John pulled his mike stand towards him.

'We don't exactly do a lot for society, do we? I know it sounds pretentious. Us lot here... we don't. We play music. Our group.

We please ourselves. And people like us… just do things for ourselves. Really, we do…'

The boss challenged the three blank faces.

'If we're honest…' He began to pick out a slow, unwinding arpeggio. 'It's a pretty selfish… endeavour.' John let the chord ring out. 'Yeh… more for me than it is for you – I realise that.' The boss looked up from his guitar. 'Not accusing anyone of anything…' He smiled. 'Except myself.'

The others nodded. Ashley began tapping skins and twirling drumsticks. Ron mopped up spilled tea from his keyboard. Justin began to tune his guitar. John continued.

'… apart from actually giving them money – "funding the protest" or whatever – which is a very easy thing to do – anyone can do that – we should… just for once… sort of… do something about it. Make a *physical* effort… then, even if things go wrong when we're over there, it'll still mean we've done something. We actually showed up. Went over there. To make a point, at least. Generate publicity for… the cause, and that'll be a good thing.'

'And publicity for us…' added Justin.

'Right. That is right, Just. For us, too…' conceded the boss.

Justin slunk back to the tea-making corner and the safety of his fuzzbox. He continued to tune, half in a trance, lending an ear to what John was saying. Ron had been deep in thought.

'Don't wanna be… cynical, man. But… that's the bit Pondy's into. The publicity? *If* we're honest. Even if we don't play, we get coverage: *"Group walk out of Rhodesia"*. Can see it now – see him lovin' it. Imaginin' everything that might happen… whatever actually does happen.' Ron began a reedy tune on the Mellotron.

"Political reasons"… *"Band refuse to play to separated audience".*

'Segregated!' shouted Jonathan, 'f' fuck's sake.'

John turned to his drummer. Ashley was busy integrating two conga drums into his new set-up.

'Ash… shall we…'

The drummer parked his cigarette in the corner of his mouth, got comfortable on his stool, rotated from side to side again, grabbed his sticks, did a little roly-poly roll around the kit and settled into a clipped ska rhythm, in tribute to last night's gig.

From somewhere at the back of the dome an excited voice – 'DESMOND DEKKER!' – as Iona and Monika charged through the swing doors looking like they'd just got out of bed, which they had, while the Sleepwalkers relaxed into the skank of 'Mu Mu Tea' at half its usual speed.

'Gimme some of that Mu Mu Tea, I only want that… uh… remedy, woo-hoo… It's my… spe-cial-i-Tea… Gimme some of that… For GODSAKE!'

John sang the nonsensical chorus, mocking his own money-making creation with an exaggerated Elvis wobble. 'Mu Mu Tea' was mutating back into a Cliff Richard coffee-bar 45. The girls threw off their sheepskins, skipped into the centre of the room, let the sunlight catch their ingénue eyes and began to sway to the beat.

'GOD…'

The boss played a deliberately wrong chord, his usual signal for the band to stop. 'I *HATE* this bloody song!' He loosened his guitar strap and opened his arms to hug the two visitors.

'But it's Monika's favourite…' Iona looked to her friend for confirmation.

'This one, deferately fabourite, 'ona.' Monika pointed at John and began to mimic his singing.

'Sorry, Mon. And sorry everyone. But I... I really cannot keep singing these songs over and over,' he put both hands across the guitar neck to deaden the sound. 'Driving me... absolutely mad. Really it is."

John glanced around the room at each face in turn. He reached for Iona's hand.

'Sorry... no vibes or anything...'

Monika, not sensing the moment at all, had a comment.

'How 'bout Flank Sinatara, John? He sing song many, many time. Same hit... many year... and Elbis?'

'Well, they're pretty good songs, I guess, Mon!' Justin cut in. 'Gotta do the hits, man... As every promoter you've ever come across always says...' [mimics gruff-voiced Northerner] '*Gotta do the hits tonight, guys!* Not that bad is it, John? Be a lot worse if we didn't have any hits to play.'

Justin turned his amp up full and blasted the room with a devastatingly loud 'Wipe Out'. As usual, the band fell for it.

'*Okay! Alright... Hey!*' John Nightly was wise enough to stop 'spontaneous jam sessions' as soon as they reared their heads. 'Sorry everyone, but... let's not get distracted.' He turned to Justin. 'Sorry Just...' And then Iona: 'Sorry, darling...' letting go of her hand. 'Let's try something else. Anything else. Don't mind... but I really honestly do hate that one – sorry, man...'

The drummer behaved as philosophically as ever.

'Always the way, man... every band I ever been in. Group never wanna play what the audience wanna hear.'

Justin agreed. 'Every band I been in as well... 1-2... 1-2...'

Justin tested his vocal mike as Ash downed sticks and tapped out a rolling rhythm on the congas. Ron continued to play a light ska figure for Desmond.

The doors swung open again.

''Mazin'...'

'Lee! Decided to join us then!'

John was irritated now. Though he wasn't entirely sure why. Not because the soundman was late. In the two years he'd been working for John Nightly, Lee had never yet once showed up on time.

The band's main communicator and vibemeister moseyed in. Still wired from last night, his manic stare registering each crew member in turn as he took up his rightful position behind the mixing desk, plugged in a couple of cables and pushed up the master fader. Behind him, lugging a 4 x 12 speaker cabinet, came Malcolm, the group's driver and only permanent roadie... and behind him... Pondy. The man himself... the real boss. Though no one, and certainly not John Nightly, would ever call him that to his face. The manager commanded utter respect from his employees. Having proved himself to be a staggeringly effective organiser, creative thinker, problem-solver and all-round strategist. A man with answers to more or less any question under the sun, including occasionally some of the questions posed by the group.

In his green cord jacket, still sporting the remains of a pink carnation from a wedding a few weeks back, his crushed-velvet flares and mismatched sandals, Pond was every inch the modern, switched-on operator. The acceptable face of pop music management. Mr ex-public schoolboy, ex-union organiser; Mr Pond was entirely suited to John Nightly's needs, with his air of utter confidence, slight huffiness and an off-the-cuff response or, as he put it himself, 'retaliation' to any question, any challenge, whether it be tomorrow's weather forecast, legal, medical or sexual advice, or next week's chart position.

'1-2... 1-2...'

'Keep going, Just... again man...'

As Lee spoke, Justin stepped up to the mike as if he were about to make a much-considered statement.

'1-2... uh... Buckle my shoe...'

'Keep it simple, mate, please... the thing's distortin'...'

'Right, uh... 1 – 1... 2 – 2... 1 – 1 – 1... 2 – 2 – 2... 1 – 2... uh...'

Justin stuck to the basics. As if in the general scheme of things it mattered a damn to anyone at all, whether or not you could hear his voice. Lee pushed the master fader to its limit, sending screeching feedback around the hall. The girls covered their ears, Monika burying her head in Iona's coat.

'That's it, guys! Should be loud enough f'ya... Better check it with the guitars.'

Everything was okay now. Seemed better now. With Lee finally installed. As with the crew and technicians on a film set, it's often the supporting players, or service people, that give a working situation its vibe or 'heart'. Not the stars, the director or the money men, but the make-up, best boys, grips, camera technicians. Technical people. It's the crew that the stars hang out with. Maybe sensing in them a more honest contentment or workaday reality; a friendlier, more relaxed time than can sometimes be had with the 'bosses'.

Lee was undoubtedly the most popular member of the Nightly entourage. Always Up – both spiritually and physically. In terms of physically being awake all the time – the guy seemingly never actually slept. Wanting for nothing more than a few winks on a tour bus or plane, his own hotel rooms were seldom troubled by his presence – Pondy reckoned they could have saved thousands by never bothering to book a room for Lee, who was always available, and reachable – at any hour – for people and their problems. The service-person sound engineer was the *star* of the band! Apart from the girls of course. Well… the girls were always popular.

That report from Cape Town, where our reporter Jonas Janis will update us during the programme. [cue BBC logo ident] Now we turn to another aspect of the situation – which faces foreign performers and artists who are hoping to travel to Rhodesia in order to perform. I'm joined in the studio by the singer and performer John Nightly, recently returned from Johannesburg, where he was due to play three concerts as part of his current tour.

John… thank you for coming in today.

[blank look…]

You've recently returned from South Africa, where we understand you were forced to abandon your plans. Can you tell us why?

[sniffs] We planned three concerts at the Shenk Assembly Hall. On the basis that the concerts would be to a non… segregated audience… Things are… changing over there and this is one thing… condition… in our contract. When we got there… we could see… well, blacks and whites were not… gonna be allowed… to sit with each other. But that was after we'd set everything up. All the equipment and that. Before the audience had been… allowed in. We… we came out on stage… couple of times… to check equipment… take a look, and you could

see they were definitely not actually sitting together. Our manager then came back and told us that there were notices outside about... segregation, so... we had to... [coughs] About an hour before the concert when we, well... had to tell the promoter... you know... that it was... it wasn't gonna happen. And... like that, and... then... It wasn't a good atmosphere. It was... it was...

And you told the promoter that you would not be able to perform to a segregated audience?

Our manager... and us... the group... had to make a difficult... decision there. Easy decision to make... but... difficult as well, because we... we were already there and we... we weren't sure what the... You know... the reaction to that – *from that* – was gonna be...

---

[1] In May 1969, the Sleepwalkers recorded a one-off single under the name the *Mayflower* for the Mosaic label (Mo119663) of an unreleased John Nightly composition, 'Kassandra's Kaftan', a song that had been rehearsed with the group but never performed or recorded by John himself, along with a self-penned B-side, 'Quoits'. Although the single disappeared without trace, pressings in the original picture sleeve currently change hands for £1,000-£1,500.

The *Mayflower* also recorded for John St. John's Tree label, turning John Nightly's rejected 'She Is Perfection' * into what now sounds like it could have been a bona fide hit. But tensions in the studio meant that the *Mayflower's* planned escape route was aborted.

Source: Record Collecting US: *Rare Record Guide*, 1999.

* see also Brocade/Alexander Telstar

John was up early the next morning. Six o'clock as usual. Part of the deal. If the resident got up early, he could claim one of the ten or so available day jobs to help with the smooth running of the Center. He wouldn't be allowed to spend all of his time watering plants, as he had done at SUMHA in England, but he would be allowed to assist in the laundry or on the visitors' terrace, serving other patients 'the healthiest toasties in California', or to sort parcels arriving in the mailroom gift-wrapped at Bloomingdale's and Neiman Marcus.

Although John was very, very ill, the attitude of the staff towards him was not always sympathetic. He didn't look ill, and when he was experiencing a 'happy' or 'confident' day he was charming and bright. He carried himself well, remembering everyone's name as he helped wash dishes in the mornings, while in the afternoons he would sit in one of the glasshouses reading articles on astronomy, or astrophysics, in US publications that he had never before had access to, from the well-stocked library in Eseme Park, just minutes away from Gold Star studios, right up there on Santa Monica Boulevard, spiritual home of Phil Spector, the Ronettes, the Righteous Brothers and the Beach Boys; a locale with which he was almost over-familiar.

Gold Star had been the delivery room for 'Be My Baby', 'You've Lost That Lovin' Feelin'', 'Good Vibrations' and 'God Only Knows'. For pop-music followers, the equivalent of the Bateau-Lavoir for painters, or the Brontë parsonage for Romantic novelists. A recording facility that became a shrine – the studio was also where John Nightly had spent nightmare weeks and months, in the summer of 1970, trying to pull the *Mink Bungalow Requiem* into some kind of listenable, presentable shape.

On an 'unhappy' day at SUMHA, the patient was either morose – on a 'good' unhappy day, or near catatonic and tending towards violence – on a 'bad' one. Johanna bore the scar on her neck from an ashtray John had slung her way only the second time they met. The cheap gift-shop glass ricocheted off the wall straight into her carotid artery, in the process transforming itself into a $70,000 ashtray. A mutually agreed sum, as the singer was not insured for 'third-party injury'. The reason the woman stayed on the job at all no doubt being the $165,000 per year for two consultations a week and an overall project spec and case archive just too good to turn down, investment-wise if nothing else.

'And these are?'

'... canna... *Canna* 'Luxor' – my very own strain! They really are a strain, as well. Take a lot of looking after, these things.' John removed a couple of dead leaves and turned the plant round to face Johanna. 'They'll grow to six/seven foot. Then come into flower... like these ones here.' He pointed to a shelf of pink and yellow bellflowers enjoying life over in the only shaded corner of the room. 'That one's a proper pink – viridian – but if you don't look after the rhizomes over the winter, the flowers won't be... *lush*, as they say. No, they won't be lush. They really only last a couple of days... then they're gone.'

The psychiatrist leaned in to inspect a particularly healthy-looking bloom. 'This one's come up, hasn't it? Since we came by before.'

'That's because of the heat and because I asked Hank to put a little something in the water in the mornings.' He paused. 'Joking, yeh! I've been really looking after that one.' John picked up a plastic watering can. 'You water in the afternoons and evenings, never the mornings, out here anyway... too hot... and... as I wasn't allowed to come in yesterday... or the day before...'

'Why was that?'

'...having a bad day...'

John tipped the yellow can, circumnavigating the rim of the pot with the funnel. Making sure that all new growth from the orchid-like creature would receive the recommended level of refreshment. He wiggled the fleshy stalk to let water drain through while at the same time dabbing at the soil with a chopstick, in order to aerate it.

'I'm recommending to Dr Marvin that we talk about you going back at the end of the year.'

No response from the dabber. Johanna remained still, waiting to see whether what she said had registered.

'Back?' The resident turned towards her. 'But we've already been "back", haven't we? We had to go back to go forward. You said that.'

The CP didn't respond. She demanded the resident be straight with her for once. The man stopped watering and rested for a moment on the ledge.

'back how far… exactly?'

'Back home.'

The patient's expression froze solid.

'home? What do you mean "home"? Which "home" exactly?'

'Your home. Your own home. Back to SUMMER there. If you like, until you…'

'Summer in England?' John Nightly seemed genuinely not to have taken it in, '… but it'll be raining all the time…'

The consultant psychiatrist looked blank. The resident wore a rather helpless smile. He put down the watering can and removed his sunhat, lifting thin wisps of old man's hair from his balding skull.

'… how can I go back? I don't know anyone there – or from there – anymore. Don't understand it, either – the place, I mean.' He peered down at the floor. 'Didn't understand it before – and it'll be different again now. I don't actually under-stand… actually what you exactly mean…'

'There's been some… positive moves. Developments. Here. Also over there. And there's a plan.'

'… plan? Over where? What plan? Not for me to do any work, I hope?'

The CP smiled. 'Not for you to do any work – not *music* work, if that's what you mean. Nothing like that. It's… it's to get you back over there.'

John remained silent. Johanna stayed positive.

'I don't know any more than that. I wanted to… sound you out. But… I'm quite confident you'll be going back to England.'

This was completely unexpected. John Nightly got up rather unsteadily to look his mistress straight in the face.

'… it's the tax people,' he declared. 'That's it, isn't it?'

Now the CP laughed.

'It's not the authorities, John. It's a friend of yours. Guy who came to visit the first couple of weeks you arrived.'

'John?'

'Yes, John – your friend.'

'RCN's organised this?'

John Nightly took a breath. The thing about Johanna, the one good thing that he appreciated and respected above all others, was that she never deceived. Never lied or raised expectations. 'Vibing up' wasn't the business Ms Zorn was in. One reason being that the consultant psychiatrist had no sense of humour whatsoever – and no sense of harmless fantasy either. However doubtful he may have been about the reality of what was being discussed, John understood very well that Johanna would only be telling him something if she was absolutely certain it had potential. This was a sounding-out. But it was also a proposition. He acted immediately to suppress and control his emotions, but inside John was heating up.

'can you… "keep me under control", though? When… *if*… I did end up…'

'I think that with the medication at the level we have… now – and that's a big difference in terms of where we were before…' she paused. 'I think we both know that we can.'

'both?' He moved towards her. 'You mean you and… Hank?'

'I mean you and I.'

John Nightly stopped contesting and started considering. For the first time in years, the boy really did have to get on with something.

John had never imagined he would ever actually go home. He'd kind of lost interest in it. The Center – California itself – suited him. Being so naturally unreal and everything. In California he had been living in limbo, in a dream state. Not a good or bad dream, but a 'nothing' dream. *That* suited him, too. For one so utterly numb, a state of absolute nothingness would have been the only day-to-day situation he could bear. Any kind of normal, everyday exchange with mankind, particularly on an 'unconfident', or 'unhappy' day, being out of the question.

The solution to a flare-up was Tryptizol – the pills that were said to have killed Nick Drake. The tricyclic antidepressant, which left the recipient in a state of confusion, though calm, had become the day-to-day answer for John Nightly. In John's case, the drug made it impossible for anyone to communicate with him. The alternatives being Percodan or – laughably – Mandrax. *Mandies!*

That really was ridiculous. Every time this particular downer appeared on the delivery sheet it brought back memories of Lenny the Bear.

Over the years, John Nightly had become something of a tranquiliser guinea pig. When the Community Care in California (CCC) conducted a routine examination of his medical records over a seven-year period they found he'd been given no less than forty-three different tranquilisers and anti-depressants throughout his time at the Center. In the Sunny State those who weren't always sunny tended to subject their pill of choice to the same rigours as the latest handbag, timepiece or automobile. Prescription drugs had their ups and downs, not only in terms of their physical and mental effect but also fashion-wise. The previous summer, Californian residents with psychotic tendencies were taking Reviron, the shiny green hexagons guaranteeing fewer 'unhappy' days than before. It was all the rage. The problem being that unhappy days were replaced by one hell of a lot of 'nothing' days.

But Reviron worked, for John Nightly at least. The next new thing was a 'whitie'. Branded Neuamyl, the tablets came in a handy flip-pack in two shades of Polaris white. Neuamyl being so cool that users would leave the packaging lying around the house, the way your friends used to leave *Led Zeppelin III* on the carpet or sofa in case of visitors.

And what a brand name. Pondy would've loved that. Chemically, Neuamyl was very similar to the blue, triangular-shaped tabs marketed by Smith, Kline & French as Drinamyl – Pete Meadon and Lee Hide's preferred upper during the summer of 1965.

Neuamyl worked too. But not on John, who in the past 12 months hadn't been in need of any helpers whatsoever. Presently, and hopefully for a good while longer, John Nightly was 'on the loose' as they say. Pill-free. The first time in thirteen summers.

A few months more and it would be time to reassess yet again and take the next (and hopefully final) step towards regular existence. Back to integration and some possible future, though Johanna hesitated to use the word. A real home in a real climate, though a far less luxurious way of life. And maybe, as his friends and fans no doubt hoped, back to music – any kind of music. After the events of this unusually sunny and most confident day, even that notion seemed possible. Thanks to the care John Nightly had received at SUMHA, this module, this position, this new creative possibility, was all plugged up and ready to go. All the boy had to do was to walk back into his cell and hit *PLAY*.

Everybody's talkin' 'bout a new way of walkin'
Do you want to lose your mind?
Walk right in, sit right down
Daddy, let your mind roll on

'Walk Right In', The Rooftop Singers, 1963
(Vanguard 35017)

Four weeks later... Week 1,339, series 29, session #1.
The consultant psychiatrist paddled through the double swing door, along the plant-infested corridor, into the box room at the end. A cul-de-sac of greenness, the patient's glass box resembled nothing so much as the subtropical dorm of a local garden centre. Not overgrown, out-there or wild but self-contained, in-here, temperate, cultivated. Safe. A real control zone for a real control freak. An exotic contradiction, the rich man's conservatory. Like the one Philip Marlowe visits in *The Big Sleep*, or the spymaster's glasshouse in *Minority Report*. Or the greenhouse in outer space in *Silent Running*. Each fake tropic existing for a reason beyond the cultivation of plants. The room, though airy and spacious, still somehow oppressive. Dead but for plant life. Humid not only with vegetation but also with the uneven inhaling and exhaling of the creature that has made its home there.

Johanna grabbed a high-back chair from a stack. She pulled it over to the left of where the resident lay, as she did twice a week during a 'series'; the inhabitant never in all this time having been kind or thoughtful enough to place the chair in position for his guest prior to her arrival.

Never a greeting passed between them, but over the years this single piece of business became the first contact-event proper, in analysis terms, of each two-hour stint. Johanna stood for a moment, admiring the bright-orange starflowers neatly arranged along the floor-to-ceiling window. The patient gazed up at her. Deigned to look up. Something was different today; something was wrong.

He frowned, trying to fathom as he continued to look her up and down. She seemed younger, for a start, he thought. More girlish… more vulnerable… flimsier somehow. He viewed not admiringly, not desirous, figuring whether or not he had any real interest in the interloper this afternoon.

In normal circumstances, outside of work, Johanna Zorn was an attractive proposition. Happily married with two youngsters, as John had been informed by one of the groundsmen the day of their meeting; she was a statuesque, big-limbed sports-woman. In normal life. And in his own previous life the patient would have been trying to dazzle her. Try it on with her. Charm and capture along with other seductions. But right now, able to think only in the moment, trying to gaze, figure and fathom all at the same time, he looked at her in a most unmanly way.

Johanna turned back towards the patient, a good deal more relaxed in the presence of her charge these past few months. Betraying a relief that there was now an end in sight, a cadence, perfect or otherwise, to these six long, drawn-out summers.

'flat shoes!'

'Excuse me?'

'Flat shoes! That's what it is! I knew there was something!' The man seemed worryingly excited. 'Never seen you in flat shoes before. Hah!' He smiled. 'It… well, it makes you look a lot less "important"… I mean… "formal".' John bit his lip. '"Superior" is what I…' He cleared his throat a little sheepishly.

Johanna sat down and crossed her legs, flower-patterned flip-flops dangling from varnished toes. 'Had a strap break on me… getting out of the car… It doesn't quite give me the height…'

'No… it doesn't. So… well then…' he mumbled. *The shrink has shrunk!'*

The patient became consumed with his own brilliance '*The shrink has shrunk!*' John repeated a couple times more.

Johanna breathed deep. Snatching an opportunity when (for once) the patient wasn't acting, she looked him up and down – trying to gaze and fathom also. There he sat, paper-thin, but seemingly healthy, full of himself today, entombed in this sunlit capsule. Lying in wait. But for what exactly?

The CP fixed on the boy's blue, blue eyes; eyes that had dazzled so many. She wondered just how much he really cared for her, looked forward to her coming, missed her when she didn't come. In terms of his inner self, quite a lot, she imagined. There had never been any person-to-person chit-chat, no close relations, not even a polite friendliness between them, but Johanna was reasonably convinced that the patient quite 'liked' her, in whatever ways there were left for him to like. If not that, he respected her. And therefore she guessed – and most probably, somewhere deep within, hoped – that he did indeed look forward to her visits.

Ordinarily, Johanna would have had the patient home by now. An afternoon at first, then an overnight; a weekend if things went particularly well. A slow fade back to the ordinariness, the regularity, day and night hours; all of the innate boredom of real everyday life, reinstating the natural ups and downs, psychological and physical, the drab timetable of existence. Essential for those for whom, in the outside world, life had become just that little bit too exciting.

Visit 1: she'd get the houseguest to make coffee, burn the toast, wash dishes. *Visit 2:* a bit of superficial gardening, clean the place, help cook dinner. *Visit 3:* repeat the practical tasks, go to the store and maybe take a couple of hours off during this final stage of the programme, bringing back a hopeless case who was otherwise 'real gone'.

Taking the patient home, male or female… There was always

a chance it might not come off. Might lead to the odd unforeseen situation or difficulty. Possible resentment of the keeper's other-world stability. The Freak might freak out, in which case a switch would be pressed and the cavalry summoned.

This home-visit final act could continue for months. Johanna would have three or four outpatients rotating at any one time. But dependency, or freaking out, was the opposite of how John Nightly was likely to react. The CP was convinced of that. John had been dependent on a number of people all his life. From Frieda to Jana, Pondy to Iona, and RCN of course. John became dependent on everyone who *walked right in*. What he needed now, and what Johanna had been building towards, was a stand-alone 'need no one' independence.

Were she being honest, the consultant psychiatrist was resigned to the fact that this degree of self-reliance would never come. Already SUMMER had entered into an agreement, a long-term one – at least as long as a major recording contract – for John Nightly to be looked after, more or less locked up, for the rest of his days. Arranged long ago; the actual 'going back'. Now all of the hard work, the ace-serving and the volleying, the wear and tear on both players, was to be rewarded.

John Nightly was about to become another Johanna Zorn success story. A case study to be added to her forthcoming lecture programme, repositioned at the top of her already impressive CV. An inclusion which would stir up even more interest in her practice, earning her a couple more notches, and lead to more exclusive highly paid high-profile work. Famous whacked-out cases were what she specialised in. Celebrity nutters, from which the CP would be able to extract an even greater monthly sum in order to remain at the very top of her tree. *Number 1*, in Santa Monica mind control. The truth was, it was as much about the keeper keeping busy as the captive staying 'level'. Crucial to Johanna's own state of mind was that she stayed as busy as a busy, busy bee.

Had Ms Zorn been killed in a hit and run or gunned down in a liquor-store midway through John Nightly's rehabilitation, John would never have walked out of the Center alive. There would've been no recovery stories and no conclusion. The end of Johanna would have been the end of John. That's how big an impact she had. For the first time since Frieda mothered and smothered, a woman had the upper hand. And although a lot had been taken out of him, Johanna did, in a way, respect, even trust, the resident. The CP considered all this as he mocked her now.

'I was thinking that… as we had quite a… a sad, or "indifferent" kind of week last week, all in all…'

'did we?' John shifted around on his lounger. 'Wasn't aware of… to be totally… *brutally…*'

'I think we did… with those particular memories… I thought this week we might go over – remember – a time that might perhaps be described as a particularly "happy time".'

'happy?' John persevered with the tone, stroking his chin as if trying to fathom one of Justin's crosswords. Johanna smiled, but in terms of progress having been made, John finally being able to leave the Center for good, she found it difficult to hide her disappointment in the resident's attitude.

'Shall we talk about a happy time? It's always good to remember a happy time.' It was as if she were addressing a 5-year-old.

'… this is true.'

'Excuse me?'

'I said it's true. Always good to remember a happy time – Jojo.'

'Shall we talk about the old days, maybe?'

'you mean the "good" old days… or… the "bad" old days?'

'We should try the "good" old days, don't you think?'

No response.

The resident slipped his finger inside the strap of his sandal, eased it off, and lifted his foot onto the daybed.

'Most certainly!'

Hearing a positive response, even a mocking one, Johanna fell silent. The resident checked his watch and counted 120 seconds before he spoke.

'exactly how "old" do you mean, though? We talking *old* old, like schooldays old? The... *reasonably okay* good old days or...' He yawned, very self-consciously. 'The really quite... *bad* good old days, which would be... "much more recent" old?'

The psychiatrist swallowed. John Nightly could be quite a comedian.

'I guess *old* old is what we mean. I didn't think you'd want to talk about the... more recent, good old...' Johanna transferred her pen from one hand to the other, 'you don't, do you, John?'

No response. John put his playful foot on the floor, using it to support him while he leaned back and balanced on the bed, at the same time staring up at the spotless ceiling.

'not yet...' he sighed. 'I think it's kind of a... a "never" to the more recent... "good old... days"... far as you're concerned.'

He repositioned himself and put both feet up on the crossbar of Johanna's chair, something he had never dared do before, coming over all 'confident' in the knowledge that he was about to take them both back to the 'old', reasonably acceptable, even 'vintage' days of yore.

The CP needed to speed things up a little.

'Let's find a music memory,' she began. 'Music memories are always nice for you, I think.'

'are they? Hmm… some are. The early ones, anyway. Earlier the better, I guess.'

'Tell me when you first became aware that people were "playing"… performing music, instead of just listening to it… That it could be… played, and maybe you realised that you had the ability to… to do that.' Johanna sat back. 'You said you had a friend who…'

'I didn't actually have any friends… so I didn't say that. Except the dog. And he didn't make a lot of noise… at all.'

Now they were at least out of the pen.

'Once upon a time…' he started, 'one day, anyway! Once upon a time I was walking home from school. It was a very hot day, always a hot day in those days… as I remember it. Lot of kids walking in front of me with tennis racquets and other bats and things… in shorts… It was a really hot day.' He squinted. 'I remember these things… all these memories, as always taking place in summer. We were walking along Mill Road in Cambridge and we got as far as the Meadowsweet Dairy. Just outside there… in – can't remember where exactly – what road that was… what year either.' He scratched his head. 'But it was…' John looked up, 'sometime in the middle of the century! It was in Cambridge as well…'

'Mill Road…'

'yeh. How'd you know that?'

'Did you know the guys in front?'

'No… no. I didn't know anybody in Cambridge, but sometimes I… I used to… tag on to a gaggle… of kids, follow them around a bit, if they were walking somewhere. I'd… walk a bit with them, behind them. I was sort of a… you know… I'd pretend I was with them, if you understand what I mean. That I had some… friends… mates, I s'pose.' He turned to Johanna. 'I used to wonder where the hell all these kids were going. People used to… those days… walk around a lot? Really did. Kids everywhere. Maybe because there never seemed to be anywhere to actually… go. Not in Cambridge, anyway.' John cleared his throat as if he'd accidentally revealed something about himself. 'I used to… get as close to them… as I could. As if I was with them… and… well, that was what I used to do sometimes.' He began to fidget. 'They were probably a bit older than me, the kids in front… a year, two years or something, but at that age… well, one year is a long time. Anyway, and… I didn't want to lose them, so when they stopped I stopped as well, and I kneeled down, so I wouldn't pass them. Pretended I was tying my shoelace, because my mother would never allow me to have "slip-ons" – slip-on shoes; they were the latest thing.' John stopped abruptly. 'I was always aware of fashion, Johanna, even at an extremely young age.'

The boy smirked then turned pale. He looked down at his shape-less Sta-Prest and orthopaedic sandals. Johanna didn't react.

'Like I am now!' John continued, 'and in the yard at the Dairy there was a girl with a skipping-rope. Using the forecourt to practise. Skipping real fast… real impressive… and the kids sat down to rest, 'cos it was so hot. They started to clap and cheer… sort of cheer her on; she started to go faster and faster… till she fell over.'

'Was she okay?'

'She was okay. And these kids got up and… helped her up, and she started to go… a bit odd. Dizzy probably. And the kids started to get up and leave. She didn't look very well, though she righted herself and started to… but in the other direction.

'So... because I didn't really know what to do... these kids were going off in one direction and she was going off in the other direction. I thought I'd follow her...'

'And she was a pretty girl?'

'Oh... she was pretty. That's why I noticed her... should think I was eight... maybe six, seven years old.'

'She got up to go...'

'Yeh, but she left something behind. A little case. One of the boys ran after her, but by that time she'd turned a corner... so the boy stopped and he looked round and there I was behind him, following behind him, so he gave the case to me. And I had seen her turn the corner, so I got up speed and ran after her, and she was there and I shouted out and she stopped and turned around and I went up to her and gave her the case and she said, "My violin!" or whatever it was, and... then I realised that there was a violin inside this case and that the girl with the skipping-rope was also the... the violin player.'

'And did she thank you?'

'She was very... polite. Well... I didn't know what was inside the case; I knew it was something... special... "intricate". Not intricate – you know what I mean... fragile... "valuable". Maybe a jewel or something. Like jewellery, I thought, in my stupid head... It was a special weird-shaped case, and now I'm thinking... for some reason I think I thought it was a telescope!' He laughed. 'Anyway, don't know why, but she just opened the case and took this bit of green cloth covering it and checked it was okay, not damaged, and sort of plucked the strings – "Hey, it works!" I guess... I was so impressed with her just... you know... the way she plucked these strings... sort of "in rhythm"... Beautiful sound... and... I'd never seen anybody do anything like that before.'

Johanna, bored out of her skull, did what all psychoanalysts do when they're about to fall asleep. She feigned an undue amount of interest in the patient's very personal and (from her point of view) potentially most revealing flashback so far.

'Did you ever see her again?'

'Saw her a lot after that… yeh. Well… that was my girlfriend… Jana… my first girlfriend… I told you about her a lot. She's an architect now.'

'So that was much later?'

'… what was?'

'When she was your girlfriend?'

'… lot later, yeh. I don't know how late that was.' John put a hand over his eyes. 'Never told her about this and she doesn't know about it either, this… particular story…'

Johanna remained silent.

'… thought it would show… weakness, you see… But that's the way you talk about things… isn't it?'

Johanna, mainly due to the extreme humidity in the room this afternoon, began to yawn enthusiastically.

'So… you never told her you'd met before… when you were small?'

John opened his mouth wide and yawned, making no attempt at good manners.

'And when did you meet Jana again?'

'that's what I said… when I was eleven or twelve… when Hank

Marvin came out.'

'Excuse me?'

'A group. I mean… it's a band. Of course it's a band! Something special… proper band. Hank's group.'

'And when did you last see Jana?'

'… we did do that bit. We've done it. We did go through that… element – in detail. I know we did. You've got it in your notes. Was a really… well, it was a bad, *bad old days* bit, I seem to remember.' The patient looked disappointed. 'I know that you… I realise that you… have a lot of clients… *patients*. I know you have to listen to a hell of a lot of rubbish. As well as my old… but… but…'

Johanna slowly began to realise she'd cracked it. After all this time. This tormented, sad individual was actually showing a lot… of progress.

'It's good that you're able to go revisit the old days like that… now…'

'… well, that's kind of in between the "old" old days and the recent old days.' John let out a breath, aware that 'good' progress had been made. 'Even that is a very long time ago, isn't it? Long time ago; and the last time I saw her… we met. It wasn't a good meeting I don't think…'

'You really can't talk about that… "element" at the moment, can you?'

Johanna was hoping that he couldn't.

'can't really… no need to either. It won't "reveal" anything, babe… and, well… you've got it in your notes already.'

'Now… if you look up there to the right John… see it up there?'

John could see it alright. It was the brightest thing in the heavens. Although his neck hurt and he was still wearing his school uniform with short trousers, beginning to feel the cold. His father removed his own scarf and wrapped it around his son.

'Is that one always in the same place, Daddy?'

'Always in the same place, John. What they call "fixed", that one. A fixed star. You've got the Big Dipper over there…' John Snr indicated towards a vertical point directly above the botanical gardens. 'Find that one first, then look about a yard to the right of that corner star over there…' John Snr fixed the position with his index finger then rotated it clockwise as if it were a radar arm. 'See where I am now?' The boy cricked his neck once again. 'And you've got it.'

John Snr squinted through his old naval binoculars, delighting in the fresh, moonlit night and this first ever outdoor stargazing trip with his young son.

'It's a saucepan, Daddy.'

'That's right, John. Like your mother's saucepans… a bit crooked! But a little bit bigger as well! You only have to remember two stars… there's *Dubhe*, on the rim of the "bowl" there, look…' Daddy pointed to the right again. 'And *Mizar*, actually a binary star… Remember what we talked about? The one on the edge of the… "handle", at the other end…'

John Snr looked to see if there might be any planets visible tonight. 'But it's not important to remember the names, John… I know you will anyway, with your memory…'

The boy stared up at the night sky, bending backwards at a most awkward angle. '*Dubber* and *Myzar*,' he murmured, 'like *My Star!*' he shouted to his father.

'That's right John, like *My Star.*'

The boy turned to John Snr. 'There's a *shooting star*, Daddy – *jetstar!*' John almost jumped out of his shoes.

'Bit unusual, that…' replied his father.

John peered further upwards. 'The really bright one is *Polaris*?'

'Yes. Same as in the book. If you went off at 45 degrees in the other direction from the bowl, just around to the right… but further round… you'd get to *Capella*. Over there on the right-hand side… Do you see?'

The boy blew his nose, swept his fringe away from his eyes, then pressed the binoculars hard to his forehead, making an indentation in his brow that would still be there next morning. John could see a very bright star indeed.

'The only other one we're going to try to remember – for tonight anyway, because I think you're getting a bit cold – is that one. You see where I'm pointing? There's a *W* shape. Way over there, across the midheaven point.' John's father gathered his duffle coat around him and checked his watch. Nine o'clock was just about the boy's bedtime. Late arrival home would be an excuse for Frieda to berate her husband while making an extra special fuss of her son when they arrived back at the house.

'*Cas-si-opei-a*… I can see it easy, Daddy. That's the best one.'

'Very easy to see, yes… Then tomorrow we'll have a look at *Orion*, if it's a nice night. That's an easy one as well. Quite a lot of stars in it… and that'll give you three good signposts.'

John's father reached for his binocular-case and picked up the pair's rucksacks ready to head back.

'What's that one, though?' The boy stopped looking with

binoculars and pointed to an orangey-yellow ball of fire. It looked shinier, more glowy than the others, and gave out plenty of local light.

'What is it, Daddy… The really bright one?'

'Ah well… that's Venus, John. Bound to cause trouble. Troublemaker, that one. Thought you'd have to pick that one out. You have to remember that the planets go along on their own trajectory, their own… "wheels", "rail tracks" in the sky. A bit like women do.' John Snr pulled up his collar and took hold of his son's hand. 'Right then… we'll have a look at that little lady tomorrow.'

October 1974: Dutch fans, trying to get closer to the Bay City Rollers, throw themselves into a canal during the group's arrival in Amsterdam. The Rollers continue their assault on the UK pop charts with 'Shang-A-Lang'. Stephen Hawking proposes his Black Hole theory and is elected Fellow of the Royal Society. David Jones dies in a nursing home in Harrow. Billy Fury (Ronald Wycherley) retires from music to open a bird sanctuary in Wales.

October '74 was also something of a pre-Zero Point lull for John Nightly. When he was readmitted to the Center in Santa Monica, March 1973, he was still a 'face' around the local area. John had been quiet for a while but interest remained at a pitch. The magicien bought groceries from a wholefoods barn on La Brea, was sighted trying on a kaftan at the Village Spree on Highland Avenue, sitting on a moped outside LA GO! (John Nightly never learned to drive) and attending the premiere of *Lost Horizon* with Rafaella. The Center's log from the beginning of the new year records that the boy rarely left the compound unless he needed to go to a regular practitioner in a regular hospital. In 1974 John Nightly was just getting used to liking being 'no one special' all over again.

Jonathan Foxley, Rolling Stone magazine (Retrospective Special Edition), May 1998. 'A Very English Genius'. Interview by John Spring.

During the period you're talking about I don't think John listened to music at all. I did try, but I don't know whether he heard it or not... I know I went to see him in California and I took him some records; Scott Joplin, John Cale, the *Paris* one[1], a Bernstein record[2]... Todd Rundgren LP ... whatever the new one was at the time. One of those records that everyone was listening to '74... '75 maybe[3]. There was a hi-fi in the room and I put it on. Him on one side of the room, just laying there on his bed, me on the other. Amazing, light-filled room, full of plants, huge window out onto a big lawn. Like a Grange... convalescent home. A bit like being at school as well – 'here's the new record to listen to', you know? There's that medley, great little bit... (sings, dada, hmm-mmn, trying to remember the bit)... his eyes lit up immediately. It was like electrons going on, because of that 'two keys at once' thing. He loved those chords... like Carole King, but... *heavy*... you know? He looked up at me: "Is it Todd?"' Jonathan laughed, "recognising it straightaway. The sheer ambition of it, the easiness of it. The extreme musicality, of course. Just like John himself. Recognised a kindred spirit there, another kind of... I don't know how you want to call it... "mad genius" is what they say, isn't it?'

He had business problems at the time, didn't he?

On top of everything else, yes. I'd actually gone not just to see him but to talk about... money, to be honest... if I'm honest. He... or his company, owed me... quite a bit... Royalties

[1] John Cale *Paris 1919* (Reprise K44239) 1973 Cale used a Leonard Bernstein scholarship to get him from the Amman Valley, South Wales firstly to Goldsmiths College in London then to Massachusetts where he studied with Copland and Xenakis at Tanglewood.

[2] Leonard Bernstein 'The Norton Lectures' (Columbia X1398) 1973.

[3] Referring to either the medley on *A Wizard, A True Star* (Bearsville BR2133) 1973 or side two of *Todd* (Bearsville 6954), 1974.

mainly. Tangled up with all the usual stuff. It wasn't just a...
'philanthropic' visit, I'm afraid.

His manager was... incarcerated?

Crazy as it sounds, for something like six weeks, I think. God
knows who he came across in there... what happened to him...
[Jonathan's eyes glaze over] I would've thought even Pondy
found it difficult to negotiate very much in prison. As if putting
someone like him in a place like that was going to do anyone any
good? He was moved to a place in St Albans. One of those
asylum/free house... 'open asylum', you'd call it now.' [becomes
more distant and distracted as he continues] This is 'off the
record', isn't it?

[journalist nods]

After he got busted a second time, they put him in the Severs
Centre. Pondy was in a pretty bad way. Not at all the 'let's-get-
on-with-it', sort of... ludicrous, but brilliant character he had
been. There was no life to him anymore. As if his whole...
reaction, had been – I mean his responses – everything, his
senses... had been dulled. Wasn't responding to anything,
except perhaps the drugs they were giving him. [checks time]

I visited him... intended to go every week... or a few times a
week, as I lived close by, but one visit was enough, to be honest
with you. He was... pretty vile to me, I remembered he always
owed me money. Very difficult to get a cheque out of Mr Pond.
Not only for the Nightly stuff but for sessions I had done for his
other bands. JCE work. Seeing him that afternoon... I don't...
I think I... I knew he would never be coming out of it... out of
there... that situation. Awful place... nothing 'free and easy'
about it as far as I could see. Abysmal. State-run... 'urine-
perfumed', as they say... graffiti and shitty [sniff]. Orderlies, the
lot... really... very *conventional*, in reality [stares at the floor].

I knew so many people in that sort of state... at that time.

Everyone was in a state! Somehow, I escaped that. Because of work I suppose. I was always working hard. Technical work as well. Orchestrating. Had to concentrate. Even if they weren't clinically… 'psychotic' or whatever you want to… they behaved as if they were. [leans forward and rests his elbows on the mixing desk]. Everyone I knew was on *Risperdal*.

What would that… do?

It's a… light antipsychotic. Everyone I knew was on it. I had a friend in another place, in St Albans, Villa 21. Jeremy, 'Jez'… Trombone player. Great friend of mine. He played with… lots of people… Cat Stevens sessions… Georgie Fame. It was drink that did him, but he was on *Risperdal*… and another 'acquaintance' of John's, the only girlfriend who managed to keep in touch with him – Raf – Rafaella, she was actually a countess, the contessa… was her correct… 'title'… In a really bad way the last time I saw her. Raf had the same character as John. I think she was… well, there was something between her and Pondy too. Jonathan swings back on his chair, visibly relieved, now that he considered it, to have survived the late-'60s onslaught.

'When I think about these things now, we could've all been in the same boat. In '65 – I think it was '65 – a lot of these things weren't actually illegal, were they? People were reading books about it. Educating themselves about drugs. But you could get the stuff. [he leaned back and put his feet up on the console, as he cast his mind back thirty years] *The Psychedelic Experience*[4]… everyone had a copy, and the Laing book[5] – the whole 'new psychiatry' thing… [takes a sip of coffee]. Then the World Psychedelic Centre[6], in Pont Street. John went there… But that got a bad reputation quite quickly. Don't know what happened to the people behind it'.

[4] By Ralph Metzner, Timothy Leary & Richard Alpert (Citadel), 1964.
[5] *The Divided Self* (Pelican reprint), 1965.
[6] The World Psychedelic Centre opened in Belgravia by Mike Hollingshead.

'We saw the Beatles film *Help!* where they all lived in the same house, and we thought – that's for us!'
Jim Dandy, Black Oak Arkansas

For a rock'n'roll household, very little music made its way through Trewin's dense undergrowth courtesy of its residents. With no communal record collection, middle-of-the-road local-radio playlists emanated from Mrs Peed's kitchen transistor and singer-songwriters from the stereogram Robert had installed in his bedroom. On the three nights a week he stayed over at Porthcreek, the CEO of Trewin Exotics was kept company by the ghosts of Gram Parsons, Nick Drake and Tim Buckley.

It was rare for John Nightly to play anything at all from his small ad hoc collection. Nothing remained from the old days, though every now and again a familiar riff could be heard leaking through the boss's bedroom door. A bit of jazz, Graham Bond or Tubby Hayes; happy sounds, indicating that the whole house was about to experience an unusually 'confident' day.

The only genuine record fan was RCN, who boasted two bookcases full of 'top-shelf classics and rarities' by the likes of Rory Storm, Johnny Kidd, and the John Barry Seven, all lovingly preserved in their original paper sleeves, anti-static PVC outers and dust-free archival library boxes. Bobby 'Boris' Pickett's 'The Monster Mash' (Garpax 44167), 'Transfusion' by Nervous Norvus (Dot 15470) and a stack of crypt-kicking 45s by the incomparable Screaming Lord Sutch: 'My Big Black Coffin' (aka 'Till the Following Night') (HMV Pop Series 953), 'Jack the Ripper' (Decca F11598) and 'She's Fallen in Love with a Monster Man' (Oriole CB1944), along with Storm's 'America' (Parlophone R5197) were among the graveyard smashes which reverberated around the damp bungalow.

Although RCN was very much the employee, and the Johns were completely at ease in one another's company, they spent little time together away from everyday business. A kind of communal method had evolved at Trewin; the family able to share their daily experience within the social group, managing to avoid eye contact when doing so by speaking to each other while at the same time staring into the television screen.

The inmates would congregate on a summer's evening to catch up on bulletins of the news and weather, with favourites like South West Television's *Helpful Hints*, in which a master furniture-maker might advise on how to get a teacup burn out of a piece of mahogany or a seamstress would instruct on the preservation of wartime pinafores and keeping bath towels fluffy. Sometimes there would be a black-and-white film, John Mills or John Barrymore; Mrs Peed's favourites, in which case she would be summoned from the kitchen by the cry of 'Black-and-white film!' and would come running.

'Is it a flashback?' the housekeeper would ask. 'I love flashbacks!' she'd cry as the drama, a tale of disenchantment fuelled by unrequited love or perhaps alcohol, would begin in the 'present' – i.e.1942 – then unwind and unfold by flashing back to the past, delighting this connoisseur of Gothic monochrome.

During the commercial breaks, Mrs Peed would serve her coagulated fudge or boil a few damsons as the community relaxed around the TV set, gorging themselves while complaining about the lack of flavour in supermarket fruit and the quality of life in Britain today. As Trewin's residents generally ate at separate times, these films, or *Helpful Hints*, anything to do with gardening – watched in awed silence – and the regional news (rather than the dramatised BBC edition) were the only activities that united the group in terms of family get-together or common experience.

If the boss bothered to engage at all until the appearance of Mawgan – or 'Jesus', as Robert referred to him – it would be for a quick teatime chat in the kitchen with Endy, who would regale him with tales about historic Cornwall; shipwrecks around Land's End, the usual smuggling stories (John's favourites), embroidered more elaborately by the housekeeper with each retelling, and tales of childhood days in the fishing colony close to where the Peed sisters had been brought up.

Sometimes Endy would have horticultural news about other estates in the area – grand houses at Godolphin or Sancreed – where she and her sister had been in service as children. And then workaday tales about local head gardeners, many of them holders of Chelsea Gold Medals and National Rose Society medallions.

One morning, during her first week in residence, the feisty housekeeper had impressed John Nightly when she took him and Robert for a walk through the side meadow. Here she was able to identify ragwort, teasel, dog-rose, toadflax and pignut, speaking knowledgeably about their life-saving and death-giving properties. Thanks to her, John was, over the coming months, finally able to put a name to many of the wildflower species he'd known as a boy in Grantchester.

Mrs Peed had a stock of tales about nurserymen selling boxes of lavender and meadowsweet to landowners in Bristol and Plymouth, which would end up in the baskets of the simplers of Piccadilly, and about the medicinal qualities of speedwell and knapweed, a cure for painful cold sores but also for a broken heart.

Endy said that in some places in Penwith they still used tonics made from the spoon-shaped leaves of ragged-robin. And that for superstitious reasons she always carried about her person the last packet of pipe tobacco produced by her father from the purplish stems of coltsfoot. On one trip, the tough-as-old-boots octogenarian pulled up a heavy clump of St John's wort to take back to the house which she said would do wonders for Robert's thinning hair.

It wasn't long before Endy assumed a kind of cure-all, problem-solving role within the group. Firstly, with regard to practical domestic matters, then, as time went on, in more of a philosophical capacity, advising and giving the benefit of her wide experience regarding what might now be referred to as 'lifestyle'. But Mrs Peed's lifestyle was the style of her parents and of generations before. Her appearance was wartime, the lady having been isolated for so long that she'd gained a kind of 'need no one' outlook. Self-sufficient, independent and in apparent rude health with all of her wits still about her, she quickly earned the respect of the family and began to be seen as something of a household guru, rather than the paid-help-cum-skivvy she'd been engaged as. In many ways Endy then became the Boss. The residents worried about abandoned coffee spoons – 'Now where's that spoon I was just about to wash up… ?' – and the remnants of late-night drinks, cigarettes (and joints). 'That's one of Mr John's, I hazard…' the house-keeper would huff and puff, aware that there were limits to the type of behaviour or lifestyle she was able to impose on her fellow residents and employers.

Soon after her arrival Mrs Peed was consulted about an infesta-tion of nocturnal hawk moths that had been busy pollinating honeysuckle sticks along the kitchen wall. The quandary being how to remove the creatures without inflicting damage on the deciduous shrub, which Endy announced was a guarantee of good luck. The problem was solved by an application of diluted Fairy Liquid, the glistening mucus making the moths lose their grip while leaving the shrub unharmed. Endy had risen at five one December morning in order to dig out a patch of enchanter's nightshade that was threatening to choke the bed of asparagus outside the pantry.

Because Mrs Peed had not the faintest idea who John Nightly was or indeed had ever been – she remembered the Beatles as 'people from the North' – the boss found her an easy companion. Endy had visited London only twice (not unusual for a Cornishwoman of her age) and had not been impressed by it. Indeed, it was difficult to find very much that would impress her. But what she did appreciate was general good manners and a stolid reserve, which was of course John Nightly's stock-in-trade. As with many people who come from a background of family disagreement and frustration, though the housekeeper would laugh and joke with RCN and Robert the relationship between herself and her paymasters was strictly business, most conversations ending abruptly with the lively matriarch's, 'Well… I'll have to get on, I suppose.' And get on she would, buzzing through the house with dustpan, brush and her faithful bottle of Dettol while humming some long forgotten melody, a Methodist hymn or battle cry, which never seemed to resolve.

'Isn't it a coincidence you being called Daly and him Nightly?'

'Suppose it is… Daly is an old Huntingdon name and there's a lot of people in Cambridge called Nightly – fairly normal Cambridge name. Not from the university, but from the town. His father came from Boston, in Lincolnshire, which is still quite local.' RCN sipped his tea. 'We thought it was pretty ridiculous when we first met, though…'

Endy continued to pick dog hairs off the carpet while RCN flicked through the *Cornishman*.

'What about the name Peed?'

'Don't start on about that! All the trouble I've had with that over the years, all the terrible names and…'

'I'm sure you've had a lot to put up with…' RCN kept his head down.

'Lot? I've had to put up with a right lot, I can tell you! I've had to bloody well put up with – oh, sorry…'

Endy got up, washed her hands and filled the kettle with water from the hot tap. She often got confused about the positions of hot and cold so that RCN would habitually find some excuse as to why the kettle had to be refilled with fresh, cold water before getting up himself to make the final cup of tea of the day.

'I don't know where the name comes from; I just wish I'd never heard of it! That's all I can tell you,' Endy continued. 'It might be Methodist – we were an old Methodist family, the Peeds – but it was difficult at school of course because "Endy Peed" sounds like some kind of… 100-legged creature. Didn't take long for them to start calling me "insect", which was actually what my husband used to call me as w… ***BUGGER ME!'***

Endy had turned on the hot tap thinking it was the cold and almost scalded herself. 'Ooh, sorry…' She immediately switched to the cold one and ran her hand underneath it to try to reverse the damage. 'Then down at Quethiock House, where I was known as "Miss Peed", of course, the children could never… They never knew if that was Miss Peed or *Miss Speed*, so that was where I picked up the nickname "Speedy" – I suppose partly because I used to move so fast in those days.'

'You still do!'

'Not as fast as I used to, though… I can tell you… I was a fast mover in those days, you know! *Oh!* Well… I mean… when I was working, I was…'

Free School Lane, Cambridge, Michaelmas Term 1967
Photo credit: Flora Johnson/Cambridge Evening News

Free School Lane, Cambridge. Saturday, 20 May 1967. 10.30am.

Back in Cambridge for the weekend to break the news to John and Frieda that Iona was pregnant, the couple stood in the vestibule of the Whipple Museum of the History of Science, located in Free School Lane, a stone's throw from KCEMS. John had spent many hours in these small rooms hidden away behind the city centre, learning all about the unsung heroes who had made so many important discoveries by studying tides, stars, wave patterns and in turn acoustics and sound. In particular, this was the scientific home of one of John Nightly's forebears, the astronomer and inventor of both the telegraph and the microphone, Sir Charles Wheatstone.

This morning, John Hilton, John's friend and former drummer with the now defunct Everyman, would be delivering this week's Saturday Lecture – *Wave Machines: Adventures in Cybersound* – a subject with which John Nightly was all too familiar.

'Hallo everyone. It really is very nice to see so many of you here today, for the Whipple Museum's sixth Saturday Lecture of the Easter term. Thank you all very much for coming, particularly with the weather as it is today.'

The speaker smiled apologetically as the thirty or so members of the audience settled down.

'We're here to talk about, and also take a look at, wave machines – whatever they might be! Particularly the work of Sir Charles Wheatstone, who, through his study of waves, and his interest in acoustics, almost by accident ended up inventing… the microphone. You may want to sit on the seats provided or find a place to get comfortable as we're going to be based in this one room for the next fifty minutes or so.' The speaker referred to his notes: 'Right then, ladies and gentleman… Today's Saturday Lecture is entitled **Adventures in Cybersound, the Work of Sir Charles Wheatstone (1802–1875)**. Let me tell you something about this extraordinary man…'

The speaker moved towards one of the peculiar-looking contraptions by the window. He cleared his throat to begin as he threw a welcoming smile in the direction of John and Iona.

'Charles Wheatstone was born into a musical family in Gloucester, and it was sound that first captured Wheatstone's imagination. In 1821 he began to try to classify vibrations – the basis of sound. He investigated vibrations in strings, columns of air and metal rods and, in the search for a simple method of demonstrating how these vibrations worked, invented the *kaleidophone.*' Hilton pointed to a diagram. 'Three metal rods were inserted into a wooden base, with reflective beads on the end of each rod. The rods had different cross-sections, with one bent to 90 degrees at its middle. When the rods vibrated in the different modes, they produced different sounds and the beads displayed different patterns. The end of the bent rod was free to vibrate in both the horizontal and vertical plane, producing a three-dimensional pattern. The instrument was first displayed at the Royal Institution on 4 May 1827, though its inventor was apparently so shy that he asked Michael Faraday to deliver his lectures for him.

By the time Wheatstone wrote his last paper on sound he had entirely categorised pitched harmonics as they applied to wind instruments, at the same time establishing himself as a major scientific figure. He applied all this knowledge to an invention that used air to make musical notes but by using a human breathing mechanism. Initially he found this difficult. Wheatstone's *Symphonium* of 1829' [indicates to another diagram] 'required lung power to supply the air to its metal reeds, with the player using keys to select the desired note. However, he then began using bellows to supply that air and, in the process, invented an instrument we are all too familiar with today: the concertina! The important innovation was the reeds being arranged radially around the end hand plates of the machine and laid flat. With twenty-four buttons for each hand, the instrument had a range of over four octaves. He also made sure his concertina was "double-acting", meaning that the same note could be played and sustained with the bellows going in or going out.

'Following on from this success, Wheatstone turned his attention to electricity. He was appointed Professor of Experimental Philosophy at King's College London in 1834, and invented a machine that used rotating mirrors and eight miles of wire to measure the speed of electricity. However, at some point an error in his calculations led him to believe that electricity was faster than light. Undaunted, three years later, in 1837, he patented the electric telegraph and with Sir William Fothergill Cooke made it available to the public. Now… let me tell you a little about Sir Charles Wheatstone's amazing life and achievements…'

item: Biographical papers: Sir Charles Wheatstone (source the Wilkins Library, Massachusetts) private papers, book 6, John Hoe bequest. David Googenbroom Collection.

Sir Charles Wheatstone (b. Feb. 6 1802, d. Oct. 19 1875), was an English physicist and inventor whose work was instrumental in the development of the telegraph in Great Britain. Around 1821 Wheatstone is said* to have devised the so-called 'enchanted lyre'. Musicians played on a piano or harp in the room above the lyre, and the vibrations, passed down a brass wire, made the lyre appear to play itself. Wheatstone served (1823–34) an apprenticeship as a musical-instrument maker. His work in acoustics won him (1834) a professorship of experimental physics at King's College London where his pioneering experiments in electricity included measuring the speed of electricity, devising an improved dynamo and inventing two new devices to measure and regulate electrical resistance and current: the rheostat and the Wheatstone bridge, an electrical circuit in truth actually invented by S. H. Christie to measure the value of a resistance. It is named after Wheatstone, however, as he was the first to put it to extensive and significant use. He worked on magneto-electricity and submarine telegraphy, and he suggested the stereoscope still used today in X-rays and aerial photographs, later perfected by the inventor of the kaleidoscope, David Brewster. In 1837 he designed, with William Fothergill Cooke, an electric telegraph system that became standard in Britain in 1840. On 10 July 1837 Charles Wheatstone and William F. Cooke patented the electric telegraph.

source: Various incl. **The New Grolier Multimedia Encyclopedia, Cable and Wireless** and the **Telegraphic Journal and Electrical Review:**

item: 'A New and Beautiful Invention', *Poughkeepsie Journal*. 13 September 1837.

An English newspaper contains the following description of a new and highly ingenious mode of applying the principles of electricity, or 'galvanism', to the communication of intelligence – in other words, to the construction of an electric telegraph. The theory is probably correct, but we fear that serious obstacles will prevent its application to an extensive scale, as appears to be contemplated by the writer: I begin…

When in London, a few days ago, we learned that an eminent scientific gentleman -1- is, at present engaged in maturing an invention which promises to lead to the most astonishing results, and to exert a vast influence on the future progress of society. It is an electric

Telegraph, the powers of which as much surpass those of the common instrument bearing that name, as the art of printing surpasses the picture-writing of the Mexicans. The telegraph consists of five wires, enclosed in a sheath of Indian rubber, which isolates them from each other and protects them from the external air.

A galvanic trough or 'pile' is placed at the one end of the wires, which act upon needles at the other; and, when any of the wires is put in communication with the trough, a motion is instantly produced in the needle at the other extremity, which motion ceases the moment the connection between the wire and the trough is suspended. The five wires may thus denote as many letters, and by binary and trinary combinations the six and twenty letters of the alphabet may easily be represented. By a simple mechanical contrivance, the communication between the wires and the trough may be established and stopped, as the keys of a piano forte are touched by the hands of a practised musician, and the indications will be exhibited at the other end of the chain of wires, as quickly as they can be read off.

In the experiments already made, the chain of wires has been extended to a length of five miles (by forming numerous coils within a limited surface) and the two ends being placed near each other, it is found that the transmission of the electric action is, so far as the human sense can discern, perfectly instantaneous. Little doubt is entertained that it may be conveyed over a hundred or a thousand miles, with the same velocity; and the powers of the instrument promise to be as great as the action is rapid. It will not be confined, like the common telegraph, to the transmission of a few sentences, or a short message, and this only in the day time, in clear weather, and by repeated operations, each consuming a portion of time; for, while it works by night or by day, it will convey intelligence with the speed of thought, and with such copiousness and ease that a speech slowly spoken in London might be written down in Edinburgh, each sentence appearing on paper within a few minutes after it was uttered four hundred miles off ! There may be practical difficulties attending its operation, as yet unknown; but we speak here of what intelligent men, acquainted with the experiments now in progress, look forward to as their probable result. If the promises their experiments hold out be realised, the discovery will perhaps be the grandest in the annals of the world; and its effects will be such as no efforts of imagination can anticipate.

item: Cooke and Wheatstone Five-Needle Telegraph System

Wheatstone's Five-Needle Telegraph System employed five magnetic needles and a lattice grid of 20 letters (omitting C, J, Q, U, X and Z). Five wires are needed to send the signals, which deflect two of the five needles at the other end that point to the letter in question. One needle is used to point to a numeral. Cooke and Wheatstone refined their invention until it used only one needle and a signal code. However, ill feeling developed between them as to who actually invented the telegraph.

The telegraph employed five iron needles which when not in use rested in a vertical position. Each needle could be moved either to the left or the right by electromagnets. To transmit a letter of the alphabet two switches were pressed which caused two needles to move and point to the appropriate letter. By pressing different combinations of switches any one of 20 letters could be transmitted.

*Unfortunately the omission of the letters J, C, Q, U, X and Z made it diffi-
cult to send some words. Alternative methods were adopted to spell words
such as Queen, Quiz or Axe. Despite its shortcomings, their equipment had
the advantage of being usable by unskilled operators. Although the five-
needle telegraph was easy to operate it required six wires. It was soon
replaced by a single needle instrument. Each letter of the alphabet was given
a code of right and left needle movements, and in this way messages could
be transmitted. However, this required skilled operators. Wheatstone also
initiated the use of electromagnets in electric generators and invented the
Playfair cipher, which is based on substituting different pairs of letters for
paired letters in the message. He was knighted in 1868.
(*Encyclopaedia Britannica*, 1966.)

John Hilton walked over to a Formica-topped table in the
corner of the room, lifted the lid of a small portable record-
player within and dropped a 7-inch single onto the deck.

We skipped the light fandango…

'You probably heard on the news this morning that it's
National Flower Power Day in New York today. Well, without
Charles Wheatstone and all of his hard work, it's likely that we
wouldn't have anything like this at all. In fact, we wouldn't have
records… because we wouldn't be able to record them!'

As the Miller told his tale…

The lecturer turned back to the audience, continuing his round-up.

'Later, Wheatstone designed a sophisticated wave-machine model
to demonstrate the action of transverse waveforms. His final
machine, which could demonstrate the addition of two wave-

forms with variable phase difference, as well as resolving a waveform into perpendicularly polarised components, received a special mention in the Great Exhibition of 1851. He was knighted in 1868 and died in Paris on 19 October 1875, after contracting a common cold.'

Her face, at first just ghostly…*

'Well… there we are!' The speaker adjusted the volume on the Dansette. 'Thank you for coming here today. I'm sorry the weather has been so bad; it always is in Cambridge, I'm afraid! But I hope that won't deter you from coming next Saturday… when we'll be looking at and discussing the work of the eminent astronomer and… Cambridge man, John Pond.

* 'A Whiter Shade of Pale' (Brooker/Reid/Fisher) © Bucks Music Ltd.

'God in a pill'

Pete Townshend, speaking about Meher Baba,
Rolling Stone **magazine, 26 November 1970**

Johanna picked up her coffee cup and indicated for the waitress to bring the check. Fleetwood Mac had been programmed four times in a row on the counter jukebox. She turned to the Horoscope page in *People* magazine.

'Here's something that might be of interest...'

No response.

'The Reagans use astrologers.'

'Well!' He lifted his head. 'Nothing surprises me about what those two ponies get up to.'

'But it's a... "trained" practitioner,' Johanna explained to her fellow breakfaster. 'Wasn't that the more "academic" astrology you were interested in? Birth charts and so on?'

'As-Tron-O-Me... not the other one...' John made a face and folded down a corner of his napkin. 'I was never really interested in any kind of charts.'

The CP failed to read the witticism.

'It's a guy Nancy Reagan's been seeing for years'[1]

'Apart from Ronnie?'

'Astrologer guy... they plan all the White House official duties by it.'

John folded and unfolded the *LA Times*. The CP laid her Amex card on the saucer without looking up from the print. 'Everything's divided into "good" and "bad" days. Well...' She looked directly at her patient. 'I've heard that one before...'

The psychiatrist eased herself back onto her stool, adjusting her reading glasses as she peered further into the page.

'Everything's arranged according to… nan… sha…'

'Nakshatras.'

'…nan-shatras… and the… *twelve lunar mansions.*'

'Loony-bins, yeh. They've got that bit right… that's certainly where the pair of 'em oughta be.'

The boy thought the news hilarious. Having watched the Reagan puppets be put through their paces enough times on the local cable as rulers of the seaside principality of So-Cal, this was hardly a very shocking 'revelation'.

'What *is* this record?'

'The song? "Rhiannon"… Fleetwood Mac.' Johanna turned to her companion: 'Where have you been for the past… fifty years?'

'*Fleetwood Mac?*' he squinted. 'Doesn't sound like Fleetwood Mac. Not any Fleetwood Mac I know…'

John took the waitress's pen from the counter and doodled over a photograph of former Governor Reagan. He traced a tiny cylinder around Ronnie's head, as in the astral diagrams of medieval astronomers.

Today was an extremely 'good' day for Ronald and Nancy Reagan. On this day, 5 November 1980, Ronnie completed his 32-year-long journey from President of the Screen Actors Guild to President of the United States. In keeping with that bare political fact, it was an unusually confident day for John Nightly.

All in all, it ranked as a very happy day, a most unusual, most convivial day. Outside, that is. Inside, things weren't quite so convivial. But they weren't impossible either. The ex-patient was experiencing quite a cylindrical day. Particularly at the moment, due to this hilarious newspaper report. It was certainly an *abnormal* day. To find this incongruous couple, she in bikini top and wrap, flip-flops and car keys, he with his multi-layers of fleece on this atomically hot morning, sitting at the bar of the old Regal Diner, downtown Santa Monica, amid the moms, dads and kids, traffic cops, florists, security guys and garden designers – the itinerant local workforce – and other consultant-psychiatrists from the local centre, being just… completely, absolutely 'normal', everything the boy had always fought against, was a most unusual and quite wonderful thing.

There was little point in John Nightly trying to behave any more politely or be any more responsive or 'nice' in general than he felt like being. Johanna had told him not to do that. Not to bother. His keeper wanted her charge to be himself. Absolutely real from now on. As real as John thought he could manage. As bad or good as he felt like behaving within the confines of this public space – 'out of the cage', so to speak. So as not to upset the toddlers and teens and delivery boys and PR men and pretty young actresses and pool guys and drivers and cops who frequented the old Art Deco dining car.

What SUMMER had achieved was to make John Nightly real again. Broken down all those layers. Stripped away and banished forever the easy charm, the well-meant smile, the fine, measured manners; the old-fashioned way of going about things drummed into him by Frieda which had initially lifted him above the competition, helped make him sophisticated – much more so than the other kids – and helped make him a star. Along with his talent of course. Although that was gone too. John no longer felt the need. The boy had no gumph or spunk left in him to create anything anymore. Nothing to get out and nothing to get up about. Pills, dope, acid, alcohol and the ensuing ego-loss and paranoia resulting from their prolonged use had seen to that. Creatively John Nightly was impotent. He just wasn't able to 'receive' musical ideas any longer. And did not expect to either. No longer a fount of creation, a guru, mystic or Master to anyone. John was just… ordinary now. As ordinary, or normal as they come; the one thing he'd spent his life fighting against.

'You know, Johanna… I used to have a very good, functioning, or "well-functioning" brain…' He took a breath as if about to say something profound. 'At least I think I did. But now… Reagan and all those guys? How do they – not "get away with it"… but *get through* it?' John shifted closer to Johanna. 'With me, it's not… Well, it's not… not as important as it used to be.'

He remembered his toastie, picked up a knife and cut into a square of butter.

'Pills… and other… all that *stuff*…' John took a bite. 'Must've… messed me up more than…' he swallowed. 'What it destroyed, you know?'

The patient cupped his hands around his coffee mug. He continued on the same tack, Johanna wishing they'd have stuck with astrology.

'What I ought to be saying is… I won't try it on, you see.' He looked directly at her. 'cos we've been… well… "seeing quite a lot of each other", I guess you… might say…'

Johanna affected an uncertain smile, not knowing quite how to deal with what might be coming and also embarrassed by her companion's turn of phrase. A gag? *Just kidding?* His idea of fun? Johanna hoped not. That would really be too unkind, after all this progress and her deciding to open herself up to him like this. Something she'd never allowed herself to do with any patient before. The CP put down the newspaper and squinted in the sunlight. John continued…

'What I mean is… maybe you've been seeing quite a lot of me… and I… I haven't actually been seeing so much of you.' John looked directly at her as the scene seemed to run out of juice and slowly grind to a halt.

He took a gulp of coffee, as if he were gulping for air. 'That's it really. What I've been meaning to say for some time…'

Johanna took a moment. She seemed relieved. 'You've helped me,' he droned on. 'And I haven't always been that… *appreciative*, have I?' He put down his cup. 'I know you got paid for it… I paid the bill, so I know it was… *well-paid* work. What you trained all those years for. You put me down for going back. I'm grateful to you.'

The consultant psychiatrist needed to get out of there. This kind of development being literally the last thing either of them needed right now. Johanna sought 'reality', but not actual emotion – not the 'from the heart'-type stuff flowing from the patient today. The kind she herself found difficult to deal with. And the way he played it. She still wasn't certain. She picked up her magazine.

'John…'

'I really thought that was "the route", Johanna. Getting high was… we all did. "God in a pill"… as someone said.'

Johanna felt sympathy for her veteran. She was moved by what he was trying to convey and found herself, against all professional instincts, feeling sorry for him.

'Maybe a pill is a kind of a guru,' he smiled. 'Or there's a weird "religion" pill – or whatever it is. It doesn't have to be a tab of speed, because "getting high" was… "getting low", really, and… I guess I went lower than most.'

'But most of them don't usually come back.'

'That's right.' The boy nodded. 'They don't… but that's because…'

It really was too much. Johanna didn't want it, and she certainly hadn't expected it. What she needed was for the patient to be kept on an even keel, although this quite tempered outburst was a further sign of John Nightly being in touch with his emotions again. Able to emote, express something; appreciation, in this case... love even. But though John himself had opened up, seeing himself – and themselves – in this situation as off duty, for the CP it wasn't like that. Johanna was still very much at work. Still getting paid. To sit there and listen to it.

For her, coffee and toasties at the Regal was no different to being in the consulting room. Johanna had a vested interest in John Nightly. A successful 'return' meant a significant financial gain for any consultant at her level. Not only from the patient directly, but also from the authority. Success in terms of the resident being weaned off the system and actually leaving the establishment brought rewards of donations from former inmates and their families. Almost uniquely for a business in any field, the SUMMER Center hoped their regular clients would leave them. One more success story, and excellent accumulative PR for the business.

At times, neither Hank nor Johanna believed the boy would ever actually 'come back'. But somehow, because of their individual skills and training and their adhering to the rules, John was at the point he was today. He lived and breathed, and retained what they calculated to be at least 85 to 90 per cent of former brain function. John Nightly was unaware that he was the longest long-stay patient the Center had ever entertained. *Top of the Pops* in 'psycho' hours.

The CP noticed the boy's eyes follow a pretty young college type as she moved along the aisle between the tables the entire length of the restaurant, attracting looks from every male diner. For a moment Johanna caught a glimpse of the young John Nightly, the boy who wandered the back streets of Cambridge seeking companionship and company. Eventually finding it in music and the gaggle of friends, personalities and hangers-on that came with it. Those interested in John because of his star potential and social potential, rather than his gift. It had been quite a journey. John and Johanna smiled at each other and got up. 'Rhiannon' was still going strong. They slid their seats neatly under the counter, put on their shades and walked out into the blazing heat.

[1] Nancy Reagan was a well-known user of astrologers, as most young players were during Hollywood's golden period. In its May 1988 issue, *People* magazine revealed that Nancy had consulted with socialite and Vassar-educated star-reader Joan Quigley, who had mapped out predictions based on both Nancy and Ronald's natal charts and advised on matters such as 'good' and 'bad' dates for world summits, congressional legislation and the bombing of Libya.

Ref: *What Does Joan Say?: My Seven Years as White House Astrologer*, Joan Quigley (Birch Lane), 1990.

'The memory of space is fleeting. When you get back, all you have left are your mind pictures'

John Pattern, astronaut

SURFING IN CORNWALL

GREETINGS FROM CORNWALL

The *Cornish Gardener*. July 2004. 'Weather Notes' by Martyn Davies.
The long-term maximum mean temperature in the South West in July is between 19°C and 21°C. In Exeter, the hottest July day in recent years was on the 21st in 1990 when the temperature reached 30.3°C. That's hot, although it has a long way to go to beat the hottest July on record in Devon on the 12th July, 1923 when 34.4°C was recorded at Killerton. But neither of those beat the national record of 36°C which was recorded at Epsom in Surrey on 22 July 1911. however, even if we don't see temperatures like those, with temperatures between 19 and 21°C you have to keep a watchful eye on the condition of your garden. With an average of 190 hours of bright sunshine a month in South Cornwall make sure you utilise that light, which is a vital part of summer gardening.

The black Jaguar made its way along the coast road heading eastwards – inland – as it left the ocean behind. A long, open carriageway, trimmed with gorse and ling, its contours following those of the cliff edge. With gleaming, translucent water on one side and a clear blue sky all around, the driver relaxed into his frayed leather seat and, using only one hand to steer the car, checked the time on his wristwatch before indicating to overtake a horsebox in front, the only other vehicle on the road this morning.

As he approached the junction to the A30, the dual carriageway that takes you over to the south peninsula, two hippie kids, dwarfed by their 9-foot longboards, waited at the roundabout ahead. The dudes stuck out their thumbs in a mocking gesture, never for one moment expecting a lift from the shiny black saloon. The driver acknowledged them with a nod as he cruised past, picking up speed now that he was on a proper road. RCN accelerated sharply, pulled down the sun guard to block out the harsh sea-reflected rays, and turned on the radio.

On the passenger seat beside him lay a pink-and-white-banded paper bag containing sweets. Shop-soiled sweets. Part of Mrs Peed's flood-damaged stock from a tobacconist in St Ives. Endy had bought twelve large jars of 'shop-soiled boiled': aniseeds, humbugs and sherbet rocks, along with a couple of boxes of waterlogged Toffee Crisps and Kit Kats. The wax wrappers lay strewn all over Trewin.

The news came on. Freddie Mercury had died of AIDS. The back streets of Kensington, where the singer lived, overflowed with grieving fans. RCN remembered going there once, to some party or other. Couldn't remember when exactly. Or what the occasion was. Maybe it was a different place altogether. It was becoming hard to recall very much from the old days, particularly detail, and dates, now that his head was full of propagation, cultivation and irrigation… and – much worse than that – the other thing that was on his mind this morning, the dreaded V-A-T. Tax-ation.

BANG!

A gull hit the car full-on. Slammed right into the windscreen. A deadening thud. Its oily trunk suckering the glass before it slid off the bonnet and onto the road. John flinched, fixing the steering wheel tight with both hands. He slowed, checking for traffic behind, pulled over onto the left-hand verge and stopped.

A glorious morning. Funnels of yellow light flooded the saloon. The driver wiped a bead of sweat from his forehead, took a deep breath and loosened the fabric around his neck. What the hell was the damned thing up to? It was lucky he had his wits about him today.

Sudden death, bird-wise, was of course not that unusual an occurrence in these parts. The previous time it had happened, in the middle of the summer, a black crow, disturbed by squirrels in the cypress trees, collided with the outside phone line connecting Trewin House to the rest of the world. The bird shot straight into the cable and pulled it down, more or less cutting itself in two in the process. The event put Trewin Exotics out of business for the remainder of the week, until BT engineers came over to fix it once they had managed to locate the heavily camouflaged entrance.

'Suicide mission?' the man had asked.

RCN turned off the engine and with it the radio, and the usual nauseating stock platitudes about Fred.

He got out, left the door ajar to let some air in the car, lit a Rothmans and allowed himself a moment to mentally return to where he had been just minutes before. The impact had squeezed a slick of black fluid from the filthy bird right across the windscreen; John took a duster from inside to wipe it off, then tossed the rag into the ditch.

It was actually chilly outside. As he looked back across the undulating rocks, the gorse fields and the ocean beyond, a flock of black-headed gulls flew overhead, searching for their friend. The nurse turned and gazed back in the direction of home. He wandered over to the dead animal, checked for any visible sign of disease, bent down, pulled a leather gardening glove from his pocket, picked the bird up by its tail and slung it into the bracken.

The onset of rheumatism and a tendency to travel even the shortest of distances by car meant that RCN's physical mobility was not what it used to be. As he lowered himself down into the beaten-up seat his knee cracked like a gun. A potato-lorry rumbled past as he prepared to get back on the road, the freight looking rather too casually tied as its pink-knotted ropes blew about in the wind along with a Cornish flag provocatively displayed atop the driver's cab. Coming up behind, a Cadogan Tate removal van transferring the worldly goods of some burned-out hedge-funder to the peace and relative calm of a coastal town. Another unwelcome foreigner from 'up country' having bought property that the locals could no longer afford. A home that would probably save a life in the way that lives had been saved at Trewin. The nurse waited for the road to clear again before he pulled back off of the verge and continued on his way.

It was always difficult to find a place to park in Penzance. And in Chapel Street more or less impossible. So RCN left the car down by the harbour and walked up the hill past the Wesleyan chapel towards the old town. Outside the Abbey Hotel a gasjet-blue coupé and a white scooter were parked precariously on the kerb. The hotel's breakfast room looked out onto the sunny street. Sitting at a table in the high recessed window he could see the outline of a woman in a shawl, her hair tied in a loose knot, almost like a living painting. There was a hairdresser opposite – Beachcomber – and John thought he might have time to pop in later on for a trim. He took off his cap and made sure to rub his boots rather furiously on the thick stubbly mat before entering the establishment. This unnecessary piece of business indicated that he was nervous, as there had been no rainfall at all in the region for five weeks. The whole of the West Country was dry as a bone.

item: 'Fifty Years': a weekly insight into people and their times.
This week the philanthropist Contessina Rafaella de Weyden speaks about living in London during revolutionary times. A presentation for Arté Channel Online by David Quickly-Jones.

Rafaella van der Weyden, we're delighted that you've been able to find time to come in and talk to us.

It's all my pleasure.

One of the things that comes across in your book as important in your life is your meeting and subsequent relationship with the singer John Nightly, who sadly passed away this week. Perhaps you can tell us how the two of you first came to meet?

This was because my father was the associate director of the Berliner Concert Orchester; and John had come to Berlin to give a concert and we were using the same concert hall and there was a cocktail… and I saw that my father was talking to this… extremely good-looking man! [laughs] And I remarked that my father wasn't bored! [laughs again] which he almost always was. And then I was introduced to this man and, and I think that, then, something happened and… [giggles]

You talk in your book about the two of you having to 'adjust' to one another?

Very much so, because I had been coming from a very… 'social' or 'society' family, as my father was a diplomat, and so our life was social or society in a way, and going out… and John was from a very small town, a pretty town in Cambridge, and it was very different for him, so he told me that as a family he had really never been out even to eat at a restaurant, not in their home town, even though there was a restaurant some doors away. Why should they do this when there was food at home, at the table, you see? [giggles again] Because of this, John, when I met him, was not really a 'people person' very much and the 'manners of society', can we say, or even the 'manners of the table'! [laughs] On the many occasions when there were the guests of… singers, actors… he would sit, his head… leaning by his elbows, seeming quite bored actually and talking in single-syllable 'yes' or 'no', unless there was anyone there who really…

He wasn't a great conversationalist?

He was not [giggles] because his… enthusiasm was for music, for talking about that and doing that, which was very like my father. But only 'in depth' – John did not want to issue comment on this week's 'sensations' – gossip 'scandals'. He was not interested in how many songs he himself was selling either, but the payments kept him happy, which they did I suppose, and he was also refusing his music to be played in films and such things. In terms of money, I think he was making a good… quite enough anyway, and of course making this money the way he wanted to… just very, very quietly living.

This attitude had a profound effect on you when you decided to begin the Foundation, which has grown to be one of the most… active and energetic philanthropic operations in the world, especially in the field of music commissioning.

In a way this was the reason I began. I had really done many things early in life, which I began to think, this is not so important, and… not so rewarding for me so much. So when my father died I did want… something which would be a 'permanent' pro-gramme in order to honour him by and this very much had to do with music, so that we could… develop long term in the fields of music and of art and so on. I would not have done that if I had not met and watched, observed, John – Nightly – when he was working and understood what his attitude was to creating his music and his very open mind into it and also for the… well, the absolute act of creation itself.

**BBC TV: *This Week*, 9 November 1968. 'Ape Box Metal':
The Albert Hall concert. Interview by David Peat.**

John... welcome to *This Week*

pleasure...

**Now... you're about to begin a tour of Great Britain with the
new LP; we've just heard an excerpt from it there – which will
of course culminate in your appearance with the Royal
Philharmonic Orchestra at London's Royal Albert Hall.
Now... what I want to ask you today is... You say that you're
intending to use 'wave power'... energy, for this one special
performance instead of the usual 'general electricity' as supplied by the mains grid?**

[John Nightly smiles as if to reassure the presenter]

Now... er hem... How exactly is this going to work?

'Oh, you look well!'

'Do I?'

The woman got up to embrace the farm manager. She put her
arms around his tubby frame and attempted the warmest of
hugs. RCN held out his arms too, but only to embrace her with
the lightest of touches. He understood all too well that
someone like himself, a person of relatively lowly capacity,
paunchily middle-aged with, no doubt, a very low level of
attraction to the opposite sex, could never be worthy of the
attention of such a beautiful creature.

'You look so well, John – tanned and brown – it's nice to see
you looking like this.'

'Red, you mean!'

Her eyes flashed as she remembered that her old friend had always found it impossible to accept even the most casual of compliments. Long ago in the past, kind words had often been met with a droll, even abrasive response. The pair smiled in agreement and sat down.

'It suits you being down here…'

'I came here first with my mum and dad. Summer holidays. You know when you get off the train? I noticed, even then, how everyone was bright red. Red-faced — and very thick-skinned; literally thick-skinned — rather than properly tanned. Same as they are now. All these old guys on the platform, with bright-red cheeks, not from the sun but from the wind — wind-tan, as they call it. "Wurzel cheeks",' he laughed, 'from walking along the coast and all that wind… well… I am now that red-faced man!'

RCN looked pleased with himself, having managed to deflect the woman's compliment with this pleasant observation and ease his general discomfort at being present this lunchtime.

To be polite, if nothing else, he ought to have paid the lady sitting opposite a compliment in return, as any other gentleman would. But he was far too shy and also quite overcome by the way she appeared before him today — even more dignified and serene than he remembered — to be thinking about etiquette. John Daly removed his anorak and draped it over the empty chair beside him while Iona looked around for a waitress.

I think the… the way that it'll work will… maybe I should start at the beginning. It is a bit complicated to explain — in a simple way, I mean — but… What we are going to be doing… if I do explain it simply, is 'harnessing' water power, natural water energy, the mass, the volume — the energetic part of the water — by connecting our… our guitars and our amps… amplifiers… and PA systems; everything… up to… well, you know… to the upper reaches of the River Thames…

'But what I don't understand, and never have done, after all this time – and it is a long time now; such a long time…' Iona untied her hair and let it fall onto her shoulders, making her look younger still than her forty-three eventful years.

'I don't absolutely understand, what is, at this moment in particular… the actual matter with him?'

Daly picked up a teaspoon and began playing with it. 'That's a very good question.'

'It is an absolutely long time, John, a long time now. Because most people with this problem, John's kind of problems, surely they can recover? Or have some type of… permanent medicine which can work, or what is it called – "regulate" them? By now…'

The farmer didn't hesitate. 'You'd have thought so.' He put down the spoon. 'But it's not that simple.'

'No, it's not. It's how we see things, though, isn't it?'

Iona picked up her glass as RCN caught a whiff of the past. What looked like fresh orange juice, the pith sparkling in the sunlight, was laced with two, maybe three shots of Scotch whisky. A waitress came over. Daly ordered a gammon sandwich and a half of shandy.

'It's a very, very difficult thing… for him to deal with, obviously… And also for us to deal with… day to day.'

'Yes. And tell me… who is "us"?'

Daly turned redder still. 'Right… Well… I suppose we've got a proper little family now,' RCN smiled. 'In a way anyway. That sounds a bit… presumptuous, maybe. No women, I mean… apart from a housekeeper… you know, she's old – "elderly", I mean – oh dear!' RCN rubbed his eyes and looked rather ashamed. 'Lady from Quethiock who keeps us all in check, you might say. You'd like her. There's the guy who runs the business, proper plantsman, Robert, reliable chap, keeps everything the way it should be plant-wise, and takes care of other stuff, well… Then there's me and… the boss.'

RCN calculated that he was roughly halfway through the allocated time. Certain questions he had anticipated having to deal with were being seen to; those he dreaded were just around the corner. 'As I say… it is difficult for everyone… But all I can tell you is that things are better now.' He coughed. 'He… is better now… generally, I mean. Day to day. Really better.' His lunch companion peered into her glass as Daly continued.

'What they did manage to sort out over there – and this was obviously a major achievement, which made things a lot, lot easier for us…' RCN spoke nervously, 'was to get him off the bad drugs – I don't mean the "bad", bad drugs…' He slid the empty glass in front of him from side to side. 'He'll never touch those again – they'd kill him if he did. I mean the bad prescription drugs – because they were doing as much damage as the other ones… in my opinion. The ones that were making him… numb. So at least, you see… as he says himself… he's not numb anymore.'

Iona lit a cigarette. She was battling hard to follow the rather long, rather too drawn-out, defensive-sounding explanation.

'You sound like him… the way you…'

Daly looked sheepish again. It sounded like a compliment, but also a criticism.

'Well, we've been with… around each other… a long time now, Iona.'

'So… this is how I understand it… and it's only in part, his condition at the moment, that is… only in part due…'

'To all the stuff he chucked down his throat. That's correct. That's what I understand. What I was told, by them, anyway.'

Iona stared at the defendant.

'The actual "condition", or whatever it is all really… this… the thing you sent me?'

'That's it.'

'Because I certainly didn't understand this one!'

Iona adopted a rather hurt expression. She didn't seem at all convinced as she sat forward in her chair.

'Because… you are a qualified doctor. You know these things. Everyone forgets this.'

The farmer turned pink.

'I've got *nursing* qualifications, Iona. But even that was a long time ago.' RCN was desperate to eat something. It was a fair few hours since Mrs Peed's cooked breakfast. 'It's all changed now; if you were to go into it in a professional way, I mean.'

He smiled sweetly and looked around to see where his order had gotten to. Iona pressed on.

'But… you can at least… understand these things… What you mean is the hormone, adrenaline?'

RCN nodded.

'So can you start again, please? Sorry, but I… I really didn't understand what you said on the telephone… and my husband, he was talking to me as usual… and I… I don't know… I could not concentrate…'

She suddenly appeared beaten down. 'That's why I thought it would be better to meet.'

[John Nightly cupped his head in his hands. He couldn't wait to get back to the Albert Hall soundcheck].

RCN was in need of immediate refreshment and was relieved to see his shandy arrive. He took a swig, raising his glass to his lunch companion.

'It's been... cliché though it might be... a hell of a long time, Iona.'

'It's a lifetime, John. Really it is... *another* lifetime.'

RCN put down the glass and swallowed – another bit of business – ready to continue with the tale.

'What they discovered in America is that John... when his body produces adrenaline... it's... There's some kind of fault in it, in his metabolism... the adrenaline metabolism as it works in the brain.'

RCN gathered his cardigan around him and pulled down the cuffs, suddenly feeling a draught. 'Let me get this right... so I tell it properly.' The fat man looked around the room and took a moment.

'John's condition... which is not... uncommon, apparently... If they don't do tests and whatever... whatever it is they do, they'd... It'd never've been discovered in the first place...'

'And this means?'

'...that instead of producing adrenaline "normally", like... a "reasonable" amount of the stuff... like it occurs in everyone else – naturally and all that – it means that in John's case he's... when his brain is producing – secreting – the hormone, it's actually making... an "unreasonable" amount... so unreasonable that it's actually *something else* – or it was. And that something else is partly, amazing as it might sound... a substance... chemical... or a compound, very close to mescaline.'

Iona raised her eyes in dismay. Not knowing quite how to respond, she turned away from the trustee towards the light streaming through the hotel entrance, where the noonday sun cast an ambiguous shadow, an almost human form, onto the arched doorway of the old abbey.

'You mean "mescaline" mescaline? The "bad drug" mescaline?' Iona looked at once disbelieving and suspicious. 'The "really bad" drug?'

RCN squinted in the sunlight. Iona looked straight at him –

John...'

– her eyes suddenly becoming watery, 'it doesn't make sense to me today.'

'I know. Sounds ridiculous... bit... comical.' RCN noticed his gammon sandwich making its way through the tables. 'The really "very bad" drug. That's what it is and that is the actual fact. Medical thing. Chemical thing.' RCN acknowledged the waiter. 'Thank you – looks good!' He took the plate from the young man and laid it in front of him. 'I saw the results – there's a copy of the whole thing up at the house. Reams of the stuff. And......' RCN removed the top slice of bread and picked up a jar of mustard. 'What I've just told you. It means that this "process" produces a kind of... *psychosis*. So that his brain is making a... Well, it's hallucinating.' Daly took a knife to spread far too much mustard onto the chunky ham. 'Like a... a... "hallucinatory" substance.'

Iona lodged her cigarette on the rim of her saucer. She lay the palms of her hands together and cupped them around her chin, trying to make sense of the whole weird tale. '*So*... the question... whether this thing – "process" – was happening *before* John got into... you know... doing a lot of things?'

'That's exactly…'

'When he was… a child, for instance?' Iona's eyes were wide open.

'The actual "problem substance", the "chemical" his brain is making, is called *adrenochrome*.' RCN took a bite. 'You can look it up in all the medical… textbooks… It's there. There was a programme on the radio about it. And it's always been there; it's not a new thing or anything. It's just… a derivative… of adrenaline.'

The woman seemed to relax a little. Her friend had been convincing and she was impressed at the ease with which he navigated the 'medical' side of the explanation.

'You're good at this, John.'

Daly blushed again. It seemed the grilling might be more or less over.

'It's in the table of "known hallucinogens", as they say. The consultant explained to me. They have… evidence that adrenochrome does occur in the normal brain. They tried giving it to patients in trials… The effects of people actually taking the stuff is that it produces symptoms close to clinical schizophrenia.' RCN pulled a string of ham from his tooth. 'So there you are. That just about sums him up and does actually all make sense. Same stuff Aldous Huxley was writing about.'

'Was it? You're much more up for it… *on* it, I mean… "with it!" – than I am.'

RCN smiled as he recalled her endearing difficulties with the language.

'We've got all the research papers at home. *John Smythies* is the name I remember – the guy who wrote a lot about the syndrome.

Couple of hundred pages sitting in a plastic bag somewhere. And stuff related to it about epilepsy and fits... "flicker" – *strobes* and all that...'

'Oh, no... not that... He was always going mad about that... that... "flicker-machine."

RCN licked his lips. 'Hmn... good food...'

'John is not epileptic, though...'

'Not... no... never has been. But that has got something to do with it, the condition. Symptoms. Like when you have a band with a strobe on the telly and they tell people not to watch it... if they're epileptic.'

'And he knows about all this?'

'He knows everything about it. Understands it a lot better than I do. Gets updates from the Center... new findings... the whole bit. Could have already been happening when he was a kid. But maybe that's what gave him all his ideas and everything as well, y'see. Maybe that was his... juice. Never know, do you?'

Iona stared at the red-cheeked, middle-aged farmer. After all these years, all these... changes... difficult times. He still had only sweet things to say about John Nightly.

'Ideas... exactly. All those ideas, damn ideas... things he wanted to do. The true problem with everything...'

...it's hardly a very radical idea. Most of the industrial revolution was powered by water, after all. What do you think kept the mills going? [the interviewee punctuated his response with a series of long yawns] *Isaac Newton made models of windmills and watermills as a child. Then you had water clocks as well. So I don't think...* [the boy thought for a second] *Even Constable's* Hay Wain – *the best-known picture in England* – *shows his father's mill, Flatford Mill, the water*

wheel… the ultimate… idyllic view of the English countryside. Well, that's
a little bit like my wave-hub!

RCN picked over the other half of his sandwich as Iona lifted
a large, rusty cake tin up onto the table.

'Could I ask you to do one thing for me, John…'

She turned the object round so the lid was facing him. 'This is
a present for John – and for you as well, of course.' Iona raised
her hand and made a gesture as if to stop him from responding.
'I know you don't want me to give him anything; and I know
he doesn't know that we're meeting today or anything like this.
I understand all this… but it might, as my husband will say…
re-kindle memories… I thought so anyway. John always used to
like it.'

Outside in the real world, Chapel Street, a funeral procession
was attempting to bypass vehicles parked illegally in front of
John Wesley's chapel. Eventually the hearse had to unceremo-
niously climb the kerb for several yards, causing astonishment
among holidaymakers and shoppers admiring the expertly
polished limousines. As it did so the funeral director rolled
down the window, stuck two fingers up in the direction of the
hotel and cursed the owner of the damned coupé.

item: Monthly Cultural Notes: June.

June brings a marked change in the garden, with regular watering and feeding becoming essential. Don't forget 'critter control', with snails, slugs and all manner of unwanted guests dropping by this month. Use cane stakes and twine on your peonies and poppies. Feed flowering cacti. Cut back Regal Pelargonium and snip your patio roses. Prick out violas and pansies sown last month. Deadhead faded blooms and place hanging baskets outdoors. Remember to strim before mowing the lawn and borders this month as growth can be 'triffid-like'!

The inability to carry out any domestic task properly, in terms of devoting the correct amount of energy to it or having suitable tools with which to complete it, was a common thread running through all aspects of John Nightly's existence.

Maybe it was the fact that he had begun his recording career trying to create 48-track tapestries on a 2-track loom, never being able to either hear or see what he was doing; unable to physically realise the sounds he imagined. Maybe it was because the Nightly family, living on a fixed income, had never received any win, windfall or legacy to alleviate, even temporarily, the grim fixtures of debt imposed by the government on all of the people of England to control them and keep them down. John's parents never experienced the luxury of spare cash or savings of any sort in order to enjoy very much… *variety*. From the basics: basic food staples, basic everyday clothes and basic British holidays – those spent sheltering in amusement arcades, fish-and-chip restaurants and pinball halls. For the Nightlys, life occurred – as it did in almost every British household of the late 1950s and early sixties – in the context of what was affordable. A quality of life possible within the economic constraints of the family income, rather than what might be achieved with a little imagination or… ambition. 'Ambition' was not exactly a byword of the times.

At his secondary school careers talks had centred not around professional careers or vocations but a *job*, a *steady* job, to occupy your time and bring in a salary – though most probably not much of one. The kind of job which might one day be needed to 'fall back on'. But John Nightly was an impatient soul. It wouldn't have occurred to him that he might ever need to fall back. Failure was not something the boy had factored in. Not because he was in any way arrogant – he was barely confident most days – but because he recognised his own ability. Understood what he had. It was greater than most men's; John knew that. And so, whenever people complimented him on how clever or 'gifted' he was, rather than put on a self-effacing, half-arsed smile and thereby, in a way, denying his gift, John would simply reply: 'I know.' A quick, dismissive acknowledgement of what talent and application had allowed him to achieve.

The boy was stifled by the numbing conformity and social-ladder-climbing he found in the little satellite village of Grantchester and at his primary and secondary schools. John longed to get away from Meadow Road and its ponies and guard dogs, its acquiescent sons and daughters, nervous curtains and unforgiving tongues. John Snr and Frieda had no cash for anything but the most basic seasonal gifts. Soap, socks and shortcake biscuit for Christmas with perhaps a toy, book or a card for birthdays. The young Nightly and his very ascetic parents were therefore used to having to make do. Improvisation was the key to advancement. The key to survival. It became the key to John Nightly's life.

John would never begin any task, musical or otherwise, with preparation. He'd just start. At Trewin, the boss would walk into the rose garden and begin pruning vintage tea roses with an old potato knife. Why didn't he ask Robert for secateurs? the nurseryman wondered. There were at least twenty pairs, old and new, lying around the kitchen/outhouse area. It would also have been worth checking with his gardener whether the roses had already been pruned…

Of course, John Nightly didn't have to ask the gardener for permission to do anything. John Nightly could do whatever he liked. He could take a rotavator to the rose garden if he so desired. But it would have been better, more sensible and, in the long run, cheaper to ask.

In his second summer at Trewin, Kemp complained that the reason that year's 'Golden Dawn' were showing approximately half as many buds as the previous season was the boss's insistence on pruning a collection of the finest hybrid teas in the South West with nail clippers.[1]

John would water huge swathes of dahlias and hollyhocks with bottles of expensive mineral water, removed from the fridge by the kitchen door because they were 'handy'. This resulted in RCN instructing Robert to hide the plastic bottles on shelves in the main garage, thereby creating a nuisance for both Mrs Peed and Mawgan every time they needed one. John's excuse was that either he could never remember where the outside tap was – there wasn't one, except for the industrial pump by the meadow – or because he hadn't been able to lay his hands on one of the tens of thousands of brightly coloured plastic watering-cans accumulated at Trewin over the years.

But it wasn't just gardening matters. Sometimes, in the kitchen, much to Endy's alarm, John would cut a slice of bread not by placing it flat on the breadboard like everyone else but holding the loaf in the palm of his right hand while he sawed vertically down into it with his left. If the knife slipped, the boss risked either a very nasty gash or possible death were the blade to pass through the loaf and into his main artery. On these occasions Mrs Peed would stand over him, teeth on edge, imploring John to *please* let her do it for him, which he would of course refuse. At which point she'd run out into the back garden shouting: *'I can't watch him! I can't look!'*

Other times, instead of taking his coffee cup to the sugar bowl, like the rest of Porthcreek, John would carry a heaped tea-spoonful of loose granules all the way across the kitchen en route to the cup. Spilling half of it in the process, which meant that Endy would have to firstly pretend she hadn't noticed and then wait for him to leave the room before she got out the vacuum cleaner to sweep up the sticky white mess.

The solution for the put-upon housekeeper was to greet her employer every morning, and indeed every time he wandered into her domain, with the words, 'I bet you'd like a nice cup of coffee... or a piece of toast... wouldn't you?'

Thereby avoiding an unnecessary outing for the Hoover and the possible sudden demise of a sixties legend.

In another annoying little habit, John would make notes and sketches on any scrap of paper that was handy, using a dead match, somehow never able to locate one of the hundreds of writing implements lying around the house. Sheets of newspaper doubled as dishcloths and safety-pins became trouser zips in John Nightly's make-do habitat. He never complained about any of it, of course, except for the odd 'Can't find a damned pen!' or 'Where *is* the watering can? I had it a minute ago...' and never, ever, not even once, would he shout or give any sense of displeasure in the direction of either RCN or his faithful housekeeper. John Nightly understood very well where his real bread was buttered.

The boss never had any problem with his other half. Without his roadie/nurse-cum-companion/minder, John Nightly, the real John Nightly – the one we're interested in – couldn't have existed. It was that simple and also most likely true in reverse. The doom and gloom of Nightly and the 'Lux Eterna', unfailing optimism, of Daly. Without each other, one would have been dead long ago while the other would be sat in a care home some-where, maybe close by, earning the minimum wage as he attended a ward of vegetation, the human kind. If not that, they'd both be sweeping the streets. The thought must have run through both men's minds many times over the past thirty summers. So generally, and with very good reason, as though a *No Moaning* agreement had been entered into long before, neither John ever complained or found fault with anything at all.

But then, there was literally nothing to moan about. Because in terms of where they were ten or fifteen years back... this was a big improvement. A whole lot better. Bliss consciousness superseding even that outlined by the Maharishi. Because this, this loony state, this soft, spineless life – no pressure, no rush – or, as Mawgan said, almost constantly, 'no worries', was reality. This way of going on, getting from one flickering frame to the next, one dislodged event to another, became Daly and Nightly's 'normal'.

And look what they had to show for their pain. Carn Point had become their true *Savenheer*, their haven, their 'normal'. At least as normal as it ever could be – for the two Johns.

The new domestic environment provided the first taste of regular living either of them had experienced. Nine-to-five normal. Weekend normal. Extended-family, TV-meal normal. Giving a damn about anyone else normal. *Boring* normal, in the very best sense.

When John Nightly was in a playful mood, which he was roughly once a year from '73 up to around early 2002, and this very subject – 'normality' and the cares and woes of everyday – came into conversation, the former megalomaniac would sit down and serenade his good friend and companion with Rodgers and Hammerstein's 'Cockeyed Optimist'. A couple of lines were sufficient. No big deal. Just a jaunty sing-along of what was most certainly the pair's least favourite song from the whole 'normal' world.

---

[1] In 2005, the National Council of Rose Breeders completed a five-year long trial into methods of pruning roses. The results showed that a randomly wielded chainsaw produced exactly the same results as meticulous deadheading and topping, laying to rest centuries of mumbo-jumbo, myth and method. (NCRG Council report, 1 September 2005.)

Life was quiet. So if any exciting event occurred – like the Friday John almost burned down the house after covering his fan heater with a damp copy of the *Cornishman* (he was trying to dry it out before reading it) – news would leak and circulate around the community faster than you could say 'the house on the hill'.

Friday was also delivery day for local tradesmen – so the 'bread man', the 'organic man', the 'apple man' and the 'egg man', along with the Penwith recycling teams, night-time truck drivers and the two 'fish men' all came under suspicion as leakers of the amazingly uneventful tale.

During the event itself, it had taken longer than it should have for anyone to notice the puffs of smoke emanating from the widely-read newspaper because Robert was outside attending a bonfire and Mawgan was in the music room on headphones and spliff, oblivious to the outside world. But the story became the talking point of Porthcreek and beyond for most of the summer, archived in the collective memory of the inhabitants of both the village itself and the wider local area. Eventually becoming dramatised, and embroidered with all manner of detail, until, as with most other stories involving John Nightly, mutating into complete fiction – i.e. it was not a copy of *Playboy* magazine, it did not happen in the middle of the night, the perpetrator wasn't on a wild acid trip and the house did not actually burn down.

In September, with the holidaymakers gone, things were quieter still. Endy and Mawg would sometimes take a mid-afternoon walk up through the fields overlooking the ocean bay. Not the grazing area along the coast path, but the couple of acres of potatoes and barley a little further up, where the cotton lavender gradually changed from a deep purple to a streaked lilac as it sloped down to the sea.

Armed with her British Birds *Handy* guide, a recent buy from the Sue Ryder shop in Penzance, Endy spotted sparrowhawks, black-tailed godwits and even a dunlin or two on the lavender slopes.

The hawks loved to build nests around the little orchard where Robert mixed red loam with tomato compost so it could be broken down to a fine tilth for sowing. Up in that part of the property there was also a patch of Japanese flowering cherry, rosary vine and blue geranium, the latter turned this unusual colour by Robert making a series of small incisions into the roots with a rusty razor blade. These aberrations, cultivated specially to adorn John RCN's new dining-room conservatory, were much admired by the bread man, both fish men, the egg man and the night-time truck-drivers.

'Silence, ye troubled Waves, and thou Deep, peace!'

John Milton, *Paradise Lost* (Book VII)

Only local people winter by the sea. So the regular inhabitants of the farmhouses along the headland brought the area's seasonal population to around forty. The coastal fields shimmered in the soft October light and the white foam roared in the distance, as always. In the low branches of the Sequoia, redpolls purred and bleated, while up above, storm petrels took flight, making bat-like changes in direction, as Endy and Mawgan tracked them in the dappled sunlight, fascinated by their instinctive navigation systems.

Every band or group has a member who is popular with every other member of the band, the 'brilliant bloke' or 'glue' within the set-up. Someone who everyone likes, gets on with and respects. In creative terms, this is not necessarily the most talented recruit. At Trewin, Mrs Peed soon became that glue, that centre. The Johns often wondered how on earth they'd managed before she arrived. How had they? With her flesh-coloured spectacles and faded pink sunhat (which she quickly renamed a 'rainhat' whenever the weather changed), she rushed from room to room creating a kind of life at the white farm somehow. Mainly because of her unflagging industry, her domestic wisdom and her obsessive attention to the very highest standards of cleanliness and hygiene. Endy wasn't getting any younger, though, and so, on the odd occasion when she would have one of her 'turns', a hot flush followed by slight dizziness, the company would gather round, suddenly become believers and offer anything in the world as long as the former housemaid from Quethiock would magically become 'alright' again, 'back to normal' as soon as possible.

Early November and the tides had changed, giving the bay a high stretch of water at lunchtime, the warmest part of the day. November brought the area's annual surfing competition, so with Julian Tregan deserting the waves at Fistral beach, and Mawgan in possession of a new balsa board, the entire household – minus the boss, of course – decided to brave the slimy, lichen-covered path leading to the old graveyard as they wandered down through the dripping caves.

Mawgan, Robert and Endy made themselves as comfortable as possible on a hard granite recess. Buttoned up top to toe, they followed the action from the safety of the rocks. Some fifty yards out, the line-up waited patiently for a big enough swell. As the water gently lapped over the competitors and their boards, Julian, ever the showman, checked his ankle-leash as he waved back towards the headland. He looked every bit the champion with his 9-foot board – a white single-fin pintail – attached to his wrist by what appeared to be an oversized curly-wurly guitar-lead.

Mawgan's ambition was more modest. As he rested on the slippery rocks beside the overheating Endy, his rubber flippers tied to each ankle in a loose-knotted bow, the *Mink Bungalow* theme swirled around in his head.

'Get yourself drowned out there if you don't tie them up properly!' Endy motioned to the kid to move closer, indicating a large hollowed-out space in the rock.

Mawgan's flipper ribbons dangled on the slime. His hair, the longest he had worn it since his arrival at Trewin, was matted with seaweed and sand. The kid looked like a member of Jethro Tull. Out there in the ocean a neat line of dudes and several respected elders – a seventy-year-old lady from Portreath had won last year's St Ives Bay one-day championship – awaited the next wave.

The sun beat down, playing tricks with perspective, phasing the sea-line, as a parade of marshmallow lighthouses appeared along the coast; the light bouncing from the vibrating sands to the topaz waves, reducing the visually complex scene to two parallel strips of tangerine and turquoise – sand and sea. The wide horizontal of the shore and the ocean beyond it reverberating in the sheer noise of the heat, resembled nothing so much as the slick graphic of a Visa card.

Mawg ambled down to the water, his half-size board tucked under his arm. Splashing through rockpools in his oversize flippers, the kid waded knee-deep through the foam, dragging the board behind him to take his place in the line-up.

'Dudes!'

A lone dude twenty yards further out shouted back along the line, as the water sparkled and swelled behind them.

'Here't comes!'

As if choreographed in some aquatic chorus line, Julian and his compadres twisted ninety degrees onto the swell in order to hit the wave head-on. Suddenly it was beneath them. Julian jumped straight on it, paddling halfway down the face; then, as the oxygen of the wave increased, he stood up straight, assuming a classic 'fencing' position as he attempted to ride it, diving left and right, flexing every muscle in his lean body to pick up the curl, utilising the energy of the water to try to slip into the tube of the powerful wave.

So elegantly poised was he, skimming along on the breaker to the delight of Endy and Robert until... in an instant... the wave beneath him collapsed, as if someone had suddenly pulled its plug. The rider was given no choice but to dismount and turn inwards on the thing, letting his board go. Julian was left bobbing up and down, abandoned in the foam, distraught to be suddenly breathless and cold – literally deflated.

Mawgan had already been licked. With nothing like the experience of his referee, Mawg had hit the big one head-on and simply crashed into it, picking up nasty bruises from the hard bank of water. The kid was left swilling around in its wash while Julian was already back at the line-up, waiting for the next one.

item: 'Wave Dragon: the first Danish Wave Energy Converter', Wave Dragon
APS press release. January 2003.
Erik Friis-Madsen got the idea to *Wave Dragon* in 1987. The *Wave Dragon* prototype
was successfully launched in Aalborg, Denmark. The Wave Energy Converter will soon
be deployed at the test site in Nissum Bredning and tested.

The launch of the 237 tonnes prototype *Wave Dragon* was a milestone in the rewarding
development and cooperation between the Wave Dragon inventor Erik Friis-Madsen,
coordinator Hans Sørensen, SPOK AsP, Aalborg University and companies from Denmark,
UK, Ireland, Austria, Germany and Sweden.

After launch, *Wave Dragon* tugged to Nissum Bredning for extensive testing activities
to optimise the *Wave Dragon* technology. Wave Dragon will be connected and produce
electricity to the grid over a longer period of time.

From 2003 to 2005 a development consortium will perform long term and real sea test
on hydraulic behaviour, turbine strategy and power production to the grid. The 4.35 mill.
$\Leftrightarrow$ project has been secured through substantial grants from the Danish Energy
Administration (1.7 mill. $\Leftrightarrow$), EU (1.5 mill. $\Leftrightarrow$) and from the Danish system operator
Elkraft System's RTD fund (0.25 mill. $\Leftrightarrow$).

Wave Dragon is a slack moored device of the overtopping type, consisting of two wave
reflectors focusing the waves towards the ramp, where water overtops into a reservoir.
The pressure height in the reservoir is converted into power through a number of variable
speed axial turbines.

In a project co-funded by the Danish Energy Agency and the EU, a model Kaplan turbine
especially designed for the low and varying heads and flows has been developed and
tested with very promising results. This and 6 new turbines will be installed on the
prototype in the ongoing Nissum Bredning project. The prototype is designed as a 1:1
(full-size) model relatively to the wave climate in Nissum Bredning. This corresponds to
1:4.5 for a North Sea Wave Dragon and a 1:5.2 scale for a Wave Dragon in a 36 kW/m
wave climate.

Due to scale effects the rated power will be 20 kW resembling 4 MW when deployed
in a relatively low-energy (24 kW/m) wave climate and 7 MW when deployed in a 36
kW/m climate. The prototype activities are expected to establish the necessary knowledge
in order to deploy a full-scale offshore *Wave Dragon* in 2006.

Contact & Information:
Wave Dragon ApS
Blegdamsvej 4
DK-2200 Copenhagen N
Denmark

He's in! He's on! He's John-nie Wal-ker! **This is Radio Caroline International on 259 metres on the medium wave-band broadcasting three and a half miles off the Frinton, Essex coast…**

Beaming up the love from the North Sea tonight. This is Free Radio. It's ten o'clock and that means it's *Johnnie Walker's Ten O'Clock Turn-on Time!* By the way, thanks to everyone who writes in and says 'thanks Caroline' for defeating the British government and keeping going – you can depend on us. We're gonna be here forever – good on yer, we're gonna be here forever! Now, anybody listening in the car? For anyone driving around Frinton – Frinton in Essex – the sea has calmed down tonight. I might just try getting out on the deck, at about 11.30, so stick your cars around Frinton, point your lights out towards the sea and get your headlights flashing – that'll be at around eleven o'clock tonight. Coming up is *Walker's One to Watch* this week on Caroline. In the old days you used to be able to see the lights of Radio London just a little way away from the ship but now it's just me and Caroline – we're out here all on our own.

[He places a purple-labelled disc on the turntable]

Now… who's gonna vote for Harold and the Labour government after they put the pirates off the air? And what d'ya get instead? BBC Radio 1? It went off the air at seven o'clock tonight! They've all gone to bed! Coming up, we got the Yardbirds, the Mamas & the Papas, but first, a big favourite out here, this is John Nightly and…

Church Lane, Trumpington, Cambridge. The home of Jani and Valerie Feather, Monday, 11 January 1968.

'Before you say anything… please let… please let me speak…' The boy's eyes stayed trained on the piano in the corner of the room. 'I'm really sorry, but I've… I've come to see you to say something in person and… and… I'll have to just… do it… say it… all pretty quickly now.'

'Is that why you're talking so fast, John?' Jana carried on sorting through her papers.

'Yeh… I mean, *no* – what do you mean?' The boy looked aimlessly around the room. '*Please*… it's taken all of my energy to… and strength, to come here and…'

'Come by foot, did you?'

'Jaan…'

'*John*…'

The boy jumped back in: 'Jaan… let me speak,' he fumbled. 'And say… 'cos I… I think, I mean – I don't "think", I *know* – I know that I will ever… I mean, *never*… I never will meet… anyone – a woman, I mean – a woman, any woman, anywhere, so… who is so… would be so… completely…… completely… *suitable*… for me, and…'

'Go fuck yourself, John.'

The girl slapped a ruler down on the table. 'I *suit* you?'

'*Yes* – I mean, no… I mean, you don't… Well, you don't…'

'I *don't* suit you… at the moment… Think I'm getting it now.'

'God… *Christ*, look… "suitable"… That isn't the word, obviously. I… it's…'

John breathed deep breaths then puffed out his cheeks in exasperation as the 'love of his life' re-ordered the carefully drawn plans on her drawing board and placed a soft cover over them. Jana would not be going back to her work today.

'How about if you save yourself all the agony and let *me* say something?'

The girl collected her pens and pencils into a tidy heap. She turned straight on to her former hero, who carried on speaking.

'...what I would like to say... it's like this, really. I say this in such a way, I mean, the way that I actually mean it. Mean every word... nuance...'

Jana fixed him.

'Why don't you just piss off and leave me alone, John. That's what *I* want to say. That's the sum of my thoughts and nuances, my... my *darling*. And go and be with your models and actresses and... ballet dancers... Contessas – all that *fucking... crap*... and leave reasonable people... people like me... *suitable* people... alone. Well alone.'

John spoke in a whisper, as if he were afraid someone might hear – though there was no one else in the house.

'...Contessinas...'

'*Contessafuckers*... is what I mean!'

Jana paused. 'I got that wrong actually, didn't I! What *I* mean... It's you that's a Contessa-fucker, isn't it? Not them! You're that alright, John. What a changed man you are. So easily influenced. So easily softened. So... smoothed out. So easily... fucked, presumably. Not at all the... bright, ambitious individual, the *bright starre*, the dedicated... loyal (believe it or not)... *village* boy... "real" boy I used to be... to *know*...'

She spoke hysterically but still nervously, before turning back to gather up the remaining items on her desk – pencil sharpeners, metric rulers and set squares – realising she had nothing at all to occupy her hands. Jana continued to speak with her back to John. 'What on *earth* happened to you, boy?' Her brain barely able to get her mouth to produce any kind of dignified sound.

'Better go off and fuck 'em,' she sniffed, finally letting go at last, 'then go and fuck them around. Like you did me. Why don't you? Probably are already. Fucking them around, I mean. What the hell are you doing here, anyway? You don't owe me any money or anything, do you? Did I put in a bill for a million coffees or… ten thousand "cheese snacks"… five hundred bus fares?' Jana swallowed and turned round to him. 'You left me alone for such a long time. What is it suddenly that… ?' She broke off. 'You really don't give a fuck for me – about me – do you?'

Jana held on to a side table to steady herself. She picked up a gold cigarette-box in the shape of a violin.

'No response? What's the matter with you then? You used to have plenty of words.' She took out a cigarette and lit up. 'D'ya hear me, John? What I'm saying here? Why don't you fuck off… *fuck off, FUCK OFF!* And be with that one, and that one… and that one… See how long they last with you? See how long they put up with it. *Contessa… Waydown* or whatever she's…' Jana took two long drags in quick succession. 'The numbness of not being with you, John. Total numbness. That's what I've been experiencing… while trying to… hate you and absolutely loathe you and… detest… and wish something bad would happen to you for all the bad you've done me… And then… hang on to you – or the memory of you – for some weird, crappy reason I don't understand. Don't know why. Have no idea why.' Jana turned back to face the wall. 'And to myself, trying to somehow hang on to myself…' she sobbed. 'Go and try it, boy. See if you can experience the things with them that you experienced… with…'

The boy, almost choking with stifled tears, awoke from his slumber.

'This is not... *God*... Christ Almighty... I mean I... I won't... I can't... I don't expect to be able to...'

'Good, John. Good. Go on, cry, cry... cry your fucking eyes out... blare like a kid...' She held her hand to her throat as if having difficulty breathing. 'You fucking arsewipe, John.'

The boy, disintegrating rapidly, blathered on. Apart from anything else, never in the ten years since he met Jana Feather had he ever heard her swear. The girl's language, a free-expression soufflé of unadulterated spite he associated with Pondy or Lee, freaked him out almost as much as the terrifying reality of the situation itself.

'I know I won't be able to... cannot experience those things again – things I experienced with you.' He looked round for a tissue. 'You know I can't. That... was the start of everything, where it all came from. *You* were the start of it... when things – influential things – got to be discovered, and...'

Jana dabbed her eyes with her handkerchief and turned away from the twerp standing before her, who blabbed and sobbed too, making little sense, really making a terrible, terrible job of what he had come to do.

'Discovering music, being with you... being really, really...'

'That's *what* it was!' The student continued to pitilessly mock.

'Your family... being with them... this isn't what I came to say, but... a normal family, getting away from mine, watching how your family... *operated*... your mother and father...'

'Operated? You've really got it sorted out, fucker... I was "suitable" and they "operated"... we must have been a very convenient family indeed.'

'I do mean "operated". Important to say it. How they related to each other. A proper… unit. A really… a loving family.'

'You can tell?'

'Godsake, Jaan… it was such a different… different to mine, you know it was… completely…'

'*John*…' Jana blew a stream of smoke in the direction of the open window. John furiously rubbed his eyes.

The architectural student, having edged closer, positioned herself a foot away from the slobbering, shaking cretin. Point blank.

'I want to ask one thing, John. Quick little thing. If you will do me the honour – the last thing you'll ever, ever have to do for me – of answering it honestly.' She moved in close. 'Let me ask you this…'

Jana wedged the heel of one foot inside the inner step of the other, the position her father had recommended she assume when about to embark on a particularly difficult task like singing a solo as a member of her school choir. Perfectly balanced, she stood bolt upright in front of her assailant.

'Did you like being with me? Did it do anything for you? Did you like being with me at all? Did you ever really… *like* me… even know me, were you ever… even a little bit interested in me?'

'What do you mean *like you?* I loved you. So much, Jaan. So… so much. I loved you… I love you now.' He twitched. 'Not "loved", I mean – *love* – I *still* love you. I *will* love you. Every day I will. For all time as well. I know it sounds… stupid, put like that. For all that time. It's true. Every day of my… you know that. I want you to know…'

'Get out please.'

The girl turned away, supporting herself by placing her hand on the family's Bechstein upright.

'Can't you just let me…'

'Get out, John.'

'Jaan… I just want to…'

Jana stubbed out her cigarette on the glass ashtray and turned back towards him.

'Get out now please… You're going to have to leave right now I'm afraid.'

A sound at the front door. A crazily familiar sound. Someone arriving home. The girl took a second handkerchief and began to hurriedly wipe her eyes. John looked back in the direction of the living-room door. He caught a shadow as it moved through the gap between the velvet drape and the damp-stained wallpaper. A familiar shadow. The front door to the house slammed tight. The imposing figure of Jani Feather – master, mentor, maestro… father – was home. John heard Jani place his violin case in the umbrella rack, hang his raincoat up on the stand and clear his throat, in the same three-way rhythm, laid out across the same clickety *1-2- &-then-3*, as he had heard so many times before.

Just a couple of summers ago, hearing this signature arrival, John Nightly would have taken his hands off Jani's daughter, jumped off the couch, straightened his clothes and quickly made himself decent enough to greet his Master. Today the boy waited in dread for the presence about to enter the living room. Jani made his way down the narrow hallway with as much dignity as he could muster. Slightly louder footsteps than usual and a further discreet cough to announce his presence were concessions to the upheaval taking place in his own living room.

In the old days, if he had not set eyes on John for even an afternoon or two the teacher would've greeted the boy with a warm, bearlike hug.

'Dr Feather…'

John… call me Jani, I told you… call me Jani, for God's sake,' the proud and generous man would reply. 'I'm not your teacher now.'

But today Jani, having noticed the Jaguar parked in the road beside Jana's cycle, continued straight past the music room, not even peering in to check on the current hair length of his former protégé, any trace of pot recently extinguished, or the general emotional state of his only child, as he would have in the past. His young genius mustered a broken-voiced greeting.

'Dr Feather…'

'John.'

Came the abrupt acknowledgement as Jani strolled right on past, the *Cambridge Evening News* and a leaflet about the St John's Harvest Supper rolled tightly under his arm.

There was no way that Jani could ever have thought about embracing or even giving the briefest of welcomes to one who had brought his own daughter so much misery. After he and his wife, and Jana, had in a way 'adopted' John, given the boy opportunities, singled him out – rescued him – as John himself acknowledged. Jani had, after all, trusted John Nightly with his most treasured possession; and had shown the extraordinarily gifted boy so much… love.

This action, the barest acknowledgement of the boy's existence, by such a respected figure, cut deep. As deep as Jani's daughter's unexpected and totally uncharacteristic aggression.

John signalled he was about to leave. His face almost on the floor.

'Wait…… John.'

Jana pushed back the hair from her face, reached out and took John's tissue from his hands. Her cheeks were raw with tears.

'I want… I just hope… you do well, John. That's all. I hope that you really do… do well. Get on well. I really, I sincerely hope you do.'

Taken aback by the sudden change towards him, the boy attempted to speak but was unable to. His lips trembled, his teeth chattered uncontrollably. He felt worthless. A complete waste of time, waste of space; a waste of a person. It was as if he suddenly saw the girl's true worth. Feeling he'd been wasting every moment of his life not spent in Jana's company. While she, clutching her tear-soaked shirt, but keeping her distance, continued.

'Don't be nasty to people, John. Don't do your worst.' She took the deepest of breaths. 'Do your best. If you do your worst… if you are… cruel… and if you don't consider your… the consequences of your actions… you'll cause chaos everywhere you go.'

She sniffled, wiped her eyes again and smiled almost apologetically.

'Remember that, boy. Won't you? You may be incredibly talented – and you are… fucking Christ you are… but so are a lot of other people. Consider them as well.'

Jana raised the dynamic of her vocal cords, while remembering that Jani was now in the next-door room.

'I'm talented too, you know. I am… I always have been. Ever looked at me that way? Considered what I'm good at… might be able to achieve? Ever thought about that, John? Considered *my* talent?' She took a breath. 'Haven't, have you? Haven't had time, have you, darling? Poor fucking sod.'

She was off again. An agonising, despairing pronouncement, sobbing uncontrollably. John had nothing more to say. Jana began to cry the whole house down, forgetting Jani, forgetting herself, forgetting Church Lane, the backstreets of Cambridge, and the world outside.

'I'm talented too, John... *I'm clever... too.* I can do things. Just consider it, you fool. Consider others.' Jana breathed in but not out again. 'We all have something to give. It's not just you, you fucking idiot.' She lowered her voice. 'We all have something to *give*. Look for it in others. If you can spare a few moments... And don't... don't go around causing all this... *chaos.*'

'I don't want to hurt anyone, you know. I don't want to put anyone down. I've no principles, no morals. I just go along. No one influences me anymore. I'm on my own.'
Bob Dylan, London, May 1965

Queen Square, Regent's Park, London NW1. Sunday, 17 January 1968.

'Do you remember Kenneth, darling?'

'What?'

'I'm going to marry him on Saturday, if you don't marry me...'

item: Monthly Cultural Notes: July.

Holidays are a problem. Ask a friend or neighbour to take care of watering duties and greenhouse maintenance. Be on the lookout for red spider mite, greenfly, whitefly, thrips, grey mould and mildew. Time to raise lawnmower blades and lower the garden veranda. Check potatoes, tomatoes, courgettes, marrow and peppers daily. Peg back wands of Guara and Poppea. Summer flowering buds make a fine show – Gloxinia, Achimenes, begonias and cannas especially.

'I came home very tired. Dinner being over […] I sat down at the piano. In a little while, soothed and feeling rested, I began to play, suddenly my wife interrupted me saying, "Edward, that's a good tune." I awoke from the dream: "Eh! Tune, what tune?" and she said, "Play it again, I like that tune." I played and strummed, and played, and then she exclaimed, "That's the tune." And that is the theme of the Variations.'

Edward Elgar recalling how the *Enigma Variations* came to be conceived, 21 October 1898

'How for some wise purpose is every bit of sunshine clouded over in me?'

John Constable's Everyday Book, 1829

From Pendeen Watch you can see all along the vast expanse of the bay; the ocean corridor from St Just and Zennor right up to Carn Point and beyond. Its sun-damaged picture-book views of creeks, inlets and zawns, platefuls of translucent blue, lead back to ancient Spanish routes. Lead way back. Back through history. The history of invasion. A time when armadas advanced up the estuaries before setting down to come ashore under cover of the many bluffs, coves and dunes in order to plunder our lands, our food and livestock, our copper and tin, and our women; the items we produced and those that produced us.

Since childhood, John Nightly had viewed himself as a character living within, and throughout, history. A figure plotted on a timeline. John would most certainly be assured of his place in the annals of popular or 'pop' music; the classical music of *Now*. Even as a kid he knew. Fantasising about past and future times. What the exact nature of his achievement within that system of events and revolutions might end up being was more tricky. But John knew he'd be there. Maybe he'd have to wait until after his time to be appreciated. The genius astronomers, composers, architects, poets… and plantsmen; John Pond and John Pierce, John Nash and John Dee, John Harrison, John Donne and John Clare. John Nightly didn't consider them as belonging to the past. Or to any time. As far as John Nightly was concerned these Johns were very much alive and in the room with him, as alive and well as his present company. Their atmospheres and ideas as vital and real as the music of the composer-inventors who seemed to him to be sharing this day and age, this dislodged atomic age and time, with himself and his wife, their fellow seekers and travellers.

Some evenings at Queen Square, John would put on Ravel's left-handed concerto or Gershwin's *Rhapsody in Blue* and try as best he could to bore Iona to death about how he felt he knew these works' composers not just as creators but as beings. Knew them and felt them so well he believed he could reach out and touch them, trying to explain to his wife in such a way that he hoped she might understand. John felt Gershwin's presence right there in the room. George was sitting in John's rattan chair, trying his best to get comfortable as he glittered and gleamed, beamed like a veritable lighthouse of invention. The man possessed with so much crude ability, such confidence, 'comet-hit'. George's great big personality, his immodest but thoroughly generous reality, was right here in sixties London just as sure as it was in those swellegent, self-assured melodies.

George and his cigar smoke often lingered in John and Iona's front room. George was the centre of attention – as always. George was enjoying his drink; George was tapping his foot on John and Iona's floor. George was pounding away on John's upright, explaining how easy it had been for him to write the *Rhapsody* and his other masterpieces – using the term very matter-of-factly. George said that… well, coming up with the stuff… it just wasn't that difficult a thing. The music came to him and out of him like a torrent. Rushed in and tumbled out faster than he was able to realise it, remember it, catch it. Certainly much faster than he could write it down.

John spoke about John Donne, sensing the poet's frustrations in the verses he insisted on reading to Iona late into the night. Donne's rough quality, his explicit tone, the inner conflict of his carnal and spiritual longings. John imagined Donne very much a modern man. Young guy of today. Pusher. Go-getter. A *Now*-man – hippie, like John Nightly himself.

John regaled Iona with endless, cobbled philosophy involving Bach, Mozart, Beethoven. The big ones. Even Iona knew about them. He ran her into the ground with it. They were all hippies too. As 'Now' as Stravinsky or Prokofiev – or Stockhausen, Terry Riley, Harrison Birtwistle, the 'progressive' composers of *today*.

Then there was Rachmaninov. Well, Rachmaninov was different. Rachmaninov was a spirit. The composer having travelled as far as it was possible to go within the confines of 'formal' harmony without entering the realms of dissonance. John described the composer's *Piano Concerto No. 3* as 'hysterical', using the word in its real sense; i.e. like hysteria – 'unmanageable, emotional excess'.

Hysteria. Heaven-like. Yes, Rachmaninov's music was exactly that. A stream-of-consciousness whirling hysterically from beginning to end. One long unravelling mess of human-ness. Of life. And morality. No immorality to be heard in Rachmaninov. Although to many this composer was another thing entirely: old-fashioned, conventional, very obviously formal and overly romantic. 'Exaggerated' was a word often used. Rachmaninov was a square. But to John Nightly, excessively romantic and reasonably exaggerated himself, Rachmaninov was *It*. Rachmaninov was God – or *a* God. A God or *Spirit** to stand alongside the composer-Gods of the Baroque and Classical eras. Just a bit more recent. John often reflected that he had missed him, Sergei, and also the glittering George, by some twenty or so years. That's all. Just a little slip in time and they could have actually met. Anyway, the 'Intermezzo: adagio' from the third *Concerto* – a careering, swivelling, swirling mass of breakers and swells, crescendi and diminuendi, human and humane, a pool of humanity, seraphic, 'hippie-ish' in both conception and execution – was the piece of music that he and Iona chose to get married to.

* 'He was not a conductor, he was not even a composer – he was a spirit' – Mikhael Pletnev on Sergei Rachmaninov. In 1999 the pianist made a recital disc at Rachmaninov's villa in Switzerland of the composer's first piano concerto on Rachmaninov's own 1933 Steinway.

Pathé London News. Saturday, 14 February 1968.
The world of entertainment was out in force today for the wedding of pop singer John Nightly and Danish fashion model Iona Sandstrand, TV's Kit Kat girl. Traffic quickly came to a standstill outside Marylebone register office, bringing calls from local residents for a ban on showbiz weddings. The bride wore an Ossie Clark teal-blue kaftan from Quorum and a pair of Moya Bowler's new Zodiac sandals in yellow suede (exclusively available at Ronald Keith in Oxford Street, W1), while the bridegroom wore a rather traditional cotton suit... in pink, mind you! (Pathé Newsreel)

Queen Square, Regents Park, London, NW1. Monday 16 February 1968.

John and Iona were married at Marylebone register office on Valentine's Day 1968. In attendance were John Snr, Frieda, Signhild, Sindre, Steinar, Iona's parents – Thorkild and Lisabet – and her brother, Kim, along with John's dog Tyko and Jonathan and Justin from the group. Monika and Patti duly fulfilled their bridesmaid duties. It was one of those sunny London mornings; soft air, low light, a sharp, edgy frost and non-stop traffic – so loud that the tiny congregation could barely hear the service.

'Like when James Stewart keeps saying he's got a sound in his head...'

'What, darling?'

'James Stewart.'

'Stuart?'

'*James Stewart*... the actor, *Glenn Miller Story*.' It didn't seem to be ringing a bell.

'What it's like. I mean – that's what I've got.' John scratched his head. 'Maybe what everyone's got. I can hear it, but I can't seem to achieve it – same problem as him.'

'Who?'

'Jimmy Stewart!' he repeated again, '*Godsake…*' John extricated a cotton bud from his left ear and examined it for wax.

'You don't mean you going deaf, darling? Not already? Like Beethoven?'

'Let's hope not…' The boy looked at his bride in exasperation. 'Godsake…'

John put down the swab and picked up his headphones. He put on both earpieces, having removed the left side so that he could clean out his head, listen to the track and speak to his wife simultaneously.

'I can't *translate* it,' he continued. 'That's what I mean. If only I could make what I hear in my head a reality, I'd be…'

John…' Iona adjusted the towel holding her head together. 'Can you shout a bit quieter, darling…'

'Being able to *create* the sound you'd imagined. More or less an impossibility, obviously, but that would really be…' he pulled the headphones tight over his head. 'The physical *reality* of sound is so different to our imagining of it.'

Iona put down her spliff and picked up a pair of large pattern-cutting scissors.

'But isn't it always like this?' she murmured as she looked around for her smoke box, 'the same it is with everything?'

John removed one side yet again. 'I can't hear you if you talk to me when I've got these on, can I?' Iona looked across and repeated her philosophy.

'It's not "like everything else", anyway – only music,' he answered, as he flicked switches on the console in order to set up a new track. John prepared the bounce, heartened by the

pleasing blend of Mellotron, Moog synthesiser and harpsichord. Seemingly more relaxed, the boy lightened up.

'That's better...' he hummed. 'Like when I think of you,
darling... well... the "thinking" is a bit different to the reality!'

His wife sat bolt upright. 'What do you mean, John?' Iona shut
her book. 'I know there was gonna be some "philosophy"
coming.' She got up from her chair. 'So we coming down to it,
don't we? Your meaning, the "thinking" is better than the
"reality",' she puffed. 'I certainly... I *definitely* understand you
now!'

The boy made an act of slowly and systematically removing
both headphones as he tossed his brand-new wife a thin,
exasperated sigh.

'*Godsake*,' he said again. 'Don't be ridiculous, my love. Of course
the thinking isn't better than the reality with you!'

'I don't be ridiculous, John. It's one of these... "psycho-logical"
things...' Iona wrapped her towel even tighter around her head.
'You speak about it. It must be true.'

John completed the balance to his satisfaction. He sat and listened
carefully to playback, checking that everything was exactly as he
intended before he erased the two original tracks that made up
the new combination. Unfortunately, a more comprehensive
explanation was going to be necessary if he were to avoid one of
the many mood swings and tempo changes that were becoming
increasingly frequent from behind the oversize sunglasses of the
'ultimate face of today's young fashion'.

'The only thing I'm saying – and this is all I'm saying...' he
broke off, 'is, well, if we, *I*... could only translate this sound – and
other elements as well – and I'm sure that's what the classical
composers had to do, because they couldn't exactly make
"demos", before recording came along. Composers obviously

had to orchestrate without hearing anything at all… without any idea what it was going to sound like.' The boy picked up his guitar, ready to add the next part. 'Keep literally everything in their heads…' He plucked a couple of strings and grimaced at the tuning. 'At least we can *mock it up*. Mock the real thing up, I mean.' He began to tune as he spoke. 'At least we can do that. Because they couldn't, you see…'

'Do you want tea, my darling?' Iona seemed somewhat placated.

'Don't know why I'm always so… so dissatisfied with everything,' John sighed wearily as he tried to remember the lyric to an old song from Grantchester days – *'Easier said than done… Found your number on my doorstep, to take one more step… It's easier said than done. Now that we've begun… Don't believe you'll make me say that I won't see you. Easier said than…'* He turned to his wife and sang directly to her as he strummed: *'Easy…'*

'John…' Iona was visibly moved by the sweet melody. 'You've got me… for starters.'

'For starters?'

The boy laughed at the colloquialism his wife had picked up from God-knows-where. 'I shouldn't be dissatisfied, should I? I really shouldn't,' he said affectionately.

The fact was that John Nightly would never be satisfied with anything. The disability being part of his make-up, part of the fun – if it could be put that way – of who he was. Dissatisfaction somehow defined him. As Pondy said and Lee Hide always agreed: 'Never satisfied!' It seemed to sum the geezer up.

Out shopping with Iona one day John had become mesmerised by a couple and their kids; an ordinary couple, walking idly along; doing very little at all – apart from just 'being' … *living*. But they were happy, John thought. They appeared happy. Without ambition or plan, apart from the intention to get from start to finish as comfortably, and as quietly, as possible. Living for that. Not thinking too much about their lives, the speed of things, their place in the world, who they were and where life was taking them.

If only he, John Nightly, could be satisfied in the same way as those 'innocents'. As he would often complain to Iona, if only *he* didn't have to *do* things. All this work. Creating this and that. Ideas going round and round in his head like a cylindrical saw. How difficult, and unrelenting, it was – particularly at the moment. If only the mercury flow would stop. Run out of juice. Give the boy a break.

Even when he'd finished recording a new song, the most exciting moment of all for any songwriter, John would forever be seeking that extra 'edge', something to lift it above the competition. Not always strictly a musical something; that edge could be sonic or mechanical. Adding more compression or distortion, overloading things a little – or a lot. Opening up the reverb across the whole track, or speeding things up by a very small increment. Though that ingredient might not exist – his collaborators pulling their hair out trying to prove to him that the track really didn't need it – John Nightly would demand it of himself.

Sometimes the boy would become desperate. At which point his colleagues were alerted that they must tread carefully, lest that first speck of doubt be followed by a rapid descent. John's mood could change faster than the wind, in which case a recording he'd just spent a week lovingly creating would be heard with dead ears. Cynical ears. Declaring to one and all that the thing was… 'worthless' and instructing Lee that he may as well wipe it all off, get rid of it – that really would be the best thing. Erase everything, and start afresh on something new tomorrow, thereby creating a cache of supposedly 'wiped' tracks, in various states of undress, that the boss would promptly forget all about. Recordings that years later the wily sound engineer would continue to make a comfortable living out of by 'licensing' encoded masters to bootleggers, downloaders and streamers. Issues about rights and ownership to both the songs and recordings tied up in one never-ending legal dispute.

It turned out that there were enough 'erased' tracks from 1967–1971 for at least three complete albums. After the eventual appearance of the *Requiem*, these 'lost' recordings began to filter through. Several of them re-mastered and remixed (the source having been a multitrack reel), appearing in expensive Digipak sleeves featuring unseen shots of John and the band taken in dressing-rooms in Bremen or Winnipeg or even shopping in their local supermarket. Sometimes personal band photographs, taken inside the studio during working sessions, cropped up inside CD booklets. It was obvious from the quality of both sound and picture and the very 'completeness' of the package that the source of these illegal recordings sadly had to be the group itself.

By September '67, John Nightly had recorded an enormous body of work for his nineteen years. It ranged from piano interludes written in his early teens to the ballet piece he was currently at work on. But the creator of this massive outpouring probably wasn't satisfied or entirely convinced by any of it and never would be. To her credit, Iona understood that that part of his character in the context of their relationship was never going to change.

When Iona first watched John working, with Lee at Regal, she encountered a different personality altogether from the guy she'd spoken with properly only a few days before. In the studio, John Nightly was the absolute opposite of the shy young boy she'd assumed him to be. At Regal, John was confident; arrogant even. Desultory about his own music and critical of the studio – although it was by far the best facility he'd set foot in. *'It'll be good when we get it done properly!'* or whatever it was he said, was an unintentional slur on his engineer and the results Lee was able to achieve. John was dismissive of most music he encountered in any situation and would promptly turn the radio off if something came on that he felt was beneath him. 'We don't want to listen to that!' he'd say, leaning over the transistor. 'Not gonna pollute my brain with that, I don't think!'

But John Nightly could afford to be high and mighty simply because he was so very talented. Iona noted the respect he received from Lee and the others being an accomplished performer on any number of instruments with a perfectly formed 'head' blueprint of the way his inventions should be recorded in the studio. With no dots, nothing written down, the music was literally in the boy's head, possessing him as usual.

His consummate understanding of all things musical was confirmed by further studio visits. John would finish what he was working on then sit down at the piano and serenade his loved one with an Irving Berlin ballad. He'd perform a Spanish lament on the guitar, mocking his own dexterity with impossibly fast runs, cascades of complex chords that he'd dash off while responding to a question about food or which club to go to later that evening. Then he'd jump on the drum kit to knock out a Stax backbeat, get up on the vibraphone and imitate Lionel Hampton, run off Russ Conway's 'Sleigh Ride' at triple speed or play a Mozartian version of that week's Number 1 – not to impress; more to prove to himself that he could do it.

John was not so much 'educated' – he spent little time at his studies – as 'self-improved'; curious to learn about anything he didn't already know. He carried a pile of books and pamphlets around in a leather bag, ready to shove un-constituted astronomy and ecology, along with the obligatory own-brand philosophy, down everyone's throat. The boy relished the role of self-proclaimed instructor. An inspiration to all who came across him. And, as long as he was in a good mood, that is exactly what he was.

So Iona was completely zapped by John. But she wasn't stupid; though sometimes, most uncharitably, her companion took her to be so. Her only real failing was to expect their life together to continue on indefinitely. The blessed union should have been a time-compressed experience, something for both to enjoy, get out of the way, then look back on with affection for the rest of their days. But the relationship became more of a 'siege'. After that, the affair retained a casualness not associated with such a binding agreement because John Nightly found himself, at just twenty summers, unable to commit psychologically to anyone or anything except music itself, his creative and spiritual centre. Iona should have realised that. Instead, she chose to ignore it. And ended up trying to get him out of her consciousness for the remainder of her days.

Queen Square, Regent's Park, London NW1. Saturday, 11 March 1968.

The newlyweds spread themselves out on the balcony. With their coffee and toast, sun-loungers and lotions, piles of magazines and of course grass – the best available in London – John and Iona seemed very much at home.

It was extremely early in the day for both of them, the reason being that neither had yet been to bed – Iona having arrived back from a photo-shoot at 4am with John walking in two hours later, zomboid after driving down from Manchester. London's most beautiful, *beautiful couple* were taking it easy.

As she gazed lovingly at her husband the new Mrs Nightly was all too aware that she was a lucky girl. The fan mail flowing into JCE, some of it of a shockingly personal nature, gave a good indication of John Nightly's pull. It was the same for Iona. Everywhere she went the girl was trailed by admirers, while appearing to be entirely innocent about the effect she had on men of all ages. At work or play, sharing an equal level of attraction, Iona and John were two 'naifs'; Arcadian spirits fated somehow to meet and to exist as one.

If John Nightly had believed in fate, he would have had to agree. His wife, with her homespun horoscopes, consultant palmists, birth charts, star charts, tarot, *I Ching* and other paraphernalia of prediction and destiny, remained certain that this very real concept had been instrumental in bringing herself and her loved one together.

Belief was the reason Iona had pursued John in the first place. When she set eyes on him walking into Sotheran's, ill at ease and lost to the real world in his Mr Byrite togs and bowl-cut hair, Iona knew right away that this was a talisman. A gift sent to her from… somewhere, God, maybe, via her friend and sidereal messenger John Pond. Somehow Pondy, in just as coincidental, fated way, had delivered to Iona the present – and the problem – of a lifetime.

As she sat swathed in a pink bath towel, perched precariously on a roof tile, her hands cupped around a macro-grain concoction made by her husband with his new Topcaff machine, the Danish teenager gazed out over her meadow. Before her a jigsaw vista of the city. Uneven rooftops, crumbling terraces, water-damaged chimneys and rusty balustrades reminded her of the illustrations in the Peter Pan pop-up edition presented by her mother on the occasion of her confirmation. The girl looked out across history – a perfect fairytale vista inside and out. The demands of commerce in the Queen's backyard meant continual development and renovation at street level but up here, as far as Iona's heavily lashed eyes could see, all around her remained more or less as it had been 100 years before.

Her husband wandered back into the box room, strummed a few chords and began to moan away. Iona picked up the book she'd begun a few nights before when, after a long session at the Bag O'Nails, she'd left John, Justin and Monika more or less comatose in the bedroom and had snuck up here to read. It seemed that everyone was into *The Psychedelic Experience*, a 'manual' based on the *Tibetan Book of the Dead*. It was the only reading material Monika possessed, stolen during one of her many trips to the World Psychedelic Centre. Little did Iona know that the 'ego-death', 'de-personalisation' and 'evil karma', referred to within its pages – words and phrases that had had no reason to occupy her thoughts previously – would soon become part of her own story, shaking her apparently perfect world. As Iona settled down, Monika's voice shouted from the kitchen.

'John! Radio! Quick! Be quick!'

But the man of the house didn't stir. He didn't give a damn if someone's terrible cover version of one of his songs – the Bellbottoms' 'Zigging & Zagging' – polluted the nation's collective brain or not. Right now it was the last thing on John Nightly's mind.

The boy took a sip of Topcaff's trademark mud and sang a long, arched melody into his Dictaphone. Having already decided that his next step compositionally would be to move away from the restrictions of song form, he offloaded one brilliant idea after another into the small plastic box.

One thing that constantly nagged was the feeling of being over-looked by the classical-music establishment. The serious press coverage awarded to so-called contemporary composers made him envious. He worried that his place in history – if he were to have one at all – would always be as a 'pop' musician. How unfair that seemed. Ridiculous that there should be any division at all in these free and easy days.

John and Iona attended the premiere of Harrison Birtwistle's *Punch and Judy* at the 1968 Aldeburgh Festival. Here was the first fully staged, fully sung, 'post-serialist' work, as John painstakingly explained to his wife, certain he could have done something similar, better himself. He could have gotten there before Birtwistle. *John Nightly* could have been the name attached to this high watermark – Aldeburgh, BBC Proms – a project stamped with cultural authority and credibility. He possessed the talent and the imagination, and the connections, but he'd spent the past two years making 'commercial' recordings. He'd made them as un-commercial as possible, of course – as his manager never failed to remind him – but they still bore the hallmarks of 'product'; blocks of music within a four-square beat wrapped in a deluxe, record-orientated sound. A confection of the people for the people, firmly based within the requirements and therefore the constraints of radio playlisting and the market.

Not subject to grants and commissions, John Nightly's work, like all product within the pop machine, existed – from the point of view of its funders and its promoters – to generate income. It had been created, come into being, for that purpose, its very success derived from sales: the absolute bottom-line, which would, in terms of chart position and subsequent coverage, justify the outlay and prove the music's worth. Otherwise, there was no game to be played. The operation of recording companies had little in common with that of the Arts Council. In the classical world, the orchestral musician, winding his way through the system, and through the ranks, would learn to play an instrument at school by reading music; he would take exams, attend music college, get his degree. If he were fortunate a career as a composer might follow, dependent upon the usual grants, commissions and bursaries. If not, there was the option of work as an orchestral player. Even with world-class orchestras this was a tough, uncompromising life. The stress and strain of touring and learning repertoire combined with film and television sessions scheduled on days off involved at least as much alcohol consumption among the professional classical world as there was to be found in rock'n'roll. If you didn't make it there, it was down to teaching: the 'fallback' career in education. John remembered the tired faces of Jani and Valerie. Eking out a living in that way, life being nothing but one continual compromise, had never been what John Nightly had in mind.

On the other side lay the great escape: pop music, the art medium of the times. Sooner or later, these two protected spheres would have to coexist within the same universe; musicians on either side seeming to have no problem whatsoever appreciating the stuff coming from the opposite direction. 'Pop' success had its compensations, though. It allowed John Nightly to indulge himself in a way he could never have imagined just a few years before.

Back in his Cambridge days, in the library at Trinity College, John had spent hours poring over the great scientific texts of the Classical era. Now he was able to fill Queen Square with expensively produced facsimiles. When he wasn't in the box room sewing the quilt that would become *Quiz Axe Queen* John would immerse himself in reprinted editions of star almanacs and celestial atlases by Brahe, Kepler, Flamsteed, Galileo and Copernicus. The great works of science, translated from the academic Latin, were now available to him or indeed anyone with the money to purchase them. The boy was not only able to read and make notes from actual calculations and theses as originally published, but he was also able to have all of the major works of reference on permanent display, laid out side by side in the small studio-room, available to him to cross-reference one with another. John had even managed to procure one of the first-edition copies of Isaac Newton's *Principia*[1]. Purchased from Sotheby's at great cost, the *Principia* was John's most treasured possession – apart from Iona. Its yellowed pages lay open on the couple's kitchen table within easy reach of stray breadcrumbs and coffee spills.

On the wall above hung one of Tycho Brahe's elaborate celestial maps created in his specially built Stjerneborg ('Star Castle') observatory. John compared Brahe's findings with modern satellite pictures. He was impatient to discover how much of John Flamsteed – the first Astronomer Royal – existed in Newton's writings. And why the great astronomer had been denied credit by his rival, who deleted Flamsteed's name from the second version of the *Principia*.

Cross-referencing the actual texts, the young enthusiast was able to resolve many questions – particularly those concerning the perspective of time and date. He contrasted the designations of Brahe and Copernicus by studying the corresponding maps, laying across them a tracing of his own modern-day star map. It was immediately obvious how Kepler, then employed as Brahe's assistant, improved on his master's findings, taking Tycho's work to the next elevated stage.

The thrill of being able to view the damp-stained title of *The Rudolphine Tables* or *Delle stelle fisse* in the exact same format as their authors would have written them was a revelation to the boy astronomer.

John had been able to obtain all four volumes of the *Principia* (Foote Society Reprint, 1965), along with a facsimile version of John Pond's *Catalogue of 1,000 Stars*, botanical indices by John Gerard, John Tradescant and John Ray as well as very early editions by another influence, John Clare (the lunatic, peasant genius who'd spent the last forty years of his life in an asylum). A bound copy of John Donne's early poetry, again an original printing, had also been acquired for him from Sotheran's by Iona. The first and last birthday present her boyfriend would ever receive from her.

[1]*Philosophiæ Naturalis Principia Mathematica* by Isaac Newton, 1687. Published and edited by Edmund Halley.

John Nightly fantasised that this *Principia* was from the batch of 40 sent by coach from London to Cambridge by Newton's patron Halley, with a letter asking Newton himself to arrange for them to be sold so that Halley, the eminent astronomer who had invested a considerable sum in publishing his friend's work, would be able to recover his investment.

The next few months were taken up with gigs. The band pleaded with their manager to try to schedule dates a little more efficiently. Not to book them into Aberdeen one night and Plymouth the next if at all possible, but the canny management still had them headlining at Hull Student Union on the Thursday followed by Exeter Tech on the Friday. These two carefully scheduled appearances were followed by a trip the following day up to Lancaster Poly.

On 10 May a special one-off date was booked at the Lyceum Ballroom, in order to try out material from the new album in front of a mainly fan-based audience. In the event, the concert was so oversubscribed that two more nights had to be added before JCE came up with the idea of adding two 'lunchtime' slots. The second daytime show being recorded for BBC's *Sounds of the Seventies* hosted by David Symonds. 'The gear's all set up, and there's no extra cost. So let's just do it!' said Pondy. And do it they did. The Nightly band ended up 'doing it' eight times in four days, kept lively by a large and quite varied amphetamine intake courtesy of their sound engineer, washed down with bottles of White Horse whiskey and Iona's exotic fudge.

The following week came the final mixing sessions for *Pitfall*. Fewer than were scheduled, as the project had long since run out of funds. The Knoll Film Company were not only experiencing distribution problems at home but were also dealing with the logistics of producing a US-financed feature in London with a Polish director and a mainly French cast. Though John Nightly, on his first-ever 'sync-to-picture' assignment, had turned in an inspired score. He was almost pleased with it himself, though there were some complaints from the producer that every now and then the soundtrack would occasionally slip into its own world – a John Nightly world – becoming a little too self-conscious or 'sad' for the film it served.

'The scene is supposed to be "terrifying", John,' Myra would announce. 'Why do we have all this tear-jerk stuff going on?'

The boy hadn't got a clue, of course. John listened politely, but failed to identify a 'tear-jerk' aspect to anything he'd delivered. When Myra innocently enquired why the composer hadn't used more 'major' chords, sarcasm would get the better of John, who would quote Tchaikovsky's line – saying he always 'saved the major chords for the sad bits'.

The composer was vindicated when *Pitfall* was released to surprisingly good reviews. All mentioned the soundtrack, a most unorthodox imagining for a mainstream feature, with John succeeding in recording the majority of it himself, at home mostly, to the chagrin of Justin, Jonathan and Ash, who complained of having to sit around doing nothing – and getting paid for it – while the boss finished his other projects.

One of the 'other' projects the boss was finishing was the young film producer herself, who was gracing John Nightly's bed in his wife's absence. With Iona now at the peak of her career, abroad for periods of a week or more at a time, John had opportunity enough to schedule a few home recording sessions followed by afterhours entertainment.

John was tripping out almost every night when he wasn't working. Taking fifty milligram sheets of acid, alone or with Myra or in 'sessions' with the Sleepwalkers or his manager.

With long, tiring journeys between gigs, seldom arriving back home before dawn, and little sleep while he was recording, John's already hollow cheeks became hollower as unsightly bags and creases began to appear beneath his sapphire eyes which now took on a staring, almost accusatory look beneath his beleaguered brow. Some mornings his eyelids appeared so heavy and hooded that he resembled a lizard – saura dinos – 'terrible lizard' or 'dinosaur' (a word that would have depressing associations later on). On the occasions when John wasn't taking the sacramental chemical, there would be an immediate reversion and the shy young charmer would re-emerge to become everyone's favourite pied piper once again.

Everyone was taking some form of 'helper', as creative artists always had; the laudanum with which Coleridge pummelled himself, the nitrous oxide – laughing gas – Humphry Davy sniffed from a silk bag, Freud's long-term use of lime cocaine. Those past times when the safest source of liquid had often been alcohol due to the fact that water was so unfit, and therefore unsafe, to drink.

Fortunately, John Nightly had never been attracted to booze. His 'drink' was fresh orange juice with one white, occasionally customised, sugar cube. The family member who became affected by a different kind of spirit was Iona, who, because she could see that she was losing her brightest starre, took to lacing everything from Typhoo Tea to beetroot juice with cornershop whiskey which lay concealed in small bottles in one of the three fridges in the Nightly household. Not only could Iona *drinka pinta thata* day she could also down several other varieties. The girl was getting through at least two quart bottles a week, more than enough liquor for someone to be concerned about. But no one was. The husband who should have been was hardly ever at home at the same time as his wife, and he was beginning not to care that much about other human beings anymore.

Like so many of their contemporaries, by June 1968, John and Iona were pretty much freaked out most of the time. If they did happen to find themselves alone in the flat, alone with each other, they tended not to stay that way, rounding up a group of friends to lend a little comfort and spread a little, if temporary, happiness.

Together the couple were a veritable pool of beauty and talent. However, great success can bring not only great fulfilment but also great destruction. John and Iona were two seeds in a seedpod of possibility powdered by the hand of fate. Life for them overflowed with potential. Fantasies, no matter how far-fetched or existential, had become fact. But still they desired more. More intensity, more cloud-cuckoos to be listened to and seduced by. As it dawned on them they'd squeezed one another and the immediate vicinity dry they looked elsewhere.

When Iona returned to Denmark for her parents' silver wedding she considered not coming back. After just three years' professional work Iona was already much too comfortable, and intelligent enough to realise that there was much more to life than waiting around.

Lighting set-ups, lens changes, backdrops, Polaroid tests; the general drill on every assignment. The company and the locations were often unbearably dull. Then, when she arrived home, Iona would be waiting again, now for her husband to show up or at least call and tell his wife the name of the town he was no longer coming back from. Leaving Iona to spend another troubled night with her spiked juices and delusions.

Eventually the girl decided that she'd waited long enough. And that realisation about her own damaged prospects was the prelude to John Nightly's own slow fade.

'I believe Elvis Presley and the Beatles and the Rolling Stones are going to answer to God. God is going to rain judgement upon earth – and this could happen at any moment with all the rock music and illicit sex and wine, women and the glasses they wear – and there will be a time of terrible tribulation when all hell will be let loose on earth...'

Reverend Jack Wyrtzen, World of Life community, in *All You Need Is Love*, (Futura Productions Ltd), 1977.

'Cut the page down the centre, then take the other and do the same.'

Justin demonstrated with the scissors as he handed the four new vertical sections to Ash. 'Now try putting page one to the left-hand side of page four and see whatcha get…'

Ashley slid the two halves together.

'The butter | in the native | Zanzibar "You get outta here!" 2,000 years old |Anglo-Saxon heritage. No budgerigar. She lies about her |chimney – "Hello Mister!"', Justin eyed up the final line: 'Put her |the oven at one hundred degrees!'

'What a loada shit, Just. We did it the other way round last time.' But before Ash could finish, the guitarist had snatched back the scissors and was cutting the page into single lines. Justin snipped off each word separately, held the pieces of paper high in the air then let them fall on the lino. 'This'll be interesting…' he whispered, while the others gathered round.

'You should only do it in "threes", though – let's see…' Ash peered down at the random arrangement.

mystery chimney

develops hat butter medley,

crop harmless budgerigars

Crazy, man! Native!

'See what I mean! It's brilliant, brilliant!' declared Justin. '*Crazy*, man… *Crazy*…' Ash looked up to see if anyone was still listening.

'Always works!' the guitarist whispered hopefully.

item: 'Look Away' by Brion Gysin, from *Minutes to Go*, with Sinclair Beiles,
William Burroughs, Gregory Corso, Brion Gysin (Beach Books). 1968.
"My Principal is no Monkey"...You figure it out. Try it yourself. Here is how you do it:
Let's see, now. No, I'm not stalling. Common sense tells you that words are meant to
mislead. It's about like this: Just talk to yourself for a minute. You hear that little voice?
Well, now argue with yourself: take two sides of a question. Dig? That's already a line.
Do it like a phone call. Broadcast something. I hesitate to advise, because I know only
for me, that something pretty saucy will often get you a sharp answer. Realize that it is
an answer when you hear it and not just you. Your first party or any party may be hard
to identify but just go on listening. Soon plenty of voices will come in and soon you will
be able to call out. Don't put this down. Lots of people want this, need it and are
damned well getting it by themselves. This ain't no monopoly, lady. Shove off, you!

Stop and listen. The state called reverie just before sleep is a good place to start. Artists
and intellectuals BEST learn a method best called LOOK AWAY. You will find that you
are broadcasting at all hours without knowing it. How else do you think ideas 'get
around', man. Well, call me any time you want and just identify yourself when you call.
Name and address, please. I'll be glad to talk to you about this or anything else you have
in mind. Crazy, man, crazy.

CUT ME UP * BRION GYSIN * CUT ME UP * BRION GYSIN *
CUT ME UP * BRION GYSIN * CUT ME IN *

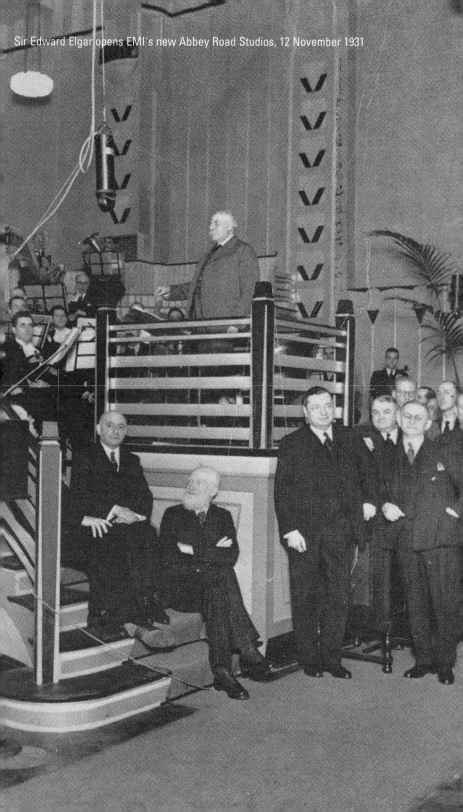

Sir Edward Elgar opens EMI's new Abbey Road Studios, 12 November 1931

'The enigma I will not explain – its "dark saying" must be left unguessed'

Edward Elgar, programme notes for the Hans Richter premiere of the *Enigma Variations*, 19 June 1899

There's a new world coming, and it's just around the bend

**'New World Coming', Mama Cass, 1970
(Dunhill/ABC4225)**

People who live by the ocean get heavy when the weather does and lighten when it breaks. The rain which had been forecast for weeks arrived in a downpour as RCN made his way back over to Porthcreek.

The atmosphere was black all round. A gothic mist rolling all the way up the north coast as John drove along, keeping a careful eye on the road. Potato trucks, school buses and local fish vans were stopped in their tracks along the waterlogged coastal canal. A queue of vehicles stretched back as far as Black Zawn, where an articulated container had run aground just off the barely sufficient 1950s-built B-carriageway.

Daly planned on stopping somewhere before he got too close to home, so he pulled off the B3306 and parked up on a mound of ocean-heather. He grabbed the plastic bag and eased himself out of the car, gazing back at the traffic built up behind him and at the torrent of water which had fallen in barely ten minutes. RCN lifted his boots out of the slub and shook his head in disbelief as he stroked the bristles on the back of his neck.

Too short. Much too short. Ever since John was a small boy the new haircut had been too short. As a teenager this had made him look younger, like a fresh-faced bobby-soxer, the kid in *Champion the Wonder Horse*, or Kookie, his schoolboy crush from *77 Sunset Strip*, a USAF crewcut being the required style of summer '61. But nowadays, hair cut too short made him look considerably older, and greyer, than before. It showed up the unsightly bump at the back of his neck and his enlarged 'pensioner's ears', which alarmed him every time he caught sight of himself in the wing mirror but was met by a ghostly vision of his father instead.

There seemed to be literally no trace left of the old John. Where was he? The hippie fixer. The quiet reliable guy who turned in early while the children stayed up all night. The idiot who stuck to Lucozade and pasties when everyone else laid in to tequila and pills and anything else that might be on offer.

Here lay the result of that unnecessary devotion. This mooching, rain-soaked figure, soft-edged silhouette alone on the rock. Fat old 'anorak man' with too-short hair. Still good for looking after people, though. That hadn't changed, though his gut certainly had. RCN was hardly able to walk some days, he was so full of beer, fags and Typhoo – buckets of it. Even worse on a Sunday after Mrs Peed's magnificent roast plate and lemon-curd slice.

Feeling a chill, John wound his scarf tight around his neck. He wiped the spray from his eyes, pulled his collar up and his cap down. The thoughts rushing through his head weren't kind ones.

Suddenly the scene lightened. The smoky skies cleared. The rain moved southwards and became finer. Magpies and jays began to squawk. There was visibility ahead. Though it was just mid-afternoon, the farmhouses along the headland already had their lights on. From the highest point of the Zawn, RCN had a clear view across Black Cliff; and beyond that Carn Point and Porthcreek. He stabbed at the gorse with his boot to see if there wasn't a covered ditch in front, then walked the couple of yards further up to the edge of the rock, stopping abruptly just inches from the overhang. Still dazzled after all these years by the Vista-Vision sweep of the pendulous landscape, he stared blearily out over the precipice.

Viewed from this height and at this angle the oceanic bowl appeared weightless. As if the tank of a huge crane lifted you up and tilted you back, face-on to the sky. Removing you. Most people who came out here hoped to experience something like that. To taste rough elements. Wished to be removed; from something.

If the hapless tourist wandered up onto the headland on a bad-weather day, then the wind chopped and howled and the rain lashed at his face. Horizontal, hard pellets of water. Visitors commented on the harsh weather but they also relished it. Smiling and nodding knowingly, like insiders, when they told the folks back home, as if they could hardly believe the conditions they'd been subjected to. With the elements swirling around them, encircling them, confusing their sense of perspective and balance, these weekenders no doubt assumed they were at the very core of nature's chaos. The bay was the cosmos itself, whipping and whirling, spinning around its life-giving hub. But the holidaymakers, up here to experience an alternative condition or 'state', away from their tidy, temperate, kind-weather lives, were interested only in egofied, geocentric cosmology. A habitual, self-obsessed way of viewing the world – and one's place in it. Life as a self-portrait, accompanied by a hastily sketched matte of supporting players. Human beings invariably see themselves as the centre of every unit, every group, every assembly, every cosmos.

Standing bolt upright, keeping still, looking out at the ocean haze while letting the elements swirl and lash all they wanted, it was easy to imagine that it was the world revolving around you rather than vice versa. Where was the centre anyway? The midheaven point? We'd all like to know that. Though of course there couldn't be just one. There were many centres and swirls, ripple-pools, panels, pulsars, energy triangles, hubs and converters. Existence as time-dependent landscape. Human beings no more significant than hairdresser's clippings and other detritus whirling through the universe from one corner of eternity to another.

RCN surveyed the view before him as he had done so many times over the years. Until, in the mist and confusion between rainwater, seawater and cyclonic curtains of smoke and storm, the exact point of the horizon disappeared as his retinas gave up and became gel against the moisture in the air. John's tired old, rheumy old eyes lost their will to focus as he shut down normal transmission and lapsed into free flow while his altered state delivered him back to some idyllic beachside with his Kiwi wife – his sun-damaged face and her continual hen-pecking his only daytime distraction – until the screams of gulls sheltering below, and the cut of an RNLI helicopter, dragged him back to his own wretched mind.

RCN wasn't an unsentimental man, but he had to be absolutely certain that all of his hard work over the years wasn't going to be wasted. He dwelled on these thoughts for a moment. The dark legacy of the day, its past and present. Characters, events, circumstances and possible outcomes. Moving forward. The conclusion of what he and Iona had discussed that morning.

Up until now, the whole unfinished tale of John Nightly had rarely involved fate. Events had taken place due to the protagonists' actions, and their choices. Decisions. Their stupid, bad decisions. RCN thought about the roads the four or five star players had taken. Stupid, wrong roads. Roads that always led to the coast. The edge of things. The limits. He thought about Iona, back in her luxurious surroundings long before now, of course. Tucked up well inland, on her inherited acres. Probably five or six miles between Iona and the sea. Compare that to Trewin. No amount of miles there. Nightly and Daly were right on the thing. Right bloody on it. Always had been. *Straightway dangerous* was their marker. The Nightly fable was about innocence, ambition, industry – pretty much in that order – and a kind of measured risk, as if they welcomed it; thrived on 'fancy over reason'.

RCN thought about the boss, waiting at home, ignorant of anything outside of the perimeter fence. Pottering, planting, plotting. The stuff he'd built around him, bubble-wrapped himself in; layers of protection from his various 'anxieties'. The boss had managed to stave off his melancholy without being able to actually rid himself of it. Dull tasks put in place to lift his untidy moods, whatever it was that actually got him through the night – and the following day. But John Nightly knew he could still count on his old friend from Huntingdon.

Daly would have loved to have erased all of these burdensome thoughts and characters from his inner cosmos. But, realising that he was actually getting very damp indeed, the anorak man lifted the large round tin out of its bag and hurled it over the edge.

John Nightly's new world view began to cause trouble with his associates during the long summer of '68, the last good summer of the decade. As usual, John was busy; a little busier than he liked. There was really no need for this wildly successful auteur to be rushing around like a gopher. He'd even begun to assume some of the practicals himself, thereby removing a good deal of his manager's workload, John Pond's part of the deal – and Pond's hold, or, as the manager himself would've put it, 'control' over his protégé's career.

Suddenly the client wanted to know where every penny was going. For no particular reason. John Nightly wasn't at all money-oriented, or money-minded. He never had been. He simply wanted to know. Having read that the Beatles knew where 'every penny was going', John Nightly thought that he should too.

John's accountants demanded royalty statements and recoupables from records that had barely left the shops. Wage slips and MU session forms were located and dispatched. Hotel bills and petrol receipts from last summer's college gigs, cheque stubs and wage packets, petty-cash and other miscellaneous (drugs and booze) expenses were ordered up and sent over.

One drizzly Saturday morning a mountain of filed invoices impaled on coat-hanger wire was delivered to Queen Square along with bought ledgers, sales ledgers and heavy cardboard box-files containing bound three-monthly accounts, all stamped with Her Majesty's dull red seal. John would never look at them.

As it was, the Beatles knew so little about where the pennies went that they were heading for bankruptcy themselves. Unbelievable as it may sound now, following the death of their manager and the creation of the free-for-all that was Apple Corps, money really was flowing out like rain, leading to John Lennon's statement that 'I'm down to my last 10,000 [pounds] and will probably be broke by Christmas.'

The magiciens, at the height of their creative powers, and with millions of dollars' worth of record and film sales, merchandising, product endorsements and box-office touring receipts behind them, they should have been spending each waking hour offloading as many of their transmissions onto tape as was humanly possible. Instead, their heads were full of financial plans and forecasts, for Beatles Ltd and Apple, budgets for launching other artists careers and for planning and producing Apple product. They'd become businessmen, but not business*like*. In physical man-hours, the group could expect to be working harder than ever – partly in an attempt to stave off their own collective despair, their own dark hours.

John Nightly began to encounter similar difficulties. Each musical exploration seemed to take longer than the previous one and could quickly turn into a logistical nightmare as the boy's nervy, wide-eyed innocence slowly transformed itself into world-weary paranoia.

John insisted on personally autographing every cheque JCE wrote out on behalf of John Nightly Ltd. Impossible if you consider an orchestral session from which each player would receive their individual MU fee – some 150 payments in all. Or the costings and budgets for a tour, involving 100 or so employees paid weekly over a four- to five-month period. Not only that, but John also insisted that the band's weekly wages be paid in absolute cash (brown envelope every Friday) that he would personally present to Justin, Jonathan, Ashley, Ron and Lee. This hands-on payday would necessarily be accompanied by a discussion about the band's clothes – the suitability of olive-green capes and magic beards for Ash and Ron ('Definitely not!' said Lee) – along with ongoing discussions about their personal lives – girlfriends' travelling arrangements and accommodation, individual members' drug and alcohol intake while performing, comfort elements of the workplace, onstage security (particularly with regard to 'electricals') – and of course their gear – instruments and amplification being the absolute preferred topic of conversation of every touring musician.

This personal weekly bestowment lasted all of six Fridays, ending only when John, carrying £14,000 in cash to be handed out on a particularly profitable payday, boarded a double-decker from Queen Square to Bond Street to be topped and tailed for a new suit. Immersed in a much too favourable *Melody Maker* review of *Quiz Axe Queen*, the paymaster managed to leave the cash – all of it – in a brown paper bag on the downstairs side-seat of the bus. He hung on to the magazine.

Realising his mistake in H. & C. Johnson & Co., Suit & Boot, John took a taxi straight to JCE and resigned from the position. With a bill of £14,000 and nothing but his own organisational shortcomings and embarrassment to show for it, this was the very last time John Nightly would ever have any involvement whatsoever in his own finances.

The end of the year approached, and the Sleepwalkers embarked upon yet another round of British dates. Universities and technical colleges, mainly – preferred by their manager because they were 'good payers' while keeping the band's profile high within the all-important student demographic. This handful of gigs being followed by a further five sold-out nights at the Lyceum Ballroom.

As expected, all went well, both with audiences and reviewers, but the Nightly band was tired, and the artist/manager relationship was becoming strained between each of the controlling arms of the operation, from John Nightly himself and JCE and John Nightly Ltd to Mosaic/EMI.

General over-indulgence was the obvious reason. John Pond still relied on two personal assistants – Sandra and, following Cornelia's departure, Daisy; 'Sand' and 'Daze' – to run his day-to-day affairs, and had settled into a daily routine of not so much 'nine to five' but more like 'four to five'. He'd arrive at the office late in the afternoon, to check on things rather than to instigate or direct them, only to leave the premises just one hour later. There were no more midnight calls to his client with inspired ideas for doing this or that and no more turning up at gigs in Harrogate or Swansea, unglamorous turning up, in order to demonstrate his continuing support.

The self-styled Svengali no longer appeared to care – not even enough to bother to *pretend* he cared in order to keep hold of his star act. For no doubt John Pond, like so many impresarios, imagined himself as being at the centre of things. Not existing to serve, enable or facilitate the artists. Pond saw himself as the tree, the source, and they, no matter how fond of them he was, were the branches – sometimes the twigs. The stars in the sky. As long as the Nightly industry generated sufficient income for his manager's percentage to fund an excessive personal lifestyle as well as business development – a string of new signings, a new production company and record label, an office in New York – Pond was content. The literal cash *flow*, or torrent, allowing the manager to prove to one and all that he really was capable of focussing on and overseeing the careers of a handful of his most happening clients while simultaneously staying up all night, boozing himself silly, downing a variety of illegal substances and screwing anything that happened to catch his eye and detain him for a few lonely hours.

Pondy was not overseeing very much at all anymore. JCE's most recent signing, Brocade – the group with the loudest buzz in years – had been launched not with a piece of plastic but via a Stateside TV series produced by Toba-Co Inc., the company behind most of the major cigarette advertising and commercial sports sponsorship in the US.

Toba-Co had approached JCE before, attempting to forge a union with Swinging London youth culture and introduce their traditionally midwestern smokes to a European market by way of the most happening English pop singer. Neither Pond nor his charge had been interested. Globally there was increasing public awareness about the link between smoking and illness; and although all of the Nightly band, including John himself, were heavy smokers the deal had seemed to everyone like an unnecessary and quite wrongheaded move. Pondy had been worried that the big hitters might go away and hit elsewhere, but had in the event been able to secure the tobacco giant's interest on to his latest signing.

The resultant TV series, *Psycho Deli*, told the story of a teacake, or 'English muffin' café/emporium, located in a free-living, free-loving suburb of San Francisco. An archetypal hippie enterprise, the action was set in what television executives in Burbank imagined to be a typically-English village store. Butcher's aprons and boaters, delivery bikes and perambulators mixed uneasily in the stage-set of a 'Victorian' bakery in which a customer entering the premises to make a purchase became enough of an excuse for a song. *Psycho Deli* was a kind of psychedelic 'tenement symphony' featuring the hapless Brocade in a series of multiple character roles with a change in both costume, and accent, every few minutes.

Introducing the five Hemel Hempstead lads as a touring band who liked the place so much they decided to open a Flower-Power delicatessen on Main Street, the series was a queasy mix of run-of-the-mill songs* provided by second-division Brill Building teams, together with a series of *Laugh-In* inspired, slapstick routines in forty-eight excruciatingly long episodes.

Deryk, Clement, Brian and Lance, a bunch of secondary-modern lookers with no previous convictions beyond the school

---

* The exception being the title song, 'She is Perfection' (Amber ABM 66038), a previously unreleased track by Alexander Telstar that became a turntable hit for the group in the US.

play were shown dealing simultaneously with both the racier elements of the Free Society and the cloddish, cliché-ridden script. The series premiered on US networks a week before the Nightly Lyceum dates, gathering some of the worst reviews in showbiz history. The group, its management and everything connected with it became a laughing stock. Not even the ruse of flying half of the British press to the West Coast for an exclusive preview of the first three episodes did anything but work against them. That exercise served as nothing more than confirmation that someone had, unfortunately, now actually seen the show. The idea of audience participation in *Psycho Deli* was based on the premise that viewers should be able to laugh with the protagonists, not at them. The press junket itself became mythical, an example of the very worst kind of pushy, paid-for promotion – only a few steps short of actual payola. Sadly this was all the Manager's doing.

Luckily, John Nightly was several layers removed from the whole thing. He missed the London opening because, as he explained to Pondy, he 'just forgot about it'; and the press and record-buying public made no connection between Brocade and the Nightly operation. Of the forty-eight episodes filmed only seven were ever broadcast in Britain.

Pond survived the incident, of course. Though he did seem to find it increasingly difficult to be anywhere near 'available for work'; that being the case, his staff grew accustomed to their boss being otherwise engaged and pretty much got on with the business of managing his client's careers without him. Pond cruised through the restaurants and clubs of London making deals and breaking them without being too concerned about whether or not a particular project was likely to happen. The important thing, the 'buzz', was that there might be yet another contract on the table, with further advance royalties to be pocketed.

But John Nightly was hot property and soon other players began to pick up the scent. It's a good deal easier to take over an act than to take one on, and various interested parties enquired after the wellbeing of both manager and star. Song publishers crossed the Atlantic hoping for an audience. In Britain, the NEMS office and former Who mentor Peter Meaden were just two who tried their luck.

Pond never studied chart positions anymore, even when they were good, appearing to have lost all interest in the day-to-day progress of his charges. He seemed unable to plan, too; or to see detail either. He had no thought for release dates, touring schedules or artwork, all of which were left to Sand, Daze and the acts themselves to sort out.

Like so many artists, John Nightly professed interest in the business side of his career without having any intention of following things through. Any kind of public relations, no matter how limited, was really just 'a waste of my time'. Engaged in the promotion of his current project, John's only thought would be to get back into the studio to begin work on the next.

item: Monthly Cultural Notes: August.

Things can get out of hand in the garden this month. Patio pots, hanging baskets and window boxes are particularly vulnerable. Houseplants need extra ventilation both day and night. Deal with any invasion of *Soleirolia soleirolii* (baby's tears) and other creeping perennials invading the lawn by hoeing out. Sow seeds in the cool of the evening or chill the earth with cold water before you sow. Fruit-bearing plants need regular liquid-feeding. If you live by the sea, gather seaweed for composting. Keep watch for slugs on bedding plants. Give roses, honeysuckle and camellias a good watering and remember to deadhead dahlias daily.

Cliff Shapiro Films, two floors above *the Jack* strip club, boasted its own self-contained recording studio. Shapiro's small track-laying room could accommodate up to twenty musicians, well enough space for the Nightly band to stretch out, rehearse their parts, have a good moan and do their thing. At the back of the studio, behind a corkboard screen, stood a simple projection set-up and a simple projectionist. Clips could be run when Morrie, brother of Cliff, said so, and not before.

Pitfall had been a success. Not an Oscar-laden box-office shatterer, but successful nonetheless. The low-budget, low-life thriller received flattering reviews all round, becoming one of a handful of homemade features doing respectable business up and down the country throughout the late summer of 1968.

As with many of the French new wave films of the period, *Pitfall* updated the crime genre by adding a psychological component while setting the story in a more optimistic, upbeat time. Its postcard of London at its swingiest, much of it shot around Soho and the West End, coupled with the good looks of its two young leads, Teri-Ann Christie and Bruno John, made the film a must-see for teenage cinema-goers, a 'thriller-diller', as Pondy termed it. Though the movie itself is now largely forgotten, location scenes regularly crop up as stock footage in cheaply produced TV tributes to the swinging decade.

While posters of Teri-Ann in her see-through cheesecloth made their way from the Apple Boutique to the school locker-room, the memorable soundtrack, which utilised a tension/release device borrowed from Michael Tippett, lodged itself in the British LP charts for a total of twenty-nine weeks, ensuring that *Pitfall* stayed in the public's consciousness much longer than it might have done without its soundtrack album – or its soundtrack composer.

Myra Knoll, just twenty-four, new to London and without any practical experience of the industry, was suddenly a hit-movie producer, achieving good-looking results on a limited budget and limited production schedule without the box-office benefit of established stars.

With this out-of-town debut the Texan heiress had demonstrated that she could both spot new talent and execute a project to a successful conclusion. Myra's hunches had paid off and so *Pitfall* accompanied *If* and *Performance* around the circuit as part of an ABC Regal double-bill. Stylistically, the film had its roots in the Italian and French cinema of the period. The movies watched by students, 'raincoats' and heads at the Academy Cinema in Oxford Street any wet weekday afternoon. The audience finding itself able to cope with subtitles as long as there was enough female nudity to nurse them through 90 quite unfathomable minutes. The producer had made sure that there was. The main characters, Pyotr and Jeanne, had been pushed in their scenes together to a level of sexual intimacy previously unseen in a British feature. The producer decided that the temporary or 'temp' French dialogue spoken between them should remain in the final cut.

These episodes, played out in the brilliant sunshine of London's parks and squares, went un-subtitled. This was a first for a British film of any kind and also the first time that domestic audiences outside of the capital would ever have watched anything that *foreign* and actually legal.

Two years earlier, on campus at UCLA, Myra had been inspired by Lelouch's *Un Homme et une Femme*. The young film student, noticing how scenes that took place in the car, on the beach and in the hotel bedroom needed little dialogue. It was entirely possible to watch the original movie in French without understanding a word of the language. When she explained her ideas about the use of music to her composer, the producer made it clear that this was a job she expected the score to do, with the same skill Francis Lai had demonstrated in *A Man and a Woman*.

John had of course come up with the goods. The movie's main

theme worked so well and swung so heavily that it was regularly heard in other contexts, becoming the main 'bed' to DJ chatter on Radio 1 as well as featuring in several Rediffusion Television commercials. Pondy, always on the lookout for 'the big one', had even presented it to the International Olympic Committee for Mexico '68 – though the response to the over-optimistic manager had been that the score was deemed 'a little too avant-garde for The Games.'

The title theme could no doubt have become an instrumental hit in its own right. In 1968, non-vocal singles were as popular as vocal tracks, chart-wise, and sat comfortably alongside any number of other chart-bound sounds in the nation's beloved *Fab Forty*. The *Top of the Pops* countdown included one-offs like Paul Mauriat's 'Love is Blue', Love Sculpture's 'Sabre Dance' and in another vein Whistling Jack Smith's 'I Was Kaiser Bill's Batman' and 'I Was Queen Victoria's Chambermaid' by pub pianist Mrs Mills*. John's own personal favourite, a record he played over and over, driving Iona to distraction, was Mason Williams' nylon symphony, 'Classical Gas'.

But the problem with film scores, as opposed to stand-alone records, was that a movie being pulled from the circuit by its distributor would pretty much signal the end for its soundtrack too. Each Friday a new line-up of film releases waited to take their place in the fleapit; so if a feature didn't fill the theatre week after week, another would replace it. For a period of almost six weeks in ABC theatres up and down Britain *Pitfall* remained the movie to see. In the Dandelion cafés and 'grad pads' of England's university towns, students mused over its social

---

* A former superintendent in the typing pool of the Paymaster General, 'sing-along' pianist Mrs Mills (Gladys) was signed by Dave Clark Five and Rolling Stones manager Eric Easton after being spotted at Woodford Golf Club by EMI talent scouts. Her sing-along singles and albums, recorded at Abbey Road Studios, became million-sellers, including 'Mrs Mills' Party' (PMC 1264), 1965, 'Let's Have Another Party' (PMC 7035), 1967, and 'Another Flippin' Party' (PCS 1753), 1972. Her seasonal offering for 1977 was 'Glad Tidings' (EMI OU2197).

message, argued about its muddled plot and fantasised about its lead actress.

Back in the basement of the Jack, Ron tucked into a Cornish pasty while Justin took the pliers to his top *E.* The others ran through a spiralling, semitonal progression, the music slithering along its uneasy path before seeming to turn in on itself, although actually ascending to a higher pitch – a trick John had picked up from studying an MFP recording of a Prokofiev ballet. In the composer's *Cinderella,* the melodies embarked upon their independent trajectories. They progressed in the direction the listener expected, but seldom arrived. Instead, they flattened and diminished, alternatively decisive and indecisive in a key-defying display. To the average listener, at sea with anything more than three chords and easy-to-chew phrases, this was distracting rather than thrilling; but to the musical listener, the bearer of the gift of listening, the effect could be mesmerising. On a journey without signposts, the serious musical audience was led down – lifted down – a sometimes slippery path, a chromatic staircase without end in an often ironic though supremely elegant arrangement of melody and harmony typical of the composer. Prokofiev gave no clues about cadences or resolves. He was beyond all that. So was John Nightly. In *Cinderella,* every phrase posed a question, seemed a stretch or opened a door. In John's upcoming Cantata – or Requiem; he hadn't yet decided which – the three independent yet individually complete LPs would set off on their own courses. By piling one inversion on top of another (the way Miles Davis created 'cool' harmony), by combining unusual instruments (the way Rimsky-Korsakov and Stravinsky pioneered sounds and effects for the orchestra), by scattering each free-thinking melody in all directions (as in Charlie Parker or Brian Wilson's 'explorations'), John intended to remove his audience to a more ambiguous musical withdrawing room. For Sergei Prokofiev, and therefore for John Nightly, a question *was* a resolve.

'What *is* that guitar you're wearing today, sir?' John asked of Justin in a momentary and quite uncharacteristic lapse into frivolity.

Justin seemed pleasantly taken aback as he spun around.

'That, sir, is a Rickenbacker *Jetstar* 325!'

Ashley jumped on to his kit to play out a mock 'Tah-dah!' – clicking his sticks together while at the same time disturbing several years' worth of dust in the dried-out cellar.

'Is it, by Christ?' replied the boss. 'Well... my giddy aunt! All the better to see you with.'

'*Hear you with...*' interjected Ms Knoll, as John opened his guitar case to reveal a freshly painted rainbow Stratocaster.

'*hear you with* – yeh... that's right,' he mumbled, while Justin smiled knowingly and continued to tune his instrument.

The boss searched his pockets for a plectrum, acknowledged the other members of the band, accepted a cigarette from Ron, then picked up a chair and placed it in front of the stage for the producer to sit down. Even in this high summer of super-fame the boy's Grantchester manners had not deserted him. As soon as Jackie, Myra's assistant, entered bearing a portable cassette recorder, the order was given to roll film.

At the back of the room, Morrie eased his fat belly out of his seat and cut the lights as John strapped on his guitar and stood face-on to the band. Arms outstretched, legs apart, John engaged in eye contact and nodded to each performer in turn as if he were about to conduct a Prom at the Royal Albert Hall. The projector started on its cranky course.

Exterior: *A silver spring day. The entrance to Notting Hill underground station. 5pm. Rush hour. Commuters pour out onto the pavement as the camera picks out a teenage girl, a 'Flower Child' in purple headband and 'hippie' dress, goldleaf stars painted on her cheeks.*

On screen, Teri-Ann crossed the street and disappeared into

The Glass Bead, a head shop tucked away behind a pub on the corner of Pembridge Road. In the studio, John began a slow, measured count – in seven, of course – *2-3-4, 1-2-3-4-5-6-7* – until the scene cut to the interior of the building. An inky line-drawing of the proprietor, a comic-book hippie, became superimposed on the screen before being lost within a haze of smoke, supposedly emanating from inside the premises, so dense and impenetrable that there must have been a whole sackful of marijuana involved, as the teenager handed over a package to the girl behind the counter. Right on cue, the editor's punch-flash appeared in the top right-hand corner of the screen, the signal for Justin and Ron to begin.

The music immediately lent atmosphere to the scene; a rising motif helping to convey the narrative without getting in the way; the traditional function and sometimes unrewarding 'lot' of the film composer. As Ashley laid into the drums, things suddenly got very loud indeed within the confines of the small basement so that both Myra and Jackie, not at all used to hearing a rock'n'roll drum kit being pelted just a few feet away, slapped their hands tightly over their ears. John immediately indicated that everyone play softer, at which point the effect of the score when it was properly synced to picture became apparent.

The next scene, a frenzied chase through the back streets of Kensington, had been shot in forward and backward motion simultaneously; again, with one take superimposed on another. Robin Hedges, familiar to TV viewers as a delinquent in *Z Cars* and *Dixon of Dock Green*, appeared as the stoned shop-keeper, looking suitably bedraggled and crazed. The previous week, during editing, Myra had expressed concerns about the scene moving too fast. This afternoon, with John Nightly's serpent-like guitar laid across it, the composer managing to slow things down as briefed, the pace slackened, almost to slow motion, creating a mood that the clip did not possess previously. Hedges and his co-star, Hazel Linden, came to a halt outside an antique shop at the top of Portobello Road. Again, the music showed a keen touch, able to modulate and lift the scene without revealing where it was actually headed.

Everyone seemed pleased as the lights went up. Morrie announced a 'toilet' break while Myra congratulated John, walking over to put her arm around him as Jackie took photographs of the assembled group for a forthcoming *Rave* feature and passed her telephone number to Justin.

Ash hit *playback* on the tape-machine and Ron began to improvise around the upcoming 'Main Title' on the piano.

'Don't spoil it, man,' John snapped. 'Haven't got to that bit yet – don't spoil it.' The over-enthusiastic pianist switched to the theme to *Daktari* while Ashley rolled joints and Morrie lined up the next reel. Myra visibly relaxed as she removed her knitted cap to let her hair fall down across her wide shoulders. A most unlikely film producer, John thought. He may not have liked his collaborator much, but as she sat cross-legged in front of him with her kaftan and scarves and oversized sunglasses and cue-sheets and clipboards, he certainly *desired* her. A married oil heiress might not be that big a deal as a conquest. But one for whom he happened to be working would be. As he considered the odds, John Nightly had to conclude that any romantic involvement with Miss Knoll was not good protocol whichever way he looked at it.

But John also suspected that his unstoppable egotism, his unaccountable need to 'score' and his lack of self-respect after a couple of whiskeys and some hashish would probably lead him astray. Another notch to add to his by now difficult-to-recall tally. Or maybe it was just something to do. A new diversion; literally a new body to experience. Sleeping with someone was a very good way of getting to know them, as Pondy helpfully observed.

The producer glanced back in the boy's direction and noticed him staring. She smiled a wholly empty smile back. Maybe she shared the same feelings, neither of them being what might be described as considerate people. They may not even have considered themselves. John Nightly and Myra Knoll were both capable of walking over others to achieve a self-imposed goal. The only difference being that John was so self-obsessed and distracted he was seldom aware that he was doing it.

'It's sounding good, honey.' Myra complimented the composer while she continued to study the club's interior.

The Jack, a 'listed building' in Soho drinking circles, was a disgrace. Its once-shimmering velveteen walls lay heavily damp-stained with beer, mould and who-knows-what. The stench of cheap second-hand cologne hit the unsuspecting punter like a sedative. It drifted through the corridors and passageways and lingered in the common parts. No – the entire place was common. Without any attempt being made to preserve any of the listed decorative elements from the club's authentic Regency interior, once-proud single-timber joists were now having to support polypropylene fixtures and fittings. Prefab skirting intervened between original Welsh-oak floors and Rococo recesses. K-Lord curtains adorned ornate hand-crafted window boxes while built-in pear-wood seating had been usurped by plastic garden seats and pub benches. The overall decorative style best summed up as 'modern vulgar'.

The front and back entrances to the club were patrolled by a couple of heavies so stereotypical they might've been assembled from a kit. 'Alright, darlin'? What time you on then?' chirped Tommy, 'the fat one' – they were both obese – as Ms Knoll landed on the welcome mat.

'Long after your bedtime, honey,' came the quick-as-a-flash response. Justin cast his eye over the small ads vying for competition on the club's noticeboard.

'This is a good one, Ash,' Justin chuckled. *Large, new chest, in beautiful condition, to view tel: FUL 603.'*

'Ya really wanna view that, Just?'

John ordered drinks all round from the Coca-Cola bar, telling the band that it would be a short break as Karmov, the film's director, was due in to take a look at the next scene.

'I have more projects coming up. Perhaps you'll be interested in another movie?' Myra inhaled from her filter-tip and checked her make-up in a tiny, bejewelled compact.

'As long as it's something… different to this one. I'm not entirely sure I'm, well… any good at this yet,' replied the composer, before deciding to qualify his less-than-enthusiastic response. 'I know I can write the music, but I don't know if it's really… entirely suitable… or… even proper *film music*, for that, uh…'

Taken aback by her collaborator not exactly leaping to the challenge, Myra raised her eyebrows in a questioning, rather deflated way.

'Maybe that's what's good about it. What you've written. Maybe it's not really *film music*. Doesn't sound like film music usually sounds.' The producer considered for a second. 'Maybe film music doesn't sound like film music anymore.'

John sent a grateful smile Myra's way.

'I have two scripts. One British – to be shot here – from a book with a title I hope we can keep.' Myra cleared her throat. *'Shipwreck at Pistol Meadow.'*

'… that is a good title.'

'Very English story,' she explained. 'Smugglers' story. Set in Cornwall, where King Arthur came from. Kind of… atmospheric… That's popular back home. Right now it is. Something dark and… English. *Gothic melodrama.* What my father would call "dirty-looking films".' Myra edged further up on her chair. 'But I want to make a realistic… hard-hitting movie. Not one about Dick Turpin.' She took another drag.

'and the other one?'

'No title yet. But I'm talking to R. D. Laing… Ronald Laing.'

'The psychiatrist?'

'"Anti-psychiatrist"… isn't it?' The barman brought a tray holding six half-size tumblers. Myra picked up her drink.

'I actually like the title *The Divided Self*… his book,' she continued. 'I wondered whether… a kind of modern, romantic story, could be written around someone trying to help someone else… who needed their help… Both needing each other… equally – as much as each other – needing the same thing from each other.' Myra paused. 'Like a patient needs their psychiatrist… and vice versa. Some kind of… mental… "tempera- mental" story…'

John signalled the band go downstairs and get on with it. He picked up his guitar.

'I'd be interested in that. I don't know about smugglers… don't know if what I would think of doing would be what you… want,' he reasoned, excusing himself in a roundabout way. 'I don't know if I can really *do* anything – in that line… Music to accompany film, or "a film", I mean… other than… what I would naturally or… normally do anyway.' He looked round for his cigarettes. 'Maybe not a "problem" exactly… but…'

Myra smiled politely and grabbed her editing notes. As she turned away she eavesdropped on the conversation going on behind; mindless chatter between individual band members about their billing on the film's poster. Unsurprised but unfazed, she got up and moved through the bar towards the stairs and back to the session.

It was hard to hear yourself think in the corridor, as the bass pedals of a Wurlitzer organ thundered up through the floor of the club, dislodging ancient plaster while helping some unfortunate grind her way through her act downstairs.

The producer continued to take in the scene. A naked light-bulb caked in fly shit illuminated the entrance to the Jack creating a fine first impression to all-comers. The girls' performance rota – '*April: 2pm, May: 3pm, June: 4pm…*' – was pinned up above statutory notices concerning the status of the club's on/off drinks licence, fire regulations – '*In Case of Fire: Move Your Arse!!!*' – and the ludicrously expensive bar tariff.

What was she doing in London anyway? Myra could so easily have stayed back home, riding out with her much-mentioned husband, surveying her father's vast estates. Helping with the daily round, as she would when she was Daddy's girl. Mending fences, not breaking them. The lush open spread of Orange County. The finely trellised lawns of White Farm Ranch, all 37 years' worth of Knoll ancestral home.

Myra and her brother Bill rode the open range until they reached deserts of epiphyllum, opuntia and giant barrel-cacti. Her brother's cattle and her father's buffalo herds grazed among redwood, cypress and overgrown yew. The adolescent tomboy had enjoyed the privileged lifestyle Bill Knoll Snr had provided for her and her baby brother by means of his and his own father's hard work. If Myra was ever going to strike oil herself, she most likely wasn't going to find it in London's armpit. Bill could make neither head nor tail of his daughter's choice of career. Why his little girl wanted to leave the family quinta and hang around in musty old England with its inedible food and its fey, unmanly types he hadn't a clue; and he was damned certain his wife wouldn't have either.

Bill had not enjoyed *Pitfall*. Though of course he'd told his daughter that he had. It was 'a tough picture'. With no real suspense or romance, and certainly no thrills. He found the two leads unattractive, skinny – 'creepy' even. And the music? He probably hadn't even noticed it. Maybe it was the music that was creepy and not the actors. Maybe they both were – he couldn't tell. Bill Knoll was a simple man, as he pronounced to everyone within minutes of meeting them, and wrote to his daughter that she ought to be making musicals, anyway. Like *Kismet, The Sound of Music* or *The Music Man*. Big films. With big tunes. The word 'music' in the title, if at all possible. So the audience knew what they were dealing with. Films that everyone liked. That the box office liked. Or maybe a Western. It didn't have to be an old John Wayne one; it could be a modern Western… like *Butch Cassidy*. Bill loved *Butch Cassidy*. Butch Cassidy summed it up. A real film, a '*real*' man's '*real*' film. The movie of the moment, with Butch and Sundance the kind of cowboys or cow*men* he himself might employ at BeeKay. That kind of movie was most definitely the way to go.

But Bill didn't know the half of it. Because while the oil executive imagined his daughter at the tennis club, or the broker's brunch, Myra was out there at the very heart of the action. Slumming it with the real down-and-outs – the artists themselves. Hanging with 'difficult' actor types in damp rehearsal rooms, accompanying arrogant and seemingly dim-witted musicians to concerts, after-hours drinking clubs and dope parties, earning herself a reputation as a regular party girl, or at least when she wasn't up at the crack of dawn on a film set – in which case her whole persona would revert and she'd be as sober and clear-headed as an executioner.

'It's really okay to get out of your head – as long as you put your whole heart into it'

John Nightly, SUMHA, Los Angeles, 1972

As the new year turned once more, John Nightly chose to disregard his manager's mostly self-inflicted problems and concentrate on making music. John threw himself into his work, ignoring his wife, his various consorts and his expensively retainered band, who wished for nothing more than to stop sitting around in London and 'get back on the road'.

John fleshed out his orchestral sketch, now re-titled *Symphony in Orange Ink*, until he was satisfied with the five short movements before handing it over to Jonathan Foxley to orchestrate. The composer checked that the combination of instruments, the timbre and the various orchestral weights and colours as chosen by Jonathan were exactly as he envisaged during three day-long rehearsals at the Royal Academy of Music with the college's second-year student orchestra.

This new piece, a strand of John's output often regarded as being overly dark or melancholic – 'misery tunes' as Iona put it – suddenly appeared driven by a fresh, youthful spirit; particularly the slow, fourth movement, its ever-ascending sequence indicating a new influence or 'spark' in the composer's own very geocentric world. A person or event he could not help but refer to in his music.

Again, *Orange Ink* received a single performance; though favourably reviewed, it lacked the much-missed input of his manager, a collaborator able to take advantage of every opportunity so that all concerned might benefit from resulting ticket and record sales. Had John Pond been engaged, the sold-out premiere at the London Dance Theatre's temporary Covent Garden space could have been replicated many times over.

With choreography by Donna Vost, and a spirited performance coerced out of inexperienced players by Jonathan, the one thing missing (as the reviews pointed out) were those big John Nightly melodies. Those *Firebird*-like themes, so rich, confident and strong – and modal – that they required neither harmonic underpinning, nor the context and framework of long-form structure. *Orange Ink* seemed to have everything going for it except those big, life-giving tunes.

But there was a good reason for their absence. The composer was saving the absolute best of everything for his next blast, his 'best shot' – a piece that was to be the culmination of everything he'd written so far, as well as combining 'all of the music I've ever heard in my life'. A kind of coming together, a distillation of fabric that had been sourced, absorbed and filtered, put through the John Nightly sieve, in order that he might complete this master project, this definitive account, highest of high points, before abandoning everything he'd ever committed to tape – the lot of it – to begin again, begin afresh, as he often talked of, 'at POINT ZERO'.

As he entered the third decade of his life, the 'Jesus decade' (again, as he himself referred to it), John Nightly wished more than anything to make his mark in the serious music world, in order that if, in his morbid sensibility, he had gotten run over by the proverbial bus, dropped dead in the proverbial street, fell out of the sky one day or fell victim to his new favourite fear – onstage assassination – he might have something of real value to leave behind. This best shot was going to be truly remarkable, something to be reckoned with, to be remembered by. 'Progressive', 'groundbreaking', 'pioneering'; those hyperbolic adjectives applied by promoters of contemporary culture to so many new contrivances would have an undeniable, almost 'human' right, as a genuine pre-emptive strike superglued to whichever title John might ascribe to this new imagining. Like the 'shuttle songs' or 'supernova symphonies', blasted into space in order to represent the best of our earth to alien civilisations, John Nightly would conceive his 'world hymns for mankind' – music for the horses to graze by, music for the bees to buzz to, music as eternal as birdsong, as incarnate as human flesh – to be as contingent and unfailing as the human spirit itself.*

Even the format would cross boundaries, push envelopes and cut edges. Three separate LPs played on three separate turntables, each in sync with one another, delivering one piece of extremely big-sounding music. Triple-Stereo indeed. A real triple-album. A trilogy. A triumvirate. A triptych. A trinity. Or 'Triplets!' as Iona declared.

A trip, and hopefully a triumph, this Black Mass or Black Symphony was going to be proper and posh. A kind of 'village cantata'. Multi-dimensional, multimedia, in its own world, on its own terms, non-concessionary and non-compromising, an all-weather *Pop Music Gesamtkunstwerk*, as John Pond christened it. A *savenheer* for the serious listener but also a 'living work' for all people – 'For Everyman. Everyone Everywhere,' Pond insisted, supergluing as many adjectives as he could summon – and, from its composer's point of view, a work approaching sacramental status. That's why he called it the *Mink Bungalow Requiem*.

---

* The 1965 *Gemini VI* space mission included 'Hello Dolly' as sung by Jack Jones. For the 1968 *Apollo II* moon mission flight director Eugene F. Krantz psyched himself up with John Philip Sousa marches. In 1972, the *Apollo 17* crew shipped the Carpenters' 'We've Only Just Begun'.

note:
5.24.2011. 'The crew of the space shuttle Endeavour will awaken today to the sound of Rush. A one-minute clip of Rush's "Countdown", from 1982's *Signals*, will be beamed from Earth to the shuttle at 6pm EST. The song was selected by mission specialist Mike Fincke and coincides with Victoria Day in Canada. Watch it live on NASA TV. This is the final flight for *Endeavour* and the second-to-last scheduled space-shuttle flight for NASA. Rush, in the meantime, are on their *Time Machine* tour, which continues Wednesday in London and will wrap up in Seattle in July.' (www.BraveWords.com)

note:
The space probes *Voyagers 1 & 2*, both launched in September 1977, carried onboard a gold record containing the sounds of the Earth – surf, wind, thunder, whale calls, greetings in 55 languages – and music by Bach, Beethoven, Stravinsky, Chuck Berry's 'Johnny B. Goode' and 'Dark was the Night' by Blind Willie Johnson. Frank Sinatra's 1964 recording of Bart Howard's 'Fly Me to the Moon' was played by the astronauts of *Apollo 10* on their lunar-orbital mission and again on the moon itself by the astronaut Buzz Aldrin during the *Apollo 11* landing.

'...y' 'ad y'straights, and y' 'ad y' 'eads', y'know.
Y' 'ad y' 'freaks' and what they used to call
y' 'freaky beaks' [laughs].
John was... 'e was what people mighta thought of as...
'e was like... I dunno...
like... 'e was the 'ead 'ead... if y'know
what ah mean...'

Lee Hide

'The record I like most right now is "Classical Gas" by Mason Williams. I love it.'

John Nightly, *Scene & Heard*, BBC Radio 1, 17 June 1968

If Myra Knoll was full of herself then Donna Vost was full of doubt. Donna experienced many more 'unconfident' than confident days, while Myra, even if she was prone to the odd moment of self-doubt, was not one to let the facade drop. In terms of personality, as well as physical appearance, they could not have been more different.

Miss Knoll was the very picture of health. Her cow-fed, Daddy-fattened childhood had produced a formidable Texan princess. Donna was the opposite. Her seldom-fed slender frame, the product of a family of Iron Curtain hoofers, was starved by choice. She followed the diet of a ballerina or champion jockey. In her case nourished not by protein or vitamin, but by book reading and play-going. Keeping to a strict macrobiotic regime, Donna's physical and mental discipline had produced a sylph-like presence. The young dancer was acutely intelligent, acutely sensitive and acutely neurotic.

But Miss Vost was no less physically attractive than her rival, and rather more conventionally feminine in appearance. It was the way she moved, on tiptoe almost, padding around the studio as if she were part-sighted, feeling her way through a semi-resistant web. For a trained soloist, able to memorise the ticker-tape choreography of both Frederick Ashton and Frederich Astaire, Donna Vost rarely gave the impression that she knew where she was headed. Either in the next few steps or in life itself.

But you'd notice her. You'd notice her alright. She was the leaf-light figure in Isadora silks smiling and swaying backstage at the Roundhouse or soul-dancing at Sybilla's. Donna would appear unannounced at whichever studio the band were booked into, kick off her flip-flops and let herself be liberated by what she heard, gently bending her supple limbs as she floated through the control room, alternating between swigs of peppermint tea and Southern Comfort. Able to illustrate and act out the music, interpreting it exactly as the composer imagined. John said that Donna moved to his music as if she'd written it herself. 'The Gazelle', Justin called her, for she did have something of the appearance of a fallow deer. The band members could only imagine what sublime pleasures might be experienced if Donna's anatomically perfect, classically trained, supplement-enriched limbs ever came anywhere near their creaky, calcium-deprived rock'n'roll sheckles.

But the combination was never likely to be, for the girl had eyes only for one: the boss, the enchanter. Donna declared that, should John ever be free to love and be loved, she would lay out all of her charms and pentacles, her love beads, her prayer beads, even her Ukrainian grandmother's beads (the most treasured beads in her possession), and plot some kind of beady, astrologically-sound seduction or enchantment.

The Gazelle had already obtained detailed charts for both herself and her intended. He was a Cancer with Saturn in Gemini, she a Pisces with Jupiter in Virgo – conclusive proof that creator and interpreter were as perfect a match, astrally-speaking, as could ever be. This taken-as-fact pronouncement she repeated to Ron, Justin, Ashley, Jonathan, Lee and even Pondy, plus anyone else who would listen, politely or otherwise, including the enchanter himself.

It was Donna who kept the boss up to date, kept him avant-garde. John Nightly used to be avant-garde, back in his Grantchester days, but the effect seemed to have gradually worn off. In Cambridge, John's enthusiasm for unmusical music, un-poetic poetry and illogical, cosmological equations raised him above the pub-and-cellar chit-chat of both Town and Gown. There remained a kind of academic tradition along the Backs; but, given that this was the seat of learning of Darwin, Donne and Newton, topics of conversation at the Cavendish laboratory were much the same as anywhere else. When they weren't making groundbreaking discoveries, research students' minds were focused on university goings-on and -off; football, cricket and rugger, James Bond actresses and institutional scandal. Most likely it never dawned on the boy that it was his very solitude that kept him 'thinking differently', naturally off-centre. It was almost more difficult to keep up to date in London. Particularly when you were being creative yourself, and away from the action a lot of the time promoting those creations.

Therefore Donna Vost appointed herself John Nightly's personal tastemaker. Taking him to evenings at the Open Space Theatre in Tottenham Court Road, jazz and poetry – Jazzetry – concerts at the ICA, or dance events at the Roundhouse. They'd go out to Eel Pie Island* to see John Mayall's Bluesbreakers or Long John Baldry's Hoochie Coochie Men. Close by was the location of Pete Townshend's Oceanic, the UK's first Meher Baba retreat. Prayer circles, 'encounter groups' and other gatherings were springing up all over the capital. Donna kept John in threads. At least for casual clothes, something Iona could never be bothered to do, as he dutifully accompanied Ms Vost to her favourite boutiques.

What John saw in the teenager was someone, the only person other than Jana, who was able to really get to grips with what he was trying to do. Donna heard the music, spoke that same language; and this of course meant everything to him.

John hammered out his inspirations and Donna, inspired, danced to them. Though she found the music itself very moving, what no doubt motivated her as much as anything else was the actual proximity to – and the possibility of closer contact *with* – its perpetrator. The girl would not have to wait long. John tried to concentrate on his crushed tritones and spread-fingered arpeggios but soon became distracted by her fluid, attention-seeking movement and ended up playing many more clusters than usual.

Whenever they did meet, to have sex – at Queen Square, as Donna shared a bedsit in Earl's Court with Marnie, her regular stand-in, or in a room at the Savoy Hotel pre-booked with a piano and a dance-friendly floor – the late-afternoon sessions comprised

* By 1970 Eel Pie Island had become Britain's largest hippie commune.

50 per cent work and 50 per cent recreation, though the affair still retained something of the feeling of an old-fashioned romance – unlike John's adventures with Myra, who would have more or less disrobed on the stairs leading up to his front door. Myra wanted to get on with it, get it over with, in a way, so she could get back to her production schedules and call sheets. Love-making sessions with his producer would be interrupted by telephone calls at awkward times, most being transatlantic, leaving the composer in abeyance. John would hold his boss in his arms while she wooed some highly touted actor or director; the wooer-in-waiting ironically much more fabulous, and famous, than that being wooed.

For a short while – autumn 1968 through to spring the following year – John Nightly appeared to have it both ways. These two opposing forces were available to him at any time of the day or night at very short notice. Short notice was good, and suited everyone. Convenient to both Myra's filming commitments and Donna's independent dance projects. Notwithstanding the odd groupie or fan he might occasionally favour, John Nightly seemed to have solved the age-old problem of how to truly combine business with pleasure – or in his case pleasure with pleasure.

But keeping several lovers at once is not at all straightforward. Being involved in two serious relationships simultaneously necessitated an adjustment psychologically. In those moments when the reality of the situation might suddenly be brought into focus, the boy would be forced to conclude that he had no real feelings for either companion. No commitment or preference romantically or morally. How did Donna and Myra deal with their own compromising situations?

Six months in there remained a kind of collusion between the three partners as to the true nature of each one's relationship with the other. Every liaison became a mini-drama in itself. Both women asked impossible-to-answer questions. An inquisition would often take place, prompting the defendant to view that particular evening's get-together as the final bout of an overlong series. Though a brilliant instigator of projects and a natural ideas man, John Nightly was a very poor closer.

Dropping a tab of lightning several nights a week, whether in the company of mistress or band, groupie or hanger-on, the boss found he was beginning to get very overtired indeed – sometimes inhumanly so. But then, everyone was. Revolution had proved to be hard work. Due to the almost round-the-clock socialising, band rehearsals and meetings were fitted in around more important events – friends' gigs, album playbacks, press receptions and art openings – resulting in everyone performing badly and becoming irritable and aggressive. A roomful of distracted, paranoid persons, out of their heads with worry about their own half-imagined, self-obsessed non-anxieties.

When the freaks should have been viewing their output objectively, from outside of their overcooked heads, the substances they were taking placed them firmly at the centre of things. The layout of the day became distorted. Wake-up calls could never be earlier than one or two in the afternoon. Bedtime occurred anytime at all within the Greenwich Mean Time spectrum.

The scene was half asleep, in a daze, mostly; running out of steam and therefore easy prey for the flanks of commercial operators looking to exploit neo-hippie culture. A decade of optimism and expectation was edging into decline. It seemed to many that the Revolution was running very late, if indeed it was coming at all.

When John and Iona attended the Dialectics of Liberation conference (Chalk Farm Roundhouse, July '67), the most significant counter-cultural assembly of the era, he did finally, – for the first time in his life – begin to consider his own physical and psychological limits; the otherwise-unexplored space between his own inner and outer self.

The conference, set up by R. D. Laing and the Institute of Phenomenological Studies, considered the effect of mental and physical 'violence' in society. Including the home-spun violence of love itself, by way of making inroads into understanding the 'oppression' of love while at the same time demystifying it. 'Education enslaves us, technology kills us!' proclaimed the handout for the fortnight-long bash. After hearing lectures by Laing and Black Power leader Stokely Carmichael, John resolved to make changes, including a real attempt to clean up and get himself together so as to be able to exploit the 'heavy creative phase' he felt was currently being 'laid on him'.

This meant that over the next few months the young millionaire took far less pick-me-ups and spent far more time at home, improvising freely on the piano, recording every thought and spark, while sampling paperbacks of Laing, Winnicott and Freud in easy-to-swallow doses. Health-wise, there was a noticeable, immediate improvement. But also, for the first time since he left Grantchester, John began to think – really *think*. And when that happened his reflections inevitably centred around his childhood.

John Nightly considered daily life firstly from the point of view of his mother Frieda. He imagined her standing on the edge of a wide bay, like a sentinel or watchman, looking out to sea at her two 'best men'. Floating impressions in the form of the lifeless bodies of John himself and his father came in and out of focus like skiffs or sailboats brought into land to be taken away again by the waves and tides. Was Frieda really better off than she would have been if she'd remained at home in Norway? A society with a good supply of strong, independent-minded, 'normal' Norwegian men instead of weak, repressed Englishmen. He imagined Nightly family life as if he were John Snr, the invigilator and guardian who had encouraged John more than anyone, giving up even the family home, converting it into a sonic adventure playground for his only child. A playground that no doubt reflected John Snr's own interests, perhaps enabling him to realise some of his own unfulfilled dreams and desires. John the son hoped that had indeed been the case.

For the first time ever, John Nightly was able to view his compliant, put-upon but thoroughly good-natured father as a stand-alone man. A whole person (temporarily) disconnected from his wife and child, rather than a service character or supporting player, a mere attachment to his family. Was this man, this individual, really fulfilled and content? Or just making the best of it? 'Doing his duty', like everyone else of a proper moral bent in these hard-up times.

In this respect, the boy's family were with him throughout the birth of what was to become his magnum opus. John sat in the stillness and darkness of the box room, his hands resting on the keys, and let his mind go as he waited for something to come. When it did, he hit the red button on his new mini cassette-machine faster than Rod Laver could return a serve. Everything John Nightly channelled during this most productive period would be collated, edited and assembled to be reordered and reorganised at a later date by Justin. Ready to be restructured, reformatted, re-recorded, prior to being orchestrated and carefully polished, finessed for human consumption. Donkeywork a lot of it, particularly the part that would have to be completed after the composer had exhausted his ideas, long after his current heavy creative phase had deserted him.

A lot of what had been discussed at the Laing conference applied to John's own beginnings. The Nightly family, as it existed in Cambridge, would have been the perfect control group. It lived in a kind of cell, sealed tightly away from its neighbours. Even the streets bordering Meadow Road were light years away from it. Few relatives visited. No friends stayed over. No birthday or tea parties had ever been celebrated. There was never more than 25 per cent school attendance for John, with hardly any interaction with children of his own age. Days were long and generally given over to work. For John Snr that meant numbingly extended hours and extra shifts. But, as he would regularly tell his workmates, 'if it means a better going-on for my wife and son...' – the unspoken reason for maximum overtime being the need for John's father to get away from Frieda's and John's specific two-hander while remaining able to bring sufficient income into the production for the group to be able to maintain its own vital seclusion from the outside world.

But there was also a great deal of love. Of a type. Residual love is what it was. The love that could apparently be produced from concerted labour. It seemed that, as far as the Nightly household was concerned, love itself was one of the by-products of labour. And apparently, like karma, it would eventually seep out, suffuse and envelope both the lovers and the loved. It was a love squeezed from tired eyes. Snuggled up between dry lips. Producing, the perpetrators imagined, in distilled form, contentment; a sort of tired, dry happiness. Another by-product. Of a kind.

As John Nightly studied his precious facsimiles, highlighting sections by placing slips of different coloured paper between the pages, he began to think about what might remain if the music were to be removed from his own psychological make-up. John no doubt realised that he would one day have to come to terms with his own behavioural imbalance, but what he concluded wasn't healthy reading. Without the music of John Nightly – removing the song from the singer – there was little more than a stain of the boy left. John remembered a comment by one of his teachers from his final school report. Rebecca Thorne, BA (Hons), MA (Cantab), John's history monitor and form mistress, had written that 'apart from being continually distracted, in a world of his own, and finding it hard to concentrate', the boy seemed 'emotionally detached, cold sometimes, hard to get through to'.

Neither Frieda nor her husband had ever mentioned this rather too frank comment. Or if they had it was glossed over and forgotten like everything else in the Nightly household relating to emotions or opinions that might affect or upset its own precarious balance. That was it! No one wanted to be affected! The dynamic between the partners having been wound up so damn tight that the group may not have been able to survive a slight momentum shift. John considered how things might be at the present moment between John Snr and Frieda. Day to day. Without John himself – the pivot, the referee, the buffer separating two headstrong contenders who were victims also. He assumed there were few words spoken between the sparrers now. They barely existed as a couple. His mother and father had somehow stayed together… but why? Too afraid to leave or even to move? Move on? Go forward, or maybe go back?

John imagined there being little human contact in Meadow Road beyond the postman and the milkman. As far as he knew, his father continued to work as many hours as possible while his mother drifted farther away. Comforted by her son's unexpected success of course. Proud of him no doubt, without actually wanting to have anything to do with it. Fearful of the whole development of fame itself and what might come after.

Frieda hadn't even gone to see the Nightly band at Cambridge Guildhall the previous July. A big gig, just two miles from home. Though John's father had, of course, making an excuse for his wife's absence when he himself appeared from behind the backstage monitors minutes before his son boarded a tour bus bound for Carlisle.

John Nightly spent the winter of that year in this considering, configuring mode. Then, as the flow dried up and more practical concerns took over, he went back into the studio and back into denial. The boy requested that JCE book a six-month lockout in the two most expensive recording facilities in London and at the same time book him an appointment with Dr Laing at his practice in Wimpole Street. John Nightly then beat a hasty retreat back into a limbo world of half-waking, half-sleeping escape.

Gorse bushes at Porthcreek
© John Daly 2002

Cornwall is yellow in spring. From daffodil acres on sloping coastal plains to the lemon tapers of the *Aeonium Heliconia* that decorate Endymion Peed's kitchen window. Fiery-orange gorse, nature's barbed wire, protects the outland pasture from walkers and hikers. The enemy. Unwashed and unwanted. TRESPASSERS. Heavy-booted destroyers of coastal fields and plots. Despised by the indigenous population, walkers are both a serious environmental nuisance and a joke, as far as the locals are concerned.

These legalised invaders – with their bulging rucksacks, ever-present *athletes'* water bottles (later found abandoned in every ditch and spill), their collections of rods and staffs to help them up the soft 3:1 gradient – could be seen, and sometimes heard, braving the track that led firstly towards and then away from the white farm. A rainforest-grade kitbag full of compasses and charts is necessary to guide these hapless meanderers along perfectly well-marked acorn paths.

'What *are* they on?' Mawg would ask.

'Private land,' RCN would reply.

Endy was in full flow. It wasn't often she felt the need, but when a gush of Quethiock logic did come it came in a flood. Subjects for discussion: the cutting down of coast redwoods, house-building on ancient grazing land and residential developments close to the beach. After that, if anyone was still conscious, she might proclaim about the decimation of the local bird population, erosion of the hedgerows and hedge banks, or closure of local services. Cutbacks in nearby casualty units meant that her friends, those in need of sugar regulation or new hips, were bumped along country roads to far-off wards and surgeries when they'd previously have been put out of their misery locally.

Then there was Penwith District Council – ah... a pause for breath was needed. PDC was a favourite punchbag. The very mention of this quango brought forth scorn and anger from the pensioner's cracked lips. Penwith being an organisation akin to the TUC or New Labour as far as Endy was concerned.

All of the above served as easy prey – delivered to anyone within earshot – coming in and out of rotation in accordance with coverage in that week's local rag. With Daly and Nightly both highly skilled at polite and also realistic-sounding excuses whenever an outburst seemed imminent, it fell to Robert or, more often than not, Mawgan to lend a sympathetic ear and complete at least fifteen minutes' worth of 'duty' as the house-keeper railed against both regional tin-pot politicians and the country's most-respected statesmen.

National trust? There wasn't any, according to Endy. Not anymore. Every snip of information leaked or spun seemed designed to promote, confuse or cover up. It did not seem designed to help or inform; to assist the common people of Britain in their daily labours and tribulations.

Getting through life. That was it. The real crux. Endy having come to the conclusion long ago that getting through life was the travail with which the general population needed assistance. Getting through life continued to be everyone's predicament. She ranted and raved against the flat-screen Blair and his chortling cohorts on the six o'clock news. Their political opponents were no better – or different – she argued, as she harrumphed and guffawed at both parties' weak excuses, rhetorical explanations, unconvincing assurances and fake condolences.

Like tinder, the lady of the house caught fire easily, needing only the merest mention of GM food, reconstituted meat or Bird Flu to spark her off and send her reaching for her stash of well-worn catchphrases: 'I said that, didn't I? Didn't I say that?' or 'There you are then! There you are indeed!!!'

Some days, it seemed that her ladyship really did have the global solution in the palm of her poor old hands. It was all there. The answer that Bush, Putin, Blair and Brown, Bin

Laden, all of the 'them' and 'they' were searching for. Being spouted from a farmhouse kitchen in darkest Cornwall as its dispatcher, facing away from her audience, and bent double over an old enamel sink, engaged in the therapeutic act of washing-up. The solution itself. At her fingertips, as it were. Simple, maybe, as she herself was only too willing to admit. But certainly preferable to all the building up and cutting down going on around her. Endy didn't get it at all. Horrific square-box housing sprang up on land where only a few months before 200-year-old Sequoia had proudly stood as long as crows crowed and nightingales sang. Make any sense? Not to anyone over retirement age it didn't. To young locals maybe. Those starting out on life; young families, those with a job dependent on tourists and holidaymakers, and walkers. Maybe it did make sense to them. But not to Endymion Peed, the Lady of Carn Point.

Everyone at Trewin – bar Mawgan, of course – was finishing up on life. If they were honest. The perfect location and living conditions providing the most pleasant of padded cells. A cushioned, secluded, sheltered 'end of things'. Everything of the very best quality. Food quality, air quality, weather quality. 'Coming up roses', as the housekeeper often reminded herself.

The lady had no reason to complain. No reason at all. She was certainly better off than any of her buddies; the widowed, aged but surprisingly able-bodied frequenters of Women's Institutes and flower societies, now manless and therefore free from all of the washing and cooking, fetching and carrying, and arguing, that had taken up so much of their existence at the beginning of life. Who, with time on their hands and pensions and allowances to be dispersed, sought refuge in the bingo halls of Redruth and Camborne, or cancer-care coffee mornings in parish halls from Black Cliff to St Just.

Today's lecture concerned drugs: top topic and pet hate. Endy saw 'drugs', whatever that term actually meant to her, as the be all and end all of decay. The reason everything had 'gone wrong'.

Why the world as she had known it – compassionate and tender, a world of blackberry tips, orchards and birdsong, the world of her beloved mother and father – had all but disappeared.

Everything was wrong now. Very, very wrong. And, as Endy concluded, it would never be brought back into rightness. *Drugs* had seen to that. And the 'maniacs', crazy, dirty men who sold the stuff to kids, schoolchildren in Padstow and Bude, or to Mawgan and his friend Julian, come to that. They 'ought to be locked up'; needed to be put away, punished along with those who brought them into England in the first place.

Didn't Sir Walter Raleigh have something to do with it? Endy seemed to remember a story about the Kickapoo and tobacco plants. Well, that was going back a bit maybe. But wasn't that the start of all this badness? She wasn't sure, would have to look it up. If she had any books to look in, which of course she hadn't. Then again… Didn't Sir Walter bring in potatoes as well? Or was that Francis Drake? Local man, as far as she knew, from Plymouth if she remembered correctly. Again, she didn't really know. Wasn't really sure. Didn't really know anything much at all in terms of social history, the ways of the world, the way that things came about or well… the actual facts of anything 'big', as she put it, if truth were told. She knew they wouldn't get very far at Trewin without potatoes, though.

'Hilles of water came about this place'

John Calve, A History of Cornwall
(the flood of January 1607)
hand-copied churchwarden's manuscript, 1666

Sitting in the darkest corner of the Ad Lib, the best seat in the house, with Monika, Kenneth and Connie, John reached inside his jacket pocket and produced a small velvet box.

The guests' eyes were fixed on John, each sensing that tonight might be an important occasion without realising that it would be the last time any of them would see John and Iona together, intact – as a couple. John laid the small, furry box on the table and poured another drink. Iona placed her hand on her husband's arm. What was about to take place would have been impossible for most couples to deal with in private, let alone to act out in company.

Under normal circumstances she might have expected a ring, the usual token of celebration and confirmation, but Iona had been given many rings, several of them by John – the only ones she had kept. Treasuring them, making sure that she wore them often, showing them off, not just on special occasions but on photo shoots as well: *blouse by Jean Muir, slacks by St Laurent Rive Gauche, ring... model's own.* But in tonight's seemingly unresolved circumstances, a ring might appear peculiar, funny... wrong somehow. 'Immoral' – as John himself may have already concluded – one of the reasons those assembled together on this significant, somewhat peculiar evening appeared so unsettled.

'Right then... friends and...' John looked up and down the table. 'I'm definitely not... gonna make a speech...'

'Thank God for that!' piped Kenneth, as he refilled everyone's glass to prepare for a toast. 'One doesn't come to a *top West End nightspot* to listen to speeches!'

'But… it's Iona's birthday.' John's eyes settled on his wife. 'Once again, darling…' he smiled mischievously and raised his glass. 'My little Danish pastry!'

John!'

'And, well… obviously… if it's a special day for Iona, it's a special day for us, her friends and… also special and… nice for us, all of us, for once… to be sitting here… all together… together at last!'

John couldn't bear either Kenneth or Connie. The agent and his fiancée were two of the most savage gossip-mongers in London. John remained tight-lipped any time the grotesques happened to be within hearing distance. He continued: 'Not having to worry about all the things we usually have to… well… *worry about…*'

Those assembled smiled at one another sheepishly as they pondered what on earth in any of their kind-weather lives, in this warmest of warm seasons, might possibly constitute a 'worry'. Monika and Connie exchanged cigarettes and consoling looks as Kenneth feigned boredom with the 'speech', and sniffed at the Ad Lib's rather undistinguished clientele.

But Iona's eyes sparkled due to the unheard-of attention she was receiving from her husband. Attention she was very unused to. Being Mrs John Nightly was not quite what her friends might have imagined. Too much of the time it meant being ignored, forgotten or taken for granted, shown off a bit and then put aside – abandoned. Iona was often left to her own devices while John, adrift on an ocean of brainwaves, worked day and night in trying to achieve… whatever the hell it was that he was trying to achieve.

Iona clutched her husband's hand and poured another Scotch, suddenly feeling wanted for once. More wanted and desired than she had by any amount of smooth-talking, propositioning photographers, art directors and male models who had attempted (and maybe even succeeded, on the odd occasion) to take her away from her troubles. John picked up the eminent box and placed it in his wife's unnaturally cold hand.

'... I only hope you like it, darling.'

Iona put down her unlit cigarette, laid the item on the table before her, cupped both hands around John's dutiful expression and kissed him full on the lips. Then, visibly consumed with expectation, she released the latch on the perfectly crafted case.

John...' she breathed as she lifted the lid. The felt miniature opened to reveal not a ring but a brooch, an emblemed Rococo arrangement with a sparkling central cut diamond. This shimmering thing – undoubtedly an *objet*, translucent as water at low tide shot through with the last sunlight of the day – had the appearance of a refined but still glamorous antiquity. And Iona was clearly overcome by not only the item's apparent almost spiritual quality but also the very gesture itself.

It was easy to imagine this pin to have been among the most valuable trinkets inside a treasure chest full of booty, lifted by smugglers and passed down to the fairest lady of the village. The brooch, laid to rest in its crushed-velvet casket, exuded the potency or draw of a special charm, a Hitchcock MacGuffin maybe, used by the director as a device, a character almost, in his Gothic melodramas, but with all of the cachet, 'morality' even, inherent in the most precious stones and settings.

Iona wouldn't have cared whether it had come from Tutankhamen's tomb or Petticoat Market. She didn't give a damn. The important thing was that it came from her husband. Crucially so, because it meant that at some point during the past week, when Iona had not been with John, he had been thinking about her, concentrating on her, what she might like, might appreciate; at least during the time it took to search for and then purchase the item. Caring for and about his wife, considering her feelings, preferences, likes and dislikes. She lifted the lustrous thing from its holder, twisted it this way and that so that it would catch the glare from the club's gaudy light-fittings and favour her before carefully pinning it onto her top.

Kenneth ordered a special dessert wine – 'I must have sweet wine!' – along with a top-up of Scotch for the birthday girl.

'Okay, people… now…' he began. 'We are all aware that the lady who we… whom we honour tonight – just like the Oscars, isn't it! – is a very special "birthday girl" indeed.' Kenneth, more than slightly tipsy, raised his glass, almost toppling his drink over the birthday girl herself as he encouraged the others on.

'So, if I may… on behalf of myself… Her Majesty the Queen Mother, the Lord Chief Justice, Lord Chancellor… my dear friend, the First Sea Lord of the Admiralty… hur-rum!' He cleared his throat and canvassed the table for a response. 'And of course on behalf of the assembled VIPs – *Visionaries*, *Imbeciles* and *Penises* of the *Arts* one and all – heartily wish our dear Iona, our very dearest Iona, dearest "pastry" and "Kit Kat" – *ouch!* he feigned injury… 'Darling… the very… *really* very happiest of happy birthdays!'

Kenneth rose to his feet and lifted his already empty glass higher still. 'My darling, as far as I… I mean, *all* of your friends are concerned… *the* most special… *theee* most fairest, *most* entrancing…' The speechmaker paused, in difficulty for a moment as he wobbled, managed to steady himself, then let out the remainder of the sentence so fast it seemed he were gasping for life… 'Woman in the world!' he quaffed, before promptly keeling over.

The party laughed and shrieked at full volume, pretending to be surprised at Kenneth's collapse, as if it had never occurred before. While Connie apologised and attended to her partner, the others leaned over to kiss and hug Iona as her husband looked on, dutifully waiting his turn. When the suddenly recovered Kenneth took the opportunity to legitimately get his hands on Iona, her husband immediately got up and pulled her away, taking his wife in his outstretched arms as she began to sniffle with the excitement of receiving something, anything – attention mainly – from her real treasure.

Beneath it all, the scene was even more dramatic than it appeared. Tonight, John Nightly, intent on returning to 'Point Zero' as quickly as possible, was in fact doing little more than biding his time, as he waited patiently, with about as much engagement as if he were waiting for a bus, for this evening, this very special evening, to be over. Cadenced – like his marriage. To finish, without tumbling to a finish in a heaving, retching mess. John was determined to avoid that at all costs, but if it were not possible then things must still be concluded. As long as it was out of the way, done and over with. That was the real mission on this diminishing, dishonest occasion.

Notwithstanding the evening's premeditated performance, for John Nightly birthdays, weddings, anniversaries, even Christmas and New Year, had always been dead days; a waste of days and of his precious time. For John, feast days were no more than an interruption to composing or recording. Tonight was a particular inconvenience as he struggled to relate to and socialise with the couple's 'dearest friends', presumably soon-to-be enemies, when he would have much rather been in the studio, dreaming up and fantasising about his new Black Mass creation.

But there it was. Over now. With all of the effort he'd put in, John felt that he had at least done his duty. Done what he must do to please and satisfy his wife and, as usual, everyone else. He'd shown up for a start, put a slightly bent nickel in the machine, engaged in the very minimum of polite conversation as had been deemed necessary – ignoring the food and wine, and the gossip, and the guests themselves; but, importantly, delivering the appropriate amount of 'appreciation' and respect to his wife by demonstrating very publicly that he cared. Presenting her with this remembrance sourced and chosen by his manager, or maybe his manager's assistant – he wasn't sure which. It all amounted to a significant exertion on the boy's part, and one with which his wife seemed delighted.

In their hearts, both John and Iona must have known full well that this 'event' was just a delaying tactic. How different it was to the first birthday Iona celebrated during their relationship, when, in the fever and frenzy – and in his particular case the utter, unbalanced craziness of his infatuation – John Nightly had made such an effort to make that day remembered as 'the best day of my life', as his future wife was fond of recalling on so many occasions. On that wondrous day John had presented Iona with her own personalised natal chart showing the trajectories of planets and stars, their movements and conjunctions, in so much intricate, attentive detail; each circle and pathway having been illustrated by the Master himself using a child's watercolour set.

As the party around him faded into the background, John took a scrap of paper from his pocket and scribbled something before folding it inside a £5 note to keep it safe.

His wife presented the brooch to everyone around the table, catching sight of her reflection in the club's filthy mirrors. Iona flexed her pretty fingers in order that those assembled might better fully admire the new accessory. She was already planning to wear it to tomorrow morning's shoot on the steps of the National Gallery.

The clip would stay close to her over the years, always be with her. More valuable than her various properties, her pets and her vast storerooms of clothes. It represented something unique. An appreciation from the man she loved and would always love. A man for whom she was still willing to give up everything to facilitate his wellbeing and contentment.

Iona studied her husband in the tinted glass. John remained quietly beside her, listening patiently to Connie, holding an un-smoked cigarette in one hand while impatiently tapping out a rhythm on the table mat with the other. Something racing through his head as ever. Something other than the primary business. A stray inspiration, perhaps, words or a tune – a title maybe. Not bothering to make conversation, believing his wife's needs to have been taken care of, her attention taken away for a moment, John began to dream and daydream, return to his preferred world, as he attempted to block out the cabaret coming from the far corner of the heart-shaped lounge.

What Iona's husband didn't reveal to his birthday girl, not being aware of it himself, was that the gift which had brought so much joy was not exactly a celebratory item. It was a mourning brooch: a token presented to the widow of a fisherman lost at sea or a tinner or face-worker killed in a mining accident. One of Pondy's ironic little touches, it may have come from the hulk of a galleon washed up when Penzance had been burned to ashes by the Spaniards. The brooch would most likely have been traded by 'belles' (local debutantes) when 'lads' (eligible young bachelors) ran through the streets of the market town on Midsummer Eve with torches dipped in tar while their lasses sold snuff boxes and crucifixes along with smuggled valuables to the good citizens of Cornwall's wealthy seaside towns.

John Beach, recording engineer, Tawny Studios, Caterham, Surrey. May 2006
I bumped into him in Teletape on Shaftsbury Avenue buying tape-machines for his home studio. The weird thing was that he greeted me warmly, as he always did, and he complimented Anna on her shoes, which most men would never notice. I helped him out of the shop and into a cab with these heavy boxes; he jumped in and was away without so much as a goodbye or thank you or anything at all. But… that was John. Normal most of the time, until something would come into his head and he'd be gone, in various ways, you could say… in this case, literally!

item: *MOJO* magazine #78. March 2004.
Brian Wilson talks to Sylvie Simmons about the reconstruction of his masterwork
Smile, *performed at London's Royal Festival Hall 24. 2. 2003 to an audience of*
onlookers and interested parties, including Paul McCartney, George Martin, Roger
Daltrey and the author.

It took me right back to the time when I made the music… [stares into the distance]
Took me right back to that time.

And was that a good time to go back to?

[considers for a moment] No, it wasn't, it wasn't a good time at all…

The political and social outlook in Britain remained uncertain. Harold Wilson's government appeared as tired as the revolutionaries. With the pound devalued, the economy rattled rather than rolled, though Wilson, a politician for the times, with his slogans and image-enhancers – briar pipe, Gannex mac and helicopter on call for the Scilly Isles – stayed optimistic, at least on TV.

The new obsession for Britain's most dynamic new businessmen – i.e. its high-achieving pop groups – was tax. John Nightly, along with other high-bracket earners, was paying 75 percent in the pound. This concerned his manager much more than it did the singer himself, but meant that the government was keeping the country afloat by taxing the efforts of those of whose behaviour it disapproved. The Beatles in particular were criticised and mocked. Whether because of day trips to Bangor with the Maharishi, or the unscheduled announcement that they had taken LSD, the group were viewed with suspicion and cynicism by the authorities; any performer with a dissenting voice or seen to wield power and influence was a potential threat to the status quo. The government painting them as undesirables while taking from them 17/6 out of every pound sterling they earned.

Britain did its best to revive itself. The *I'm Backing Britain* campaign faltered when it was revealed that the promotional T-shirts were manufactured in Portugal. Progress in this 'year of protest' was halted by the actions of everyone from the IRA to the ANC and the LSE. Student Demonstration Time was here to stay. The previous decade's all-night party had finally been raided, the only thing left to look forward to being one huge convective cloud of a hangover (this would turn out to be the 1970s). Either that or some kind of bio-dynamic rejuvenation. In nature, a plant that grows rapidly during summer rewards its gardener by showing an almost daily improvement before shedding its flowers and foliage in autumn to be comatose through the winter. It will return the following spring to divide and spread, repeating the cycle to a second receptive audience.

That's not what happened to the Revolution. Instead, cynicism set in. The gardeners tended the plant. They did everything they could to save it. But firstly, they were somewhat disillusioned themselves already and secondly, the individuals who had broken through, whether they be boogie men, boxers or boot makers had become a little too successful themselves. Realising that wealth is entirely relative and often short-lived, they reckoned to take stock in order to preserve what they had already accumulated.

The Apple boutique was a case in point. The beginnings of a planned global operation, the shop began with ideals – John Lennon referred to it as a 'psychedelic Woolworths'. In the beginning, goods were sold as normal; but soon the right-on shop assistants thought it either embarrassing or ideologically unsound to mention the matter of payment, so customers were often allowed to take whatever they fancied free of charge.

But the Beatles were more closely linked to the counter-culture than their fans, their detractors or their shop assistants realised. They were funding it. Donating large sums to Release, *IT, Oz*, CND, Legalise Cannabis, Amnesty, Black Power and other organisations within the culture of protest. Somewhere it had to stop and soon Apple, the fruity, surreal corps set up as a tax dodge, ended up needing one.

Festival culture took over. Woodstock, the Isle of Wight and Monterey, 'free states' in themselves, wanted free entrance to their borders, but it was not to be. These were expensive to put on; hippie-capitalist concerns. As soon as the organisers got organised the performers no longer played for free – and the organisers did not organise for free. The audience paid and the acts and their managers received the long- and short-term benefit.

In terms of the *Age of Aquarius*, the phenomenon needed to be given at least as much poetic license as the lyrics to Rado and Ragni's astrological anthem. Drug busts and arrests on 'obscenity' charges became weekly occurrences that featured on the teatime news alongside the much-caricatured Love-Ins,

Sit-Ins, Bed-Ins, Be-Ins, Peace-Ins and Do-Ins. Another new world. Some referred to it as the New Enlightenment.

In the symbolic language of astrology, a glyph – the recognised mark for Aquarius – represents the waves of the ocean. But this particular glyph amounted to an ocean of possibility polluted by a drug-fuelled opacity, a real pea-souper, impossible to navigate. New Enlightenment is what it wasn't. What it should have been was more akin to a spring equinox, a kind of astrological Zero Point, a new beginning building on changes in society having taken place over the past two or three summers. Those experiencing mind expansion felt they had waited patiently; but instead something of an autumnal solstice arrived, along with a period of realisation that the revolutionaries may indeed have been wasting their time.

Mind-expansion helped John Nightly in one sense, it did literally expand him. With all that sugar-cube and alcoholic snacking John put on the extra five or six pounds that brought him up to a prime welterweight. Though it certainly did not make him fighting fit, this New (supposedly Aquarian) Age expanded both his mind and his body, along with, as John himself put it, his 'ability to engage more meaningfully within and without his own *Self...*'

a Pelican Book

Encounter Groups
Carl R. Rogers

Group psychotherapy sessions were popular in the early 1970s

'Dr Laing?'

'Call me Ronnie,'

The conjuror opened the door to 21 Wimpole Street himself, shook John Nightly firmly by the hand and indicated towards the back of the house as he led the way barefoot on the cold slate floor through to his consulting room.

'So… what's it all about?'

The boy looked up.

'what's… what do you…?'

The psychiatrist continued walking. He turned back to John.

'This. What's it all about?'

Laing was so full-on, immediately on it, though quite freaky at the same time that the boy couldn't help himself.

'Alfie!'

There was no response. John paused, then repeated in a softer voice, *Alfie* – that's what it's all about…'

John Nightly, innocent as ever, sought an appropriate, light-hearted response. But Dr Laing, lank-haired and sunken-eyed, at least as haunted-looking as his visitor, seemed not a bit impressed by this sparky, almost perfect word association. He bent over, picked up a dog-end from the carpet and tossed it into one of two glass ashtrays sitting at either end of his desk.

'Good one, yeah. I know the song, obviously.' Laing appeared weary. 'What I meant, though…' The conjuror sat down, relaxed into his armchair and moved aside a pen and a small notepad. 'I know a bit about you. You're very… successful, and therefore I guess… somewhat fulfilled, possibly.' He folded over a page. 'I'm assuming that you're about to tell me… *all of your troubles?*'

John was noticeably uncomfortable about the man's approach. He'd read the books, particularly *The Divided Self*, and expected its author to be commendably serious, clear about things – as he'd been led to believe by other happy customers. But John also hoped Laing would be, somehow… *as lyrical a speaker as he was writer* – and certainly more sympathetic, in his approach.

Both *The Divided Self* and its follow-up, *The Politics of Experience*, were elegantly written, 'poetic' even. Not reading at all like any kind of textbook or, as many had expected, simply the philosophies, rants and raves of its author, but in a style that John Nightly could only describe as 'purely philosophical'. Spiritual almost. *'If I could turn you on, if I could drive you out of your wretched mind, if I could tell you, I would let you know…'**

John had devoured both paperbacks, pristine copies of which were kept underneath his bed, in a spot safe from borrowing hands, along with his songbook and a small pad in case he happened to awaken one night with some particular inspiration. But so far the boy was unsure about the man himself. Laing looked John Nightly straight in the eye for the first time.

'Let's talk about groups,' he offered.

The boy smiled at Ronnie's old-fashioned terminology. The good doctor picked up a packet of cheroots. 'Groups of people…'

'… oh…'

'Social groups… maybe your… your school friends… or the people in your group, your "band" – your co-workers. The same thing – that's a family, too.' Laing shrugged his shoulders.

'… well. I've… I've been thinking about…'

The psychiatrist continued. 'And school, other "families". Were you happy at school?' He leaned forward, lit up without offering one to the client, threw the match in the general direction of the ashtray and sat back. Laing prompted again: 'More or less?'

John took a deep breath. 'It's a lot to… go into…'

'Presumably that's why we're here?'

Laing, possibly realising his rather bleak welcome may well have put the boy off, laughed half-apologetically as he loosened up, smiling what John Nightly took to be something approaching an almost genuine smile. The boy shuffled uncomfortably, putting himself very much in the physical position of the underdog – or in this case the paying customer. 'I always found it quite difficult to make friends at school, so…'

'Were you a sportsman?'

'… oh… no, not at all… I wasn't particularly… healthy – "athletic", I mean – as a child. I wasn't "ill" either, but I… I wasn't that way inclined, I…'

'No permanent… group of friends? Not on the sports field… or… in the bicycle sheds?' Laing waved his notepad in the air, not having written anything down as yet.

'… I was a real… "corner of the playground" kid…'

John smiled shyly and waited for comfort that wasn't forthcoming. Not having taken any kind of counselling or analysis before, he was unsure when to speak and when not to; he had not quite understood that it was the patient who did most of the talking.

'Go on…'

Dr Laing, sitting comfortably on his chair, encouraged the boy to reveal whatever it was that John Nightly had no intention of revealing.

'Cat got your tongue already? That's no good.' Laing acted hurt. 'Okay! I'll tell you about my playground, then. My archive, my… well-filed catalogue of… insecurities… and other animals…'

* The concluding sentence from *The Bird of Paradise* (Penguin) 1967

item: Monthly Cultural Notes: September
The first days of autumn arrive and the colourful summer display begins to fade. Temperatures alternate between hot and dusty or breezy and cool. September is the best time to establish or repair a lawn. Plant spring bulbs and hardy annuals for next year. Gather fallen leaves and burn those that are diseased. Leave berries on shrubs for blackbirds, robins, mistle thrush and house sparrows. Visit local flower societies and botanical gardens for ideas on next year's planting. Sow radish, lettuce and spinach in frames. Plants that are frost-sensitive need to be prepared for the coming winter.

The Speakeasy, 48 Margaret Street, London W1. Later that same day.

'My father told me to be wary of men like you.'

'You mean extremely talented… uh rich young men?'

The girl stared right into John's sweet blue eyes.

'No, John… *English* men.'

'… Dickens, Shakespeare… Churchill. Steer clear of those… unreliable, un… imaginative types… Those are the English guys he was referring to, aren't they?'

Myra didn't even smile. 'Guess so… freaky, obsessed, difficult-to-please… controlling…'

It was the kind of lively exchange John always had to win – insisted on winning. Everyone must surrender to John Nightly. The boy was insufferable. And quick. He couldn't be beaten. No one had ever beaten John, or had what you might call a proper conversation with him either. Nothing 'serious'. It always had to be funny with John Nightly. Every compliment deflated, each kind word questioned, reflected, returned, shot right back at the complimenter. The game played fast. Though often dimmed by the endless sleepless nights that came with the job, the boy's mind was still quick.

'We have enough of the fall guys at home. It's the talent that's difficult to… come by.' Myra took a swig.

'Well… we better get on and come upon the talent that's waiting for us back at the studio then. Or they'll start to charge extra…'

'Are you going to charge extra, John?'

'… if only I could… charge you extra, Myra… you're certainly in a strange mood today, babe…'

Myra put her glass down on the bar. 'If you don't mind... could you not call me that... certainly not in company.' She needed to exert a rub of power. 'At the moment, right here, right now, John, I'm your producer... I'm not your... *babe*... babe.'

John gave a little sympathetic half-smile to the self-assured young woman hitched up on the stool opposite. Without saying a word, he leaned forward, looked her in the eye and placed his hand on her thigh. Myra showed no reaction as his fingers made their own way up inside the line of her skirt. Then she pulled away, picked up John's hand as if it were a damp rag and placed it firmly back on his knee. Had they been at Queen Square, or more likely back at her own flat in Cheyne Walk, she'd have let it go – all the way, he was certain. This little taunt being the prelude, a small guiding star, to a whole new cluster, maybe a lifetime's worth, of... problems – in the long run.

There was polite applause at the far end of the bar as a drummer ambled out onto the Speakeasy's tiny stage, followed by the rest of his band. The club's MC appeared and tapped the microphone... '1-2, 1-2... Okay, people... Good to see so many of you here at this... inhospitable time, what with the weather and everything out there, so...' [pause for any kind of response which wasn't forthcoming] 'Anyway... sure to be blowing up a storm inside as well as out... In a moment or two... today the fabulous Speakeasy is very proud to present – and let's have a very big hand for them – I give to you... ha, ha... No really! The absolute one and only *AYNSLEY... DUNBAR RETALIATION!*' As the quintet launched into a thunderous drum-heavy riff and the film producer immediately searched her bag for cotton-wool.

As it turned out there was nothing very good about what developed between Myra Knoll and John Nightly following that exchange. Over the next 12 months, as John's career zoomed and he struggled to cope with trying to conceptualise a masterwork while at the same time keeping afloat what amounted to a full symphony orchestra, Myra juggled the organisational, promotional and distributional requirements of films in pre-production with her own overactive social life.

Both parties should have owned up that sex was what the two of them were all about. Sex and comfort. Their only mutual interest. If only these two semi-intelligent beings had not confused the side matter of physical love-making with deeper feelings. Some sort of commitment, some kind of hold on one another. Maybe in altered defenceless moments they forgot themselves and let the epithet 'love' become attached to their mutually beneficial arrangement. It was an emotion that neither one had any knowledge or experience of whatsoever.

The late '60s social playground gave two individuals like these license to do whatever they chose. Behave in a way that previous generations could not have done because they would not have been minded to. With both of them married, Myra usually in production and on location, therefore away from her husband for months at a time, and with John away from Iona every few weeks, there were plenty of opportunities to exploit one another, which they did. It suited them both. Much as it did countless others in similar situations during an era of apparently free love, which often seemed an automatic and convenient excuse for the most negligent personal behaviour. As another year drew to a close, the composer and his employer rose to the challenge and made an almost Academy Award-winning job of being quite the most appalling pair you could ever wish to meet.

'When I am open I am the *Artist*.
When I am closed, I am John Nightly.'

Letter sent from Los Angeles, 13.6.75 to Jonathan Foxley
(courtesy Neil Winters archive)

Indica Bookshop & Gallery, Southampton Row, London WC1. Monday, 17 November 1969. 10.30 am. John Nightly interviewed by Hiroshi Murakami for *Pop Star Real One* magazine (Japan)

And eh… what you fabourite corour, Missa Nightry?

… oh… [gazes into the distance] Orange, I should think… or it was when I last looked. [visibly a wreck, searches his draw bag for skins and prepares to roll one] Never really thought about it… Think my favourite… right now anyway… maybe… black…

[The editor scribbles furiously in his notebook, barely able to keep pace with his own enthusiasm]

Pitchblack… jet black – black with pitches! [John Nightly laughs and burps at the same time]

Eh… *brack one*… [Hiroshi responds philosophically, as if he has just been handed the secret of life itself] And eh… you fabourite TV a-star?

Actor? Oh… I only watch telly in the afternoons… so… my 'favourite'… probably… Sooty.

[The journalist responds with a series of knowing nods]

Suttie… [scribbling, pressing hard with his pen] What it is exactery? Engerish pop-a-star?

That's it… wears a suit, orange as well… so, a connection – of sorts. One piece fur, hence the name, and… he's orange so, quite… 'bear-like'… [John play-acts a little too disrespectfully] He… well… Sooty doesn't actually say that much…

Aha! This one… compretery sirent bear… in suit? [Spoken as if this too is a revelation; Hiroshi frowns as he scribbles some more, trying to fix the indecipherable image in his mind]

… do you think we could… [John, so rudely patronising one of his very biggest and most loyal markets, desperately wishes to move on]

And you fabourite a-drink?

oh… again… it's difficult. When I was a kid, I used to really like, was kind of addicted to… Kia-Ora.

[A further snippet totally unfathomable to the Japanese super fan]

Key A-or-A?… this *nice* word! [Attempts to write down the impossibly assonant creation; double-checks that his cassette recorder is turning round] And… *addict?* Eh… [Looks up] Who this Qui or-A?

It's a drink. Mainly used by children… but… that is actually orange as well – weirdly enough.

Aha… this orange one also! You rearry rike orange thing…

Seems like it. *Kia ora* – the actual words – mean 'wellbeing' in Maori. [John is at least interested in this] New Zealand language. Read that in a leaflet… from the Kia-Ora Children's Club – sorry, 'crub', I mean!

Ehhhhh… So *Key A-or-A Crub*, this your fabourite drink and mean Well Bean? [The interviewer has cracked it] It strange thing…

Well, it is… that's exactly it… [John, a little guilty at the deception, continues; he lights up and takes a drag]

Went to a couple of places with my manager last night… and we had… well, Bolivian rum and Bacardi and Coke… *Coca-Cola*… quite a lot of whiskey, bit too much probably… and that was… a very good drink, *'mazin'* drink, I'd say, and a… a good night, good night out – maybe a bit too good". The boy cleared his throat and mimed lifting the lids from his hooded eyes.

And book? What you read, Missa John?

Yeah… that's a bit more… might be a bit more… 'revealing', mightn't it? [Coughs and clears throat, ready to be serious (and quite possibly pretentious) for a moment] Books… well… currently I'm writing… working on… a piece of music partly inspired by William Blake… [Looks doubtfully at Hiroshi] An… *old poet*… and his… his sort of… 'enlightened' ideas. So last night I was reading a book of poetry called *Children of Albion*, which I just bought. I'm sure you get it in here… [motions towards the shelves] Poetry doesn't have so many conventions and… structures as other writing… that's why I particularly like… 'free'… unstructured stuff – and it's shorter!

This interest me today! [The journalist squints, suddenly with full comprehension] And eh… how 'bout poetry?

Pardon?

Missa John Nightry… now last thing… what you eh… you faborite music? All-time-one, prease…

… oh God…

[The interviewee has had enough; he flicks through a mind-file of what might be termed his most 'un-favourite' records]

Mrs Mills is… she's pretty good…

Miss Mirrr?

… the miller's daughter. In terms of 'absolute' favourites, though, that… that's easy. It would always be Gustav, *The Planets*. When I was little. But there's… a lot of other things I like now, more modern things… What exactly *am* I listening to? [Pulls out a neatly folded sheet from his bag] Can't remember the name of the thing…

[Hiroshi looks blank]

You might not know it… but… in terms of pop… in terms of favourites… [An image of John Snr and the family's tiny front room in Grantchester flips into the boy's head] Gotta be Mrs Mills…

Brian Wilson called George Gershwin's *Rhapsody in Blue* his 'theme for life'. *The Planets* and *The Firebird* were John Nightly's themes. They didn't just 'speak' to him; they kidnapped him, called him like sirens. Pulled him away from whatever he was doing, through the mirror, down into the tunnel. As a child John would lie on the floor next to John Snr's record player while he held the stylus over a particular few grooves of Stravinsky's ballet suite. The boy would put the arm down on the same section of music over and over again as his brain dissected and analysed exactly what was going on harmonically, melodically and structurally and what that meant philosophically and spiritually. The turned earth of these compositions had helped form the basis of John Nightly himself, not only his music-making but his psychological make-up.

Like many composers, much of what John wrote was based on a spark. Two or three notes or 'events' that could be adapted and developed. He often worked from the same spore or cell, admitting that he'd been 'writing the same piece of music all my life'.

In addition to these dangerously influential works, John was attached to his own pet *system of three*. He beat it out with his fingers whenever he drifted off for a moment or someone bored him. Lyrically he would employ this 'natural way' more often than not, the first word consisting of one syllable only. John viewed the world as a spiritual triangle, seeing groups of three, a stressed metre or rhythm across three beats – a natural balance of three – in almost everything he encountered, whether or not it was there. From *the Father, the Son and the Holy Ghost* to *Births, Marriages & Deaths*. Even as a child he understood that musical structure seemed to have everything to do with this naturally occurring principle. A song was comprised of three distinct parts: verse, chorus and middle; each one based around a three-chord pattern, with three primary chords in each key, C-F-G and E-A-B in a major key or Am-Dm-Em and C#m-F#m-Gbm in a minor, conforming to the more Dorian-based blues mode of the times. As with the colour chart of primary and secondary colours in visual art, there was a corresponding group of three 'secondary' chords, most usually the relative minors, or majors, depending on the key – or 'home' itself. Verses and choruses almost always occurred three times each during a song, the song itself lasting roughly three minutes; in the words of the detractors, a 'three-chord wonder' or 'three-minute wonder'. He liked the three-beat grouping of words: 'Please Please Me', 'She Loves You', 'Don't Be Cruel', 'Do the Twist'; 'the *swing* of the words, the *waves* of the notes'... and so on and so on. And on and on and on.

Sonata form, concerto form. And such as King's College Choir, *Nine Lessons & Carols* and *Peter Grimes, Billy Budd, Owen Wingrave, Gloriana*. John Nightly wasn't the only composer into this 'three' thing. Every song John had written so far employed a three-word title: a trio of chiming bells. As a teenager he had striven to achieve stylised compositional features equivalent to those of his peers. Mahler's unresolved suspensions, Ravel's tight clusters, Stravinsky's piled ninths, Richard Rodgers' semitonal motifs, Delius' 'folk harmony', Ellington's piano tumbles, Steve Reich's skyscraper rhythms, Cage's rejection of structure, Bernstein's grasp of zeitgeist, whatever it happened to be, Bacharach's daring melodic leaps and his technically 'atonal' pop songs. Even at a young age John had been able to identify each composer's handwriting. And now, with a major new work occupying his mind as nothing had done before, he vowed to take this 'learning', this 'natural, existential musicality', to another level.

The plan was to have three different movements – *mouvements* – one per LP. The music itself in 3/4 time, or a multiple of it.

LP 1 *(Mink)* would contain the rhythm,
LP 2 *(Bungalow)* the poetry and 'fractional collage', and
LP 3 *(Requiem?)*... he had yet to decide.

Probably just sound, washes of sound, a 'sonic pasture' on which to project the more conceptual propositions. The third record completely non-rhythmic, so as not to clash – in the wrong way – with the other two.

The boy continued to gather inspiration. To be patient and receptive. What he was planning was a Requiem Mass that wasn't really a mass at all – or a requiem – more a gigantic choral symphony, or tone-poem, involving some 400 performers. John wasn't concerned that there was, as yet, very little actual text, or music. The good thing being that there would never be anything at all forced, or coerced, about the concept. Concept! That's exactly what it was at the moment. The composer not having written one note of anything. All he had in his mind were storm clouds, coastal grey, Zawn black, sunset orange, Sooty orange, Mrs Mill's vamping, Ravel's intensely romantic voicings, Stravinsky's neo-classicism, Glenn Miller's expressive colours, Gershwin's easy populism, Debussy's starlight, Ellington's introspection – and the Beatles sales figures! Doom clouds, boom clouds, gathering all around. Various accumulating masses, each with different intentions. He knew he would rise up and punch through. Rise to the challenge. To zoom again. Get back to that one and only elusive Zero Point. Get back by going forward. He just needed to get on with it.

Right now, only one thing was certain: the *Mink Bungalow Requiem* would be in waltz-time.

John Nightly Sex M
Cambridge, England, Great Britain 07/15/1948 12:00 −
Julian day 2432747.96
Adjust -1.00 ST 6.33 Lat. 52.13 Long. -0.08

Donna Vost Sex F
Cambridge, Mass., USA 09/17/1950 05:00 −
Julian day 2433541.92
Adjust 5.00 ST 4.50 Lat. 43.01 Long. 73.23

Ten minutes later, when he could take no more, John got up
from his chair mid-sentence, shook hands with a still confused
Man from Japan, and wandered out into the sunshine of
Russell Square for his weekly rendezvous with Miss Vost.

Each Tuesday, for the past six months, the top-of-his-game
composer had met his precious young choreographer in the
corner seat at the Kardomah coffee house in the Strand. Here
they would put movement to music in preparation for the
world premiere of the *black mass*.

Observing Donna persuade a troupe of teenagers to walk in
patterns around Piccadilly Circus for a BBC documentary,
John warmed to her plan of beginning this next project, not with
conventional choreography but with co-ordinated real movement:
walking, running, jumping, jerking, sitting, starting, stopping.
Natural kinetics, she called it, set in motion by the 'movers' as
the music ran its course, the resultant work developing through
each performance.

Most afternoons the pair would work on layouts and tempos,
the composer asking about every dance format from the Baroque
Chaconne − a stately dance in 'three' time − to contemporary
'group-walking'. Donna knew enough about both to be able to
interpret whatever her master envisaged. At the end of each
session, with step-diagrams and patterns folded into John's
songbook, they would repair to the Savoy to have brainstorms,
have tea and have each other.

Donna was no doubt infatuated. But she fooled herself, imagining some improbable scenario in which she might take the place of Iona in John's life rather than just his bed. Donna could never hope to replace Iona, either emotionally or logistically. John Nightly's existing domestic set-up entirely suited him. Allowing him security *and* freedom. Any kind of permanency was unthinkable from his viewpoint, so this convenient session had become an undeniably exciting but also genuinely warm and loving way to pass a midweek afternoon.

Donna drifted through the Savoy in her ishka, her veils of cheese-cloth, ribbons and string tied into her hair, a 'spirit' ballerina. She was voraciously driven and, like her lord and master, on a kind of quest. But regularly struck down by various no doubt psychosomatic disorders along with the habitual dancer's injuries; she was beginning to cultivate something of a permanent frown which threatened to stamp her young forehead with unsightly creases.

In rehearsal with the group, soaking up inspiration from all quarters, she managed to catch each nuance of John's imagining while encouraging everyone else's contributions. She was able to solve the conundrum of how to make passages of physical time-frame equate to musical bars; the problem facing choreographers of every discipline. Trying to match time, space, dynamics *and* meaning with expressive movement. What she and the composer ended up with wasn't *dance* exactly − it wasn't intended to be; not as people understand it − but it was completely rigged to the music and also emotionally affecting. Donna had managed to translate the composer's generally unformed ideas into something cohesive. In terms of a choreographic style, the *mouvement* was more to do with soul-walking or 'dance-walking'. As if ten people happened to be walking down a street as individuals, then, after being aware of each other, began to be influenced by one another's pace and rhythm. The result a co-ordinated shuffle between a group of 'movers', relating to some common source − a church bell, plane overhead, children playing, the traffic's loop...

The choreographer, like her composer, was herself unable to read dots and had her head stuffed full of numbers. With a highly sophisticated musical memory, rather like that of a concert pianist, Donna had coded what seemed like acres of orchestral interludes and links; helped by the sketches blocked out on those Tuesday afternoons, which would form the basis of the choreography for John Nightly's 'walking ballet'.

Aged just 23, *the gazelle* was to be in charge of a chorus of at least 40 professional hoofers, on a different stage almost every night for the planned 70-date tour covering most of Europe and Japan – to include the biggest attended concert ever planned – finishing up on the West Coast of America. The prodigiously talented Miss Vost shouldered the overall responsibility of pulling everyone through.

John was confident she could do it. During the course of rehearsals, he found himself more and more attentive and admiring, quite knocked out by what she had achieved. Her grace, the way she handled herself, stood up for herself, held herself: back straight, head in air; the way she bent and stretched, or the way she sat, cross-legged on the floor, sliding across to demonstrate the next move; her soft flat shoes, the layers of thin garments that clung and sometimes fell from her slight, perspiring body. As rehearsals progressed, the composer found himself a mere spectator as Donna explained to much more experienced feet the 'head attitude' necessary in order to perform this 'enlightened and enlightening piece'.

Because of this free exchange, the resultant choreography was ahead of its time – without being recognised as such in the real world of contemporary dance, due to being linked to what was seen as a hugely overwrought commercial enterprise, although dancers working on other productions in the capital would have died to be a part of this company. The spirit of experimentation present at *MBR* rehearsals was unheard of in the often tunnel-minded world of modern dance. As were the wages! For John Nightly, able to afford the best, not only demanded the best but also gave the best – to the outrage of his manager. The maestro had no real interest in the huge royalty income he was generating and reasoned that if you paid well you got well; JCE therefore ended up paying each performer almost double the going rate. At last, professional dancers were able to pay the rent *and* eat. *The Mink Bungalow Requiem* became the talk of the town, and not only in the dance world. As full-tour rehearsals got underway, the payroll rose to £2,000 a day just to continue to kick things into shape.

John and Donna found that it was seldom necessary to explain or discuss very much. They communicated by doing, not by considering. If Donna was lost on a particular step, John would rush over and beat out the rhythm for her, taking off his shoes, putting his hands inside them and getting down on the floor-boards to tap out a kind of spoof routine. If the Master lost his way during a section, Donna would tiptoe over to the piano and remind him of it in her inimitable one-fingered style. Her brain must have decoded the music in exactly the same way as John's had encoded it; a sense of absolute knowing existing between them.

But while there was no way she was ever going to betray the Master, Donna Vost fully intended to exploit any work opportunity that might follow on from her new insider connection.

So the composer was disappointed when his choreographer invited potential future bosses – directors, managers and patrons, even other composers – to dress rehearsals, walk-throughs and costume checks without bothering to ask him. Then again, the era was one of collaboration rather than competition. In those looser days artists hung out with their peers while they were physically creating. Everyone was invited and often did join in. The benefit resulting from letting people attend these particular run-throughs being that word – good word – about the *Mink Bungalow Requiem* quickly got around. It was, as John Glade, the *Times'* dance critic, described it after attending a rehearsal at Ms Vost's invitation, *incredible people walking together in rhythm. Somehow sacred gestures, at the same time sometimes absurdist. A pagan Enid Blyton!*

Ridiculous as that sounds I was transfixed by what I saw, and could not get the haunting themes out of my head. I for one am absolutely crazy to see the real thing.
Sunday Times colour supplement: 'Here's to the New Decade', Sunday, 10 December 1969

This was all JCE needed to obtain funding for what Pondy called the venture's 'uniquely innovative' element: sea electricity. The utility chosen to power the entire opus.

A few weeks after the London Electricity Board backed out following the sudden realisation that every one of the performers, along with the organisers, were 'long hairs', rehearsals were halted in an attempt by JCE to stem the flow of cash pouring out of the operation. The company held its collective breath.

It didn't have to wait long. In November '69, John Nightly's stock was high. His manager, with a shortlist of partners lining up to get involved with anything the star put his name to, was able to announce that every item of equipment used on the tour would be adorned by an ocean-blue E-Lec logo – a cartoon-like lightning-strike proclaiming the unhindered progress of nature's most powerful force.

By the time of the release of *Ape Box Metal* and its subsequent world tour, it was possible for the Nightly band to try out selections from the new work on an unsuspecting audience. Most of *Ape Box* was on tape anyway, it being the third in the trilogy of albums to combine already-recorded and live sounds. The group, having long since realised that their job would be made far simpler if they played along with pre-recorded tracks, rather than attempting to create the music from scratch, found it easy to switch gear between the reality of live performance and what had been recorded in the studio.

This taster-plate, particularly the interludes, seemed to concentrate the faithful more easily than had been anticipated and by the end of the fifth and final concert the crowd was brought to its feet.

Bootlegged tracks began to be played in student common-rooms while a BBC teatime *Dombey and Son* licensed one of the incidental links as its theme tune. John happily gave permission, the passage being something he hadn't considered as particularly significant to the work as a whole. It gave the boy a kick to see his composer credit – *music by Alexander Telstar* – come up at the end of each episode.

But the project faced competition from elsewhere during those heady weeks of 1970. The musical *Hair* continued to attract the crowds, the songs as familiar as anything on a Simon & Garfunkel album, while Kenneth Tynan's *Oh! Calcutta!* recently opened at the Roundhouse, had the benefit of full onstage nudity. *Oh! Calcutta!* drew a sell-out house every night.

Pitted against this, in normal circumstances, the *Mink Bungalow Requiem* might have struggled to find an audience and sustain sufficient attendance over that first month to allow PR worker bees to exploit reviews and bring in the second and third waves of audiences, including the much-wanted coach parties – permed and tinted grandmothers from Redcar and Grimsby booked into a West End matinee as part of their London Weekend; every theatre manager longed to see coaches from Lancashire pull up at their doors.

There was no doubt that *MBR* was very much an untried phenomenon in Theatreland. On the other hand, JCE could count on a solid fan base in Britain of at least 150,000 real-live believers. Happily, advance sales for the UK dress rehearsals – three nights at Friars Aylesbury followed by a further three at Hatfield Poly – sold out 'before they went on sale', according to a temporarily reinvigorated Pond.

As well as rehearsing for these engagements, John spent time in the studio piecing together the music to be performed. This was a mammoth task in itself as sessions at Sound Techniques, Olympic Studios and Regent Sound, orchestra under the supervision of Jonathan Foxley, took place amongst a feverish round of pro-motion, awards ceremonies, interviews and guest appearances.

There were other appearances. Closeted meetings with HM Customs and Excise, which John Nightly learned of by accident after finding a claim for unpaid tax on his manager's desk laid open for all to see. Unknown to the star and major shareholder of his own empire, the Inland Revenue had been investigating irregularities at JCE for the past 12 months. It seemed that cash pouring in and out of the company's bank account was being listed in a separately named profits-holding into seemingly unrelated businesses at various addresses in the South West of England. Mining operations that had gone to the wall ten years previously continued to receive heavy investment from a London account.

Taxable profits on John Nightly royalties had been set off against failure in second-investment businesses that no longer existed. Of course John knew nothing about it. But the discovery was the stray spark that would eventually lead to the downfall and collapse of the by now pre-eminent management. One year on, John Carter would be facing imprisonment for fraud; but right now John Nightly was blissfully unaware of both the economic storm that was about to burst and also the damage being done to his relationship with Iona. There was also his own mental state.

Many of John's associates were already gone to the woods, but perhaps not quite so far gone as John himself as he paced around Queen Square, watching a feature about his new pop/rock opera on the TV news while stuffing packet after packet of cheese thins into his gob, chain-smoking and listening to Erik Satie over and over – no doubt mindful of trying to keep oncoming storms at bay.

You should never go back – that's the thing. Seems like a long time ago now since we went out with our little torches. To look at the sky. We woulda been seven or eight... not much more than that. We really knew our stars then, had our little maps... star maps – used to get 'em free in comics – and we looked for patterns we recognised... constellations. Little bit of red plastic over the lens to stop the glare. John's dad showed us that. We were real serious about it.

You have to wait at least fifteen minutes for your iris to adapt to the dark anyway. It'll open to let more light in, but it takes that amount of time. After another hour, the retina adapts as well and you can see everything you're looking for, with the naked eye. Like the old naked-eye astronomers, before they had telescopes. After that amount of time... you can also get bloody cold!

We had our sandwiches and we'd just walk for a bit, find a spot, sit down and gaze up at the sky. Wasn't exactly Jodrell Bank! But it was pretty amazing – was in those days anyway. No light pollution, y'see. Thing was... 'cause we heard Jodrell Bank was sited in a botanical garden* we used to head up in the direction of Bateman Street, where the Cambridge Botanic Garden was... [Justin guffaws loudly to himself] *Really! for no reason... just our little kiddie brains...*

If, like we did, you spend a lot of time looking at the sky and seeing amazing stuff, you do start to wonder... all this, y'know? Movement and... Does make you think... what the hell is it all about. [raises his eyebrows, in a mock-serious moment] *And that makes you think about everything.*

We'd read the... schoolboy versions of what Einstein and Newton had discovered. When the Hawking book came out it blasted us, man. In a way because he came from Cambridge. [smiles] *John had even done a bit of work for him when John was at school... He was from... the same direction we were.* [laughs] *Or so we thought! I did anyway... in my... schoolboy brain.*

All I know is... I'd love to go back and walk down that road and look up at those stars again... with John, I mean. Any night of the year. Don't matter what the weather's like.
Justin Makepeace, *Guitar Hero* Magazine. Zed Publishing, May 1995

---

* The Jodrell Bank observatory, built in 1945 by the astronomer Bernard Lovell, is situated at the Manchester University Botanical Gardens in Macclesfield.

Maharishi Mahesh Yogi talking to Leslie Smith, BBC Radio 4. Transcript: 14 October 1969.

Well, now. Suppose I came to you and I said, please tell me how to meditate 'transcendentally'? What advice would you give me?

I'll suggest to you one syllable…

A *syllable*?

By syllable, I mean some sound…

Like 'rose', for example?

No, no, not like 'rose'. Some sound which will not have any meaning. Its value will be just the sound. Because… because…

Give me an example of such a sound…

No, because… because… the thing is that when we say 'rose' the mind goes on the rose and the mind floats on the horizontal… what we call 'thinking'… Contemplating on something is the horizontal activity of the mind.."

Well, now, can you give me an example?

Examples we don't give because… because each personality has his own suitable syllable…

'And Jesus said to them
When you make the two one
And when you make the inner as the outer
And the outer as the inner
And the above as the below
And when you make the male and female into a single one
So that the male will not be male
And the female will not be female
When you make eyes in the place of an eye
And a hand in the place of a hand
And a foot in the place of a foot
And an image in the place of an image
Then you shall enter the Kingdom'

'The Gospel According to Thomas'
(Nag Hammadi Library)

Meher Baba and Meredith Starr (Herbert Close) at the Coombe Martin retreat, East Challacombe, Devon, 15 September 1931

Vanna Aquila Suri, by day Centrepoint volunteer, by night Wardour Street groupie, sat cross-legged on the pine floorboards of her Cricklewood bedsit.

Placing a pick-up arm on the grooves of 'Lavender Girl', Vanna wound the disc slowly backwards, trying to maintain a smooth, steady motion as the peripatetic needle grated its way through each crescendoing high and diminishing low.

She took a pencil from her mouth to scribble half-words on a scrap of Basildon Bond as she nodded her head in acquiescence to the wisdom being dispatched, and squinted, seemingly in some pain, while listening attentively for 'messages' — the odd word or sound, a combination of syllables buried within, as her friend Jasmine had indicated.

The polytechnic dropout was fifty-four seconds into the track; the point, just before — or after — chorus three, where Jas had heard John Nightly croon the words 'Vanna come Nightly', a distorted, drunken-sounding love-instruction from idol to fan. One of several karmic threads concealed by its author along with other *clues* deep in the jagged crevices of the vinyl.

The former Davina Woods, 21, recently decamped from Sheffield, was certainly a John Nightly obsessive — a true follower, the perfect *chela*. But in her own mind Davina was much more. Davina *was* John Nightly. The actual item. Not merely fan or even fanatic, but a kind of sacred conduit. The word 'clone' had not yet come into general use, but it would have been the word to describe her. For Davina saw herself as absolute; a completely integral part of His being. Inner woman to outer man. Shaman and 'she-man'. He, Him, *It* — the thing itself. Guest+Host=Ghost. In this case Ghost to the Maker — female half.

Her friends agreed. For, as effectively as she had transformed herself from social worker to socialite, Davina had become, within her natural habitat — the university common-room or pub corner seat – the entire Student Union's first port of call on all things astrological, and illogical.

Davina would peddle her Vedic horoscopes and natal charts involving 'solar arcs in transit', 'lunar returns', 'Nakshatras', 'ascendants', 'cardinals', 'conjunctions'; a sort of cosmic kebab – *yours for only 19 shillings and 11 pence, including fully personalised reading* – to the highly impressionable only. Naturally divine, with O Level passes in PE and needlework, Woods was suddenly an authority on Zen spirit, pre-life and post-life possibility, spiritual praxis, universality and *the Way* – all heavily related, when given half the chance, to the creative works of John Nightly.

No one could deny that Vanna was in touch with the vibrations of the age, imagining herself as her Master's companion along the undulating carriageways of life. But in the past months she had come to believe something more. Some nights, in the depths of her euphoria, the girl from Eccleshall imagined her whole being to have been somehow absorbed inside the Master, the physical person, the man, becoming a part of her Master's very essence; the soul of him, what there was left of it – the male half – and no doubt wished, wish upon wish upon wish, that he could somehow be inside her.

Like the record she manipulated, Vanna was herself slowly unwinding. She loped along Cricklewood Broadway having 'head conversations' with her idol, ignoring the internal cross-talk that had troubled her since childhood, waiting for a word from Him, wherever he might be. Rehearsing potential episodes, learning her lines. How she and her unwitting Master would exist in the regular, everyday world, do their thing at the butcher's or the laundrette. How serendipitous and significant for them to bump into each other at the zebra crossing or bus-stop? She fantasised how, when in her Master's company, she would deal with the little things, introduce herself to others and how her Master/Lover might refer to his new 'other half'.

She might even be accepted as John Nightly's 'lady'. Not conjuror's assistant but more Zen Mistress to Zen Master. Though even Vanna had to admit this was unlikely. That being the case she fancied herself as a kind of 'head' academic, an authority on her loved one's creative achievements and his… spiritual outlook; John Nightly's 'life view' – what he did, what he got up to. Hopefully an 'authorised authority' – the first port of call on all things Nightly. Popping up on radio and television whenever any discussion of the Master's work or his personal ups and downs came up. Or down.

Davina was certain that every word, every note of Nightly's torrential output, had been the result of some cosmic birth – literally 'divine' and aimed directly at her. The entire Nightly oeuvre had been conceived and created for Woods. Her friends thought so too. Told her so. Nightly's life's work, its tapestry of ciphers and signifiers, numerators and predictors added up to the ultimate astral chart; full of hope and optimism for the poor deluded young… nutcase – as Pondy would've no doubt suggested.

Tonight, the low-roller would be in the presence of the Master once again. 'Live' this time, the seventh so far. A fan-club-only concert at Chalk Farm Roundhouse, using one of the tickets given to Centrepoint volunteers. John would perform his famous song about her, his lavender girl. Tonight she would, for the first time, be properly close to her idol and other-world paramour. Close enough to touch. Tonight Davina planned to do something new with John Nightly. Go that little bit further, cross the line. Step through the mirror into a veritable pothole of jiggery-pokery; from open-eyed reality to wettest dream.

Man-Force, God-Force, John-Force. Vanna and Johnna were both Seekers. Two parts of the same *One*; Single Universal Parent. Mother of God. Atom Heart… Two halves of the same lemon. Whipped up, whirled up, maybe washed up, on a five-mile stretch of golden sand. Both completely… rama-lama-ding-donged, she hoped. Krishna'd out. Like a burned-out Sibelius, a retreating Dylan.

Life's like that. Sometimes it feels as though it's all coming at once. Flashes of the past, or 'before', long before; ignitions, premonitions of things that may come along next. Life is hardly ever still – or moving in one horizontal, equatorial dimension.

A different situation altogether to her previous relationships with gurus[1]; for she'd had a few. David Philip Johansson being the first. The primary-school teacher who had recognised her particular talents and encouraged Davina to 'use her imagination'. Marking her thirty-page essays 9/10. Taking time with her, worrying about her, making sure to place her in workgroups with other kids, leaving her to her own devices as little as possible.

Davina's child psychiatrist, Dr John Woodley, was another. Someone she enjoyed telling her troubles to, guiding her – 'saving her' – through her early teenage years. Woodley in turn being a devotee of J. G. (John Godolphin) Bennett. Vanna had spent time at Bennett's Coombe Springs community at Kingston upon Thames, two months of a ten-month course, just after arriving in London.

Then finally, a proper guru: foreign, Eastern, one that her friends had actually heard of. Meher Baba (compassionate father), later to become spiritual muse to Pete Townshend, had temporarily showed Vanna *the light*… Illuminating the way so that John Nightly, her final and absolute saviour, could make his entrance.

But let's not judge too harshly. Maybe Vanna and Davina came from a background much harsher than yours. When you come from abuse, rejection and deprivation, as do thirty-seven per cent of all children born to families in the north of England[2], you go to extremes. You discover your own Enlightenment. In

---

[1] Guru. Etymologically 'darkness' (gu) and 'light' (ru). Leading the follower from darkness into light.

[2] Statistics, General Medical Report, 'Cycles of Abuse in the System', p. 379, rep. ed. A Freely, September 1970.

the late months of 1970, full of disappointment and alienated from reality and also themselves, many people offered just that. Maybe the gurus from India and Tibet, like the evangelists from California, were more of an everyday occurrence on their home territory than they were in Eccleshall. Like princesses in Persia or Malaysia – or Golders Green.

Maybe those gurus seemed more removed. Aloof and special, as an alternative to the violence of our own domestic environment: to our extremely loving parents – our 'owners', as the law would have it – and to conventional, left-brained schoolteachers – our 'trainers'. Or set against the brand of enlightenment as touted by the government and the state – our actual 'keepers'; the only ones able to exert any real authority over the people, more often than not against the will of the people.

Perhaps in India these becalmed, half-sedated holy men were really more akin to the parish priest, pub landlord or local GP. It might be possible to have some kind of exchange, swap them over, transplanting the pub landlord to the rivers of Rishikesh. Maybe the Maharishi Mahesh Yogi would have exactly the same effect as Derek the landlord down at the Dog and Duck? How might Derek fare in the Himalayas?

Mawgan didn't think so. He and his friend Julian had gurus too. Surf guys. Kelly Slater or Greg Noll; grade-school athletes riding those big swells out in Waimea Bay whose physical strength had endowed them with true wisdom. Mawg knew they were special. Just last week he and Jules had watched the DVD of *Riding Giants*[3], incredulous at both the power and grace of the boardmasters. Staying on top of the wave was hard enough. How on earth did they get inside and then underneath it?

Endy couldn't fathom it at all. She could figure surfing on top,

[3] d. Stacey Peralta (2004)

of course. Had seen it with her own eyes, during the war when she and her sister travelled to Newquay to watch the American servicemen. If they stayed on for more than ten seconds people would clap and cheer. But these new boys. Walking not *on* but *inside* water. How on earth? Though as Mawg pointed out, it wasn't actually 'on earth'.

Neither were the sparkling clusters that both John Jnr and John Snr were fixed on. The Nightly family was well aware that Life often necessitated a suspension of belief. As in Hitch's fantasies, Endy's flashback matinees. Events that special never do take place in real time. A movie being nothing more than time-compressed reality; as with John Nightly's entire career, taking place on the other side of the lens.

Real life is the stuff behind the lens, the set-ups, the lighting, the pulling and focussing. What happens on the other side is that magic, the fantasy that in turn creates the person, or 'personality', as opposed to the already existing Self. The star and collapsed star, the Newton/Hawking genius – 'other Self' as opposed to 'Self'. One generation or 'clone' along. The seventh seal having been broken, the seventh son born, and the seven... brides of seven brothers... ah... Endy's all-time favourite film matinee. Was it on today? She asked Mawg.

As Jani would often teach, it's what happens on the other side of music composition that matters. According to Ronnie: *violence* > *experience* > *behaviour* > *phantasy / creation* is what makes us. What we create, creates us. Gives us personality. Changing our names, our physical and psychological selves, the groups and worlds we choose to exist within. The unreal makes us real. The imagined makes us real. Makes us new.

Johanna Zorn was an expert on both sides of the line, as Laing had been. According to Johanna, John Nightly's *Self* was so buried, so submerged, she wondered if it would ever re-surface; come back, come home. Bring him back.

Frieda suffered similar problems. John's mother may have been a frustrated talent long before her son came along. Maybe Frieda, a charismatic 'comet child' herself, would have been a singer-songwriter, poet or novelist had she been given the chance. Never having had the opportunity to express herself or present her gifts; she may never have discovered where her abilities lay, may never have known what the hell her gift was. That made her frustrated, and that made her crazy.

Frieda sent her husband into hiding. John Snr's escape, or retreat, was to remain at his place of work of a day or evening for as long as possible in order to escape the turmoil and abuse he suffered at home. John Nightly spent his childhood against such a background. What he regularly described as 'idyllic' or 'quite perfect' was quite the opposite. The young boy was smothered – violently so, to the extent that he was sometimes barely able to draw breath.

Music became John's way out. He had only to pick up his guitar or sit down at the piano and he would immediately feel able to exist again. Music transported John Nightly to that other side – as Alice said. And in that place he found like-minds. There would never be any need to return home. When JPG & R visited the Maharishi's retreat, they were literally *in retreat*. In 1696, aged 53, Isaac Newton published works about religion and philosophy rather than science. He became director of the Royal Mint, a job given as a sinecure, which Newton took seriously. In his sixth decade he needed to make money (literally) and enjoy life. It was Newton's work in this capacity (rather than his contributions to science) that earned him a knighthood.

Irving Berlin, Frieda's favourite, the greatest songwriter of the century, maybe of all time, gave it all up to become… a painter. Not because he was in a dry spot. Berlin's recent musical-theatre works had been stellar successes. He was hardly coming to the end of his life either – he was only half way through. The songwriter would live for another 50 years, dying at the age of 101. But Berlin didn't know that at the time.

There were other breakdowns and stoppages – and 'comebacks'. Sinatra made a habit of it[4]. Horowitz came back in the same place he bowed out[5]. Most often a breakdown was not due to lack of success, but rather to too much of it. Laing re-termed the breakdown a 'breakthrough'. When the author John Fowles decided to completely rewrite/revise and then republish *The Magus* in 1977 the book was already an international bestseller. *The Magus* was first published in 1965, but Fowles admitted he had been writing it 'since the early 1950s'.

Jean Sibelius, continually industrious throughout the first 50 years of life, struggled for the next 30 to complete just one work – an eighth symphony. The score was eventually burned in the garden of his home, Ainola[6]. Richard Wagner spent twenty-five years off and on writing *Parsifal*, during which time he completed *Tristan und Isolde*, *Die Meistersinger* and the *Ring Cycle*. Van Gogh first picked up a paintbrush aged 27. Ten years later he had killed himself.

[4] Following half a lifetime's worth of farewell concerts and comebacks, Frank Sinatra sang in public for the very last time on the evening of 25 February 1995 for the guests of the Frank Sinatra Desert Classic Golf Tournament near the singer's home in Palm Springs. His final song to the world being *The Best is Yet to Come*.

[5] Vladimir Horowitz made his US debut as a pianist at Carnegie Hall, on 12 January 1928. He retired from performance on 25 February 1953, bidding farewell at the same venue before making his comeback on the same stage 12 years later: at 3.38pm on Sunday, 9 May 1965, welcomed by a standing, shouting ovation from the 2,760-capacity crowd. In 1982, Horowitz began using prescribed antidepressant medications. Amid reports that he was drinking, his performances suffered. He retired, 'for good', but in 1985 returned, again at Carnegie Hall, and was back on form. For the LP release of his 1965 comeback, CBS engineers edited out the momentary slips and ambiguity that marred the pianist's first comeback. What they failed to remove were the whoops, gasps and tears, the audible weeping that greeted this transcendent performance, including Horowitz's demonic reading of Scriabin's *Sonata No. 9*, the notorious *Black Mass Sonata*.

[6] Sibelius' wife Aino recalled later, 'After this, my husband appeared calmer and his attitude was more optimistic. It was a happy time.'

John Constable passed through the glass. Though we may like to imagine otherwise, *the Hay Wain*, his and British paintings' all-time Greatest Hit, was painted not in front of his father's mill in Suffolk but at his Keppel Street painting-room in London, a short walk from Tottenham Court Road. Constable asked his friend John Dunthorpe, a local handyman, to make a sketch of the scene for him and *the Hay Wain*, a master-rendering of both imagination and technique, mixed fantasy with actuality. Re-ordered and refigured, the mill repositioned, the sky elongated, the vertical light drawn to fall at the very centre of the scene; the hay-wagon itself compressed. The result 'perfectly artificial' like a Photoshopped jpeg or 24 bit audio. The painting failed to sell, and it took the French to make the English aware of the genius they had borne[7]. Constable travelled to the other side to create his most commercial 'six-footers'. He'd cut and edit, redraw, 'improve'. His true self, the self of the oil sketches and drawings, lay in the chest of drawers beside his bed in Charlotte Street; out of sight, unexhibited, unseen, until after the artist's death.

Or Daphne Mpanza – the abuse she suffered due to her colour, instead of being celebrated for her talent. Daphne became one of the African continent's most significant educators, taking deprived but gifted children on scholarships to Britain and the US, just as she herself had lodged with Jani and Valerie. And Jana... Jana, the original facilitator of John's spark. Jana's mistake was to continue to expect life to be as simple and straightforward as she had experienced it to be so far. Jana believed in giving her all, and became disfigured by the person she had patronised; never able to hear one note of John Nightly's music or to trespass upon one syllable of his name after he abandoned her. Jana became one of the world's most innovative architects, a pioneer of eco-friendly and sustainable practices, perhaps able to build

[7] Exhibited at the Paris Salon of 1824, *The Hay Wain* was singled out for a gold medal awarded by Charles X of France, a cast of which is incorporated into the picture's frame. The works by Constable in the exhibition inspired a new generation of French painters, including Delacroix.

physically what she had been deprived of building emotionally. Or Iona. Iona had another face, a 'second Self', too. Though it took her twenty years to walk through the narrow gate that opened into the meadow leading down to the widening coastal path. And RCN himself, a presence never developed, never printed out. RCN had escaped once; but then returned, went backwards, flashed back, committing the sin of actually 'coming back'.

Robert Kemp, repressed and frustrated, a more printed-out Englishman would be hard to find. Robert was certainly old before his time, and growing older – fifty last birthday. Likely he would remain unfulfilled, unless he behaved uncharacteristically bravely. And finally Endy, content with her lot, happy to serve others who were undoubtedly happy to be served. Maybe Endy did experience a kind of genuine satisfaction. As one who was never tempted to even gaze through any kind of glass except with the intention of cleaning it.

'Do one thing for me,' whispers the blind Fredo to his young companion in *Cinema Paradiso* as Toto prepares to leave for active service. 'Never come back… never return.' The most important line in the movie for Mawgan Hall, who watched an old VHS of the film one night from Trewin's home-cinema selection. Fredo's wisdom would have resonated with all the inhabitants of the house.

The grads and undergrads who sat for hours in the Dandelion, mixing small amounts of Mary Jane into their roll-ups. How many of them would make proper use of inherited gifts? Discover their true abilities? How many of those visionary tea-drinkers were to end up as college administrators or local councillors, all Terylene slacks and a comb-over? How many get the chance – have the guts – to travel… really travel?

'I am a Traveller –,' sang John Nightly; 'I am a Traveller,' sang the audience. Get up out of your armchairs! Out of your beds! Out of your heads! Go somewhere. Do something. With your lives, your precious lives. For God's sake don't waste it. Don't waste it! Renounce the television, the telephone, the radio, the computer. Renounce the councillors, the government and the state. Do not spend time with people you do not want to be with for any reason. Do not erase time, remain in places, situations and circumstances where you do not want to be. Move! *Move!* That's what he meant. That's what they meant.

Trewin Farm, Porthcreek, Carn Point, Cornwall. Monday, 1 September 2006.
'There's one for you. And one for you!'

Mawg laid an A4 sheet on Endy's lap and handed the other one to John. The housekeeper got up to rinse her hands before putting on her glasses.

'And what's this when it's at home?' Endy squinted at the beautifully laid-out page.

'Natal charts... he's done your horoscope for you,' mumbled the boss amid his peanut-butter and burned toast.

The glossy laser print didn't resemble any zodiac Endy had ever come across in the *Daily Mail* – none of the usual crabs or scales – but her employer understood exactly what it was. Mawgan bent down to attend to Alexandre.

'Just downloaded it. It's your natal star chart Endy. Position of stars at birth and... loads of other stuff... tells you everything you'll ever want to know about yourself.'

'I don't think I want to know too much about myself, Mawgan. Dangerous, that is.'

Endy was oblivious to the implications of her comment. The man sitting opposite her had spent the past thirty or so years trying to discover just one little snowflake of something about himself.

'... seen a lot of these before, but I guess that was... well, thirty years ago now.' The boss adjusted his specs. 'They were a bit... fancier than this. Of the more "mystical"... variety.' John held his chart upside down, fixing on a couple of familiar patterns.

'You can see a lot more detail online, man. Remember we had a look when I first got the machine? They do a 100-page readout if you want it.' Mawgan went to get Alexandre's biscuits.

He shouted from the larder: 'I did Karen's this morning... Amazingly accurate... weirdly "real".'

While Endy, glasses lodged on the tip of her nose, turned her chart this way and that, trying to make sense of the hieroglyphics, the kid grabbed a packet of Cappu-grain.

'Good subject for a bit of music, John...'

The boss poured himself a glass of Ribena, sat back in his chair and folded the chart in two perfect halves, tucking it safely inside the *Cornishman*. Having no interest whatsoever in his natal pattern or in anything to do with the future in general, he figured he had given the item the required amount of attention so as not to disappoint his much-treasured friend.

Things were a bit like that now. Everything John Nightly did had to be figured and regulated. Time-allocated. The last thing John wanted was to erase any more time than he had done already – whatever amount he calculated he had left, each day already feeling like it was being somehow erased. Then again, neither did he want to appear ungrateful or impolite. If someone was considering his welfare, displayed kindness or decided to give him something, he wanted to appear grateful. But it had to be limited to the group. No PR or 'fan' stuff anymore – just family.

This was a big change. The lost art of giving and receiving. John Nightly had always been a good 'giver', an excellent giver; no doubt about that. At times generous to the point of his own detriment. But he was a rubbish 'taker'. Whatever else his faults, John was not naturally a selfish boy. He was lost, yes, a dreamer, certainly, needed attention and time to himself, time inside his own mind of course – had always demanded that – but always been willing to be jolted out of his dream if someone needed help. As had been the case so many times over the years. Particularly towards the end of the golden decade. The end of various people's 'situations'. So many *friends* had needed all sorts of assistance. And he had given it, or his manager had. Made the calls, spoken to whoever he'd been asked to speak to, signed the cheques. A place to crash, some kind of job or introduction. But mostly it was just pure cash money. Money did after all sort out most things for most people. And in rock'n'roll as in any creative endeavour, they – the artists – seemed in need of a pretty much constant supply.

Amazingly, John Nightly had never been in that situation himself. The cash rolled in more or less from day one – and when it rolled out again, some more rolled in. The reason being that the product on sale, whether it be exotic musical creations or exotic plants, was a great product.

Trewin Exotics, eighteen years in business, was now, as stated in the current edition of the Exotic Plant Grower's Register for England and Ireland, the third-largest supplier of exotics in the United Kingdom. If the business had been run by a media-friendly power couple who could be photographed for the Sunday supplements with their water features and obelisks and too-cool kiddies instead of a couple of reclusive anoraks who resembled child molesters more than anything else, they'd have been Number 1. Top of the Pops – in the plant trade. So, taking into account the anonymity and the total TV-unfriendliness of its founders, Trewin Exotics was doing just fine. Established as a mark of quality in the industrial plant universe, it was also a properly fattened cash cow.

When wholesalers and exporters saw the tiny orange label *Trewin* – the lettering copied from the title page of Calve's *Survey of Cornwall* – and the logo – a medieval woodcut of the haven-towne church – attached to the lip of each pot, they knew it meant quality of the highest order. The two Johns had even gone to the trouble, expensive though it had been, of having the tags sewn, like a designer label you might find inside a man's bespoke suit. That was the idea anyway, rather than add another gummed label to the batch that would end up stuck to the pots once they had left the haven.

Plant stickers drove Endy crazy. Particularly those from the local garden centre. When she needed geraniums or chrysanths or anything that Trewin didn't actually grow, Robert would bring back the healthiest specimens he could find. Endy would then spend a good half-hour steaming the labels from their pots. Cursing and damning under her breath, using words few people outside the local area would recognise.

Under Robert Kemp's direction no plant ever left Carn Point in anything other than tip-top condition. Each item going through a rigorous checking process before it was loaded up on overnight transport to foreign parts. Trewin lorries even boasted a primitive onboard irrigation system. Approximately twelve hundred stems could be watered at a time, a couple of hours before they were due to be unpacked and delivered to centrally located haulage warehouses before their final resting place in overlit supermarkets or handy Express stores.

It had been a hugely rewarding experience for all of them, building up such a highly regarded business. But hard work, too. With Trewin's numbered canna strains being listed in the monthly gardening magazines and catalogues, the nursery was beginning to make a name for itself in history.

That was its real achievement. Difficult enough to reach the top in just one career during a single lifetime, but to achieve that in two entirely different fields? Hard to think of anyone who had managed it while having a proper day-to-day involvement in both businesses. Daly and Nightly had. The two Johns could be truly proud of themselves. They couldn't be famous, or appear on *Gardeners' World* or *BBC Breakfast*, like the wizards of Trelissick or St Michael's Mount, but they could be proud.

The founders' very anonymity was a triumph. It proved that it was still possible to create a successful business simply by delivering an honest product. Nor was Trewin dependent on a personality or celebrity-for-hire who promoted or endorsed the item while having no direct involvement in what was being offered. What the two

Johns had managed to produce were simply just fabulous plants.

Success brought happiness. And in summer 2006 the inhabitants of Trewin were experiencing the happiest of times. A bunch of ill-matched misfits who had once found themselves in turmoil, more or less at the end of the road, had been somehow revived. Put back together again. Back on track. Trewin even had its own registered charity, donating half a million pounds per year to local causes. Playschools in Penzance, hospices in Helston, charities in cut-off communities along the coast… They would never know where the money came from. What they did know was that, for the past decade or so, regular funding kept coming through, unattached to the dread of community grants and government allocations. New roofs for schoolhouses, safer school buses and an increase in the amount of care workers were benefits felt in underprivileged areas of the county. The coastline from Zennor Head to Zawn Point was in so many ways a richer environment than it had been before the weirdos moved in.

From his telescope high above Black Cliff, John Nightly could not only observe the relative movements of celestial bodies but could also, if he so desired, turn the refractor on himself. There he would have seen the effect of his coming to live at the sandy towne. A bleary, fish-eyed version of his craggy, deepening features and his ungainly stance booming out of the telescope's precision-tooled shaft with the cartoon haven – all spires and seagulls, mermaids and red-faced men – in the background. Compressed and distorted, like all of his favourite '60s recordings. The effect the place had had on him, and he on it.

John would have observed a house of freaks, a gang of gypsies, space cowboys descended on the headland from… they weren't quite sure from where. The area of West Penwith and Kerrier had literally given him and all of them their lives back. Restored them like an elderly gardener might rescue a dying plant. By providing a proper environment in which to grow. By giving love, plenty of light and a permanency of place. *Miracle-Gro* indeed. Each wave that lapped upon the shore at Carn Point was, for the Nightly household, a wave of renewal. Each sun that rose over the Black Cliff to smile upon Trewin provided one more priceless 'extra' day. A day most of them surely never expected to see. A day that provided an opportunity to do good, to *be* good, for themselves and for others. Endy, Mawg, Robert, John and John were grateful for the sun and the waves. They used those days well. They honoured those days. What a pity it was all about to end.

Stephen's Achievement

There used to be a café
The Dandelion
Cambridge '72
Mill Road before the bridge
The poor part
Where nobody goes

Curved glass shopfront
Victorian ash
Beyond the yellow wood
A kind place
Of Students
Guitarists
Poets
Philosophers
Pop philosophers
Head in book
Head-in-air

Heads
Would sit all day
And muse
There were a lot of places in Cambridge like that then

Underground print
Pamphlets from London
Oz, IT, Ink
A few holy teas
Himalayan-grain coffee
Dope cake if you knew…
We used to go there a lot
We used to be there a lot
We used to 'be'…

John Nightly had a corner at the Dandy most days
Michaelmas '72 to Lent '76
And a pile of beetsuger
In his Hollywood dream

Another statistical dropout
Still at the university
Like most of them
Sponging off the system
While lecturing everyone
That it wasn't working

Happy to while away his time
Too young to consider the wastage of time
Old enough not to worry about what anyone else thought
Too messed up to care

At night
Through the passing of the years
And the yellow
He went to the Dandelion often
The café was where
Events having taken another turn
He would've ended up

With Jana
And Justin
And one or two other music-minded frendz

Laing said:
We only dream of where we want to be…
From '72 to '76
John Nightly himself
Was secure in California
dreaming
While his dreams were insecure in Cambridge

If events had taken another turn
it would've been the other way around
What if John Nightly had not chosen a career
In… Pop?
What if he'd stayed at Cavendish with his friend Hawking
And all the other genius research students you've never heard
of?

Maybe right now he'd be sat in his rooms
Giving another irrelevant lecture and
Trying to figure out
How to get into the pants of the 18-year-old sitting opposite

In his spare time
Maybe he worked to crack
Some scientific code
Which would lead him into immortality
(like his friend)

Stephen's achievement
Is now compared
To that of Isaac Newton
Instead of Mick bloody Jagger!
For God's sake.

In these dreams
John often wondered
About the other side
Which was the sunnier place?

Bright-yellow days on the quadrant of King's
Or soft orange skies in the Metropolis of Angels?

No seasonal planting in a place without seasons

Both Cambridge University
And the SUMMER Centre
Spent a lot of money on gardeners

In England
They were young apprentices
In old hands
Schooled in John Gerard
And his Herball
The fantastic Tradescants
And the plants they hunted

The Americans were mainly
Pool guys or 'maintenance'
Beefcake jardiniers
Often employed
Because the lady of the house
Liked muscle in a man
And liked to fantasise

But Cambridge gardeners were employed by the Bursars
Or maybe the Masters, the Fellows or Deans
Muscle wouldn't count for a great deal
So their arms were thin like guitarist's...

Cambridge gardeners were old men
Mostly
Headful of seed catalogues, surveys and tables
Employing young men
Like John Nightly
If he'd have stayed

To do this heavy work

1 April 1971 was April Fools' Day in more ways than one. It was the appointed day on which John Nightly and his manager had arranged to meet in order to talk through the problems within their business relationship. When Pondy arrived at Queen Square, John was absent. Instead the manager encountered Iona on her way out of the apartment.

'*Majoun!*' Pond opened his arms to her. 'I don't suppose you have any of that fabulous cake of yours?'

Iona let herself be embraced despite everything.

'I'm afraid I don't,' she replied without quite surrendering. 'The pigeons have had it. *Majoun** is very popular with the birds of Regent's Park.'

Pond smiled and let go of her reluctantly. He peered rather timidly into the flat. 'Is he around?'

'John is out… he will not be long.' Iona picked up her scarf and prepared once again to exit.

'… is he… alright?' The manager, uncharacteristically subdued, pulled a packet of Rizla from his bag.

'In a daily way?' Iona answered matter-of-factly.

'In any way. *Is he okay?*'

Iona took a breath, gave up and put her coat down on the hall chair. 'Are *you* okay, John? Are you alright? This is the question … *n'est-ce pas?*' Pond seemed genuinely taken aback.

'I'm as okay as everyone else…' He looked on a cluttered table for a box of matches. 'Not sure what you mean by that?'

'You do know what I mean by this, John. What I mean is, are you really doing your best for things? Right now? For John…

as well as for yourself…' She sighed and lodged her car keys on the table. 'I hope you are. Because John needs it. He needs it now. I think you both need it.'

Iona took a cigarette from her bag. She sounded tearful. Pond reached to steady her arm. 'Darling… everything really is fine. It honestly is…' He tried hard not to slur his speech. 'Or will be… when we've… you know what I'm… well, that's why I'm here.'

He sounded almost reassuring. 'We do probably need to… sit down and… Like we used to.' Pond unwound the scarf around his neck. 'Me and him never do sit down anymore.'

'This is probably because you're so… so bloody out of it all the time.'

'… ah…' The manager tried to support himself against the wall.

Iona appeared rather out of it herself. As if she'd said something she actually meant. Her old friend looked at her guiltily, as one might look in on a scene rather than being actually involved in it.

'That's what you… or "everyone" thinks?'

'How can they think something else? All they have to do is look at you. Speak with you. Do you know? Do you know what's happening?' Iona took a taper from a candle holder on the wall.

'We are both working. Very hard, me and him. John sits in that room all day and all night. He is so tired by it. And when he comes to our bed he looks like… a *fantôme*… as if part of him is not there anymore… a bloody ghost.' Iona threw herself down on the hall chair. 'And when he's not doing that you drive him up and down the bloody… the English road. Driving him crazy. Far places… Scotland… and that makes him, all of them, more tireder. My husband doesn't need to do this thing anymore.'

The manager needed to get through the next few minutes somehow. Determined not to be beaten up too badly, he summoned the tiny pocket of courage left in him.

'I do not, and cannot, make John, or anyone else, do anything they don't want to do – no one can. I'm sure you know that better than anyone, my dear.' Pond looked Iona straight in the eye. 'Financially, he may not "need" to do that kind of stuff literally right at this minute, but promotionally… and press-wise – vibe-wise as well – he does need to do it. They all do.' Pond levered himself off the wall and began a slow mooch up and down the corridor. He stopped halfway, turning back towards her. 'Same as in your business. Exploit it while it's there, yes?' Iona let her bag fall to the floor, taking it all in while also being taken in – at least momentarily.

'We have to honour touring commitments… which are booked long in advance, as you know. Unless we're the bloody Rolling Stones…' Pond shuffled back and crouched down before Iona. 'Because we have to behave. Like a normal band, if that's at all possible, in the circumstances. Not like a band who've had everything handed to them on a plate from… day one.'

Iona needed to leave. 'John… if this is like it is, then you have to behave like a "bloody manager", I think.'

It was the first time ever that Iona had questioned him. Pond slid down the wall on his back to rest on the calico mat, hoping the girl had the wherewithal for him to roll something. 'As far as I know, I am – and will be, until further notice – the "bloody manager".'

Iona sighed, put her arm on her friend's shoulder and came to rest somewhat sympathetically beside him. 'Maybe you are, John. You are still the manager, for sure, but a manager who is never there, who does not know what is happening to his friend's… life. When he is supposed to be leading things. You are not "directing" anymore, are you? You've stopped doing that.' She looked round for her keys again. 'It seems you... you quickly...' She paused once more. 'You lost interest in your best person.'

At that moment there was a familiar knock on the door. Iona made a vexed face, handed Pondy a small silver packet from her bag, then walked to the far end of the hallway to let her husband in. Just once, once in a while, she thought, couldn't there be one time ever when John might remember his keys? But as she turned the lock a tall gentleman in a navy overcoat, standard issue, placed his boot across the threshold. There were two other gentlemen in abnormally plain clothes standing behind him.

'Good afternoon...'

The tall man smiled and looked past Iona down the length of the entrance hall. 'Detective Sergeant Seagrave.' The man held out his visitor's card. 'I'm sorry to disturb you without notice, but I'm afraid I'm going to have to ask you to let me take a look around.' He placed his hand on the door to draw it further open.

At least a million things flashed through the girl's mind. The first was Prison. Iona imagined herself locked up with Pond, incarcerated somewhere underground, with rats. A dank Victorian locker. The pair of no-gooders, caught in the act. Sentenced to life imprisonment for sharing a spliff beyond the bicycle sheds. The second was Time; there wasn't very much of it. Just seconds away Pondy was sat rolling one. Concocting the evidence that would be used against them. Less than another few minutes away, her husband was on his way home – and he had a habit of stopping off in the park to roll a joint before walking in smoking it. Iona had no idea how much stuff either John had on them. Neither was she sure how much they had hidden around the flat. A reasonable amount, certainly. A 'significant amount', no doubt.

If she were up to date there was a block of 'normal' under the sink, a roll of Monika's best Moroccan Black in the toilet-brush holder, a medium-sized bag of Gold Seal suspended from the sewage pipe outside the back-bedroom window and some tabs from a while back Sellotaped to the trap door leading to the attic.

It was… quite a lot. A good stash. Enough to suggest that they were dealing – which of course they weren't – rather than just 'using' or that it was, in the oft-quoted legal phrase, *for their own purposes.*

Pondy remained uncharacteristically silent for once, so Iona made the good move of asking DS Seagrave in and leading him and his plain men into the closest room, her husband's music studio, hoping that they might be temporarily distracted by the flashing lights, buzzers and bells, the Bedouin furnishings, the putrid aroma of incense and patchouli, the little mini-altar with light-stained photographs of Indian men and classical composers smiling amid jars of tulips and daffodils, before ushering them through the connecting door and along the hallway into the adjoining room – the couple's space-age kitchen. The room in the flat furthest away from Pond.

But it made no difference. As one stone-faced officer walked out of the kitchen, Pond walked in. Genuinely pleased to see visitors, the always-affable manager held out one hand to greet him; the other contained one of the largest spliffs the constable had ever set eyes on.

* love potion' in Arabic.

The Hay Wain Beefeater Grill, motorway services, A12/A120 Colchester, Suffolk. 15 July 1971. 4.30pm.
John and Justin were slumped at the counter. Justin with his baked beans, distracted by Tony Blackburn at one end of the restaurant and the BBC test card at the other. John poured a lukewarm mu from his flask, the way of macrobiotics a little at odds with the Hay Wain's popular 'sizzles and griddles'. Zigging and zagging the student universe required sustenance. John opened a ball of kitchen foil to reveal a lovingly-made adzuki rice ball, prepared by a loving Iona just over a week ago. The Yardbirds' 'For Your Love' came on, followed by the highly rotated 'Layla' into 'You Really Got Me' into Vanity Fare's 'Hitchin' a Ride'. 'If only we could...' mumbled Justin as he slipped further down the bench. 'Really need to get off the... old beaten track, as they say... and bloody go... bloody home.'

'Home to where?' asked John, trying to get the rice ball to his mouth without it falling apart. 'Home is anywhere you are, man. Sometimes I feel I've been put in one of those tumblers... rollers... the things with the handle you wind up, for a sweepstake or... lucky-dip and everything in it... tumbles round... Including me.'

'Sweepstake tumbler.'

'That's it.'

Justin opened the *Melody Maker.* 'Keith Relf's left Renaissance,' he announced. 'I remember seeing him doing "Dazed and Confused" with the Yardbirds. Five minutes later they're Led Zeppelin!' [1]

John gazed at his watch, hoping tonight's gig might have suffered a lightning strike or flood while they'd been in the café, there being no longer any need to get back on the motorway. The café proprietor switched off the transistor and turned up the TV for the teatime news. John and Just angled themselves side on to the television screen where the gap between programmes was being filled by an interlude film. 'That's your track,' said

Justin. 'Must have known you were coming!' as Satie's *Gymnopédie No. 1* accompanied images of hayfields and windmills. 'Revolutionary bit of music, that...' he continued, mid-burger. 'Doesn't go anywhere, does it? Doesn't move. Just sits there. That's different. Must've been very different at the time.'

'... all been done before. By Chopin' [2] replied John. 'There's nothing new on this earth, Justin – 'cept maybe a "higher consciousness burger" down at the Co-Op...'

'That "Layla' riff's something else, y'know,' [3] replied Justin, suddenly feeling faint, having recently recovered from a bout of hepatitis A – 'hippie-itis', as it had become known in doctors' waiting-rooms. 'I think these beans might be a bit weird,' he said, ladling a third helping onto his plate.

' "Layla" is in the... Dorian mode. "You Really Got Me"... that's... uh... Mixolydian.' John yawned. 'Well, this is one hell of a birthday party.'

---

[1] Led Zeppelin performed initially as the New Yardbirds, with Relf as vocalist.

[2] Probably referring to Chopin's *Berceuse in Db, Opus 57*.

[3] The vocal melody of Albert King's 'As the Years Go Passing By' written by Fenton Robinson.

'*Perfectionist*', '*control freak*', '*mental*', '*psychotic*', '*genius*'... All had been applied to John Nightly over the years. The inference of each having overtaken its literal meaning long ago. Though whenever any application had occurred in John's presence he had denied it, of course. Renounced them all; the good, bad and the just plain ignorant.

John Nightly had never considered himself to be a genius, in any sense, and he didn't believe he was *psychotic*. Maybe he was just a tiny bit *mental*. Maybe he didn't mind admitting that one. In both senses of the word.

Had anyone ever gotten a straight answer out of him, John might have agreed that the best way to describe him these days would be... 'sensitive'. In rock'n'roll journalese – the buzz language of dead-eared commentators who, as Pondy so rightly stated, never do write about the music itself – he would most likely have been referred to as 'psycho-delicate'. Though John was nowhere near as sensitive or delicate as he used to be. These days, John Nightly was quite desensitised. Quite numb.

The rock'n'roll thing was what had done it for him. Trying to keep up with it was a full-time job and not at all what he had expected. Not a job about writing songs, making records and people either liking or not liking them. That had very little to do with it. It was really about all this other stuff. The stuff that somehow got compacted and entwined with the creating part.

John Nightly had embraced life. He'd given it all he had, took whatever life had ungratefully slung back and, remembering the parables and philosophies that had been inflicted upon him as a child, had utilised the gift bestowed to the best of his ability. But when the game had played itself out John stepped backwards into a vat of psychological manure. It took at least ten years to un-stick himself. *Psychotic?* No, that wouldn't be right at all. Nor would *control freak*. Except possibly in terms of a determination for getting things the way he wanted them. And... *genius?*

'The Seashore Test' (1944), *Psychedelic Drugs: Psychological, Medical and Social Issues,* Dr Brian Wells (Penguin Education), 1973.

One of the most celebrated, and earliest, of the attempts to study the effects of psychedelic substances on the creative process was that of Aldrich (1944). This study is of particular interest for the way it illustrates how far test measures can depart from the realities of the situation which they set out to assess and how, when the results are reported elsewhere, they continue to get even further away from the point. Aldrich's study was entitled 'The effects of a synthetic marihuana-like compound on musical talent as measured by the Seashore Test', the stated purpose of the experiment being to investigate a popular claim that the use of marihuana causes jazz musicians to 'ascend to new peaks of virtuosity'.

The circumstances of the investigation were as follows: the subjects were 12 male prisoners, two of whom were professional musicians and all of whom were regular users of marihuana, who had been imprisoned, ostensibly, for violation of the Marihuana Tax Act. There were three once-weekly sessions in which the subjects took the Seashore Tests; only on the third occasion was a drug, Parahexyl, used. The tests, presented on gramophone records, involved the subject in distinguishing between pairs of notes as to their difference in pitch, loudness, time and timbre, and in identifying similarities, differences, and changes in simple patterns of sound. Broadly speaking, the results showed that most subjects made gains, due to practice, between the first and second tests but slipped back to a lower level on the drug-involved final test – despite most of them feeling that they had done better on this last trial.

Queen Square, Regent's Park, London NW1. Bonfire Night, 5 November 1971.

'You know when we were at the Revolution and Antony came up and kissed you and you took hold of his hand and brought him over to meet me?'

'Antony?'

'*Antony.* Tony… come on…' John kept his eyes fixed directly on Iona's. 'He came in and he came straight over to you and… he obviously knew you very well.'

'Of course he knows me.' Iona was a competent actress. 'We were out together. But I told you this…'

'Yeh, but… what I… when I saw you actually take his hand, in that… way… and then look at me like you did while you were talking to him…' John paused. 'I don't know whether you gave me that… sort of weird – it was weird – that look to make me jealous or, perhaps to see if I was looking… or… if I was alright with it… or… maybe to reassure me that I was, even at that very small moment, the only person in your world, or… But… at that very moment with his hand, his… horrible hand in yours. Well… all I wanted to do was to kill him.'

'*John…*'

'It's a… freaky… thing to say. But I mean it. I wanted to kill a man. Destroy somebody; a person who I knew nothing about. I'd actually never set eyes on him before that night. Didn't know whether he was a… kind man, or… "decent", which he probably is…'

Iona's face lost all expression as she looked down at the floor, fixing on a pattern in the carpet that may or may not have really existed.

'Anyway. That's the depth of it. That's all I've got to…' John took a breath as Iona began to sob. She turned at right angles to her husband and emitted irregular yelping noises.

'I'm saying this – bothering to say it – because that is the depth of my love for you. As I said to you, so many times, and you used to make fun of me – still don't understand why – because it was so completely true. You kept asking me if I loved you. You asked me that all the time. And I always said the same thing back, didn't I?'

'You said you "a-dored" me.'

'I said I "worshipped" you. Even better than "adored". I said that I couldn't strictly "love" you because worshipfulness and… adoration… was a bigger thing than love. Whether or not you think that's funny is irrelevant.'

Iona didn't really understand.

'That word "love" isn't big enough, you see. Isn't big enough at all. For what I felt. Didn't you get it? Didn't I tell you? "Worshipped" is much better… It's much more…'

'It means… it means something else, though, John.'

'It's more actually descriptive,' he pressed on. 'Of the actual situation, darling. But it's completely unconditional, you see? Like a dog.'

The boy sat down on the opposite side of the room, as far as it was possible to physically get from his wife. 'I adored you and looked up to you and… and worshipped you and wanted to be so close to you literally all of the time, like a dog wants to be close to his owner. Do you see? Like when you see a dog tied up outside a shop and they can't stop looking and wanting the owner to come out, come back to it. It's just looking into the shop all the time and howling. I don't know if dogs have a time factor… I don't know if they understand… *Time*, you know?

Don't think they do. Obviously it's *difficult*… impossible really… for them to understand *Time*. How can they possibly know when their owner is coming back to get them?'

'John…'

John was off on one of his things. Whether or not dogs understood the concept of *Time* was not what concerned Iona at this moment.

'… anyway… Iona…' The boy hesitated. 'Just that little thing is funny as well…' He lifted his head. 'It's so weird for me to actually say my wife's name.'

Iona did not respond.

'That's funny… strange.' John leaned back and breathed out. Breathed out a long, patient breath.

'… p'raps that's it. Said it now. I think I have just said what I came to say. Hope I have. And I had to come. Because there won't be any more of this now. Any more misery, I mean… any more of anything. For either of us… ever again.'

Now they were both sobbing. John could hardly get the words out.

'The depth of my love for you… during that long… amazing, period. And since I messed up the wonderful situation we had…'

'After I… messed it up…'

Iona slumped on her hard-backed chair. Expecting John to lean over and comfort her, make things just a little bit easier than they seemed right now. It didn't cross her husband's mind.

'I can't tell you why… because I don't know that either. And since there are no excuses for my behaviour… what I've done, the only way out of this now, for me anyway… is never to see you again. And never to hear from you… never hear about you either – if I can help it. So please – and for you never to hear from me… obviously. It has to be this way, my… Because I won't be able to bear it otherwise… and then… well… I won't be able to concentrate on any music or anything. And if I can't concentrate, then something… bad, something quite bad might… well…'

Iona stood up and used her cardigan to wipe her eyes. 'And… Myra?'

'That's nothing to do with this… or us. Nothing to do with anything to do with us.'

'Is she downstairs?'

John appeared found out. As if he'd brought his new girlfriend into his parents' house, knowing she would not be welcome.

'She's waiting for me in the car. She doesn't know anything about what we're saying.' John appeared calm. As if he were trying to conclude the deal and appeal to Iona. 'But she… Myra is nothing… "nothing"… what I… nothing. Compared… I mean… I don't mean… I didn't mean to say that at all. Not "nothing"; what I mean is… Myra is an independent person. She's nothing to do with this… "us"… I…' he paused. 'She's special… like all humans… but compared to you…' He paused again. 'That's really bad. Sorry…'

'What do you want me to do?'

John looked at his wife one more time. Stared at her, realising it might be the last. Iona had asked him not to come this afternoon. And now yet another bad thing was part of their history.

Suddenly, the beautiful Danish model, most desirable of females, covered her eyes with both hands and let out a shocking, almost deathly wail, a 'last breath' kind of sound that seemed to encompass all of the pain that she had been caused by this cold inhuman man in a few very short minutes. And all of the pain, that she had brought upon him. Iona continued to wail and howl and squeal as if in uncontrollable terror, attempting to cry and to stay vertical at the same time. Looking as if she were about to pass out, she placed her hands on the chair to steady herself and then lifted up her cardigan and vomited small bits of sick and phlegm into it.

John took one last look at the apartment, the three-deck audio system still taking up most of one side of the large reception room, three televisions side by side – BBC1, BBC2, ITV – on the other. The Kasbah-style decor, canvas mats, embroideries and endless knick-knacks that comforted Iona and made her feel at home. Every corner and cranny filled with canna plants.

He dragged his hair away from his eyes, wiped tears using the back of his hand, wiped his nose, ignored Iona. Picked up his car keys, took a deep, deep breath, turned around and walked out. No kiss, no smile. Not even a look. John made his way down to the car, his new partner waiting patiently there. He had no intention of trying to explain to Myra what had just happened to a previous, incredibly famous, perfectly matched, absolute couple. Myra didn't ask. She guessed what had taken place, having been through it herself, though in a much more sanitised way, by telephone to her displaced husband. Myra took John's hand and kissed the back of it in a tender, most unusually (for her) understanding way. John wiped his eyes again, gave Myra a kind of apologetic, side-on smile and put his foot down hard.

Two hours later, in perfect driving conditions, John turned over the XJS while taking a bend on the B3396, the Plymouth road to Truro. He was travelling much faster than he should have been when the Jaguar hit a bank, swivelling round onto an oncoming articulated vehicle that buckled up on itself, flipped over and came to rest on its side, straddling the entire width of the small carriageway. John and Myra's car lifted up and rolled across the verge, both passengers being shaken like jelly before being compressed inside it.

John sustained two broken legs, a broken collarbone and injuries to his head and chest. When they found him, the steering wheel was embedded in his shoulder; his back was holding up the vehicle's collapsed roof. It took two hours to slowly cut him free. He was then taken to Taunton General Hospital, where he remained for the next four months. The driver of the lorry died the following day after several operations to remove lengths of steel from his neck and chest. Myra's head had been forced through the re-enforced windscreen. She was killed instantly.

NBC News: *The Midnight Report with Dan Glubner.*
12 November 1971: The News Today
Stars of stage and screen were in attendance in Beverly Hills today at the funeral of Rachel Myra Knoll, heiress to the Knoll electricity fortune. Miss Knoll was the daughter of power magnate Bill Knoll and his wife, Isola. A successful film producer in her own right, Ms Knoll died when the car in which she was a passenger was involved in a fatal accident when it spun off a small road in England. Her companion, rock singer John Nightly, who was driving the car at the time, escaped unhurt. The Knoll family have begun legal proceedings against Mr Nightly, who, it is claimed, may have been under the influence of illegal substances at the time the tragedy occurred. Mr Nightly did not attend the funeral.

Trewin Farm, Porthcreek, Carn Point, Cornwall. Harvest Sunday 2006.

'I like everything to be nice and clean. That's all I ask. Everything to be clean – then I'm happy.' Endy rinsed her dishcloth, 'Happy as a sand boy, I am. *Shipshape*... like my father used to say.' She looked up, ready to answer a non-existent question in the empty early morning silence. 'Why did he say it? Because he was on a ship, I should think.'

What the housekeeper was saying made a lot of sense, as usual. It *was* good to have everything shipshape. Alexandre appeared puzzled by her ladyship talking to herself as he loped to the sink to angle his head towards her while Endy bent over the washbasin and applied her favourite cream cleaner to the already sparkling enamel.

'Did I tell you that when I was a little girl they used to call me Thomasine?'

Mawg looked wary, no doubt fearing a further assault.

'Don't think you did, Endy...' the kid muttered, resigning himself to at least ten minutes' worth, as he balanced the full weight of his body on the back legs of his chair. 'Why was that, then?'

'Well...' The housekeeper was delighted to be asked. 'It was because I was... considered to be a bit... "bolshie" in my younger days, or whatever they call it these days.' Endy lifted Alexandre's front legs down from the washer. 'C'mon, boy, there's nothing for you in there. They thought I was a bit like Thomasine, you see.'

Both Mawg and Alexandre appeared flummoxed. Endy smiled her most excited smile and turned towards them.

'Thomasine! *Thomasine Bonaventura!*'

The kid copped a mouthful of Joosi Juice. 'Great name for a band!'

RCN wandered in, needing to get to the basin quickly to wash paraffin from his hands. Endy rambled on.

'Oh, she was very famous, Thomasine… The shepherd girl who became Lord Mayor of London. Came from Week St Mary.'

'What?'

Week… Week St Mary… up near Trigg.' Endy picked up the dishcloth again and worked it over her shrivelled fingers. 'Little Thomasine was toiling in the fields one morning when a grand gentleman, a really grand one, on a horse…' The narrator mimicked holding the reins of the grand gentleman's horse… 'Noticed her and… well, he was *dazzled* by her. Completely taken over… by her beauty, I suppose. Liked the way she looked, you see. He wanted to…'

'We get it, Endy…'

'Anyway…' Endy let go the reins and picked up leaves of eucalyptus blown into the kitchen by the wind. 'He took Thomasine off back to London with him then after he died she became the mayor – or mayoress, I should say. Lady Mayoress of London… Lady Percyval.'

'He *kidnapped* her?' RCN liked to tease the committed washer-upper.

'"Kidnapped"…? No, not kidnapped. This was a very grand gentleman.'

'What's the place again?' Mawg was polite enough to at least pretend to be listening. 'Weak… what did you say?'

'Week St Mary, Mawgan. W-E-E-K. Up near Trigg, on the north coast. Everybody knows Week St Mary!' The housekeeper spoke emphatically, slightly rattled at the lack of local knowledge. '*Week*: "dairy-farm", *St Mary*: eh… well, "St Mary".

Everywhere round here's to do with saints. They had the first Free School in Cornwall there, the Spring School – which Thomasine, Lady Percyval, paid for.' Endy paused for breath. 'Anyway… that's why they called me that…'

RCN couldn't resist spoiling her fun.

'Thought you said you used to be called a lot of… "nasty" things at school, and that was how you got your name?' He went to the sink and picked up one of several small offcuts of soap. The housekeeper seemed flustered.

'Ah, well… that's right… but… but that was at my junior school, in Quethiock.' She straightened herself up. 'I'm talking about my other school now – before I went into service…' RCN turned on the cold tap and began to swill his hands.

'So you actually had… quite a bit of schooling then? I was under the… impression you'd hardly had any schooling at all.'

Endy turned off the water for him, passed RCN a towel, took a J-cloth out of its box and wiped the rim of the sink. She turned to the kid.

'Shall you… want me to make you a packed lunch tomorrow, Mawgan? I'll be up with the birds… so I can make you a nice sandwich. And a nice bit of cake… if you want me to…'

If spring is the season of hope, the kindest season, then autumn is certainly the cruellest. It's the season of no hope. The season of suicide. The 'wolf months' of the year.

Though most prominent '60s 'makers were still in the spring of their years by the mid- to late '70s, many had already given up, having realised that the scene as they had known it – the one they had helped create – had treated them in an extremely fickle way.

Run down and pretty much dried out from a lack of optimism, self-belief and much-needed funds, the former shaker-makers were becoming just a little too mature in years to be able to continue with the lifestyle they had been privileged to lead. None too keen to step back through the glass into the reality of responsible adulthood and the new social clime, their retinas found it hard to adjust to twilight after years in the limelight.

With Joe Meek (3. 2. 67) Brian Epstein (27. 8. 67) Brian Jones (3. 7. 69) Jimi Hendrix (18. 9. 70) Tubby Hayes (8. 6. 73) Gram Parsons (19. 8. 73) and Mama Cass (29. 7. 74) already gone, Graham Bond threw himself under a tube train at Finsbury Park, 8 May 74. Nick Drake overdosed on anti-depressants, 3 September the same year. Pete Ham was found hanged in his garage, 23 April 75. Tim Buckley mistook heroin for cocaine, 26 June 75. Paul Kossoff suffered a mid-flight heart attack 19 March 76. Phil Ochs hung himself in his sister's house in Far Rockaway, Queens, New York, 9 April 76. Keith Moon overdosed on the sedative Heminevrine, 7 September 78 (he was taking it to control his drinking), Terry Kath shot himself in the head with a pistol while demonstrating it was unloaded, 23 January 1978 and on the 14 May the same year Keith Relf was electro-cuted while tuning his guitar at home. The Final Academy had been delivered back to its Maker.

On the night of September 27, 1972, the same night John Nightly booked himself into the Sumha centre, Beatle employer and proto-rocker Rory Storm – the former Alan Caldwell – took an overdose of sleeping-pills in an alleged suicide pact with his mother Violet*, while mod guru Peter Meaden ran out of stories and committed suicide with pills on 5 August 1978.

John Pond, in and out of rehabilitation centres and addiction groups through the early years of the '70s was, by the time of his sudden demise, still making enough to keep himself institutionalised by exploiting what he could of the John Nightly catalogue, until a heroin speedball got the better of him in the VIP toilets of a Paris nightclub, when he also left without saying goodbye during the early hours of 10 October 1978.

In keeping with common themes running through rock'n'roll's back pages, it had seemed at the time of his death that Pond was about to re-enter the scene for the first time during the new era – in the field of TV production, where he'd been in discussion for a series of acoustic-only performances with '60s legends/ has-beens, including Lee Hide's old mucker from Berwick Street Market, Marc Feld, until Marc's car was found wrapped around a horse-chestnut tree on Barnes Common on the morning of 16 September 1977.

By 1980, the new world had arrived. The '60s was now two generations away. The decade was not well thought of. The Beatles, the Rolling Stones and the Who were shunned. Sixties superstars being out of favour, in cotton wool, in cabaret, or dead. Peter Green was found running around a supermarket in South London giving away £5 notes to alarmed customers. The guitarist

* After disbanding the Hurricanes, Rory Storm worked as a DJ at the Silver Blades ice rink in Liverpool and in Benidorm where he was also a water-skiing instructor. Having returned to Liverpool to be with his mother following his father's death, he developed a chest infection and took sleeping pills. On 28 September 1972 Storm and his mother were both found dead at their home 'Stormsville'. The post-mortem reported that Storm had alcohol and sleeping pills in his blood, but not enough to cause death. It is thought his mother may have committed suicide after finding her son's body.

The Hurricanes released just two singles, the second of which, 'America' from *West Side Story*, was produced by Brian Epstein – who also sang backing vocals on it.

had grown his fingernails so long that he could no longer get his hands anywhere near his green Gibson Les Paul, which somehow ended up in a second-hand guitar shop in Richmond. Brian Wilson, burned out by his family, the record industry, LSD and his own unfathomable genius, retreated into his sandbox and spent the next six years in bed. John Lennon, too famous to go anywhere near a help centre, retreated to his Dakota white cell with his Japanese therapist, exiled in New York before being murdered after signing an autograph for his killer on 8 December 1980.

Pete Townshend, Eric Clapton, George Harrison and Robert Stigwood were all associated with the setting up of a clinic at Broadhurst Manor in Sussex by Dr Meg Patterson in order to promote her controversial Black Box treatment. The method somehow alleviated withdrawal symptoms from heroin by attaching electrodes to the ears. It was never claimed to be any kind of cure.

At Coombe Springs in Kingston upon Thames, J. G. Bennett, follower of *The Fourth Way*, prince of psycho-seekers and former disciple of both Gurdjieff and Shivapuri Baba, founded a hippie monastery just outside Central London; while down the river at Richmond, close to the old mod hangout Eel Pie Island, Pete Townshend celebrated his own personal guru, Meher Baba [1] by setting up the Oceanic, a temple on the upper floors of his private recording studio. Just as Tycho Brahe built his Uranienborg and Bernard Lovell built Jodrell Bank, Townsend built his Oceanic and Bennett built his Djameechoonatra [2]. All observatories of some kind, it remains for us to reflect as to what was actually being observed. In the US, Scientology chief L. Ron Hubbard got into the act by

---

[1] Meher Baba (1894-1969) took a vow of silence and was said not to have spoken at all from January 1922 to his death, preferring to use 'alphabet boards' to deliver his Universal Message.

[2] John Godolphin Bennett (1897–1974) was an English mathematician, scientist, military-intelligence agent and philosopher. His *magnum opus* was the constantly written and rewritten *The Dramatic Universe* (1956–1966). The Djameechoonatra was a 'Western tekke' built of nine sides and orientated towards Gurdjieff's grave. The voices of both J. G. Bennett and Shivapuri Baba featured on Robert Fripp's 1979 album *Exposure* (EG Records, EG101).

running the drug rehabilitation programme Narcannon while the Betty Ford Clinic catered for Sunset Boulevard's most high-profile collapsed stars.

John McLaughlin abandoned his Mahavishnu Orchestra[3] – the album *The Inner Mounting Flame* was a Nightly-band favourite of the period – but continued his devotion to Sri Chinmoy along with other followers Carlos 'Devadip' Santana, Larry Coryell and Wardour Street organmeister Brian Auger. If Chinmoy was the 'jazz-rock guru' then there was also a Rolls-Royce guru in the shape of tantric master Bhagwan Shree Rajneesh, who was said to have acquired more than 100 Rolls-Royce saloons in his quest for knowledge.

It seemed that every survivor suddenly had their own personal holy man, leading to a veritable glut of gurus, Sufis, swamis and yogis. A cult of personality grew up around such masters of wisdom as Chinmoy follower Frederick Lenz (Zen Master Rama), former cable-TV executive J. Z. Knight (Ramtha, the Enlightened One), Harvard psychologist Richard Alpert (Baba Ram Dass) and American 'televangelists' Jimmy Swaggart and Jim and Tammy Faye Bakker.

Cat Stevens retired from music and took up the Muslim faith, becoming Yusuf Islam (this conversion taking place after he was overcome by a wave while swimming off the shores of Malibu), while George Harrison continued to fund Krishna Consciousness with his support for the Radha Krishna Temple and (much later) its 'political wing', the Natural Law Party. All a very long way from Methodism.

For the old establishment, shaken by the almost-revolution of the 1960s and impatient to reclaim their mind territory, it seemed only a short stroll from the Community to the Cult – Maharishi to Manson to Koresh. But Rishikesh to Waco had been a 30-year trek. Manson and Altamont were the seventh seal of the '60s. As

3 Mahavishnu is an aspect of Vishnu meaning 'Great Creation'.

the '70s dawned, so the mood and the methods changed and, for some, a pill or a rope seemed the only way out. R. D. Laing[4] and his *Politics of Experience* – 'no one can begin to think, feel or act now except from the starting-point of his or her own alienation' – from almost two decades earlier seemed more prescient than ever.

When David 'Lord' Sutch, the loony in leopardskin beaming out from every By-Election Special, hanged himself in his garage in South Harrow on 16 June 1999, another link with the pre-Beatle world was severed. The hapless Sutch contributed nothing whatsoever to the fraying string ends of rock but his Monster Raving Loony Party surely embodied the true spirit of both England and the '60s; the obstinate, absurdist, irascible and whimsical outlook of the characters who inhabit the worlds of Wonderland, Woodhouse and Monty Python. The knowledge that anyone with a £500 deposit to lose could found their very own political party spawned thousands of other one-man start-ups, decried in the press but often fighting for worthy, mainly localised causes. Political satire still came cheap.

Suddenly there were loonies everywhere, courtesy of MRLP rivals the Rainbow Alliance. Green loonies, eco-loonies and Euro-loonies provided easy final-item fodder for TV news editors, with loonydom reaching its PR peak when Prime Minister Margaret Thatcher, waiting for the returning officer at the Finchley count on the night of the 1987 general election was filmed deep in conversation with a man with a bucket on his head – the venerable Lord Buckethead, of the Gremloids Party[5].

---

[4] Laing recorded an album, *Life After Death* (Charisma CAS 1141), 1978, for the famous Charisma label, the record company of both Genesis and the Nice, under the direction of pop Svengalis Ken Howard and Alan Blaikley, songwriters for the Herd and the Tremeloes. Michael Tippett's 1970 opera *The Knot Garden* was inspired by Laing's book of poetry *Knots* (Tavistock) 1969. Celandine Films produced a mime-based film (1975) with Edward Petherbridge.

[5] Other notable *loonies* were Tarquin Biscuit-Barrel (Cambridge Raving Looney) and Johan Sebastian La-Di-Da Bark (Knighthoods Free With Corn Flakes) Party.

But now, in the new, New Age, another species of guru sprung up, one which illustrated how far things had regressed in the opposite direction, away from the counter-culture and agit-pop revolt, the good, 'good old days' of yore. The early '80s saw the birth of the financial guru. Mark McCormack's *Things They Don't Teach You at Harvard Business School* (Bantam Dell, 1984), was a compendium of negotiation tips by the 'street smart' sports promoter and founder of International Management Group (IMG). Others followed, with lifestyle gurus, diet gurus, fitness gurus, dating gurus and, for the first time since Einstein, a popular scientific guru when cosmologist and self-anointed genius Dr Stephen Hawking published *A Brief History of Time* (Bantam, 1988), achieving a worldwide sale of 9 million copies for the apparently unreadable tome. Hawking appeared on TV chat shows and performed his own 'gigs' at the Royal Albert Hall, even turning up on Pink Floyd's *The Division Bell* [6] as *ABHOT* famously became known as the book that 'everyone bought but no one actually read'.

John Nightly read it. *A Brief History of Time* was a critical text, one of the few to trouble his addled brain cells during his first ten years – the '80s Me Decade – at Trewin, interrupting the constant flow of manuals and free sheets. It was impossible for a kid like Mawgan Hall, enlightened son of enlightened parentage, to understand how society at large had shifted from the cliff-edge of universality far inland to the safety of the old material world. The Kid could find little mystique in his own present day, only the hard wall of science. The prevailing strand being 'science law', the factual high watermark against which all things that cannot be explained and therefore do not exist must be measured. 'If you can't see it, it's not there' was the establishment diktat of Thatcher, Reagan, Major, Clinton, Putin, Blair, Bush and Brown, imagination not being one of the prevailing assets of our political masters. As John Nightly once commented to his young companion, 'You can't see music; sometimes you can't physically hear it, Mawgan... but it's always there, isn't it? If you're there.'

---

[6] Hawking's synthesized voice promoting the benefits of 'talking' on the Cambridge band's 1994 album (EMI TCEMD1055) which reduced Dave Gilmour to tears when he first heard it, was sampled from a British Telecom TV commercial.

Trewin Farm, Porthcreek, Carn Point, Cornwall. Sunday, 10 September 2006.
'Russ Conway's died.'

Endy was lost in her *Daily Mail.* John looked up from the *West Briton.*

'… didn't know he was still alive.'

'It says he was living in Eastbourne… *"suffered from alcoholism and had gone bankrupt".* They all do that, don't they?'

'… what?'

'Go bankrupt *and* "suffer from alcoholism".' Endy could barely read the fine newsprint even with her new glasses. 'Oh… I am sorry…' The housekeeper managed a look of embarrassment for all of two seconds. 'Lovely pianist, he was.' She held the newspaper away from her eyes so it caught the light from the open window, allowing her to admire the photograph of Russ in his heyday at the BBC Steinway. John lifted his head from the bric-a-brac ads and removed his glasses in preparation for further detail.

'Only record we had at home,' Endy continued. *"My Concerto for You."* Lovely, that was…'

John cleared his throat.

'It says he used to go hunting elephants in Africa to get ivory for his piano keys.' The housekeeper picked up her teacup and turned to the boss for a response. John got up from his chair.

'…well, I don't suppose he could do it in Eastbourne…'

item: Monthly Cultural Notes: October

There is still work to do in the garden even though the heat has gone. Move geraniums, fuchsias, camellias and cinerarias onto the patio or into sheltered corners. Clip and deadhead all shrubs, removing any yellowing or diseased leaves. Bring in azaleas and begonias for winter bloom. Tender specimens may need protection outside with newspaper or straw. Complete all trimming of evergreen hedges. Wait for frosts to hit dahlias, cannas and other tubers before lifting. Use stored or recycled rainwater wherever possible. Wrap aeoniums and phormiums in acrylic sheets for overall protection.

The Continental Hyatt House Hotel, 8401 Sunset Boulevard, West Hollywood, Los Angeles, Room 313, 10th Floor, 11 May 1972.

'That's correct, sir, patient is out on the floor.

[pause]

I have done that, sir, and we are awaiting paramedics.

[pause]

I don't believe there has been drug use. But I'm informed by persons in the room that there is history.

[longer pause]

Yes, I will.

[longer pause]

No, not that one, sir – the big concert tomorrow night.

[pause]

I will wait for them, yes. Thank you.'

The thing was a mess. How can it be told simply? Without giving entirely the wrong impression about the level of unhindered panic, unremitting fear and sheer, lashing terror that had come upon John Nightly with such a mighty blow – crash, bang, wallop – right in the centre of his skull that, well… [pause] Let's try…

The singer and his associates were at the Continental Hyatt House. Fourteen rooms – half of the tenth floor – taken up by band and entourage. More or less a small travelling village, in the manner of a medieval hamlet, with all the skills and services on board to serve, nourish and sustain its people. Two long, five-star-studded corridors, six security guards, seven housekeepers and a goods lift separated the group from the regular residents and other bands – the Who, Barclay James Harvest, the Mothers of Invention, Colosseum and the touring cast of *Godspell* – were also staying at the Hyatt, the famed 'Riot House', that weekend.

Travelling with the community, but in much less expensive accommodation, were their colleagues and workmates. Seventy other *Mink Bungalow* regulars: orchestra, chorus, sound and lighting crews, dancers, girlfriends, groupies, roadies, humpers, record-promotion men and retail reps along with another 50 or so technical people, *tekkies*, most of them specialist construction engineers more used to working on North Sea oil platforms. The company even included a team of quantity surveyors from the East Anglian Water Board.

The tekkies were waiting to begin placement and assembly of a unique wave-based energy triangle out in the bay, some twelve miles south-west of Malibu Beach, set at a precise 32-degree angle facing in towards Westward Beach. The location scouted and decided upon twelve months earlier, on the occasion of the Nightly band's previous visit during the second leg of the tour to promote *Ape Box Metal*. At that point, a team led by Jean-Claude Marx had taken a 'copter high above Malibu, specifically the area around Point Dume; a location renowned for its powerful waves as well as for being something of a container, or soup crater, of energy.

Accompanied by local engineers and a federal-government advisor they surveyed the area from Zuma right up to Surfrider Beach, alongside the pier. The pinpoint location determined that afternoon, 17 August 1971, when an application for a temporary hub as an experiment in more environmentally friendly sources of power than oil and gas was received by the office of the Governor of California.

The Zuma hub was to involve more or less the same construction, with slight modification, as used just a few weeks before in Akiro Bay, Japan; buried deep within the microcosmic paradise of the Fujiyama reef, for the historic Kyoto eco-concert. The get-go for Zuma being received by JCE in London at the end of October that year at which point construction began on the heavy engineering of the triangle itself in the Wallsend shipyards of G. & W. Woodbye & Sons that mid-December.

So, here they were. The team from the Water Board, all chips and beer, ready and waiting to supervise a gang of local good ol' boys in the erecting and positioning of the resultant sea-powered generator into two homemade (in Sheffield) mounts. The exercise involving close co-operation between the British team and several local marine-crane operators. A further group, AFL-unionised metal-workers, pipe-layers and arc-welders, waited alongside for the go-ahead from the harbourmaster to install this basic construction, originally designed by John Nightly himself using Meccano parts, a red and yellow maquette having been presented to Jean-Claude to replicate into the real thing.

A simple concept then. Two angle-iron girders coming together in an arrow formation – an isosceles triangle – to first capture and then harness the immense force of waves crashing into the Southern Californian coastline. This raw power to be channelled into a 'gate' of energy convertors, already positioned and buried under the sea bed, which would transform the waves into mass, and the mass into energy – electricity – which would, in turn, run the concert, the music.

So… you're on the West Coast of America, you're touring your masterpiece and 'life's work', which also happens to be your new album, just released in the territory with more than half a million advance orders. You're at the pinnacle of your career, which, up until now, has never been at any point other than a pinnacle. The pinnacles just keep getting higher. Steeper. Making it easier for you to lose your balance and fall. But that hasn't happened and so, on the face of it, everything is, or really should be, must be, very much *okay*. Even close to 'mazin'. As one of the many assembled that day might've put it.

The current state of John Nightly must surely have been, from the outside at least, almost off the scale, nearing paradise-level. Even the little things were good; the singer approaching Messiah status within his own rapidly expanding universe. John Nightly was in a good place surrounded by well-meaning people, with an endless supply of anything he required or fancied either already on the table in front of him or waiting to come in and visit him to do his bidding and perform – like performing seals – if he so desired. LA's most-desired groupies were gathered in the downstairs lounge, with another, younger, apprentice party outside, attempting to gain entry into the hotel itself. John

Nightly was with friends and carers, including his own very loyal and respectful band. Jonathan, Justin, Ron and Ashley had been nourished by the boss's patronage day and night coming up for five years. Accumulative nourishing, fed and watered by an almighty hand. The material rewards of that long-term engagement apparent in their threads and car keys, the wallets in their tour bags and the women on their arms. There was the boss's own personal support crew: hairdressers, wardrobe, make-up, chefs, tailors, candlemakers. All here for John Nightly. Doing their thing, so that he could do his. Doing their best for him. Loving him and what he did. Been around each other a long time now. So in terms of a family situation, easy-going in every respect, it couldn't get much more relaxed or comfortable than this. Not for a rock'n'roll tour.

That's how it looks from here, then, from the outside. Hanging out in the premium and deluxe suites and ante-rooms along each velvet-lined corridor. Eating papaya, coconut, mango and other fruits that don't make it as far as Huntingdon or Macclesfield in the Hyatt's Venetian-themed restaurant while swigging exotic brandies and bourbons in the hotel's well-stocked bars. Visited by a constant stream of 'laydees', willing victims who would not usually consort with an HGV driver from Birkenhead who failed his Eleven-plus and is penniless in the real world, or give a second look to an itinerant layabout from Hull who, had he not displayed a precocious skill for humping 4 x 12 speaker cabinets up and down narrow stairwells without a word of complaint, would most likely by now be working on Britain's roads, if he weren't safely locked up for the good of the general public by now. The *MBR* touring party consisted of a vast crew partying on, pleasuring themselves at the expense of their host and his patrons.

But from the inside… *Room 313*, the master bedroom of the Hyatt's Presidential Suite, with its Chippendales and Chesterfields and its fake-Regency bureaux, gilt-embossed stationery and utter, utter emptiness, things aren't quite that way. Certainly not since John Nightly and his representatives happened to catch a ten-minute item on NBC concerning today's particular difficulty.

To sum up, after long consultations with Los Angeles Port Authority (LAPA) officials and local councillors, the American Federation of Labor and Congress of Industrial Organizations (AFL-CIO) – the Musicians' Union of the bridge-building world – have decided that their members will now not be able to work alongside the team from the Water Board. This unfounded and unexpected decision is sudden and final. A surprise, since an agreement was signed some six months ago, confirming the arrangements as they stand today.

It can only be concluded that something has changed on the inside track. There has been an intervention. Someone has stepped in, someone of power has had a word and there's no changing that word, that decision. The news from the Nightly legal representatives – as ever, doing their best under 'very difficult legal conditions' – is both depressing and unhelpful.

So... here it is in conclusion. The real, real deal. How things lie, if you are inhabiting (or would indeed for some reason wish to be doing so) the human form of a being personally and professionally known as John Nightly.

1: There is a warrant out for your arrest. 2: Your future father-in-law has accused you of 'murdering' his daughter. 3: You've just heard yourself described as 'drug-addled' and 'subversive' on the 9pm News. 4: You have 140 tonnes of iron parked closeby, a very heavy metal triangle that will now not be lowered into its mounts so that the ocean power your career depends on can be harnessed. 5: Some 160,000 people have bought tickets for an event that will now have no electricity with which to power it. 6: There are less than 24 hours to go to the concert. 7: No way can the concert go ahead and at the present moment you're not feeling 100 per cent.

What to do? Some would turn on the television and simply forget all about it. Some just wouldn't worry anyway. They'd claim it was nothing to do with them – 'speak to the manager', they'd say, and then go out and party even harder. But John

Nightly wasn't drinking at the moment. He wasn't in the mood for partying. He no longer had a manager.

John Nightly didn't do any of the above. He took on the responsibility. He worried. That's why he was laying face down on the carpet with three LA County police, the county sheriff, the hotel doctor, two porters, his road manager, his guitarist, his new girlfriend, his old girlfriend and the conductor of his orchestra all sitting right there with him, loving him, vibing him, willing him, being there for him, holding his head, hands, arms, legs, feet... holding their breath. John Nightly did not look particularly well. He looked like he could do with a night in.

As far as anyone knew, it appeared that John may have suffered some kind of collapse, or seizure, while alone in his room. Not because of drugs: he had laid off those in the past few months; been quite 'clean' generally, since Pondy went AWOL. John's alcohol intake was also non-existent. The boy's current state must have been due to stress – panic, grief, despair. John had it running through his blood at the moment, what with Pond, Myra, Donna all gone. The deepest, baddest grief. The kind of distress a person might find it hard to recover from.

The internal telephone rang. A call from the Hollywood Roosevelt. Lady Jane, one of the Valley's most desired, and her friend Irish Becky, wanted to come over. Justin took the receiver. He explained that right now, just right at this very minute, was not a great time, but that they should... yeah... call again tomorrow, or later tonight maybe, when things might be... back to normal a little – if they happened to still be in the vicinity.

A knock on the door. Room service arrived and was turned away. Another knock. The housekeeper came in with John's suits, ironed, pressed and wrapped in the requested white tissue, box-fresh for tomorrow's performance. If only the star himself had been. A chambermaid arrived to turn down the bed. It had the makings of a Marx Brothers set-up in Room 313.

All these events occurred. But the subject of the events, the reason they could occur in the first place, the reason Justin, Ashley, Ron and Jonathan were all here tonight and not at home in their cul-de-sacs watching television, still lay face-down on the floor.

The subject wasn't dead, he wasn't unconscious, he wasn't comatose… yet. As far as anyone could see, the subject was just… petrified. Literally petrified. Not stoned, but stone. Nightly was frozen solid. That's what happens when a person has been crying and screaming, open-mouthed at the limit of their voice, into their phlegm-covered hands. Into the mattress, into the pillow, the curtains, sofas, daybeds and other upholstery, trying to dull the sound for normal folks, screaming into their blue-eyed little-boy soul… Bellowing into themselves, their whole being, their whole bag.

There he lay, the Grantchester boy. His stick-thin body contorted and locked in a kind of slow-mo spasm, right there on the Hyatt pile, resplendent with its large HH insignia. His eyes manically fixed on one small dot, an important, crucial dot, though a mere speck, up there on the ceiling. Just like he'd been told to. 'Focus on something physical.' Because you have to fix on *something*. And right now, this small piece of detritus – fly shit, something that had gotten flicked up there, just a trick of the light; maybe there was nothing really there at all – right now, this small fleck of imagination – midget crap, or a urine stain from the room above – became the single most important item in John Nightly's life. It was his whole world. The dot that isn't there at all is a dot that may one day save you.

After various comings and goings, and umm-ings and ahh-ings, stuff coming into the room and going out, cod-philosophical comments from the band and natural-born sympathy from the girls, John Nightly began to tremble; slowly at first, then uncontrollably, like chattering teeth in the coldest fenland winter, but it wasn't just his teeth. The boy's whole body was doing the Shake, just like Iona and Monika had done down at the Marquee. *Do The Convulsion!* That's it! Shaking, twisting, jerking, Mashed Potatoeing, blabbering on. Just like them.

1-2-3-4-5-6-7
1-2-3-4-5-6-7
1-2-3-4
1-2-3-4
1-2-3-4-5-6-7

'What the hell's he doing, Just?' Justin wasn't feeling too well himself anymore.

'He's counting, Ash…'

And that's how Justin found him. Shaking and sobbing, like an infant child, the old lady on Newlyn beach in a Walter Langley watercolour, her husband, the centre of the world as she had always understood it, lost to the waves. An abandoned relic of a person left clutching a rag handkerchief, staring into an unfocused, empty abyss. Langley was able to capture it. The panel of grief depicted in the fisherwoman's face was the same unquantifiable pain John Nightly was experiencing right now.

Justin checked his stopwatch – another seven seconds. Multiply by 16, add 49, divide by 60 and you get a waveform time per minute. Over a two-hour duration that will change of course. There'll be fluctuations. Need to add another three seconds every nine minutes, then a further four, so seven in all at the end of each 90-minute period.

But even using this simple, stabilising equation an allowance still needs to be made for natural Greenwich shifts and also of course, leap seconds. It was how both the old John Pond and the new John Nightly arrived at their conclusions about time inconsistencies in the turn of the earth. In terms of the calculation of waves and tides, for the astronomers of the old world the solution was to add one extra day every 218 years. In the final reckoning for John Nightly, a fixable resolution would be at least another lifetime away.

Trewin House, Porthcreek, Carn Point, Cornwall. Monday, 2 November 2006.

Robert had spent the afternoon mixing millet and oatmeal with packets of Bill Oddie's Really Wild Bird Food.

'Come to a bad state when they have to get Bill bloody Oddie to sell us bird food.' The disgruntled nurseryman poured Bill-sanctioned seeds into gourd pods ready to be hung on wires across the back lawn.

'I like him on them bird programmes, though.' Endy was a long-established fan.

There was an enormous amount of bird noise today. Sparrows and gulls and other commoners could be heard from right across the compound, the disturbance carried along by a strong westerly breeze which howled through the outhouses and slip paths, sweeping through the long canna stalks, bruising a new crop of roses and making it difficult to stay the huge barn doors, therefore taking Robert Kemp much more time to load up trucks and vans with the week's cuttings.

'Bloody wind last night. Never known it so bad. Not at this time o'year, anyway. Funny how it's all calm now.'

RCN piled more sugar into his mug while Robert continued filling the pods, packing them tightly into an old potato box; seed grenades ready to be dispatched to the frontline.

'I'll need to get there in a minute, Endy… need to fill up this can,' Kemp shouted from the back steps. Mawgan was beginning to feel restless. 'I'll go and do a bit of work, I think. See if all the tapes and stuff are numbered properly. Check through my notes…'

It was just about time for Mawg's evening smoke. The kid looked inside his tumbler at the residue of his Cappu-grain, gave Alexandre a cursory pat and shuffled back to the music room.

Robert's next mission was to deal with pests. He dropped a large canister into the sink and squirted in Fairy Liquid.

'There you are, Endy… the best deterrent for greenfly in the world. *Detergent that really deters!*'

Pleased with himself, Robert lifted the can out of the bowl and attached it to his knapsack sprayer. A solution of Fairy Liquid and tap water, roughly one part Fairy to ten parts tap, is just about the most effective way to relieve your roses of fly. Using a sprayer loaded with nothing more deadly than this household staple it is possible to rid your buds of crippling aphids almost as soon as you notice them. RCN wandered out onto the patio with canes and string to tie up some of the taller wind-damaged plants.

'Ex-ter-min-ate! Ex-ter-min-ate!' shouted the nurseryman as he followed RCN into the garden.

Endy raised her eyes to the heavens, pleased to have headed off both Robert and RCN and to have the kitchen to herself again.

'He's a funny one… that Robert,' she murmured to Alexandre as she wiped over already spotless surfaces yet again and looked around for the next task to occupy her time.

'To achieve great things, two things are needed: a plan, and not quite enough time.'

Leonard Bernstein

'Men are born with various manias.'

Robert Louis Stevenson (1850–1894)

item: Monthly Cultural Notes: November.

If ants have been nesting in your lawn, then November is the time to re-turf or re-sow. The time for seed collecting and slip-taking. Consult your catalogues and order for next year's display. Plant needle evergreens and ovate-leaved shrubs for ground cover. Prune and fertilise bungalow roses and honeysuckle. Cut down Evening Primrose and Japanese spiraea but not *Spiraea prunifolia* (bridal wreath) which will remove its early spring buds. Clean and disinfect greenhouses and sunhouses. Remember to feed the birds and top up their baths.

I'm doing well with my orchids.
Never tried them before. They like
shade, and regular temperature.
The nurses picked out purple
and white from the ones you
sent, as they were delivered one
one day when I was really
busy with things— Got them next
to my window. Thanks for the
letter about Jane. It was nice
of J. to let you know.
I should send something, but
have been really busy lately.
I hope J is really well.
Have to get on now. John.

BBC News 24. Tuesday, 11 August 1998. Published 08:16 GMT 09:16 UK, 'Total eclipse will bring chaos to Cornwall'. Reporter, Clinton Rodgers.

Planners in rural Cornwall expect chaos when eclipse-hunters descend on the county next year. Traffic gridlock, food and water shortages, sanitation problems, lack of accommodation and additional stress on the emergency services are anticipated when 1.5 million people arrive to see the first total solar eclipse over Britain for 72 years. Co-ordinator Brigadier Gage-Williams (Eclipse Planning) told civic leaders he was confident that problems would be overcome: 'We're advising people to book early, come early, stay long and leave late to avoid problems.' Brigadier Gage-Williams said an application had been made for army help but he was confident 'it's all under control'.

The last time there was a total eclipse over part of Britain was in June 1927. It passed over the north of the country, where 3 million people watched; an audience that triggered the largest-ever recorded movement by train in England. This time only Cornwall and parts of Devon will be able to experience it, on 11 August 1998. Six times the usual number of people who visit the region during the height of the summer season are expected. Ron Morrison-Smith of the West Country Tourist Board is confident but admits there will be problems: 'There is a major problem for the emergency services and traffic management – and also for toilets and water and fresh food. When services for 1.5 million extra people and the 500,000 extra cars that will carry them are sorted out, there is still the problem of accommodation. It is a major, major problem.

The two Johns shuffled along Robert's new shingle path, now diverted through the summer cacti garden, where agave and moon-clover had colonised the rockery on both sides. A bonfire had been prepared at the top field where orchid lavender and echeveria had cleverly turned from lilac to tussock-purple in an attempt to shield themselves from the harsh midsummer sun.

At one time both the sun and the moon would've waited for John Nightly. Not any longer. For once in their lives the two rhythm guitarists were in a hurry. They shunted up the steep gradient of the path, not without a little huffing and puffing, until they reached a clearing beyond the grass. The boss walked on ahead, stopping at the canna sheds to check on overnight growth, while RCN brought the car round. The Jag turned on a sixpence, picked up its owner, and Daly and Nightly drove off across the freshly-turned fields.

10.16am. As they climbed the slopes away from the ocean, overnight fog began to clear and they caught their first sight of people, with their attendant camper vans, motorbikes and scooters – the preferred carriages of hippies, travellers, downsizers and eclipse-watchers. This ragged, dew-soaked congregation lined the coastal shelf as far as Zennor Quoit.

In the opposite direction, looking out across Doom Point, there was nothing at all. Just what they were looking for. So RCN reversed up and started back the other way, the Jag driving another mile or so before the Johns found what they thought might be a suitable spot, parked up and got out.

A family of crusties, weighed down with telescopes and camera bags, all weak smiles and good-for-nothing vibes, came towards them. Both Johns acknowledged them with stony faces as a drift of smoke, indicating more campers, came up from a ledge below. The weather was still misty, with a fine, almost horizontal drizzle as they ploughed on towards Black Cliff.

10.46am. With exactly one hour to go, thick cloud appeared on the horizon, descending like a stage curtain ready to clothe a command performance. The wind picked up. Darkness crept along the headland from the direction of Redruth. The flanks of visitors and their car radios fell silent as they huddled in groups, cowering in heavy coats and anoraks in the very middle of summer, their tents and shelters like inflated mushrooms strewn across the rocks. The wind dropped and suddenly all was black. Torches and Jiffi lighters illuminated the granite. The encircling bay and the sea chamber were suddenly transformed into a vast auditorium, stadium rock, or John Wesley's crater, as the congregation waited for something – anything – to happen. Hopefully some kind of whirling black mass; celestial music, the creak of the mill-wheel, maybe even the long, measured, West Country vowels of the Miller himself.

As in any situation where one or two are gathered together, assembled worshippers waited not for what was about to be delivered but for what they hoped to see in it and what they expected to get out of it. The impressionable among them would experience not the reality – the sun and moon in odd conjunction, very temporary unseasonal weather, fellow travellers like themselves coming together to worship – but some kind of *Messiah* or *Magus* event. A mindbender, holy-star power – *message* – if there was one. Some sense to be knocked into them out of all this chaos.

A couple of quick flashes from an automatic camera then suddenly thousands. Like ground fire from *ack-ack* positions. The Johns pressed their binoculars hard into their foreheads. Having no more dreams left in them, they concentrated not on what might develop but on what was now taking place behind the façade; the curtain of dense cloud that obscured almost all of the view out to sea. More flashes, and more massed cheering from the bedraggled assembly framed as silhouettes against the disappearing black-water.

Then 'it' happened. The sun and the moon seemed to appear from nowhere, converge directly upon the mass, become one, reach a point of absolute conjunction, two pendulum worlds, as perfect a fit as hand and glove, ring and finger. A magnetic pull away from everyday worry and oppression. Gulls called to each other and flew from the cliffs. Kittiwakes scattered, scared out of their birdbrains by instant and total darkness. The two gods of sun and moon, most ancient super-powers, passed over, did their thing and separated. Visitation and divine alignment. A Cornish rhapsody. Two become one, and a message no doubt for all present.

Then, just as suddenly as it had begun, the thing was over. The freaks hit their car horns and cheered, applauding the two great gods as the Johns removed their binoculars and rubbed their indented skulls. They yawned as if it were a habit, looked out across the bay, the leaden sky, the starless, mid-morning twilight. They glanced at one another and chuckled.

'Lot of fuss over nothing,' said RCN. Further along the headland, backpackers were lined up along the old tinners' path, consulting maps and seeking wastepaper bins for illegal cans and bottles. Up ahead, farmhouses already had their lights on while behind them, along the dual carriageway, flickering torches and beams from mobile phones pointed the way home. Above the ocean's roar and the sea-polished rocks the cloud curtains opened, the sky becoming tinged with yellow, a slab of double-black as black as the Dandelion's homemade carob cake streaked with precious philosophical student gold. 'Said on the radio Hawkwind were supposed to play…'*

Suddenly daylight. Things moved quickly on. There was music. A rave beat leaked from somewhere over near the Zawn. Booming out from a proper rig. The Johns gathered themselves together and began walking back to the car.

'… well… we made the effort…'

'Not a lot to see though… and bloody cold… for the time o' year.'

'… let's get back.'

* Hawkwind played at St Michael's Mount in 1971.

item: John Nightly: *Melody Maker* interview, 13 March 1971 by Chris Bell.
I like the whole idea of randomness. Tristan Tzara used to pull words out of a hat and make up a poem. It's no big deal in terms of how I think about words or anything, but it leaves me free with the words. Otherwise, writing songs is just one big… crossword. [takes a match and lights another cigarette, takes a first drag and continues]

I'd be trying to fit words that don't go into musical spaces because they don't want to. [snaps the match in half] Trying to balance the weight – the beat… of the syllables – the weight of the music, and the beat and the meaning of each note of the tune.

[journalist nods sympathetically and continues doodling]

Even if I could achieve… the technical feat… I still need things to… make sense as well… [flicks ash into his saucer] Whatever that means, so,.. by writing down some kind of 'sense' to start with… cutting up and… that will free me up… make the writing freer… and that's how you get… words. *Ape Box Metal* or *Mink Bungalow*… [Thinks for a second] I don't just make them up because they sound nice. [sniffs and clears his throat]. It's kind of… there has to be…

Did the title *Principal Fixed Stars* come about in that way?

That's from a paper… research paper… by an old astronomer – John Pond. It's the first ever star atlas… from around the… mid-1500s… *Delle stelle fisse.* Written by Alessandro Piccolomini.

[journalist looks suitably impressed]

And *Mink Bungalow?*

It came from the house I stayed in with my… then girlfriend… when we first went to Los Angeles. The realtor – estate agent – billed it as a *Spanish villa*… but my girlfriend said it's like a bungalow – old people's bungalow. And the lady we rented it from was a Mrs Mink, originally Minski… she was related to the Protopopovs – the ice dancers. [stubs out his cigarette. Yawns and apologises for his tiredness]

Every time I think about the place… the record we played – listened to all the time we were there – was 'Jesus Was a Cross Maker'. [whistles the tune; interviewer nods again]

Phoebe loved that song. I can't think about the house without hearing it. And Billy Fury, hah! Thats what I was playing, 'Halfway to Paradise' – like me! and *Parsifal,* unbelievable bit, the 'transformation' bit. The chords. Amazing chords – and tune. Shouldn't tell you that… [the boy smiles sweetly as he fiddles with the piece of string wound around his wrist] *Ape Box Metal* came from the chimpanzee they sent into space. That was an easy one.

And *Quiz Axe Queen?*

From the experiments with telegraphs Charles Wheatstone did. But it doesn't matter about the source. I like all these titles anyway – as titles. Because it all connects... doesn't sound like a cut-up. You've got this nice balance of 'three'... naturally... in a natural way. Inherent in it, which I... I love the sound of and... that's why I always use it.

From around the time of the third US tour, mid-July 1971 onwards, the Nightly live set tended to be configured in two halves, the first being a slow burner. Ashley would begin with a short prologue, one chord held down on the Mellotron with his left hand while he played the 'Lux Eterna' theme on an electric harpsichord with his right. Then a waltz treatment of 'Lavender Girl', a specialty that went down particularly well with stoned audiences.

The atmosphere was somewhere between evangelist convention, mime theatre with a budget and rock'n'roll funfair. Everyone – performers and audience – would be settling down, sunset would come and night would begin to fall. Without any announcement, dressed head to toe in white, and in complete darkness save for a solitary guiding torch, a silent, slight figure, a magicien – *the* Magicien – would emerge from the shadows.

With his guitar set unfashionably high – the way Merseybeat groups held their instruments – the only Mahavishnu it could've been was John Nightly, if not John McLaughlin, who also cut a dash onstage and off in white cotton slacks and polo-neck, Royal Navy haircut and twin-necked cherry-red SG.

In his soft white suit, loosely tied cravat and felt bolero – one of three or four per night to be sacrificed to the crowd – John would've been watching the build-up from behind the PA. Getting in the mood, swaying in time to the music before stepping out. As candle-lighters tiptoed around the stage, making sure to avoid the perilous tangle of cables and wires, and dancers put their arms around each other to give good-luck hugs, there would be a gradual realisation among those gathered that the 'presence' they'd come to pay homage to was now... among them.

As Ashley continued to improvise, forcing Stravinsky on Irving Berlin, zigging and zagging in and out of *The Planets*, weaving in and out of Debussy, a dash of Pretty Things here and Russ Conway there, the twinkling, skywide star-curtain would appear from smoke-filled scaffold. As it descended, the lighting of candles would gradually replace the late-evening sun as the auditorium was transformed into a revolving celestial sphere, backlit to reveal the performers, each bathed in their own radiant glow, while the band took up their positions and dancers trespassed upon the edges of the stage. As if Tycho Brahe had been the set designer for *Jailhouse Rock*.

After a few minutes or so the preamble would grind to a halt, the circular section of the platform would stop revolving and – **BANG!** – the assembled community would launch into 'The Miller'…

Meet me at the Corn Exchange…
And bring me eggs that are free-range
Please don't think me very strange
If I prefer a toasted cake or sop… o… nge…

… followed by tracks from the first two albums, those the star himself could still bear to perform. Although, truth be told, as soon as John Nightly had a song recorded he instantly lost all interest in performing it or even hearing it again. Listening to his own recordings made their creator feel physically sick. The only enjoyment John Nightly had ever gotten from his own music was in the actual creation of it. The spark that begat it; and the reaction to that spark. There might be some kind of secondary pleasure in the sales accounting of each record and the accumulation of income, an absolute indication of the level of acceptance from the audience in response to what its originator had given, but the real buzz occurred in solitude. Nowadays, the creation of music was the only activity that could lift the Magicien from his despairing aloneness – or, as he now often referred to it, again after Laing, his 'perpetual solitude'.

'Free School Lane', because of its easy, repetitive groove, closed the first set, bringing the audience to climax even though the festivities were barely halfway through. At the end of that 40 minutes, the heavenly backdrop depicting the fixed stars of the sidereal zodiac opened from the centre to reveal, like a megalomaniac conjuror's act, more than 100 string players, their violins, violas, cellos and double-basses bowing as one for the intro to 'Lavender Girl'. This effect having been conceived as being 'too much' for the audience, who would lift up their arms, cheer and chant, reach out and generally go apeshit crazy at the sight of such a spectacle, making the anticipation for the remainder of the evening almost unbearable.

Thirty minutes or so later, intoxicated by the balm of various fragrances, the incense wafting in from the wings, the lavender and sandalwood phials smashed on the stage, cheap joss sticks in the crowd, the musky aroma of scented candles planted in the undergrowth, and at least one complete bottle of Southern Comfort, John Nightly would step up to the microphone.

'I...' he would say, 'am a traveller...'

'I... am a lost child...' The audience would respond – as one – before the band attempted to reproduce whatever they could manage from the nascent work in progress, the still-untitled *(Black) Requiem.*

Another 40 or so dancers, choreographed by Donna, climbed to the edge of the upper deck as the lighting designers used stage beams to silhouette the chorus against the starry backcloth.

This overblown conceit was the reality of live performance of the era. The greatest show on earth. Something of a circus, but a state circus at least. Had they believed it possible to include dancing horses, elephants and hot-air balloons, the Nightly production would've. Whether in a small club, a ballroom, Student Union hall or polytechnic canteen, a makeshift festival stage or a huge arena like this one, Ashley, Justin, Jonathan, Ron and the others delivered a genuine one-off excitement, a level of live performance the audience did not expect to be bettered by any other act of the time. No other band or group being able to afford or be stupid enough to try to stage it. The stops were well and truly pulled out. It was a performance more akin to

Diaghilev or Billy Smart than rock'n'roll. That was what was good about it.

At the end of the night there would be 'encores', as many as the audience could get out of the assembled crew – John Nightly having taken to not performing any of his own songs at all as 'requests', but instead an alternative 'bouquet of love songs'. Usually in the form of a cabaret-club medley consisting of 'I Know Where I'm Going' by Roger Quilter, snippets of the Yardbirds' 'For Your Love' or the Fourmost's 'Hello Little Girl', with a nod to Mahavishnu's 'Meeting of the Spirits' topped off with a crowd-pleasing singalong of Sutch's 'My Big Black Coffin'.*

Security Notice: *Because of the use of lighted candles in the performance, the stadium manager requests that the audience refrain from smoking, lighting fires or using paraffin cigarette-lighters, incense or joss sticks in the main auditorium and the surrounding area.*

* From time to time John Nightly encores of the period also included Phil Och's 'There But for Fortune', Astaire's 'Top Hat', with the full complement of cane-tap gunshots courtesy of Miss Vost and the RKO film projected onto the group's backdrop, along with a rather too heavy-handed reading of Badfinger's 'No Matter What'.

Being back in LA was like being in space – though if anything more isolated. In the outer cosmos there are (as far as we know) no people, while in Los Angeles there are too many faces to first get into, then out of, your mind.

The news was that the Magicien was 'catatonic' – the term used to describe a medical condition which through no fault of its own had acquired a tinge of glamour; if there could be anything at all glamorous about a schizophrenia so debilitating that it can lead to unconsciousness.

In John Nightly's case it was natural to assume burn-out to be a delayed reaction to the industrial amounts of weed, alcohol and various pastel-coloured toxins the boss had seen fit to inflict on his system these past few summers.

Onstage that evening, as the Nightly band faced their audience, John Nightly gazed out and saw not row upon row of adoring good-vibing heads, but flank upon flank of bad-vibing pirate skulls shooting plumes of smoke. Warrior dandelions and thistles the size of telegraph poles like the ones from his father's garden colonised the terrain. He saw ploughed acres in rainbow strips. He felt the heat of the guano, the composited remains of the nightdreams of a deluded generation.

As he zoomed in and out he encountered distorted faces, the fat-bellied jowls of the maddest, most obsessed super-fans. Distended, tip-burned heads, seeming to devour themselves; heads that would never flower. Then out of nowhere, heavy horses came thundering towards the stage, and therefore towards the band, charging from a flickering, fiery mount – a crazed DeMille rhapsody, targeting players and dancers. The chariots eating up the entire stage, devouring the poor innocent English boys and washing over them, drenching them. Obliterating Justin, Ashley, Jon and Ron, boys from small towns promoted well above their social expectation. Clueless about life in general and no doubt thankful to be in the privileged position the gift of music had bestowed upon them. The TV news would report the unfortunates literally wiped off the planet by killer gulfweed, hair-weed, grizzle-weed.

Last week in Madrid was the worst yet. Killer stalks, the same ones that haunted John's father, creatures that would sneak up overnight between cracks in the suburban brick, needing to be weeded out almost daily – need to weed, as they say in gardening mags. Here were those same beady eyes, not bashful, not subservient, but utterly confident, driven, right up there in front, leering like anorak uncles, on the scaffold with the tweeters and woofers and bins, their rusted, corrugated leaves and jaundiced ovaries dangling most unhealthily high above the performers.

In Grantchester, John had been well trained. Pinching the bastards out as soon as he saw one taking root. The child hated touching the furry, flesh-crawly things. Unpleasant to the touch, somehow malevolent, taunting him from inside their padded, upholstered gullets. Consumptive presences. Their faces hidden among a tangle of hard yellow knots. Or were they just fans? Justin asked, as he uncorked another bottle of '69.

The boss stared out front, then looked back to the band. 'Stop watering them, Ash! Stop watering!' he cried, in this suddenly frail and sexless voice – as documented on bootlegs of the concert. In the posted clip – *www.freefall.com/nightlyend/smonica/snatcher71* – as they launch into 'Free School Lane', John doesn't so much sing his heart out as scream it, his voice becoming unrecognisably hoarse, before, thank God, he is coerced away from the mike in a most graceful display by Justin as the band rolls into the newly extended overture to *MBR*.

At first the audience seems excited by the committed performance; whatever is going on is exciting. *Is* passionate, undressed, direct. Uncontrolled. Human. Very un-John Nightly-ish.

But, that night, John Nightly was seeing something neither his colleagues nor the audience could see – an apparition indeed. At the end of the mercifully short clip the crowd emerge from their communal stupor and begin shouting, cheering… jeering. 'C'mon… c'mon… then!' they cry, encouraging the Master to shout harder, scream louder, go further, be more passionate still, make more of a fool, more of a human, of himself.

But, because the singer fails to respond to or even acknowledge this encouragement, neither hearing nor seeing them, failing to engage with the audience at all for the duration of the concert, a wave of puzzlement soon comes over them. The packed stadium of long-term devotees, knowing and possibly under-standing a good deal more about John Nightly than he ever will himself, realise that something is deeply, desperately wrong.

Back in the auditorium, the band had stopped performing. They were still playing, but had stopped giving out. There was the sight of Justin, cast as sentinel stage left, a position he had never previously occupied (it being reserved exclusively for the main attraction, as Pondy dictated). Right-hand man, suddenly up there on equal terms with the Master. Justin's eyes fixed on John. Ron, resplendent in cape and bicorn hat, abandoned his Mellotron and crept across the stage towards Jonathan and Ash. 'Keep playing!!' he shouted, as the drummer struggled to keep things in order by reverting to a completely uncharacteristic backbeat. Tying down the groove, grounding it. Bringing John Nightly's agitated, un-rhythmic rhythms right back to rock'n'roll basics. A flashback drum-wise through the group's progressively experimental journey as seamlessly as he could manage.

A few more minutes, and the delicate, ornate metre of 'Lavender Girl' had been reduced to a slow-burning mechanical tick. The group's leader left clutching the mike, as if, God forbid, electrocution had welded him to it, his faithful Stratocaster hanging limply across his shoulder blades.

The boss stared out to face his audience, while at the same time staring into the sub-natural abyss. John mouthed something. Numbers… a count-in, or count-out maybe. Random numbers, as Ashley yelled to everyone from the other end of the wide platform, held his sticks high in the air, indicating that the band and orchestra take note, before executing a very long, very clichéd drum roll twice around the kit, the staple rejoinder for an assembly of musicians to call it a day, song-wise. This swift, extremely unsignature riff brought the song, and also the careers of all those on stage, to a most unscheduled and uncharacteristically, somewhat-corny end.

But Lee was way ahead of them; and so, during Ashley's solo, and the extended drum wind-up, the Revox had been faded up through the house speakers into the stadium itself. A muffled orchestral segment from *MBR*; the funereal 'Adagio Mortada', seeped out into the ether, washing over the open-mouthed gathering like a chemical purifier or detergent. What had just occurred had been unsettling to watch, if you were in your right mind.

That final night at the Estadio Quinta, John Nightly must have known that these evil Manga weeds were not real. He must have. There was so much opposition in that very worshipful assembly against evil itself. Forty-seven thousand well-wishing, ticket-bearing freaks in communion with their main man. Sending him their best, willing to be seduced by his fakery, wanting him to take them home, duped by his phoney courtship and tin-pot philosophy. Like the tinners in John Wesley's pit congregations, John Nightly's assembly had come to worship.

Justin, unable to deal with emotion any easier than the average band member, tried to comfort: 'Not to worry, man… just a… a flip-out; weird one. Really… y'know…'

And that was it. The extent of the wisdom that John Nightly's closest associate, oldest and no doubt most-treasured countenance had to offer his lifelong buddy and patron. 'Don't cut yourself up, man,' comforted Ash. 'We're here right beside you… standing on the same stage, John. Your mates… your old mates, band mates. Listening to me, John? We can't see any weeds… because there ain't no fuckin' weeds. No… horses and no carts neither.' Justin took another swig. 'Nothing like that out there. All there is, is a bunch of fans. Record-buyers… supporters of the band.

John…'

Justin took his friend's guitar, liberated it from John's neck, making sure the volume was off before he leaned it carefully against the speaker cabinet. The machine rocked from side to side, refusing to be silenced. Like the boys themselves, unwilling to finish its days quite yet. The machine protested by emitting a low, morose hum. Regenerating feedback that pumped through the circuitry of the amp and the guitar's expensively customised pick-ups. The instrument continued to complain and moan for several minutes, but its cry for mercy was lost in the creak of broken topsoil and turned earth beginning to both envelop and encase a panicked frontman.

'We can't see anything, man,' repeated Justin, waving one arm out into the universe as he wrapped the other around his companion for the night, the unnatural blonde otherwise to be found behind the stadium's hot-dog counter… 'Can we, babe?' But the young woman was visibly shocked, and silenced, by the state of the backstage persona of the most famous individual she'd yet been in the presence of.

This frighteningly recent episode was one of a million other flashbacks that sped through John Nightly's mind-files as he lay face-down on the carpet. Weeds in the audience, weeds on stage. Meetings with the taxman, deaths in the family, specks on the ceiling. It had come to this. Whacked-out on the floor where Kennedy, Johnston, Nixon and God knows how many candidates, dealers, pushers and hookers had slept or slumped. John Nightly was making a very close inspection of the carpet. Soon, very soon now, he would indeed be returning 'home'.

Although no one realised it at the time, that night at the Hyatt, the leading man in no fit condition to continue, it really was all finally over. Laid to rest. The auditory hallucinations had sealed it. Paramedics arrived and stopped the fight. John Nightly was cut off. Never to be switched on again. John would never sing for money again. He would never have any kind of a relationship with an outsider again. The boss would rather let go the ropes, give up and perish, than have to make any kind of effort towards engagement. Given the option, it was an alternative he would happily consider right now. If he, or any of the others, were able to break into the de-oxygenated soul that lay frozen before them.

But what of the 'practicals'? As the manager, were he still any kind of manager at all, would doubtless ask. What exactly were the practicals? They had to be considered, of course. And as a five-man Los Angeles district PM unit carried the now unconscious boss out of Room 313, the assembled crew considered the practicals extremely... practically.

The most pressing practical being that Ash, Justin, Ron, Jonathan, Lee and Jean-Claude would have no option but to seek alternative employment, wherever it could be found. All were professionals, and as such, week to week, needed to make a living from their profession.

Mosaic/EMI, its shareholders and directors, would have no alternative but to take the hit. Loss of income from this extremely profitable, easy-to-deal-with multi-stream sales generator would be difficult to bear. Company share price was guaranteed to suffer. The John Nightly infrastructure – agents, bookers, promoters, publishers, label bosses, marketing men, PR executives, legal teams, income-distribution processors and royalty-calculation societies, all of whom depended on his earnings as a significant part of their annual turnover – would readjust; maybe, in some cases, collapse.

The fans would disperse, find another ten-a-penny, hyped-to-death rock'n'roll fabrication. General interest would evaporate, and sooner or later, three, four... five years down the line, income would dry up, at which point he... he himself, god of all things – boss, shaman, magicien, revered seer and peer, devoted school chum and... all the rest of it – he... would dry up.

Thirty-two years old. Stopped... like a .42-calibre slug fired into arc-iron, beached like a sperm whale, dried out like a California raisin. No use to anyone anymore. The world too small a place. The most deserted oceanic hideaway, the farthest arctic cabin too close a place. Nowhere to go. Nowhere to run, to 'get back'. Nowhere to go to try to right things. Except inward maybe.

That's exactly where he went.

During the next weeks there was some, albeit temporary, recovery. John remained in Los Angeles. In bed mostly. No doubt he whittled and worried. He did not fiddle, fornicate or philander. The boy kept himself to himself, fixed on many ceilings and floors. Considering his position and his options. Mentally, spiritually and physically, John Nightly was becoming quite unrecognisable.

John's straw hair, now more *scarecrow* than *swan*, poked out of his head like the dandelion stalks he had been trying to avoid. His Dutch-boy cut had collapsed into a kind of crow's nest. The whites of his eyes, and the craters beneath them, were riddled with thin, red veins. Like many so-called music fans who stop listening, stop tuning in at a certain point in their life, it was as if John had also become cobwebbed. The boss never seemed quite clean or very hygienic anymore; his scaly, glazed skin no longer protected and covered his innards but seemed to leak from them, like skin on custard. This odd, unhealthy look, coupled with his dead-eyed countenance and worsening manners, lent him a kind of instant 'feel-bad factor' whenever he entered a room.

After six weeks of it John Nightly got up from his bed one endless day, took one step forward, and 32,000 steps back. He looked himself up and down. He dusted himself off, straightened himself out and cut off his ragged corners, checking that whatever remained of him was operational before he folded himself in, sealed himself up and disconnected his tired, spongy brain. John Nightly flicked the switch, pulled the plug on his own internal power supply, let the battery go flat, went completely off air and stopped broadcasting. Closed down altogether, taking the only route open to him. He then, from the general public's point of view, vanished for almost forty years.

The Twilight Grotto of Tito and Hanna Robst

Local Zarathustrians Tito and Hanna Robst opened their beautiful, recently refurbished modular residence to the local community of Elmo for the first time last weekend as part of the Elmo Open, the popular twice-yearly event where residents of the small Wisconsin town are invited to open their gardens to the public on two weekends per year. The Robsts proudly unveiled a new 'Disney-inspired' candlelit grotto dedicated to the preachings of Zarathustra and the Avestan way of life and also as a celebration of the music of seventies rock singer John Nightly from England, Great Britain. The Robsts have spent two months preparing this 'contemplative' and 'calming' corner of their garden adjoining their rose-covered English bungalow. For further information go to Wisconsin.gov (e-government portal) or by post 1113, 6th Ave, Elmo, Wisconsin, W1 54481, USA.
Hyperlink: The American Folklore Society, afsnet.org

item: Brian O'Hara, the Fourmost (12 March 1942– 27 June 27 1999).

Brian O'Hara, former singer and guitarist with the Fourmost, a 1960s Liverpool group managed by Brian Epstein that had hits with songs written by John Lennon and Paul McCartney, has been found hanged at his home. He was 58. Liverpool police found O'Hara in the Wavertree area of the city. The group, originally known as the Blue Jays, had half a dozen hit singles from 1963 to 1965, including 'Hello Little Girl' and 'I'm In Love' by Lennon and McCartney. The Fourmost appeared in the Gerry and the Pacemakers film *Ferry Cross the Mersey.*

THE STORY OF JOHN NIGHTLY

SCREENPLAY / LOCATIONS

Cambridge – University & Town	1958-1965
London – Soho, Regent's Park, Mayfair	1966-1970
Los Angeles – the Summer Center	1972-1982
Cornwall – area surrounding Porthcreek	1982-2006

OPENING TITLE

Cornwall – a vast expanse of ocean is seen from the air. Bright sparkling colours. A sunny midsummer's day with high, rolling waves. The camera swoops and glides like a bird high above the water. Close-ups of the inside – the 'tubes' – of the waves, as they roll in. The volume of the waves is deafening. Orchestral music rolls with the film, rushing along in tempo with the wind and the ocean.

The camera circles the cliff edge to locate a lone character perched on top of a precipice facing out to sea. A thin, slight figure, 60 years old, huddled together as if freezing cold on this blisteringly hot summer's day, knees drawn up to his chin, windcheater zipped right up to his neck.

Close-up we see he is shivering in the sun, his teeth chattering. He gazes out to sea immobile and lost; the camera floats over him and glides down to the road running behind him, parallel to the coast. A delivery truck, a white fish van, makes its way slowly along the narrow B-road, supplying fresh fish to the houses and farms dotted about the coastal plain.

VOICEOVER

A close-miked, world-weary, but still youthful voice...

'You know in a dream? When something really bad, or something really

good is about to happen? And you try to move, to run? To get out of there as fast as your legs can carry you? But somehow, no matter how hard you try, you just can't seem to move fast enough? As fast as you need to. You're running and running, but you're just not getting anywhere. Well… my life was a bit like that…'

Suddenly the wind turns and the bird is dragged away, carried backwards high up into the sky. The music also unwinds and plays the symphonic extract backwards, Britten's *A Ceremony of Carols*, as we spin back through the film at tremendous speed – a typical film flashback – in black and white. Looking down the tube, out of this spiralling tunnel we can just about make out a figure coming towards us. A young boy, five, maybe six years old, with a school cap and a satchel, running, running, along a pavement, as fast as his legs can carry him. It is an idyllic, sunny late afternoon in a suburban tree-lined Cambridge street sometime in the mid-1950s.

The boy cannot wait to get home as he turns through a wooden gate into a gravel drive leading up to a house where an attractive woman, his mother, waits at an open doorway. They greet and hug as though they haven't set eyes on each other for years, though the child left home for school only that morning. As she releases him from her arms, he rushes past her down a corridor into another room, a modern open-plan lounge that looks out onto a tended garden. There is an upright piano which the boy jumps on and plays although we don't hear what he plays as the orchestral music still carries over. The camera closes in on his hands and now we do hear John Nightly's music – simple piano chords that fade in as the orchestra gradually recedes.

When the camera pulls back from the same hands we see the same character but 20 years later a young man sitting at a grander piano in a large recording-studio where there is a band rehearsing, recording. John Nightly is dressed in a white YSL suit and silk scarf, very much in 1970s mode. He gets up from his white piano, stares into the control-room and mouths something to the engineer. He walks towards the control-room and pushes the heavy, soundproofed door. As it opens, the camera peers inside the room, John Nightly looks in and sees himself, a young teenage ex-schoolboy sitting nervously, foot tapping like a jackhammer, as he waits in a typically dismal showbiz office.

SCENE 1
Interior: London, Carnaby Street; Monday, 12 January 1966

Seen from the boy's POV, a small office with two pretty secretaries. John is daydreaming about a recent live appearance in Cambridge, his group having won the annual music competition at a local public house. We see and hear the performance going on in his head.

Girl

'Had a cup of tea?' – a secretary interrupts the boy's concentration

SCENE 2
Exterior: London, Carnaby Street

A TV reporter on the streets of London's Carnaby Street. She is 16-17 years old, a little over-enthusiastic in her 'swinging' commentary...

'This is London...'

SCENE 3
Trewin House, Porthcreek, 1982

A hand picks up the telephone....

'I'd like to speak with Mr Nightly, please...' a voice announces at the other end.

'Carn Point Lighthouse is situated on one of the most dangerous and dramatic stretches of coastline in Britain. For years CPL has been warning mariners of the treacherous sunken and exposed rocks near Pendeen Watch. Its lamp has the intensity of 300,000 candela, and a range of nineteen miles.'
www.lighthouse.org

item: The Times, London. 7 March 2004.
West Penwith in Cornwall is set to become the international centre for wave-power generation if a bid to install one of the world's most advanced wave-energy technologies is successful this Friday. A sea-based power plant will gather the energy generated by the massive swells that regularly batter Cornwall's west coast, and is intended to be the first of five plants designed to transform the energy of the seas around Britain into electricity for the national grid. Speaking at a public meeting in Truro yesterday, Lars Vardom, chairman of WavCon, the company behind the wave-power generator, said: 'Wave plants are the mains power of the future. We believe that the plant will be 100 per cent effective, so that if people want to look at successful sea-power systems – which is going to be a major factor in energy generation in the future – they will come here.' A prototype wave generator built by Wave Boom is now successfully completing trials at Limfjorden in east Denmark. Other companies, including Wavedom and Seagrove Systems, are also developing plans for construction of other wave-power plants in the UK.

'He paints the wayside flower, he lights the evening star...'

Endy is in full flow. Sunday teatime means *Songs of Praise* to some 13 million Britons. Endymion Peed is one of them. The housekeeper sits, as she always does, deep within the springless depths of Trewin's tulip-patterned couch. Alexandre beside her, both of them at one with the TV congregation, oblivious to the real, unholy chaos beyond their own little hidey-hole. The *singing housekeeper*, swept away by the sight of BBC believers joining together on her favourite Methodist anthem. The exact same sound that makes the two Johns feel 'physically sick' should they happen to pass by the living room at 6pm on a Sunday.

'We plough the fields and scatter, the good seed on the land...'

'I love this one', whispers Endy. 'Oh, I love the harvest hymns, Sandy... good old John Wesley hymn, this is.' She ruffles the grey-flecked coat of her dopey friend.

Next door, the men of the house do their best not to listen. RCN is on the telephone trying to track down grass seed, while Robert deals with a pile of export documents to meet new European Community guidelines. As for Mawg, he lays half-comatose on the carpet, lost in his own Xbox reality, shielded from normal life by the religion of Nintendo while being protected still further by his ever-present 'full-spectrum' headset.

But what of John? The boss is... well, no one knows exactly where he is – in any sense – but he is around. Occasionally the old rocker will wander off on his own, but not very far. He liked to sit, on a humid, late-October eve, among the flowering cacti and pelargoniums set along the back corridor of the farm-house. If he isn't there, seemingly content and self-contained, he might be in the kitchen, reading the local paper, scouring the classifieds for bargains he doesn't need, checking auction lists of sales that have already taken place, or maybe just burning some toast. Perhaps he'll be in the study, taking a casual look at one of his 'favourites', as he thumbs through the scientific, astronomical and cosmological treatises lining the shelves of RCN's makeshift office.

Stephen Hawking is a favourite. Stephen Hawking is well-thumbed-through, Hawking's ideas following on from those of the other Cambridge geniuses John has studied all those years before. The way things are simply put, with the book using everyday language. The way it all seems so obvious and somehow natural. Stephen never tries to put it on.

The last time John Nightly had visited Cambridge, at the very height of his megalomania, he'd heard the man himself speak at a hastily arranged lecture in Caius cellars. As usual, the place was packed. John Nightly recalled the feeling of expectation, the familiar click-clack of stick on slate as Hawking made his way along the dank passage. Even at 21 years old, the future guru already had a reputation as an enlightening speaker, creating a buzz about himself and his ideas long before *A Brief History of Time*. Neither was there anything at all 'difficult' about the legendary but little-read tome. A kid could understand it. All you had to do was tune in and hang on. Be receptive – as receptive as a child. John could certainly do that. Both Mawg and RCN had taken on *ABHOT* and managed to survive it, no doubt emerging cosmically enriched at the other end.

Some days, if Mawg was in domestic mode, off-duty during an enforced break from technology, taking Alexandre for a stroll or catching up with a pile of sci-fi downloads, John might wander into the music room and hit *PLAY*. Not meaning at all to interfere, but simply to check exactly where his collaborator was at. Whether the kid had completed all of his 'tasks'; these being instructions from the boss, a list of which was drawn up at the end of each session.

John Nightly couldn't re-jig or update anything himself of course. Not even to turn up the volume or delete an instrument. John had no idea about how anything actually worked. But he could listen, absorb, memorise *and* obsess, with that photographic sound memory of his unbelievably still intact. Now, more than ever, the boss was coming back to the kid with suggestions, managing to keep whole swathes of music logged in his right-hand brain, just as he was able to in the old days. 'Harpsichord needs to be louder there', 'Let's add another bar at the start of that', 'Turn up the brightness – on everything – no, just turn up everything!' he instructed. Sometimes struck by inspiration while stargazing out on the lawn or downing one of Endy's homemade pasties.

The kid had certainly done a job on the music. And on John Nightly. Every move of the cursor was there to serve the Master. Mawgan was talented enough to be making music in his own right, of course. He had more than the necessary skill and imagination, if he'd wanted to do it. It must have been what he was aiming for eventually. After all, he was still only twenty-one, three years into the project, as it neared its eventual end – the 'end of the end' – as RCN cheerfully referred to it. Both Johns were no doubt looking forward to hearing what their young friend and colleague would be getting up to on his release.

But the first thing the kid needed was a good, long break. Mawg's girlfriend, local hippie-chick Karen, model daughter of model-mother escapee from the Swinging age, had made an excellent job of charming the misfits of Trewin. A florist and flower-arranger by trade, Karen had quickly engaged with the 'family' by quizzing Robert about flowering cycles and Endy on Peed-patented Fairy Liquid mixtures. The teenager planned to get Mawg down to the small cottage they'd recently taken near Sennen Cove, financed by an inheritance from her grandfather and the £60,000 advance on royalties that RCN had given the young man in return for three years of his life. A suitable reward for overseeing a project that the nurse believed had the potential to generate at least ten times that amount, maybe 100 times, with the release of the *MBR* monster mash now set for the following July.

They were almost there. Really very little to be done now. The thing lay in wait back there in the guest bedroom. Having been rescued, watered and fed, it sat patiently on three Apple displays; a picture of health, lush as Eucalyptus. Reassembled, remodelled, remixed, reheated, redeemed. The *Mink Bungalow Requiem* had been spoiled rotten by long-term TLC. Sonically brought up to spec, polished and digitised, bits duplicated or copied – though never chopped off. Every second of John Nightly's original vision had managed to survive the thirty-year-long journey. It really was a fully fledged triple-album monstrosity, the sort of thing that really shouldn't be kept in the back bedroom, once again recognisable and identifiable as the same monster its creator remembered it as from three decades back in time.

Foyle's bookshop, Charing Cross Road, London WC2. Monday, 8 May 1988. Jean-Claude Marx, author of *Exclamation Marx! 60 Stories from the 60s* (Random House, 1988) featured author.
'His problems got far worse after the failure of the... *Requiem.*' Jean-Claude stares at the untouched stack of signed copies on the table in front of him, '*Ape Box* had sold this crazy... ten million albums or something, but they still couldn't get a single

play on the new one.' J-C leans over and straightens the pile, 'And how could you? You're trying to get them to play a record that doesn't have anything on it which is actually 'play-a-ble'. Long passages of... sound effects and... God-knows-what!' The author seems put out, for no particular reason. 'Bits and pieces of this and that. "Random-chanced", he called them.' He looks disgusted, 'and then expect it to be played on US radio? Or any-where else for that matter!' J-C takes a sip of water as he notices an unusually well-dressed woman who has just entered the shop.

'No "real songs" on the record at all. No "concessions", you see. To people. People who buy records! The shortest piece lasted twenty minutes! J-C pauses and takes a deep breath, 'there were... beautiful things, of course — I don't say there weren't — things they recorded in London... in the church — those orchestral pieces — the links, they were genuinely beautiful. [nods his head in agreement with himself] I used to... almost to have tears when they played them over the system, even at soundchecks and things. In those huge auditoriums with all that power. Like God coming out of the speakers. The "Lux Eterna"... That was... was a real — very much the 'real thing', as people say. But the rest of it... [gesticulates wildly as he travels back in time] Then... the real terror, when "reality struck"! J-C's eyes become wild now too, 'bankrupted by the whole fusion-power... farce. Stupid fool. Fool! Who the hell is travelling across the United States with a 200-piece rock group, 4,000-piece orchestra and 5,000 groupies? [lots of shuffling in the room] Then tries to power the whole thing up using water and candles!'

J-C picks up a wine bottle, checks the label, turns his nose up, and pours himself a glass.

'No lighting at all apart from that, you see. Just candles. Millions of candles! Couldn't damned well see what you were doing! My engineers and electricians were going absolutely crazy. You can't fix a plug or wire, or sort out a fault in candlelight for God's sake!'

The store's event manager shuffles in his chair, preparing to curtail the 'interview'; tonight's featured author puts down his empty glass, takes another disgusted look at the empty bottle and continues.

'Wave Power was something that *I* put together for *him*, something that no one else was doing… using. And that, I'm sure, was part of the attraction and the attention for us. To be the first… which he, John, always wanted to be. Literally nobody else in the world had it and even we didn't know if it was efficient – in terms of being 'stable' or even 'safe' power. We didn't know! We're transporting these huge girders around on trucks. They have to be set up along the coast.' Jean-Claude gets up from his chair. 'Madness! In an extremely mad, bad way I'm afraid,' he laughs, laughing 'at' as well as 'with' the memory of the whole (in retrospect) ludicrously doomed enterprise; a fresh bottle appears on the table and is waved away by the event manager.

'Even with the music you get pitching problems all the time because the level of power is not stable. Everything is flat! That's one of the reasons we all use electricity in the first place. Sta-bi-li-ty! He knew that, of course. Knew that very well. If anyone understood that, John did.'

The speaker sits down again, rather exhausted already, even before his unscheduled outburst. 'I can't think about it anymore. The man went through hell. But self-inflicted hell in a way also, I believe. To some extent, maybe we all did.'

'We had this guy, mu-si-co-logist, come in and give a sort of lecture on the Requiem Mass. Not the Bungalow one, but the normal one, Mozart, Fauré, er… as a musical format. So that we mortals could 'understand' it. Hah! [pours himself a full glass of water and grimaces]

'He – John – thought it was important that we all know about it. Because as usual, of course, the man was suddenly an expert! Anyway… we all soon became quite 'au fait' – expert too, about the old Requiem Mass. And the choreographer, Donna… sweet girl. As usual there was something going on… some "stuff" there.' J-C raises his eyebrows. 'Poor girl, you know… couldn't see what she was doing. None of the dancers could see what they were bloody well dancing towards! Where exactly was the end of the bloody stage? [Settles down a little, possibly feeling that by now he may have made his point]

'I was always told it looked good from the arena. *Incroyable!* was what everyone said. But it was dangerous as hell. Then of course the "bad thing" happened, and we lost a guy… Sacha… beautiful young guy… who fell from the rig… and that was because he could not see what he was doing, or even exactly where he was. And that really affected him – John. Destroyed him, certainly. You don't usually have people die when you do entertainment.' J-C smiles sourly and motions to the woman, now fixed on her own reflection in the bookshop window.

'Our friend really was a poor thing after that. For a long, long time. But again, he was, or "is", wherever he is, whatever he is doing, still an artist. He's an artist and so he can recover from these things… rescue himself… as long as he has his *Art*. But I think what did it for John more than anything else was when we got back. When the… career side of things began to… dis… deteriorate. And the horror-movie people[1] approached him for the music, the Requiem music, for some… *horrible horror.* That affected John because there was nothing he could do to stop it. So they used it… this extremely beautiful thing. They sped it up and hacked it about… this amazing piece of music, composed for entirely another purpose, became the bloody tune to bloody *Blood of Dracula!* Or whatever it was.

Then after that, when they got back to England, they asked him to write a song for that… Europe song thing. You know… Eurovision! is what I mean[2]. Then the bloody record company

[1] *Drac's Blood,* a Cameo Films Production. d. John Luseinger, UK/Italy 1974.

went down. He did something with a circus in London... TV gig. I think was the last thing he ever did do, wasn't it?". J-C acknowledges the woman again and smiles a little too sweetly, 'After that it was totally over. Totally! And he went into a... a kind of – I don't know what exactly – terrible desperation, I presume.'

2 John Nightly himself did actually suggest his publishers submit a track – 'Jesus Lover', an anti-religion, anti-fan song based on the Wesleyan hymn 'Jesus Lover Of My Soul'. The song was rejected by the UK Eurovision selection committee.

The winds and waves obey him,
By him the birds are fed...

Oh God... Endy was still singing along. Robert sat thumbing through the paper. 'That one could have been written for the boss...'

'I hope you're saying that in a respectful way, Robert. This is a John Wesley hymn.'

RCN looked up from his bowl of crumble, a little surprised by Endy's uncharacteristically bumptious remark.

Much more to us, his children,
He gives our daily bread...

'Next week's *Songs of Praise* will come from Royston in Huntingdonshire and will be presented by Alex Sanders. Next on BBC 1, the *Antiques Roadshow*, followed by our Digital Premiere for D-Day, the wartime romance *The Way to the Stars*, starring Michael Redgrave and Rosamund John. That's in three quarters of an hour here on BBC 1...'

The housekeeper immediately brightened and got up to make tea. 'Rosamund John... that's a name you don't hear very often nowadays. That's the film with the poem in it.'

Everyone looked blank. Mawg decided to drag himself away from the excitement and wandered off next door to do a bit more work.

'You *know*...' insisted Endy. *'Head in air', See his children fed...'* That one. Surely you know that? That's a lovely film, that is... always reminds me of my mother...'

'Does sound familiar...' Robert picked up his teacup.

'Oh, it was famous in its day, Robert... meant a lot, that film.

To a lot of different people. Like a lot of things…'

The housekeeper took a pin from inside her bonnet and clipped it onto her pinafore.

Anders Jonsson, long-term John Nightly super-fan, interviewed on Radio Free Denmark. March 1979.
What it was in real? As a form, you mean? It was grand, wasn't it? Grandiose. It was a mad one of those things. In a fantastic way, though. Very glorious. The Bungalow was three records, LPs, together in one art work where one played all three simultaneously, for which one needed three record-players or… hi-fis… Quad in those days. Line each one up, then set all three off at the same time, at which point all types of… noisiness and bizarre sounds would come loose. Of course, he had been doing this kind of thing for a very long time. I went to his flat in London to see Iona… when he was recording *Quiz Axe Queen* – '68 that should be. He had the theme to the *Bungalow* then and he played it to me on the piano. Put the tape on, one chord repeating, over and over, and played along with it. Even like that, it sounded good, really good. I thought, this is something new! Something really new!

Later, when he had a more… permanent set-up with three proper decks up there along with his three TVs, all on at the same time as well, with – of course – all three channels… and the new one, BBC2. He would get all his girlfriends to come in and put the records on 'as directed' and basically subject all of his friends, anyone who visited the flat, to this... terrible chaos noise – as far as they were concerned it must be.

Then they came to record it properly – the Quadrophonic as well – I remember going to the big studio and a lot of it was piano versions and love-making sounds and all this... sex noises and everything, all mixed up. That day he had nine decks, arranged all in different parts of the flat, like 3+3... and these big, huge... tree-plants, with beautiful colours. It was a big old-time flat, and we were all going around, listening to all the different bits in the different rooms. Really... tripping out with our minds and with sounds. But... but this was long after people had stopped tripping out! And that in itself was a big... huge problem. Honestly, the whole music was physically very out of sync... because there was no way of synchronising it with all these record decks running alone from each other.

In a way, of course, that might have been what he wanted. Maybe it had been constructed like that, to be truly 'freeform'... *FREE MUSIC!* [gets very excited] But sometimes it just didn't work at all. it just would sound like a mess a lot of the time. Of course it was influential, because soon after you had... 'Revolution 9' and all the love-making records and noise things on records – Tangerine Dream and things like this. Can and progressive things and all these things as well. But I don't think any of them – and the Pink Floyd things, because they came from Cambridge at the same time – would have happened without John Nightly.

He made arrangements with the HMV London studios in Abbey Road, with the conductor Lawrence Collingwood and the London Symphony orchestra, with gramophone personnel to transport a speaker-relay system to Marl Bank and set it up in an adjoining bedroom, with the Post Office for connecting lines.

Edward Elgar, aided by a supply of morphine, tunes into his own recording session at Abbey Road from his deathbed. 22 January 1934.

Trewin Farm, Porthcreek, Carn Point, Cornwall. Thursday, 1 July 2006.

'There'll be plenty of food at the studio for him. A whole canteen of organic this and that. Lots of healthy vegetarian musicians, no doubt.' RCN raised his eyebrows and finished drying his hands.

'Oh… oh, dear me…' Endy stopped what she was doing. Fixed as she was on the new white loaf she'd just cut into. 'There's a… well, there's a hole in this bread…' She picked up the loaf. 'Goes right through, that does.'

'*Hole in the bread,* then,' Mawgan rocked back and forwards on his chair.

'But that… well, that sometimes means…'

'Death in the family, Mawgan.' RCN put Endy out of her misery. He turned to the housekeeper. 'That's what you mean. Isn't it, my dear? All those old wives' tales and superstitions' RCN sat down at the kitchen table and waited for the telepathically requested fresh pot of tea, his head already in the local rag.

'Not superstitious are you, Endy?' Mawg was in a mischievous mood today.

'There's nothing suspicious about that, Mawgan,' the house-keeper replied – at which point everyone laughed, including the lady herself. '*Super-stitious!* You know what I mean! But that is…

well... that's the deepest hole I ever did see. Dear oh dear oh dear...' Endy put the tin-fresh loaf down on the draining board. 'We won't be eating that tonight, I can tell you. I'll put that straight in the bin.' She looked forlornly out of the window. 'It just means we don't have any white bread for me to make you a sandwich for tomorrow...'

'He'll have plenty of grub – I told you.' RCN turned to the kid. 'That'll be the least of your worries, my dear Endy...'

EMI Recording Studios, 3 Abbey Road, St John's Wood, London NW6. Monday, 2 July 2006.

Mawgan sailed along the freshly mown corridor hung with multiplatinum trophies. The Pink Floyd, Sir Edward Elgar, Paul & Linda, Daniel Barenboim, Leonard Bernstein, Stokowski, Hollies, Patrick Moore, Russ Conway, Mrs Mills, the Pretty Things, Sir Adrian Boult, Sir Malcolm Sargent, George Martin, Ravi Shankar, Peter and Gordon, Yehudi Menuhin, Freddie Mercury, Glenn Miller, the Fourmost, John Barry, Benjamin Britten, Michael Tippett, Radu Lupu, John McLaughlin, Johnny Kidd, Anthony Newley, Lionel Bart, Imogen Holst, The Action, John Taverner, Cliff, the Shads... all Abbey Road regulars. The dude completed a full two laps, taking it all in.

'Hi!'

A tiny olive-skinned lady in a white dress, hair dyed a little too dark for her skin colour, stood in silhouette at the end of the passage. Small and ornamental. The genie in the lamp.

'Mawgan?'

'... oh... hi...'

'I'm Carrie, Jonathan's wife? It's nice to meet you today,' the tiny lady extended her hand.

'... and you...' Mawg smiled bashfully. 'And thanks for..."

'Jon asked if you wouldn't mind waiting just a few moments in the restaurant? They're still at work out there but he'll be through in just a moment.'

'... no worries.' Mawgan made sure to appear unworried as he pulled down his hoodie until it covered his T-shirt and belt. Atypically, the kid suddenly felt a little underdressed, out of his depth perhaps in such refined surroundings.

'... had a cup of tea?'

'... uh... yes... yeh... thanks.'

'... well, would you like another?'

'I'm uh... alright, at the minute, thanks.'

The white lady indicated toward a heavy soundproofed door. She walked ahead of Mawg, leading him down a connecting staircase into a low-ceilinged, light-filled room, the studio restaurant, which looked out onto a cottage garden. Some 100 or so bodies were packed into the busy dining area. Discussing the session and the sunny weather. Worse-for-wear orchestral contractors stood at a bar in the corner, their eyes fixed on a huge TV screen relaying satellite football. They cheered and jeered as fortunes changed. Beside them a group of five or six neater-looking men were sat around a table scribbling furiously.

'What are they doing?'

'Oh... they're copyists,' the lady smiled. 'Copying parts for Jon. On film assignments the picture tends to be changing all the time... right up to the last minute, so we're working right up to that time – literally, until we actually put it down – "record it", that is. They're constantly having to modify the orchestral parts so that it fits the edit...'

'But can't they do that on a computer?'

'They can… or they can do a *bit* of it,' she elaborated. 'They can change it and make the inserts on the computer. But the players still need individual parts… pieces of paper to read from, so…' Carrie looked up at the football screen. 'Tricky job… as with all these things.'

Mawg surveyed the busy dining area. 'And they do that while there's all this noise going on?'

'They can do that on the back of a bus, Maw-gan. These guys can read batshit.'

'Hi, darling…'

A very tall, very bald man appeared behind the genie.

'Maw-gan?'

The kid got up. 'Jonathan?'

The tall, bald man, having the appearance of a GP or local-government canvasser, bore no resemblance whatsoever to the crazie in pink loon-pants who peered out from the gatefold of *Quiz Axe Queen*. Jonathan shifted a bunch of papers from his right to left hand so he could greet the dude properly.

'Nice to meet… really very nice.' He looked Mawg up and down. 'Very nice to see you.' The man swapped hands again and took a breath. 'So… this is a big thing, isn't it? Shall we… sit down…', Jonathan looked up and down the crowded room. 'Though where exactly, I'm not quite…'

The maestro nodded to the many familiar faces squeezed around the tables. With the orchestra on an MU break, the canteen overflowed with cellists, flautists, oboists, percussionists… and copyists. Members of the Royal Philharmonic who had been performing Jonathan's soundtrack in Studio 1. Carrie manoeuvred the three of them into the garden then went off to get tea for everyone in order to allow a plot to be hatched.

'So… John knows nothing about this?'

'Oh, he does, yeah… he knows everything – more or less…' Mawg remained in upbeat mood. 'But he thinks it's coming out without the interludes. Then after me and RCN… the other John…'

'Daly?'

'John Daly, yeah.'

'He's still around?'

'Sure he is. That's the only reason John… John uh… Nightly's still around. I mean John… Daly… he sorts out… well, he sort of does everything for the boss really…'

Jonathan paid close attention.

'I'm amazed he's… hung in there so long.' He put down his papers. 'And is he well?'

'RCN? Oh, John's fine.' Mawgan looked around him. 'He's a pretty chilled guy…'

'That's good to hear… and… sorry, but… before we go on to talk about it all… do you mind if I ask? We will get on to the main stuff but…" Jonathan edged closer to the kid. 'What sort of… "state" is John himself in? Really in…'

'The boss? He's fine too.' Mawgan considered, "well, he's *kind of* fine. I mean… he's not that fantastic at the moment actually. Not in terms of… 'normally well', I guess. He's not well in that way… but… it's like… *he's* like… he's really into doing this. This job… 'project'. We've been working on it for like… two years… probably nearly three.'

'You've been with him all this time?' Mawg nodded.

'And you've actually managed to get him back into it… music?'

'Yeah.' Mawg gazed around the room. 'More or less…'

'That's amazing… *awesome.*'

Jonathan was being signalled to by the guys at the bar, one of whom pointed to his watch. Time was getting on. The kid continued.

'I'll be glad to get it done, to be honest. And to get it out. 'Cause I think it's like… we're like… we're on the edge of it at the moment… Maybe even starting to lose it a bit. Or we will do. If we don't do it now. If we don't get it *sorted* now. I think so, anyway…' Mawg drew back his hood. 'But the thing is… I've spoken to John – John Daly – it was sort of… It was his idea, really. Or both of ours, I s'pose. We just thought that if we could get the orchestral bits – sorry, *interludes* – recorded again, it'd make the whole thing really complete, and it's like… we're only gonna do it once.'

Jonathan looked at his watch. 'Will John be there?'

'Nightly? No… John Nightly won't be there. Definitely not… no way. We want it to be a surprise. But also… me and John – Daly, that is – we sort of… We went through it. And there's no way that John will wanna be there anyway.' Mawg paused. 'There might be an area somewhere in the future where he might have "wanted" to be there. In the future…' the kid scratched his head. 'Somehow he might… but I… I think when he adds it all up… getting him down to London and…'

'Can he travel?'

'No, no. He can't travel. No… he – John, the boss, I mean – doesn't go anywhere. He's out in the garden but…' Mawgan fidgeted with his unopened notebook. 'Up on the rocks some-times. But in terms of him actually being there – "showing up", kind of thing – and everyone sort of looking at him and that…' Mawg picked up a teaspoon. 'Ain't gonna happen, y'know. Gonna be much too much for him. It's never… well, y'know what I mean…'

The kid sensed his moment was up.

'John Daly's got a budget and all that. He will work that all out with you. That's no problem. It's just… it's like… it just depends on…'

Mawg began to lose it a little. Wondering whether Jonathan might be just that little bit too grand, bit too 'employed' generally to take on what would likely turn out to be quite a frazzled, chaotic situation.

'It's like… in the first place, if you've still got the parts really. The music parts and… and also… if you think that you would like to do it – we're all kind of all really hoping that you will… *would*, like to…'

The kid picked up a serviette, folding it in halves until he couldn't fold it anymore. It was apparent that Jonathan was in two minds. Mawg lifted his hoodie, threw back his unruly dreads, smiled a little too unconfidently and rested his case. Carrie, pushing through obstructive instrument cases, chairs and umbrellas, arrived on cue with tea and treacle cake. Jonathan got up to take the tray from his wife.

'Darling… we're going to record the Interludes!'

Jesu, lover of my soul, let me to Thy bosom fly
While the nearer waters roll
While the tempest still is high:
Hide me, O my Savior, hide,
Till the storm of life is past;
Safe into the haven guide;
O receive my soul at last

'Jesu, Lover of My Soul', Charles Wesley, 1740
from the Primitive Baptist Hymnbook (1887 edition)

item: Monthly Cultural Notes: December.
The December gardener reaps the benefit of preparation in autumn. Bring cyclamens, primulas, and cinerarias into the living room for Christmas decoration. Attention switches to the greenhouse. Keep the air moving with good ventilation and heat where necessary. It is essential to keep greenhouse soil dry if plants are not in flower. A satisfying, quieter time, then, but a difficult one. December is not the coldest month, but it is the darkest.

With the final recording session about to take place, the one thing remaining to be done before the *Mink Bungalow Requiem* could finally be set free was the disc mastering, which Mawgan himself would supervise with RCN.

The mastering of any record is the final step towards its proper completion. Transfer from a professional recording format to a domestic one needs as much care and attention as any other stage of the operation. Not only to convert the music from tape to disc, but also to ensure that it arrives at its destination bigger and brighter than it was when it left home. A procedure that involves listening, checking and adjusting, then listening, checking and adjusting again (and again), all the time referencing favourite records that have been as life-enhancing to your own ears as you hope your record might be to others; tracks which have proved to be life-givers, seducing on the radio or dance floor, as you A/B between your offering and songs as familiar as the wind, flick between your little symphony and the absolute behemoths of rock'n'roll. How do you compare with Lennon, Led Zep or the Floyd, those who are beyond us, the standing stones of rock culture? Words and music that are etched into our collective psyche, a few random seconds bringing back time and place, people, past lives and our own former selves, the way we were. Songs that not only tuned us up, made us grow, but that also distracted and diverted us, revolutionised the way we think, the way we behave. Or, on the other hand, the toothpaste squeeze of today? The flat-pack pop of this week's top downloads, indie bands sponsored by luxury brands, the panto-rock that these days passes for the behaviouristic revolution in aesthetics known as rock'n'roll?

On the final turn of your journey you will polish your creation, shape and tone it, dust it off sound-wise, adapting it to the formats on which it will be listened to: radio, iPod dock, streaming, hi-fi and lo-fi, headphones, earphones, iPhones, car speakers, DJ decks, festival PA systems. Although you went out of your way to make a record that would sound 'individual', you're now going to try to make it sound like all other records, part of the musicalised correspondence, the ongoing archive that is Recorded Music Sound.

A&R executives refer to it as a 'sit-right' quality. More often than not this stands for a flattened dynamic. Elimination of the peaks and dips, the headroom and vast bandwidth of frequencies – removing the 'hi-fi' itself, the life and soul, the very gut of rock'n'roll – to make the track sound good and loud, louder than the rest, and therefore more 'commercial', more 'sellable' in the outside world.

A *Radio 1 Sound* is what it is. Pluggers lining the corridors of Broadcasting House use the phrase repeatedly, as they boast to one another about having a *Radio 1 Sound* in their record bags and a hit on their hands. A Radio 1 Sound*, or 'radio-friendly record', strikes a hard-to-achieve balance – some would say compromise, between overall impact, roundness of tone, consistency of volume, 'rightness', 'wrongness', 'wow' factor, 'now' factor and sheer 'ordinariness'. A necessity and a problem ever since, sometime around the mid '70s, pop music's collective ambition seemed to diminish, to almost go into reverse, following the parting of the ways between *rock* and *pop*. The watershed creating a new tributary, a kind of 'concept-rock', a more thoroughly conceived, sometimes ill-conceived, more considered, more technical, more rehearsed, 'better' performed, more expensively produced, altogether shinier stream running alongside two mainstreams. This more conceptual state is the antithesis of coffee-bar skiffle, rockabilly, Merseybeat, the groups of the Blues Boom, the Brum Sound or any other primitive or provincial subgenre. Concept rock is Self-conscious. More linked to non-musical forms – performance art, theatre, mime, dance, spiritualism, Evangelism, Belief – than normal rock. Conceptual rock thinks itself more worthy than basic rock'n' roll. Through its mercury channel flows the glistening debuts of Queen and Roxy Music, King Crimson and Jethro Tull. A new beginning for the Bowie re-heated Mott the Hoople following

---

*In February 2012, BBC Radio 1 recorded 12.66 million listeners aged ten and over.

their mentor's own eventual infiltration of the student common room and the surrender of T. Rex to the demands of Woollies sales reps after many years of loyal service to the cause. The *mouvement* creating another new New World for ELO, Todd Rundgren, Alice Cooper, Focus, Sparks, 10cc and others who took the road less travelled, at least for a while, as opposed to the jammed-up B-carriageway of hard rock and metal[1]. In terms of presentation, this strand looked back to the antics of Screaming Lord Sutch and Johnny Kidd, while musically it recast pop in the mould of classical music; more melodic, more chromatic, thematic, more harmonically unusual, more structurally complex and more gimmicky while being seemingly more lyrically philosophical. It put the jump-leads on rock'n'roll itself, but could not perform the same feat on the movement's chief protagonist.

That third summer of the '70s had been John Nightly's eventual Zero Point. The point at which the ailing superstar jettisoned both his mind and his body from an existing cocoon, preferring the uncharted waters of oblivion to the more logical step, career-wise, towards the new popular genres and formats, pop rock, art rock, space rock, made-for-radio, adult-orientated (AOR) pop and stadium rock. Each one of the Nightly recordings had been conceived with the idea of recording-studio as instrument. With the refinements in the recording process, 24 tracks available instead of four, a galaxy of FX, more budget, and therefore more time – too much time – and a willingness to experiment with sound itself, much more was now achievable and therefore conceivable.

The fans' enthusiasm for a more deluxe listening experience meant this was also the point at which the door opened for anyone with a tin ear and a cast-iron bank account to take part in another new phenomenon – ironically, one that threatened

---

[1] 'Each song is a pastiche of the previous one. With glazed eyes fixed on the stage, seat holders rise up as one, they rock backwards and forwards like seaweed…' Roy Carr reviews Black Sabbath, *NME*, March 1973.

the act of music appreciation itself. Sound reproduction – the quality of 'sonics' – had always been a major component of rock. The very progenitor of the music. Now rechristened the demon *audio* it became much more; almost a concept in itself. The era of the self-proclaimed audiophile had dawned.

Those who had been unable to decode the musical fabris leaking from the matchbox speaker of their Dansette were now able to invest in and enthuse about *audio* to their fellow non-hearers. Talk of tweeters, bins, woofers and subwoofers along with all manner of super-decks, amps and pre-amps, compressors, limiters and equalisers taking mono into stereo, stereo to Quad and Quad to surround sound seemed to almost take the place of consideration of tunes and words. By the time the pop machine had been repackaged yet again, stadium rock had taken off and John Nightly had been taken away, it was as though rock'n'roll had never happened.

Suddenly we were all rewound, back in the pre-Beatle world. The part-word *pop* once more stood for disposability and instant appeal. The Pop Music Product was again aimed squarely at the new decade's teenage (this time 'teeny-bop') audience. Success – the desired outcome linking each new release with eternity – seemed not at all dependent upon the product being viewed as being hip or influential or even on being actually liked by the public at large, but rather on its potential to be literally 'successful': i.e. money-making, unit-shifting at retail and 'instant' in broadcasting terms. Radio-friendly enough for the BBC Playlist – an all-too-select selection of tracks on rotation in any given week, injecting content via Telstar and the BBC's own satellites into every home in Britain. The new *Radio 1 Sound* was as instant as a popper or a suitcase containing a million dollars.

When mastering, in the midst of this tricky weighing-up, the creator listens in absolute silence; absolute detail and denial – a kind of communion. Because this is the final time. Your very last chance. The proofs of your novel, final cut of your movie. The genuine 'end of the end', as RCN still liked to remind everyone. 'Let's stop before it gets any better!' as Pondy used to say. The creator must do his best to hear with new ears at an endpoint where what sounded rapturous now sounds rudimentary. Once-thrilling chord changes rise and fall in the distance; strings that aroused the hairs on the back of your neck pass without notice. A perfect word or phrase, one that once meant so much, seems inconsequential. Familiarity and repetition have dulled the experience, put out the spark.

Hearing anew is an impossible task. So the mastering technician is implored to be particularly diligent, to pay special attention. Everyone must listen now. Not just the artistes themselves, but the studio maintenance man, the lady from the canteen, the boy who comes to service the machines. Anyone who happens to pass by the isolation tank is press-ganged and put to good use. What is sought is objectivity. A box-fresh ear. Trying to imagine that you know nothing whatsoever about the masterpiece that is now so much a part of you that you must deny it. Your own cosmic string is about to be cast off. Time to finally let the infant go.

And so, RCN and Mawg were sat at what appeared to be a flight deck in Mastering Room 13 at EMI's Abbey Road complex along with a cleaner, a tea lady and tape-op intern. On the sofas at the back of the studio, barely able to sit upright without flopping over, were a group of overweight, late-middle-aged men formerly known (sometimes) as the Sleepwalkers. The John Nightly Love-Rock band: Justin, Ash, Ron and Jon, even Jean-Claude, and the man with more opinions than most, Lee Hide. Life-crash survivors together in the same capsule for the first summer since '72. The new recruit felt like a '60s throwback himself.

'Over the past thirty-four years the word regarding the Mink Bungalow Requiem *has altered dramatically. When the Virgin Record Guide published a listing for John Nightly in 1984, the work was seen as the overblown excess of a drug-addled mind, but at the time of its reissue and reassessment in 2006,* MOJO *described it as 'possibly the most ambitious, genuinely imaginative work ever produced under the vague mantle of Pop'.* The Mink Bungalow Requiem *is a true fusion of '60s beat, acid pop, love rock, cut-*

ups, mash-ups, (cock-ups), contemporary-classical, mid-20th-century avant garde, romanticism, musique concrète, concrete poetry, electronica, folk rock, art rock, space rock, serialism and exotica. The only thing it doesn't contain is any element of "jazz". Truly a work of genius.'

'Well, that's what it says…'

RCN handed Mawgan the review but the kid wasn't interested. Mawg got up from the Master's chair without acknowledging the nurse, pulled down his cardigan sleeves and gazed out onto the rose garden. Expressionless and blank, he picked out a small, plastic watering can from a selection on an overcrowded shelf and wandered through to the sun room.

'The crows are all over the dahlias again…'

Mawgan slid open the door and stepped out onto the dew-soaked lawn. Before him, not the rockeries and canna sheds, Robert's bonfire and Endy's washing-line, but a vast auditorium of life. The grass shimmered beneath his feet as Mawg lifted his head to look out above the trees to a place beyond the sanctuary where he felt something else might exist, a kind of 'good' place somewhere up there, maybe influencing bad places. A control zone that sort of 'sat right' and felt right, evened things out and felt good. In this good, green wood everything you tried to get to work actually worked; success waited around every corner, reward around every bend. Everything and everyone, every worm and every bluebell, had 'flow'. Everything really was… well, shipshape. As Endy always said things ought to be.

Just a few feet ahead of Mawgan's warm toes was the edge of the world and Mawgan stepped off it. In this new reachable zone things immediately felt better and more resolved. It looked nice for a start. There were lush flower meadows of seagrass and chamomile. The drill of pigeons and blackcaps made him feel at home. Japanese kamikaze pilots rained from the sky like floating chrysanthemums as Mawgan slid along on a battery pack powered by chicken shit and came upon an iron gate where a shingle path led visitors to a garden centre, a real one, wedged between the headland and the tape head. The reception area was not the customary car bay with storage tubs for fertiliser and swings for the kids, but rather a bay of blue-green pasture scattered with brush heads of valerian ready to explode and seed the meadows with deliriously happy seeds. Beyond that, a wide transept of stained glass – cockle white, storm red, eclipse yellow – set against a bank of orange crushed velvet, *Terry's Orange Gold*. Always good to have a sponsor for life, he thought, as he kicked off his sandals and dipped his toe into a dense floral sea of mayweed and mesembryanthemums – or sand daisies, Robert Kemp's favourite B&Q value filler.

Then a decision. Up ahead, a fork in the road, connecting this reachable 'seen' world to the unseen. To the right... Carnaby Street, to the left... Carn Point. Along that right-hand path, the most 'happening' path that ever existed, a number of ship-wrecks, lives lost in submerged reefs, washed up in the narrow zawns and clefts between fast-wind and rewind. John Speedy Keen, 21 March 2002. Lisbett Ann Nightly, 9 December 1967. The boy pressed *PLAY*, took the left-hand track, as he always would, and came upon an ancient way-mark, engraved on granite, that once read *5 miles*. Weathered over the years, and with part of the numeral 5 having been eroded, it now announced that he had come upon a place called *Smiles*. Which was true.

Another familiar sight, the old branch-line track, and a signpost pointing towards the parish of Morvah ('sea grave'). *Keep to the Paths*, it said, *Keep to the Paths*. 'Keep to the paths,' he murmured as he carried on not keeping to the paths. Now the world became entirely more familiar. All around him a recharged ocean, no heaviness at all, no lives lost, only happy seed explosions and maypole smiles. If all was silent before, now there was sound. Pye full spectrum, f4 waveband. The kid could just about make out the yelps of surfers echoing around the Shepperton tank, basking in the gas, the groove, the pure fix of summer. Fistral Beach regulars expecting another wave, another burst, another cave-in. Fragrant musk from the Santa Rosa floribunda ('Stanwell Perpetual'), blush-pink and fading to white, wafted like incense through the halting places and waiting rooms of these swinging, swaying worlds, these pendulum worlds. Up ahead there was a farmhouse, hanging like a bauble on John Wesley's tree, suspended right in front of the kid's nose; a picture postcard, with smoky edges, like those Victorian photo-cards in St John's Hall, Penzance. In flickering black-and-white cinemascope a door opened and a little girl holding on to her sun bonnet for dear life ran into the yard to put out nightjars for wasps and slugs.

Further on, woodruff and field madder (lady's bedstraw) smelling of new-mown hay, phased in and out, twin-tracked, twin-necked, diode-connected, guiding him, guarding him, encouraging him further, leading him on. Spores of dandelion and daystar danced before the dude along the lazy, hazy, crazy coastal path of summer, no longer sand and pebbledash but crazy-paved, the whole vista, the whole awning, now become visionary and transcendental, perpetual and evergreen in the powdery summer afternoon.

In this particular seaside postcard it would always be a sunny day, 'delightfully situated', like the holiday homes in Johnson's estate agents in Saint Ives or the tinners' cottages at Black Cliff in the classic John Hinde postcards of West Country coastal resorts. Many smiles came his way, beamed their beams towards Mawg, regarding him, rewarding him, thinking about him, until a shallow breeze lifted the seedheads of the dandelions into the air and into the wind, over the cliffs and into the ocean deep. The 'lantic sea. Into the sunshine.

The kid walked a little further and came to a final clearing and a glade. There was a cappuccino pond stuffed with tape grass and frog-bit (water soldier), the reeds suspended in the water, three-petalled, male and female on separate plants, flowers white, a shy flowerer.

It became time to say goodbye… *Goodbye*… and then something brushed past him, something or someone, passed by from day into night, something warm and tender, well-meaning, innocent, kamikaze; with his honour intact. A vagrant comet indeed, spirit wind, someone definitely in the ascendant. A 'knowledge' man, like John Snr or Jani or Alexander Telstar – for it was he – cascading in and out. A life-giver, Jesus-lover, whose motion with the firmament most certainly agreed, a brush with… a kind of universal truth, via the dude's diminishing understanding and acceptance of his own infatuated, geocentric world.

6 April 1945. That was the date, the date of the highest number of kamikaze pilots killed in action in one single sunny afternoon during WW2. The Battle of Okinawa, *Operation Kikusai*. The young men who went to their deaths were referred to as *kikusai* (floating chrysanthemums) by their life-takers and their undertakers. Stick to the rules. Stick to the rules, they said. Don't look down… And they didn't; they looked up, like John and Justin had done so many times at Cambridge Botanical Gardens. *Beware the cliff edge. Do not wander up onto the coast path after dark. Follow the Acorn route. Keep children supervised.*

BANG!

A gull flew straight into the BT line behind him, cut itself in half and brought down the cable as both bits of the bird, nicely singed at each end, tumbled out of the sky. Kamikaze. No other explanation for it. Except bird flu, LSD maybe, or general Blair-world. Unless it was the fault, like everything else round here, of Penwith District Council.

'I put the black plastic bags out but it don't scare 'em anymore…' RCN put the kettle on and searched for teabags. Mawg turned back and acknowledged his old and good, his most-treasured friend.

'I have to go and do the watering now.'

John Nightly died peacefully in his room sometime during the late afternoon of 1 July 2007, just fourteen days before his fifty-ninth birthday. John was found by his old and good friend RCN after failing to come in to get his 5pm kick-start coffee, as he had done every teatime for the past 9,205 teatimes.

After the dramatic though in some ways quite fitting deaths of many of his fellow travellers, John Nightly's was a most unviolent, unglamorous passing. An almost embarrassingly *normal* way to go.

John hadn't bothered to lay on anything special, like Pondy, Myra, Donna and the others. The conjuror had abandoned his tricks, literally 'passing over' in the euphemistic condolence of coffee-morning volunteers and Methodist lay-preachers. No story value in that. No PR buzz, no 'tragic passing' local freesheet headlines.

The end of the end, as far as it went, was unremarkable in terms of column inches that might be used to maximise posthumous record sales. No use at all in terms of a fitting rock'n'roll end, double-clicked, copied and pasted before being alphabetically listed as a stop-press departure on death-watch weblogs.

These acute and admittedly hard-edged practicals were the first thoughts that passed through John Nightly's keeper's mind. RCN was shocked, very shocked, but not surprised. In a way, he'd been waiting for this day a long time; maybe not 'waiting' exactly, but sort of expecting it, wondering what would happen when it did finally arrive. Suddenly, the nurse needed to think clearly and focus on the scene before him. Time stopped temporarily in the small back bedroom, it's climate more suited to force-fed triffids than to a prematurely aged, fifty-eight-year-old single male. RCN drew back a curtain and opened the steamed-up window in order to un-stick the air.

In terms of 'mechanical' practicals, the Master's limbs seemed set within an awkward compass, his left arm locked at a hard

90-degree turn, his right, bent like supple willow, carefully folded around his summer-weight duvet. One of those classic, exhibit-like positions in which the subject could only be, well… dead, unfortunately.

On the flower-patterned quilt beside him lay the master's cheap reading-glasses – four-quid Specsavers specials – a half-empty tumbler of whiskey, a marker-pen for marking, a highlighter for highlighting and a copy of the local gazette, John's absolute favourite read, open at the weekly classifieds: *Garden Furniture, Bric-a-Brac, Tools.*

So there he lay, the real boss… only Master and Teacher. Slumped in this most uncomfortable of poses. It occurred to RCN that his old friend might have been trying to get off the bed, maybe grasping for something, mid-position or halfway through a quite-desperate motion, perhaps, when the moment of absolution came upon him.

Maybe John Nightly had suffered some kind of minor heart attack or stroke. Reaching out, possibly for the first (and last) time in his life, for something or someone… attempting to lift himself up in the midst of being struck down. RCN considered that John must have felt very ill indeed to even think about asking anyone else for help. Although the Master's expression, such as it was – a placid, empty face – was utterly calm. And that's what RCN was fixed on, John Nightly's facial appearance. Wanting to be absolutely sure that his old friend had not suffered, as so many do, when death comes unexpectedly and there is simply no one there.

In these situations, it is tempting for those who are left behind to imagine the exact circumstances of their loved one's passing. There may have been a few seconds, minutes even, of unease, struggle. An intense few moments that the remaining loved ones hope and wish had never existed, but can't help wondering about. The bit of life they never saw. That part of the mystery, maybe the only part, of someone's existence that could never be known to another.

Bizarre really, because the Master's twisted mouth and permanent frown, the deep single furrow or 'zawn' above his brow, were gone; vanished without trace – like their host. The stress, all the weight of living, of being this bloody difficult, impossible-to-deal-with individual, this character, this intense, geocentric persona, had miraculously disappeared from his face, the boy's face. Now, John Nightly was dead *and* calm. Now he was simply human again. Calmer in death, much calmer (apart from this crooked, bony old arm), as far as RCN could see, than he had ever been, or his friend had ever known him to be, in life.

The nurse stood a while. Lingered in a kind of timeless surveillance over his boss. Stood and stared. Wanting to take just a moment, a little time for himself, before going in to tell the others what had occurred. The remaining John most definitely needing a few moments to consider, and assess, exactly what the new situation might be. There would be some cobbling together certainly. A story... something.

But first RCN wanted to think a little about his old friend. Just for a moment or two. Not to 'say goodbye' or any low-grade cliché like that. How can you say goodbye to someone who isn't bloody there? Someone who's just bloody well gone and left you without bothering to say goodbye themselves? That was the nurse's very first thought. What came into his head right there and then? Together with his initial overall emotion; anger.

Selfish as it may sound, unqualified anger is often one of the first reactions following a death. Particularly when someone very close has just disappeared into thin air, popped off for good, in the middle of the night. Like a schoolgirl elopement, teenage runaway, or a bullied child unable to face it any longer.

But also, RCN wanted to remember.

Daly, only half-awake himself after a troublesome night with his poor old back, bent down and touched his friend lightly on the shoulder in a most affectionate way. Something he would never have done had John Nightly still breathed. He lay his hand on, then suddenly, and completely unexpectedly, uneven breathing and sobbing began to overtake him, before – taken unawares by his own unguarded emotions, and worried that Mawg or Endy might wonder where the both of them were – the nurse stifled his tears, cleared his throat and swallowed. Holding back, like a good Englishman, in case emotion might get the better of him. Lest he might show his imperfection, his common humanity.

RCN perched on the corner of the bed and examined John's position thinking he might do something to try to correct it.

Better he do that, he thought, one who knew the deceased – and technically qualified, after all – than some young apprentice in Penzance; the 'laying-out' guy, undertaker's mate, who didn't know John Nightly, wouldn't have had the faintest idea who he was, who he had been, and what he had managed to achieve in his reasonably short existence.

The laying-out guy might therefore not operate at the very top of his game. Might not move the boss with the required degree of respect, the correct amount of loving care and attention, bearing in mind the achievements of the dead person in his arms – the jargonised *TLC*, as everyone, even Endy, called it now.

RCN imagined the trainee wanting to get away of an evening, get off early, rushing to meet his girl, get to the pub, watch a match, then take her to his bed, to the pub car park or outside toilets, the usual place for a quickie, followed by a kebab on the way home.

These were the thoughts that might end up rushing through the mind of the young apprentice as he lay his black-gloved hands on the boss. The remaining John didn't like those thoughts. Considered they might be… completely inappropriate and therefore decided to change things around a little so as to minimise the actual laying-out process for the presumably preoccupied apprentice.

RCN leaned over and lifted his friend's arm. Gently, carefully, using both hands, stretching it out, correcting this most awkward of positions, making the boss a good deal more comfortable than before, he imagined. He picked up John's specs and laid them to the side.

There was the boss's watch, a Rolex *Antibes*, one of the very few possessions he'd kept from the old days, the strap entwined with the piece of braided string that the Master wore around his wrist. A leftover from the heady days of gurus and philosophers. Days of belief. In the old days the string would have been a fine orange braid; maybe it glistened with gold thread or flax. Now it was just twine, a length of gardening or tying string that John would fiddle with when daydreaming, or while taking his coffee and biscuits, shooting the breeze for a while at Endy's impressive kitchen table.

More thoughts came, and suddenly events seemed to be gathering... rushing, swirling. He and the house itself seemed in a rush, in a spin, as if, well... As if he'd done something wrong in some way. A rush of guilt, maybe, although he definitely hadn't, wasn't, did not... RCN was absolutely certain he had not transgressed in any way whatsoever. Had he? Certainly not in terms of anything to do with the boss. Only right things. Only right things for John Nightly. All the way along. All the way down. All his bloody life. RCN was positive he'd seen right by his friend, his good and brilliant friend. Done his very best in every mechanical, managerial, facilitatingly practical, and yes, 'emotional' way possible.

Arranging things only for the good of Nightly. Not anyone else. And certainly not for himself. That had most definitely always been the case. So... no guilt then, and therefore, suddenly... once again, all was calm.

RCN was certain and could take comfort in the fact that he had done his duty, what he'd been paid to do, both on and off the pitch; and, to be honest, he had made a very good living and gotten a great deal of satisfaction from the job entrusted to him.

The nurse quickly snapped himself out of it, rubbed his forehead hard, looked around, and made to go and tell... well, who exactly was there to tell... when you came to think about it... first?

Endy? Robert? Mawg? None were really close, were they? Not now. When it boiled down to it. Or really... well, 'connected' to either himself or the Master, in any way at all.

The fact was that the two Johns, old anorak guys, as they

existed up to then, hadn't… didn't actually have… any friends. If we were being honest. And we might as well all be honest now.

The fact that this huge, this whole huge, messy whole, huge old thing, Trewin Farm, Trewin Exotics, whatever the hell you wanted to call it, this whole caboodle of make-believe, with its cavalcade of freaks and flora, this ludicrous, ridiculous assembly, was nothing more than… well… a fake. In so many ways. Business arrangement, really. A very formal, very professional, very profitable and now increasingly efficient – even a little too slick at times, he thought – business arrangement. A damned good business arrangement as it turned out. As of course the assembled cast must all recognise.

Sounded a little bleak maybe… putting it like that. Bleaker than usual, anyway. But the fact of the matter was that RCN definitely must look on the bleak side now. Being the only person in charge, only decision-maker, after all.

Then, as he heard Alexandre loping along the corridor, and Endy's clock radio come on in the kitchen, it suddenly dawned on him… what, with John Nightly gone, these people had no connection at all with either himself or each other anymore. When it boiled down to it. They were all workers. Employees. *Service-people.* That's what RCN thought, and that's why he had something of a mild turn himself, and became confused, coming over slightly dizzy all of a sudden. Most likely a bit of delayed shock; that's all it was. Though he was pleased to sit down and rest for a moment on the corner of the bed beside his old friend.

Both John Daly and the residents of the white farm would have to rethink everything now. That was certain. Things would change. No doubt about it. They'd change immediately. For as soon as he turned and walked out of the room there would be no 'day to day', no 'regularity' anymore. No one in the background to kow-tow to. No Mr Dick to foil Betsey Trotwood. No one at all to, in a way – in a weird way – keep the thing together

– the whole thing – rocking and rolling along the bumpy coastal plains.

John just hoped it wouldn't be chaos. Didn't think it would. But you never know with unexpected and unplanned situations, do you? Then it suddenly occurred to him... Iona... Oh, Christ! He would have to tell Iona right away. She was the connected one. One hell of a phone call to have to make. A call he had hoped would never have to be made. And, of course, well... it would immediately give her the excuse, the one she'd waited so long for, to actually step inside the compound. Trespass. Check out the crazies. See where and how her husband had lived, and now died, and ask herself why he never wanted his wife anywhere near him, his fellow travellers, or his place of residence.

Because now, with John gone, there was no longer any excuse, no reason whatsoever why this beautiful woman – the only real, 'legitimate' member of the family, at the end of the day – shouldn't visit. The wife... surely the wife had a claim? A right to at least put in an appearance?

RCN began to think through the true practicals. Horrible ones at that. The death notice, music-magazine announcements, the dreaded funeral and the arrangements associated with it. Sandwiches and stuff. The 'going back' after. Burial/cremation, what was it they'd decided on? He thought he remembered cremation being talked about. Couldn't be sure of anything at the moment. And the obituaries, of course. There would be some – sympathetic he hoped; and accurate in terms of the Master's contribution. But, whether good or bad, obituaries tended to seal you up, fix you, before being filed away for future reference by rock'n'roll history men. The very last 'last word', as it were.

The true practicals were certainly hard to bear. The residents would no doubt find it hard. It wouldn't be just, well... that the Master was dead, or even that someone, an individual, had passed on. But that the 'weirdo' had died, to the outside world, at least: to the fish man, bread man, the fresh-fruit people, vitamin man, people up in London, the undertaker, and his apprentice. And to the inside world… as if… some kind of neat way of living – paradise, in a way – was coming, had come, to an end.

Abruptly. Demi-paradise at least. Still a pretty good sort of paradise he reasoned, as he wiped away a last tear and looked around for a piece of toilet roll to blew his nose on.

A final arrangement slipped in. The funeral. Now he remembered. RCN had decided long ago that when the time came it really must be as simple as possible. As unfussy and quiet as such an occasion could be. Invisible… if it could be so. Thing was, when he thought about it, although RCN had known the day would arrive, he'd never considered that things might be the other way around; and, although he had tried to get on to the topic several times over the years, his old friend had always headed him off. They were both of them experts at heading off.

'I don't want anything… "death-wise",' the master had said. 'Nothing special! Well, nothing at all really. Don't actually want a funeral… It's not necessary anyway, legally, I don't think – that you have to have it, *do* it. So… you just take me somewhere, with a priest or whatever… Whichever way you want to do it, and… get rid of me.' The Master looked at RCN and smiled. 'You remember the story about Gram Parsons? His manager…' RCN smiled back. 'You can decide it, anyway,' the Master continued, 'but no "publicity" funeral, whatever happens. And no funeral with people you or I haven't seen for thirty years, and definitely no band or anything. *God!*' John Nightly clasped his hands together. 'Or… local tradesmen… business people. No publishers or copyright people either… nothing like that. No *representatives*. And definitely no bloodsucking flower-importers. They'll come anyway… if there's a buck to be had. Christ… makes you think how bad it really could turn out…'

John Nightly had never asked RCN to actually promise anything before now. Never any need to 'promise you'll do this or that'. Whatever his old friend considered necessary… well, that's what RCN was going to do. No need to discuss it any further. RCN would take care of the Master's needs in death as he had done in life, and that was all there was to it.

The nurse sighed and got up from the bed.

But there was a will. Both Johns had seen to that. Done them together, at Johnston & Reed in Penzance. Each witnessing the other's hand. So… things were more or less sorted, in terms of actual 'law of the land' practicals. Even charitable donations had been fixed and allocated. RCN would receive John's shares in the business; Endy, Robert and Mawg would all be okay. John Nightly had seen to that. Seen them right. Well right; of course he had. As of course they knew he would.

RCN would have to turn his attention to what might happen next. Long-term next. The fact that none of them had anywhere to go to, for a start; apart from Mawg. Then with the record about to come out… Bad timing, you might say. Sad that the author, the auteur, wouldn't see the final result after all this work. Sad for the outside world anyway; but then, maybe the author himself wouldn't actually give a damn. John Nightly knew full well that Mawg had done a great job. A wonderful job. Things sounded the way they should. Much better than they ought. However much money they were paying him, it wasn't enough. As the Boss had often told the kid himself.

But there was a lot to do. And so, RCN thought he better go… and bloody well do it. Walk out of that room and get time started again. Press *PLAY* again. Forward-wind somehow. Move it.

He took a last look back at the boss, still thinking about the apprentice and the apprentice's girlfriend and the stuff going on in his head, then leaned over the magicien, brushing the master's hair slightly to the left, roughing it up a little before smoothing it back over to cover his visible bald patch. RCN picked up John Nightly's hands, hands that had created magic and chaos in equal measure, arthritic and yellowy now. He straightened them out and placed them together, fixed them, the left over the right, arranged very naturally, too naturally maybe, as he moved back, careful not to trip over zygocacti and spider plants and bird feed and upset the Master's universe. John Nightly was starting to look like a... Well... a 'horizontal angel'... one of those you see in Westminster Abbey on top of a tomb. RCN couldn't remember the word for it, 'medieval stone knights' or something, with ridiculously detailed carved swords and chains. Anyway, the boss looked a lot better now than he had done a few moments before or for a good thirty years and so RCN drew the curtain closed and walked back down the leafy corridor into the white kitchen in order to relay the news.

The birds were expressive. As much as a squawk or a croak can be. RCN was used to an early-morning outburst somewhere above the house. A high-pitched shriek – literally *Sreeeep! Sreeeep!* – that seemed to go on forever. The nurse listened intently, distracted by the glissando of the wing-ed messenger. Was there a pattern to it? A message? Or was it a warning, a panic call?

The noise waned as the caller lost interest or achieved his aim, noted that his warning had been heeded. *Beware! Beware!* Sparrowhawks are coming. Maybe already here. *Beware! Beware!* The bird crowed to his brothers and sisters… *Sreeeep! Sreeeep!*

'Don't feed the sparrowhawks, whatever you do. You'll never get rid of them!' cried Endy. But RCN was more philosophical.

'They hide up there and wait for the smaller birds to fly in. It all goes quiet… There's no breeze; it's as if the wind stops for them. We used to sit and watch it happen. The wind accommodates those birds… not the other way round. No bleating or shrieks anymore… no bird or tree noise at all. Those sparrowhawks are concentrated. Then a pause… literally no sound… nothing. Me and John look at each other. What's going on? All is silent. All is just expectation.' RCN put his hands around his cup to warm them. 'Like the intro to 'Gimme Shelter': forty-one seconds of the most… the greatest seduction – as he would've put it – on record.'

The anorak man, pleased with his comparison and his posh words, took a sip from his cup and became even more excited about telling his story. 'All that incredible view. We're looking out beyond the bay. The sun beats down so strong you can hardly look up…'

RCN shook his head and brushed a heap of dandruff from his jacket. 'Then nothing… nothing at all. Everything still as a post. The world – or our little bit of it – stops. You forget about everything. Forget that you're waiting even. Then

BANG!

There's a sound... high up... very high. Slash... like a... a kamikaze cut. Slash through thick air...' He laughed. 'All hell breaks loose... a mass of birds, clouds of 'em... Crow flies out of one of the cypresses... you wait another second... or two... and a very beautiful, very dead, sparrowhawk falls to the ground.'

'It is bliss consciousness that makes a man rise to Universal Love. Life is all bliss.'

Maharishi Mahesh Yogi, 14 October 1969.
BBC Radio 4. Talking to Leslie Smith

Trewin House, Porthcreek, Cornwall. Thursday, 12 July 2007.
'Did you say Tregidden? There used to be a little Christian
Bible Chapel up there.'

The housekeeper finished rinsing the last breakfast plate.

'There was one at Zoar too. They had the *John Wesley school
rooms* at Zoar.' Endy glanced at Mawgan as he idled in the
entrance to the larder while flipping through a magazine.

'What I'm talking about is what you would call a… "pop
singer", Endy.'

'I gathered that, Mawgan. You're always talking about a pop
singer. *Pop-yowlers*, they used call them in my day.' The housekeeper wiped the sink enthusiastically.

'When exactly was "your day", though? If you don't mind me
asking.' Endy looked a little taken aback at her friend's
uncalled-for cheek.

'I had my day, Mawgan, I can tell you. I had a lot of days…
Not just one.' The boy half-smiled back.

'This particular… "pop singer", though… He was a special
one.' Mawg closed his copy of *MOJO*. 'Gram Parsons, Gram –
probably Graham – was his name, a sort of… country singer,
Country & Western, I mean. You like a bit of country music?'
The housekeeper carried on with her tasks. 'And Tregidden
was the place he stayed when he came to England.'

'Not a Cornish name, that,' said Endy, dismissive as ever. 'And
Tregidden? Whatever did he want to go up there for? There's
nothing up there… except for this chapel and…'

'He was in… eh… a bit of a state. That's why.' Mawg stepped
back into the kitchen. 'Maybe… a hell of a bit of a state…'

Julian stood in front of the kitchen window admiring himself while finger-combing his hair.

'As if I couldn't guess what sort of "bit of state" that man was in...' Endy wrung out her cloth and turned to the two boys, ready to be of service – put the kettle on, pour some juice or make a cheese sandwich. Anything to please him and them. Keep the boys happy and content, and of course healthy, while keeping her own mind occupied.

'He'd been... well... he was friendly with... the Rolling Stones...'

'Rolling Stones? Don't mention them to me, Mawgan... I'd get them to roll... If I ever came across them I would. Why, they've never—' *'Never done a day's work in their lives!'* chorused both boys before collapsing in laughter. A momentary break of cloud in an otherwise overcast day. The housekeeper remained in cantankerous mode as she finished up.

'Here we go...' murmured Julian, to the duded-up kid, maintaining respect for the pensioner while at the same time motioning behind her back as if to go, get outta there and get on with it; as Mawgan tucked in his shirt, combed his hair with his fingers, tightened his new black tie and investigated Endy's shoe-polishing box.'

Four days later…

Mawg threw the pieces up in the air. He did so rather over-enthusiastically and the paper landed mainly in Endy's washing-up, bringing mock huffs and puffs from the housekeeper as Julian picked out a square of foolscap lodged in her hairnet.

'There you go, Endy… might be an important word, that…'

'I don't know what you two are up to, but I know I don't want it in my washing-up!'

The words floated through the kitchen, coming to rest in plant pots, the dog's bowl, on top of the breadbin and inside the toaster. Any promising conjunctions or patterns? Any wisdom? Any hymn?

Mawgan stared down at the floor, presiding over a promising clump, while Jules laughed his head off at Endy's apparent disgust. In the living room, RCN and Robert no doubt wondered what all the fuss was about. It was good to hear laughter, that much laughter, just days after the funeral.

The kid turned to the dude. 'Got one!' he cried, as he fixed on a group of five or six squares. 'Got anything?'

Julian angled his head this way and that, accommodating upside-down glyphs and torn syllables to see if anything might actually fit. Mawg went first.

'Lemon… Scarecrow… Approximately…'

'Lemon scarecrow… Okay, staggering! Staggering, man!' Jules was not impressed. 'I can definitely better you there, Mawg.' Jules turned his head back. 'So…

Hazard… Mongoose… Mongoose… Bis… uh… cuit…'

'Mongoose, mongoose, biscuit?' Mawg moved over to his friend's side of the kitchen. 'How come there's two mongooses? Only supposed to be one of each word?'

But Jules was resigned. 'That's right,' he said, nodding his head in agreement with himself. Thing is, it doesn't really work. Not really. 'Cause the way things are now, *in the world today*, everything sounds, sort of... *alright* somehow anyway; everythin's sweet.' The dude moved to another patch. 'There ain't no "random" anymore, man...' He bent down.

'Heaven... Bent... Sideways... See! Everything – just about everything – makes sense.'

'Don't be daft, Jules.' Mawg took another bite of toast, crunching into the peanut butter as Jules picked up his sweater, willing to give the game one final shot before heading to the beach.

'Now *this* is quite nice...'

Jules gazed down at three squares that had arranged themselves in a bracelet on the flagstones. He pivoted and swivelled on his hips so as to be able to read all three at once. Outside, a curtain of mist appeared to have descended almost unnoticeably. The rose garden seeming to glow in the sudden imposed goldness. Black crows squawked as if they knew something; and a strange lull, a kind of dead stop, a restraint, came over the house.

'Wave... Orange...'

Mawg froze as if struck by lightning – 'What y' say?' – while Jules, fixed in this anglepoise arrangement, repeated more slowly...

'Wave... Orange...'

'LOVE...' Mawg completed the trio in a soft tremolando without daring to turn round and face his friend.

'How'd you know that?' The dude turned back towards the kid, then bent down again to check the words.

'Wave... Orange... Love"

That's what it says, "Wave Orange Love". Jules cast round for his bag and his board. 'Not bad, that...' he murmured, as he turned to go.

'There is a new song, too complex to get all of first time around. Poetic, beautiful even in its obscurity, "Surf's Up" is one aspect of new things happening in pop music today. As such, it is a symbol of the change many of these young musicians see in our future.'

Leonard Bernstein, November 1966.
CBS News Special, 'Inside Pop – The Rock Revolution'.

Canvass the town and brush the backdrop
Are you sleeping, brother John?

'Surf's Up', The Beach Boys, 1966/'71.
(Brother/Reprise RS-6453)

'English Nature. That's what it was!'

item: The Rural Stations Project, History/Activities: 1955–2006.
The Rural Stations Project, an initiative to improve the appearance of railway stations throughout the United Kingdom, was born out of Scope, the organisation for people with learning difficulties, and the creation of the Conservation Corps way back in the 1950s. The idea being to involve volunteers in practical conservation work by planting trees and shrubs and also by supplying much-needed aftercare. The first ever Conservation Corps project was held in 1966 at Box Hill in Surrey when 42 volunteers, including the naturalist David Bellamy, cleared dogwood to encourage the growth of juniper and the area's distinctive chalkland flora.

In 1970, the Conservation Corps changed its name to the British Trust for Conservation Volunteers (BTCV) and the new name and new logo was launched to coincide with HRH the Duke of Edinburgh becoming patron. In the '90s the organisation began other initiatives such as the first Woodland Action Week, with broadcaster David Jacobs planting the Trust's second-millionth tree at Two Storm Wood in Richmond Park, Surrey and the group running its first National Pond Campaign. BTCV also joined forces with Dr William Bird of Sonning Common Health Centre in Berkshire to introduce their Green Gym project. Other related initiatives include the Community Railways Scheme, the Riviera Project and Sustrans.

Scope is currently using gardeners with learning difficulties on a pan-Cornwall venture to supply hanging baskets, planters and seats to mainline stations from Penzance to Gunnislake as well as some of the branch lines. The Riviera Project was commissioned as a major study by the Rail Forum with a brief to formulate a framework for the regeneration of Cornwall's railway stations, and Sustrans, the sustainable transport charity which complements bus infrastructure improvements such as the much-talked-about Corlink service between Bodmin and Padstow which has branded buses, real-time information boards and links to demand-responsive services. Cornwall became the first county to be selected as a Centre of Excellence for integrated rural transport in March 2001 after demonstrating its ability to address issues of rural travel in an innovative way.

Getting around – being able to move easily between the inland, agricultural B-roads jammed in the summer by coach tours and container vans and the wide coastal plains with their little buses and branch lines – remains an ongoing problem for the people of Cornwall.

So English Nature was what had done it. Put the idea into John Nightly's head. A new oak bench replacing one put there in 1947 in memory of the village's war dead had appeared on the platform at Porthcreek. Paid for by English Nature, the plaque announced that it was part of the new *Rural Stations Project.*

Not a 'legacy' exactly, but something the boss had mentioned more than once. On the rare times the Johns had occasion to visit one of the bracelet chain of stations along the branch line – to collect a shipment of plant feed or to recover lost mail – they would often be shocked by what greeted them. These once well-maintained stopping points appeared desolate and forgotten. Barren outposts of brick and mortar. Closed ticket offices and cold platforms welcomed the uninitiated day-tripper. But little do most passengers realise that once they brave the unwelcoming climate of the stations themselves they can look forward to travelling across some of the country's most beautiful coastal routes, as Brunel's broad-gauge track starts off in a deep cutting at Trenile then hugs the cliff edge all the way to Zawn Point.

At Whitesand, station platforms and outbuildings that had previously felt the touch of loving hands seemed now to have been vandalised not only by successive governments but also by local schoolchildren left abandoned in the cold on their way home to isolated farmhouses.

The rafters of the wayside chapel at Corncrake, once hung with wreaths and banners, were now painted over with several coats of unsuccessful colour and lay shrouded in creeper and vine. The flowerbeds at Kingsand were trampled flat. At Lantern Bay, two stations up – with the advantage of the first sight of the ocean – the small waiting-room had been closed since 1980, while at Trenile itself, once grateful recipient of all freight in and out of the Trenile Clay Mine* a scrap-metal yard and car-crusher were the first sights to greet visitors after the locomotive turned the bend into the station.

Waiting at these lonely halts, rail commuters must have bemoaned the lack of planting and floral colour on the railway banks of England's most outstanding coastal route. Further up, the branch-line stops of St Day and Gull Rock had managed to survive the Beeching Report of the 1960s and the holiday-makers of every long, hot summer since but not local vandals or the Strategic Rail Authority. The St Day ticket-office stood covered in graffiti while Japanese knapweed continued its colonisation of the once-prizewinning flowerbeds and of Cornwall in general.

And so, on the morning of Friday, 1 July 2008, the anniversary of John Nightly's passing, three lorryloads of cannas and hostas, strelitzias and geraniums, with a back-up of architectural, fast-growing echium and boxes of Mrs Peed's favourite wildflowers, were lifted onto the platform at Porthcreek.

Packed and crated at Trewin during heart-attack-inducing heat the previous evening, the specimen-quality plants waited patiently as RCN, Robert, Endy, Mawg, Jules and Karen, with the help of two volunteers from the Rural Stations Scheme and a St Eina churchwarden, began planting the things so densely that just one month later each stopping point erupted in a swirl of crazy-colour, its Day-Glo effect so intense that it threatened to dazzle and possibly derail each unsuspecting train driver arriving there.

* On 26 July 1966, the Cornish China Clay Industry received the Queen's Award for Industry.

item: The *Cornishman*. 9 September 2008 (Chrysanthemum Day in Japan)

'Branch Lines Go Psychedelic!'
Stations along the Trenile branch line have benefitted from a gift contained in the will of sixties pop legend John Nightly, who lived for many years at Porthcreek until his recent death. Lorries carrying expensive exotics rolled up at 6am last Tuesday morning as part of an initiative by Scope, the association for people with learning difficulties. A group of volunteers planted beds along the branch-line route.

A spokesperson for the Strategic Rail Authority commented that it would do what it could to maintain the plants but the amount of watering needed, particularly with the recent impositions of hosepipe bans in the county, 'might prove a big job'.
Jon Speedwell, 'Man About Cornwall'.

'Faster than witches' it wasn't. Robert Louis Stevenson got that completely wrong.

As the Riviera Sleeper shunted its way through Liskeard, Bodmin, Lostwithiel and Par, the boy, unable to take the air-con any longer, was out of his cabin and slumped in the window of the deserted buffet car. Facing forward on the sunny side, feet up on the seat opposite, head full of last night's free bar, he attempted consciousness in order to consider his situation.

Mawgan was deeply in love. With Karen – and with Cornwall. Entranced by the wild, restless nature of this mysterious county and the wild, restless nature of its natives. As the train climbed the hilly ground, lifting its passengers high above the green pasture, the mass of detail in every lobelia plot, the red-painted paddle boats tied to each jetty, the assembly of birds picking over every tilled field, he imagined daily life in the settlements below; the reality that might lie along those dusty tracks strobing in and out of view behind railway banks.

The diesel picked up speed over the Liskeard valley, steam rising from the pampas below, rhododendron and claxus pines glistening in the perfectly horizontal light. The patchwork of radial fields at Lostwithiel, the town with the most beautiful name in England – literally 'lost forest' – reminded him of his mother's patched jeans. This now-insignificant stop was once the busiest port in the South West, an exporter of tin and wool, boasting its own tannery and creamery, until the river silted up and the village died, to be reborn 100 years later as a 'must-visit' for antique-hunters and tripadvisors. Nowadays, Lostwithiel is mainly known as the connection for branch lines taking surfers to Newquay and walkers to the Looe valley.

Mawgan slumped further in his seat. Cottages with a pony and bathtub keeping each other company in the yard were dotted about the line from St Austell to Truro, the final stretch of the journey. Their gardens pruned to buggery by gardeners with nothing better to do. Plots cultivated by leaseholders who watch for new growth each day. Further up, valleys of sheep and cattle. They seemed happy enough at six in the morning, grazing with their offspring beside the old Great Western tracks.

A few miles further still and sunlight. The hard glare of a new summer. Mawgan had been well educated by the plant-hunters of Trewin. Before coming to the South West he would have been pressed to name much more than the common daffodil. Now, both the proper Latin forms and Endy's old wives' alternatives tripped off his tongue. 'There's Aeschynanthus,' he'd say – or in Endy's terms 'lipstick vine' – casually dropping it into a conversation with Robert. 'Didn't we ought to cut that verbena down… ?' Though Mawgan had never yet been motivated to cut anything down himself. But the family at Trewin was tight-knit. It was a batch, a group – a genuine band of persons, not just humans – with a common group personality. Or at least it had been, up to just a few months back.

Now of course, things would never be like that again. Nothing would. Everyone understood that. Though the vegetation would die off and regenerate, the inhabitants of Trewin weren't quite so sure about themselves. The business of growing exotics was now as much of a local fixture as the quarries and the pits had been. And the tin mines, the Methodist chapels, the hidden coves, the low clouds and hanging mists, the sparrowhawks, the ants, the winding lanes and trails, the constant cacophonous but somehow comforting bleat of the gulls… And the magical promise of the coast path.

The wild west. Wild West indeed. The wild west had been invaded. By nannies and the nanny state. The upside being that every area of land worth exploring was 'protected', an Environmentally Sensitive Area (ESA) or a Site of Special Scientific Interest (SSSI), if the planning authorities wanted to take notice. If they didn't, there'd be a Jetstar garage or a Tesco/Sainsbury's/M&S sitting where wildflower meadows, grazing land and bird settlements used to be. At this particular moment Trewin Farm ought to have been designated a Psychologically Very Sensitive Area (PVSA). Because of what had occurred. At the moment, he wasn't even sure if the white farm really existed. Or if it ever had. The kid didn't know anything about anything. No one did. Nothing definite.

Mawg picked up last night's paper. The area surrounding Penwith and Kerrier was in the news again. Its fragile ecology under pressure because of the impact of holidaymakers, caravanners, developers, local planners, county planners, local councils, county councils, local government, national government, even the environmentalists themselves. Mawg tossed the thing onto the seat opposite. He didn't get it. Didn't at all realise the consequences of recent events. What had just happened to him – to all of them. But he knew one thing about it, about Cornwall. He knew that he would never leave.

Obituary: Jana Feather-Areia. Died 14 February 2004, aged 56.
Jana Valerie Feather was born in Cambridge, England, on 18 June 1948, and attended the St Mary's Girls school in the town. In 1966 she won a scholarship to Girton College, where she read her Architecture and Fine Arts Tripos, resulting in her Master of Arts degree and diploma in Architecture. In 1970, at Clare Hall, she prepared her PhD thesis on planning and urban design in Central America, going on to become a leading expert on sustainable methods applied to public buildings, and also on recyclable power. She married the Chilean musician Juan Carlos Areia and lived with him in Santiago before moving back to England and Cambridge in 1988, where she lectured at the School of Architecture until her death. Dr Feather was also lecturer in Architecture at the Open University. In 1996 she became UK chairman of ECHO, the international action group for research into tidal changes and their consequences. Her father was the distinguished educator and musician Dr Janislav 'Jani' Feather; her mother the celebrated cellist Valerie Gyorsarev. In later years Jana Feather-Areia specialised in the design of acoustically humanised buildings, her memorials being the concert hall at Rialka, Chile, the Bashawitz Temple Auditorium, Houston, Texas, and the Santa Rocha Center for the Performing Arts in Caracas. She was a trustee of the Sandz Museum until 2000 when she first became ill.

Waterstone's bookshop, Charing Cross Road, London WC2. 24 August 1994. Iona St John Firmin reads from her memoir, *Iona & Friends*.

The day I met John he was the heavenly person I had ever set my eye on. John was out-of-this-world... He was out of the other-world as well! [laughs nervously] He did not know what... day it was. He was charming... in his fresh-pressed suit and scarf, which was copied by all the fashion designers and really became a big 'style'... for Swinging London, as they said – although we never did that, behaved like Swinging London. [laughs] we never knew it was there... we were wrapped up in ourselves, in those days – and those 'old time' manners which had been put into him by Frieda, his mother Frieda, a beautiful woman, physically... exquisite... Because of her, he had this sand-blond hair and a little, little bit... Norwegian speaking... A 'lilt', as they said. Which of course made girls wild and made him, John, literally... irresistible to all the women he met... Sadly, I suppose in a way, that is the case.

[Iona speaks more softly] I think myself lucky to spend these years with John... the years we spend together. He could have anyone he wanted, but... nonetheless at that time... he wanted me. [looks round for her glass]

[In the revised version of the book, commissioned by her publishers to add more spice and 'sex-up' the story, Iona expands on some of John's more personal habits]

My husband was... unusual... in other ways also. When he moved into Queen Square and for the first time lived by himself, I went to the bathroom one morning to see a large pile of folded-up toilet sheet. John had folded each paper he was going to use eight times over before he used it. Carefully folded over, these... piles of paper, waiting to be used. The sides and tops perfectly lined up, and sat neatly on top of each other. I didn't mention this to him. But later on he told me Frieda has insisted he always fold the loo sheet eight times. Eight times for... hygiene reasons, when he used the toilet. His mother was a big influence on John... [picks up the glass of golden liquid]

Ten minutes later:

I said to John... this is the doctor you have to go and see. John looked at the note: 'Dr Sansar Miller, 17 Clitterhouse Crescent, NW2'. I said she will be your... saviour. Because I sure he will be and it was then he went to the macrobiotic diet... which I had already adapted... a long time ago. He went to it in a big style, cutting the carrots up in triangles because in the book it said that carrots... as a vegetable, liked, preferred, to be cut as a triangle, and that of course they might then feel better about themselves and do you more health good... Perhaps they would be healthier for you, if you cut them the way they liked to be cut...

Dr Niels Hansen, Christiania, Copenhagen, Denmark. June 2006.

Situated right in the heart of Copenhagen, Christiania occupies an old army barracks that was squatted when vacated by the military in the early 1970s. The land is owned by the Danish Ministry of Defence. The commune itself standing on the site of a 17th-century fortress constructed to keep out the Swedes. No cars, no tarmac roads, no street lighting and therefore no light pollution. It's possible to see many stars and many star clusters in Christiania.

Niels, an experimental film-star, now town councillor at the commune, is sitting in the smoky fug of the Moonfisher Bar on the main square of the 34 hectares that make up Copenhagen's Freetown. 'Black Sheep from all the Classes Unite' is the motto of the village.

'When John came here in... '72, to kind of... try to... sort out his life, I think it was just to... just get away from England and all the stuff about the accident. But also to try to get him away from the SUMHA rehabilitation.

At first, things went well. Christiania was new then and we hadn't developed the... problems we have to deal with today.

John was writing and composing all the time and had written a new piece of music. It was a gentle piece, a kind of hymn piece; to Iona, there's no doubt.

What they intended was to make a performance of it here at Grey Hall, where Dylan had played. That year, in exchange for agreeing to pay for electricity and water, the Danish government finally conferred on the commune the status of 'social experiment'. It took some of the pressure off us but it also meant that many people were just sitting around getting stoned all the time. I think John began to experience strong feelings of paranoia again, and started to spend more and more time in the... what we call, refer to, as the *pharmacology department* – the hash market.' [Niels opens his smoke box] New Age was actually... new then... and people were coming here to try things. Other ways of... living... of doing.'

Niels put down his soggy joint and peered into the smoke, as if attempting to decrypt or decipher something that might be in there. But in a way... I always thought that John himself was in a kind of a... a kind of downbeat place at that time... personally I mean...

item: 'Star Trends', by Sacha Gomez, GIRL magazine, (Vol. 5, No. 87). 10 November 1967.
Jasmine Sansar Mukti (Dawn Miller). Birthdate: 26 April 1948, Bolton, Lancs.

Born on 26 April, Jasmine is a typical Taurean. Strength of will and obstinacy – look at the eyes in the photograph – and practical knowhow are her zodiacal characteristics. Her natal horoscope shows the moon in Sagittarius, denoting a quickness of mind, and a keen intuitive nature associated with Sagittarians. She is wise, generous with her time, and has a measured sense of self. Jasmine has recently taken the names Sansar ('world') and Mukti ('freedom') as is the custom in India; possibly giving an indication of her wider interests when she leaves her university. In the coming week, Monday and Wednesday are good days for shopping!

14a Down End Road, London SW11. Monday, 18 December 2008.

'Like the thing Leonard Bernstein said about music. On his TV series…for schools, wasn't it?'

Justin had the three decks lined up ready to go. He put on his reading glasses, adjusting them by gently tapping back and forwards along the bridge of his nose, all the time squinting and frowning as though he were twenty years older than his actual age. He double-checked that he had the correct sides of the LPs while at the same time lining up that morning's roll call of pills.

'Me and John watched it one day in America when they were first trying to get him back to… normal health, I suppose. He was such a fan – of Bernstein. Thought he was really "the man" y'know, man. Always managed to get himself out of bed to watch that show.'

Justin shuffled to the sink, pausing momentarily to look out over adjacent rooftops before downing the tabs in one with a tumbler of water. A shared bedsit in the eaves of a terraced house in South London was most definitely not what the guitarist and former stargazer might have been expecting as a final resting place, but he seemed quite chipper.

'John loved the fact that you had, like, the most… "profound" musician in the world, but that he'd always be talking about pop music or… the Pointer Sisters.' He laughed, 'at least at that time anyway, or… Mahavishnu, the sort of… "un-profound" stuff. While realising of course that the whole thing, everything we were doing, stuff that everyone like us… was doing, was actually very profound indeed!' Justin looked to his friend for a response, but none came. 'You remember the programme, don't you?'

RCN nodded, at the same time wondering exactly where they were headed. It was quite an epistle this early in the morning, and he had to be getting on.

'Bernstein was decked out in his Levi's suit. This kind of… profound, or whatever, guy… in jeans and that…' Justin leaned over the amp and switched it on.

'There was the bit where he came on at the end of the series and they did this… Q&A… and the interviewer asked him these stupid questions.' He began to half-heartedly act out the part, putting on a typical 'cinema-trailer' voiceover…

"It's been a truly wonderful series, Maestro, and I should like to ask you this one final question…" The question was something like, *"After all of this teaching, all these weeks spent… analysing… explaining things – educating, Maestro – can you tell us, and I hope this won't sound too simplistic…"* And they cut to Bernstein, who has on this sort of expression – *What the hell's this imbecile on about? And why on earth am I still sitting here?* Bernstein had this fag in a holder… sort of superior… super-clever, supercilious and that…'

Justin moved over to Deck 1 and lined up the needle. 'So the guy says… *"Maestro, let me ask you this…"'* Justin for some reason now fell into a half-Russian, half-Indian accent… ' *"What exactly is music, Maestro? What is it really? And how do you… how can you… really describe it?"* Whatever it was he said… it was or coulda been at least a… a fairly stupid question…'

RCN sniffled and snuffled in his woollen cardi as he nursed his habitual cold, tipped a third lump of sugar into his tea and stirred it once more for luck. He motioned that his friend continue.

'And he says – the interviewer I mean – *"Because when this music – inspiration – comes to you, wherever it comes from, when it does come… can you… tell me… explain to me, what do you try to do with it?"*

'So… Bernstein sort of… looks straight at the guy. Straight *through* him… raises his eyes to the heavens, confirming his true feelings for the human being sitting in front of him.' Justin began to elaborate with his hands. 'That he was… y'know, he was basically a guy who didn't understand a fuckin' thing about anything – you remember this, John?' RCN shifted position on the sofa-bed and picked up the newspaper in anticipation of Justin's imminent concluding of the tale.

'Remember the programme, yeah.'

' *"Do with it?"* says Bernstein, like… becoming even more irritated. *"Yes, do with it,"* says the interviewer, becoming more y'know… confident. *"When inspiration hits, and some music comes to you, what do you do with it?"*

'So, the camera stays on the Maestro, and the Maestro nods, as if to say, Okay, you imbecile, I will actually answer that. *"As little as possible,"* says Bernstein, most definitely looking pleased with his answer, a half-smile coming from his eyes as he takes another drag from his ciggie, coughs then suddenly looks… extremely sick.' At which point, as noted by RCN, Justin appeared to do the same, he stood up straight to get his balance and cleared his throat…

' *"So… in conclusion then, my question is, as I say, after all this… this going through things, all these weeks of explaining to us, teaching, educating' us, Maestro… I ask… What exactly is music? What really is the…"*

' *"Waves of love,"* says the Maestro. *"Waves of love…"* ' Justin paused, swallowed and began to tremble slightly as he repeated the words. ' *"Waves of love,"* the Maestro says again, much softer this time, before he, Bernstein, takes yet another drag and sort of… puffs it out all over the screen, and stares down at the floor. As if the Maestro was suddenly… overcome by his own… *genius brilliance*, you know?'

The old codger that Justin had become lined up Decks 2 and 3, balancing each stylus rather precariously on the record's outermost grooves before he himself wiped away an unwelcome tear, got up the courage to look RCN in the eye, raised his eyebrows in a kind of apologetic 'So there you go!' way, and flicked the switch.

'That IS what it is, man. That's exactly what it is. *Music* y'know – John? You know? The only… literal thing it can be. Can't it? *Waves of Love?*'

The nurse nodded philosophically as the *Mink Bungalow's* opening credentials, the most perfect seduction known to man, muffled in and out of sync, as it always had. Sludgy and uneven in texture, despite surface noise and static, poor stereo-imaging and the odd rumbling floorboard, John Nightly, even on a dusky, damp morning in deepest Balham, still managed to flood the room with eternal light and wisdom.

'Weirdest chords I've ever heard…' slurred the guitarist, following a deep intake of breath before taking a Bernstein-like drag himself, as he turned his head towards the speakers and began to physically vibrate, letting his very being fade into the music, letting himself be thoroughly consumed by it. 'And they're still fuckin' weird!'

RCN breathed heavily and sighed as if he literally could not take one more second of this unabashed, unhindered and certainly uncalled-for display of emotion. An upset this early in the morning, and also at this strange location, this uncomfortable and somehow (it had to be said) reasonably unwelcoming, tiny-roomed home.

The nurse got up from the sofa-bed and walked over to the window by the sink. What a sight it was that greeted him. Not the soft, late-afternoon haze of his Cornish idyll but a series of filthy, good-for-nothing backyards and their utterly inappropriate extensions. Ken Livingstone's vision for London. Cold, grey… afraid, a-feared… money-grabbing, money-generating, money-orientated. A vision very unlike that of Lady Percyval, the Wesleys, Justin, RCN… or Leonard Bernstein. Not at all 'profound', except for the snap of footsteps in the street and the song of the sparrow on the next-door roof. The visitor sighed again and pulled a face before he too paused, looked down at the beer-stained floor, over at his old acquaintance, then inward at himself – his very being; shirt buttons popping across RCN's belly, waistline so tight even he himself was surprised his faded old jeans hadn't burst their seams. He opened the door to the fridge.

'There's juice in here from 2005!' RCN shouted to the guitarist over the meandering masterpiece.

'Yeah... but it's the *end* of 2005!' replied Justin, quick as a flash, as RCN affected another deep breath, as deep as he could manage, pulled a another face, signalling his discomfort, giving his friend a sympathetic gaze before slumping wearily on Justin's Oxfam recliner, hoisting himself up with no little trouble onto its unmatched, scratched and soiled, plastic cushions.

'But what he didn't say, Just..." RCN mumbled, as his own rheumy old eyes began to well up. 'Is that... sometimes... sometimes...' RCN looked directly at his host. 'You get a tidal wave.'

item: Transfer deposit from: Royal Bank of Scotland, Market Jew Street, Penzance, Cornwall TR18 2QR.
Account in the name of Mr J. Nightly.
Account Number 3357049
Sort Code 60-41-34
Amount £8,529,000 (conversion from dollar account)
Beneficiary Coutts Private Bank, 25, Berkeley Square, London W1A 4WW

Transfers per amounts listed
Date 14 November 2007
Reference Will, donations
Tax reference Nightly, J. North London office, 844-302-32

To Greenpeace: £2,000,000
To The Elephant Trust: £500,000
To The SUMHA Centre: Brampton, Huntingdonshire: £400,000
To The Carbon Trust: £500,000
To St Danes Hospitals: F. Centre Project Trust: Trondheim, Norway: £300,000
To The Cinnamon Trust: £300,000
To Mr R. Kemp (details as advised): £100,000
To E.P. Peed (details as advised): £100,000
To Mr M. Hall (details as advised): £100,000
To Cornwall Tree Trust: £300,000
To St Eina Roof Appeal: £100,000
To St Stephens Nursing Trust: £300,000
To Rural Stations Project: £50,000
To St Eina Churchwarden's Appeal Fund: £100,000

Saturday house-clearance sale. Pears Auction House, Penzance. 17 March 2009
Lot 113 An illustrated plastic goose
Lot 704 A kite spinner
Lot 022 A cane bin
Lot 403 A Thunderbirds Supermanionation puppet of (Alan)
Lot 349 A box of books
Lot 299 A box of books
Lot 401 A padded tartan dog
Lot 413 A boomerang
Lot 399 A coloured print of The Hay Wain after John Constable, framed
Lot 556 A 1970's rocket lamp
Lot 586 Two pairs of field-glasses
Lot 599 A rocking-horse
Lot 922 A John Speed Map of Cornwall (reproduction)
Lot 223 A box of 78 rpm records (artists incl. Beatles, Jim Reeve, Starship and Will to Power)

"Anemone hortensis"
(stellata) [Starry Anemone
from Cap S. Martin, Mentone
April 5. 1878.
(see p. 13.)

The following timeline features persons or events that might be seen to have had an influence on the characters in the story.

300BC Aristotle publishes *On the Heavens* (proposing geocentric cosmology)

120BC Ptolemy (in The Almagest) creates a more accurate model of the universe based on Aristotle's theories

1100 Cornish saints establish prayer circles around the area of Black Cliff and Porthcreek, Kernow, (Cornwall)

1230 John of Hollywood (Johannes de Sacrobosco) publishes his *Tractatus de Sphaera*, the first printed astronomical handbook

1450 May 9, Thomasine Bonaventure born in Week St Mary, North Cornwall

1473 February 19, Mikolaj Kopernik, 'Nicolaus Copernicus', the founder of modern astronomy, born in Torun, Poland

1498 Thomasine Bonaventure marries Sir John Percyval, Lord Mayor of London

1511 St John's College, Cambridge, founded by Lady Margaret Beaufort, mother of King Heny VII

1514 Copernicus proposes heliocentric cosmology

1527 July 13, John Dee, astrologer to Queen Elizabeth II, born in Tower Ward, London

1530 December 23, Thomasine Bonaventure dies in Week St Mary, North Cornwall

1540 Alessandro Piccolomini publishes *Delle stelle fisse*, the first star atlas

1542 November 12, Dee enters St John's College, Cambridge

1543 May 24, Copernicus dies in Frauenburg, Poland, having received an 'altered' copy of his *On the Revolutions of Heavenly Spheres* on his deathbed

1545 May 1, John Gerard born in Nantwich, Cheshire

1546 December 14, Tycho Brahe born in Knudstrup, Skåne, Denmark

1552 July 15, John Speed, historian and cartographer, born in Farndon, Cheshire

1555 May 28, John Dee arrested for 'calculating'

1564 February 15, Galileo Galilei born in Pisa, Italy

1567 June 9, John Parkinson born in Nottingham

1570 April 15, John Tradescant the Elder born in Suffolk

1571 December 27, Johannes Kepler born in Weil der Stadt, Germany

1572 January 28, John Donne born on Bread Street, London

1573 Brahe publishes *De Nova Stella*

1576 Construction begins on Brahe's Uranienborg observatory, his 'Castle of the Heavens'

1577 Brahe draws the first circular natal star charts (for the children of King Frederic II)

1577 Dee publishes the *Perfect Arte of Navigation*

1584 Brahe builds Stjerneborg, 'Star Castle', his underground observatory

1586 Donne attends Cambridge University

1592 Brahe produces his *Catalogue of 777 Stars*

1597 John Gerard publishes his *Herball*, or *Generall Historie of Plantes*, the first botanical catalogue in England

1600 Kepler becomes Brahe's assistant

1601 October 14, Brahe dies in Prague, Bohemia

1601 Donne produces his *Songs and Sonnets*

1605 Galileo publishes his *Dialogo de Cecco di Ronchitti da Bruzene in perpuosito de la stella Nuova (or concerning the New star)*

1607   Donne publishes his *Divine Poems*

1608   March 26, John Dee dies in Mortlake, Surrey

1608   August 4, John Tradescant the Younger born in Meopham, Kent

1608   December 9, John Milton born in Cheapside, London

1609   Johannes Kepler publishes *Astronomia Nova*

1609   Galileo builds a series of refracting telescopes

1610   Galileo publishes *Sidereus Nuncius (The Starry Messenger)*

1610   July 25, Galileo discovers the planet Saturn

1610   Kepler publishes his *Conversations with the Sidereal Messenger* in support of Galileo

1612   John Speed publishes his first map of Cornwall

1612   October 23, Gerard dies in London

1612   December 28, Galileo records Neptune as an 'eigth-magnitude star'

1614   January 1, John Wilkins, clergyman and founder of the Royal Society, born in Fawsley, Northamptonshire

1615   April 11, Donne made Doctor of Divinity, Cambridge University

1616   February 24, in Rome, the Sacred Congregation of the Index condemns the Copernican system

1618   May 27, Kepler completes *Harmonies of the World*

1621   Kepler publishes *Epitome Astronomiae*

1621   Donne becomes Dean of St Paul's Cathedral

1621   The first botanic garden, the Oxford Physick Garden, founded in England

1624   Jean-Baptiste de La Quintinie, Louis XIV's gardener, born at Chabanais, France

1625   Milton attends Christ's College, Cambridge

1627   Kepler publishes his *Rudolphine Tables*

1627   November 29, John Ray born in Black Notley, Essex

1629   Parkinson publishes *Paradise on Earth*, the first modern gardening book

1629   July 28, Speed dies in Cripplegate, London

1630   Tradescant the Younger appointed 'Keeper of His Majesty's Gardens'

1630   November 15, Kepler dies in Regensburg, Germany

1631   March 31, Donne dies in London

1632   Galileo publishes his *Dialogue Concerning the Two Chief World Systems* (Ptolemy and Copernicus)

1632   August 29, John Locke born in Wrington, Somerset

1633   Thomas Johnson revises and enlarges Gerard's *Herball*

1635   John Bate publishes *The Mysteries of Art and Nature* (the book pored over by the young Isaac Newton)

1638   Galileo publishes *Dialogues Concerning Two New Sciences*, (the genesis of modern physics)

1638   John Wilkins publishes *The Discovery of a World in the Moon*

1640   John Parkinson publishes his *Theatre of Plants,* describing more than 3,000 plants

1642   January 8, Galileo dies in Florence, Italy

1642   Christmas Day, Issac Newton born in Woolsthorpe, Lincolnshire

1644   John Ray attends Catherine Hall, Cambridge, (then Trinity College)

1646   John Falmsteed, the first Astronomer Royal, born in Dewby, Derbyshire

1648   John Wilkins publishes *Mathematical Magick*

1656   July 4, John Parkinson dies in London

1656   November 8, Edmond Halley born in Haggerston, Middlesex

1657   John Milton begins work on *Paradise Lost*

1659 John Wilkins becomes Master of Trinity College, Cambridge
1661 June 5, Isaac Newton attends Trinity College, Cambridge
1662 April 22, Tradescant the Younger dies in London
1663 Newton buys book on astrology at Sturbridge Fair, Cambridge
1663 Wilkins elected Fellow of the Royal Society
1664 John Forster publishes *England's Happiness Increased*
1665 Newton leaves Cambridge to escape the Great Plague
1666 John Calve publishes his *Survey of Kernow* (Cornwall)
1668 Newton invents the reflecting telescope
1669 Newton elected Lucasian Professor of Mathematics, aged 27
1669 Ray contributes the 'Table of Plants' to Wilkins' *Essay Towards Real Character*
       the first systematic work in botany published in England
1670 Flamsteed attends Jesus College, Cambridge
1672 November 16, Wilkins dies in Chester, Derbyshire
1674 November 8, Milton dies in Chalfont St Giles, Buckinghamshire
1678 de La Quintinie designs the Potager du Roi gardens at Versailles
1680 Flamsteed publishes *Doctrine of the Sphere*
1686 Ray publishes his *Historia Plantarum*
1686 Newton presents his *Philosophiae Naturalis Principia Mathematica* (Book 1), to
       the Royal Society (publication paid for by Halley)
1688 November 11, de La Quintinie dies at Versailles
1689 Locke's *An Essay Concerning Human Understanding* is published
1690 *The Spoure Book* is published
1692 Newton suffers nervous breakdown
1693 March 24, John Harrison born in Foulby, Yorkshire
1695 November 10, John Bevis born in Old Sarum, Wiltshire
1699 March 23, John Bartram, 'America's first botanist' born in Darby, Pennsylvania
1703 June 28, John Wesley born in Epworth, Lincolnshire
1703 Newton elected President of the Royal Society
1703 John Broughton becomes the first to use the word 'psychology' (in his book
       Psychologia: the nature of the rational soul).
1704 Newton publishes *Opticks*
1704 October 28, Locke dies in Oates, Essex
1705 January 17, Ray dies in Black Notley, Essex
1705 Newton becomes the first scientist to be knighted
1705 Newton's Cambridge lectures (1673–1683) published
1707 December 18, Charles Wesley born in Epworth, Lincolnshire
1715 May 3, 'the most celebrated eclipse ever seen in England' passes over Cornwall
1717 Harrison becomes choirmaster and bell tuner at St Saviours Church,
       Barrow-upon-Humber
1719 December 13, Flamsteed dies in Burstow, Surrey
1724 John Michell, geologist and astronomer, born in Nottinghamshire (date unknown)
1727 March 31, Sir Isaac Newton dies in Kensington, London
1729 John Flamsteed's *Atlas Coelestis* published posthumously
1732 October 6, John Broadwood, piano manufacturer and innovator born Berwickshire
1738 John Bevis sets up private observatory at Stoke Newington
1738 John Wesley publishes *A Collection of Psalms and Hymns*
1740 Expansion of deep copper mining in Cornwall heralds the Industrial Revolution in Britain

1742 January 14, Edmond Halley dies in London

1744 John Claridge (the Shepherd of Banbury) publishes his *Rules to Judge the Changes of the Weather*

1748 Bevis produces his *Uranographia Britannica*

1749 Michell attends Queen's College, Cambridge

1752 January 18, John Nash born in Lambeth, London

1753 September 10, John Swan 'John Soane', born in Goring-on-Thames

1761 Michell elected Member of the Royal Society

1761 Harrison invents the H4 marine chronometer

1767 John Pond born in London (date unknown)

1770 Harrison publishes *Concerning Such Mechanism*, on the manufacture and tuning of bells

1771 November 6, Bevis dies in London from injuries received when working in his observatory

1773 August 22, John Wesley preaches to 20,000 miners and fisherman at Gwennap pit, Redruth, Cornwall

1776 March 24, Harrison dies in Red Lion Square, London

1776 June 11, John Constable born in East Bergholt, Suffolk.

1777 September 23, John Bartram dies in Kingsessing, Pennsylvania

1780 John Wesley publishes *A Collection of Hymns for the Use of People called Methodists*' ('a little body of experimental and practical Divinity')

1783 Michell describes Black Holes ('dark stars') in a paper to the Royal Society

1786 John Bevis' *Uranographia Britannica* published as Atlas Celeste

1788 March 29, Charles Wesley dies in Marylebone, London

1791 March 2, Wesley dies in London

1793 April 21, Michell dies in Thornhill, Yorkshire

1793 July 13, John Clare born in Helpstone, Northamptonshire

1795 October 31, John Keats born in Moorfields, London

1799 February 8, John Lindley, botanist, born in Catton, Norwich

1800 February 19, Constable attends the Royal Academy Schools, London

1810 March 1, Frederich Chopin born Zalazowa Wola, Poland

1811 October 27, Franz Liszt born in Raiding, Austria

1811 Nash maps out his design for Marylebone Park (Regent's Park), London

1812 July 17, John Broadwood dies in London

1815 June 5, John Couch Adams born in Laneast, Cornwall

1818 Nash builds his 'garden city' from St James's to Regent's Park

1820 December 18, John Constable begins work on *The Hay Wain* in London

1821 February 23, John Keats dies, aged 25, in Rome

1821 September 12, Charles Wheatstone exhibits *The Enchanted Lyre*

1821 John Clare publishes *The Village Minstrel*

1827 John Clare publishes *The Shepherd's Calendar*

1833 May 7, Johannes Brahms born in Hamburg, Germany

1833 November 12, Alexander Borodin born in St Petersburg, Russia

1834 Lindley the father of modern orchidology', publishes *Ladies' Botany*

1835 May 13, John Nash dies at East Cowes, Isle of Wight

1836 September 7, Pond dies in Blackheath, London; is later buried in Halley's tomb

1837 January 20, Sir John Soane dies in Lincoln's Inn Fields, London

1837 March 31, John Constable dies on Charlotte Street, London

1837 July 15, Chopin visits England

1843 June 15, Edvard Grieg born, Bergen, Norway

1845 John Couch Adams discovers the planet Neptune

1848 October 31, Chopin plays the final concert of his life, at the Guildhall, London

1849 British psychiatrist John Charles Bucknill uses electrical stimulation to treat asylum patients with melancholic depression

1849 Pendeen Church in Cornwall built on the model of Iona Cathedral, Mull

1852 Liszt revises and completes his *Transcendental Studies* (S.139) for solo piano

1861 Couch Adams becomes Director of the Cambridge Observatory

1862 January 29, Frederick Delius born in Bradford

1862 August 22, Claude Debussy born St. Germain-en-Laye, France

1864 May 20, Clare dies in Northampton General Lunatic Asylum

1866 Brahms composes his *German Requiem*

1867 Grieg founds the Music Union in Christiana

1869 April 3, the first performance of Grieg's Piano Concerto 1

1873 April 1, Sergei Rachmaninov born in Novgorod, Russia

1874 September 21, Gustav Holst born in Cheltenham, Gloucestershire

1876 John and Charles Wesley's *The Methodist Hymnal* published

1879 March 14, Albert Einstein born in Ulm, Germany

1882 John Sowerby publishes *British Wild Flowers*

1882 June 17, Igor Stravinsky born St. Petersburg, Russia

1882 Greig begins work on a second piano concerto unfinished at his death

1886 July 21, Franz Liszt dies Bayreuth, Germany

1887 February 27, Borodin dies in St. Petersburg, Russia

1888 May 11, Israel Baline, 'Irving Berlin', born in Tyumen, Siberia

1889 March 12, Vaslav Nijinsky born in Kiev, Russian Empire

1890 December 29, Meredith Starr (Herbert Close) born Hampton, Middx

1892 January 21, Couch Adams dies in Cambridge

1894 February 25, Merwan Sheriar Irani (Meher Baba) born in Poona, Persia

1895 November 1, David Jones born in Brockley, Kent

1895 November 16, Paul Hindemith born, Hanau, Germany

1896 October 28, Howard Hanson born in Wahoo, Nebraska

1896 December 17, a tsunami washes away the embankment and main boulevard of Santa Monica, California

1897 April 3, Brahms dies in Vienna

1897 June 8, John Godolphin Bennett (J.G. Bennett), founder of psycho-kinetics, born in London

1898 September 26, Jacob Gershovitz, 'George Gershwin' born in Brooklyn, New York

1899 January 7, Francis Poulenc born in Paris

1900 Nijinsky joins the Imperial Ballet School.

1900 Sigmund Freud publishes *The Interpretation of Dreams*

1900 September 10, James Hilton born in Leigh, Lancashire

1903 October 3, Vladimir Horowitz born in Kiev, Russia

1905 March 23, Canon John Collins, the founder of Christian Action, born in Hawkshurst, Kent

1905 Einstein presents the Special Theory of Relativity in his paper *On the Electrodynamics of Moving Bodies*

1905 September 5, Arthur Koestler born in Budapest, Hungary

1906 July 8, Philip Johnson born in Cleveland, Ohio

1906 August 28, John Betjeman born in Highgate, London

1907 April 12, Imogen Holst born in Richmond, Surrey

1909 Grieg's Piano Concerto 1 becomes the first ever to be recorded

1910 Halley's Comet puts on a bright show

1910 January 16, Gustav Mahler conducts the premiere of Rachmaninov's Piano Concerto 3 in New York

1911 May 11, Raymond 'Mr Teasy-Weasy' Bessone, born Wardour Street, London

1911 July 9, John Wheeler, theoretical physicist born, Jacksonville, Florida

1912 September 5, John Cage born Los Angeles

1913 November 2, Benjamin Britten born in Lowestoft, Suffolk

1914 Gustav Holst begins work on *The Planets*

1915 James Hilton attends The Leys School, Cambridge

1916 January 19, Brion Gysin born in Taplow, Buckinghamshire

1916 April 22, Yehudi Menuhin born in New York City, New York

1917 December 11, first performance of Poulenc's *Rapsodie Negre*

1918 March 25, Debussy dies in Paris

1918 The Astronomical Congress recognises 88 star constellations

1918 August 25, Leonard Bernstein born in Lawrence, Massachusetts

1918 August 29, (Mrs) Gladys Mills born, Beckton, East London

1919 May 16, Wladziu Valentino, 'Liberace', born in West Allis, Wisconsin, USA

1919 May 20, Nijinsky admitted to the Bellevue Sanatorium, Zurich

1919 December 30, David Valentine Willcocks born Newquay, Cornwall

1920 April 7, Ravi Shankar born, Varanasi, India

1920 November 15, first complete performance of *The Planets*, Queen's Hall, London

1921 Einstein elected Member of the Royal Society

1921 Jones arrives at Eric Gill's Ditchling artists' community.

1921 July 18, John Glenn born in Cambridge, Ohio

1922 Collins attends Sidney Sussex College, Cambridge

1923 March 4, Patrick Moore, astronomer and musician born in Pinner, Middlesex

1925 July 10, Baba takes his vow of silence

1925 September 2, Trevor Herbert Stanford, 'Russ Conway', born in Bristol

1927 October 7, Ronald David Laing born in Govanhill, Glasgow

1927 Poulenc composes his harpsichord concerto *Concert Champetre*

1928 January 12, Vladimir Horowitz makes his debut at Carnegie Hall

1928 May 12, Burt Bacharach born Kansas City, Missouri, US

1929 April 5, Robert George Meek, 'Joe Meek', born in Newent, Gloucestershire

1930 *The Atlas Celeste* published in Cambridge, England by the International Astronomical Association

1931 November 11, Edward Elgar opens EMI's Abbey Road Studios, St John's Wood

1931 Meredith Starr (Herbert Close) sets up the retreat centre at East Challacombe, Coombe Martin, North Devon

1933 Comic actor Will (W.T.) Hay discovers the white spot on Saturn

1933 November 3, John Barry born in York, England

1933 Hilton's *Lost Horizon* published

1934 February 23, Elgar dies at Marl Bank, Worcester

1934 March 9, Yuri Gagarin born in Klushino, Russia

1934 May 25, Gustav Holst dies in London

1934 June 10, Delius dies in Grez-Sur-Loing, France
1934 July 15, Harrison Birtwistle born in Accrington, Lancashire
1934 Betjeman's *Cornwall Illustrated* published
1934 Hilton's *Goodbye Mr Chips* published
1937 March 6, Valentino Tereshkova born in Bolshoye Maslennikovo, Russia
1937 October 28, Graham Bond born in Romford, Essex
1937 July 11, Gershwin dies in Hollywood, California
1937 Hindemith publishes *The Craft of Musical Composition*
1938 June 15, Leonard Lewis 'Leonard of Mayfair' born Notting Hill Gate, London
1938 July 15, John Bates, fashion designer, born in Northumberland
1939 December 23, Fred Heath, 'Johnny Kidd', born in Willesden, London
1940 June 1, Rachmaninov begins work on his final composition, the Symphonic Dances
1940 July 7, Richard Starkey, 'Ringo Starr', born in Liverpool
1940 October 9, John Lennon born in Liverpool
1940 November 11, David Sutch born in Kilburn, London
1941 Hilton publishes *Random Harvest*
1942 January 4, John McLaughlin born Doncaster, South Yorkshire
1942 January 8, Stephen Hawking born in Oxford (300 years to the day after the
        death of Galileo)
1942 March 9, John Cale born in Garnant, West Wales
1942 June 18, James Paul McCartney born in Liverpool
1942 June 20, Brian Douglas Wilson born in Inglewood, California
1942 July 24, Heinz Burt born in Detmold, Germany
1943 February 25, George Harrison born in Liverpool
1943 March 28, Rachmaninov dies in Beverly Hills, California
1943 July 15, Jocelyn Bell born in Belfast, Northern Ireland
1944 January 28, John Taverner born in Wembley Park, London
1945 June 7, premiere of *Peter Grimes*, Sadlers Wells, London.
1945 December, Bernard Lovell begins work on cosmic rays and ionised meteor trails
        at Jodrell Bank in the University Botanical Gardens, Macclesfield
1946 October 29, Peter Greenbaum born in Bethnal Green, London
1945 July 14, John Pond born in Keynsham, Bristol
1946 Bennett sets up his community at Kingston-upon-Thames 1947
1947 July 12, John Wilkinson, 'Wilko Johnson' born in Canvey Island, Essex
1947 Nijinsky moves to Surrey, England with his wife Romola
1948 May 5, Iona Sandstrand born Herning, Denmark
1948 June 18, June Jana Feather born in Trumpington, Cambridge
1948 June 22, Todd Rundgren born in Upper Darby, Philadelphia
1948 July 15, John Nightly born in Grantchester, Cambridge
1949 John Collins named as Canon of St Paul's Cathedral
1950 April 8, Nijinsky dies in London
1953 Cambridge scientist John R. Smythies publishes 'The Mescaline Phenomena' in
        the *British Journal for the Philosophy of Science*
1953 February 25, Vladimir Horowitz performs in public for the last time
1954 Karlheinz Stockhausen becomes the first composer to have a work – *Electronic
        Studies #2* – published in score with pitch specified in Hertz and volume in decibels
1954 December 20, James Hilton dies Long Beach, California
1955 April 18, Einstein dies in Princeton, New Jersey

1956 Bennett publishes the first volume of *The Dramatic Universe*

1956 Bennett begins work on the Djameechoonatra, a nine-sided auditory hall based on the enneagram symbol

1957 *The Sky At Night* is first broadcast

1957 International Geophysical Year (IGY)

1957 Bernard Lovell and Charles Husband develop and build the Mark I radar telescope

1957 September 20, Sibelius dies, Jarvenpaa, Finland

1957 September 26, *West Side Story* opens on Broadway

1957 Sputnik 1, the world's first artificial satellite launched from the Baikonur Cosmodrome, Khazakstan, Russia

1957 November 3, Sputnik 2 launched; Soviet 'Muttnik' Laika becomes the first dog in orbit

1957 November 4, Laika dies in space

1959 R. D. Laing publishes *The Divided Self*

1959 Koestler publishes *The Sleepwalkers*

1959 John Taverner becomes organist at St John's Kensington

1960 August 12, John R. Pierce's Echo 1 satellite launched

1960 May 22, a wave up to 35 feet high kills 1,000 people in Chile, causing damage in Hawaii, the Philippines, Okinawa and Japan.

1961 February 13, *West Side Story: Symphonic Dances* international release; Nightly purchases the CBS recording in Miller's, Cambridge

1961 May 5, the first suborbital space flight by Alan B. Shepherd Jnr in *Freedom 7*

1961 April 12, Gagarin becomes the first man in space

1961 J.G. Bennett visits the Shivapuri Baba in Nepal

1962 January 11, Beatles national-TV debut on *Thank Your Lucky Stars* with Brian Matthew

1962 February 20, 9.47am, John Glenn blasts off Cape Canaveral to become the first American in orbit

1962 October 12, Hawking arrives at Trinity Hall, Cambridge

1962 May 30, Britten's *War Requiem* premieres at Coventry Cathedral

1962 July 10, launch of Telstar, the first orbiting communications satellite

1962 August 9, 'Telstar' by the Tornados released (Decca F11494)

1962 Britten's *War Requiem* released (Decca SET252)

1963 January 30, Francis Poulenc dies in Paris

1963 April 13, John Bates invents the miniskirt

1963 June 16, Valentina Tereshkova becomes the first woman in space

1963 November 26, John and Jana attend Beatles concert ABC Regal, Cambridge

1963 Pierce receives National Medal of Science for contributions in theory, electron optics and travelling wave tubes

1964 John Cale awarded Leonard Bernstein scholarship to study in the US

1964 March 28, Radio Caroline begins broadcasting

1965 Bell begins PhD at Cambridge University

1965 May 9, Horowitz makes his comeback at Carnegie Hall, New York

1966 January 31, Luna 9 becomes first spacecraft to land on the moon

1966 Meher Baba issues his 'Don't Worry, Be Happy' card

1966 May 16, *Pet Sounds* (Capitol T 2458) released

1966 July 15, John Nightly's eighteenth birthday

1966 August 5, *Revolver* (Parlophone PMC7009) released

1966 October 7, Johnny Kidd killed in car accident, Manchester

1966 October 15, *Principal Fixed Stars* released (Mosaic PO195738)

1967 January 13, Jimi Hendrix plays the Bag o'Nails

1967 February 3, Joe Meek murders his landlady and then commits suicide

1967 March 15, *The Story of Simon Simopath* by Nirvana is released

1967 July 15, Jocelyn Bell discovers CP1919, the world's first pulsar (the 'Cambridge Pulsar), at the radio astronomy observatory.

1967 July 15, the Dialectics of Liberation conference opens at the Roundhouse, London

1967 March 18, Torrey Canyon disaster, Lands End, Cornwall

1967 May 18, *Sgt Pepper* (Parlophone PMC 7027) released.

1967 May 22, Ravi Shankar opens his Kinnara Music School in Los Angeles

1967 August 14, British government announces all radio stations transmitting off the coast are silent

1967 August 24, Trancendental meditation lecture Hilton Hotel Ballroom, London, J.P&G, John, Iona and Monika attend

1967 September 30, BBC Radio One is launched

1967 October 1, *Quiz Axe Queen* released (Mosaic PO195746)

1967 October 17, Premiere of *Hair* on Broadway

1967 John Daly leaves for New Zealand

1967 December 5, the Apple Boutique opens at 94, Baker Street, London W1

1967 December 29, John Wheeler coins the term 'Black Hole' (collapsed stars) at a talk at GISS, the NASA Goddard Institute for Space Studies

1968 February 14, John & Iona marry at Marylebone Registry Office, London

1968 March 27, Yuri Gagarin dies Kirzhach, Russia

1968 Cornelius Cardew's experimental music class, Morley College, the beginning of the Scratch Orchestra

1968 July 4, Round the World yachtsman Alec Rose returns to Portsmouth following his 28,500 mile adventure

1968 June 8, Birtwistle's *Punch & Judy* premiere at Aldeburgh

1968 September 13, John Nightly, *Scene & Heard* interview with Miranda Ward

1968 October 17, The Pretty Things *S.F. Sorrow* released

1969 January 31, Meher Baba dies Meherebad ashram, Ahmednager, India

1969 First performance of *Jesus Christ Superstar*

1969 March 2, John & Yoko perform at Lady Mitchell Hall, Cambridge

1969 May 23, The Who release their rock-opera *Tommy*, dedicated to Meher Baba

1969 July 15, John Nightly's twenty-first birthday

1969 July 16, Apollo 11 takes Neil Armstrong to the moon

1969 September 24, Deep Purple and The Royal Philharmonic Orchestra conducted by Malcolm Arnold perform Jon Lord's 'Concerto for Group and Orchestra' at the Royal Albert Hall, London

1969 October 17, John and Donna attend the Nice's *Five Bridges Suite* live, Fairfield Halls, Croydon

1969 November 22, the *White Album* released (Apple PMC7067)

1970 February 14, *Ape Box Metal* (Mosaic PO281928) released

1970 February 23, Leonard Bernstein records the Verdi Requim at the Royal Albert Hall in Quad

1970 March 21, The Who release *The Seeker* b/w *Here for More* (Track 605036)

1970 September 1, John Nightly begins composing MBR, source: *The John Nightly Diaries* edited Michael Ede (Harmon Books) 2002

1970 September 7, John Nightly completes composistion of *MBR* and returns to

Cambridge for one week.

1970 September 25, Apple Records issues John Taverner's *The Whale*

1970 October 16, *Jesus Christ Superstar* album released in the UK (Decca DSXA 7206)

1971 April 6, Stravinsky dies in New York

1971 April 28, Hawkwind play St. Michael's Mount, Cornwall

1971 May 4, Heiress Myra Knoll is killed instantly when car driven by John Nightly overturns near Taunton, Somerset

1971 August 1, Concert for Bangladesh

1971 September 5, John attends free gig at Grantchester Meadows with Raphaella

1971 September 8, Leonard Bernstein's MASS premieres at the Kennedy Center, Washington

1971 October 12, the album of *Jesus Christ Superstar* (Columbia C31042)) released

1972 Stephen Hawking elected fellow of Gonville & Caius, Cambridge

1972 January 2, six weeks of rehearsals of MBR begin at Hornsey Secondary School, North London, before moving onto The Rainbow, Finsbury Park

1972 February 14, *Something/Anything* by Todd Rundgren (Bearsville 2BX2066) released

1972 May 5, *Mink Bungalow Requiem* performed in front of an audience of 400,000 people at the Ongaku Center, formerly Pleasance Memorial Park, Kyoto, Japan. The largest musical gathering in history.

1972 May 19, *Mink Bungalow Requiem* US premiere at the Shrine Auditorium, Los Angeles, California

1972 May 28, Outdoor Amphitheatre, Los Angeles, *Symphonia da Requiem for Group, Orchestra and Choir.* The final performance.

1972 May 6, the Dorothy Ballroom closes

1972 September 1, John Betjeman appointed Poet Laureate

1972 September 27, John Nightly books into the Sumha Centre, Huntingdon, Cambs

1972 December 7, Sixth and final manned Lunar landing

1973 March 7, John Nightly attends premiere of *Lost Horizon*, National Theatre, Westwood, Los Angeles

1973 John Nightly moves to the SUMHA Centre, Santa Monica, California

1973 August 23, Donna Ekaterina Vost dies in New York

1974 March 11, Stephen Hawking elected fellow of the Royal Society

1974 October 29, David Jones dies, Calvary nursing home, Harrow

1974 December 13, J.G. Bennett dies Sherbourne, Glos

1976 August 16, a tsunami kills more than 5,000 people in the Philippines

1977 The Duke of Edinburgh elected Chancellor of Cambridge University

1978 February 24, Mrs Mills dies in London

1978 October 10, John Pond collapses and dies in a Paris nightclub

1979 Stephen Hawking elected Lucasian professor at Cambridge University

1980 December 8, John Lennon dies in New York City

1981 February 26, Howard Hanson dies Rochester, New York

1981 September 28, John Daly returns to England

1981 October 17, John Nightly leaves Sumha and returns to Grantchester

1981 Dec 13, Cornelius Cardew killed by hit and run driver in Leytonstone, London

1981 John Bevis's *Uranographia Britannica* finally published 233 years after it was written

1982 April 9, Nightly & Daly move to Porthcreek

1982 May 13, Mr Teasy-Weasy Raymond receives the OBE for services to Hairdressing

1983 March 1, Arthur Koestler overdoses on the barbiturate Tuinal in a double-suicide pact with his wife Cynthia

1983 June 18, Sally Ride becomes the first American woman in space
1983 August 17, Steinar dies
1984 March 12, Imogen Holst dies Aldeburgh, Suffolk
1984 May 19, Sir John Betjeman dies Trebetherick, Cornwall
1984 August 17, Sindre dies
1986 January 28, US Space shuttle Challenger explodes killing all seven crew members
1986 July 13, Brion Gysin dies, Paris
1989 August 23, R.D. Laing dies, St.Tropez
1989 September 22, Irving Berlin dies in New York aged 101
1989 November 5, Vladimir Horowitz dies New York City
1990 A new 32 metre bowl telescope at Cambridge forms part of the European Very-
      Long-Baseline-Interferometry (VLBI) Network. The world's most sensitive VLBI array
1990 October 14, Leonard Bernstein dies in New York
1991 The VLB1 array becomes Merlin: Multi-element-Radio-Linked-Interferometer Network
1992 April 17, Mr Teasy-Weasy Raymond dies Berkshire
1994 March 30, Stephen Hawking appears on Pink Floyd's *The Division Bell*
1995 *A Brief History of Time* enters the all time best-selling paperback list in the
      Guinness Book of Records
1996 January 5, John Nightly snr dies at home in Cambridge
1997 April 17, Alan Hale and Tom Bopp give their names to the comet which is one of
      the brightest ever seen
1997 September 6, Jean-Michel Jarre performs *Oxygene* to 3,500,000 in Moscow – the
      world's largest ever rock concert
1998 September 2, Frieda dies, Grantchester, Cambridge
1999 June 16, Screaming Lord Sutch found hanged, South Harrow, London
1999 August 11, 9.57am BST. Daly and Nightly drive to Zennor Quoit and experience
      total eclipse blackout during the final solar eclipse of the millenium
1999 November 12, Yehudi Menuhin dies in Berlin
2000 November 16, Russ Conway dies in Eastbourne
2001 April 28, Dennis Tito becomes the first 'space tourist'
2001 November 29, George Harrison dies in Los Angeles
2003 March 3, Mawgan Hall arrives at Porthcreek
2003 October 23, Michael Brown, Chad Trujillo and David Rabinowitz discover UB131,
      the '10th planet'
2004 February 14, Dr Jana Feather, RIBA, dies in Locasa, Peru
2006 August 26, John Nightly wins horticultural medal at Porthcreek Annual Show2007
April 17, official opening of the 'S-shaped' Stephen Hawking Building, Caius
      College, by HRH Prince Philip
2007 July 1, John Nightly dies, Carn Point, Cornwall
2007 July 15, Release of the *Mink Bungalow Requiem*
2008 April 14, John Wheeler dies Hightstown, New Jersey
2008 May 7, Alexandre dies
2012 December 11, Ravi Shankar dies in La Jolla, California
2013 November 12, John Tavener dies at Child Okeford, Dorset
2015 September 17, Sir David Willcocks dies in Cambridge
2016 March 11, Keith Emerson commits suicide in Santa Monica, CA
2016 November 30, Leonard Lewis, 'Leonard of Mayfair' dies in Putney, London

John Nightly Discography

Albums

1. *Principal Fixed Stars* - 1966 - Released 15 October, 1966
2. *Quiz Axe Queen* - 1967 - Released 1 October 1967
3. *Ape Box Metal* - 1970 - Released 14 February 1970
4. *Pitfall* (OST) - 1968 - Film soundtrack, d. Joseph Karmov, released October, 1968. p. Zuba films, Knoll Entertainment Co
5. *Easy Jack* (OST) - 1969 - Film soundtrack, released October 1969
6. *Theatre*: - 1970 m- Hyde Park, London Dance Centre summer season, 1970
7. *Mink Bungalow Requiem* - 1972 - (unissued) re-issued 2008
   MBR tracklisting:
   Alpha Beta Prelude
   Allegro Castor
   Adagio Mortada
   Vega Fluxus
   Dromeda Mink Interlude
   Fantasia Capella
   Rigel Epilogue

Grantchester Love Chronicle: a six song suite 1965 (unissued)

John Nightly songs recorded by other artists:
Zigging & Zagging b/w *The House with Toytown Bricks:* The Everyman: October 1966
Mu Mu Tea b/w *Milk Break:* Vanessa Frye: December 1966
Zigging & Zagging b/w *Black Sheep:* The Bellbottoms: March 1968
Lavender Girl b/w *The Loon:* The If: June 1968

Peachfruit Love Parchment: (originally from the *Ape Box Metal* album - covered by Star Castle on the album *We Are The Rock & Roll,* Warner Reprise (W33PTR 930) 1988.
Easier Said Than Done recorded by Alexander Telstar, Dizzy Records, (Daze133) 1968.

Orchestral and dance works:
Six Second Echo: (for double string orchestra and two transistor radios) 1965
De La Stelle Nova '67: 1967
Symphony In Orange Ink: 1969
Silhouette: 2008 (published posthumously)

Bibliography

I have frequently referred to and quoted from many sources, including the following:

Music, Poetry & Art

A Collection of Hymns For the People called Methodists, the Rev John Wesley, MA (London Wesleyan-Methodist Book-Room) 1780
Son to Susanna, The Private Life Of John Wesley, G. Elsie Harrison (Penguin) 1937
The Wesleys in Cornwall, The Journals of John and Charles Wesley, John Pearce (Binton Bingley) 1964
Elgar, His Life and Works, Vol 2, Basil Maine (Bell) 1933
Elgar, W. H. Reed (J.M.Dent & Sons Ltd) 1939
Edward Elgar, A Creative Life, Jerrold Northrop Moore (OUP) 1984
An ABC of Music, Imogen Holst (OUP) 1963
What to Listen for in Music, Aaron Copland, (McGraw-Hill Book Co) USA, 1957
Benjamin Britten: His Life & Operas, Eric Walter White (Faber) 1983
Conversations with Igor Stravinsky, Robert Craft (Faber) USA, 1958
Memories & Commentaries, Igor Stravinsky, Robert Craft (Faber) USA, 1959
Chronicle Of My Life, Igor Stravinsky (Victor Gollancz) 1936
The Unanswered Question, Leonard Bernstein (Harvard Lectures)
Findings, Leonard Bernstein (MacDonald & Co) 1982
The Infinite Variety of Music, Leonard Bernstein (Weidenfeld & Nicholson) 1968
The Joy Of Music, Leonard Bernstein (Simon & Schuster) 1954
Gershwin: A Biography, Edward Jabonski (Simon & Schuster) 1987
The Gershwin Years, Edward Jablonski & Lawrence D. Stewart (Robson Books) 1974
Fred Astaire, His Friends Talk, Sarah Giles (Bloomsbury) 1988
Steps In Time, Fred Astaire, autobiography (Heinemann) 1960
The Fred Astaire Dance Book, Fred Astaire (Pocket Books Inc) 1965
The Electric Kool-Aid Acid Test, Tom Wolfe (Farrar edition) US, 1968
The Kandy-Kolored Tangerine-Flake Streamline Baby, Tom Wolfe (Mayflower) 1965
The Blue Plaque Guide, Victor Burrows (Newman Neame, London) 1953
Diary Of A Genius, Salvador Dali, autobiography (Hutchinson & Co) 1966
The Life & Remains of John Clare, J. L. Cherry (Warne) 1873
Art & Love, Eric Gill (Golden Cockerill Press/Douglas Cleverdon, Bristol) 1927
Frederick Delius, Sir Thomas Beecham (Hutchinson) 1959
Delius: As I Knew Him, Eric Fenby (Bell) London, 1936
Jesus And The Christian In A Pop Culture, Tony Jasper (Robert Royce) 1984
An Exacting Heart: the Story of Hephzibah Menuhin, Jacqueline Kent and Marie-Louise Walker (Viking) 2008
High & Low, John Betjeman (John Murray) 1959
John Piper, John Betjeman, Penguin Modern Painters (Penguin) 1944
David Jones, Robin Ironside, Penguin Modern Painters (Penguin) 1942
David Jones, Writer & Artist, Keith Alldritt (Constable) 2004
John Donne, John Hayward (Penguin Poets) 1950
John Donne, Complete Poems, Everyman's Library (J.M.Dent) 1956
Letters to Severall Persons of Honour, John Donne 1651. Edited by John Donne, Jr. Facsimile, with introduction by M. Thomas Hester.

A Collection of Letters, Made by Sir Tobie Matthews, John Donne Kt, 1660.
The Metaphysical Poets, Helen Gardner (Penguin) 1957
Penguin Modern Poets 2, Amis, Morase, Porter (Penguin) 1962
Penguin Modern Poets 12, Jackson, Nuttall, Wantling (Penguin) 1968
Not In Our Stars, Phyllis Bottome (Faber & Faber) 1955
Ariel, Andre Maurois (John Lane/The Bodley Head) 1924
John Nobody, Dom Moraes (Eyre & Spottiswoode) 1965
Under Milk Wood, A Play for Voices, Dylan Thomas (JM Dent) 1954
Selected Poems, John Pudney Guild Books (The Bodley Head) 1947
Ten Summers, John Pudney Guild Books (The Bodley Head) 1944
Everyone Was Working, Alison Oldham (Falmouth College of Arts) 2003
John Nightly: Shaman/Magus/Messiah, Neil Winters (Redpoll Books) 1978
Out Of The Wood, British Woodcuts & Wood Engravings, 1890-1945, Simon Brett
(British Council) 1991
John Constable, Phoebe Pool (Blandford Art Series) 1964
Constable: The Natural Painter, Graham Reynolds (Cory, Adams & Mackay) 1965
Constable: Paintings, Watercolours, and Drawings. Catalogue (Tate) 1976
John Constable's Correspondence: ed. R.B.Beckett (Suffolk Record Society) 1962-70
John Constable, William Vaughan (Tate) 2002
Constable, Michael Rosenthal (Thames & Hudson) 1987
A Smattering of Ignorance, Oscar Levant (Gardens City Publishing) New York 1942
The Unimportance of Being Oscar, Oscar Levant (Putnam) New York 1968
The Memoirs of an Amnesiac, Oscar Levant (Putnam) New York 1965
George Formby: A Troubled Genius, David Brett (Robson Books) 2001

The Sixties

British Beat: Chris May & Tim Phillips (Scion Books) 1974
Swinging London: A guide to where the action is: Karl Dallas (Stanmore Press) 1967
In The Sixties: Barry Miles, Pimlico (Random House) 2003
Brion Gysin: Tuning to the Multimedia Age, Edited by Jose Ferez Kuri (Thames &
Hudson) 2003
Belles (Paris: Two Cities Editions, 1960/San Francisco: Beach Books) 1968
All You Need Is Love, Tony Palmer (Futura Publications) 1977
Beat Music, Derek Johnson (Hardar) 1972
Give The Anarchist A Cigarette, Mick Farren (Pimlico) 2002
Chapel of Extreme Experience, A Short History of Stroboscopic Light, John Geiger
(Soft Skull Press) 2003
Bomb Culture, Jeff Nuttall (MacGibbon & Kee) 1968
High Priest, Timothy Leary, (World Publishing Co) 1968
Revolution In The Head, Ian Macdonald (Fourth Estate) 1994
A Chorister's Pocket-Book (Royal School of Church Music) 1967
Chopin's Musical Style, Gerald Abraham (OUP) 1939
Chopin, an Index to his works, Maurice Brown (Macmillan) 1960
Frédéric Chopin, Selected Correspondence, Arthur Hedley, Heinemann 1960
Dinner with Lenny, Jonathan Cott (OUP USA) 2014
The Leonard Bernstein Letters, edited by Nigel Simeone (Yale) 2014
Ravel: Variations on his Life & Work, H. H. Stuckenschmidt (Calder & Boyers)

London 1966

Arnold Schoenberg, H. H. Stuckenschmidt (Calder & Boyers) London 1970

Tchaikovsky, Michel Hoffman (Calder & Boyers) London 1969

Wagner Opera, Audrey Williamson (Calder & Boyers) London 1970

A Cellarful Of Noise, Brian Epstein (Souvenir Press) 1964

Apple To The Core, The Unmaking of the Beatles, Peter McCabe & Robert D. Schonfeld (Martin Brian & O'Keeffe) 1972

Love Me Do, The Beatles Progress, Michael Braun (Penguin) 1964

Here are The Beatles! Charles Hamblett (Four Square) 1964

Yellow Submarine, Max Wilk (Times New English Library) 1968

The Psychedelic Experience, Ralph Metzner, Timothy Leary and Richard Alpert, (Citadel) 1964

The Big Scene: Groups, & Groupies, their Trips & Kicks, Robin Squire, (WH Allen) 1968

Generation X, Charles Hamblett & Jane Deverson (Tandem) 1964

Fashion In The Sixties, Barbara Bernard (Academy Editions) 1978

Courreges, Valerie Guillaume (Thames & Hudson) 1998

Seventeen Watts, Mo Foster (Sanctuary) 1997

The Tapestry of Delights, Vernon Joynson (Borderline) 1995

Diary Of A Teddy Boy, Mim Scala (Review/Headline Books) 2000

Creative Music Production: Joe Meek's Bold Techniques, Barry Cleveland (Omnibus) 2001

The Legendary Joe Meek, The Telstar Man, John Repsch (Woodford House) 1989

Minutes to Go, with William S. Burroughs, Gregory Corso and Sinclair

Belles (San Francisco: Beach Books) 1968

The Process (New York: Doubleday) 1969

Oeuvre Croisée (The Third Mind) with William S. Burroughs (Viking Press) New York (John Calder) 1979

The Sixties: Life: Style: Architecture, Edited by Elain Harwood & Alan Powers (20th Century Society) 2002

Poems from Poetry & Jazz In Concert, ed. Jeremy Robinson (Souvenir Press) 1969

All Dressed Up: The Sixties & the Counterculture, Jonathon Green (Jonathan Cape) 1998

Los Angeles, Reyner Banham (Allen Lane) 1971

Hef's Little Black Book, Hugh M. Hefner & Bill Zehme (Harper Entertainment) 2004

X-Ray, Ray Davies (Overlook Press) 1994

An Attempt At Exorcism, Edwin Brock (Scorpion Press) 1959

With Love From Judas, Edwin Brock (Scorpion Press) 1963

Hyde Park, William Shakespeare (Folio) 1625

Before I Get Old, The Story of the Who, Dave Marsh (Plexus) 1983

Hippie, Hippie, Shake, Richard Neville (Bloomsbury) 1995

Hippie, Barry Miles (Cassell) 2003

Eric Gill, Fiona MacCarthy (Faber) 1989

Kitaj, Marco Livingstone (Phaidon) 1985

The Sleepwalkers, Arthur Koestler (Hutchinson) 1959

Starmakers & Svengalis: Johnny Rogan, (Queen Anne Press/Futura) 1988

Bob Dylan In His Own Words: compiled by Miles (Omnibus Press) 1978

Rock & Pop London, (Handbook Publishing Ltd) 1997

Madcap - The Half-life of Syd Barrett, Tim Willis (Short Books) 2002

Crazy Diamond, Mike Watkinson & Pete Anderson (Omnibus Press) 1991

Owning Up, George Melly (Weidenfeld & Nicholson) 1965

The Hippies, edited by Joe David Brown (Time Inc) New York 1967
Waiting For The Man, Harry Shapiro (Helter Skelter) 1999 (Quartet) 1988
Wouldn't It Be Nice? Brian Wilson with Todd Gold (Bloomsbury) 1992
Cannabis: A History, Martin Booth (Doubleday) 2003
Out Of His Head: The Sound of Phil Spector. Richard Williams (Abacus) 1972
It Ain't Necessarily So, Larry Adler (Collins) 1984
Nova: edited by David Hillman (Pavilion) 1993

Occultism in rock'n'roll www.iluminati-news.com (Gary Gomez)

The Seventies

Plays & Players, June 1972 (Hansom Books) 1972
More Locations of America's Pop Culture Landmarks, Chris Epting (Santa Monica Press) 2004
A British Picture, Ken Russell, (Heinemann) 1989
Halston, Steven Bluttal (Phaidon) 2000

Cornwall, Climate, Tides & Environment

Galileo and the Theory of the Tides, Eric J. Aiton, (Isis 56) 1965
Vanishing Cornwall, Daphne Du Maurier (Victor Gollancz) London, 1967
The Climate of London, Luke Howard (unbound) 1818
The Shell Guide to Cornwall, John Betjeman, John Piper, (Faber & Faber) 1964
The Cornish Smuggling Industry, Paul White (Tor Mark Press), 1997
Birds of Sea and Coast, Lars Jonsson (Wahlstrom & Widstrand/Penguin Nature Guides) 1977
Seabirds, J.Fisher and R.M. Lockley (Collins) 1954
Shipwrecks around Land's End (Richard & Bridget Larn (Tor Mark Press) 1989
A New Dictionary of Birds, A.L.Thomson (Nelson) 1960
Woodland Management for Birds (RSPB Management Guides) paperback 2004
That Must Be Julian, N.R. Syme (Peter Lunn) 1947
The Handbook of British Birds, H.F. Witherby, F.C.R. Jourdain, N.F. Ticehurst and B.W. Tucker (H.F. and G. Witherby) 1938-1941
John Speed's Atlas of England & Wales (King Penguin) 1951
Circular Coast Walks of Cornwall, Charles Adams (Moor, Dale & Mountain Press) 1997
A History of Cornish Methodism, Thomas Shaw (D. Bradford Barton) 1967
The Wesleys in Cornwall, ed. John Pearce (D.Bradford Barton) 1964
Gardens of Cornwall, Douglas Ellory Pett (Alison Hodge) 2003
The National Trust, Coast of Cornwall (Des Hannigan, John Dyke)
Researches about Atmospheric Phenomena, Thomas Forster (Cornish Local History)

Cambridge

From Our Cambridge Correspondent: Mark Weatherall (Varsity Publications) 1995
The English Town in the Last Hundred Years, Rede Lecture Pamphlet (Cambridge University Press) 1956
John Milton, Kenneth Muir (Longmans, Green, and Co. Ltd) 1965.
Down Your Street, Cambridge Past and Present, Sara Payne, (the Pevensey Press) 1983
Coroners' Records in England and Wales Second Edition by Jeremy Gibson and Colin

Rogers (Federation of Family History Societies)
Prospect of Cambridge, Edwin Smith & Olive Cook (B.T.Batsford) 1965
The Kings College Choir Book, ed. Jonathan Rippon & Penny Cleobury (Phillimore & Co) 1997
Kelly's Directory of Bedfordshire 1898
National Index of Parish Registers (Vol 9, Pt 1: Bedfordshire and Huntingdonshire) compiled by Cliff Webb (The Society of Genealogists)
England: on Five Dollars a Day, Stanley Mills Haggart (Arthur B. Frommer Inc) 1964

Botany & Gardening

John Ray, Naturalist: His Life and Works, C.E. Raven (Cambridge) 1942
Memorials of John Ray, W.Derham (London) 1946
Makers of British Botany, S.H. Vines, Robert Morison, 1620-1683 and John Ray, 1627-1688, edited by F.W. Oliver (Cambridge) 1913
John Ray, a Bibliography, G.L.Keynes, (London) 1951
Historical and Biographical Sketches of the Progress of Botany in England, Richard Pulteney (London) 1790
The Spoure Book
John Gerard: The Herball or General Historie of Plants, Imprinted Facsimile, (John Norton) London 1957.
Observer's Book of British Grasses, Sedges and Rushes, compiled by W.J. Stokoe, (Frederick Warne & Co Ltd)
The Handbook of British Flora (Bentham & Hooker) 1949
Annual and Biennial Flowers, A.P.Balfour (Penguin) 1959
British Wild Flowers, John Sowerby (Schmidlin) 1948
The Flowering Plants of Great Britain, Anne Pratt (loose binding) 1825
Syme's English Botany (unknown binding) 1863
Roses F.Fairbrother (Penguin Handbooks) 1958
Wildflowers of the Cornish hedgerows, Trevor & Endymion Beer (Tor Mark Press) 2000
The Enemies of the Rose, John Ramsbottom and G.Fox Wilson (National Rose Society) 1957
Gardening The Modern Way, Roy Hay (Penguin) 1962
Lawns, R.B.Dawson (Royal Horticultural Society/Penguin) 1960
Hardy Herbaceous Plants (Royal Horticultural Society/Penguin) 1960
Dahlias, Stuart Ogg (Royal Horticultural Society/Penguin)1961
Chrysanthemums, Edward T. Thistlethwaite (Penguin) 1960
The London Gardener (London Historic Parks and Gardens Trust) 2000
The City Gardener, Thomas Fairchild (Unknown) 1722

Astronomy, Astrology, Space Adventure, Science & Architecture

The Observer's Book of Astronomy, Patrick Moore (Frederick Warne & Co Ltd) 1962
Guide To The Sky, E.A. Beet (Cambridge University Press) 1933
Instructions to Young Astronomers, H.P.Wilkins (Museum Press) 1957
Through My Telescope, Will Hay (Reed) 1935
Outline Of The Universe, Vol 1, J.G. Crowther (Pelican Library) 1931
The Nautical Almanac, 1829, Her Majesty's Nautical Almanac Office (HMNAO)
Catalogue of 1112 Stars, John Pond, 1833
Alchemy, Astrology and Ovid: A Love Poem by Tycho Brahe (P.Zeeberg)

The Star Almanac For Land Surveyors 2003 (RAL)

The Astronomical Almanac (US Navel Observatory/Rutherford Appleton Laboratory) 2004

The Lord of Uraniborg: A Biography of Tycho Brahe, Victor E. Thoren (Cambridge University Press) 1990

Astrology: Evolution & Revolution, Alan Oken (Bantam) 1976

The Correspondence of John Flamsteed, the first Astronomer Royal, Vol 1 & 2, Eric G. Forbes, Lesley Murdin and Frances Willmoth, (Institute of Physics Publishing, Bristol and Philadelphia) 1995 & 1997

Sphaera Mundi: Astronomy Books in the Whipple Museum 1478-1600, J. Bennett & D. Bertoloni Meli, Cambridge 1994

Black Holes, John A. Wheeler, Phi Beta Kappa Society Journal: The American Scholar (Vol. 37, no 2, spring) 1998

Black Hole Physics: Basic Concepts and New Developments, V.P. Frolov and I.D. Novikov (Kluwer, Dordrecht) 1998

Rotation, Nut charge and Anti de sitter space, Sdr. Stephen Hawking, Feburary 1999

Black Holes & Baby Universes, Dr. Stephen Hawking (Dove) 1999

The Cambridge Lectures, Dr. Stephen Hawking (Bantam) 2000

The Large-Scale Structure of Space-Time, Dr. Stephen Hawking & G F R Ellis, (Cambridge University Press) 1973

Introducing Stephen Hawking, J.P.McEvoy, Oscar Zarate (Totem Books) 1995

Stephen Hawking, A Life In Science, Michael White & John Gribbin (Viking) 1992

Music To Move The Stars – A Life With Stephen Hawking, Jane Hawking (Macmillan) 1999

The Charters & Statutes of the Royal Society of London (London) 1717

The Science of Musical Sound, J.R.Pierce (Scientific American Library) 1983

The Whipple Museum of the History of Science. Catalogue 6. Sundials and Related Instruments, D.J.Bryden, 1988

The Sun in the Church: Cathedrals As Solar Observatories, J.L.Heilbron (Harvard University Press) 1999

The Forgotten Star Atlas: John Bevis's Uranographia Britannica, Kevin J. Kilburn

The Mysteries of Art & Nature, John Bate (Thomas Harper/Ralph Mab) 1635

M. Pasachoff, and Owen Gingerich (Williams College) Williamstown, Mass, USA

Flamsteed's Stars: New Perspectives on the Life and Work of the first Astronomer Royal, ed: Frances Willmoth, (Boydell and Brewer) Woodbridge, 1997

An Account of the Revd John Flamsteed, Frances Bailey (London 1835)

Philosophiae Naturalis Principia Mathematica: Sir Isaac Newton, 1687

Sir Isaac Newton, E.N. da'Andrade, (William Collins & Sons) 1954

The Library of Isaac Newton, J. Harrison (Cambridge) 1978

Sir I. Newton, Correspondence, ed. H. Turnball (Cambridge 1959-1977)

The Role of Music in Galileo's Experiments, Scientific American, 232 (Jan-June 1975)

Telescopes, Tides, and Tactics: A Galilean Dialogue about the Starry Messenger and Systems of the World. Chicago (University of Chicago Press) 1983

Compendious Rehearsal, John Dee (1592)

Perfect Arte of Navigation, John Dee (1577)

John Dee: the World of an Elizabethan Magus, Peter J. French (London 1972)

Tudor Georgraphy, E.G.R. Taylor (London 1930)

Mathematical Practitioners of Tudor and Stuart England (Cambridge 1954)

My Head is a Map: Essays & Memoirs in Honour of R.V. Tooley (London 1973)

Results of Astronomical Observations made during the years 1834, 5, 6, 7, 8 at the Cape

of Good Hope. J.F.W.Herschel, London, 1847.

Neville Maskelyne - The Seaman's Astronomer, Derek Howse (Cambridge University Press) 1989

Joannis Kepleri Astronomi Opera Omnia. 8 vols. Johannes Kepler, Edited by C. Frisch, (Frankfurt and Erlangen) 1858-1871

Gesammelte Werke, Johannes Kepler, edited by Max Caspar, Munich (Beck 1937)

Mysterium Cosmographicum -The Secret of the Universe, translated by A. M. Duncan, New York (Abaris Books) 1981.

New Astronomy, translated by William H. Donahue.Cambridge (Cambridge University Press) 1992

Kepler's Conversation with Galileo's Sidereal Messenger. translated by Edward Rosen, New York (Johnson Reprint) 1965

The Six-Cornered Snowflake, translated by Colin Hardie, Oxford (Clarendon Press) 1966

Somnium: the Dream, or Posthumous Work on Lunar Astronomy, translated by Edward Rosen, Madison (University of Wisconsin Press) 1967

The Harmonies of the World [Book V], translated by Charles Glenn Wallis. Great Books of the Western World. Vol. 16. Chicago (Encyclopaedia Britannica) 1955

The History of the Telescope, Henry C. King, London (Charles Griffin) 1955 New York (Dover) 1985

The Watershed: a Biography of Johannes Kepler, Arthur Koestler (Garden City: Doubleday) 1960

The Copernican Revolution, Thomas S. Kuhn, Cambridge (Harvard University Press) 1957

Space in the Sixties, Patrick Moore, Pelican 1963

Tycho Brahe's Nose, Joseph Ashbrook, 'Sky & Telescope' issue 29, #6, 1965

The Conquerors: Space, Leonard G. Rule (Max Parrish & co Ltd) 1966

Flat and Curved Space Times, G F R Ellis & R W Williams (Oxford University Press) 2000

Brief Lives, John Aubrey (ed. R.Barber, (Boydell Press) 1982

John Dee, Charlotte Fell-Smith (Constable & Company) 1909

Radio Round The World, A.W. Haslett (Cambridge University Press) 1934

Norton's Star Atlas, A.P. Norton (Gall & Inglis) 1910

Signpost To The Stars, F.E. Butler (George Philip & Son) London, 1945

NASA, 50 Years of Space Exploration! (Madacy Entertainment Group Ltd) DVD 2003

National Geographic Magazine, 'Exploring Space' (National Geographic Society) Washington DC, PO Box 98/99

John Lautner, Alan Hess (Thames & Hudson) 1999

An Introduction to Information Theory, Symbols, Signals and Noise, J.R.Pierce, Dover paperback (1980 revised)

Chambers Biographical Encyclopaedia of Scientists (1983)

Observation of a Rapidly Pulsating Radio Source, Antony Hewish, Jocelyn Bell Burnell, J. D. H. Pilkington, P. F. Scott, and R. A. Collins (Nature) February 24, 1968

Discovery of Pulsars: A Graduate Student's Story, Nicholas Wade (News and Comment -Science) August 1, 1975

The Sidereal Messenger of Galileo Galilei (translation by Edward Stafford Carlos, MA)

A Discussion with the Sidereal Messenger (Florence, 1610) Johannes Kepler Narrative, Johannes Kepler (Florence, 1611)

A Discussion with the Sidereal Messenger (Florence, 1610)

Kepler's Works, ed. C. Frisch. Frankfurt a. M. (1858-71)

Prodromus dissertationum mathematicarum continens Mysterium Cosmographicum de

admirabili proportione orbium cœlestium. Tübingen (1596)
Astronomia nova (Commentaria de motibus stellæ Martis) [Prague] (1609)

History, Philosophy, Psychology

The Life of John Locke, Peter King, Bristol (Thoemmes) 1991
John Locke: Problems and Perspectives, John Yolton (Cambridge University Press) 1969
John Locke and the Compass of Human Understanding, John Yolton (Cambridge University Press) 1970
Freud & The Post-Freudians, J.A.C. Brown (Pelican Books) 1961
Uber Psychoanalyse, Sigmund Freud (Vienna) 1920
Two Short Accounts of Psycho-analysis, Sigmund Freud, trans/ed. James Strachey (1962)
The Divided Self, R. D. Laing (Tavistock Publications) 1960
Self and Others, R.D. Laing (Tavistock Publications) 1961
Sanity, Madness & The Family (The Families of Schizophrenics) R.D. Laing & A. Esterson (Tavistock) 1964
The Politics of Experience, R. D. Laing (Harmondsworth) 1967
Knots, R.D. Laing (Penguin) 1969
Do You Love Me, R.D. Laing (Pantheon Books) 1976
Laing & Anti-Psychiatry (Penguin) 1972
The Child, The Family, and the Outside World, D.W. Winnicott (Pelican) 1964
Bishop Trevor Huddleston: 'Naught For Your Comfort (Doubleday) 1955
Macroguide No 6: The George Ohsawa Macrobiotic Foundation (San Francisco) 1970
The Psychology of Moral Behaviour, Derek Wright (Pelican Books) 1972
On The Bhagavad-Gita, translated by Maharishi Mahesh Yogi (SRM Publications) 1967

www.duversity.org (J.G.Bennett)

Endpapers

Everyman, David Jones, engraving, 152 x 178mm, Golden Cockerel Press, 1929. courtesy of the David Jones Society

Plates

Golding Constable's Flower Garden John Constable, oil on canvas (13 x 20ins) 1815
Ipswich Borough Council Museums and Galleries, Suffolk
Corner of Carnaby Street and Foubert's Place, 1967 (Eric Wadsworth/The Guardian)

Music

The Planets, London Symphony Orchestra, Sir Adrian Boult (HMV ED290 7251) 1948
Gustav Holst conducts the Planets (Pearl GEMM CD 9437)
Imogen Holst conducts Gustav Holst, English Chamber Orchestra (Lyrita SRCD 223)
L'Oiseau de la Feu (The Firebird), Igor Stravinsky, original 1910 Edition (Eulenburg)
The Firebird Igor Stravinsky, New York Philharmonic Orchestra, Leonard Bernstein (Columbia Masterworks 5182) 1972
Piano Concerto 1, Edvard Grieg Clifford Curzon (Decca SXI 2173) 1959

Piano Concerto 1, John Ireland (Chester Music, score) 1930

Concerto pour Piano en Sol Majeur, Ravel, Arturo Benedetti Michelangeli, Philharmonia, conducted Ettore Gracis (EMI CDC7b 49326 2) 1957

The Composer and his Orchestra, Howard Hanson, The Eastman-Rochester Orchestra (Mercury Living Presence 434 370-2) 1957

Hanson Conducts Hanson, Symphonies 1 & 2, The Eastman-Rochester Orchestra, The Eastman School of Music Chorus (Mercury Living Presence 475 6181) 1958

Piano Concerto 3 Sergei Rachmaninoff, Jorge Bolet (Decca LDR71) 1988

More Rounds & Canons, compiled Christopher Le Fleming (Mills Music Ltd) 1964

Bobby Shaftoe, Shirley Collins, (Library of Congress 900762) 1959

We Plough the Fields and Scatter, John & Charles Wesley, from 'A Collection of Hymns' (London Wesleyan-Methodist Book-Room) 1780

Then Play On, Fleetwood Mac (Reprise RSLP 9000) 1969

Telstar, The Tornados (Decca F11494) 1962

Rosalyn, the Pretty Things (Fontana TF469) 1966

London Social Degree, from the LP 'Would You Believe' Billy Nicholls (Immediate IMCP009) 1968

A Whiter Shade of Pale, Procul Harum (Deram 13) 1967

Excerpt From A Teenage Opera, Keith West (Parlophone R5623) 1967

Man Of The World, Fleetwood Mac (Immediate IM 080) 1969

Matthew & Son, Cat Stevens (Deram DM 110) 1966

Cinderella Rockefeller, Esther & Abi Ofarim (Phillips BF 1640) 1967

Classical Gas, Mason Williams, Warner Bros (WB7190) 1968

Eloise, Barry Ryan, composed by Paul Ryan (MGM1442) 1968

The 59th Bridge Street Song (Feelin' Groovy) Simon & Garfunkel (Columbia US) 1966

Feeling Good, Anthony Newley, Newley/Bricusse (Concord Music) 1965

Jesus Was A Cross Maker, Judee Sill, (Asylum AYM502) 1971

A Wizard, A True Star, Todd Rundgren, Bearsville (BR2133) 1973

Todd, Todd Rundgren (Bearsville BR85501) 1974

Friday On My Mind, the Easybeats (UA UP1157) 1966

Shapes Of Things To Come, the Yardbirds (Columbia DB7848)

The Five Bridges Suite, the Nice (Charisma CAS1014) 1970

Sorrow, The Merseys (Fontana TF694) 1966

Baby You've Got It, the Action (Parlophone R5474) 1966

Pet Sounds, the Beach Boys (Capitol T-2458) 1966

Surf's Up, the Beach Boys (Reprise REP1058) 1971

Surf's Up, the Beach Boys (Brother-Reprise US RS6453) 1971

Lonely Woman, Modern Jazz Quartet (Atlantic 8122-75361-2) 1972

Revolver, the Beatles (Parlophone PMC 7009) 1966

Sgt Pepper's Lonely Heart's Club Band, the Beatles (Parlophone PMC 7027) 1967

The Beatles, the Beatles (Apple PMC 7067) 1968

Abbey Road, the Beatles (Apple PCS 7088) 1969

Free As A Bird, The Beatles (Apple 7243-8-825787-2-2) 1995

American Crucifixion Resurrection, the Four Seasons, from the album 'Imitation Life Gazette' (Phillips PHS 600-290) 1969

Sonny plays Alfie, Sonny Rollins, HMV (CLP3529) 1966

Star's End: for two Rock Guitarists & Orchestra, David Bedford (Virgin V2020) 197

Mikrophonie 1, Karlheinz Stockhausen (CBS 32 11 0044) 1964

Beat Music '71 for Orchestra & Electric Instruments, Roger Smalley (Faber) score, 1971
The Whale, John Taverner, Apple (Sapcor 15) 1968
Sunshine Superman, Donovan (Pye 7N 17241) 1966
Goin' Back, Carole King & Gerry Goffin, (ODE EK34 944) 1970
Wuthering Heights, original soundtrack by Alfred Newman (score) 1939
Concerto De Aranuez, Rodrigo, Angel Romero, Victory Allssandro & the San Antonio
Symphony (Mercury Living Presence, Mercury 475 6184)
Rachmaninov, Piano Concertos 2 & 3, Byron Janis, Antal Dorati, Minneapolis Symphony
Orchestra (Mercury Living Presence 470 6392)
Vertigo, Bernard Herrmann (original soundtrack) 1958
Silver Treetop School For Boys, the Beatstalkers (CBS 3105) 1967
Apache, the Shadows, composed by Jerry Lordan (Columbia 45-DB 4484) 1963
Cinderella Rockerfeller, Esther & Abi Ofarim (Phillips BF1640) 1967
SF Sorrow, the Pretty Things (Columbia SCX6306) 1968
A Clockwork Orange, Walter Carlos (CBS Masterworks KC31480) 1972
Butch Cassidy & the Sundance Kid, Burt Bacharach (A&M SP4227) 1969
On Her Majesty's Secret Service, music by John Barry (UAS 29020) 1967
Debussy's Greatest Hits (CBS MS7523) 1970
The George Gershwin Songbook, William Bolcom (Nonesuch 871284) 1973
Mass: a theatre piece for Singers, Players, Dancers. Leonard Bernstein with lyrics by
Stephen Schwartz (Columbia Masterworks M231008 Quadrophonic) 1971
Horowitz at Carnegie Hall – An Historic Return (Columbia M2I 328) 1966
Horowitz Plays Rachmaninoff (Columbia M-30464) 1972
Horowitz Plays Chopin (Columbia M-30643) 1973
Horowitz Plays Scriabin (Columbia M-31620) 1974
Vladimir Horowitz – the Last Recording (Sony SK 45818) 1991
Piano Concerto 1, Grieg, Arturo Michaelangelo Benedetti (Phillips BH4510) 1959
Sidesaddle, Russ Conway (Columbia 7XCA 24644 49) 1959
Roulette Russ Conway (Columbia 7XCA 24839 45) 1959

Societies and institutions

NASA
The Royal Society for the Protection of Birds,The Lodge, Sandy, Bedfordshire
California Department of Industrial Relations, Division of Apprenticeship Standards
455 Golden Gate Avenue, San Francisco, CA 94102
Field Iron Workers and Training Program, CA 95823
International Association of Bridge, Structural, and Ornamental Iron Workers, AFL-CIO
1750 New York Avenue NW, Washington, DC
HM Nautical Almanac Office
The Oceanographic Research Institute
The Ruthorford Appleton Laboratory, Chilton, Didcot, OX11, OQX
The National Science Foundation
The National Maritime Museum
Southampton University (e-print Archive mirror)
The Department of Applied Mathematics & Theoretical Physics (Cambridge University)
The American Association for the Advancement of Science (AAAS)
The International Astronomical Union (IAU)

The Market & Coastal Towns Initiative, Cornwall (MCTi)
The South West of England Regional Development Agency (RDA)
The Mechanical Copyright Protection Society
The Performing Rights Society
The Joe Meek Appreciation Society
www.meeksville.com
The Laing Institute (Theodor Itten)
The Laing Society
The American Folklore Society (afsnet)
HYPERLINK "http://www.coastal.ca.gov/ventura/malibu-maps"www.coastal.ca.gov/ventura/malibu-maps (Malibu - Emma Polansky)
The Royal Society, 6-9 Carlton House Terrace, London SW1Y 5AG (Christine Woollett, John Pond article source)
Indiana University, Department of History and Philosophy of Science
The Scientific Book Club
The Cambridge Collection (Mike Petty)
The Garden History Society
The Royal Horticultural Society
The Royal Astronomical Society
The High Energy Astrophysics Science Archive Research Center (NASA)
British Astronomy Association
The Department of History & Philosophy of Science (University of Cambridge)
The Galileo Project (Richard S. Westfall)
The National Trust
The Arts Council South West
Penwith District Council
The Museum of Cornish Methodism
The Wilkins Library, Massachusetts.
The John Clare Society
The Peterborough Natural History Society

Clubs and Boutiques, Arts Labs and other enterprises

Le Bisquit, 16, May St, Mayfair, London W1
Beachcomber Bar at the Mayfair Hotel, Berkeley Street, London W1
Jim Haynes New Arts Lab, 182, Drury Lane, London WC2. Films, plays, music, art, restaurant
IT International Times, 22, Betterton St, London WC1, 836-3727. 1s 6d fortnightly
Middle Earth, 43, King St, London WC2. (Paul Wardman)
OZ, 38a, Palace Gardens Terrace, Kensington, London W8
Malyard, 12, Ganton St, London W1, GER 1848. Mens and women's hats and caps (George Malyard)
Mary Davies, 12, Queen St, London W1 GRO1696. Irish Tweed dresses, skirts, long skirts, long evening dresses, slacks, men's woollen shirts (Cecily O'Brien)
Mary Fair, 18, Baker St, London W1, WEL 8618, from 8gns to 120 gns (Suzanne Peet)
Vanessa Frye, 6f, Sloane St, London SW1 BEL1909. £2.10s - £35 (Vanessa Denza, Madeleine Frye)
Bus Stop, 3, Kensington Church St, London W8. 69s 6d to 99s 6d
Early Bird, 20 Park Walk, Fulham London SW10 (Angela Lynes)

Spectrum '70, Gloucester Rd, London SW7. Day dresses £2.19s to £10, party dresses 5gns to 35gns (Fiona Brown)
Apple, 94, Baker St. London W1 (486-1922). Exotica from Simon and Marijke.
Forposter, 22, Cole St SW3 (589-2468). Posters 7s 6d to £12
Gear 35, Carnaby St, London W1 (GER 1891)
I Was Lord Kitchener's Valet, Piccadilly Circus, London W1. Piccadilly, previously Portobello Rd, (Paul Cafell)
Kleptomania, 22, Carnaby St, London W1. Shirts, old clothes, old things
Leonard, 6, Upper Grosvenor St, London W1 (629-5757) Hairdresser: cut, shampoo and set £2.15s to £4 10s (Leonard)
Liza & Despina, 46, Davies St, London W1 (GRO 7631) (Mrs Sassoon/Mrs Shaw)
Vidal Sassoon, 172, New Bond Street, London W1 (MAY9665) Hairdresser

Newspapers and Journals

The Cornwall Review
The St.Ives Times & Echo
The Cornish Gardener
The Cornish Country Gardener (Anthony Edwards)
The West Briton (XXX publications Ltd
The Falmouth Packet (1829)
The Penzance Gazette, (1839)
The Penzance Journal, (1847)
The Cornish Telegraph, (1851)
The Falmouth & Penryn Weekly Times, (1861)
The Cornish & Devon Post (1877)
The Cornishman (1878)
Disc & Music Echo
Rolling Stone
New Music Express
Melody Maker
Nova magazine
Town magazine
The Studio magazine

Miscellaneous & special thanks...

(NASA). National Geographic, 'Exploring Space', (Jerry Ross) April 26th, 2004 national-geographic.com
References to Cornish place-names are in the main taken from 'A Popular Dictionary of Cornish Place-Names' by O.J. Padel (Alison Hodge) 1988

I am indepted to the pages of Varsity and the compendium 'From Our Cambridge Correspondent' by Mark Weatherall (Varsity Publications Ltd) for insights into Cambridge student life during the 1950's and 60's.

Charles Wheatstone lecture source: www.prairienet.org

Alex Burns at disinformation.com for research on J. G. Bennett
I would especially like to thank Kenneth Silverman, silvrmnk@is2.nyu.edu,
of New York University who transcribed the Poughkeepsie article on Charles Wheatstone
from an actual copy of the Poughkeepsie Journal of 13 September, 1837 for general use
online.
BTCV, Freepost CS780, Conservation Centre, Balby Road, Doncaster. DN4 0RH
information@btcv.org.uk
Scope, 6 Market Road, London N7 9PW, England, UK, cphelpline@scope.org.uk
Brion Gysin source: www.cequel.co.uk/acclarke/shc.html
Meher Baba information: Box 1101, Berkeley, California 94701.
Meher Baba in Rolling Stone, source: WD Keller, www.wdkeller.com
Dr. Anita M. S. Richards, AstroGrid Astronomer
MERLIN/VLBI National Facility, University of Manchester
Jodrell Bank Observatory, Macclesfield, Cheshire SK11 9DL, U.K.
Kate Perry, archivist, Girton College, Cambridge
Joan Lyall, Documentation Officer, Colchester and Ipswich Museum Service
Isaac Newton: PR Quarrie: The Library of the Earls of Macclesfield, catalogue, 'Science I-
O' (Sothebys, London)

Song Lyrics

ACKNOWLEDGEMENTS

My deep thanks are due to my friend and collaborator Julian Balme at Vegas Design for the inspired design and layout of this 'sea of words'. To Bob and Roberta Smith for painting the cover the words are delighted to have. To Mark at Mecob for making the words shout from the cover.

A big thank you to Ian Neil and his team at Sony Music for clearing the song lyrics. Thank you to Yuri Zupancic and James Grauerholz at William Burroughs Communications and Charles Buchan at the Wylie Agency for their help regarding use of texts by Brion Gysin. Thanks to Steve McDermott and David Lindsey for the use of the Cambridge Free Festival poster – design by 'Steff' – from 1969.

Thank you to John Mitchinson, Mathew Clayton, Anna Simpson, Jimmy Leach and ALL of the saviour dudes at the very good ship Unbound who have spent many more of their waking hours than they expected helping me turn nineteen boxes of 'real gone' manuscript into one 'real live' adventure story of the mind.

And, not least, thank you to EVERYONE who believed in and pledged for this unbound, unknown quantity. I hope that – as Yusuf Islam said – "it works for you".

Thank you also to John Nightly himself; The Magicien, the Master – Baba – the Presence. The man that he was and might have, would have been.

Finally, thanks to all the future ex-pop stars parading our streets, those same magiciens who, thirty years later, might be stacking shelves, digging up the roads and driving us around in mini-cabs when they should be creating.

This lone book is dedicated to you all.

Tot Taylor, July 2017

SUPPORTERS

Atosa Anzalchi
Peter Ashworth
Domo Baal
Agnes Meath Baker
Leslie Balfour-Lynn
Adam Barker-Mill
Carolyn Barker-Mill
David Barrie
Niklas Bartha
David Bellingham
Candida Benson
Ilaria Benucci
Roger Bevan
Denis Blais
Lukas Pohl Blondez
Mikael Bokström
Francesca Boschieri
David Breuer
Bill Brewer
Alla Broeksmit
Elizabeth Brooks
Louisa Brown
Martin Brunt
Christopher Bucklow
Jo Cannings
Xander Cansell
Anthony Charles
Nandita Chinkaudhuri
Jason Clark
Mathew Clayton
Michal Cole
Chris Coleman
Sophie Coller
Philip Connor

Clare Conville
Aldo Coronelli
Steve Cox
Paul Cuddeford
Rohan Daft
Virginia Damtsa
Spyros Damtsas
Nick Davey
Elena de Leaniz
Bridget de Leon
Anna Dent
John Dilworth
Anna Dorofeeva
Jessica Duchen
Annabel Duncan-Smith
Irshaad Ebrahim
Emma Elles-Hill
Tony Elliott
Sarah Elson
Ayelet Elstein
Robin Epworth
I-S Eruths
Graham Fink
Raffaella Fletcher
Lobet Florence
Johnnie Frankel
Jacintha Franzen
Lavinia Freitas
David Galbraith
Hilary Gallo
Melanie Gerlis
Anna Geva
Dorothy Glee
Gus Goad

Yulia Golubeva
James Gordon
Leah Gordon
Jos Hackforth-Jones
Jenny Hall
Jane Hamlyn
Bryony Harris
Frances Hatch
David Hebblethwaite
Cherine Helmy
Sally Henderson
Lee Henshaw
Linda Hewson
Rilo Hire
Pete Holidai
Tetchie Homma
Barbara Hoogeweegen
Denise Hooker
Marianne Hosford
Mark Howden
Mark Hudson
Simon Hui Kin Onn
Sun Hulbert
Veronica Humphris
Maxim Jakubowski
Kristina Jarosova
Cameron Jenkins
Amanda Lloyd Jennings
Samantha Jennings
Tristan John
Uma Kaur
Dermot Kavanagh
Michael Kelly
Kai Keup
Dan Kieran
Paul Kinder
Sigrid Kirk
Anna Kuznetsova
Idun Larsson
Jimmy Leach
Trender Lee
Aishleen Lester
Liliane Lijn
Laetitia Lina
Kristina Lindell

Philip Lines
Jonathan Lockwood
Jade Lu
Henry Lydiate
Cajsa MacDougall
Seonaid Mackenzie-Murray
Roxanna Macklow-Smith
Ian MacMillan
Budge Magraw
Sharon Major
Gautam Malkani
John Mallison
Louise Marchal
Ursula Matussek
Sabine Maurer
Clair McCarthy
Andrew McMillan
Al McWalter
Alex Meitlis
Jan Mesdag
Charles Miller
John Mitchinson
Mini Moderns
Diarmid Mogg
Dave Morley
Alan Morris
Eric Mouchet
Alison Myners
Markus Naegele
Priscilla Nasrallah
Carlo Navato
Robert Nedelkoff
Mark Nevin
Quentin Newark
Cat Nilsson
Bernard O'Neill
Georgia Odd
David Ogilvy
Ada Ooi
Pablo
Tris Penna
Penny Pepper
Miho Pickering
Thierry Planelle
David Plumb

Uscha Pohl
Justin Pollard
Brian and Irina Porritt
David Quantick
Philip Rambow
Christof Reichelt
Jill Richards
Ellen Richardson
Liam Riley
Dave Rimmer
K Robbins
Greg Rook
Dominik Rothbard
Iain Rousham
Ruby Ruff
Simon Rumley
Barry Ryan
Matt Ryan
Tim Salavat
Gustavo Sanchez
Francoise Sarre
Alan Searl
Ian Sephton
Serma
George Shilling
Thom Soriano
Josh Spero
Cornelia Staeubli
David Stark
Bernard Starkmann
Lane Steinberg
Justin Stine

Kevin Stone
Richard Strange
Emma Swift
Judith Taylor
Teeny
MC Thijsen
Roger Thorp
Lala Thorpe
Robert Torday
Miles Tredinnick
Rita Tweeter
Nia Valenti
Dea Vanagan
Julio Vega
Errollyn Wallen
Yuxi Wang
Stan C Waterman
Rick Wells
Stefan Wesley
Ray Weston
Hannah Whelan
Joshua White
Keith Whittle
Paulina Wilhelmsen
Nutty Williams
Derek Wilson
Lucy Wilson
Alec Worrall
Patricia Wynn
Hui Yang
Adrian Zolotuhin